W9-AAE-080

the SEDUCER

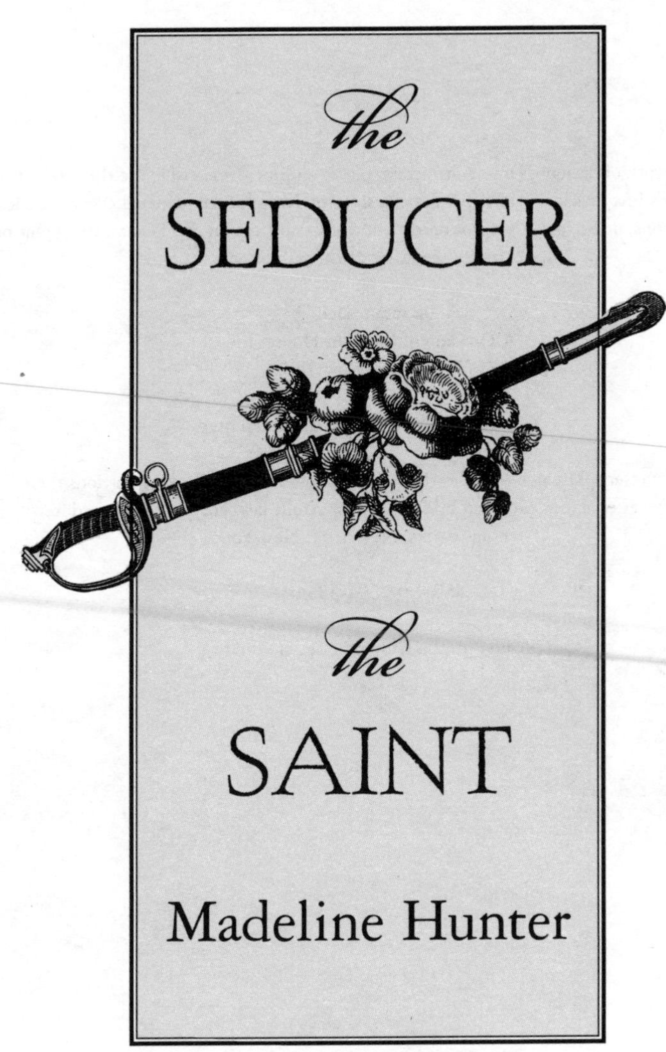

the SAINT

Madeline Hunter

BANTAM BOOKS

Bantam Dell
A Division of Random House, Inc.
New York, New York

ISBN 0-7394-3864-6

Printed in the United States of America

CONTENTS

the SEDUCER

chapter I

~ 1818

The Devil Man had come.

Madame Leblanc had threatened to send for him, and it appeared she had done so.

Diane watched the carriage slow to a stop in front of the school's entrance. Green and gold, with abundant carving, it was drawn by four white steeds. A prince might use such a carriage.

He had not always come in such grand style. There were times he rode a horse, and once he had walked. One year he had not visited at all. Madame Leblanc had come close to sending her to the Dominican orphanage for the poor before a woman had arrived instead and paid for her keep for a while longer.

A bilious sensation churned in Diane's stomach. A guardian who only visited annually out of duty would not appreciate being summoned because of a disaster.

The brave plan she had hatched suddenly struck her as hopeless. Facing the inevitable, she had concluded that fate decreed a future that she had been too cowardly to embrace on her own.

Watching the carriage, her fragile courage abandoned her. The sanctuary of this school might be lonely and small, but it was safe. The quest that beckoned her could wait.

Maybe with time it could even be ignored.

The Devil Man stepped out of the carriage, resplendent in a midnight-blue cloak and high boots. The wind blew through his dark hair. He was not wearing a hat. He never did.

He had not always looked so rich. She vaguely remembered years when he had appeared almost rustic. There had been the time, ages ago, when she had thought him ill. Rich or poor, their meetings always followed the same pattern. He would glance at her, barely, and ask his questions.

Are you being treated well? Do you have any complaints? Are you learning your school lessons? How old are you now?

He did not care about the answers. She told him what he wanted to hear. Except once. She had been whipped for a transgression she had not committed and the humiliation was very raw when he visited. She impulsively complained to him. Amazingly, she had never been whipped again. Before he left he forbade it, much to Madame Leblanc's frustration. From then on she could not be physically punished without his permission.

Which was why he had been summoned today.

He strode to the entrance. She barely caught a glimpse of his face, but she saw enough of that severe countenance to know for sure who it was.

"Denounce me and I will kill you."

The sharp whisper pulled Diane out of her thoughts. She spun around.

Madame Oiseau, the music teacher, glared at her from the door, which she blocked with her body. Short and slight in stature, she still made an effective barrier. Her eyes glowed like two tiny coals in her fine-boned face. Her dark hair appeared mussed, as if she had rushed through her morning toilet.

"Do not doubt that I will do it, Diane. Take the punishment, keep your silence, and I will be your friend. Otherwise . . ." She raised her eyebrows meaningfully.

A chill slid through Diane, as if evil breathed on her nape.

"No one will believe you," Madame said. "And when it is over, we will both still be here. You are smart enough to make the right choice." She opened the door. "Come down when you are called. I will bring you in."

Stunned, Diane watched her leave.

She glanced around her spartan chamber, seeking reassurance from the familiar objects. She had an odd fondness for the hard bed and old coverlet, for the wood chair and simple desk. The wardrobe needed painting and the pink washbowl had gotten very chipped over the years. The physical comforts were few, but time had made the narrow room the center of her life. It was the only home she could remember.

She pictured herself living in this chamber for a few years more. Not happy, but content. Not such a bad future, even with what she faced today, even with Madame Oiseau nearby. The alternative stretched in front of her like an endless void, dark and unfathomable.

The old questions began intruding, robbing the chamber of its meager comfort. Questions from her childhood, eternally unasked and unanswered. *Who am I? Why did I come here? Where is my family?* For a few years she had stopped wondering, but recently the questions had returned, louder and more insistently, until they ran in a silent chant echoing in a hollow part of her heart.

The answers were not here. Learning the truth meant abandoning this little world.

She only needed to grab the opportunity that fate had created.

Should she do it? Should she throw herself at the mercy of the Devil Man?

". . . if she goes unpunished, I must insist that she leave. I cannot have the virtue of my girls corrupted. . . ."

Madame Leblanc rambled on in severe tones. Distracted by thoughts of the unfinished business he had left in Paris, Daniel St. John only half-listened.

Something about a book. Of course the girl would have books. It was a school.

He forced his attention to the gray-haired, buxom schoolmistress and broke her incessant flow. "Your summons said that this was serious, madame. I assumed she had taken ill and lay on death's door."

It had been a bizarre stroke of luck that the letter had found him in Paris at all. He certainly had not planned to interrupt his visit there to make this journey. He was annoyed that he had been bothered for such a minor matter. "If she has broken the rules, deal with it as you normally do. As I pay you to do. There was no need to send for me."

Madame lowered her chin and glared at him. "This transgression requires more than bread and water for a few days, m'sieur, and you gave strict orders she was not to be punished with the rod without your permission."

"Did I? When was that?"

"Years ago. I told you that such leniency would lead to grief, and now it has."

Yes, he vaguely remembered the earnest expression on a gamine-faced child, asking him for justice. He could not recall giving instructions about it. If he had known it would prove this damned inconvenient he would not have been so generous.

He straightened in the chair, prepared to rescind the order. His gaze fell on the willow rod lying across the desk. The memory of tearful eyes and a choking voice accusing Madame Leblanc of unwarranted brutality came back to him again.

"You said something about a book. Let me see it."

"M'sieur, that is not necessary. I assure you that it is of a nature to be forbidden, to say the least."

"That could mean it is only a volume of poems by Ovid, or a religious tract by a dissenter. I would like to see it and judge for myself."

"I do not think—"

"The book, madame."

She strode to a cabinet. Using one of several keys on a cord around her neck, she unlocked it and retrieved a small, red volume. She thrust it at him and retreated to a window. She took up a position with her back to him, physically announcing her condemnation of the literature in his hands.

He flipped it open, and immediately saw why.

Not literature. In fact, no words at all. The thin volume contained only engravings that displayed carnal intercourse in all its inventiveness.

He paged through. Things started out simply enough, but got increasingly athletic. Toward the end there were a few representations that struck him as totally unworkable.

"I see," he said, snapping the book closed.

"Indeed." Her tone said he had *seen* more than was necessary.

"Call for the child, madame."

Satisfaction lit her face. "I would like you to be here when it is done. She should know that you approve."

"Send for her."

Madame Oiseau escorted Diane in.

As expected, a visitor waited in the headmistress's study. The Devil Man lounged in Madame Leblanc's chair behind the fruitwood desk. Madame stood beside him rigidly, a bulwark of censure. Two items lay upon the spotless desk. A willow rod, and *the book.*

Typically, Daniel St. John barely glanced at her. He appeared a little annoyed and very bored. She half-expected him to yawn and pull out his snuffbox.

He did not really look like a devil. She had given him that name as a young girl because of his eyes. Dark and intense, they were framed by eyebrows that peaked in vague points toward the ends. Those eyes could burn right into you if he paid attention.

Since he never did, she did not find them so frightening anymore.

His mouth was set in a straight, hard, full line, but then it always was. Even when he smiled, it only curved enough to suggest that whatever amused him was a private joke. Along with the eyes and chiseled face, it made him look cruel. Maybe he was. She wouldn't know. Still, she suspected that women thought him very handsome, and maybe even found his harshness attractive. She had seen Madame Oiseau flush and fluster in his presence.

He was not as old as she had once thought. He had grown more youthful as she had matured. She realized now that he could not be more than thirty. That struck her as peculiar. He had been an adult her whole life, and should be older.

It was easy to forget how hard he could appear. Every year the months hazed over her memory. Seeing him now, she knew that her plan had been stupid. He would never take on more inconvenience, and she would be left here to await Madame Oiseau's vengeance.

"M'sieur has learned of your disgraceful behavior," Madame Leblanc intoned. "He is shocked, as one would expect."

He quirked one of his sardonic smiles at the description of his reaction. He tapped the book. "Is there an explanation?"

Madame Oiseau moved closer, a physical reminder of her threat. Madame Leblanc glared, daring her to make excuses. The Devil Man looked indifferent, as always. He wanted this to be done so he could be gone.

Diane made her choice. The safe, cowardly choice. "No explanation, m'sieur."

He glanced up at her, suddenly attentive. It only lasted an instant. He sank back in the chair and gestured impatiently to Madame Leblanc.

The two women readied the chamber for punishment. A prie-dieu was dragged into the center of the room. A chair was pushed in front of it. The headmistress lifted the willow rod and motioned for the sinner to take the position.

The Devil Man just sat there, lost in his thoughts, gazing at the desk, ignoring the activity.

He was going to stay. Madame Leblanc had insisted that he witness it.

Diane had known remaining here would mean punishment. Madame Leblanc firmly believed that sins deserved whipping, and she did not reserve the rod for her students. Several months ago a serving woman of mature years was caught sneaking out to meet a man and the same justice had been meted out to her.

Burning with humiliation and praying that he remained in his daze, Diane approached the prie-dieu. Stepping up on the kneeler, she bent her hips over the raised, cushioned armrest and balanced herself by grasping the seat of the chair.

Madame Oiseau ceremoniously lifted the skirt of her sack dress. Madame Leblanc gave the usual exhortation for her to pray for forgiveness.

The rod fell on her exposed bottom. It fell again. She ground her teeth against the pain, knowing it was futile. They would whip her mercilessly until she begged heaven's pardon.

"Stop." His voice cut through the tension in the room.

Madame Leblanc got one last strike in.

"I said to stop."

"M'sieur, it must—"

"Stop. And leave."

Diane began to push herself up.

Madame Oiseau pressed her back down. "It appears her guardian is so outraged that he feels obliged to mete out the punishment himself, Madame Leblanc," she said in oily tones. "It is appropriate for such a sin, no?"

Madame Leblanc debated in a string of mumbles. Madame Oiseau walked around the prie-dieu. The two women left.

She heard him rise and walk toward her. She hoped that he would be quick about it. She would gladly accept any pain just to be done with the mortification that she felt, positioned there, half-naked.

The skirt fluttered down. A firm grasp took her arm. "Get up."

She righted herself and smoothed the sack gown. Biting back her humiliation, she faced him.

He sat behind the desk again. No longer bored. Definitely paying attention. She squirmed under his dark gaze.

He gestured to the book. "Where did you get it?"

"Does it matter?"

"I should say it does. I put you in a school that is almost cloistered. I find it curious that you came by such a thing."

Madame Oiseau's threat rang in her ears. She could do it. She could kill someone. And when it happened, the Devil Man would not care at all. He would be grateful to be spared the journey each year.

"I stole it."

"From a bookseller?"

"I stole it and Madame Leblanc found it among my belongings. That is all that matters. Madame says that excuses and explanations only make the sin worse."

"Does she? What nonsense. Do you understand why Madame was so shocked that you had this book?"

"The women are undressed, so I assume that it is about sins of the flesh."

That seemed to amuse him, as if he thought of a clever response but kept it to himself. "I believe that you stole this book, but I think it was from someone here. Madame Leblanc?"

She shook her head.

"I did not think so. It was the other one, wasn't it? The one more than happy to leave you alone with me." He speared her with those eyes. "Tell me now."

She hesitated. He really didn't care about her. This was the first time in years that he had even really looked at her.

He was definitely doing that. Sharply. Deeply. It made her uncomfortable.

He had helped her that time when she complained. Maybe if she told him, he would agree to keep silent and things could continue as before. Or perhaps if he complained, Madame Leblanc would believe him, and Madame Oiseau would be dismissed.

There was something in his expression that indicated he would have the truth, one way or another. Something determined, even ruthless, burned in those devil eyes.

She much preferred him bored and indifferent.

"It belongs to Madame Oiseau, as you guessed," she said. "There is a young girl, no more than fourteen, to whom she has been showing it. The girl told me how Madame Oiseau described the riches to be had for a woman who did such things. I went to Madame's chamber and took it. I was looking for a way to bring it down to the fire, but Madame Oiseau claimed a brooch had gone missing and all the girls' chambers were searched. The book was found in mine."

"And the brooch never was found, was it?"

"No."

His eyes narrowed thoughtfully while his gaze moved all over her, lingering on her face. He was trying to decide if she spoke the truth.

"How old are you now?"

The annual question, coming now, startled her. "Sixteen."

"You spoke of your friend who is fourteen as a young girl."

"She acts younger than that."

He scrutinized her. He had never looked at her so long or so thoroughly. No one ever had.

"I brought you here, what, ten years ago? Twelve? It was right after . . . You were a girl then, but not a little child." His gaze met hers squarely. "How old are you?"

Her foolish plan was unfolding in spite of her cowardice.

Only she did not want it now.

"Sixteen."

"I do not care for young women trying to make a fool of me. I think if we let down your hair from those childish braids, and see you in something besides that sack, that we will know the truth."

"The truth is that I am sixteen."

"Indeed? Indulge my curiosity, then." He gestured at her head. "The hair. Take it down."

Cursing herself for having attracted his attention, she pulled the ribbons off the ends of her braids. Unplaiting and combing with her fingers, she loosed her hair. It fell in waves around her face and down her body.

His sharp eyes warmed. That should have reassured her, but it had the opposite effect. Caution prickled her back.

"How old are you?" His voice was quieter this time, with no hard edge.

He had her very worried now. "Sixteen."

"I am sure not. I suspect that you concluded it was in your interest to lie. But let us be certain. The gown, mam'selle."

"The gown?"

"The gown. Remove it."

chapter 2

She faced him, with her chestnut hair pouring down her lithe body. Her lips parted in confusion and her soulful eyes widened with shock. With that expression she looked almost as young as she claimed to be.

"Remove it," he repeated.

"You cannot tell my age from . . . At sixteen I already . . ."

"A female does not stop maturing so early. There is a difference between the voice of a girl and that of a woman, and yours has a mature resonance. There is also a difference in their bodies, especially in the hips. The ones that I just saw struck me as too rounded for sixteen. Remove your garments so that I can check if my fleeting impression was correct."

Her face flushed a deep red. Sparks of indignation flickered in her dark eyes. He half-expected her to start disrobing and call his bluff.

Then the fires disappeared and her gaze turned cool.

She suddenly reminded him of her father. There was no reason why the hell that should bother him, but it always had, and he abruptly lost interest in the game he had initiated with her.

"I am twenty years old."

She did not sound like someone who had just been outflanked. Her tone suggested that she had made some decision.

A tiny spike of caution stabbed him.

"Does Madame Leblanc know your true age?"

"She never asked my age when I came. I was small and unschooled and put with the youngest girls. However, she can count the years."

"But she never raised the question of your future with me."

"It was not in her interest to do so. You continued paying the fees. I progressed through the curriculum quicker than most. Three years ago I moved to the front of the schoolroom and began teaching what I had been taught."

"Very convenient for Madame Leblanc. However, you also never raised the question. In fact, you have lied to me about it before, and just did again."

"I have seen girls leave at eighteen. I did not think you would let me stay here if you knew I had come of age. So when you asked, I gave you the same age for several years before getting older again."

She had been very clever, Daniel realized. More clever than one expected of a young girl.

He made the annual trips to this school with dark, soul-churning resentment. They served as sharp announcements of duties delayed and hungers unfed, of time passing and of quests unfulfilled. His responsibility here only reminded him that there would be no peace until he finished what he had started years ago. Even as he talked with her each year in this study, he blocked most of his mind to her.

She had seen his self-absorption as indifference and taken advantage of it.

She blushed prettily at her admission of guilt. "I apologize for the deception, but this is the only home I have known. I have friends here, and a family of sorts."

Home. Family. A small, wistful smile accompanied those words.

She had been willing to take a whipping to keep what little she had of both those things.

He instantly wished that he had not let curiosity follow its course. Looking at her pretty face, he had forgotten whom he dealt with. For a few moments there he had been a man toying with an attractive woman and enjoying her dismay far too much.

"We will forget this conversation, mam'selle. You can indeed stay. We will say nothing about your true age, and I will continue sending the fees. In time, Madame Leblanc will probably begin compensating you for your duties and you will officially move to the front of the schoolroom."

She strolled around the chamber, absently touching the glassed bookcase and the velvet prie-dieu. "It is tempting, I will not deny it. But the book . . . Madame Oiseau . . . It cannot be the same now. Sometimes events conspire to force one to do what should be done." Her ambling brought her back to the desk. "No, it is long past time for me to leave here. I must ask for your help, however. Very little, I promise you. I am a good teacher in the subjects expected of a governess. If you could aid me in securing a position, I would be grateful."

"I expect that is possible. I know some families in Paris who—"

"I would prefer London."

She said it quickly and firmly enough that his instincts tightened.

How much did she remember?

"I think that I can get better terms in London," she said. "They will think that I am French. That should count for something."

They will think that I am French. Clearly she had remembered the basics.

"Paris would be easier."

"It must be London. If you will not help me, I will manage on my own."

He pictured her arriving in London unprotected and unsupervised. She would get into trouble immediately.

And get him into trouble eventually.

"I cannot permit that."

"What you will permit is not of consequence, m'sieur. I am in this school by your charity, I know that. But I am of an age when I daresay that you have no further obligation to me, nor I to you. If events have forced courage on me, then I shall be courageous. I must find my life, and I intend to go to London."

I must find my life. His caution sharpened to a sword's edge.

As often happened, that produced a mental alertness that instantly clarified certain things. His mind neatly transformed an unexpected complication into an opportunity. One that might salve the hunger and finish the quest.

It stood facing him, waiting for his response. Proud. Determined. But not nearly so confident as she posed. Not nearly so brave.

Sometimes events conspire to force one to do what should be done.

How true.

How much did she remember? It would not matter. And if, as he suspected, she hoped to learn all of it, it would be over before she even came close. In the meantime he could keep an eye on her.

He studied her lithe frame and the body vaguely apparent beneath the sack. He pictured her in a pale gown of the latest fashion. Something both alluring and demure. Her hair up and a single, fine jewel at her neck, with those soulful eyes gazing out of her porcelain, unpainted face. Lovely, but young. Fresh and vulnerable, but not a silly schoolgirl.

Yes, she would do. Splendidly, in fact.

"I will speak with Madame Leblanc and explain that you will leave with me today. We will discuss the details of finding you a position when we get to Paris."

Diane folded her few garments and stacked them in the valise that Monsieur St. John had sent up from his carriage. They were all too childish for a governess to wear. She would have to find some way to rectify that.

From the small drawer of her tiny writing table, she removed an English Bible. It was one of two remnants of her life before this school.

She thrust her hand to the far back of the drawer and grasped a wadded handkerchief. She let it unwrap and its contents fall onto the desk. A gold ring rolled and rolled before stopping, poised upright. A scrap of paper fluttered down beside it.

For several years she had worn the ring on her thumb every night when she went to sleep. Then the day had come when her tenuous hold on childhood memories failed, when they became fractured snippets of images and sensations. The ritual of putting on the ring no longer made sense and she had ceased doing so.

She did not have to read the words on the paper. They were from the Devil Man, the only note he had ever sent her. It had come with this ring one year on the feast of the Nativity, explaining that the ring had been her father's and that he thought that she might like to have it. She doubted that he even remembered making the gesture.

It had been years ago. The second or third Nativity that she was here, perhaps. She couldn't remember exactly.

She tucked the ring and note into the valise. She would have to ask Daniel St. John how he came to have it.

And her.

The door to her chamber opened and Madame Leblanc entered. She marched to the window and peered out with critical eyes. "Take your time. Let him wait."

"If he waits too long he may leave without me."

"He will not leave without you. Trust this old woman when she says that. I am not ignorant of the world, or of men." She turned abruptly and pointed to the bed. *"Sit."*

Diane sat obediently. Madame paced in front of her, shaking her head.

"Sometimes this happens. One of my orphans leaves to be a governess or to live with a relative, but I know that there is more. I can sense it. Holy Mother forgive me, I do not welcome giving the advice that I am about to impart, but I would fail in my duty to you if I did not."

"There is no need, madame. Your training has been most thorough."

"Not in this." She crossed her arms over her substantial chest. "Property and jewels, secured to you. That is what you must demand. Legally secured, so there can be no misunderstanding."

"He has no reason to be so generous."

"He will have a reason. He has realized that you are of age . . . and that book. Now he thinks that you are amenable. . . . I should have considered that, but in my disappointment at your sin, I did not."

"You distress yourself for nothing. He has agreed to help me find a position and I will be safe."

"He intends to find you a position, Diane, but not the one that you think. He wants you for a mistress." She looked down severely, but her expression instantly softened. "You look at me so blankly. You do not even know what that means, do you?"

She could believe that she looked blank, for she wasn't very clear on what that meant, except that it was sinful.

"The book, Diane. The terrible images in the book. Those are the duties of a mistress, and with no benefit of marriage."

The odd engravings flashed through her mind. She felt her face turn hot. "Surely you misunderstand."

"I have over fifty years on this earth. I know a man's sinful interest when I see it. Oh, his cool demeanor hides it better than most, but hear what I say to you now. You must protect your future. Property and jewels. Make him pay dearly for every liberty that you grant him."

Diane wiped the pictures from her thoughts. Madame might have fifty years, but they had not been very worldly ones, and she always spoke badly of men. "I am sure that you are wrong."

"He is rich. He will seduce you with luxuries and kindness, and then . . ."

Diane rose. "I thank you for your concern, but my association with Monsieur St. John will be brief."

Madame helped buckle the valise. "Do not forget to say your prayers. Every night. Perhaps then, when the offer comes . . . Maybe."

Diane lifted the valise. It wasn't very heavy. All the same, carrying it out of this chamber would not be easy. Nor would leaving Madame, for all of her strictness.

"I thank you for your care, madame."

Impulsively, the formidable woman enclosed her in an embrace.

She had never done that before. No one had, for as long as Diane could remember. It evoked ghostly sensations, however, of the security and comfort of other, long-ago embraces.

It took her breath away. The warmth and intimacy astonished her and moved her so much that her eyes teared. The human contact both salved the odd hollow that she carried in her heart and also made it ache.

The little cruelties over the years did not seem very important suddenly. Madame had been the closest thing to a mother.

The moment of tenderness made Diane brave. She turned her head and spoke in the older woman's ear. "The book. I stole it from Madame Oiseau. She shows it to the girls."

She broke away and turned to the door quickly, catching only a glimpse of Madame Leblanc's shocked face.

Madame Oiseau waited for her down below. She slipped an arm around Diane's waist and guided her to the door.

"I underestimated you." She smiled slyly, as if they had suddenly become great friends. "Who could have guessed that such a shrewd mind worked beneath that demure manner. Well done, Diane."

"I think that you overestimate me now."

"Hardly. But you are too young to appreciate the victory waiting for you. Too ignorant to reap all that you can. You must write to me for advice. We can help each other and grow rich from your cleverness."

"I do not want your help."

"Still proud. Too proud for an orphan with no past. Much too proud for the bourgeois merchants and lawyers to whom most of the others have gone."

They passed out to the portico. A crisp wind fluttered the edges of their muslin caps.

Daniel St. John lounged against the side of the carriage, his eyes fixed on the ground.

Madame cocked her head. "An exciting man. Maybe a dangerous one. Not born to wealth. Beneath his elegant and cool manner there is too much brooding vitality for that. He has managed to be accepted into the best circles, however. The women would permit it, to keep him nearby, and even the men would be intrigued." Her eyes narrowed. "Make him wait."

First Madame Leblanc and now Madame Oiseau. "Since I am already out the door, it is too late to try and do that now."

Madame laughed. It brought those devil eyes up, and on them.

"Perhaps you do not need much advice," Madame mused. "Your ignorance will deal with him just as well."

A gesture from Daniel sent a footman over to take the valise. Madame retreated to the door. "Remember what I have said. Write to me."

The footman opened the coach door. Daniel held out his arm, to usher her in. He did not appear *too* dangerous. Actually, right now, with the breeze tousling his short, dark locks, he looked rather young, and almost friendly.

Who am I? How did I come to be here? Where is my family?

Down the three stone steps she trod, her heart pounding with trepidation. She walked across the only solid earth she knew, toward a sea of uncertainty.

The Devil Man waited for her to join him there.

chapter 3

The Parisian town house should have surprised her more. That was Diane's first reaction on seeing its buff stone facade and elegant pilasters, so different from the rough, cold, limestone pile of the school. She should have been overwhelmed. Instead she found it oddly comforting.

Perhaps that was because arriving at its door meant that she no longer had to share a carriage with Daniel St. John.

It had been a long, silent journey. He had initiated very little conversation and she had been too nervous to ask any questions. Most of the time his sharp gaze stared at the passing countryside, his mind clearly working at something.

Several times she looked over to find him watching her in a way that made her wonder if his distraction had to do with her. The carriage would suddenly seem very small during those inspections. Worse, she found it impossible to look away. He probably had thought her bold to observe him as frankly as he did her.

The house nestled between others equally restrained and delicate in their classical style. The whole street was lined with such buildings. The whole district was.

Daniel gathered together some papers he had sporadically perused, and stuffed them back into a portfolio. Her glance caught sight of a familiar, thin red binding beneath the stored sheets.

"You stole it." Surprise made her blurt the words.

"An accusation of theft is a peculiar way to break your silence. Madame did not warn me that you were impertinent."

"The silence has not only been on my part. You have said nothing to me since we left the school, either."

"I have spent most of the journey trying to decide what to do with you."

"You are going to find me a position as a governess. Remember?"

"Of course. A governess. Now, regarding your accusation, what have I stolen?"

She gestured to the portfolio. "The book. You still have it."

"Ah, the book. It seems to have left the school with me. A fortuitous oversight, don't you think? In time, I suspect that it would have disappeared from Madame Leblanc's locked case and found its way back into that other one's hands."

"You did it to protect the other girls, you mean. That was very kind of you. I warned Madame Leblanc about Madame Oiseau, but I do not think that she will believe me."

"Since Madame Oiseau has her ear now, she probably will not."

"You should burn it. It has no value or use to anyone."

"I am grateful for your instruction, but wonder if you have judged its value correctly."

He slipped the thin volume out of the portfolio.

It appeared that he was going to open it, *right in front of her.*

"We have stopped, m'sieur. Shouldn't we get out now?"

"In a moment. We must decide the disposition of this book first," he said. "The binding is the best leather. The engraved plates are tipped in. It is well made and not cheap. It is an error to say it has no value, I think."

"I was not speaking of its binding and such, but the images."

"It could be that some pages hold maps or poems, instead of erotic engravings. Burning it may be rash." He opened the cover, to check.

The notion of perusing those pages, here, now, almost knee to knee in this carriage, horrified her. "I assure you that it contains only those images."

"Really? How do you know that?"

She felt a flush slide over her face.

"To know for certain it only holds images, you would have had to page through every leaf before trying to throw it in the fire." He looked up at her. "Did you?"

Her face scalded. She *had* paged every leaf, with a combination of curiosity and shock and appalled fascination.

"Did you?" he repeated.

"Of course not."

He smiled that private smile. "That is a relief to hear. If you had, I might regret stopping that whipping back at the school."

That only made her think of that whipping, and what he had seen. She suddenly remembered that one of the images contained a woman in a somewhat similar pose.

She wanted to sink through the floorboards. It did not help that he was watching her reaction with interest.

And that book . . . Now he thinks you are amenable.

Oh, dear.

Just then a footman opened the carriage door. Daniel stepped out and handed her down.

"I did not realize that Paris had such elegant rooming houses," she said.

"It does, but this is not one of them. This is my home." He began strolling to the house.

She looked up at the buff facade, and then at the Devil Man, and then to her valise being held by the footman. The suggestive talk about the book of engravings ran through her mind and collided with memories of Madame Leblanc's warnings.

It occurred to her that she had not thought out the details of this adventure very well.

He stopped and glanced back curiously to where she stood rooted.

"I, um, thought that I would be staying in a boarding house." In truth, she had not given any thought to where she would be staying, but living in his house now struck her as a very stupid thing to permit.

"That is not necessary. There are plenty of chambers here."

"Yes. Of course. I see. However, I will feel that I am imposing."

"Nonsense. Besides, sticking you in some tiny chamber in a rooming house or hotel would be inconvenient for us. Come with me."

Inconvenient?

Very nervous now, she joined him. Together they walked up the eight white steps toward the front door.

"For the sake of simplicity, we will tell the servants and my friends that you are a cousin, come to visit from the country."

"Am I? A cousin? A relative?"

"No."

It wasn't much, but it was a beginning. At least now she knew what she was *not* to him.

Under the circumstances, however, the lack of a blood tie was not good news. Nor was the evidence that he had concocted a deceit to explain her presence in his home.

The door opened. The house beckoned. She stepped inside, worrying that she abandoned her innocence in doing so.

Daniel shrugged off his cape into a waiting servant's hands. "Where is Mademoiselle Jeanette?"

"In the south sitting room, sir."

Daniel guided her toward the curving sweep of a marble staircase. "I will present you to my sister."

Relief broke in her. If Daniel St. John's intentions were dishonorable, surely he would never bring her here, where his sister lived too.

She felt like a queen mounting those stairs. Their breadth and elegance made one walk a little taller and straighter. Her feet sank silently into the deep pile of a strip of pale, flowered carpet running down their center.

The sitting room astonished her. Entering it felt like walking into a corner of heaven.

Dazzled, she took it in through a series of flashing impressions. Not square, but octagonal. Everything pale and creamy. Large mirrors on four walls reflected the light pouring in the one long window. Gilt tendrils framed them and snaked along the cornice like so many delicate vines. An oval painting on the high ceiling was set amidst shallow coffers. Discreet, elegant furnishings, small in scale and upholstered in pastel tones, dotted the space.

An incredibly beautiful woman, about forty years old, with black hair and white skin, sat in a chair near a diminutive fireplace.

Not only a sister, but an older sister. A mature woman. That reassured Diane even more.

Diane expected clouds to billow around her feet as she crossed the room. Then she caught a glimpse of herself in the mirrors and immediately fell back to earth. Her worn cloak and muslin cap and silly braids blurred by, reflected four times over. She looked like a peasant in this chamber.

"Jeanette, this is Diane Albret."

"You brought her back with you." It wasn't a question, but its inflection carried a note of surprise.

"It was necessary."

Jeanette took Diane's hand and gestured for her to sit on a padded bench nearby. "You are most welcome here, my dear."

"I thank you, mademoiselle. I will not impose very long. M'sieur has offered to help me find a position as a governess in London."

Daniel settled into a chair. It instantly accommodated his lean length and casual pose, no doubt because it knew better than to resist. He dominated the whole chamber the same way. Even the gilt tendrils seemed to restrain their exuberance out of deference.

"Actually, it will be several weeks before I journey to London, so those plans will have to be delayed. I hope that you will not mind too much." He spoke absently while he brushed the cuff on his coat. Delaying her plans was the least of his concerns and, whether she minded or not, of little true importance. "In the meantime, my sister will see to your comfort, and you will have the opportunity to visit this city. Paris is not a place that one merely passes through unless there is urgent business waiting elsewhere."

"It was not my intention to require your hospitality so long."

"It will be no imposition. Will it, Jeanette? You will enjoy taking her about, won't you? Enjoy your stay with us. The tedium of a governess's life awaits you. After years in that school, you owe yourself a respite of pleasure before shackling yourself to such a miserable existence."

He made the future she had chosen sound dreadful. One could not argue against his reasoning.

Especially since the only argument she could think of made no sense. She could hardly explain what she didn't understand herself. But that long, silent carriage ride had imbued their association with a certain . . . intimacy. The conversation about the book increased the familiarity and added a tinge of danger. It had made her uncomfortable then, and despite the reassurance of Jeanette's presence in this house, it still did. The notion of spending weeks in the home of Daniel St. John unsettled her.

Jeanette slid a long silk shawl off her lap. "Daniel, call for Paul. Our guest looks very tired. I will take her to her chamber so that she can rest and refresh herself."

Paul turned out to be a thick, tall pillar of a man. The elegance of his blue servant's livery could not hide his earthy solidity. The neat grooming of his reddish hair did not soften his craggy features.

Carefully, with a gentleness that looked peculiar for his bulk, he slid his arms under Jeanette and rose, holding her like a baby.

"To the Chinese bedchamber, Paul. Diane, will you come with us, please."

They mounted another flight of stairs, not so grand, but impressive still. A bank of tall windows on the top landing overlooked a garden. They stopped at a heavy, large door that Paul easily opened despite his burden.

The chamber smelled of cedar. Decorated all in blue and white, it reminded Diane of the porcelain urns displayed in the better shops' windows in Rouen. It contained many similar pieces, only these looked much nicer. She knew without being told that they were very precious and that if she broke one she would want to die.

Paul settled Jeanette on a chair by the hearth and bent to build up the fire. Then he retreated, taking up a position outside the open door.

"As you can see, I am lame," Jeanette said. "I suffered an injury some years ago. Thanks to Paul's strength, however, I need not be an infirm recluse. Everyone is accustomed to seeing him carry me and it will cause you no embarrassment."

"It will be my presence that will cause eyebrows to raise. Your brother said that I am to claim I am your cousin. Your friends will be shocked to learn that you have such poor, ill-mannered relations."

Jeanette beckoned her forward and gave her a more thorough inspection than she had down below. "Not so ill-mannered. That school taught you the basics, and you will quickly learn the rest. Your appearance, however . . . I will send my maid to do something with that hair before the evening meal. We will begin on the rest tomorrow."

"There is no need. Please. I will remain in this house until it is time to sail to England."

"My brother has affairs to attend to here. Although this is one of his homes, he makes his life in England and his visits here are always very full. If you are hovering in the shadows, he will be displeased by the reminder that he inconveniences you." Her smile suggested that giving Daniel St. John displeasure was not the path of wisdom.

A servant arrived with the valise.

"I will leave you to rest. My woman will come later, to help you unpack and dress. Again, I extend my welcome to you. I am glad that you have come to us."

Paul carried her away. The door closed. Diane sat in the chair that Jeanette had just vacated and inched it closer to the hearth. The abundant warmth flowing from the fire felt delicious.

She stared at the flames. She dared not look anywhere else. The chamber was too much. The porcelain urns waited to be broken. The front of this house had not overwhelmed her, but its interior certainly did.

Several weeks, Daniel had said. Maybe longer, Jeanette had implied. Then a life of tedium.

She was not sure that briefly tasting this luxury would be a good idea. Dwelling amidst such wealth could make what had come before, and what would come after, a source of discontentment.

He will seduce you with luxuries and kindness, and then . . .

Ridiculous. A man like this had no need of such as her. Nor would the next few weeks be the product of his kindness. It simply was not convenient for him to travel to England right now.

The fire's heat worked its way down to her bones, killing the chill that she had known most of her life. She closed her eyes and enjoyed the sensation. The warmth surrounded her like arms, comforting her.

A memory came to her suddenly, of another long carriage ride, split by a journey on a boat. Of fear and loneliness finally defeating her during an interminable night while she huddled in the corner of a moving, black space. Of arms reaching for her in the dark and pulling her close so that she cried into a wool coat.

Perhaps that buried, childish memory accounted for the familiarity in the carriage today.

No, not entirely. For one thing, she was no longer a child and he neither treated her nor spoke to her as one anymore. It was that abrupt change that made her uncomfortable with him. Still, the memory eased her misgivings a little.

She dozed off into a vision of a garden filled with golden vines.

She sat on the chair in front of the hearth, waiting to be called to the meal. Her hair felt a little unsteady, piled up as it was on her crown. After the maid had finished, her reflection displayed a stranger, someone older than her own image of herself.

The door opened, but no servant had come. Daniel stood there.

"Jeanette asked that I check on you, to spare her coming up. You are comfortable here? You have been settled in?"

She rose to face him. "Actually, I have been wondering if there is another chamber."

"This one does not suit you?"

"I would prefer something simpler. Smaller. I am not accustomed to such as this."

"The smaller ones are above and used by the servants. We can hardly put you there."

"I don't see why not."

"Because you are not a servant. You are a guest."

He stepped into the chamber and looked around curiously, as if checking its proportions and seeing its opulence anew. His expression changed to one of comprehension.

He strolled over to a table near the canopied bed. It held one of the beautiful urns. "Come here."

She did not move. She could not, and not just because the chamber intimidated her.

The space was not so large that one could ignore that it was a bedchamber. Her bedchamber, and he was in it and really should not be, even if it was his home. No one had ever taught her that lesson. She just knew it. An odd quickening in her blood, a different flow in the air, a heightening of the familiarity from the carriage—his presence produced a barrage of effects that warned that this was not correct.

"Come here," he repeated, lifting the precious urn.

When she did not obey, he walked over to her. "You cannot spend the next weeks chained to that hearth. Eventually you must move."

"It is warm here. It is the only comfort I welcome or need. In fact, it is a wonderful luxury."

"No fire in your chamber at school? No, I suppose not. And small ones in those that were lit elsewhere, I expect. Madame would justify the discomfort as good for the soul."

He stood near her, the urn casually cradled in his hands. "Take it."

She hesitated. He placed it in her hands. It was much lighter than she expected. Fragile.

"Now, drop it."

She stared at him in shock.

"Drop it."

She glanced down to the hearth tiles on which they stood. "It will break."

"Drop it."

"No."

His hands came over hers. They rested there a moment, the warmth of his palms enclosing her hands, the rough pads of his fingers grazing her wrists. The touch startled her. A deep wave of intimacy flowed through the contact.

She looked at him in surprise. Something unfathomable flickered in his gaze. That startled her even more.

They stood a long time with his hands cupping hers over the urn. Too long. Or maybe not more than an instant. She couldn't tell. Her awareness of him and of their physical contact filled the moments so totally that she had no sense of how much time had passed.

His fingers moved. He pried her hands loose.

The urn slipped away. She watched, horrified, as it fell to the tiles and shattered.

"Now you have broken one and do not have to be afraid of doing so again. They are just objects, Diane. Soulless, lifeless objects. They have no value unless they serve us with their function or beauty. Only a fool is ruled by them."

He spoke quietly and gently. More gently than she ever remembered, as if he were sharing an important secret.

He still held her hands, his pressing thumbs making strange pulses throb in her palms. New lights entered his eyes and the pulse spread. To her arms. To her blood. To her breath and the fire and the air. To the whole chamber.

Another timeless instant. An astonishing one. Compelling and confusing. A little frightening, but touched with dangerous excitement, such as one felt when peering down from a great height.

He dropped her hands abruptly, breaking the spell. He turned on his heel and aimed for the door. "Break one every day if you need to. Tear the chamber apart if it suits you." His voice came harshly, making her wonder if she had imagined what had just happened.

He paused at the threshold and looked back. A little tremor of that pulse passed to her again. Like an echo. Or a distant voice calling.

"Your intentions, Daniel. I would hear them now."

"You say that in an accusatory tone, Jeanette. I am wounded."

"It is not in anyone's power to wound you."

"Perhaps not, but if anyone could, it would be you."

That made her retreat. She relaxed back in her chair and her face lost its strict expression. "Why did you bring her here?"

"I told you, it was necessary." He explained the little drama at the school and the discovery of Diane's true age. "I suppose that I never considered that the years passed for her as well as us. And she appears very young, unless you look closely."

"Perhaps you also found it convenient not to see that she was grown and had to be dealt with."

He ignored that. "She was building up her courage to leave the school anyway. It was just a matter of time. London, she said. To find her life."

"Oh, dear."

"Exactly."

Jeanette's face came to him five times over, the real one multiplied by the mirrors. He did not care for this old-fashioned sitting room with its flimsy furniture and relentless reflections. His own tastes were more restrained, but this was Jeanette's bower and she had decorated it to create a private world. She had filled it with the light and beauty of her childhood, and he neither begrudged her the expense nor the opulence. He would build her an entire palace filled with golden tendrils if that would crowd the darkness from her memories.

"Do you intend to keep her here forever? She thinks that she is going to London."

"She will, eventually. I merely need some time to finish arrangements regarding Dupré first. Then I can turn my attention to England, and to Tyndale."

Jeanette's dark head tilted back in surprise. Concern veiled her green eyes. "Daniel . . ."

"Do not worry. And do not interfere."

She thoughtfully rearranged the long shawl around her shoulders. He waited while she contemplated the little she knew and surmised the rest. He never explained much to her, but she always saw it all.

"She is very lovely," she said. "Unpolished, but that is easily remedied. I will see to it."

"Do not make the shine too bright. It will obscure what is naturally there."

He did not have to say more. She would understand.

Wrapped to her satisfaction, the shawl's long silk ends crossing just so, she drew herself a little straighter. "So many years had passed, that I thought you had given up on it. That it was over. But if you are making arrangements for Gustave Dupré, I suppose not."

"It is only over when it is finished."

"And when you turn your attention to England, you think that you see a way to finish it for good? You plan to try and take down Andrew Tyndale? I do not like it. I do not want it. He is the brother of a marquis. It is not worth the risk. You could lose everything, even your life."

"I won all that I have so that it *could* be finished. It is definitely worth the risk."

"I will not see this girl harmed for my sake."

"It is not only about you. If you think so you are mistaken, and have forgotten too much."

"I forget nothing. Still—"

"I told you not to interfere." He caught a glimpse of himself, eyes and face suddenly hard, in the damnable mirrors. He forced the rancor down. "She will not be harmed in any way. I will not permit that."

"As always, you are very sure of yourself. Perhaps, as always, it will be as you plan. So let us put aside my larger concerns. I will not worry about them until I have cause to. However, the woman in me finds herself also wondering about something much smaller and more ordinary."

Jeanette rarely worried about small, ordinary things. He saw to it that she did not have to anymore. "What is that?"

"You have asked me to look after her. She will be my responsibility and you are a legendary seducer. Therefore I am duty bound to repeat my first question, but in this smaller, more ordinary context. What are your intentions?"

He laughed, to indicate the question was completely absurd.

She did not react. She knew him too well and had probably seen that it was not absurd at all.

"She has her father's eyes. Do you think that I could pursue her, always seeing that?" It was what he had told himself several times during that long carriage ride. Except sometimes she looked at him in that steady, unflinching way and he forgot to see the resemblance for a very long while.

Like just now, upstairs in the Chinese chamber.

"That hardly reassures me," Jeanette said. "But if you plan what I think, you need her innocent. That will check you, should you ever be tempted."

"Now you truly wound me. I do not corrupt young women."

"There are some things even you cannot plan, Daniel. Things that even you cannot control."

"Perhaps, but my appetites are not among them. I am not a total devil." He rose to leave, annoyed with her insinuations. That he had, in fact, been recently moved by something difficult to control did not help his mood.

She laughed. The mirrors showed them facing each other, her shaking her head in amusement and him looking down, a tall dark tower bespoiling this little, glittering, pastel world.

"Ah, Daniel," she said with a sigh. "I am not implying that you are a devil. I am suggesting that you are a normal man. But perhaps that is a bigger insult."

chapter 4

Gustave Dupré plucked two tomes from their shelves and carefully placed them on his desk, angling and opening them to create a haphazard arrangement that spoke of scholarly disarray. It was important for a certain type of visitor to understand that this was the study of a busy man whose advanced intellect did not like distractions of a mundane nature.

He awaited such a visitor now.

He fondly surveyed the many leather bindings on their mahogany shelves while he chose the next book. It was an unsurpassed scientific library, the envy of everyone who knew him. Hadn't Fourier himself come to borrow from it? He had enjoyed making him wait just a bit before receiving him, especially since it had been Fourier who all those years ago had found the flaw in the mathematical proof that Gustave had expected to secure his fame.

Yes, he had enjoyed humbling Fourier. Only a little, of course. They were brothers in science now, equal in status and repute. Another proof had secured that for Gustave, one which even the great Fourier could not pierce.

Adrian, his new secretary, entered the library. "His carriage is here."

Gustave settled himself in the chair behind the desk. "Bring him here when he comes in."

"Do you want me to stay?"

Gustave bristled at the impertinence. Did Adrian dare to suggest that he, Gustave Dupré, could use the counsel of a young pup barely out of university?

If so many of France's own sons had not been killed in the war, he would not have been forced to resort to this English upstart. The young man had been so bold last week as to correct the Latin that Gustave had used in a treatise. Ever since, Gustave had detected a lack of deference.

Presumptuous that, since Adrian was of suspect blood and a mongrel in appearance. The boy was fortunate to have any position at all, let alone that of a secretary to one of the greatest scientists on the Continent.

On the other hand, this visitor had made reference to foreign texts. No doubt such a person considered Latin foreign.

"You may stay. You might learn something." His own writing of Latin might make some slips, but his reading of it was unsurpassed. Perhaps he would have a chance to put this secretary in his place.

Adrian left and returned shortly, carrying three bound books. A tall man, about thirty years old, followed him in.

Daniel St. John accepted Gustave's welcome and took the chair beside the desk. Adrian deposited his burden and moved away to the wall.

Gustave examined his visitor. For a man who had made his wealth in trade, St. John was well turned out and carried himself with an arrogant dignity. Well, money could do that, up to a point, just as learning could. He had heard of St. John, but they had never met.

"It was generous of you to see me," St. John said.

"Your letter describing some rare books intrigued me. I doubt anything will come of it, but I decided that they are worth a look. Tell me where you found them."

"One of my ships was in the eastern Mediterranean. The captain, as a favor to the Turkish sultan, agreed to provide passage to Egypt for a member of the royal court. Unfortunately, the minister died while on board. These were found among his belongings."

And Daniel St. John had not sought to return them to either his passenger's family or the sultan. No wonder the books were being offered privately and quietly.

"I have heard of your library," St. John continued. "And although I cannot begin to make any sense of it, the top book appears to deal with something scientific." He flipped open the cover of the thin volume. "See here. There are drawings and numbers, and not just words."

"This is not a printed book. It is a manuscript."

"Yes. Didn't I mention that?"

He had not. What a fool.

Gustave pulled the volume closer. The writing was not Latin, but Arabic. Hell, he didn't know any Arabic.

He studied the mathematical formulas and the pictures. He paged forward.

A tiny image near a corner caught his eye. It showed rows of cylinders, connected by lines. Now, that appeared familiar. His blood began pulsing for reasons he could not name. It reminded him of how he had felt when he neared completion of that ill-fated proof.

He forced a bland expression. It would never do to reveal his interest. St. John would probably charge a fortune for anything someone really wanted.

His presumptuous secretary craned his neck to get a glimpse. Feeling a spurt of the teacher's largesse, Gustave called him over.

"Arabic," Adrian said with astonishment.

"Brilliant observation."

"I have taught myself some." Adrian's finger went to a line of jottings. "I can translate part of this for you."

Gustave snapped the cover closed, almost crushing the intrusive finger. "M'sieur St. John, would you excuse us for a short while?"

St. John graciously retreated. When the door closed behind him, Gustave turned on his employee. "Do not *ever* presume to instruct me, especially in front of others. I took you on despite your ambiguous history and your lack of fortune, but there are others waiting for your place."

"My apologies. It is just that I thought it might help if you knew what the manuscript was about."

Gustave opened the pages to where he had been. Those cylinders . . . Why did that look so familiar?

Well, what was the good in having a secretary if you didn't get your money's use out of him. "Fine," he said to Adrian. "Tell me what you make of it."

The young man frowned over the dots and dashes. "I do not think it is only scientific, but also mechanical. It appears to have something to do with iron."

Gustave's heart took a huge leap. Rushing blood prickled his scalp and extremities. He stared at the pages, flipping them again and again.

Suddenly he understood why that drawing had appeared familiar. He possessed another manuscript that contained a similar, less developed image, and that also spoke of iron. He could picture it on the top shelf behind him, thin and worn, untouched for years, filled with the ambiguous, incomplete scratchings of a man running out of time.

The excitement almost burst his heart. He thought he would swoon. It was all he could do not to jump up and grab that old manuscript, to be sure he was right.

He only controlled himself because Adrian was in the room. He would need the secretary's help with the Arabic, but he must not let Adrian know what this text might really be about.

If he was correct, the name Gustave Dupré would be immortalized for all time.

He would also become one of the richest men in the world.

• • •

A low fire crackled in the hearth. A tray sat on the table beside the bed. Diane could smell the cocoa steaming in its cup. On her third day here she had come upon Daniel drinking some in the garden and he had pressed a taste of the thick, rich fluid on her. He had found her delight in it amusing, and ever since a cup had been brought to her each morning.

A little ritual had developed to open each day. She would drink the cocoa while the hearth fire warmed the chamber. Then the maid would return and help her to wash and dress. She would go down to the breakfast room, where Jeanette would join her and they would discuss the day's plans. Daniel was never there. By the hour she emerged from her chamber, he was long gone into the city to do whatever it was he did.

Some mornings the ritual altered a bit. If Jeanette was delayed coming down, Diane went for a walk. No one had forbidden that, but she snuck out of the house through the servants' entry anyway, and felt very daring and mature as she strolled among the city's crowds.

She lifted the fragile cup and the deep aroma beckoned her. She sipped the bittersweet substance.

A girl could get accustomed to this.

She gazed at the cocoa. Richly colored, deliciously flavored, very expensive. It trickled down one's throat in a thick flow, bringing a sense of well-being. Like so much else in this house, it was a luxuriously sensual distraction.

Yes, a girl could get accustomed to it, and when she took a position as a governess, the renewal of deprivations would chafe at her.

She threw back the bedclothes and hopped down. She would not lie abed like some queen and await attendants today.

She did for herself and it did not take nearly as long as it did with the maid. She brushed out her hair and secured it in a little knot on her nape and examined the effect in the mirror. It was not very elegant, but it would do.

The breakfast chamber was not empty as she had hoped. Her anticipation of sneaking out for a walk died.

Paul sat at the table in a pose very relaxed for a servant. Beside him, finishing the last of his meal, was the dark presence of Daniel St. John.

Their conversation drifted to her as she passed through the threshold and walked to the sideboard.

"All is in place," Daniel said. "I should hear today exactly when to move. Is it ready?"

"Only the details need to be added, once you get the draw—"

Her back was to them, but she knew she had been noticed. She imagined Daniel's hand rising in a gesture that cut the sentence off.

Sounds scraped behind her. She helped herself to a plate of rolls and allowed herself the luxury of one little sweet cake. She turned, expecting to find the table deserted.

It wasn't. Paul had left, but not Daniel.

He subjected her to a lazy inspection. His gaze lingered on her hair just long enough for her to wish it had been dressed properly.

She could not stand there like some child caught pilfering food. She took a place across from him.

He poured her some coffee from a silver urn on the table. "Your visits to the city are amusing you?"

"Are you being treated well? Do you have any complaints? Are you learning your school lessons?"

That brought his gaze on her very directly.

"The questions. From the school," she explained, too aware of how his attention still flustered her. "You continue to ask them, in a way."

"And are you being treated well?"

His cadence made it clear that they now spoke of *his* care and treatment.

"Very well. I am learning my school lessons too. It is a type of education that your sister gives me, is it not? The visits to this fine city and its many sites. The dancing lessons twice a week. The gentle instructions in comportment. Even the many visits to shops are classes in taste."

"Does this displease you?"

"Only a nun would not enjoy it. I will be the most accomplished and elegant governess in England."

"A refined manner can only enhance your chance to get a position."

"I seek a position with a well-to-do family, not a duke."

"Well, perhaps you will obtain a better one now."

Perhaps she could, but that would not do. She had not been born in such an elevated world. The answers that she sought could not be found in it.

Then again, maybe he was not referring to a position as a governess at all. Madame Leblanc's warnings kept echoing in her mind as this largesse and training were heaped on her. She had concluded that was nonsense, but sometimes this man looked at her in a way that made her remember the breathless moment in her chamber that first day. Nothing would change in his expression, but a tiny flicker of time would expand into another mesmerizing eternity.

Being alone with him here was making it happen again.

She forced her gaze down to her plate, to break that spell. "Anyway, I do feel, sometimes, that I am still in a school."

"A more comfortable one, I hope. Indulge my sister. She has never had a protégée before, and it is giving her great pleasure."

That would be reason enough to set aside her misgivings. However, she could not shake the notion that she was not really Jeanette's protégée, but his.

"Paul is English, isn't he?" she asked, to turn the conversation away from her. "You were both speaking English when I entered."

"He is."

"Are you? He speaks French with an accent, but you do not."

"I am a citizen of the world, but I am French by birth. I have spent many years among English-speaking people. Both languages are natural to me and I probably think of myself as more English than French now."

"That must have been awkward during the war."

"I spent little time in either country during the war. I was normally in the West Indies or the East."

Most of the time, but not all of it. Once a year he returned to France and visited a school in Rouen. She doubted that he had come back specifically for that.

His willingness to speak of himself emboldened her. She had been curious about him for years.

"Your name. St. John. Madame always pronounced it in the French way, *Saint-Jean,* but I saw it written once and it was English."

"I was blessed with a name that is very adaptable."

"So was I. Albret. Madame always spoke it *Al-brey,* but I knew she was wrong and that the 't' should be clear, because I am English."

"What makes you think so?"

What made her so sure of that? It was not only the fragments of old memories, and of crossing the water as a girl. She could not swear to which language had been spoken in those shadowy bits of her life. "I dream in English."

"Your dreams did not lie. You are indeed English. Did you speak English at the school?"

"Madame was a great supporter of Napoleon and refused to hear it spoken even as a lesson."

"Have you lost it, then? Except in your dreams?"

"I have a Bible that is English. I read it aloud every night."

"Of course. The Bible."

He seemed to withdraw, as if mention of the only thing that she had brought with her to France had opened a door that he wanted to keep closed.

She forged on. This was the only chance that she had gotten in two weeks to ask her questions. "How did it happen, m'sieur? How did you come to bring me to France? You say you are not a relative to me."

She did not get her answer. Just as she finished speaking, Paul appeared with Jeanette in his arms, and Daniel deliberately turned his attention to his sister.

Paul settled Jeanette into a chair and prepared a plate for his mistress.

"You will be happy to know that soon we will get Diane out of those hideous sacks. Her final fitting is today," Jeanette said.

Paul placed the plate in front of her. "Unfortunately, mademoiselle, we will have to delay this excursion. M'sieur has requested that I do an errand for him," he explained.

Jeanette shot her brother a sharp glance. "Well, it can wait until another day."

"That is not necessary," Daniel said. "I have no plans for the afternoon. I will accompany you."

No one seemed surprised by the suggestion. Evidently, Daniel carried his sister about the city on occasion.

Jeanette turned from her meal. "Your hair, Diane. Go and have it done so that we can see how the gowns will properly look."

Diane had forgotten about her hair. She excused herself.

Daniel rose and joined her. They strolled along the corridor toward the grand staircase. "My sister is too strict. You hair looks charming like that."

Her heart fluttered at the compliment, gallant lie though it was.

"We will speak English henceforth so that you grow accustomed to it again. You will need that when you go to London," he said, slipping into the tongue of her dreams.

She was glad for evidence that the journey to London had not been forgotten. "When I said that I dreamed in English, you seemed to understand. Do you dream in French?"

"Not always. However, there are other times when my thoughts are only French."

"Which ones?"

They had reached one of the doors off the corridor, and he stopped. "When I am in danger. Only French comes to me then."

The calm mention of danger stunned her. He spoke as if it were a common occurrence.

He opened the door. She caught a glimpse of a man's study.

An amused, reflective expression entered his eyes. "And when I make love. Now that I think of it, I always do that in French."

• • •

"Too much lace, Jeanette. Have them remove the froth at the hem."

"If you keep this up, Daniel, it will be another week before she can leave the house in the evening."

Diane stood on display in the modiste's sitting room in the Palais Royale, decked out in dark violet silk. She might have enjoyed the sibling warmth their bickering revealed, if she had not been the doll over which they fought.

That was what she felt like. A doll being dressed. Not a fine one with porcelain face and hands as befitted these gowns, but a simple cloth doll who would never look quite right in them.

Daniel seemed to understand that better than Jeanette. The sister's own tastes tended toward the dramatic, and the designs had been commissioned accordingly. Now Daniel was demanding that they all be pared of half their embellishments.

He stood at the window of the upper level sitting room, his sculpted face looking very handsome in the diffused northern light. He contented himself most of the time with gazing out at the activity below in the gardens. Each time she emerged from the modiste's back chamber in a new ensemble he would glance, take it in, take *her* in, and issue his order as he returned his attention to the passing city.

He looked again, since his sister had resisted. "I doubt that it will take the women long to remove it. It can be delivered in a day or so. Isn't that correct, madame?"

The modiste quickly concurred. Daniel's presence had turned the proud artist into a submissive servant.

No one had ever asked Diane's own opinion of the garments.

She walked over to a long mirror and peered at herself. The dark violet set off her pale arms and neck. The square neckline's low cut revealed more body than she had ever left uncovered. The cream lace made her skin even whiter, and the high waist emphasized the swell of her breasts.

Dark eyes looked out from a delicate, almost childish face. Those eyes appeared too large and a little frightened, and revealed that the stranger was hardly a worldly woman, despite the sophisticated finery.

The mirror faced the window. A reflected movement caught her eye. Daniel no longer looked out at the city, but at her. Since he stood off to one side, he did not realize that she could see him doing so.

His expression stunned her. Something had entered his eyes and veiled his features. Something vaguely dangerous and utterly mesmerizing. It both hardened him and softened him at the same time.

Her heart rose to her throat. She could not look away, even though something inside her warned her to run as fast as she could.

She smoothed at the silk, to hide her reaction. In the reflection, his gaze slowly drifted down to the forbidden lace at the hem, then up again. It reached her hair, piled artfully in an evening style appropriate to this silk. Her hand instinctively reached for it.

Jeanette must have seen her gesture. "There is too much of it. While attractive like that, the fashion now is closer to the head. We will have it cut."

"No." The command, and it was definitely a command, came from the only man in the chamber.

Diane turned. "I think that I prefer the lace on the hem. I would like to keep it."

Jeanette cocked an eyebrow in the direction of her brother. The modiste began explaining how the lace had been a mistake.

Those devil eyes flashed awareness that he had just been challenged. "If it is what you prefer, of course it can stay. It is your gown, after all. You can have anything you want."

Diane returned to the back chamber to don the next extravagance. She really did not care about the lace. Nor would this garment truly be hers. This fitting was making that clear in ways that she could not define very clearly.

She thought of the various items that would start pouring into her wardrobe. Outfits for morning and afternoon, for calling on friends that she did not have, and for attending dinners for which she did not receive invitations.

She suspected that the friends and invitations would be arranged and chosen as carefully as the gowns themselves. Soon she would be wearing this wonderful wardrobe. From morning until night, she would be the stranger in the looking glass.

Someone's doll.

She remembered Daniel's expression in the looking glass, and how magnetic it had made him. If he had lifted his hand and beckoned her, she might have been incapable of not obeying whatever he requested. She had no evidence that he required anything at all from her, but still . . .

He will seduce you with luxury. . . .

She gazed at the pile of gowns. She should march out there and refuse them all. She should leave that house. She should . . .

The modiste's assistants held out a yellow muslin walking dress. The buttery fabric was more lovely than silk. They began to slide its narrow length onto her body.

Daniel would like this one. Its simplicity would please him.

Those thoughts popped into her head, evoking a smile.

Her reaction dismayed her.

chapter 5

The day after the visit to the dress shop, Jeanette took to her bed with a headache and Diane found herself with nothing to do. It was a fair, brisk day, but not very cold, so she borrowed a book from the library and went out to the garden to read.

She had only turned two pages when she sensed an intrusion in the garden's peace. Looking up, she found Daniel watching her. He stood in front of a row of dormant rose bushes, their bare branches creating a frame of angled, thorny lines around his dark form.

He strolled over. "Are you reading for pleasure or because you are bored?"

"A little of both."

"Then the pleasure can wait while we relieve the boredom. I have decided the day is too fine to spend on business and have called for the carriage. We will visit the Tuileries."

She looked down on her old cloak. "I must decline. My new things have not arrived."

He took the book from her hands. "It is only a carriage ride. You do not need to look like a duchess."

She accompanied him through the house, thinking she would rather not ride alone in a carriage with him again. She had never entirely recovered from the long journey from Rouen.

The carriage waited in all its splendor. Daniel settled across from her and the wheels rolled.

That sense of familiarity, of intimacy, instantly rushed over her with the closing of the door.

She would not let their closeness unsettle her this time. She would demand some information, and he could not get away. It had been convenient of Jeanette to get a headache on a day Daniel was not occupied with his affairs, and Diane did not intend to waste the opportunity.

He glanced at her, barely, to assure himself of her comfort, and then turned his gaze out the window to the passing city.

Not this time, Monsieur St. John.

"How did you find me?"

"I was passing the landing and looked out the windows and saw you in the garden."

"I am not speaking of finding me in the garden. I refer to years ago. How did you come to be my guardian?"

He turned his attention on her. "I am not your guardian, at least not legally."

"That only makes me more curious."

"I expect it does. I knew your father through business. One day I received a letter from him, written hastily. He said that he was called out of the country suddenly and asked me to see to your care until he returned."

"It was kind of you to agree."

"I could not refuse, since he had already left by the time I received the note."

"You must have been a good friend, if he made such a request."

"Not really. I always suspected that he turned to me because I was in London and available."

So her father had left her to the care of a casual acquaintance, a very young man who had probably resented the obligation.

"You must have been very young for such a charge."

"In some ways. In others, not young at all."

She had not expected the story to be this embarrassing. "Why didn't he send me to his family?"

"I believe that he was estranged from his family. As to your mother's family, I do not think that was convenient either. She was dead, and your father never spoke of her."

That made sense. Diane had vague memories of her father, of his dark hair and blue eyes. Mostly she remembered the anticipation of his occasional visits and the joy of his attention. She had no such recollections of a mother. There had been an old woman, however, whom her mind's eye saw a bit more vividly than it did her father. Apparently that was not her grandmother.

"Why didn't you return me to my father?"

"I could not. I arranged for an older couple to care for you, but when no word came, and no one had news of him, I realized that I would have to make other arrangements. What with the war . . ."

His quiet tone told her the truth that his words avoided.

Stark reality hit her in a series of shocks, as though someone kept punching her chest.

Her father was dead.

So was her mother.

She tried to block the onslaught, but the blows kept coming.

She had no family.

There was no reason to search for her life, because there would be nothing to find.

The blankness that existed inside her would never be filled the way she had dreamed. Now that void quaked, as if a mournful cry had shouted and just kept echoing.

Admitting the truth left her horribly bleak. She dropped her gaze so Daniel would not see her reaction.

"His name. What was my father's name?"

"Jonathan."

"Was he a farmer?"

"He was in shipping."

"I remember the country."

"He owned a home in the country, where you lived."

She glanced up. Her brimming tears blurred his face. "Owned? The home is no longer there?"

He clearly hesitated. "He suffered some reversals right before this happened."

The blurring got worse. She saw mostly water. Even the home was gone. Nothing at all waited for her in England.

Her throat grew terribly thick and hot, and her chest dreadfully heavy. She wished that she were back at school in her narrow, familiar chamber. She wished that she was anywhere else except riding in this grand carriage with Daniel St. John.

The silent cry kept echoing. She had never realized before how vast the void was, how vacant. Childish dreams had kept it small, but she would never be able to ignore it again.

That notion defeated her. She gritted her teeth against the tears, but they flowed anyway. The cry got louder and louder.

A movement broke the rhythm of the rocking carriage. A body sat next to her and strong arms eased her close.

She huddled against him and cried out her heart into a wool coat.

He should have lied to her.

He should have told her the elaborate fantasy that he had concocted. It would have kept her looking in all the wrong places, but she would have still had hope.

Facing her earnest, soulful eyes, he had been unable to do it. There had been glaring omissions in his telling, but only one part had been untrue, and he had told that lie to spare her the worst of it.

He held her while she cried, offering the small comfort that a stranger's sympathy provides. Her weeping touched him more than he wanted. He knew the cold isolation that comes from realizing one is totally alone in the world. The difference was that he had been a boy when he faced it, and time hides these things. It never goes away, however. If not for Jeanette, he would have lived with that emptiness his whole life.

He should have lied and let her search for a loving family, lost by some quirk of fate. He should have let her believe a little longer.

Her tears subdued to sniffles. She straightened as one last tear meandered down her cheek. He watched its path on her lovely skin and something besides sympathy branched through him.

The image of her yesterday in the modiste's mirror entered and possessed his mind. So did his reaction, and the little fantasy of that violet silk slowly sliding down her body.

He brushed his lips against that tear.

She turned glistening eyes to him. Cautious, curious eyes. The kiss had confused her, as if she sensed that more than sympathy had provoked it.

Her lower lip still trembled from her efforts to contain her emotion. He came very close to kissing it too.

The carriage stopped with a jolt that brought him to his senses.

Silently cursing himself, leashing both the empathy and the desire, he slid his arm away and opened the door. He stepped out and handed her his handkerchief. "Wipe your eyes. We will walk, and you will feel better."

The familiarity seemed less dangerous suddenly. That little kiss had not frightened her as much as it should have. There had been kindness in it, just as there had been kindness in his embrace.

There had also been something else, however. In him, and in her. Something of what she had seen in the mirror, and of how she had reacted. Like a thin watercolor wash, it blurred the edges of their relationship and changed its tone.

She dabbed at her eyes and wondered if Daniel St. John knew how to make things crisp again.

He handed her out of the carriage and they strolled together. The gardens had enough boxwood and ivies so that all was not barren. Others had taken advantage of the day and a line of carriages waited for the many visitors who dotted the landscape. Despite the air's briskness, an earthy scent announced the arrival of spring.

"Jeanette does not have a headache, does she?" The truth came to her quietly, as if the intimacy in the carriage had opened new insights into this man. "Nor did you see me in the garden by accident. You arranged this, so I could ask my questions."

"I have known that you are curious. Anyone in your place would be. If I have avoided telling you before, now you know why. I fear that I have ruined your dream of visiting England."

"It is not your fault. Even without the dream, I will still go there. It is the place of my birth."

With the ensuing steps and silence, he managed to indeed make things crisp again. He put them back where they had been. She was sorry to feel the mood pass. It had made the blankness a bit smaller for a while.

The new king, restored to the throne by France's conquerors, was in the gardens today, surrounded by an entourage of nobles and ladies. So was the Duke of Wellington, also surrounded by ladies. Daniel identified them for her and pointed out other notables, both famous and infamous.

Daniel included some of those among his friends. He might make his main home in England, but he was well-known in Paris. Aristocratic men in tall hats and hard collars and young dandies decked out in patterned silk waistcoats paused to chat. He introduced her as his cousin from the country. With one glance at her poor appearance, his friends accepted her insignificance.

Elegant, beautiful ladies favored him with warm smiles and appreciative gazes. Twice, women with more worldly expressions engaged him in conversation. Their female companions occupied Diane while Daniel was eased away for some private words.

Something in the way he looked at the second one, and in the way she looked back, made Diane think about that book of engravings. A shocking image entered her head of Daniel doing those things with this woman.

And then, in a flash, she saw him doing them with *her.*

She banished the image, but it made it very hard to continue strolling beside him. She sneaked a glance at his profile. The sensation of that little kiss returned, making her cheek tingle. She felt the rough warmth of his hands on hers that first day in her chamber, and time began stretching into a little eternity again. . . .

"Diane!"

The call pulled her out of the shameful reverie. A young woman, gorgeous in rose wool and golden hair, bore down on her with arms outstretched. A solid, fair-haired man trailed behind her.

"Diane, it is me! Margot!"

Margot had left Madame Leblanc's school the previous year.

Diane accepted the embrace and held Margot back for inspection. The rose wool was very fine, and the brimmed bonnet expertly made. Expensive jewelry finished the effect. Margot appeared beautiful and sophisticated, the equal of any lady in the Tuileries.

This time it was Diane who got eased aside as the companion occupied Daniel.

Margot bent her head close. "Holy Mother, Diane, that is the Devil Man. Have you left the school to live with his family now?"

Diane grimaced. She had always referred to Daniel that way, and the girls at school had taken it up. "For a short while. I will be seeking a position as a governess once we go to England."

Margot rolled her eyes. "What a hellish life. Wait until you see what it means."

"You left to be a governess and it seems your life is not at all hellish. It appears that you have done very well."

Margot's hand went to her necklace and then her hat. "M'sieur Johnson is very generous. You say that you journey to England? M'sieur lives in London, although he has bought me a small residence for when we visit here."

"Then perhaps we will see each other in England."

"Oh, it must not wait for that, especially if you will be jailed as a governess when you are there. You must visit for an afternoon and tell me about all of the other girls."

"If M'sieur Johnson is English, do you have many English friends here?"

"But of course. Paris is full of Englishmen these days. Would you like to meet some? Should I invite you to one of my *petits salons*?"

"I think that I would like that." Daniel had said that her father had been in shipping. Presumably some of the Englishmen in Paris now had moved in the same circles. One of them might know more about Jonathan Albret's family than Daniel seemed to.

There would never be the dramatic reunion she had dreamed of, but finding a family, even if the relatives were distant ones, would be something at least. There would be a few roots tying her to someone, somewhere.

Their escorts strolled over. Margot dipped her head to Diane's ear again. "The Devil Man was frightening when we were girls, but he is very exciting after one grows up. My heart is racing. It is a wonder you do not faint away when he looks at you."

Monsieur Johnson must have seen Margot's appreciation. He took her arm and politely but firmly disengaged her, to continue walking.

"A friend from school?" Daniel asked as they headed back to the carriage. "It must be pleasant to see her again after meeting so many strangers."

"Very pleasant." She pictured Margot's jewelry and gown. "M'sieur Johnson is not her husband, is he?"

"No. My sister can explain such things to you."

She suspected that Daniel, as a man, could explain them better. "I wonder why not. He appeared affectionate. Actually, he looked captivated."

"There are many reasons for such arrangements. He may already have a wife, who is ill, or insane, or cold. Or far away, an Oriental bride. Or perhaps he does not find your friend suitable for marriage."

She thought of the feminine attention Daniel had received this day. She guessed that some of those women had been his Margots. Maybe the last one still was. Only he had not been as enthralled with them as Monsieur Johnson had been with Margot. "Do you have a wife who is ill or far away?"

"Your question is impertinent. But, no, I do not."

"Then you must be one of the men who has not found a woman suitable for marriage."

They reached the carriage. "I am a man who considers himself unsuitable. In declining to marry, I am saving some woman a great deal of misery."

chapter 6

The wardrobe arrived. So did the invitations.

The garments made all the difference. Jeanette's friends began treating her as more than a child and became less guarded in their conversation. One day Daniel accompanied her to the Tuileries again and this time the men flattered her and the women eyed her more closely. Someone who wore fine millinery was no longer insignificant.

Only Daniel did not seem to notice. She might have still been in sacks and braids for all the attention he paid her. He was always polite, but one would have thought the intimacy in the carriage had never occurred.

Despite her newly purchased status, she did not really feel comfortable at the salons and dinners that she attended with Jeanette. And so, when Margot's letter arrived, inviting Diane to visit, she was grateful for the opportunity to spend some time with an old friend.

Dressed in her yellow muslin, she went down to Jeanette's sitting room to tell her hostess of her plans for the afternoon. She found Daniel there with his sister. An unpleasant mood permeated the room, as if she had walked in on an argument.

"You look lovely, Diane," Jeanette said, giving her an appreciative appraisal. "Doesn't she look lovely, Daniel?"

He stood by the window, half-blocking its light, looking out. He glanced over his shoulder. "Yes, very lovely."

"I think that I will stay in today, Diane," Jeanette said. "The last week has exhausted me. You won't mind, will you?"

"Not at all. As it happens, I received an invitation from a friend and would like to call on her. She lives nearby and I think that I will walk."

That pulled Daniel out of his distraction. "You intend to visit Margot? I do not think that is appropriate." His tone implied that the matter was settled and she would not make her visit.

"I appreciate your concern, m'sieur, but Margot and I will be talking about old times, not new ones. I think that I have intruded on a conversation, so I will leave now and return in a few hours." She let *her* tone convey that she would indeed make her visit, even if it displeased him.

"You intruded on nothing important," Daniel said. "In fact, we were discussing you. I will be attending the opera tonight, and you will accompany me. Please be back from your visit in time to prepare for it. Also, if you are walking there, take a servant as an escort."

Diane took her leave, glad to escape the tense mood in the sitting room. She doubted that they had really been discussing her. She truly was unimportant and would not account for an argument.

She also could not ignore that she had not been invited by Daniel to attend the opera, but ordered to do so.

The crowds at the Palais Royale irritated Gustave Dupré. He had been spoiled by the way the war had thinned the population of Paris. Now, with peace, with defeat, the classical arcades surrounding the gardens bulged with not only French but also English and Prussians of every class. In particular, it appeared that the soldiers of the occupying army had nothing to do except stroll through Paris. On a fine day such as this, with the sun alleviating the northern bite still in the air, it would be difficult to find a seat in a cafe or on a bench in the gardens.

It surprised him, therefore, to spy several empty benches. They were in a prized spot, too, where one could watch the fashionable ladies stroll close by, but be spared the noise from the restaurants. Only one man sat on the middle one, reading a book.

Gustave hurried over and settled himself on the stone seat. Cane upright between his knees to support his hands, he basked in the sun. He tried to do that every day it shone. He was convinced that it stimulated his mind.

Today he also hoped that it would calm him. Before tomorrow came, he would know if he was right about that manuscript he had bought from St. John. He would know if his life would change forever.

Two lovely, young women approached. Gustave waited for them to take the free bench, or perhaps even sit on his. To his surprise, something made them turn away.

Gustave checked his garments. Perhaps his breeches . . .

"You are not falling out, Dupré. It is me they avoid."

Gustave's head snapped around. The face of the man sitting on the next bench lifted out of the book that he read. Framed with strands of long dark hair and decorated with an old-fashioned mustache, it broke into a cynical smile.

No wonder all of these benches had been left useless. Gustave began collecting himself, to rise and go.

"Don't be an insufferable hypocrite," his neighbor snarled. "It would be unwise to insult me."

Gustave froze. He eased back down. He gazed toward the arcade with determination, so that anyone watching would know that he was not welcoming any association with the man on his left.

"No greeting, Dupré? No acknowledgment, for old time's sake?"

"I do not greet traitors."

"My, you draw some very fine lines. No doubt your rational analysis has found a way to put some things in one category and similar ones in another."

"Do not try to drag me into your current fall, Hercule. Everyone knows that you sold information to the English. It is why even they despise you now. They gladly took what you offered, but they will have nothing to do with a man so dishonorable."

"Napoleon was going mad, Gustave. He was going to destroy France in his hunger for power. The man who went to Elba was not the same man whom we made emperor. He had lost all notion of reality."

"So, you are a physician now."

"I am a soldier who worshiped a hero, only to watch him become a tyrant. I do not regret what I did. For one thing, it means that I can always find plenty of room wherever I go these days."

Gustave almost snapped that Hercule had not done any of it for France. He had done it in a perverted quest for glory. He had been stupid enough to think that the English would celebrate him when it was all over. "How you can dare to stay in Paris, where everyone knows, is beyond me."

"I stay in Paris to try and learn how it is that everyone knows. I dealt with only one man, a colonel who died at Waterloo. I am curious to know with whom he spoke, and who betrayed me."

Gustave tapped his cane with irritation. He rose, assuming that leaving now would not be the insult Hercule had threatened about. "Good day to you. If we meet again, do not expect me to address you."

"Of course not. After twenty-four years, there is no reason for that to change." Hercule's laugh followed Gustave as he walked away. So did his final question. "Oh, I forgot to ask you, Dupré. How does your famous library grow?"

Margot's house was small but attractive, in a good neighborhood not too far from Daniel's. Margot herself appeared beautiful and mature in a blue dress and silver necklace. *Property and jewels, secured to you.* Whether Margot had ever received Madame Leblanc's instructions, she had clearly followed them.

Diane sent her escort back to Jeanette's house. She and Margot spent an hour reminiscing, then decided to walk in a nearby park.

"I have brought you here because I want you to see something," Margot said. "I meet a new friend here sometimes. Her name is Marie. There she is, with those two children. Marie is a governess to the family of a man attached to the English government."

"From your tone one would think she is dead."

"She may as well be. We only speak here, since she is never free to call on friends or receive them. She cares for those children morning until night, and after they go to bed she is given other work, darning and such. When I left the school I was a governess for several months, so I know of what I speak. Fortunately, I met M'sieur Johnson one day in a park like this and was rescued."

"Then Madame Oiseau did not arrange for you to know M'sieur Johnson?"

"That bird of prey? She offered, but the girls who make use of her service get much less, since their protectors are also paying Madame. In fact, I was insulted and shocked by her suggestion. Three months living Marie's life and the shock wore off."

Diane tried to picture herself in this governess's place. The notion of no time to herself, of little contact with other people, dismayed her. For one thing, how could she ask about her relatives if she never spoke with anyone?

She tried to convince herself that Marie's drab appearance had no effect on her reaction, but she found herself fingering her buttery muslin beneath her cloak.

An English officer approached Marie. Whatever he said got an immediate reaction. She turned abruptly and began marching her charges away. The officer's laugh could be heard all the way to where Diane stood.

"Of course, some of the men one meets in gardens are not gentlemen, whatever their births. Some are not so considerate as M'sieur Johnson," Margot warned. "It is important to be able to tell the difference."

Margot turned the conversation to more pleasant topics. They discussed shops and milliners, and Diane described the wardrobe that had arrived. Margot raised her eyebrows appreciatively at the litany of luxury.

Margot took her hand and began walking out of the park. "We must return. I have invited a few friends to meet you and they have probably arrived already. Englishmen, as you requested."

A small group of carriages lined the street outside Margot's house. One looked too familiar. It belonged to Daniel, and Daniel himself lounged against it.

"M'sieur St. John has come to collect you himself. That is *very* considerate and gentlemanly. And, like the rich gifts that you have been describing, unnecessary."

"Perhaps he thought I would be late returning. We are to attend the theater tonight."

Margot's eyebrows went up again.

"I must go now."

"No. Come in and meet my friends."

"I should—"

"Come in. Let him wait."

Margot did not invite Daniel in. She barely acknowledged him. She ushered Diane into the house, where her friends were drinking wine.

They were an attractive assortment of young people. The four men were English. Monsieur Johnson was not present.

Margot drew Diane to a bench seat in front of the window. Glancing over her shoulder, Diane could see Daniel still leaning against the door of his carriage. Margot brought over one of the men and practically pushed him into place on the bench too.

Margot introduced him as Monsieur Vergilius Duclairc, the brother of an English viscount, then left them alone.

Monsieur Duclairc was a young man, and handsome in a dark, roughly chiseled way, with startling blue eyes.

"Do you live in Paris like these other countrymen of yours?" Diane gestured to the three other men fawning over the women.

"I am only visiting for a short while, to view the sites and attend the theater. I am not one of the vultures who has come to feast on your defeated nation, mam'selle."

To feast on the women made desperate due to that defeat, his tone promised.

"Do you know Margot well?"

"We met through friends a few days ago and she was kind enough to invite me today."

Diane glanced to where Margot, despite her conversation, was keeping an eye on the window seat. "To meet me?"

"I do not know. It appears that may have been her intention, doesn't it?"

Yes, it did. First Madame Oiseau, and now Margot. Perhaps her friend thought of it as a form of salvation.

Monsieur Duclairc certainly was up to Margot's standards. Diane's speculated on what it would be like to be his Margot. She felt her face getting red and an unpleasant sensation knotting her stomach.

"I think it was to meet me so that I could ply you with questions. I will be going to London soon, to take a position as a governess."

"If you have questions about the city, I will be glad to answer them."

"Those are not the sort of questions I mean. I will also be looking for someone's family. Perhaps you have heard of them. The name is Albret."

"Your name. Your relatives?"

"Yes."

"I do not recall ever meeting or hearing of someone with that name. I am very sorry. Is it a London family?"

"I do not know for sure. One of their sons was in shipping. Perhaps, as the brother of a viscount, you did not move in the same circles."

"Perhaps. However, there are ways to search for people if one knows the names. The owner of a ship would have to file certain documents. If he bought insurance, the brokers would have the location of his home, for example. That would be a place to start."

Monsieur Duclairc appeared interested in the idea of unlocking a puzzle. Diane asked him how to locate the brokers who insure ships.

As he began replying, a hush fell over the room and his voice suddenly sounded very loud. A shadow loomed in front of them. She looked up, right into the crisply annoyed face of Daniel St. John.

Monsieur Duclairc appeared startled for an instant. Then a smile broke. "St. John. A happy surprise to see you. I did not know you were in Paris."

Daniel's own smile could have cut steel. "Nor I you, Duclairc. I see that you have met my cousin."

Cautious eyes slid in her direction. "Your cousin?"

"My cousin."

"I had no idea, I assure you."

"I hope not."

Margot had moved to a position where she could observe. Her eyes glittered with triumph. Diane suddenly understood. Poor Monsieur Duclairc had only been a pawn in her friend's game. She had sat them here by the window where Daniel could see the yellow muslin beside the dark coat.

Daniel held out his hand. "Come, Diane."

He beckoned her like an errant child.

"My apologies, M'sieur Duclairc. My cousin forgets sometimes that I am of age."

"Duclairc is well aware that you are no longer a schoolgirl, my dear."

She ignored him and his hand. "You say that you are visiting Paris to attend the theater, M'sieur Duclairc. Perhaps we will see each other again. Thank you for your advice about London." She went over to Margot, kissed her friend, and aimed for the door.

Daniel did not follow immediately. She glanced back and saw him speaking quietly with Monsieur Duclairc. She got the impression of two men clarifying a few things.

Daniel caught up with her as she descended to the lower level. He gripped her elbow firmly, and not entirely in support. "Do not ever do that again."

"Do what? Visit a friend?"

"Keep me waiting."

"I did not ask you to come for me, nor did you indicate that you would. You cannot expect me to terminate my plans merely because it is convenient for your capricious impulses."

"I had the carriage out and came so you would not have to walk back. It was getting late and you have to prepare for tonight."

"I may not choose to attend the opera tonight. It isn't as though anyone invited me."

Acknowledgment of that flickered in his eyes, but his expression barely softened. "Then I invite you now. Indulge me."

It wasn't a true invitation. Not really. She had that sensation of being a doll again. It increased her irritation and embarrassment at being hauled away like this. "You were not invited to Margot's *salon* and it was rude of you to come in. Your sister has taught me that well enough, along with everything else."

His expression turned severe. "I came in because it was obvious that your friend was parading you in front of Vergil and the others as a potential mistress. It was ignorant of you to visit here, and stupid of me not to stop it." He opened the carriage door. "It is time for my sister to explain a bit more to you than how to look elegant. But I will give the first lesson. There are men who enjoy being a pretty woman's puppet and who find Margot's kind of game amusing. I am not one of them. I tell you again—do not ever keep me waiting."

chapter 7

She kept him waiting.

Daniel paced the library, dressed for the evening. First, word came down that Diane would be delayed because the maid had created a mess of her hair, and then a small tear was found in her gown.

"She is doing this on purpose," he said to Jeanette, who read a book near the hearth.

"It is her first time to the theater and she wants to be perfect. Have some consideration."

Jeanette might be fooled, but he was not. This was a deliberate challenge, a woman's way of getting back for the argument this afternoon.

"She is not to visit that woman again. It was not just coffee between old friends. Others were there."

"By others, you mean men." Jeanette looked up from her book. "If you had warned me about this Margot I would have discouraged the visit, but we had no authority to forbid it. Perhaps it is just as well that she went. She cannot be sheltered from such things, here or in London. Her lack of fortune will make her vulnerable. I will not have her ignorant, Daniel. That could lead to catastrophe."

"Then speak with her as frankly about this as you do about silks and bonnets."

"I fully expect that visiting Margot taught her a great deal."

"Perhaps not as you anticipated. Margot might be a bad influence."

"If an afternoon with a man's mistress is a bad influence, I can only imagine what weeks with me have been."

"Jeanette, do not—"

"I am finished with this conversation, dear brother. Rest assured that I will instruct her on the proper protection of her virtue." She made a display of turning the page of her book, but not before she cast him an arch glance.

That look said it all. Jeanette knew. She saw it in his forced indifference to Diane. She recognized tonight's impatience for what it really was, and had recognized his pique upon his return this afternoon as more than a guardian's concern.

He remembered the irrational anger that had built while he watched the yellow muslin nestled close to a dark coat. A good thing it had been young Duclairc. His mood had been black enough that he might have thrashed another man. Whether Duclairc had believed the "cousin" part would not matter. He would retreat in either case.

But what of the others? And there undoubtedly would be others.

He reminded himself that it was the plan and he should be glad of his success. His own reaction was merely an unforeseen complication, and he would conquer it.

Diane entered the library. No trumpets blared, no floral scent filled the air, but he knew of her arrival at once, despite her silent step.

He looked over and his mouth went dry.

She stood a bit stiffly, charmingly unsure of her effect. The violet gown and cream lace made her skin appear to be pale porcelain. Her abundant hair was piled in a loose style that begged to be undone by a man's hands. The other women at the opera would create a riotous bouquet. Amidst their full blooms, Diane would be one discreet rose, its petals barely parted in a teasing lure of what was to come.

It was the plan, and it had succeeded.

Only the wrong man had become enthralled.

"She will do, Daniel?" Jeanette asked.

"Of course, but there was never any doubt on that. However, I should probably bring my sword to protect her from the admirers."

It was the sort of thing a cousin would say, blandly gracious and politely flattering. He doubted it sounded as cool as he had planned, because a deep flush crept up Diane's neck to her cheeks. For an instant, while he approached to escort her to the waiting coach, her gaze met his in that provocative, cautious way that she had.

That was the truly hellish part of this. Not only Jeanette knew. Diane did too. She might not understand it, but she felt it. It frightened her.

As well it might.

It took her the whole way to the theater to recover from that look.

It had only lasted a moment while he walked toward her, but her heart had stopped for what seemed forever. When her pulse began again, it pounded all the way to the opera, because the commanding magnetism still poured out of him like a beckoning force.

The opulence of the theater and the rich finery of the crowd stunned her. She could only look and look, and was sure she appeared as a wide-eyed child.

It was a night of dazzling drama and brilliance. She floated beside Daniel in a dream. His friends visited the box, some whom she had met, like Vergil Duclairc, but most of whom she had not. At the lavish dinner between acts, she spied a few of Jeanette's friends with men other than their husbands. Unlike Daniel and herself, they were obviously not in the company of their cousins.

The surroundings mesmerized her enough that Daniel ceased to do so. The continuous assault on her senses made her heady, and the flatteries of the men's glances and greetings left her feeling bold. After the meal, she and Daniel found themselves alone in the box for the first time all night.

"Why did you bring me here?" she asked.

"Jeanette will not come. She is not shy about her infirmity, but being carried into a theater is too conspicuous even for her."

"Why not bring your Margot? It appears that other men have done so."

"I brought you because I thought you might enjoy it. You have not been to the opera before, have you?" He paused. "I realize that in your case innocence does not mean ignorance, but that was another impertinent question, and I think that you know it."

"I have discovered that I get frank answers when I am impertinent."

"Then perhaps you should ask such questions of my sister. It is more appropriate for her to explain the ways of the world to you."

"I have questions that Jeanette cannot answer."

The second act began then. Its flamboyance distracted her. The beautiful music flowed into her in an emotional torrent. With experience, she suspected she would not react so completely, but this was her first time and she possessed no defenses against the stirring assault on her senses.

She almost forgot about the man sitting to her right. She might have done so completely if he had forgotten about her too. But he watched her periodically. She could feel him do so.

"What questions?" The low query came well into the last scene.

She kept her gaze on the stage. "Since you ask, I have been wondering about something all night. This afternoon you said that Margot had been parading me as a potential mistress. For what purpose are you parading me, m'sieur?"

• • •

No, she wasn't ignorant, despite all those years at that school. She was too smart for that.

She took it all in, seeing clearly despite the blinding brilliance. Her delight was childish, but her assessments very mature. Behind her glittering eyes he could see her mind fitting everything in its place and absorbing the realities flickering beneath the candlelight.

That made it harder. Ignorance would have thoroughly discouraged him. He could have pretended she was still a schoolgirl, for all intents and purposes. But the worldly understanding gave her a woman's presence and provided a foil to her innocence that proved dangerously provocative.

Perhaps he had sensed it that day at the school. His instincts must have told him. It was why she was so perfect for the role.

It appeared that she might be too perceptive, however. *For what purpose are you parading me?*

As he escorted her out, he realized that the answer to her question was not the one that he thought to be true.

He had enjoyed the evening more than he could remember doing in the past. Even the company of a favored Margot, as Diane so neatly referred to mistresses, had never pleased him as much.

He was not just parading her for her education, to provide a bit of polish and to put her at ease with wealth and high society. He was doing so because he was delighted to have her company and to be seen by her side. The world might think of them as cousins, but he knew they were not. He was incredibly proud of her, and had reacted to other men's responses to her in a way that was immediate and personal. And possessive.

This was not how it was supposed to be. He contemplated that as they left the theater to await the carriage.

A crowd filled the area. Not only the attendees milled around, but also city dwellers who came to gawk at the coaches and gowns. Some of the latter shouted insults at the many foreign men exiting the theater, often with Parisian women on their arms. The top reaches of French society had survived the war fairly intact, but the common people of Paris still felt the deprivations and resented the occupying conquerors.

He guided Diane to the edge of the crowd as he saw his carriage inching down the line toward them.

"Sanclare." The furious word, snarled like a curse, pierced the noise. Daniel swerved as a ragged, bearded, fiery-eyed man lunged through the crowd.

Instincts shouting, Daniel grabbed Diane to shield her from the danger. Someone jostled her out of his grasp and she stumbled right into the attacker. The assailant swept her aside and kept coming, snarling the word again.

A knife rose. Daniel grabbed the arching arm and swung his fist with all his strength. The knife clattered to the ground as the madman doubled over. Daniel kicked the weapon away.

It happened so quickly that others nearby had only reacted with dumb astonishment. Now pandemonium broke loose in the crowd. A circle of onlookers formed around Diane. Ignoring the internal voice that warned him to hold on to his attacker, Daniel pushed through the bodies and dropped to his knee beside her.

She was badly shaken and breathless with shock. A streak of horror froze through him when a woman cried that the knife had cut Diane's arm. While other men cleared a path and shouted for the coach, he lifted her in his arms.

In the light of the coach lamp he saw that the cut was not bleeding badly and was only a scratch. The trembling body that he carried, however, said that she was hardly unscathed otherwise.

He got her into the carriage, stripped off his cape, and tucked it around her.

"Who . . . why . . ."

"A madman, perhaps angry with the English. He probably thought me one from the cut of my clothes."

She pulled the cape closer. "I am so cold suddenly."

He lifted her onto his lap so she would know she was safe. So *he* would know she was safe.

She took deep breaths to calm herself. "I feel so stupid. I was not badly hurt, but I cannot . . . I feel as though death just brushed against me. . . . It is foolish to be this unsettled, but . . ."

Death *had* just brushed against her. The thought of how closely, chilled him. He could feel the realization of that sink into her as well, frightening her more.

Her cheek was barely an inch from his face. He brushed his lips against it. "Your reaction is not foolish. It is normal. But you are safe now. We are in the carriage, going home, and he is gone."

She nestled closer and he embraced her more tightly. Slowly, like a lowering veil, her shaking subsided.

He inhaled the scent of violet water and grew too aware of the feel of her body. His concern and relief became colored with other reactions. Their mutual awareness of his embrace filled the carriage, making the silence inaudibly crackle.

He pressed a kiss on her silky hair, to reassure her. For an instant she went very still. Then her head turned up to him. He could not see her expression in the dark, but he had no trouble imagining its cautious confusion.

If not for the danger they had just faced, he might have resisted. If fate had not put her in his arms, he would have heeded the voice of reason chanting the hundred reasons why it was a disastrous mistake.

Instead, he took the step that would complicate everything, and perhaps undo plans laid a lifetime ago.

He kissed her.

She should have guessed the kind of kiss it would be. Even before his lips touched hers she should have known it would not be one of comfort. The mood in the air and the tightening of his arms warned her. So did the little infinity that spread to surround them while he looked at her.

He would have stopped if she had turned away. She did not doubt that. But his embrace felt so safe and the kiss did too. Startling, but sweet and gentle at first.

Not for long.

It changed in ways she could not ignore. The warm press grew insistent, then demanding. She permitted it because she did not know how to refuse. A new, awed part of her did not want to.

Her reaction, the thrilling excitement and deep inner flush, explained so much. Everything. Why being alone with him unnerved her. The reason his dark gaze made her flustered. The power behind his magnetic presence. The kiss was a little fulfillment of a nameless expectation that she had been experiencing with him for weeks.

It mesmerized her. The intimacy felt so wonderful. It awoke parts of her body and heart she had not known could feel this alive. It was the most astonishing, transforming thing that had ever happened to her.

He didn't stop. The one kiss became many, each one burning into her, startling her again. On her lips and her face and her neck. A series of pleasurable shocks left her senses jumbled in a chaos of amazement.

The little infinity just grew and grew until what was happening became a dream taking place in the eternal darkness of a silent carriage. Nothing entered her mind except the wonder of it.

His teeth edged her ear, sending alluring chills through her body. His embrace wandered down her side, pressing through the thick cloth of his cape. "Are you still afraid?"

"No . . . yes . . . a little . . ."

"Of me now?"

He caressed her face, and his hand smoothed lower, to her neck. She could not believe what the meandering caress did to her.

"That is probably wise."

She could not heed the little warning. The sensations streaming through her skin distracted her too much.

So did the next kiss. If his words suggested she stop this, his actions demanded that she not. The searching strokes of his fingers on her skin lured her into a wonderful madness. His passion was all in his actions—she was the one whose gasps and sighs filled the carriage.

He touched her mouth. He coaxed her lips open. Fingers sliding into her hair to hold her firmly, his teeth played at her, teasing with nips. His tongue flicked to touch hers, then entered.

The invasive intimacy sent deep, visceral thrills down to her hips. It served as a stark announcement of what they were doing and a bolder warning than his words had given.

The warmth of his embrace and the beauty of this small joining defeated her. She had never been held in any way in her life, let alone like this. Never been wanted by anyone. Never felt so alive in her essence. A poignant sigh of relief choked her. She wanted to nestle forever in this human connection.

He kept taking more. More of her body and will. He had her in a tiny place full of pleasure, where her selfness got blurred away.

"Are you still cold?"

She shook her head. They could be lying in the snow and she would not be cold.

He peeled away his cape and let it drop to the floor. Kissing her deeply, his fingers unlaced the tie of her cloak and pushed its edges back from her body. A chill shook her that had nothing to do with the temperature.

His chest crushed her arm. Without thinking, she slid it away and up around his shoulders.

A twig might have snapped, so clearly did the mutual embrace change him. His kisses became insistent and his caresses bolder. Her body reveled shamefully in its discoveries. The breast not pressed against his chest itched resentfully from the lack of contact. The whole of her silently urged his hand to move in different ways.

As if he heard, his caresses stroked lower. With long, warm lures through the thin silk, he touched her body with scandalous intimacy. Tilting his head, he kissed to the skin above her gown, then to the gown itself. The heat of his breath beckoned and she arched toward it. His mouth teased at her breast, nipping through the silk, closing on the tip.

It made her crazy. She had never thought anything could feel so good and necessary. The pleasure, and the desire for more, totally conquered her.

And he gave more. His embracing arm shifted her, so he could encompass her more securely. Even as he aroused one breast with his mouth, his hand slid up to titillate the other. He coaxed cries out of her and encouraged her to relinquish herself to the delicious euphoria.

She could not resist what was happening. She did not know how to. She did not *want* to.

He paused and gazed at her. She sensed a brittle tension rise in him, waver, and then soar higher. His hand swung back and knocked on the carriage wall.

He kissed her deeply and caressed her with a possessive hand that knew no restraint. The little pause had given her back a bit of sense, however. Reality intruded for an instant. She saw starkly what was happening and could not ignore the scandalous implications of how he now handled her.

He took her breast in his mouth again and stroked higher on her legs. She tottered on the edge of total abandon again. Her body desperately wanted to succumb and something uncivilized in her soul did too. The pleasure promised her that it would be wonderful. But another voice, barely surviving, warned it would be dangerous.

She forced her arm to drop from his shoulders. She leaned away. "We must not. You know we must not."

It took all of the strength she had. Too much of her rebelled at the denial and prayed he would not accept it.

He looked at her. His hand still rested on her thigh, raising anticipations she dared not acknowledge. Even as he stopped he lured her.

If he kissed her again she would be undone.

He released his hold on her body. "Of course. You are right. The danger got the better of us both. People often forget themselves at such times."

He eased her from his lap to the seat beside him and slipped her cloak around her again. Her heart twisted. He had offered an excuse for them both, but mostly for her.

He rapped on the wall again. He did not pull away or move to the other seat. He even kept his arm around her. It felt as if he did that out of kindness, so that she would not feel too embarrassed.

She sensed him putting distance between them despite their closeness. Before the carriage rolled to a stop, she knew that he intended to keep what had happened within the time and space in which they had just existed.

She should be grateful, but as he handed her out and escorted her to the door, a heavy sadness lodged beneath her heart.

The candles in the entryway barely illuminated his face as he walked her to the staircase.

"You should go to your chamber now, Diane. Have a maid clean your arm."

His actions were as cool and courteous as ever, his words calm and bland. His composure astonished her. *She* could barely breathe.

She hurried up the curving steps. Halfway to the top, she glanced back. Daniel had not left. He watched her with an expression that caused her legs to go liquid.

He did not appear nearly as contained as he had acted and sounded. A male speculation flickered in his eyes, dangerously.

She suddenly understood the meaning of his first rap on the carriage wall. That knock had been a signal for the vehicle to keep moving and not return to the house. If she had not stopped him . . .

Face burning, she climbed the steps more quickly, a little worried that she would hear his step behind her.

She had come perilously close to being ravished in that carriage.

chapter 8

Daniel moved silently and invisibly through the dark streets of the sleeping city. He tried to contain his thoughts to the matter at hand, but they kept flowing back to the sweet passion of a young woman in a dark carriage.

He cursed under his breath. It was inexcusable that tonight of all nights he had let pleasure distract him. He could have destroyed everything in one reckless impulse. If he had remained in that carriage, the delay would have jeopardized not one but two goals.

He never lost control to anything, least of all lust. Now he almost had, and it infuriated him.

He tried to hang on to his anger, but the memories kept returning, cooling his rancor with their sweet breeze, luring him away from his determination.

He paused in the shadow of a doorway. He would never be able to complete tonight's work like this. Thoughts of Diane's sighs and softness would make him careless.

Cursing again, he forced himself to a different path. His legs carried him, but his spirit rebelled.

He found his way to a place he never visited except when he needed the starkest reminder of who he was. His carriage never passed by this square and he rarely walked within three streets of its location. He avoided Paris itself because of this place. He resented like hell that he had to come here now, to stoke the fires of his resolution and to punish himself for briefly forgetting the reason he even stayed alive.

He leaned against a wall and gazed at a very specific spot in the darkness. He knew exactly where it was, how many paces away. It was just another group of paving stones among many others, its horrible history scuffed into oblivion by thousands of feet.

Memories assaulted him. Old ones, too vivid considering their age. Memories of horror and of dreadful helplessness. Ugly sounds and uglier sights, and eyes reflecting the onset of terror in one final glance.

He did not stay long but it might have been a lifetime. It *had* been a lifetime. He avoided this particular place, but his soul was never very far from it.

He aimed toward the destination almost forgotten while he held Diane in his arms, and toward the purpose almost abandoned to the impulse to possess her.

The house was dark, full of night's repose. Daniel scanned the facade up to the small garret windows set above the eaves. A tiny, flickering light peeked through the gloom from one of them.

He walked through the alley to the house's rear. He stripped off his coat and dropped it behind a bush. Feeling for the deep joints of the corner quoins, he edged his way up the wall.

No waistcoat impeded his movement. His black shirt would reflect no moonlight. He was a dark form inching over a dark mass.

He reached the second level and felt for the window to his left. His fingers clawed under the slight protrusion where it had been left slightly ajar. He carefully eased it open, swung around it, and entered the chamber.

The lowest embers still burned in the fireplace, but he did not need them. He recognized his destination from its bizarre profile atop a long table. Slumped into a chair beside it was the sleeping form of a man too anxious to go to bed, but too exhausted to stay awake.

Daniel examined the apparatus. Two cylinders rested on a wooden frame and wires extended into a pan of liquid. Using a stick of wood, he lifted the wires from the pan, memorizing their correct positions. He dipped his fingers into the liquid and his touch closed on a solid, squarish piece of metal. He felt its shape, noting the one blunt corner and the vague incisions along the surface.

Reaching into his pocket, he removed another piece of metal with identical markings. He switched it for the one beneath his fingers, replaced the wires, and strolled back to the window.

He slipped out and found his toeholds on the rusticated quoins. He pushed the window closed. By morning it would be locked.

He dropped to the ground and headed back through the dark streets. His part was done. Vanity would take care of things after this.

Now, he would finish the rest of it.

The garbled curse of a madman echoed in his mind. It must be concluded quickly, too, because time might be running out.

• • •

Everything had changed and Diane could not pretend it hadn't.

Daniel acted as though the lapse in the carriage had not happened, but the return of his polite indifference could not put them back where they had been this time. What they had done hung in the air during the meals and brief periods when she shared his company, and occupied her thoughts even when they were apart.

She could not suppress a new susceptibility to his presence. The magnetism was always there, making her heart pound. He did not even need to look at her for one of those infinities to begin. She kept expecting him to walk over and kiss her again. She worried that he would show up at her chamber door.

Worse, she was not entirely sure that she would refuse him that kiss, or even more. Not if he made her feel what she had in that carriage.

Which meant that she could not in good conscience stay in his house any longer.

During her social rounds with Jeanette, she let it be known that she would not be adverse to a position as a companion or governess if any of Jeanette's friends knew of such a situation. She made it clear that she would prefer an English family. That way she might eventually be brought to England and in the meantime might meet people who had known a family named Albret.

She went down to the breakfast room a week later to find Daniel making one of his rare morning appearances. Jeanette and he sat quietly together. Diane joined them, but silence descended after the initial courtesies.

Finally Daniel excused himself. "When you are finished here, Diane, I would like you to come to the library. There is something that I need to say to you."

She did not hurry her meal. He was probably going to apologize and make more excuses for them both. She would prefer to avoid the topic altogether.

Jeanette called for Paul. As the servant lifted his mistress in his arms, Jeanette looked down at her. "My brother has set aside important business to speak with you. Please do not make him wait too long."

She might have left him waiting forever but for that pointed request.

She found him in the library, sitting in a chair by the hearth. Another one had been moved near it, for her. He appeared distracted when she entered, much as he had on that journey from Rouen.

She thought of how often she had seen that expression, even at meals sometimes, even as he conversed with Jeanette. His air of indifference was partly explained by the impression that part of his mind was always occupied elsewhere.

He brooded over something and she doubted it was Diane Albret. Business? Shipping? She did not think so. It was deeper and older. It was something much more personal. It was always there, a dark force rippling through his body and presence like a barely contained energy.

She sat. He glanced over, then returned his gaze to the fire.

"My sister tells me that you have been asking her friends to inquire about a position for you."

"It seemed the sensible thing to do. There are many English families here."

"Most are attached to the army or government. It may be a long time before you go to England."

"Then I will have to wait. From the looks of things, it will also be a long time if I stay in this house."

"Not at all. I informed Jeanette this morning that we will be leaving for London in several days."

That stunned her. There had been no indication of such plans. It seemed odd to announce a departure so suddenly.

"I would like you to reconsider this decision to go off on your own. I would also like to propose a small change in your plans once we arrive in England."

"What kind of change?"

"An appealing one, I hope. A better position for you than that of a governess."

She braced herself. She could not believe he was going to be this bold.

"My sister has grown fond of you. She will be accompanying me this time. She will not be comfortable going about as she does here. A companion will ease her isolation."

She gazed at this handsome man, confidently relaxed in the other chair. No wonder Jeanette had been so quiet at breakfast. His sister probably suspected what he was up to.

Maybe Jeanette did not just suspect. Perhaps she knew. That was a sad notion. Diane had grown very fond of Jeanette. It had been a little as she imagined having a sister would be. She did not care for the idea that maybe Jeanette had been deliberately grooming her to be Daniel's lover.

From what Daniel was proposing, and considering what had passed between them in the carriage, that was the true position waiting for her in England.

That did not shock her as much as it should. A part of her had been waiting for this overture all week. Maybe all month. Still, she wished it weren't true. It tainted all of the kindnesses and soiled all of the generosity and made what had happened after the opera a calculated seduction.

It also rankled her that Daniel thought she was so stupid that she wouldn't see this ruse for what it was.

"We would continue in England as we have here?"

"Yes."

"I would be free to go calling, and have friends? You would provide for my wardrobe and other needs?"

"Of course."

His utter calm annoyed her. He might be at least a little chagrined. "What happens to me when your sister returns to Paris and you no longer have need of me?"

"By then you will have several options, including the original one of being a governess. No doubt you can be a companion for another lady. You might marry, which is not a likely prospect if you are a governess."

Daniel St. John was no Monsieur Johnson, it appeared.

"If I accept this position, I will be unsuitable later as a governess, or companion, and especially as a wife. After this position, no one would ever consider me for one of those, and you know it. You could at least have the decency to do as other men, and offer me property and jewels or some settlement."

He looked over with a startled expression, and then with an amazed one. She definitely had all of his attention now.

"You have misunderstood me, Diane."

"I understand very well. I have always understood in my heart, but ignored the evidence. You have been overly generous and introduced me to luxuries and comforts beyond my dreams. I own a wardrobe the daughter of a count might envy. I am presented as a lady and live like one. Madame Leblanc warned me of things before I left with you, and I understand now that she was correct."

"I can see how it might look to you, especially after what occurred in the carriage."

"*Indeed.* I may not be very worldly, but neither am I as stupid as a cabbage."

"I assure you again that you have misunderstood."

His eyes held amusement, and also a charming warmth.

A dreadful thought poked at her. Perhaps she *had* misunderstood?

"You really speak of my being your sister's companion, and no more? That is all that you will expect of me?"

"That is all that I will expect of you."

Humiliation flooded her. It was bad enough to accuse him of such a thing, but to have been wrong . . .

She covered her face with her hands and laughed at herself. "I . . . Oh, dear . . . This is very awkward . . ."

"There is no reason for you to feel awkward." He spoke, and looked, more kindly than she had ever seen him. "You wonder about my intentions. I don't blame you. The last weeks must have confused you. What was the point of this generosity? Why turn you into a lady if you only sought to be a governess?"

"It *has* been peculiar, and exactly what Madame predicted."

"Then I fulfilled the prediction last week. I promise you, this is not a grand scheme to get you into my bed."

She blushed hotly and was grateful when he rose and went to the fire.

He gazed at it. "I should probably admit that the generosity has not been without benefit to me, as will be your presence in my household in London. I am a man of affairs. Wives and women relatives are very useful to men such as myself. My sister's infirmity means that she cannot attract the attention of men whom it would be profitable for me to meet. You will, in London as you have already done here. There is nothing sordid to it. It is the way of the world. With a lovely cousin in society, my circles will expand, that is all."

"Do you expect me to encourage these men?"

"Not at all. It will happen without any effort on anyone's part. Admirers will appear. I will meet them and their fathers and uncles. Cards will be played at clubs, business will get done, and you will be none the wiser."

She wiped tears of embarrassed laughter from her eyes. "I thank you for explaining this. It certainly gives the last few weeks more sense. After what Madame said . . . well, it appeared as though . . . and then the opera . . . but I see that was truly a result of the danger. It is reassuring to know that you do not think of me in that way."

He turned. "I did not say that I do not think of you in that way."

Her giddiness disappeared with one sharp intake of breath.

"There is no reason to be afraid, Diane. That we took a first step does not require me to take any more. You are very lovely, and, like most men, I will notice and react, that is all."

"If I continue living in your home, that may be quite a lot. You say that you will expect nothing more of me. I want total honesty now. Will you *request* anything more? Was Madame correct? Are you thinking to ask me to be your mistress?"

"It is not my intention. As to what I think, I cannot always control that."

His ambiguous response hardly reassured her. Nor did his expression. Her heart pounded with caution and an excitement that she did not want to acknowledge.

"If I did ask, what would you say?" He spoke as if he voiced an idle curiosity.

She stared at him, dumbfounded.

"Because if I thought that you would say yes, I might be badly tempted."

"I want a promise that if I stay with Jeanette you will never yield to that temptation."

"I cannot give such a promise. Like most men, I usually leave the progression of such things to the woman, as I did with you the other night. You did not really want to stop and it could have easily ended differently. One more kiss, one more caress—that I did not take that step should reassure you now more than any glib promise."

"You astonish me. You say in one breath that you expect nothing of me, and in the next that if you did I would not resist you."

"You demanded honesty and I am giving it."

Too much honesty. It was embarrassing to have her weakness so bluntly described. Nor did his indication that the future of her virtue lay completely in her hands, reassure her.

Because she *had* been weak, and he unsettled her so much that she did not know whether she could be strong again.

She dropped her gaze to her lap, where her fingers twisted together, much like the confusing snarl of her reactions and emotions.

"Diane." It was a quiet call for her attention. One word, commanding and gentle at the same time.

She looked up. He stood before the hearth, dark and dangerously handsome. The flames peeked around the sides of his legs as if the fire had given him his substance. His gaze compelled her attention.

Her childhood name for him leaped into her mind, more appropriate than she had ever guessed. The Devil Man. A prince of temptation.

"Diane, do you want me to take that next step? Do you want to be my lover?"

Shock almost stole her voice. "I certainly *do not.*"

He came over to her. She shrank against the chair in a vain attempt to keep some distance.

He lifted her chin in his hand and gazed into her eyes, rendering her incapable of resistance. His rough thumb swept across her cheek and a scandalous thrill snaked down to her heart.

"You are lying. You are not at all certain."

He dropped his hand and walked to the door. "Consider my sister's offer. It is a chance to have some kind of life. And you are safe from me, for many reasons."

chapter 9

"Diane, this is the Countess of Glasbury," Jeanette said.

The visitor sitting in the London drawing room had dark hair and fair skin and eyes that sparkled with warmth. She was much younger than Jeanette, not much older than Diane herself. She did not appear nearly as proud as the French countesses whom Diane had seen in the Tuileries or at the opera.

The eyes might be friendly, but they inspected her all the same. "What a lovely young woman you are, Diane. She will be a magnet for attention, Jeanette. I expect that my brothers will fall in love as soon as they meet her."

"As it happens, one of them has already met her," Daniel said.

Diane turned to the window. She had not noticed Daniel when she entered the drawing room.

"One of the countess's brothers is Vergil Duclairc, whom you met in Paris," he explained.

"You have met Vergil? That is wonderful. We expect his return from Paris any day, so there will be one familiar face for you."

Diane doubted the countess would be so enthusiastic if she knew the circumstances of that first meeting, and the purpose of Margot's *petit salon.*

"The countess has agreed to be your chaperon when you attend assemblies and balls," Jeanette explained.

"Only until we can coax you to attend them yourself, Jeanette," the countess said. "I will be giving a dinner party this week, on Thursday. Daniel, perhaps you and your cousin would join us. I will have the invitation sent at once and expect your acceptance. It would have been extended earlier if I had known you were returning to London." She leaned toward Diane, as if making a confidence. "It will not be a large group. You should find it an easy introduction."

She took her leave. Diane tried to absorb that she had just become a protégée of an English countess. It made no sense. In Paris, Jeanette moved in elevated circles, but not the highest ones. Her friends had been wealthy and a few had been *petits* aristocrats, but she had not been among the women who dined with nobility.

"The countess is very generous," she said. "I think that I will be imposing. I do not belong at her dinner party, and everyone will know it."

"It will not be as you expect. The countess is a bit *outrée.* That I am her friend shows that," Daniel said. "She prefers the more democratic circles to the strictly fashionable ones, which is just as well, since the best ones do not accept her."

"Why not?"

"She separated from her husband."

"Insufferable hypocrites," Jeanette snapped. "A woman leaves a disreputable husband and she is punished. Not even for another man did she leave. And the women who cut her by day are jumping from bed to bed by night. The English are *such* a people. It still astonishes me that you can live among them, Daniel. At least in France we do not use this pretense of high morality to wound others when we are no better ourselves."

Daniel ignored his sister's outburst. "The countess is one of several women of her standing who have a very mixed group of friends, Diane. You will find your evenings diverting enough, even if you never get into Almack's."

Jeanette rolled her eyes. "Thank God for that. The worst of the worst."

"Perhaps the countess was correct, mam'selle, and you will agree to accompany me some of these evenings," Diane said.

"I do not care for English society. There is no reason for you to suffer because of my whims, however, and my brother has seen that you will not."

He had not only seen to her diversion. He had seen to it that she would be paraded about, to attract the men who could benefit him.

Diane was determined to keep the reasons for all this generosity in mind.

Jeanette appeared agitated. She had been out of sorts since they set sail from France on one of Daniel's ships. It had gotten worse when they arrived at this London house a day ago.

"Perhaps you would like to get some air in the garden, Diane," she said. "I wish to speak with my brother about something."

It was the most direct dismissal that Jeanette had ever given. Diane excused herself.

Something had changed since coming here. The relationship between brother and sister had gotten brittle.

. . .

"Do not ever do that again," Jeanette hissed.

Daniel heard the scathing tone and saw the fiery eyes. He regretted her distress, but could not help thinking that Jeanette in high dudgeon was better than Jeanette floating through life in a haze of Parisian memories.

"Do not *ever* invite your friends to call on me like that. Receiving the countess in Paris was one thing, but this is another. I agreed to come here, after all these years, for Diane's sake and yours, but I made very clear that I would not leave this house. I will not have these women cajoling me, be they countesses or wives of shippers or your lovers."

"There is no harm in accepting calls, even if you do not go out. It is not healthy for you to become completely reclusive."

"Do not tell me what to do. Do not dare. Never forget that I am the one woman in the world who is not in awe of you. Paul and Diane will be company enough."

"And when someone calls on Diane? It is bound to happen eventually."

"You *swore* that Tyndale would not come here."

"He will not, but I expect others will."

"Then I will be the gray presence in the corner, reading a book."

He had asked a great sacrifice of her, in demanding that she come this time. It pained him to see her grappling with the emotions that England evoked.

He went over and laid his hand on her shoulder. She looked up at him. The anger slid from her face, revealing the real emotions that absorbed her.

He patted her shoulder in reassurance. She tilted her head until it rested on his side, and his touch became an embrace.

"I am not being fair," she said. "It has all fallen on you, and I should not complain of a bit of discomfort. I only hope that it will be finished quickly."

"As quickly as it can be, darling."

She sniffed. He was glad that he could not see her tears, or her attempts to swallow them.

"There is one thing, Daniel. I said it at the beginning, and I say it again now. I will not have her harmed in any way. She has become quite dear to me. And I know that you want her, but it cannot be."

It cannot be. He had not needed Jeanette to tell him that. It chanted in his head by night and day. Mostly by night.

In Paris it might have been, and almost was. He had been sorely tempted to put aside everything else to make it so. He still was, sometimes, when he saw her as he had today, entering the drawing room, so delicate in her soulful beauty.

It was easy to forget everything then. Who she was and how he knew her and that she might be the means for quickly fulfilling a lifetime goal.

He left Jeanette and went to the garden, seeking Diane even though he should not.

There was no point. *It could not be.*

He went anyway.

The garden was larger than the one in Paris, and less formal. It suited the house and the Mayfair street lined with other impressive facades. Its plantings, natural and free in the English style, pleased him.

There were neighbors on the street who did not like that he occupied this premise. Those who, unlike the Countess of Glasbury, cared a great deal about how he came to afford it. He knew that he had appeared a *parvenu* when he took possession of this house, a case of a shipper plopping himself among his betters where he was not wanted.

He did not care about such things and would ignore them even if he did. He was here for a reason.

He found Diane sitting on a bench under a leafless tree, wrapped in her old school cloak. She owned better ones now and he wondered why she had called for this one instead. It did not even cover her properly, and only reached halfway down her legs.

He paused and watched her. She should have had a cloak at school that fit her better. He had left money every year for her care, but had never investigated if it actually was spent on her comfort. Apparently much of it had not been, if at twenty she still wore a cloak probably bought when she was thirteen.

Welcomed or not, she had been his responsibility. He had not taken care of her very well.

Which was another reason why *it could not be.*

He strolled toward her.

She watched him approach, with eyes that appeared almost as accusing as Jeanette's had.

"You forced her to come here, didn't you?" She hit him with the question even before he got to her. "I am not here to accompany her. *She* is here to accompany *me.*"

After an attack like that, sitting beside her was out of the question. "She is here because I needed Paul with me, and she has grown dependent on him."

"Then Paul must be more than a manservant who helps an infirm woman."

He had anticipated some pleasant conversation and the guilty pleasure of her company, not this incisive probing. The same notion struck him as it had at the opera, that, despite her inexperience, her perceptions were very sharp.

"Paul is much more than a manservant. I have known him for years, and on occasion he performs other duties than aiding my sister. He is one of the few men whom I trust completely. In fact, I would never let a mere servant assist her as he does. Now, are there any more questions or accusations that you want to pose?"

She cocked her head. "Yes. What is that noise?"

She spoke of a low, distant rumble that emerged on the breeze periodically. It had become so commonplace that he did not hear it anymore.

"A demonstration. They happen with some frequency now. There is dissatisfaction with government policies."

"It must be a very large one if we can hear it. The ones in Paris were not so loud."

"In Paris there was an occupying army to make sure they were not."

She glanced away, to a prickly hedge that cut the garden in half. "The countess appeared very familiar with you. Is she your Margot? Do not worry that your answer will shock me. Paris, and the gossip of Jeanette's friends, jaded me very quickly."

"Why do you ask?"

"I am curious."

"Why are you curious?"

She shrugged.

"If I say that she is, will you be jealous?"

"Of course not."

"I can think of no other reason for the question, Diane."

She blushed deeply. He watched the flush lower and thought it would be very nice to follow its path with his lips.

She noticed his gaze and that wary look entered her eyes. It was not as cautious and innocent as it had been during the first days in Paris.

She gave an almost coquettish smile. "I would not be jealous, but reassured."

The bold reference surprised him. He expected her to never again mention her suspicions of his intentions.

He came very close to telling her that it did not work that way, that a man could have ten Margots and still pursue another.

"The countess is only a friend. As for reassurance, my word will have to do. Now, if your questions are finished, allow me to pose a few of my own. Is your chamber adequate? Are you content?"

"Do you have any complaints? Are you learning your lessons?" She used his own inflections as she repeated the old school questions, and even dared to mimic his voice.

She glanced at him with an impish expression that made him laugh. She laughed too.

It was an astonishing moment, a little slice of euphoria. He did not doubt that she poked fun at more than his questions. She saw the deeper absurdity. They maintained these little formalities of host and guest, of guardian and ward, to contain the danger.

But she was drawn to the danger. With her impertinent question she had fluttered around its fire, not even realizing how flirtatious her reference and her smile and her laugh had been.

"My chamber is quite adequate and I am content enough. I am curious about this social life that you have planned for me, however. A mixed crowd, you called it. Not a small circle, I hope."

"Not at all. Why do you ask?"

"A small circle would not suit me, nor would one that was only composed of the highest society. I am here for a reason besides being a companion for your sister and a lure for your business."

"What reason is that? To make a marriage?" He said it lightly, hoping she would laugh again.

"To find out about my family."

That was not something he wanted to hear. He might have even preferred to hear she looked for a husband. "I thought that you had concluded there was nothing to find."

"My parents may be gone, but my history is not. I intend to begin searching for it tomorrow."

Hell. He imagined her polite questions to all those people in that mixed, fluid circle of the Countess of Glasbury. Possibly, eventually, she would get enough of an answer to cause the very problems he hoped to avoid.

"For example, Mister Duclairc said that if my father was a shipper, his ships might have been insured. I intend to find out if they were. Where would I go for that? As a shipper yourself, you should know."

Was it his imagination that she watched him very closely as she waited for his answer? Maybe so. Maybe not. For an instant her eyes reminded him of her father's. That had not happened for a long time.

The flirtatious pleasure he had been taking in their exchange died. Seeing the resemblance brought down a wall that laughter could never scale. Even desire could not.

He welcomed the barrier. It was good to be reminded of the primary reason why *it could not be.*

"Certainly I know where to go. If you can wait a few days, I will take you to the offices of the insurance brokers myself, so that you can make your inquiries."

Her expression lit with delight. "You will help me?"

"Of course. You had only to ask."

She had never appeared so happy. He half-expected her to embrace him with gratitude. It both relieved and disappointed him when she did not.

He took his leave, and she favored him with a dazzling smile full of newborn trust and belief. It provoked vague considerations of ways to make her look at him like that forever.

Paul was waiting for him inside the house. He handed over a letter that had come.

Daniel read the message. "I will be riding out to Hampstead this afternoon. I want you to stay here with my sister, Paul. It will be some time before she is comfortable here without one of us nearby."

"She may never be comfortable without us. Not here."

No, not here. Daniel looked out the window. Diane still sat in the garden, lost in her thoughts. He wondered what occupied her mind. Dreams of triumph in London society? He doubted it was that.

"Remind the servants here about Diane's chamber, Paul. It is to be the same as in Paris. The fire is to always be built up during the day, even when she is out. She is never to return to a cold hearth."

The two men went at each other with sabres, performing a rigorous dance of danger.

Daniel watched from the threshold of the Hampstead dining room. Stripped of furnishings and rustic in its Tudor charm, the chamber rang with the clash of steel.

He did not much observe the tall, thin, graying swordsman, the one dressed in old-fashioned breeches and a waistcoat of blue silk. That one's moves created fluid lines of poetry, and his cool dark eyes remained impassive.

It was the other, the one with fashionably cut blond hair, who riveted his attention. Dressed for fighting in only a shirt and trousers, he slashed so viciously that an unpracticed eye might assume he would win. His expression reflected determination and nuances of ferocity. Daniel suspected that if an accident occurred in this practice, and blood was drawn, this man would not mind. As long, of course, as the blood was not his.

The practice ended. The blond man wiped his brow with a towel and walked toward Daniel.

There was no acknowledgment, because they had never officially met. The brother of a marquess and a member of Parliament, Andrew Tyndale arranged private times for his practices so that he would not have to mix with the assortment of younger men and *arrivistes* who frequented the Chevalier Corbet's fencing academy.

Daniel subtly examined Tyndale as he passed. The man owned a face that inspired trust. A face that made powerful men listen, and bishops nod in agreement, to the considered opinions that uttered from its mouth. That face had guaranteed Tyndale an unassailable reputation. If rumors ever started about him, one had only to see those honest eyes to know the rumors were untrue.

That was what had happened two years before, when a Scottish farmer accused Tyndale of violating his young daughter. Before a scandal could develop, Tyndale had convinced everyone who mattered that he had been on a shoot twenty miles from the girl's farm.

Daniel did not doubt that the accusation had been true, however. He knew that Tyndale had a taste for innocent girls. It had come to his attention that the respectable member of Parliament made use of a scrupulously discreet procuress who found him virgins on a regular basis. Daniel also knew it was not a fear of disease that caused Tyndale to favor innocents.

Unsheathing his own sabre, he approached the chevalier.

"He is good," he said, gesturing in the direction that Tyndale had gone.

"Too hungry, however. A cool head is everything in a real duel, when life hangs in the balance."

"So you have always taught, Louis."

"Skill is not enough. The mind plays its role, and sangfroid is essential."

"A very French sentiment." Daniel swung his arm to limber up. "Very *ancien régime.*"

Louis smiled. "What do you expect?"

"Nothing less. Have you thought about going back now, what with the restoration and Louis Philippe on the throne?"

"It has been too many years. An old French chevalier can do better in England. Assuming, of course, that we do not see a revolution here now. That would be comic, no? For me to escape one as a young man, only to die in another when I am old."

"There is unrest, but I doubt that revolution threatens Britain."

"I am not so sure. This government is stupid. This Corn Law, for example. It is never good policy to starve the poor. Does the world never learn?" He gestured, waving politics and the world away. "Enough. Let us begin. I am a bad philosopher but an excellent teacher of the sword. I will stick with what I know."

Daniel prepared himself. Louis was being falsely modest. He was quite the philosopher, and his mind could slice to the heart of a problem as quickly as his sabre could destroy a man's arm.

Daniel was glad Louis would not join the French aristocrats flocking to Paris to reclaim their rights now that Bonaparte was gone. Over the years Louis had become both a counselor and a conscience. He would want his friend nearby in the weeks ahead.

Louis handed over the box containing the pistols. His expression spoke his distaste of them. "Horrible things. Crude and unsatisfying."

"True," Daniel said. "But also effective and useful."

As Daniel carried the box out to the park behind the old house, a rider trotted up the lane. Daniel recognized the young man with the English face and the dark, foreign eyes.

He had last seen him in Gustave Dupré's study in Paris.

"What are you doing here, Adrian?"

"Vergil and the others are supposed to meet me here."

By Vergil and the others he was referring to the aristocratic young men who congregated at Louis's for practice before heading back to London for gambling and drink. They had dubbed themselves the Hampstead Dueling Society and Daniel had become something of a peripheral member.

"I did not mean what are you doing *here,* but in England. We agreed that you would remain in France for at least another month."

"Dupré let me go. He decided he does not need a secretary at the moment."

Daniel continued into the park with Adrian in step beside him. "That is convenient. Now he won't become suspicious when you eventually leave on your own."

"I thought so, although it leaves me without employment."

"That will be rectified once it is learned that you are back. Castlereagh will find something for you to do."

They stopped in a clearing beyond a screen of trees. Daniel handed over a sheet of paper and Adrian carried it to a tree twenty paces away.

"Head or heart, Daniel?"

"Head."

Daniel flipped open the box. Nestled atop the pistols was a little blue velvet purse. Cursing under his breath, he tucked it in his pocket.

He knew that it contained one hundred pounds. When he had given Louis this property ten years ago, he had refused any payment. The old chevalier had other ideas, however, and with regularity the pound notes would appear, but never put in his hand. Whether intended as rent or toward purchase, Daniel did not know.

"Ready," Adrian said.

Daniel handed him one of the pistols and loaded his own. They faced the tree, where the paper had been attached at the height of a man's head.

Adrian fired. The ball hit low and wide, chipping off a chunk of tree trunk.

"You are still a terrible shot."

"I would have hit his shoulder."

"His left shoulder, which means he can still fire back. You must hit the head or the heart, Adrian. The head or the heart."

Daniel raised his own pistol and aimed. "Why doesn't Dupré need a secretary anymore?"

"Didn't I explain that? He won't be writing treatises for a while. He has come to England."

Daniel's gaze snapped to Adrian as the pistol fired. The shot missed, wildly.

Adrian pointed to the pristine white paper. His dark eyes glinted. "It appears that you missed, Daniel. Remember, the head or the heart."

"My presence in his household became a burden," Adrian explained as they strolled back to the house. "It was obvious that he harbored a great secret and important plans. He feared that I would learn of them."

"But why come to England? He should be preparing to announce his discovery in Paris, to remind the world of the brilliance of the French mind."

"I'm not convinced that he plans to announce it in Paris. He was not writing a treatise and even missed several important scientific assemblies."

"Did he bring the manuscript with him?"

Adrian shrugged. "Perhaps he plans to arrange a demonstration here. Reminding the world of French brilliance would be even more effective if you did it in the capital of France's conqueror."

If Adrian was right, it would be perfect. The humiliation of failure would be twice that in Paris. It would be a fitting punishment for a man whose vanity had obliterated his humanity.

Unfortunately, he doubted Dupré intended such a thing. More likely he had something very different in mind, and Daniel suspected what it was.

Vanity had succumbed to a more powerful vice.

Greed.

Daniel contemplated whether that heralded trouble.

The Dueling Society was dismounting from horses when they arrived at the house. Vergil Duclairc hailed them and came over with Julian Hampton, the young solicitor whom Daniel now used for business affairs.

"Will you be joining us, St. John?" Vergil asked.

"I have had my lesson. I must return to town." It was the truth, but he would not have stayed in any case. He avoided being absorbed into this group, much as he envied their camaraderie. He really had little in common with them in terms of history or goals or occupation.

As with his social circles and his neighbors in Mayfair, he moved among them, but was not really a part of them. Furthermore, they were children of their class, and when the time came that would matter more than any friendship with the likes of him. They would never side with him against one of their own. If he permitted these friendships to grow, there would have to be betrayals eventually.

Vergil and Hampton aimed to the house. Daniel caught Adrian before he followed.

"If you can resist the offer of a mission from the Foreign Secretary, I would appreciate your services for a while longer. Find out where Dupré is staying. Keep an eye on him if you can."

chapter 10

The trouble with money was that one never had enough of it.

Andrew Tyndale considered that unfortunate truth as he sat in his garden, sipping tea. He did not need to peruse any accounts to know things were getting leaner than he liked. A continual balance had run in his head since the day he came of age.

Fate had dealt him a cruel blow in making him the brother of a marquess instead of the marquess himself. Worse, his older brother had proven not only stingy, but robust and virile. Three strapping nephews now stood between Andrew and the title.

He never stopped resenting that, but he had learned to make his own way. He wielded more power in the Commons than his brother did in the House of Lords. Through shrewd investments and a profitable marriage, he had built his own wealth. Of course, it had all depended on the bold move he had made as a young man. Without that, he would not have had the money for those investments. Katy would have never considered him without that fortune he had unexpectedly come upon.

Memories of Katy slid into his head. She had been waifish and pretty, with a childish manner. For a few months he had felt like a different man. Unfortunately, he had discovered quickly that she was also stupid and tiresome, and that being a different man wasn't very interesting. She whined when she was unhappy, which meant that she whined a lot. By the time she died, he had been relieved to be free of her.

The butler approached with the morning mail. Andrew flipped through the invitations. He paused at one with a familiar penmanship.

As expected, there were no words, only a date. A very special diversion awaited him tomorrow night.

The inside of his mouth thickened as he imagined the gift. Mrs. P. had better have found one who was truly a virgin this time. The last girl had not been, he was sure, despite her cries to the contrary and Mrs. P.'s reassurances. He set the letter aside and suppressed the anticipatory arousal making his loins stir.

The butler returned, looking dismayed. "There is a gentleman who has called. I told him you were not receiving, but he is insistent."

"It is an uncivilized hour to call, so he cannot be a gentleman after all."

"Of course. However, he claims an old association." He held out the salver.

Andrew snatched the card with exasperation. When he glanced at it, his awareness took a little jolt. He had not seen the name, nor the man who owned it, in over twenty years.

He debated continuing the disassociation. Curiosity got the better of him. So did suspicion and concern.

"Put him in the library. I will see him."

Gustave Dupré examined the shelves in the library. They held a predictable collection of classics and a few modern masterpieces on natural history. It was the sort of intellectual showcase owned by men who considered themselves educated, but who never bent any bindings after they left university.

These bindings were very expensive, as was the room and house in which they were displayed. Andrew had done very well for himself. But then, he had the kind of mind that would always find profit in a situation, and pursue it. He liked money more than was tasteful. The best blood might flow in his veins, but his heart was that of a tradesman.

Gustave ruefully admitted that Andrew also had the talent for executing plans with precision, and for instilling the kind of trust in people that assured the plans would work. Gustave himself lacked that ability and quality.

Which was why he was here today.

"It is surprising to see you, Dupré. We agreed never to meet again."

Gustave turned abruptly. He disliked being caught unawares, and remembered that Tyndale could be slippery in that quiet way of his. He remembered that those plans sometimes worked out differently than people expected, because Tyndale often kept bits of information to himself.

Well, not this time.

"I decided to visit London. After all, half of England is visiting Paris," Gustave said.

"If you have left your own library to peruse mine, there must be a better reason than taking a holiday."

The reference to his library made Gustave uncomfortable. It was bad form for Tyndale to speak of it. The temptation to return a similar allusion to Tyndale's own gains almost overwhelmed him.

Gustave decided to get to the reason he had broken the old agreement. "I have made a major discovery. One that will change the world as we know it." It was the first time he had put that into words and they rushed out with all of his pent-up excitement. He had intended to sound very bland, as if, for him, such a discovery was an everyday occurrence.

Tyndale barely turned a hair. He withdrew his snuffbox and took a pinch. "It cannot have been all that significant. If it had been, I would have read of it. Another proof?"

Gustave felt his color rise at this further allusion to the past. "You have not read of it because I have told no one."

"Why not? Your reputation is your greatest concern. Accolades are to you what land is to other men."

And what pound notes and virgins are to you. "I have not revealed this discovery because it has a practical application. A revolutionary one." That got Tyndale's attention. Gustave paused for effect. "This discovery will make the men who possess it wealthy."

Tyndale absorbed that while he took another pinch of snuff. "How wealthy?"

"It cannot be calculated, it would be so massive. However, exploiting this discovery will require money."

"And so you have come to me. Why not offer it to some of your own countrymen?"

Gustave smiled, feeling rather clever. Almost as clever as Tyndale could be. "Because I know that you will not dare to cross me."

Tyndale's eyes turned icy. "Is that a threat, Dupré?"

"It is a reminder."

"How much will this discovery require?"

"I calculate five thousand to start, to convince industrialists of its practicality."

"Five thousand, out of hand! You misunderstand my financial position."

"Once you learn what is at stake, you will find a way to get it."

Tyndale appeared unimpressed. His attention began drifting. Gustave considered that he had not handled the discussion very well. He should have dangled the prize more specifically before mentioning the five thousand.

Tyndale looked at him, scrutinizing. Gustave watched the notion of massive profit reclaim his interest.

"Tell me about this wonderful discovery of yours, old friend."

Gustave hesitated. Putting it into words would mean losing some control. He had no intention of being one of those men who never saw a franc from his scientific work. He knew from experience that Tyndale could not really be trusted either. For a moment he wondered if the threat of exposure about what had happened years ago was enough to keep this man honest.

He took a deep breath. He would tell Tyndale about the discovery, but never let him know the details of how it was accomplished.

Crystal goblets and silver forks.

Balls and parties and afternoon calls.

Punch and cocoa, cakes and tea.

The Countess of Glasbury kept Diane busy every day, every evening. The countess, or Penelope as she asked Diane to address her, might be *outrée* to some, but most of London's drawing rooms opened to her. Diane met duchesses and poets, impresarios and earls.

The season had started and London was busy. In the grand houses of Mayfair and Grosvenor Square, in the theater boxes and dining rooms, a colorful pageant of privilege played out.

It was enough to turn a girl's head.

Enough to silence the questions and obscure the void.

Enough to make her not mind that Daniel's help in finding her family kept being delayed. Her disappointment every morning at discovering him already gone from the house got quickly drowned in the preparations for more calls and parties, in the intoxicating attention of men young and old, in the illusion that she was accepted and that this was her world.

But it was an illusion. Diane admitted that to herself one evening as a maid dressed her hair for a ball. Looking into the glass, watching the piles of her thick tresses being scrunched and pinned, the frivolous joy disappeared in a blink.

She stared at her own features and, as she had so often at school, scoured her mind for memories of similar eyes and lips. Sometimes when she did that, phantom images would come to her of these eyes looking back, but not reflected in a glass.

The people she met all belonged to someone else whom she met. There were connections of birth and marriage, of schools and politics. She belonged to no one. Certainly not the countess. Not even Jeanette and Daniel, despite the lie that she was a cousin.

She dismissed the maid and opened her window to the early spring chill. Twilight was falling and pink and gold lights glowed in the garden below. In the distance a disturbance rumbled, with sharp notes carried on the wind.

It was another demonstration. The drawing rooms and theaters might be a pageant of gaiety, but in the streets another drama dragged on, one of frustration and discontent. The sacrifices of war had been shouldered stoicly, but after several years of peace the people were rebelling against the continued privations.

She had grown accustomed to that sound, but tonight it might have been the blare of a horn calling her to her true fate.

She felt her hair and fingered her gown. She filled her mind with beautiful, exciting images from the last two weeks. It did not help. She might have been back at school, standing beside the chipped washbowl, wearing braids and an old sack gown.

The void swelled, bursting out of the place where she restrained it. It grew until it filled her heart. Its vacancy quaked with a loneliness so intense that it brought tears to her eyes.

All the parties in the world would never fill it, never make it go away.

Diane barely had time to catch her breath at Lady Starbridge's ball. Young men lined up to be introduced and to ask for a dance. The Countess of Glasbury did her duty as chaperon.

Daniel kept his eye on the spot near the terrace windows where the countess held court. He saw her discourage a gentleman known to be a rake. Instead she favored the fourth son of a baronet, a man of little fortune who would not find a shipper's cousin too far below him.

His reaction to that was quick annoyance, and he had to look away in order to swallow the jealousy. It was getting harder to do that, but he could hardly tell the countess that Diane should not be pushed at eligible men. Playing matchmaker was part of the fun of being a chaperon.

Diane accepted the offer to dance and swept into his view. It was a waltz, and the fourth son of a baronet smiled as he spun her around the chamber. Diane looked so happy, so lovely, that Daniel could not take his eyes off her.

His view of the dance turned into a daze of colored gowns and flickering lights, of hazy bodies and floating movements. Only one figure remained clear and sharp. Diane became a detailed, beautiful woman sliding amidst a watercolor.

Suddenly another figure loomed crisply. Across the room a man stood out, immobile and vivid, intruding on the hazy dream. His eyes followed Diane too. He examined her so completely that he did not notice Daniel watching.

The rest of the chamber lost substance. Even Diane grew dim. Daniel saw only the man and the tiny calculating lights barely visible in that gaze.

So. It had happened.

Diane had caught Andrew Tyndale's attention.

A rebellious yell swelled in Daniel's chest. He clenched his teeth against it and kept his gaze on the only other person who now existed in the room.

Other images came to him, of that face and those eyes in another chamber, in another time. Of a sincere smile and soothing voice offering salvation. Of trust born of desperation. Of good people forgetting that sometimes evil doesn't announce itself, and that devils have the same forms as angels.

The memories killed the rebellion and evoked other emotions, bitter ones, and a resolve so cold it crystallized his blood.

You do not know me, but I know you. I know what you did. I know what you are.

The music ended. Tyndale's gaze followed a path toward the terrace windows.

Tearing his attention away from Tyndale, Daniel found Diane again. It was her progress that Tyndale watched. Tyndale began walking toward the countess.

Daniel enjoyed one instant of dark satisfaction. Then abruptly, unaccountably, he lost total hold on the resolve and the memories. A chaos of primitive energy made him move.

Tyndale could wait. It all could wait. It had waited years. Decades. Another month or two would not matter.

He reached the windows before Tyndale. The fourth son of a baronet had not left and was chatting with the countess and Diane. Daniel positioned himself so that the three of them formed a protective circle around Diane, one that Tyndale could only breach by being rude.

The countess introduced Daniel to Diane's fawning dance partner. He pretended he was glad to make the acquaintance of ruddy-faced, plump-cheeked, round-eyed Christopher Meekum.

Diane immediately excused herself to go to the withdrawing room. The countess decided to go too. As she brushed past, Diane tilted her head toward Daniel.

"His older brother is involved with canals up north," she whispered behind her fan.

She was alerting him to the business that might be done and the benefits in knowing this admirer. She was trying to fulfill her side of the bargain.

She had no idea that she would do so, only not the way she expected.

A hot pain seared his chest as he watched her walk away. For an instant he hated himself as thoroughly as he did Tyndale.

"I wonder why they always do that," Meekum mused.

"Do what?"

"Withdraw together. Have you ever noticed that it is never just one. I mean, I never take a companion when I, well, you know."

"I am glad to hear it. As for the ladies, I suspect that they go together so that they can talk in privacy."

"Think so? What do you suppose they talk about?"

"Us."

"Us?"

"Men."

"Well. Good heavens." Meekum absorbed the astonishing suggestion. "I wonder what they say."

"Nothing good."

That astounded Meekum even more. He repositioned himself to face Daniel more squarely.

"You are in shipping, I hear." He was one of those men who said everything in a hearty, jovial tone. In the best of situations, and this was far from being one, Daniel found such men irritating.

"Yes."

"What do you ship?"

"Whatever is legal and pays well, except opium and slaves."

"Well, I've heard there is good profit in the former. Don't know much about the other."

"There is always good profit in human misery."

"My family is in transportation too. Just investments, needless to say. Not like you, of course."

"Of course."

Meekum became flustered and coughed a few times. Daniel doubted it was because he realized he had just been insulting.

"Your cousin is, uh, a delightful young lady, St. John." He beamed and flustered some more. "I would like to call on her, if you will accept my attentions."

"I am not the one who has to tolerate them. If she is willing to accept them, however, it is beyond my powers to stop it."

"Splendid! You can't know how happy that makes me. She is so lovely, so fresh and sweet, unlike some of these girls. Many of them are too proud for their own good, is what I say."

"Yes, she is very charming. Which is what makes it all so very sad."

"Sad?"

"Tragic. You see, she doesn't have any fortune." Daniel shook his head. "I expect that she will never marry."

"No fortune?"

"Not a pound to her name."

"Nothing?"

"Utterly penniless."

Meekum scratched his head and pondered the bad news. "But you are . . . that is, everyone just assumed . . . surely you intend to help her out there?"

"I would if I could. It vexes me that my hands are tied. Her brother feared that she would be sought only for her fortune if I settled anything on her, and he made me promise never to do so. He wanted to be sure that if any man offered for her, it would only be because of love."

Meekum's smile flashed and fell, flashed and fell. "A noble sentiment, but perhaps a bit rash."

"That is exactly what I said. Well, he was quite a dreamer. He died before releasing me of the promise, so here we are."

The ladies were coming back. Meekum watched Diane approach. "Zeus, that *is* tragic."

"Yes. Isn't it."

As soon as Diane and the countess rejoined them, the music began again.

"Another waltz," the countess said.

The fourth son of a baronet looked forlornly toward Diane.

"Would you honor me, countess?" he asked.

The countess happily agreed.

"And you, Diane? Can you spare one dance for your cousin?" The words were out before Daniel had decided to say them.

She flushed just enough to indicate they both knew all too well they were not cousins. With a crooked smile, one that made him want to nip her lips, she nodded.

The room receded again as he led her around. They twirled in the wash of colors blurring by. He could tell that she tried not to look in his eyes, but eventually she did. After that, the dance became a very private place in which nothing existed but the two of them. Not even the past that he avenged or the future that he plotted intruded.

Daniel left the library and made his way upstairs. The house was silent with the night. He pictured Diane sleeping in her bed, sated from her triumphant ball.

He wanted to go there, wanted it more than he had ever expected to want to visit a woman's chamber. He could not, of course. For many reasons, it could not be.

Admitting that he wished it *could be* led him to a different chamber, not far from Diane's.

He pushed open the door and entered the sitting room. It was not all pale and glittering like the one in Paris. The woman who used it now had not decorated it. He had forced her to leave her pastel dreamworld and come to his careful, calculated, real one.

Pulling open another door, he entered Jeanette's bedchamber.

He walked over to the bed, and the dark shadow on it.

He froze.

The shadow was too large. Too wide. As his eyes adjusted to the dark, he realized that two bodies slept in the bed.

"Do not wake him," Jeanette whispered.

Daniel was not sure he could speak, let alone wake anyone.

"Hand me my dressing robe from that bench," Jeanette instructed, sitting up.

He did so, and she slipped it on.

"Let us go into the sitting room," she said.

He lifted her in his arms and carried her to a chair in the next chamber.

She settled herself, posing like a queen. Daniel lit a brace of candles.

"You are shocked," she said.

"I am surprised."

"Why? Because Paul is base born, or because I am lame?"

"I don't know *why* I am surprised, I just am."

"That must be an unusual emotion for you. You have gone through pains to never be caught unawares."

It was an unusual emotion. Not an unpleasant one, he had to admit.

"You are to say nothing to him about this discovery of yours, Daniel. He reveres you, and any indication that you are displeased or angry would wound him."

"What could I say? You are not an innocent child."

"Hardly."

"I did not mean—"

"We both know what you meant, and I am not insulted."

They sat in silence as she waited for him to tell her why he had sought her out.

He found it hard to explain. He wasn't sure why he had come here. It had simply seemed a very necessary thing to do while he drank port in the library and tried to assess what he had experienced during the last few hours.

"Did he see her tonight?" The question came low and gentle. Just like Jeanette, to know without being told.

"Yes."

"Was there an introduction?"

"Not yet." There would be soon, however. He didn't doubt that. Only his continued interference tonight had delayed it.

"Are you having second thoughts?"

"No." Except he was. For all the wrong reasons. Ones that would pass quickly, leaving him disgusted with himself and still owned by memories that could not be escaped until they were killed.

"So, you have come to me to rebuild your resolve," she said. "Well, light more candles, brother. Shall I raise my gown so that you can see my lifeless legs? Will that help? It is my role in this now, isn't it? It always has been. To be the reminder, lest you forget."

"That is a hell of a thing to say."

"Is it? Then why did you return to France every year during the war, when doing so was dangerous and difficult?"

"To see you. To make sure you were safe, and cared for."

"I do not doubt those reasons. But can you say truly that there was no more? That seeing me, visiting Paris, even going to that school, was not necessary to feed your anger and keep it alive?"

"Not at all."

"Oh, Daniel. How a man who is so ruthlessly honest in so many things can be so blind to himself—you only put the girl in a French school to have another reason to force you back."

He rose and turned away from her accusations. "I put her there because I knew I would be returning anyway to see you, damn it. Should I have kept you both here in England? Would that have pleased you? You are afraid to even leave this house."

"Keep your voice down. You will wake Paul."

"I don't give a damn if I wake him. Hell, he is sleeping with my sister. I'm not about to be concerned if he loses a bit of rest."

"Good heavens, you *are* shocked. That would be charming if it was not so ridiculous."

Was he shocked? Was that the source of the seething annoyance churning in his gut?

"No, I think I have it wrong. You aren't shocked. You are resentful. You assumed it owned me, too, this need for revenge. Was I supposed to accept my life was over? Wither away as I waited for you to finish it? Was I supposed to forego happiness as you have? Or perhaps you assumed that because of these legs I had no choice."

"So, you are free and I am a slave, is that it?"

"I am not free. Bring him to me and I will shoot him through the heart and gladly hang for it. But don't expect me to live what time I have been given with no purpose except waiting for the chance to fire that pistol."

"My God, you are crippled because of him. How can you live with any other purpose?"

She threw up her hands and shook her head. "Take me back. You only came here to convince yourself to use that girl as a lure. I can see that I have once more been all you hoped I'd be."

"I came here to speak with my sister, that is all."

"Take me back. Quietly, please."

He lifted her and carried her to the bed. Paul slept on, his craggy face nestled amidst the pillows, his naked shoulders visible above the sheet.

Jeanette removed her robe and cast it to the floor. Daniel turned away.

"Daniel."

Her whisper caught him at the door.

"Daniel, there are many ways to be crippled. I would forget everything if I could feel my legs move again. If having your heart stir tempts you to do the same, do not feel guilty."

chapter II

"Of course, the manufacturing possibilities are not the main interest. I am a scientist first."

Gustave nodded in response to Sir Gerome Scot's earnest reassurance. Scot was a brother in science, and politeness was in order. Scot was also paying for the meal that Gustave now ate in a private club at Scot's invitation.

He really did not give a damn about experiments with chemicals, however. His mind was on other problems.

He was behind schedule already. Tyndale wanted a demonstration of the discovery prepared quickly, and so far Gustave had made no progress at all in arranging one.

It would have helped if it could have been a small demonstration, such as the experiment he had conducted in Paris. But no, Tyndale wanted to skip that stage. He demanded something larger, that could be used to procure a patent and attract industrialists.

He needed to purchase materials and chemicals. He needed to find a building, out of the way, where no one would get curious. He needed to make his way around London quietly and subtly.

Scot droned in French, as any civilized and educated man could. Even the servants in this exclusive club knew enough to see to Gustave's comfort. Unfortunately, once one stepped outside the highest levels of society in this barbaric land, no one spoke French, let alone Latin. And Gustave knew no English.

The situation was impossible. He needed to step down considerably in the world to make things work, but he could not communicate with the men he needed to approach.

Scot launched into a tedious explanation of yet another chemical process. Gustave tried to look interested, but five minutes into the conversation something caught his eye. A young man had entered from another room, looked around, and then made his way to a table to join a friend. It was his past secretary, Adrian Burchard.

Scot noticed his distraction. He glanced in Adrian's direction and smirked. "Looks out of place, doesn't he?"

"Yes. What is he doing here?"

"He is a member. Can't exactly turn down the son of an earl, can we? Even if his paternity is obviously only legal."

The news was startling. Adrian had never claimed to be an earl's son when he applied for the position in Paris. Who would have guessed such a thing, what with those black Mediterranean eyes.

"So, his mother . . ." Gustave raised his eyebrows meaningfully.

"Obvious, isn't it? Noble of Dincaster to accept the boy at all, that's what I say. Well, he is a third son, so there is little chance he'll inherit, I suppose. He has the sense to keep a low profile, not that it is really possible with those eyes. Been on his own since he left university, I hear. Not a penny from the earl, which is as it should be. He does some minor work for the Foreign Office on occasion. Secretary and such, now and then. There are those in our government who are not too particular about one's true birth, I'm sorry to say."

Adrian had claimed to have been a secretary to some diplomat or other. It was a detail Gustave had assumed was a lie and generously overlooked.

"How interesting." Actually, how useful.

Gustave doubted that Adrian had announced to anyone in this club that sometimes he served as a secretary for men less illustrious than ambassadors. No wonder he had rarely left the house in Paris, and spent his evenings up in that garret chamber.

He kept his eyes on Adrian during the rest of the meal. He timed his own finish to coincide with the secretary's. He arranged to leave the club at the same time as the foreign-looking son of an earl.

Adrian's expression registered some surprise as Gustave joined him to wait for their hats. There was no acknowledgment of their prior association, however.

That was all Gustave needed to know.

He followed Adrian out to the street and skipped a few times to catch up. "You choose to be rude to your old employer?"

"I was surprised to see you, that is all. Are you enjoying your visit?"

"I find myself too busy. I think that I released you precipitously. The aid of someone who knows this city would be useful to me."

"There are many secretaries and clerks available. If you ask your friends, they will find one for you."

"I need one who speaks French."

"That should not be too hard."

"I would prefer someone I know." Gustave smiled. "Like you."

They had reached a corner. Adrian stopped and faced him. "I am not looking for employment at the moment."

"It would not be official. It would not be public," Gustave said, letting him know that he understood what his concerns really were.

Adrian's gaze darted around the street. It came to rest on a building across the way. "I regret that I cannot help you."

"It would be very private. I myself desire discretion. Our mutual need of it will ensure the arrangement will not be known."

"Sorry. I cannot."

"I think that you can. I think that you must."

"Must?"

"Surely you do not want me asking for assistance from other scientists, and confiding that my own secretary is too proud to assist me."

Adrian darted a sharp glance at him. His annoyance slowly lifted, replaced by resignation. "I suppose I could help you, unofficially, that is."

"Good. It is not every day. Indeed, once a few difficult matters are seen to, I will not need you much at all. The same wages, shall we say? A fortnight's worth?"

Adrian's jaw stiffened as if talk of money was an insult. Here in England, where he was known as an earl's son—even one of suspect legitimacy—it would be.

"Fine. Now, I will give you the first assistance that you require, since you clearly need it. Across the way is a man with a beard who has been watching you since we stopped here. He is probably a pickpocket, and has identified you as a foreigner."

Alarmed, Gustave pivoted. As soon as he did, a bearded man, poorly dressed in an old frock coat and hat, began walking down the street.

"Be alert for such things, m'sieur. England has the best thieves in the world."

"Miss Albret?"

The call came from a coach passing on the street. Diane took in the startled blue eyes of Vergil Duclairc at the window.

Beside him, in the shadow, she spied the perfect profile of his friend Julian Hampton, a young solicitor to a handful of select clients including Daniel and the Duclairc family. She had met Mister Hampton at the countess's dinner. He was a dramatically handsome man who possessed a crystalline reserve. She had spent the evening expecting him to speak in poetry, should he ever deign to speak at all.

She marched on, resuming the mental scolding she had been giving Daniel St. John ever since she watched him leave the house this morning.

She sensed a small commotion of horses stamping and snorting. Suddenly Vergil was walking beside her.

"Miss Albret, are you alone? Did your escort lose you? Stay with me and I will find St. John's footman."

"I lost no one. I have something to do and I am going to do it. Now, good day to you."

She turned a corner, leaving him behind.

He caught up. "You are alone? But you cannot walk alone."

"Of course I can. I have been doing so for the last quarter hour or so."

A coach moved into view beside them. Mister Hampton's carriage had turned around and now rolled alongside.

Vergil stepped around and blocked her path. "Miss Albret, we will give you our carriage. The coachman will take you wherever you wish to go. I must insist on it."

He was starting to get stern and authoritative.

She was not in the mood to take instruction from anyone today, least of all a man.

"Miss Albret, either you ride in the coach or you accept my escort on foot. There will be hell to pay with your cousin in either case, since he warned me off, but if you would, please . . ." He aimed his arm toward the coach.

"I am walking because I want to walk. I cannot stop you from accompanying me if you persist. As for my cousin warning you off, he will not be worried. He probably knows that you are enthralled with some opera singer and have no interest in me. Not that I care what Daniel St. John thinks or knows or worries about."

Vergil blinked with surprise. Whether her indifference to Daniel's opinion startled him, or the evidence that the whole world knew about his opera singer, she did not know.

"You speak very frankly, don't you?"

"My apologies, but I have been speaking so politely and vapidly these last weeks that the stored up frankness just overflowed this morning."

He went to the coach and said something through the window. The vehicle picked up speed and turned away at the next street.

Vergil strode alongside her as he tried to shield her from the jostling bodies. "Where are we going?"

"Where you told me to go, to one of the partnerships that insures ships. I learned of one called Lloyds in the City."

"That will be a long walk. Surely St. John would have taken you."

She gritted her teeth. Daniel had promised to take her "in a few days." That had been two weeks ago.

Of course, he saw no need to hurry. What did he care? He wasn't the one adrift in the world, with no history, no family, no home. He did not carry an emptiness in his heart that ached to be filled with something, *anything.* He could put her off until he had absolutely nothing else to do, which would be never.

They had been walking half an hour when the bulk of a horse cast a shadow on them.

"You took your time getting here, St. John," Vergil said.

Diane stopped in her tracks. Her gaze traveled up the mass of gray horseflesh to the rigid rider blocking the sun.

"I did not want to trample anyone," Daniel said. "Hampton is following, and if you retrace your steps you will meet his coach. Thank you, and my cousin apologizes for the delay this has caused you. Don't you, Diane?"

"No apologies are necessary," Vergil said as he turned away.

Daniel dismounted. "What am I going to do with you?"

"Staying out of my way would be the wisest choice today." She began walking again.

He came along, leading his horse. The crowd parted like the Red Sea as the huge steed approached.

"A woman does not walk alone in London. Didn't my sister explain that?"

"I see plenty of women walking alone."

"That is different. They are poor and have employment to attend."

"So am I. So do I."

He ignored the first part. "What employment?"

"I am going to Lloyds."

"Ah, so this rebellion is the result of a little temper because I have not tended to that yet."

She stopped and faced him, so furious that her eyes hurt. "Do not mock me. This is why I am here. This is why I left the school. Not to amuse you, and not for your sister, much as I love her. If I wait for you to tend to this, I will grow old first. If I did not know that I am completely insignificant to you, I would suspect that you lied in the garden to put me off."

She turned on her heel and walked away. He fell into step beside her.

"Go away."

"I must insist on accompanying you. The streets are not safe, and it is too far to call for Paul or someone else."

She ignored the man beside her, but no one else did. The two of them, and the snorting, huge horse pacing alongside in the road, garnered a lot of attention.

"We are making a spectacle," Daniel said.

"The next time I will dress in my school clothes. When I did that in Paris, no one ever noticed me."

"If you wear your school clothes, no one will answer your questions. In fact, no one would today, except for the fact that I will be with you."

He might have explicitly said *you are nothing without me. I have made you.*

"You think so?" Her lips pulled tightly against her anger. "We will see."

Lloyds was in the Royal Exchange, which reminded her of an English church with its classical temple portico. The cavernous square space inside was crowded with merchants and men of business, and its sides lined with goods. Daniel took her arm so she would not get swallowed by the crowd and guided her up some stairs into a large chamber full of men.

"This is Lloyds," he said. "The brokers are along that wall. I will introduce you to Thompson. He knows me."

She did not shrink into Daniel's shadow, much as she wanted to. She approached Mister Thompson's desk as grandly as she could and looked his clerk right in the eyes.

The young man flushed and stammered and dropped his pen on the floor when she smiled at him.

Diane slid Daniel a sidelong glance, only to find him sliding one back to her at the same time.

Mister Thompson was delighted to see Daniel. Daniel introduced her and tried to impose his authority on the interview, but with another smile she demanded Mister Thompson's attention.

He was glad to give it to her. His scalp blushed beneath the strands of his sparse white hair. Forgetting the hovering presence of Daniel St. John, he beamed across the desk as she made her request.

"I am seeking information on a relative of mine, Jonathan Albret. He was in shipping some years ago, fifteen or thereabouts. I am hoping that if your partnership ever insured one of his ships, that you will have something to aid my search."

"Well, we can certainly see what we have. I can have our clerks check, and send the information to you."

"Would it be possible to do it now? I would be very grateful. I have been searching for many months."

Daniel emitted a sigh. "Mister Thompson is very busy—"

"Not too busy to aid a damsel in distress." Mister Thompson's face fell into a mask of sympathy. He gave orders to his clerk, and huge bound tomes began arriving.

Mister Thompson leaned over her shoulder to explain how the entries were made. "Do you know the names of the ships or their masters?"

She looked at Daniel, who shook his head.

"No, only the owner's name."

"Ah, that makes it more difficult. We must examine this column here, but there will be no order to it. Here, you do this one, and I'll do the other and my clerk will manage the third."

She smiled up with gratitude at his very close face. He flushed to the edge of his receding hairline.

"Mister St. John, if you have other business in the city, I am sure that Mister Thompson and his clerk will assist me," Diane said.

"Have no fear, St. John, your cousin will be safe with us."

"I will stay here," came the firm reply.

There were only three tomes, so he just sat in a chair near the window while Diane and her two smitten assistants paged through them.

Two hours later Diane had irrefutable evidence that her father had insured no ships through Lloyds during the six years before he disappeared.

She had walked into the Royal Exchange feeling bold and confident and certain of making progress. Now, as she closed the heavy binding of her volume, a wretched discouragement gripped her.

Mister Thompson noticed. "I am so sorry. We could search further back if you want."

"No, thank you."

The two men looked at her with expressions that said they'd each cut off a leg to spare her this unhappiness. That only made her feel guilty for her little flirtations.

"Come, Diane." Daniel's voice was right behind her.

She did not want to look at him. He would probably be annoyed that she had caused so much trouble to no purpose.

Forcing her disappointment down, telling herself that there were other insurance partnerships and this was not the end of her hopes, she accepted his escort down to the street. As he untied the lead of his horse, she saw his face.

Not annoyed. Something else tightened his expression and burned in his eyes.

They walked west in silence. That relieved her. She was too disheartened to meet any scolds with the self-righteous challenge she had thrown at him a couple of hours ago.

She could practically hear the scold anyway. It came to her in the indifferent tone of the old school questions. *Are you contented now? Will this be enough for a while? Is it sufficient to have wasted the afternoons of three men on your great quest?*

As they neared Temple Bar, the chaos and rhythms of the streets abruptly changed.

People walked a little faster. The poor and common ones streamed toward the river, while the carriages and better dressed people hurried in the other direction. Daniel stopped and peered down the narrow lane, cocking his head.

A rumble could be heard vaguely on the breeze.

"Another demonstration," Daniel said. "Near Parliament. The session should have started for today." He took her arm and aimed in the direction from which they had just come. "We will have to go another way. Unfortunately, it means passing through an unsavory part of the town."

They found a quiet lane, empty of people. The shops had closed their doors.

Daniel led the horse over to a mounting stone. "There is no telling what we will meet. It will be better if we ride. Get up on this block and I will help you onto the horse, behind me."

She stepped up. "I have never ridden a horse before."

"Then today will be a first for many things, won't it?" He mounted the horse, then leaned toward her. "The first time riding a horse, and the first time flirting until men gave you what you want." His expression tightened again as he said the last part.

His arm circled her waist, bringing him distressingly close. "Also the first time for displaying your legs to all of London. This will only work if you hitch up your skirt, since you must ride astride. Do it now and I'll lift you up."

She obeyed. With a swing she was behind him, her skirt scrunched up to her knees.

"Cover yourself as best you can with your cloak. Then hold on to me so you don't fall off."

She resisted the final command, and grabbed the back of the saddle instead.

She almost bounced off, and the animal was barely walking. She gingerly slid her arms around Daniel's body.

It wasn't an embrace. Not really. The connection, the warmth, instantly overwhelmed her, however. Just as Madame Leblanc's parting hug at the school had left her breathless, just as Daniel's scandalous handling in the carriage had weakened her, this hold, even lacking intimacy, caused an immediate reaction.

The void engulfed her and then cried with relief, almost moaned, as the softest, most human contentment flooded it.

See, not completely alone, her heart whispered. *There are other ways. Other homes, and other loves, beside those of family.*

It had been wise to ride back and not walk. They passed through rude streets. The people loitering in them had been stirred up by the demonstration they had not even joined. Daniel trotted along at a fast clip, ignoring the shouts aimed their way.

Suddenly he stopped the horse. Peering around his body, she saw that a crowd had formed on the street ahead of them. Daniel turned their mount, but bodies were pouring into the crossroad they had just passed too.

Muttering a curse, he turned once more and trotted forward. "There must have been some violence near Parliament. Word must have spread on it. Hold tightly now."

She held on very tightly. Faces around her wore ugly expressions that deformed the humanity of the group into the snarling masks of a mob. She remembered the attack outside the opera in Paris, and worried that some of these poor people had knives.

Using the bulk of the horse, Daniel pushed through. A few men tried to stand their ground and only jumped aside at the last minute. Curses and vulgarities flew directly at them.

"Why are they angry at us? You are not in the government."

"They are angry at anyone who can eat without counting the pennies left."

The faces sneering at her did not look so inhuman suddenly. "If they are hungry, I suppose that excuses such behavior."

He turned his head to glare back at her. "There is *no* excuse."

Just then a man grabbed the horse's bridle. Another grasped Diane's exposed ankle. Horrified, she tried to shake him off, only to have him laugh.

With a snarl, Daniel kicked her attacker so viciously that the man flew and fell back into the gutter.

Diane caught a glimpse of Daniel's face while he reacted to the threat. For an instant he appeared so hard and cruel, so primitive and ruthless, that she almost released her hold of him and veered back. Then she blinked, and the look was gone so quickly that she wondered if she had imagined it.

Daniel moved the horse to a faster gait. The crowd split. There were no more challenges.

Soon the crowd thinned and disappeared, along with the poverty of the buildings. The familiar low rumble still flowed on the breeze, but all other evidence of unrest ceased.

"You must get down now," Daniel said, stopping the horse. "Others must not see you like this."

They walked the rest of the way to his house. He didn't say anything, but she sensed that he wanted to. Not pleasant things, of that she was certain. His silence had a dark edge to it.

"Come to the study, please."

She felt as she had at school, when summoned to the headmistress's office. She hated that reaction in herself. She resented being at such a disadvantage, and not even knowing why, or what it was that he expected of her.

At least he did not sit behind the study's desk and examine her as if she were some errant schoolgirl. Instead he went to the window and, as he so often did in her presence, looked out, instead of at her.

She resented that too.

"I know that you are unhappy about today. I am sorry for that." He sounded sincere enough. So why did she sense that he wasn't entirely sorry at all?

"Perhaps you should not dwell too much on finding lost relatives, Diane. The disappointment—you are young and have a life to build. The past can be a chain, and you have been spared that."

"You do not understand."

"I think that I do, better than you know."

"If you did, you would never call the past a chain, as if it imprisons a person."

"It can."

"Then I want some of those chains. I want to be tied to a family, good or bad. I want to be able to say my grandfather lived in this town and my uncle had that trade." She heard resentment and pleading in her voice, but could not stop either. "I want to know that someone cared about me when I was born and was sad to leave me and thought about me sometimes. I want to know that somewhere there is some cousin or aunt who wonders what became of me."

The chamber rang with her declaration. It echoed for a long time before the silence swallowed it.

"Is that all? I want to leave now."

He turned. "No, that is not all. You must not go out alone again."

"In Paris we agreed that I could continue here as I did there."

"I did not know that you walked alone in Paris. Take an escort in the future."

"Are we finished *now?*"

"No. I realize that these last weeks you have learned the power that a beautiful woman has. However, the way that you flirted with Mister Thompson and his clerk today was too bold."

"It was not bold at all. It was very subtle. I have seen duchesses do far worse."

"You are not a forty-year-old duchess."

"No, I am a twenty-year-old penniless orphan. If a smile will get the Mister Thompsons of the world to open their books, it is a small price to pay and the only currency I have."

"I would have gotten the books opened for you."

"I preferred to do it myself. Tell me, m'sieur, is our arrangement producing the results you had hoped?"

"What do you mean?"

"Am I attracting the attention you expected? Are you meeting the men you hoped to meet? Is business getting done over cards and at clubs? Is your investment in me bringing returns?"

"What a thing to ask. You astonish me sometimes."

"I prefer you astonished to scolding. If all is happening as you wanted, I do not think your lessons are appropriate. Count your winnings, and leave me to amass my own."

She left, and with each step the little fury she had known since he confronted her on the street grew. She approached the staircase almost trembling with frustration and an inexplicable sense of insult.

Two Oriental urns stood on the ends of the banisters. Unlike the ones in her chamber in Paris, these were rose and green and covered with flowers. She looked at them, propped on display for all to see, announcing the urbane taste of the man who owned them.

Who owned her, too, in a way.

She lifted one of the urns. The thinness of the porcelain proclaimed the craftsmanship as clearly as the decoration did.

Cradling it in her hands, she reveled in its feel.

Expensive. Perfect. An object of exquisite beauty.

She released it from her grasp. It crashed to pieces on the marble floor.

The sound echoed down the corridor. Doors opened and servants rushed out and gaped. Daniel emerged from the library, curious.

She stood amidst the shards, barely containing a naughty euphoria.

The servants stared from her to Daniel.

He walked over with the oddest expression on his face. He pointed to the broken urn.

"That was Ming."

"You give your vases pet names?"

"Ming Dynasty. At least three hundred years old. As a pair they were priceless."

"You said to break one. Every day if I wanted."

"Those were the ones in your chamber."

"It matters?"

He headed back to the library with an expression of forbearance. "That you broke anything at all is what matters. It does not bode well for me, does it?"

chapter 12

"They have not concluded, my lady. I expect it will be at least an hour." The footman spoke through the coach's window before his face disappeared.

Penelope looked apologetically at Diane. "I hope that you don't mind waiting for them."

"Of course not." That was the most disarming thing about the countess. Even though she had befriended a shipper's obscure cousin, she acted as though Diane should not be grateful and even had some right to "mind."

"Well, I do. Not this delay. If my brother asked me to wait all afternoon, I could not complain. However, it vexes me that I am such a coward. I resent that the earl can do this to me, but I am helpless against the fear."

"That you are attending this party at all shows you are not a coward."

They were on their way to a house party in Essex, at the invitation of Lady Pennell. Penelope had arranged to stop at this old house in Hampstead, to meet her brother Vergil so they could all travel together.

Under normal circumstances, the countess would not have required such an escort, but this might be a very awkward party. Her husband, the Earl of Glasbury, would be attending. Her family was coming out in force to support her. Her eldest brother, the Viscount Laclere, intended to ride up to stand at his sister's side too.

"We could watch," Penelope said. "It is a fencing academy owned by the Chevalier Louis Corbet. Some say it is the best in England, despite the fame of Angelo's on Bond Street. At Angelo's fencing is a sport. Here it is said the chevalier teaches it as a skill for war or dueling. We might sneak a peek."

"Is it permitted? Do women watch at this Angelo's?"

"Of course not. However, I have discovered that once a woman has walked out on her husband, there is little else that she can do that will really shock anyone."

Diane had realized some time ago that Penelope considered her new freedom worth a little public censure. Not that she really exploited that freedom. Unlike some women who might brazenly take lovers, Penelope's sins were of a different nature. She mingled with people a countess normally would not, and embraced as friends others who had fallen far lower than herself.

According to Jeanette, the countess was tainting herself beyond redemption. The people who mattered would more easily forgive a love affair with a married man than democratic friendships. It was just a matter of time before some of the drawing rooms still open to the countess, started closing.

Pen led the way to the house's entrance and nudged the door open. They followed the sounds of clashing steel to a large chamber off the hall. Peeking around its doorjamb like children spying at a ball, they saw three pairs of men dueling with swords.

"It looks very dangerous," Penelope whispered. "They are not even wearing padded shirts. One wrong move and there will be blood."

Diane had not considered the danger implied by their garments. She had only noticed the lack of them. Not only did they not wear padded shirts, they wore no shirts at all. The room swam with the images of six naked, strong torsos.

She had never in her life even seen one before.

"I did not realize that your cousin would be here," Penelope said. "The gray-haired man he duels with is the Chevalier Corbet."

Diane had picked out Daniel at once. He faced them, but all his concentration remained on his opponent, as well it must.

"He and the chevalier are clearly the most skilled. My brother's moves are less daring. More studied."

Diane was not noticing the various levels of skill. She could not take her attention off Daniel. He appeared very handsome. Unlike the grimaces of exertion on the younger men's faces, his remained calm, almost cold, as he met the chevalier's attack.

He looked magnificent. Strong and confident and lean and muscular and . . . wonderful. The lightest sheen covered his skin, and taut muscles sculpted his arms and shoulders and chest. He was not the biggest man in the room, but there was no mistaking that every inch of him was finely honed and potentially dangerous.

Her gaze drifted over those muscles, fascinated by their chiseled hardness. The way his torso tapered to his hips compelled her attention. A flush swept her, and forbidden memories of his caresses in the carriage entered her head.

What would it feel like to lay her palm on that chest? It appeared so hard, and yet surely the skin would be warm and soft. . . .

"Hell, Pen, what are you doing in here?" Vergil Duclairc's yell snapped Diane out of her shameful speculations.

They had been noticed.

The sparring ceased immediately. Vergil and three other men strode to the side of the room and grabbed shirts.

Daniel did not. He lowered his sword as he looked to the doorway. His gaze caught Diane's before she could duck behind the jamb.

She felt her color rising. Something in the way he looked at her suggested he had known she was there. Much as she had seen his reaction in the modiste's mirror, he had seen hers, despite his attention on the chevalier's sword.

Unlike Vergil Duclairc, he had let her watch.

His expression reflected neither embarrassment nor shock. His eyes merely acknowledged what she was seeing, and the fact that she had not looked away. And still wasn't.

"Jesus, Pen, what are you thinking?" Vergil suddenly loomed in front of them now, blocking the view of the chamber. His shirt hung loosely off his shoulders, no more than a quick cover to hide his nakedness.

Beside him stood a perfectly beautiful young man with brown hair and a winning smile. Properly clothed, he had been lounging on a bench at the side of the room.

"I had no idea that you fenced without clothes," Pen said.

"Only when we practice defensive sparring. It is to accustom us to the vulnerability—see here, *you* are the one who needs to do the explaining, not me."

"We were just curious about the practices. Thank goodness you were not completely naked, as in Elgin's Greek metopes. And to think I always assumed that was artistic license on the sculptor's part."

Vergil sighed with exasperation. "You know very well that you should have left at once. Furthermore, to bring Miss Albret . . ."

Penelope glanced to Diane. "Oh, dear, I have been remiss. We will go now and wait in the coach. Do not hurry on our account. I insist. Finish as you planned."

Taking Diane's arm, she aimed for the building's entrance. "Vergil can be a bit stuffy. It was always in him, but is getting worse as he grows older. I don't know where he gets it, since our family is not known for such things. Rather the opposite. He means well, but it can be tiresome."

"I agree, Pen. Having just listened to a scold that lasted our entire way here, I have to say that Vergil's stuffiness has swelled considerably since I last saw him. Although sneaking a peek like that really was scandalous of you."

The response came from behind them. Diane glanced back to see the beautiful young man following. The humor in his limpid eyes suggested he found scandalous behavior great fun.

Out in the yard, Pen gave him an embrace and a kiss. "Diane, this is my youngest brother, Dante. He is only eighteen but has already lived a lifetime of trouble. I was surprised to see you in there, Dante. It was kind of you to come down from university to stand by me."

"I am glad to stand with you, but I confess that I had little choice on the coming down part."

Pen's face fell. Her sigh sounded as exasperated as Vergil's had just been. "You mean that you were rusticated? Not *again,* Dante. No wonder Vergil scolded. What was it this time?"

"Just a small matter." Dante shot Diane a glance, to remind his sister they had company.

"Since it appears that we have some time before we leave, I think that I will take a stroll in the park," Diane said.

Pen had become absorbed in her youngest brother and did not object as Diane walked away. Her last sight of them as she turned the corner of the house was Dante speaking with a sheepish expression, and Pen moaning at what she heard.

Diane was well into the woods before she realized that she had never taken a walk in the country before.

The school had been on the outskirts of Rouen, but its surroundings were hardly rural. Outings had been into the city, not away from it. In Paris, and now in London, she enjoyed the parks but never ventured away from the cultivated areas. This Hampstead house might not be circled by farms, but the land was large enough and so overgrown that the setting appeared rustic.

She strolled down paths, surprised that the experience did not startle her more. People spoke of nature as a transforming place. Instead it felt quite familiar to her. Perhaps that was because it was silent and lonely, and her heart was very accustomed to both those things.

Not completely silent. The crack of gunfire pierced the quiet at regular intervals. Not too far away, someone was shooting at game.

That did not startle her either. She knew at once what the sound meant. She knew that it belonged in this place and that she should not go near it.

She turned onto a new path and saw a clearing up ahead. A cottage came into view as she neared the break in the trees.

She paused. The image of that cottage, framed by tree trunks and hovering branches, was so familiar that her breath caught. She had the odd sensation that she had experienced this moment before.

It was not the first time she'd had that eerie feeling. She knew that everyone did sometimes. This was more distinct than ever before, however. She believed that, if required to, she could describe the cottage completely without seeing the rest of it.

She tried to do that. When her mind failed her, when no obscured details emerged, she laughed at herself and walked on.

The cottage, thatched and old, with plastered walls and visible timbers, appeared well maintained. Someone lived there.

As if summoned by her curiosity, the door opened and an old man stepped out. His clothes were simple but clean, his beard long and white. He noticed her.

"Is the chevalier taking women students now?" He chuckled at the notion as he carried a pail to a well.

"I am only visiting. I am not learning to use a sword."

"You speak like him. French, are you? Don't get women here much."

She moved closer. The sensation of a moment relived, grew. "Who are you?"

He looked at her in surprise, then laughed. "I'm George. I keep the grounds, best as I can with these bad legs. I've been here most of my life, since before the chevalier had the place. Hell, I was here when that wastrel had it, before Corbet. Lost it gambling, he did, which I could see coming. Just like I can see those young bloods who come for their dueling lessons probably losing most of what they have to women and cards." He cranked until the pail emerged from the well. "One bold question deserves another. Who are *you*?"

A profound disappointment stabbed at her. "I am no one." It was out before she realized it, a response born of the peculiar desolation suddenly breaking her heart.

She turned on her heel, to be away from this place that made her feel so odd and unknown.

"Do you know your way back?" George asked.

She halted. She had not paid much attention to the paths she had walked. That had been careless.

"Lucky you didn't get lost. You take the first path that branches right. It will bring you to the side of the woods, and just follow it up to the house. There's other, faster ways back, but that is the clearest. You stay along the trees this side of the meadow, though. That firing you hear is one of those bloods practicing with pistols on the other side."

"I thought it was hunting."

"Not much hunting done in these parts anymore. Too many houses being built. Used to be country here, but the city is closing in."

She thanked him and followed the path as he had instructed. When it turned to flank the meadow, the sun burnt away the sensation of déjà vu.

She could not see the house, but she aimed toward it, trusting George's directions. A few early wildflowers dotted the small meadow. By summer, they would blanket it.

She wondered if she would meet the chevalier. If she did, maybe he would invite her to visit again. She imagined herself running barefoot under the sun in this meadow. The fantasy was so vivid that she felt the grass and earth beneath her feet.

The shooting had stopped, but suddenly a crack split the silence. A faint buzz sounded near her ear at the same time. A *thud* to her left made her snap her head around and cry out.

She froze, stunned. It took several moments to comprehend the reason for her reaction.

A gun's ball had whizzed past her.

The chill of fear breathed down her neck. The same shock she had experienced after the opera now immobilized her.

A man emerged on the other side of the meadow. He saw her and broke into a run. As he came toward her she saw only blond hair and a distraught face.

"Are you hurt? Were you hit?" The questions called out as he neared.

She wasn't sure. She did not think so. She shook her head.

"Thank God. A hare startled me and my aim went wild. No one walks these grounds, so when I heard your cry my heart stopped."

Her senses returned. "I am quite safe. I do not even think it came close. I cried out because I was startled, that is all."

He exhaled with relief. "Please allow me to escort you back to the house. Proper introductions will have to wait, but my name is Andrew Tyndale, and I will never forgive myself for my carelessness."

He appeared solid and honest, and a gentleman. With the worry gone from his face, his expression was contrite and concerned. Diane judged him to be in his late forties.

Allowing him to escort her seemed a sensible thing to do. "Thank you, if you would. I am a little shaken, I will confess."

As they walked in silence, she sneaked a few glances his way. He was an attractive man, with a strong jaw and deep-set blue eyes. His countenance bore an open quality, as if he did not dissemble much. She guessed that he had been quite dashing when young. The Roman style of his blond hair and the fashionable cut of his coat suggested that he still thought himself so.

She had met many men of his age since leaving the school. Some ignored the passing years and pretended they were still young, which made them more foolish than clever. Others so thoroughly gave in to the march of time that they might have been sixty already. Andrew Tyndale appeared to have struck a balance. He wore his maturity frankly, but his fitness and fashion announced he was not passé.

He smiled at her. It was a warm smile. It gave his face a countenance that inspired trust. "As I said, proper introductions will have to wait, but since I almost killed you, may I know your name?"

"Diane Albret." She pronounced the "t," as she had ever since arriving in England. She kept hoping that someone would recognize the name if pronounced that way. To claim her true heritage, she had also been trying to purge her speech of French words and her accent, even if both were considered quite fashionable here.

"You are French?" he asked, indicating, as George had, that the accent still marked her.

"I am English, but I grew up in France."

"You were far from home, then, during the war."

Yes, very far from home. She did not know why, but she sensed that he would welcome her confidences on that. He would be far more interested in what that had meant to her than Daniel had been.

"Are you a relative of the chevalier?"

"No. I am here with Lady Glasbury."

"Ah, now I know why you look familiar. I think I saw you with her at Lady Starbridge's ball last week. Is the countess a friend of the chevalier's?"

"I do not think so. We are waiting for her brother to finish his practice."

"You must mean Vergil Duclairc. One of the Hampstead Dueling Society. That is what they call themselves. Not fencing society, but dueling. They practice for the challenge that will never come, and fantasize that they are corsairs."

"You are not a member, I gather."

"I am too old to find fantasies appealing."

"But you make use of the chevalier's academy too?"

"His skills are unsurpassed, and he will use the military sabre, as I prefer. I like that he will spar without padded garments. Unlike the young men in there now, however, I keep my shirt on, and carry a fresh one to don when the practice is done."

He laughed as he made his little joke. She almost did, too, until she remembered that doing so would indicate she had seen them without their shirts.

"The day is fair and the meadow very lovely," he said, giving her a fatherly smile. "Let us walk across it and up to the house by the path in the opposite woods. There is a charming brook where some crocuses are in bloom."

"No one else will be shooting, will they?"

"No, and I know how to stay clear of their range if they should start."

She felt very safe with him, even if he had almost shot her. She wanted to walk across the meadow, so she agreed.

As her hem brushed against dried grass, she decided that she rather liked Andrew Tyndale's company. She might have one day strolled like this with her father if he were not dead. Andrew Tyndale did not frighten her at all, being so old, nor make her unsettled. He treated her as he might a niece or daughter.

He did not create little eternities in which she forgot how to breathe.

"My apologies for my sister, St. John. Living independently has started her doing some very peculiar things."

Daniel smiled at Vergil's exasperation. Doing very peculiar things was something of a Duclairc tradition, and Vergil, with his respect for the appearance of propriety, was the odd one in his family.

"As a married woman, of course, it was not too shocking. Your cousin, however . . ." Vergil tied his cravat in the dressing chamber's mirror. "I will remind Pen of her responsibilities there."

"I would not make more of it than it was. I'm sure if your sister had known, she would have never intruded, let alone allowed my cousin to."

Vergil nodded, relieved to receive absolution for his sister. "Damned decent of you."

Daniel was not feeling at all decent about the whole little episode. Lady Glasbury's behavior could be excused. His own could not.

He had known they were there, long before Vergil called out. He had noticed them as he caught Louis's sword on his own. He had seen Diane watching him. He had been far too conscious of the expression in her eyes.

He had darkly enjoyed every damn second of what had felt like an hour, preening like an animal showing off for its mate.

She was making him ridiculous.

They walked out to the yard where the countess's coach waited. Vergil walked over to it with an expression that said the countess was in for a little talk, in any case.

It turned out to be a short one. He came back to Daniel. "Your cousin is not here. She went for a walk, to permit my sister some privacy with Dante while the tale of his bad behavior could be told."

"I will go and look for her."

"You said that you had an appointment to attend before you joined us in Essex. Allow me, since we will be delayed until she is found anyway."

The appointment was vitally important, but it could definitely wait. Daniel did not want Diane walking these woods.

As he turned toward the house, a little commotion ensued as two of the academy's other students emerged from the house. They piled into a coach and the equipage pulled away.

Its absence revealed a horse tied to a post.

"I did not realize that Tyndale was still here," Daniel said.

"He went to shoot just as we arrived. That was his gun we heard as we practiced."

No sooner had Vergil spoken than his eyes lit with concern. Daniel's heart sank with worry too. It was rare for anyone to walk in the park, and those practicing with pistols did not worry about such things overmuch.

"Surely, if she had been hurt—" Vergil began.

"You and Dante search the meadow and right woods," Daniel said, striding toward the back of the house. "I will go to the target area."

She had not been hurt. Daniel knew that when he heard her laughter.

He followed the sound until he could see her sitting on a log beside the brook. A little pile of crocuses had been heaped into her lap. A man offered her one more.

No pistol ball had found her.

Andrew Tyndale had.

Diane smiled as she accepted the flower. There was no cautious wariness in her eyes. No sense of danger. Of course not. Daniel could not see Tyndale's expression, but he could imagine its open honesty.

No one but Daniel had witnessed the ferocity in those eyes when Tyndale sparred with Louis.

Nor had anyone else seen the other sparks as Tyndale watched Diane from across a crowded chamber at a ball. Daniel had, only because he had been carefully watching for them.

Tyndale sat down beside Diane and pointed to another flower that he held. She puckered her brow as she peered at it and received some lesson in horticulture.

She had to lean closer in order to see the flower well. Daniel did not miss Tyndale's sly awareness of the subtle move.

Would the bastard try it now, here? Had age made the man that rash and bold?

The flower slipped from Tyndale's hand and floated away in the brook. Laughing at his clumsiness, he reached for another from the pile in Diane's lap.

Daniel watched that hand, and the arm brushing Diane's body, and Tyndale's eyes, and he knew for sure that, given enough time on that log, things would get much less innocent.

Instincts that he did not know he owned urged him to move. Primitive emotions of protection and possession shouted in his head. They surged so suddenly and violently that they almost overwhelmed him.

Other instincts held them in check. Those of the cat who sits in utter stillness and awaits the movement of its prey. Those of a man who plans a lifetime to achieve a goal.

That goal waited for him on the log. Five minutes, maybe ten, and it would be finished. Almost. The means of completion would be within reach, however.

He had expected it to take weeks. Months. Instead, fate had done it quickly.

Finished explaining the flower, Tyndale turned and poked its stem into Diane's hair near her ear.

A bit of the wariness that Daniel knew well flickered over her expression. For an instant she scrutinized the face of the man beside her. She relaxed and smiled, reassured.

Daniel pictured that wariness returning. He saw her horror when the assault came. He knew how far he would have to let things go to have an excuse to kill Tyndale for it. The shout to protect her grew and grew as his head saw it all unfold.

A storm broke in him. The urge to step out of the trees appalled the man he had fought to become. Images flew in his mind of all the reasons he should wait for this bastard to damn himself. Memories assaulted him that chilled his spine whenever they surfaced.

Head in turmoil, blood pulsing, he stood torn between the forces raging in him.

Diane bent down to pluck yet another crocus. Tyndale's gaze, hardly fatherly, wandered down her body.

The lasciviousness of that gaze caused streaks of lightning in the storm. A decision that Daniel had never expected crystallized at once.

She had suffered enough in this. He would find another way.

chapter 13

Daniel stepped out of the trees.

Diane saw him as she bent to pluck a purple crocus. The sound of his step made her head snap up. She straightened quickly.

Her girlhood name for him popped into her head. The Devil Man. She had not thought of him that way in weeks, but she did now.

His expression appeared amiable. He strolled forward casually. All the same, she sensed a threat in him, a coiled danger. His eyes definitely held the lights that said nothing distracted him this day.

"Here you are. We feared you had gotten lost. The countess is waiting." Daniel's gaze came to rest not on her, but on Andrew Tyndale. "You and I have never met. I am Daniel St. John. Miss Albret is my cousin."

Mister Tyndale rose. "I must apologize for not bringing her back at once. Her pleasure in the flowers delayed us."

"Actually, I did get lost and Mister Tyndale was good enough to show me the proper paths." The lie blurted out. For some reason, it seemed a good idea to give one.

"It is kind of you to try and overlook my inexcusable carelessness, Miss Albret, but the truth must be told or your cousin will find our association improper. I was shooting and a ball went wild, St. John. When I heard a woman cry out, I ran to investigate. Your cousin was not harmed, I am relieved to say, but she was badly shaken. Pausing a moment by this brook so she could collect herself seemed an appropriate thing to do."

"I thank you for taking care of her. There was no way for her to know that these woods could be dangerous. If I had realized she would have an opportunity to explore them, I would have mentioned it. I should have in any case, as a precaution, upon learning she would be stopping here with the countess." He stepped toward Diane and cleared the way. "You have my gratitude."

It was a dismissal, and just short of being rude. Mister Tyndale graciously took the hint and strode up the path through the trees.

"You are to have nothing to do with that man in the future. Ever."

Daniel's back was to her as he issued the command.

"I think he is very nice, and sadly distressed by the accident with the pistol."

It came out more of a challenge than she had intended.

He turned. When she saw his expression, a lump formed in her throat.

"There was no accident. He saw you walking alone and shot in your direction, to have an excuse to meet you. There is no way that someone using the target area could send a ball over the meadow."

His accusation raised her irritation. He was becoming as tiresome as Penelope found Vergil, only Daniel St. John had no right to these lessons and scolds with her. He was not her brother, or even a relative. She resented the way he impugned poor Mister Tyndale, who had been so worried and contrite for his error.

"Perhaps he used a different target area. A hare startled him and—"

"A *bear* would not startle that man. He is reputed to be one of the best shots in England. Thank God for that, since he dared such a ruse to get to you."

"You are ranting like a madman. Mister Tyndale was in every way a gentleman. Not to mention that he is old enough to be my father."

"Christ, you are ignorant. Do you think a man's age makes any difference in such things?"

"Yes, I do. His behavior was impeccable with me. I enjoyed his company. I think that he would be a good friend to me."

"He wants more than friendship, trust me on this."

She laughed. "That is what Madame Leblanc said about you. Almost the same words."

"And she was right, damn it."

He suddenly was closer. Right in front of her. She had to tilt her head to see his face.

New sparks entered his eyes. The deep ones she had seen that first evening in Paris when he broke the urn. The steely ones he had displayed when he confronted Vergil at Margot's salon.

He was jealous.

She had no experience with jealousy, but she did not doubt she was right. A stupid part of her was flattered. A bigger part was furious.

"Do you warn them all off? Do you spend your time at those parties and dinners following me around, letting them all know that I am penniless and orphaned and not worth their attention?"

"I let them know that if they do not treat you properly, they will answer to me."

"But you count on none of them wanting to pursue me properly because I have no fortune, don't you?"

He did not respond, but she had learned enough of how the world worked to know she was right.

The absurdity of her situation hit her with force. Her head pounded with indignation.

She gestured to her garments and laughed bitterly. "But you have spoiled me, St. John. Ruined me. Look at the doll you have bought. Do you expect me to sit on the shelf forever, being pretty? When this is over, what choice is there for me? Should I be content to be a governess now? Or a lady's companion? After all these grand diversions? I have been calling on *duchesses*. Since there is no proper way for me to live this life in the future, I think I had better consider the alternative."

"What do you mean by that?"

"Margot has returned to London with Mister Johnson by now. I have been remiss in not calling on her."

She turned on her heel. She managed three smug, angry steps before he grabbed her arm.

"The hell you will." He swung her back to him. Against him.

His embrace enclosed her. Shocked her. She managed one squirm of resistance before the warmth of his body and the demand in his eyes began defeating her indignation.

She fought the enticing intimacy even though her heart ached for it. Maybe that was what she had meant by threatening to become a Margot. Perhaps if she did, the loneliness and the void would be obscured for a while.

As Daniel was obscuring it now.

"You are not to have anything to do with Tyndale." He spoke gently this time. Seriously. It sounded more a warning than a command, but she still had enough sense left, enough hold on real time and place, to resent it.

"He does not think of me in that way. *He* is a gentleman."

"All men think of you in that way."

"I doubt that is true. I think—"

His kiss silenced her. Its firm demand proved that at least one man thought of her that way.

The kisses came slow and hard and merciless. They were full of the danger she had sensed when he emerged from the trees, and of the jealousy she had perceived in his accusations. They were the kisses of a man provoked, ignoring rules and proprieties, laying claims he did not even want.

She knew all of that, but her heart and her soul could not resist. The warmth weakened her as it always did. That he cared enough and noticed enough to be jealous was something, at least. Even lust required attention. Even base hunger meant she was wanted in some manner. The way he aroused her body only weakened her more. Slow caresses reminded her of the physical joy he could give.

She succumbed to the daze. She forgot where they were, and that she should stop him. The hated void shrank, died, liberating a happiness she did not deserve. She clung to it hungrily, but even in her rapture she knew it was false and would not last.

His hand moved under her cloak. Kisses burned her neck, biting at her pulse. A caress on her breast made her gasp. Her soul knew that he would not stop, that he was more removed from the world than she.

His fingers stroked her nipple, sending pleasure shivering through her.

"You are to have nothing to do with him," he said again. "With any of them."

A tiny rebellion sparked in her mind, but he obliterated it with another kiss. His embrace commanded more than lured. She lost her grip on her feeble resistance as his power swept her away. She kissed him back, not knowing why, just agreeing without deciding to, because the reactions of her body and heart demanded it.

His embrace wandered, caressing her boldly. She moved into his touch even while the path of his hands startled her. Over her stomach and bottom, down to her thighs, he pressed and claimed all of her. His touch moved more shockingly, teasing through her gown along the cleft of her bottom, venturing toward the pulse that maddened her, making the pleasure sink and throb.

A voice called his name, seeking him. She heard, but he did not. It penetrated her stupor and reawoke her alertness to their surroundings. Frightened, she twisted her body to escape.

He lifted his head and froze as the sound of Vergil's voice approached on the path.

She broke free and jumped away. With the separation, confusion inundated her.

"You said you would not. In Paris, you promised—"

"I promised nothing."

Suddenly Vergil stood at the side of the little clearing. He looked at her and then at Daniel.

She could tell that Vergil suspected what he had interrupted. Daniel undoubtedly could tell too. He appeared unfazed, however, as if what had occurred was worth the expression of disapproval flickering beneath his young friend's lowered lids.

Vergil tried to hide the awkwardness. "Tyndale said you found her. Good. Pen would like to be off soon, however. She wants to arrive at the party before the earl."

"Of course. It was rude of me to delay the countess." Diane had no idea how she found the voice to speak. She cobbled together enough poise to walk away from Daniel's scorching gaze and accept Vergil's escort to the waiting coach.

"He is being very cautious," Adrian said as he led the way down the street. "If I did not know what he was up to, I most likely wouldn't have a clue from what has happened."

Daniel walked beside him along the quiet lanes near the river. They were not in London, but across the bridge in Southwark, in a poor quarter of ramshackle buildings and warehouses.

He tried to pay attention to Adrian's story but it was hard. His mind was full of Diane. His head and body were still back at the brook, succumbing to the raging desire that his decision about Tyndale had unleashed. He had wanted to kill Vergil for interfering, but was also grateful for it. If left alone much longer, he would have laid Diane down and—

"He needed me to find this building, of course. No one who owns such insignificant property can speak his language and he can't speak theirs. He also had me take drawings to get the cylinders made. He was able to procure the chemicals on his own, I suspect, since he required nothing of me there."

"Fortunate that he stumbled upon you," Daniel said, forcing his attention to the matter at hand.

Adrian chuckled. "I walked right in front of the man three times before he did. He is always looking at the ground, ruminating on the great questions of the universe, one assumes. I never expected him to blackmail me into working for him, however. I merely thought it would be easier to keep a watch if he expected to see me about." He stopped at a building, little more than a large shed tucked low and deep between its neighbors. "Here we are."

"You'd think the crown jewels were inside." Three big shiny locks festooned the door.

"I considered having the locksmith make me extra keys, but did not want to take the chance Dupré would find out. No problem, however. Keep a watch now."

Daniel blocked him from view. Glancing back, he saw Adrian remove a thin metal stylus from his coat and begin picking the top lock. "Where did you learn that?"

"From a colonel in the guard with our embassy in Turkey. It is a useful skill for a diplomat's secretary to have."

The first two locks clicked open in rapid succession. Daniel threw back his arm. "Wait. I see someone."

Adrian turned and folded his arms. Daniel peered into the shadows across the way where he had noticed a movement. "I had better check. Wouldn't do if Dupré had someone watching this place."

"Unless he found a French spy, I don't know how he would arrange it. But go ahead."

Daniel walked out of the rubble yard in front of the building and aimed for the shadow.

As soon as his destination became clear, a man darted out and hurried down the street. In the few moments before the man turned away, Daniel caught a glimpse of a beard and dark hair beneath the hat.

He returned to Adrian. "Just some poor sod, curious and idle, as one would expect in this area."

Adrian worked the final lock. He pushed the door open.

The interior of the building was as poor as the outside. Years ago someone had plastered the walls, but time had turned them cracked and gray. A little light came in through a high small window, despite the new shutters and lock that covered it.

Against one wall was a table covered with a row of metal cylinders, each connected by wires to a liquid-filled pan.

Daniel strode over and peered into the pans. Each one held a chunk of metal of good size. "Is it operational?"

"I think so. I haven't stuck my hand in one to find out."

"There must be a hundred pounds of iron here."

"Since I arranged the purchase, I can say it is exactly that."

Daniel took in the remarkable contraption. "This must have cost a good deal of money."

"My purchases came to over a thousand pounds. The chemicals had to have been hundreds more." Adrian pointed to the iron bars. "You will notice that they are of even size and shape. I added that requirement. I had no idea what you intended, but should you plan anything, I thought the standardization would be convenient."

"Good man," Daniel said, although he also had no idea what he intended to do, if anything.

"I can't see how he had the funds for this himself. The house in Paris was his family's, and I don't think there was any great inheritance beside it. He has little income, except some fees from the university there. Let us say this cost fifteen hundred. He paid out of hand, and I sensed there was more if needed. Where would he get money like that?" Adrian said.

Daniel surveyed the experiment. No, not an experiment. It was too big for that. Too elaborate. This was more a working model, to assess costs and potential.

His suspicions had been correct. Dupré had not done this for other scientists, but to impress men from the world of manufacturing.

Fifteen hundred pounds out of hand, Adrian had said. A significant cost. One that Dupré could not manage alone, that was certain.

"How many keys did he have the locksmith make?"

"Two sets."

"He has taken on a partner," Daniel said. "The question is, who?"

chapter 14

H*ave nothing to do with him.* It proved impossible, because Andrew Tyndale had also been invited to the party.

Nor was it a large group that gathered at Lady Pennell's house for the weekend. At most, thirty attended. As one of the most notable ladies who enjoyed broad circles, Lady Pennell had invited a mixed group, including a famous actor and a popular novelist as well as members of Parliament, an earl, two barons, and a viscount.

No women from the most selective circles came, of course. Lady Pennell was not favored by the arbiters of society, even if their men found her gatherings more interesting than drinking punch at proper affairs.

"Thank goodness my brothers agreed to attend," Pen said as she and Diane settled into their chamber. Pen had insisted that they share one, even though their hostess had planned other arrangements. Since it had a small sitting room, they would hardly be crowded.

"I did not realize the party would be this small. The earl cannot be tactfully avoided, I'm afraid," Pen muttered.

Diane suspected no one could be avoided. Not the earl. Nor Mister Tyndale. Nor Daniel St. John, when he arrived this evening.

Have nothing to do with him. Daniel had issued that warning about Andrew Tyndale, but her heart now did so about Daniel himself. Their embrace and kisses in the woods had badly shaken her, and her thoughts had dwelled on them ever since. She suspected that the pact made in Paris had been irrevocably broken.

The implications frightened her. So did her reactions. Not only worry had occupied her since she took her place in Pen's coach. A wistful yearning filled her too. She miserably admitted that she was intrigued and excited by Daniel, and none of her should be, not even a tiny bit. Contrary to her rebellious threat at the brook, becoming a Margot would mean a life she could not live.

Pen busied herself instructing a servant in unpacking her wardrobe. Diane's own garments waited for attention later.

"It was kind of Lady Pennell to invite me," Diane said. Of all the invitations she had received, she found this one the most peculiar.

"She likes to surround herself with interesting people."

"I am not interesting."

"That is not true. However, I will admit that my coming influenced your invitation, as did the hope it would encourage an acceptance by your cousin."

"So Lady Pennell finds Daniel interesting?"

"Most women do. Not only his wealth and style made his way in society, but also the fascination of influential women. Actually, I think that Lady Pennell has a bit of a *tendre* for him now. He is handsome and confident and mysterious. His bearing and presence have raised all kinds of speculations over the years."

"What kind of speculations?"

"As his cousin, you will probably find them humorous. When he arrived out of nowhere several years ago, there were rumors that he had made his fortune through piracy on the high seas. Others whispered he had used his ships for special services for the navy. Some insisted he was a French émigré as a boy, from the revolution, and has blood much richer than he claims." Pen laughed and raised an eyebrow. "Which means, of course, that you do as well."

Diane forced herself to laugh too. "If we did, I should know, shouldn't I?"

"Well, as I said, it was all speculation. No one really knows his history, so stories are created." Pen gave her a quizzical, encouraging glance.

Diane could hardly satisfy Pen's curiosity about Daniel, since she herself knew very little of his history. Admitting that would reveal the lie about their relationship. That would definitely give everyone something to speculate about.

To avoid further conversation on the topic, she left Pen to the unpacking and went into the little sitting room to wait her turn.

A serving girl arrived with a tray of refreshments. As she set it on a table, she eyed Diane with blatant curiosity.

She headed back to the door, but stopped. She flushed and curtsied. "My apologies, Miss Albret, but may I ask you a question?"

"Of course. What is it?"

"I come from Fenwood, and the vicar there is named Albret too. Are you related to him?"

Diane stared at the pretty girl, with her muslin cap and lovely skin and bright blue eyes. She found herself unable to respond, because her heart began beating so hard and fast it pained her.

"My apologies," the girl said. "It was inappropriate for me to ask, it is just that I found it curious, what with you being French and all. . . ."

"I am not aware of relations in this town you mention, but if some are there, I would like to know. Where is this place?"

"Why, not more than a couple hours' cart ride from here. It is a village near Brinley. Mister Paul Albret has been vicar there forever, since before I was born."

Diane could not believe her good fortune. If this servant girl had been even a speck less bold . . .

"What is your name?"

"Mary."

"I am grateful that you spoke to me, Mary. I may have never learned of this possible relative otherwise."

"Oh, I doubt that. There're lots of us from the area, serving in the houses of this county. You'd have met one of us eventually."

"Mary, is this vicar in residence there now? If I sent a letter of inquiry, would he receive it, do you think?"

"He lives there. Always has."

"Did you know his children?"

"Before my time, they was. Two girls and a boy, seems to me, but they all left years ago. I've never heard of them coming back. My family doesn't know the vicar well, since we are Wesleyan."

The sitting room with its classical mahogany furniture suddenly felt confining. The notion of being imprisoned in this house with this party struck Diane as a terrible inconvenience. The answer to the relentless questions in her soul could be waiting a few hours away.

"Thank you, Mary."

Perhaps she would find a way to visit this town that Mary spoke of. Meanwhile, she could at least make contact with the vicar and see if he knew anything.

While Pen fussed with the wardrobe in the next room, Diane sat at the writing desk and began composing a letter.

"One would think this was Parliament and a vote had been called," Pen said. She sat beside Diane in the drawing room after dinner.

Diane squeezed her hand sympathetically. Although distracted by thoughts of a partly written letter, and by distressingly insistent memories of kisses in the woods, Diane could not miss the social drama unfolding.

The party had not been arranged to create a confrontation between the Earl and Countess of Glasbury, but the presence of both of them affected everything. Expectation rippled through the guests. During dinner, glances darted to the end of the table where the estranged couple sat too near to ignore each other.

As soon as the men had rejoined the ladies, two groups had subtly formed. The guests announced with their placement and conversation which side they had chosen. Diane eyed the larger cluster around the earl, and the presence of Andrew Tyndale by his side. Daniel, who had arrived shortly before dinner, mingled with the group near Pen. The Duclairc's solicitor, the brooding Julian Hampton, stood nearby too, observing but rarely participating.

The Viscount Laclere lent his prestige as he had promised, but it was Vergil who literally stood at Pen's side.

"They have abandoned me. It was to be expected, I suppose." Pen whispered the observation as her gaze directed Diane to the women across the chamber. Few ladies rallied near the settee.

Pen's expression and poise said that nothing untoward was happening. Diane felt her friend's embarrassment, however. She saw in Pen's eyes the realization of the full cost of separating from her husband.

Pen suddenly stiffened. The Earl of Glasbury, a slender man of middle years with gray hair, thick eyebrows, and a slack mouth, had crossed the divide and was aiming their way.

Pen's circle eased back to allow room for private combat. Everyone made a display of not noticing, even while dozens of eyes managed to keep his progress in view.

"At least no one is licking lips in anticipation," Pen whispered.

"What impressive restraint."

The earl's gaze narrowed on Pen. He struck Diane as the sort of man who enjoyed looking down on people, as he did his wife now.

"How are you faring, my dear?"

"I am faring quite well."

"Indeed you are. The whole town speaks of it. You have become the envy of every mindless female of little wit and less discretion. You have your own house and carriage. You have the freedom to behave scandalously. You have the pleasure of nurturing a tradesman's *cousin.*"

Diane did not miss the emphasis and its insinuation.

Daniel heard, even standing ten yards away. His lids lowered, but he did not otherwise react.

"See here—" Vergil began.

"Thank you, but I will handle this, Vergil." Pen had shrunk as the earl approached, but now her spine straightened. "It is unwise for a shameless libertine to impugn another man in such a way, my dear."

"Also dangerous," Vergil added.

The earl sneered. "The world has gone to hell these last years, what with countesses and duchesses being so indiscriminate. As if money and a handsome face make a man."

Pen smiled. "Better money and a handsome face than sour, degenerate old blood."

"It is a wonder that you came, if you despise Lady Pennell's circle so much," Vergil said.

"One hopes that her parties will be more agreeable after tonight. Besides, I came so that I could see my wife. It is time for this embarrassing estrangement to cease."

"You wasted your time, then. I will not return to you."

"If I decide that you will, there will be no choice. The law—"

"Do anything to coerce the countess, and the law will know all of it." The threat did not come from Vergil. Julian Hampton had strolled over to listen, and now interrupted with a very quiet voice.

The earl glared at him. "She wouldn't dare."

Hampton gazed over the assembly, both seeing all and seeing nothing. "Of course she will. You believe it, or you would have never agreed to the terms of separation I negotiated. Now, I had planned to spend these days in town, not being bored at a country party. It seems to me that this house and group are large enough that you and the countess need not speak again. Indulge me on this, so that tomorrow I can take my leave."

He strolled away, to speak to no one.

Livid, the earl left too.

"My apologies for how he insulted you and your cousin," Pen said. "Also for the way he spoke so freely in front of you."

Diane knew he had spoken so freely because he considered her too insignificant to waste discretion on. Just as men like him did not see the presence of servants, he had disregarded her.

Vergil leaned and whispered in Pen's ear, but Diane heard anyway. "Where is your chamber?"

"In the eastern wing. I insisted that Diane share it with me."

"Good girl. I will come visit, in any case."

The drawing room was emptying when Vergil approached Daniel. "Hampton and I are going to play cards. Why don't you join us?"

"I think not. I rarely gamble with friends."

"Indulge me, St. John. I am facing a long night, and since Hampton never talks, it will be unbearable."

Daniel reluctantly agreed. Vergil could ill afford to lose at cards, which meant that Daniel would have to arrange to let him win. He did not mind that, but it made the game less interesting.

He joined Vergil and left the drawing room. They did not enter the library as Daniel expected. Instead, Vergil pointed him to the staircase. "Pen's chamber has a sitting room. No reason to make the servants stay up to accommodate us, and if we play there, that will not be necessary."

As they mounted the staircase, another man headed down. Andrew Tyndale blandly acknowledged them both as he passed.

Daniel stopped Vergil. "Why not invite him too? Four will make the play more diverting."

"Best not to."

"Duclairc, we are going to play cards in that sitting room to protect your sister in case the earl arrives tonight with dishonorable intentions, am I right?"

Vergil's face hardened at having it so bluntly laid out.

"How much better if one of the earl's friends is sitting there with us. Less chance of things getting out of hand should your suspicions be correct."

Vergil grudgingly nodded. He followed Tyndale down the stairs, calling for his attention.

Daniel watched the invitation being given. This night of cards might be interesting after all. He did not like to win against friends, but he had no such compunctions about enemies.

Vergil returned with Tyndale in tow. Hampton was waiting at the top of the second landing. The four of them trailed through the east wing to Pen's sitting room.

"Now, you must all promise not to get drunk and raucous and keep us up all night," Pen admonished as they moved a table and chairs into the center of the room. In expectation of their arrival, she had called for wine and whisky.

"Us" turned out to be her and Diane. Daniel had not realized they were sharing a chamber. He guessed that having her companion nearby was another attempt on the countess's part to thwart any attempt by the earl to claim his husbandly rights while they spent the night under the same roof.

It also meant that Daniel would have Diane nearby on this night. The chamber was not large, and her proximity instantly heightened the tension that had been silently stretching between them since he arrived at this house. The whole evening he had felt her awareness of him, and of what had happened, even if she pretended he did not exist.

She continued ignoring him now. She sat at the writing desk, scratching something onto a paper, showing no interest in the men as they settled down to play. The countess perched on a bench. It appeared that the women would stay a short while before retiring, to make it appear a private party.

Daniel took the chair at the table that allowed him to watch Diane, even though she would distract him. He did not want Tyndale in that position. Watching Tyndale watch Diane would distract him worse.

His sly move served little purpose. Diane completed her task and joined the countess on the bench. That put her in an excellent location for Tyndale to smile at her and for her to smile back.

Diane also smiled at Vergil and Hampton. The only person whom she did not favor with attention was Daniel himself. She went to great pains not even to look his way, as she had all evening.

He wasn't fooled in the least. They might have been alone, embracing, so taut was the connection between them. She may not want that, she might even resent it, but it was undeniably there, affecting the air and time and light.

"Your play is off, St. John," Hampton said as Daniel lost another ten pounds to Andrew Tyndale.

"Perhaps it is not that his play is off, but that Mister Tyndale's is on," Diane offered.

Tyndale enjoyed the flattery to an unseemly degree.

Daniel caught Diane's gaze as it swept past him. He held it and allowed himself a brief, intense, and vivid memory of their embrace by the brook, one full of her sighs and yielding, of what had happened and what almost had. Her color started rising, as if his gaze communicated the image and the sensations.

"Why don't we raise the stakes?" Daniel asked. "You gentlemen should benefit from my weak play."

"Certainly. Might as well make it worth our time," Tyndale said.

Hampton offered no opinion, but his glance toward Daniel held speculation. "Perhaps the ladies would like to retire. We can continue on our own."

"Goodness, no," the countess said. "Not when the real fun begins. Besides, I need to be here to drag my brother away before he ruins himself."

Vergil sighed. "Hell, Pen, it isn't as if I am Dante."

"Speaking of Dante, the last I saw he had Mrs. Thornton making silly cooing noises as they perused some book," the countess said. "Where is he, Vergil?"

"I believe that he has retired, madame." Hampton's tone suggested that the less asked about the circumstances and location of Dante's retirement, the better. He began dealing the cards. "Fifty pounds, gentlemen?"

Tyndale and Vergil nodded. Hampton glanced to Daniel for agreement.

The high stakes appeared to distress Diane, and not because she feared her benefactor might see the worst of it. Daniel got the distinct impression that she worried only for Tyndale.

Her manner provoked him. Every cool expression denied the truth and rejected the way they were totally together in those embraces and still were in this chamber. Worse, she now deliberately encouraged Tyndale, despite the warning she had received.

An edgy annoyance grew in his head. He kept it in check, but it affected him anyway. He had foregone the dream of a lifetime for the pretty woman now fussing over her would-be assailant. He had sacrificed it for her and for something that could not even be, and she acted as though he meant nothing to her, even though she melted whenever he touched her.

He turned his attention to Tyndale.

"Why not a hundred?" he said.

Tyndale's lids lowered appreciatively, but his response was interrupted as the door of the sitting room eased open with a squeak.

A new visitor slipped in. His rump appeared first. He backed in as he checked the corridor to make sure he had not been noticed.

Hampton set down the cards and crossed his arms over his chest. Vergil appeared angry enough to kill, so much that Daniel put a restraining hand on his arm. Tyndale smiled with amusement.

Their visitor closed the door with great, silent care. He turned.

It took the Earl of Glasbury a moment to realize he had not surreptitiously entered an empty chamber, but interrupted a little party. He stood immobilized with surprise, his slack mouth open in astonishment.

"Did you want something, dear?" the countess asked.

The earl's mouth flapped.

Everyone waited, letting him twist in the breeze. Even his friend Tyndale enjoyed the moment more than a friend ought.

It was Hampton who let him off the hook. "No doubt you heard about our private gaming from a servant and hoped to join."

"Yes, that's right."

Not completely off the hook. "It is fortunate the servant's gossip was correct, or this might be misinterpreted and cost you dearly."

The earl flushed a deep rose. Composing himself, he looked down his nose at the assembly. "The gossip was in error. I was told the table would include more interesting players."

"So long as there is money to be lost, we are not fussy about the stripe of the man losing it," Daniel said. "Therefore, you are free to join us."

The earl straightened with indignation at the insult. His hand reached back for the door latch. "I think not. I am very fussy myself regarding the stripe of the men I associate with. Excuse my intrusion."

"Sleep well, my dear," the countess said sweetly to his departing back.

Diane appeared very concerned for Tyndale's erratic progress over the next hour. Her face lit with delight when he won and fell when he lost.

That raised the devil in Daniel. In response, he dragged out the destruction he had every intention of wreaking.

As play got more rash, Hampton, commenting that the night would end with one man's fortunes greatly diminished, bowed out of play completely, lest the man accidentally be him.

Down three hundred, Vergil bowed out too.

Daniel used the opportunity to lose a thousand very quickly to the only opponent left.

"Your luck had improved considerably, St. John," Tyndale said as the cards were dealt once more. "It appears the tide has turned again, however."

"I find that my luck is always erratic. Also, the countess is a great distraction."

"As is your cousin," Tyndale said jovially, giving Diane a smile.

As far as Daniel was concerned, a gauntlet had been thrown.

"If we are such distractions, it is time we retire." The countess rose, and everyone else did too. "Make this chamber your own, gentlemen. Thank you for your company."

Diane followed her into the next chamber. Daniel heard the vague sounds on the other side of the wall that spoke of women preparing for bed. He allowed himself the fantasy of imagining Diane undressing and washing and having her long hair brushed, and lost another two thousand pounds as it unfolded.

Finally the sounds stopped. A maid slipped out and away.

Daniel pictured Diane huddled on her side, her lids closed and her lovely face in repose.

He wiped the image from his mind. He turned every bit of his attention on Tyndale. "Shall we get serious now? What do you say to two hundred?"

chapter 15

"Diane, what are you laboring over?" Pen called.

"A letter." Diane had written two last night and not been satisfied with either of them. The long one that explained her entire history certainly would not do. Nor would the one that dissolved into begging pleas. Now she hurriedly scratched a simple request for information regarding one Jonathan Albret, the shipper, if the vicar of Fenwood happened to know of him.

She provided her address in London and sealed the letter before she could start fussing over it. She carried it into the bedchamber where the maid was finishing Pen's hair.

"How can I have this posted?" she asked.

Pen took the letter and thrust it at the servant. "Give it to the butler. Go now. I am done here."

The woman left. Pen peered in the mirror and tweaked one of the loose curls framing her face. "What a dreadful day I am facing. An excursion to the sea, no less. It will be biting at the coast, no matter how fair the day is here. The men are leaving earlier, to fish before we join them, but I will have to be near *him* most of the day, and, after last night, he frightens me more than ever."

Pen was referring to the earl, but her words spoke of Diane's own discomfort. After last night, Daniel frightened her even more than before too. Or rather, he made her frightened of herself.

It had been both horrible and wonderful, sitting in the outer chamber while the men played cards. She had barely looked at Daniel and he had only glanced at her, but the physical sensations he had aroused by the brook had returned when he entered the sitting room. The hands that held his cards might have been caressing her body, and the mouth that sipped at wine might have been kissing her neck and breast.

He had known. That one hot look had said so. He had toyed with her, too, keeping the memories alive, making it worse. She had been helpless to stop it and too weak to claim a headache and leave the way she should. The physical stirrings and vivid awareness of each other were too compelling, too delicious, to deny.

The notion of spending the day in such a state dismayed her. She needed time away from him, to collect her emotions. Time to try and put things back in order.

"I am not feeling very well, Pen. I think that I should stay here and rest."

Pen turned from the mirror with concern. "What ails you, dear? If I have caused you to get ill by keeping you awake until all hours—"

"It is nothing serious. I am merely very tired."

"Perhaps I should stay with you, just in case. . . ."

"That is thoughtful, but it is not necessary. I am not ill. I think that I will get some air and then come back and sleep."

Pen debated it. Finally, she shook her head. "If I stay, everyone will say it is a ruse on my part, in response to last evening. No, I have to brave this out. I will stand my ground although the day promises to be dreadful." She laughed, bitterly. "To think that I did not seek a divorce in order to spare *him* the scandal. Well, Mr. Hampton warned me that it is always the woman who pays."

Andrew Tyndale watched from the window as the carriages rolled down the lane. His gaze locked on a very expensive one. Four black horses led it, finer by far than the cattle that Andrew himself owned. It galled him that Daniel St. John could afford such luxuries.

It galled him even more that, as of today, St. John had the means to purchase many more of them.

Twenty thousand pounds worth.

How in blazes had it happened?

Andrew had been asking himself that question all through the early hours of the dawning day.

He never lost big at the gaming tables. He despised men who did not know when to walk away, men who risked too much and saw ruin as a result. He did not even enjoy cards very much. He much preferred games where luck played no role. Games he knew he would win, because he made the rules.

It had been the girl's fault, he decided. She had distracted him badly while she was there. She couldn't be more than seventeen, he judged, but she had a poise, an air, that suggested a luscious sensuality waited beneath her demure innocence. It had been a very long time since he had a refined one, and that had increased her appeal. The girls Mrs. P. found were ignorant, stupid calfs. He much preferred well-bred fillies.

Yes, she had distracted him badly. He had been in a state of arousal while she stayed in that room. Actually, he had been that way a lot since he first noticed her at that ball.

Somehow, their contest had become about her. He hadn't realized that at the time, but thinking back . . . Her smiles when he won, her concern when he lost, her cousin's disapproval—it had all played a role, he was very sure now.

Still, twenty thousand pounds? No pretty face could do that to him. He had been up so often during the night, by vast amounts, that realizing how much he had lost in the end had shocked him.

Worse, this gentleman's debt had witnesses no one would doubt.

The carriages grew small in the distance, heading to the coast. He had begged off the fishing excursion, claiming illness, even though St. John would see it for what it was. He didn't give a damn about that. He had bigger problems than the opinion of a shipper.

An ugly fury split in his head, as it had many times since he left the countess's sitting room. He saw again the glint of triumph in St. John's eyes as Hampton worked the tally. The devil probably looked like that when he won a man's soul.

There was only one explanation, of course. The lowlife bastard had cheated. How, Andrew was not sure, but that was what had transpired.

The carriages had disappeared and the drive was deserted.

A movement close below, near the house, caught his eye. A slender form with unfashionable piles of chestnut hair walked into view.

As he watched Diane Albret, a way out of the dilemma occurred to him. It had a touch of righteous justice, and it would work too. St. John had the arrogance and pride that ensured it would.

For all her polish, the girl was an obscure nobody. St. John was, too, when you got down to it. After it was over, the people who mattered would agree that St. John had been a fool and Andrew greatly wronged. Furthermore, the twenty thousand pounds would no longer matter.

After all, dead men can't collect on private debts.

After Diane got some air, to clear her thoughts, she returned to her chamber. She stayed in the room until she heard the activity outside that said the women were leaving to join the party at the coast.

They would not return until early evening. That meant that she had a long day to herself.

She had already decided how to spend it. While walking outside, she had taken a hard look at her life. She had not been pleased with what she saw.

She had admitted to herself that for all Daniel's reassurances, she was not safe from his interest.

She went to her wardrobe. As she slipped into her half boots, she admitted that she was not safe because of her own reactions. His kisses might be scandalous, but no more than the way she permitted them.

Well, she was not the girl who had left Madame Leblanc in Rouen. She had learned something of the world in the last months. She knew that Daniel had made some decision about her yesterday beside that brook, and that the next time those kisses would not stop.

And there would be a next time. She did not doubt that.

She retrieved her cloak from the wardrobe. She wished that she had brought her old garments from school, and not only because they would help her to look less conspicuous. It would embarrass her to complete today's mission wearing the things purchased for her by a man who was neither a relative nor a guardian.

Everyone knew what that usually meant.

She had been unbearably naive to believe Daniel when he said it did not in their case.

Suitably dressed for her outing, she made her way through the silent house. It was time to remember why she was even in England. If she discovered the life she'd had before Daniel St. John entered it, perhaps there would be something to anchor and sustain her when she severed her ties with him.

She hoped so. She wasn't sure that she could do it otherwise. The very notion pained her so deeply, left her so bereft, that she had sat in the garden, blocking it from her mind. Eventually she had accepted what she had to do, however.

She needed to abandon his house, and his sister, and his gifts and generosity. She needed to run away from his warmth and embraces.

She needed to leave him.

She marched on, her eyes misting, the hated void sitting fat and vacant and heavy in her heart.

A few servants wandered the house's corridors, and she asked one to find Mary. The pretty girl met her in the kitchen.

"How does one find your town?" Diane asked.

"Are you thinking to go there, my lady?"

"Someday, perhaps."

"I only know how to get there from here. You take the west road to Witham, and turn north aways, then go west again at Brinley."

"It is two hours away, you said?"

"Maybe a bit longer. The roads are only dirt once you get to Witham. Don't know how far it is from London."

Diane left the house by way of the servants' entrance near the kitchen. It seemed only right to do that, as she had those first days in Paris. It was not the doll of the wealthy Daniel St. John sallying forth today. It was the penniless orphan too obscure for anyone to notice.

Two hours by cart, Mary had said.

A person could walk faster than a cart rolls.

Diane headed west on the road. She should return well before Pen and the others got back from the coast.

An hour later, she knew why people chose slow carts over faster walking.

She had put on her half boots, but the fashions sold in Paris shops were flimsy at best. The thin-soled ones on her feet did not appear likely to survive a day on the road.

It got worse once she turned onto the dirt road at Witham. Ruts and stones gouged the bottoms of her feet. She tried to ignore the discomfort and scolded herself for being so soft. That was what luxury did to people, Madame Leblanc had always taught. It made them soft and weak and prone to sin.

How true. How very, very true.

She pictured Madame intoning her moral lessons. She tried to accept the pain to her feet as punishment for enjoying Daniel's kisses. She told herself that every touch had been wrong and sinful and spoke of a man not to be trusted. A seducer. A predator. A devil.

Her heart would not accept it. She did not feel sinful when it came to Daniel.

She was contemplating that new truth when the sound of an approaching carriage penetrated her attention. She angled off the road, to let it go by.

To her surprise it rolled to a stop right next to her. Andrew Tyndale sat in a curricle, holding the ribbons, looking at her with surprise.

"Miss Albret, what are you doing here?"

"Oh, just walking. What are you doing here?"

"I decided to visit a friend in the country for the day. Allow me to take you back to the house first, however. I fear you have walked farther than you realize."

"Please, no. You have things to do. I could not think of delaying you."

"It will only be a small delay, and insignificant in any case. Please allow me to assist you."

"I would never forgive myself for causing inconvenience. I will be fine. Truly. I enjoy long walks. Adore them. You go on your way, as planned, and I will—"

He climbed out of the carriage. "I would not think of it. Let me help you in."

It was too much. Every time she worked up her courage to pursue her goal, some *man*, determined to help and protect her, interfered.

She ignored Mister Tyndale's offer and plopped herself onto a large boulder alongside the road. She propped her face in her hands and stared down at the toes of her mangled shoes.

"Is something wrong, Miss Albret?"

"Everything is wrong."

"I don't understand."

She looked up at him. His eyes were not deep and unfathomable and dangerous like Daniel's. They were transparent and kind and very sympathetic. His open expression made her feel better at once. There was no mystery to this man, no confusing darkness, no brooding distraction.

She had worried a bit for him last night. Seeing him playing cards with Daniel, he had struck her as no match for the Devil Man and doomed to lose. Since he appeared in good humor, evidently it had not turned out so bad.

"I am not just walking for pleasure," she said, the confidence slipping out without any real decision. "I am going to a village called Fenwood. I learned that I have a relative there, and I decided to call on him."

She braced herself for the polite suggestion that she should have told her hostess or Pen so one of them could arrange for a carriage to take her. She did not want to explain that she did not want anyone knowing she was doing this. She would have to pretend that she was too stupid to have thought of such things.

Instead his expression cleared, as if her explanation made all the sense in the world. "Is this relative expecting you?"

"No. I only decided to go this morning. I have never even met him. There was this estrangement . . ."

"Are you sure he will receive you?"

She hadn't thought of that. The vicar could well be a relative, but one who wanted nothing to do with Jonathan Albret's daughter. She saw herself standing at the vicarage door as it was slammed in her face.

"There now, it will probably turn out as you expected." Mister Tyndale smiled so kindly as he reassured her that she had to smile back.

"My visit can wait until tomorrow," he said. "Why don't I take you to

Brinley? It is near Fenwood. You can wait there, and I will carry a message from you to your relative. If he is agreeable, then you can go make your visit. This way you will not have to walk back, either, and we will return to the house before the others."

A merry, conspiratorial note entered the last sentence. He thought that she was hiding this visit from Daniel because the estrangement was his doing.

Mister Tyndale's misinterpretation was convenient, however. She could hardly explain that she really wasn't Daniel's cousin and that this relative was hers alone. Also, it might be best to do it as Mister Tyndale suggested, and have a request brought to the vicar first.

"You are being very kind and generous, Mister Tyndale."

"Not at all, Miss Albret. Not at all. That is what friends are for." He gestured to the carriage. "Shall we?"

"I love the sea," Hampton said. They were the first words he had spoken in an hour. "It is the best example of the sublime. I am actually glad I did not go back to town today."

"I hate the sea," Daniel replied. He had never understood this poetic nonsense about the sublime, but if the sea was an example of it, he hated the sublime too.

"An odd sentiment, St. John," Vergil said. "The sea made your fortune."

Daniel did not care that it had made his fortune. He had spent years bobbing over its waves, but he disliked it intensely.

He hated its unpredictability and its vastness. He detested the way it made a man feel small and at the mercy of fate. He resented how its rhythmic waves had a way of washing up truths from the depths of one's soul.

Of all the things men did to pretend they could impose human will on the sea, sportfishing had always struck him as the most idiotic. It was a form of dueling, only the opponent was primeval in nature.

He stood on an outcropping of rock between Vergil and Hampton, their long poles part of a whole ridiculous array of them. Along with the other men of the party, they pitted their puny skills against the most eternal force on the planet. A few fish had actually been landed, to great cheers and excitement.

Vergil had caught a huge slick one. Hampton had not, but had been so lost in contemplation he had not shown the slightest boredom.

Only young Dante displayed restlessness. He sat on the ground beside his brother's legs, showing impatience with the sport and not at all impressed by the holy sublime either.

"When do you think the ladies will get here?" he asked.

Yes, when the hell would they get here? When would she get here? Daniel had forced himself to not look to the road for their approach, but his ears kept listening for the sound of carriages.

"I would have thought you'd had your fill," Vergil muttered as he shot an annoyed glance down at his brother's head. "You do realize, I hope, that if some husband ever calls you out, you are a dead man."

"Speaking of which, it may be time for him to begin lessons with the chevalier," Hampton said. "Considering his taste in athletic endeavors, it would be money well spent."

Dante looked up, suddenly more boy than man. "You don't really think I'd get called out, do you? It isn't as if any of the old farts really care, after all."

"Being cuckolded by a boy not even out of university might make even a jaded man care," Vergil said.

"Hardly a boy. You aren't so much older than I am—"

"Old enough to know a thing or two about discretion—"

Daniel stopped hearing their bickering. Another sound absorbed his attention.

Carriages approached.

Finally.

He made a display of watching his line instead of looking to the road as he ached to do. Through sound alone he judged her approach as he fought to conquer the rising, almost maddening, expectation.

Gritting his teeth, he stared at the sea, but that meant the damn waves did their worst, forcing memories of passion and pleasure to eddy through him. Possessive urges flared from the hot coals of desire that had been burning in him for weeks.

He closed his eyes and forced containment on his reactions. He was being more boyish than Dante. More reckless. He did not even know what to say when he saw her again. He wasn't sure what he *wanted* to say.

"Ah, the ladies have arrived," a voice down the line of men called.

Daniel waited until the carriages stopped before drawing in his line. Servants began laying out cloths and baskets on the grassy hill beyond the road.

He spied the earl looking sharply at one carriage. Following the direction of his glare, Daniel saw the countess being handed out.

Two other ladies followed her. Daniel waited for one more head to appear at the opening. A beautiful one, with soulful eyes that could make a man forget himself.

Instead, the footman closed the carriage door.

Daniel surveyed the party, searching for Diane.

He made his way toward the countess. She stood amidst three women who were managing to talk around her and through her. Taking her leave as if she had been included, she met him halfway with a smile of gratitude.

"How kind of you to arrive to save me, Mr. St. John."

"I would be happy to be your company, but I am wondering where my cousin is."

"She stayed back at the house, to sleep. It was thoughtless of me to keep her up so late last night, and she felt very tired this morning. I confess that I was tempted to call off as well but . . ." She glanced meaningfully toward the earl, and then at her companions from the carriage. "One must keep up appearances and be brave, and all that."

Daniel would have much preferred the countess giving in to her inclinations to hide. Her bravery meant that Diane had been left unchaperoned. There was no reason for the countess to be concerned about that, but Daniel certainly was.

Another member of the party had not shown the countess's courage. Andrew Tyndale had also begged off this excursion.

Which meant that Diane was not entirely alone in that house with the servants.

"I apologize, but I will not be able to be your company after all. Your brother will see to you, I am sure. I feel obliged to return to the house, to make sure my cousin is not ill."

"I am sure she is not. Merely tired—"

He turned on his heel and strode toward his carriage without waiting for the rest. He noticed Vergil and Hampton catch sight of him. Their quick frowns and deliberate interception of him at the carriage suggested that he was not hiding his concern well.

"I am returning to the house, Duclairc. Your sister could use your attendance right now."

"You are going back? Why?"

"My cousin stayed behind. She is ill, and I should see to her."

"I'm sure if it was serious that Pen—"

"I will go and check, in any case." He gestured to his coachman that they would be off.

Vergil's hand caught Daniel's arm as he stepped into the carriage. "I think that I will come with you. Dining *al fresco* bores me."

Daniel looked at that hand and then at Vergil. The disapproval Vergil had shown at the brook flickered in his bright blue eyes.

"You sister needs you by her side, and I require no assistance."

"All the same—"

"Allow me to return instead," Hampton said. "The sudden intrusion of all of this noise has ruined the day for me. I think that I will ride back to London after all. You won't mind getting me to my horse, will you, St. John?"

Hampton, who rarely smiled, did so now with a benign firmness that said Daniel would not be returning alone to the house and an unchaperoned Diane.

Hell. It was unlikely Vergil had confided his suspicions. Hampton must have sensed what was between them last night during cards.

Who else had seen it? The countess?

Tyndale?

He should thrash them both for the insult of implying he couldn't be trusted with her.

Except, of course, that they were right.

He leapt into the carriage. "Come along if you want. Damned if I care."

chapter 16

Diane waited impatiently, rehearsing what she would say when she met the vicar. Visions of a tearful reunion played out in her mind, little dramas written over the years as she lay in bed at school.

She worked hard at stopping their progress. The vicar might not even agree to see her. He might not be a relative at all. He could be such a distant one that he had no interest in an association.

Despite telling herself all that, the anticipation kept building. For a half hour after Mister Tyndale left, she was able to contain it, but as more time passed it grew and grew.

She went to the window for the twentieth time, to look down the street for the carriage. Brinley was not a large village, and this was a very tiny inn. Mister Tyndale had generously paid for a chamber so that she would not have to wait in the common room.

It was a humble but pretty chamber. Muslin curtains draped the window and bed. Cheery yellow pillows decked the simple blue coverlet. It was the sort of room she had assumed she would have when she went to Paris with Daniel. Instead, he had put her inside a blue-and-white porcelain vase.

A carriage came into view. Even when it was still a dot, she knew it was Mister Tyndale. Her heart raced. She tried to compose herself, struggled to tame the hope. She could not, and finally she bolted to run down.

Mister Tyndale was already at the chamber door when she opened it.

"Was he there? Did you see him?"

"He was there."

"What did he say? Will he see me?"

"I am very sorry to have to disappoint you, Miss Albret. He knows nothing of you and is sure there is no relationship. He is a crusty old fellow and saw no advantage in having the meeting that you sought."

The excitement disappeared as if a fist had punched it out of her. Its instant absence left the void emptier than ever before. It became so big that it might have enclosed her.

She walked to the window and looked out, to hide her reaction. Tears wanted to flow. They backed up in her chest and throat, the lack of release making her miserable.

"It pains me deeply that this has distressed you so."

She felt a warmth on her shoulder. His hand rested there, a small offering of sympathy. The fatherly gesture helped a tiny bit.

"I blame myself. I should have pled your case better."

"If there is no relationship, there is no purpose in the meeting. I thank you for going and sparing me the embarrassment of intruding on a stranger with no ties to me."

She turned to him and his hand fell away. He appeared so worried that she felt guilty. "I will be fine. It is just that I have so little family, I had hoped to discover more, that is all."

"Well, you still have your cousin."

"Yes. My cousin."

Except he wasn't a cousin and she would not have him any longer. She realized that she had pinned a lot of unacknowledged plans on this old vicar. Without admitting it, she had counted on having a place to go when she left Daniel. Now she wasn't sure where she would go or how she would live.

"You are distressed. I worried that you would be. Before I left, I asked that dinner be prepared for us. I just took the liberty of asking for it to be brought up here so that you do not have to dine below where others will see and watch."

"That was very thoughtful of you. I confess that I am not sure that I could hide my emotions well, and can do without the company of others."

He smiled gently. "Will you accept mine, at least? It may help if you are not totally alone. Some conversation might distract you."

"Oh, I did not mean you. You have been so considerate and helpful, that I . . . well, I welcome your company. Although I am not very hungry."

"You must eat something all the same. It would not do if I brought you back faint from hunger."

Right now she did not want to go back at all, ever. She would have to, of course. Eventually. Before she did, however, she wanted some time to steady herself and assess what this disappointment meant to her future.

The innkeeper arrived with his wife and daughter, carrying trays of food. They moved the small table near the window and dragged in another chair. At a subtle gesture from Mister Tyndale, the woman untied the muslin bed drapes so that the function of the room became obscured.

"It smells very good," Diane said, going over to inspect the meal after they all left. There was fowl in some sauce, and potatoes and bread. A bottle of wine waited as well.

"Simple country food," Mister Tyndale said. "I prefer it to the exotic dishes served at some London parties."

"So do I."

He gestured to her chair. She settled down. "I think that you are one of the kindest people I have met, Mister Tyndale."

He smiled modestly as he poured some wine. "Any gentleman would do the same, Miss Albret. Now, let us see about improving your spirits so that you are smiling once again."

For an hour he distracted her with conversation. His voice and consideration acted as a balm. The disappointment retreated until it became no more than a thin veil tinting her mood.

"Miss Albret, forgive me if I am prying, but today's events appeared to affect you deeply. Was it important to you to discover other family? Are you unhappy with your situation?"

The question, asked as she pricked her fork into a cream tartlet, made the veil flutter.

"I would not say that I am unhappy, but I have been thinking that it may be good to make a change in my circumstances." She was not sure why she admitted that. It simply was out of her mouth, a result of the familiarity and ease which the day had bred between them.

"I think that you may be right."

"What do you mean?"

His expression became serious and thoughtful. "I risk your displeasure in saying what I am about to, but as a gentleman concerned for your welfare, I see no choice. There has been talk, I am sorry to say."

"Talk?"

"Do not be alarmed. Very little, and mere speculation. Well, what with St. John appearing out of nowhere, with no history, rich as sin and most likely by ill-begotten means. There are rumors that he literally seduced his way into those circles you now enjoy. Now a cousin appears, also with no history . . . the way he warns men off, the way he danced with you at that ball . . . what can I say? There have been some whispers."

The Earl of Glasbury had insinuated as much, so she was not too shocked. All the same, she suddenly liked Mister Tyndale a lot less.

He misunderstood her silence. "Miss Albret, please forgive me for asking this, I know it is really not my place, but you are so innocent and young—has your cousin in any way importuned you? I have been worrying about that since last night. While we played cards I sensed that you were afraid of him, and that his interest in you was not entirely proper."

"You are mistaken, I assure you."

His expression cleared at once. "That is a relief, and what I hoped to hear. When you spoke of thinking that it would be wise to change your situation—"

"I did not mean that I needed to escape my cousin," she lied, uncomfortable with the direction this conversation had taken. Mister Tyndale might be kind and fatherly, but he wasn't *her* father. "I referred to more practical things. I have no fortune, and little future in the circles I have been visiting. It has been enjoyable, but it may be good to find a more realistic path. I do not want to be one of those poor relations who is forever dependent."

"An admirable sentiment." He set his elbows on the table, clasped his hands, rested his chin on them, and looked at her very directly. "I want you to know, however, that if you are ever in need of any help, I would be honored to be of assistance."

It was a comment very typical of Mister Tyndale. Kind and solicitous. And yet . . . Diane could not suppress a little twinge of caution. His blue eyes appeared as open and honest as always, incredibly concerned, but for the smallest instant she thought she had seen a tiny, alarming spark.

"I would like you to think of me as your friend," he continued. "I will admit, at the risk that you will laugh, that I hope that one day you will think of me as more than a friend."

The table suddenly seemed very small and his face very close. A pleasant, sincere face still, but more of those sparks entered his eyes, changing everything.

Astonishment rendered her immobile and speechless.

Suddenly his arm spanned the table and his hand cradled her chin. "I know that there is a great difference in our ages, but that is not so unusual. I have admired you since we first met. I hope that you will at least consider my affections, and that your cousin will not object if I present myself as a suitor."

Suitor!

She just stared.

He rose from his chair and leaned over the table.

Her confused mind could not comprehend why he should do that.

He showed her why.

Nice, kind, sincere Mister Tyndale kissed her, and moved his body around the table as he did so.

• • •

"There is no proof that he followed her."

Hampton offered the reassurance as the coach careened around a bend in the road. "He did not call for his carriage until long after she had left, and he may have taken a different road entirely."

"If he did, we will learn of it soon enough and you can tell me I was a fool," Daniel said.

They had arrived back at the house to discover both Tyndale and Diane absent. It had taken an insufferably long time to locate anyone who knew where Diane had gone. Finally, the housekeeper had produced a girl named Mary who had related the information about the vicar in Fenwood.

Daniel had not had any time to wonder what Diane might discover from the vicar. The groom who had prepared Tyndale's carriage had arrived soon after, and the conviction that Tyndale had followed Diane had lodged in Daniel's head with determination, leaving room for nothing else.

He kept his gaze on the countryside rushing by, looking for evidence of her, or Tyndale. Or both of them.

"Do you suspect this was because of last night?" Hampton asked. "He seems a decent fellow. Everyone says so. I would not expect him to get back at you through her."

Except he wasn't a decent fellow. He would delight in getting back at someone this way, because he had a weakness for innocent girls with refined manners and white skin and dark hair. He especially liked it if they were helpless and dependent on him, and devoid of protection.

The coach rushed through Witham and turned onto a dirt road. It had to slow then. The delay made Daniel furious.

Hampton appeared remarkably calm, but then he always did. It annoyed Daniel that the solicitor did not appreciate the danger that they rushed to avert.

"If you are so sure of Tyndale's decency, I don't know why you insisted on accompanying me."

"Since we are almost there, I will tell you why." Hampton gestured lazily at the pistols hung on the coach wall above Daniel's head. "I am here to make sure you do not take one of those with you when you step out of this carriage."

"If I am inclined to kill a man, I can do it with my bare hands."

"I do not doubt that you can. In fact, I suspect that you have. However, you will not today."

They entered the outskirts of Brinley. Daniel called to the coachman to go slowly.

Hampton checked one side of the lane, while Daniel checked the other. Near the other end of the village, Daniel spied a small inn with a familiar curricle tied up in front.

He was out of the coach before it stopped, with Hampton on his heels. Inside he found the innkeeper and asked for the man who owned the curricle.

"Not here." The man replied, turning away.

Daniel grabbed him by the front of his shirt and lifted him until his toes scraped the floor. "Where is he?"

Stunned, the innkeeper merely pointed above.

"Is he alone?"

The head above his gripping hand shook.

He dropped the man and strode to the stairs.

Hampton grabbed his arm. "Do not do anything rash."

Daniel shook him off and took the stairs three at a time.

There were only two chambers on the second level. One door stood open, revealing a deserted room.

He threw open the door of the other one. A vicious anger drowned his mind as he took in the scene of seduction.

Tyndale bent over a seated Diane, holding her face in his hands, kissing her. Her back pressed against the chair and her arms clutched at his. Resisting him? Embracing him? In the second before the door crashed against the wall, it wasn't clear. Nor did Daniel care.

Tyndale looked up and stepped away from the table. Diane's expression registered surprise, and then horror. She turned away and covered her face with her hands.

Not thinking, not caring about anything, driven by emotions too black to consider the cost, Daniel turned his total attention on Tyndale and took a step toward the man he planned to beat bloody.

A hand on his arm stopped him. He tried to shrug it off, but it would not budge. Furious, he turned on Hampton, to knock him away if necessary.

"Do not forget who he is. Would you swing for this?" Hampton said quietly.

A thin slice of rational sense returned. Tyndale watched, not the least bit concerned. Diane's hands fell. She sat there looking at no one, her humiliation palpable. They all stayed in their places in a crackling silence, a *tableau vivant* of ruin and compromise and anger.

"Miss Albret, would you leave us, please." Hampton spoke in his solicitor's voice.

She began to speak, but stopped. Daniel could not imagine what she thought she could say. Excuses for Tyndale? Accusations he had duped her? It did not matter. The situation spoke for itself. No man brought a woman to a chamber in this way if his intentions were honorable.

She hurried out and Hampton closed the door. Tyndale strolled to the table, took his seat, and poured himself some wine.

"It was just a kiss," he said. "She did not mind at all, so why should you?"

Daniel wanted to strangle him.

Hampton physically took a position between the two of them. "You have compromised her by merely bringing her to this chamber. She may not have comprehended that, but you certainly did. Now a solution must be found."

"I suppose I could offer some compensation, if it was not too high."

"This is not some milkmaid you pay off with a few pounds," Hampton said.

"For all intents and purposes, it is." Tyndale sipped his wine and thought it over. "Surely you are not suggesting that I do the right thing by her? I suppose that I might consider that, if she had any background or fortune—"

"I'll be damned before I allow such a thing," Daniel snarled.

"You cannot expect me to take her penniless, St. John. Surely her reputation is worth a few pounds."

"You also have a reputation," Hampton reminded.

Tyndale laughed. "For all of her silks, she is nobody. For all of his wealth, so is your friend here. I think that my reputation can survive this little misunderstanding."

"What sort of settlement did you have in mind?" Hampton asked.

"I'll not see her tied to him, and with him profiting—"

"Last night's debt disappears, for starters. That and another twenty thousand might do it."

"Forty thousand pounds is a rather large settlement," Hampton said.

"I think that I am generous to consider the matter seriously at all."

"I think that I am generous if I let you live," Daniel said.

Tyndale nibbled at a remaining bit of tartlet. "Is that a challenge?"

"No," Hampton said emphatically. "He is angry, as you should expect. Your manner is only provoking him more. Do not forget that I am a witness to this, and I am not a nobody."

Tyndale turned and studied Daniel. "You are extremely distressed by a simple kiss, St. John. You are as protective as if she were a sister."

The room disappeared. So did thoughts of any settlement, except one.

It was the only resolution he had ever wanted with this man. He had planned for it, lived for it, and then, because of Diane, discarded it. But now here it was, all the same.

Sometimes fate conspires to force one to do what must be done.

"There will be no marriage, no settlement," he said, pulling the door open. "My second will call on yours in London tomorrow."

chapter 17

It was as if someone had died.

Silent sobriety shrouded the house. Diane knew the reason for the dismal atmosphere. Her behavior had not only smeared her own reputation, but also that of Daniel and his sister. The whole household would suffer for her stupidity.

Men visited Daniel, wearing the faces people put on at wakes. Mister Hampton came several times the day after Diane and Daniel returned to London, and Vergil Duclairc called too. There were others, men she did not know. Finally, late in the afternoon, a gray-haired man of noble bearing was shown into Daniel's study. Diane saw him pass the library where she was reading a book.

She went into the hall and looked at the study door. Daniel had spent most of his time there since they returned. He had barely spoken to her since finding her at the inn. On emerging from the confrontation with Tyndale, he had only asked if she was unharmed. Her assurances had not softened his expression and he had not wanted to hear her explanations.

He had not even ridden in the coach on the way back to London. He had climbed up with the driver, taking the reins in his own hands.

They had returned at once. Mister Hampton had their things packed and sent back to the city in the countess's carriage.

The man did not stay long in the study. He swept out, serious and subdued, looking like a character in a stage tragedy.

The door to the study remained ajar after he left. Diane strolled by and peered in.

Daniel was positioned as he so often was, near the window, looking out. He appeared very alone. Very isolated.

She slipped into the room.

"I would like to speak with you," she said. "I think that I should return to France. This scandal will not affect you so much if I am gone."

"That will not be necessary. The fault was not yours."

"The fault *was* mine. I should have realized—"

"People more wise and worldly than you have not realized."

He sounded so distant. Her heart sickened at the way he still did not look at her. He had cut off whatever familiarity they had. Closed a door. She had become a responsibility again, nothing more.

It was what she had wanted. She had decided that this friendship and its intimacy had to end. Now, experiencing the chill of its death saddened her more than she ever expected.

"It was not what it seemed," she said, hearing her voice catch. The truth would make no difference, but it suddenly was vitally important that he hear this. "He helped me on the road, and went to see if a vicar in Fenwood would meet with me. I merely waited in the chamber for his return, not for . . ."

He turned to her. "And then he had the meal sent up, and you dined, and to your shock you discovered that he did not think of you as a daughter or niece."

"Yes."

"And then he alluded to affection and love, and even marriage."

"Yes. How did you know?"

"And then he kissed you. And you permitted it."

"I was astonished and shocked. It was so unexpected—"

"It does not matter."

"It *does* matter." And it did. Right now, it mattered more than anything in the world. "Nothing scandalous happened. You saw that when you came in."

"I am not sure what I saw when I came in. I do know that if I had not arrived, Tyndale would not have stopped with a kiss, and that your agreement to be in that chamber would have absolved him of the worst accusations."

She did not know what to say. She had been unbearably trusting and stupid. "Surely, if I left, no one would care about this. No one would know."

"Oh, it will be known. Such things have a way of getting around. Do not concern yourself about that too much, however. I am dealing with it."

He said the last part firmly. The silence of the house and Jeanette's retreat to her chambers lined up in Diane's memory. So did the little procession of serious visitors.

A terrible suspicion poked into her mind.

"That man who was just here. Wasn't that the Chevalier Corbet? He has never visited before."

Daniel strolled over to his desk. It was stacked with ledgers and books. "He is an old friend and has agreed to do me an important favor."

"What favor?" She strode over to the desk and surveyed the evidence of a man putting his affairs in order. "Holy Mother, what have you done? Did you challenge Mister Tyndale over this?"

"Of course."

"*Of course?* I am not even your real cousin. You have no responsibility for me, let alone this dangerous gesture. There had to have been another way to salvage your pride, short of trying to kill him."

"There was no other way that I found acceptable."

"And what if *he* kills *you*?" The idea made her stomach clench. If he died over this, over such a little thing, she would never forgive herself. The guilt would hound her forever.

She had decided to leave him, but not like this. Not in such a permanent way. Knowing he was in the world somewhere would have made it easier. Instead, she might suffer a loss that her heart already knew it could not absorb.

"Do not be concerned. You will be cared for if I fail. I have spent the morning arranging trusts for you and Paul and some others. You will not be destitute."

"I do not want your money. I do not want this challenge to go forward. It is reckless and unnecessary. For all you know, I was glad of his attention. Perhaps he was sincere in announcing his intentions as a suitor. Maybe I welcomed that kiss and the chance to catch the second son of a marquess."

He absently restacked some ledgers. "Maybe you did. It is sounding that way."

A spitting denial rose to her lips but she swallowed it. Proclaiming her innocence, describing her revulsion at Tyndale's insistent kisses, would only add fuel to the fire.

It broke her heart that Daniel might think she wanted that seduction, but her own pride was of little consequence now. She could not have him fight this duel. She could not risk his death. Let him wonder whether he protected a woman unworthy of such chivalry. It might lead to his standing down from the challenge.

"This is not only foolhardy, it is hypocritical. Your own behavior with me has been much worse than Mister Tyndale's."

"I am aware of that. However, at an essential level, it was very different in ways you cannot understand."

"As the object of the behavior, I see no difference, except that his ultimate intentions may have been honorable."

"I am very sure his were not. Nor were mine. In any case, one of us will pay for his misuse of you, and perhaps for much more."

"When is this duel to occur?"

"Louis is meeting with Tyndale's second right now. I expect it will be soon."

"Does Jeanette know what you are planning to do?"

"Certainly."

He had told his sister, but not the woman for whose honor he fought.

"I assume that she begged you to change your mind."

"Unlike you, Jeanette knows better than to try."

"Perhaps that is because she does not know the whole story."

She turned on her heel, to go and recruit an ally.

His voice, lazy with distraction, followed her to the door. "Actually, it is because she *does* know the whole story."

"You must stop him." Diane stood in front of Jeanette in the sitting room and said it as a command.

"No one can do that now."

Jeanette appeared resigned and frail. Her white skin showed faint lines that Diane had never noticed before.

Diane began pacing. A mix of frustration and deathly worry throbbed inside her head. "Daniel's reaction was too extreme. A duel! There had to be some other way—"

"There was. Mister Tyndale offered to marry you if a settlement came with you."

"Your brother would rather die, or kill, than pay a few pounds?"

"The settlement was extremely large and intended to insult both you and my brother. However, that is not why Daniel refused."

"Then why?"

She stroked the ends of her shawl. "He would never put you in a situation where you felt obligated to marry a man in order to avert this challenge."

"It should have been my choice, not his."

"Well, he made it. Besides, Daniel would never let Tyndale have you in any way, even in marriage. He would definitely kill the man before he permitted that."

Diane laid her hand on Jeanette's shoulder and looked in her eyes. "Daniel said something about your knowing the whole story. Is there more to this?"

"I will tell you this. I do so in the hopes that you do not blame yourself. Paul has indicated that Mister Tyndale may have taken you to that inn deliberately, intending to provoke a duel with Daniel. The night before, he lost a large sum to Daniel at cards. His obligation to that debt would disappear if Daniel died."

"That is a drastic way to settle a debt."

"It is an effective way. Mister Hampton, the solicitor, presented this theory to Daniel. My brother considers it irrelevant, of course. However, it would explain why the settlement Tyndale demanded in order to marry you was so outrageously high. It included that debt, you see."

So, she had been a pawn. The kindness on the road had merely been a man seeing an opportunity. Perhaps he had even followed her, hoping to find a way to compromise her so that this could all unfold as it did.

Being Daniel's doll had been one thing. Being Mister Tyndale's dupe was another. She had fallen into the lure like the stupid, ignorant fool she was. Worse, Daniel might die because of it.

"This theory would only work if Mister Tyndale was confident he would win the duel," she said.

"He is reputed to be an excellent shot."

One of the best shots in England, Daniel had said that day by the brook.

"We must stop this, Jeanette."

"No one can do that. Trust me on this. I know my brother as no one else does. He will meet Tyndale, and he will do so with the goal of killing him."

Diane waited until the house fell silent and then rose from her bed. Hours of turmoil and guilt had resulted in a decision.

The emotions of the last few days had prepared her for this choice. Maybe those of the last months had. The desolation of contemplating Daniel's possible death had revealed the truths in her heart.

She removed a dressing gown that she had never worn from the wardrobe. A frivolous, impractical design of deep rose satin and cream lace, it had been made in Paris on Jeanette's whim, even though Diane had insisted she would never wear such a confection.

She pictured how it would look over her simple nightgown. The image in her head was comical and ridiculous. She would appear to be a child decked out in her mother's clothing.

Deciding this was no time for modesty, she shed the nightgown and slipped the rose silk over her nakedness. It covered her almost as much as a ball gown would, but the front was slit high and the sensual flow hugged her curves. Lace framed the scooped neckline, feathering at the top of her breasts.

A knot twisted in her stomach. She was about to do something that anyone with any sense would call a stupid, scandalous mistake.

Worse, she might fail. He had been so indifferent in the study that she had no confidence her plan would work. She had to try, however. Jeanette had said that no one could get him to withdraw the challenge. There was a small chance that was not true.

Plucking up her courage, she left her chamber to go and bargain with the Devil Man.

chapter 18

She eased open Daniel's chamber door. Light poured through the crack.

Her knees wobbled. She paused while she forced some calm on herself.

She hoped it would not be too horrible. He was not a stranger. Her good intentions should keep it from being wanton, no matter how anyone else saw it. No matter how *he* saw it.

She pushed the door open farther and slipped in.

The chamber's open, spare elegance surprised her. The furnishings possessed an Oriental flavor. The bedposts and boards were angular and fretted, and the wardrobe was inlaid with flowers and birds. A chest near the bed had abundant carvings in three colors of wood.

The exotic touches did not overwhelm the chamber. This was not some Asian fantasy. These appeared to be objects he had bought on his travels and simply put to use.

Daniel sat in a chair near the cold hearth, reading a book by the light of a large brace of candles. The chair faced her and she could see the full-sleeved Japanese robe that he wore wrapped and sashed. It was dark blue with a white pattern and reminded her of the chamber she had used in Paris.

His bare legs stretched out from where the robe parted and fell on either side of his knees. A deep V of skin could be seen above the spot where the sides of the robe crossed his chest.

It appeared that he wore nothing beside the robe. That made the implications of what she was doing more stark. She had expected to find him in a frock coat and boots, or already asleep in a darkened room. Not sitting here, with all this light, almost naked.

He looked marvelous, a man of action temporarily at rest. Despite his relaxation, the magnetism beamed off him invisibly, affecting her as it always did, unsettling her and making her more alive than normal. The candlelight sculpted his handsome face into severe planes in which his dark eyes glowed like black stars.

He had not heard her enter. She stood in front of the door, so afraid and nervous that she had to force her voice out.

"What are you reading?"

He barely reacted, but she could tell that she had startled him.

"Poetry."

He looked up.

Her dressing gown suddenly felt extremely thin and very wicked. It did not seem to cover nearly as much as it had in her chamber.

He gave her a long, slow inspection full of male interest. A tense, reawakened vitality rolled across the chamber to her.

"You look very beautiful. I have not seen your hair down since that day at the school." He vaguely gestured at the gown. "It is lovely."

"Jeanette chose it for me in Paris."

"Did she suggest that you wear it tonight?"

"No. Why would she?"

He smiled that private smile of his. "So, it was your own idea to put that on, let down your hair, and come here. Why?"

Her face burned. She had not expected to announce her intentions verbally. The gown and her presence were supposed to do that.

"Have you come to tempt me, Diane?"

"Yes."

"If you think to beguile me with your beauty and then leave, I warn you now that it will not happen that way."

"I know that."

He forced his gaze away from her and to the low fire. "You do not even understand what you are offering."

"I am not ignorant. I know what is expected."

"You do not know what *I* will expect. Go back to your chamber."

She almost obeyed.

She walked toward him instead.

"I do not want this duel to happen. I want you to stand down."

He watched her, not pleased. Despite his annoyance, she noticed him glancing to her legs as they poked through the slit in the gown with each stride.

"If you have come to me like this, you must want him to live very badly. You would prefer his other solution? Marriage to you?"

She stood beside his bare legs and looked down into dark eyes that contained dangerous depths. Those eyes frightened her years ago. Now they entranced her. "I only care that there is no duel."

His gaze drifted over her, briefly and thoroughly. "It is not only about you."

"No, it is also about you and your pride."

"So, you seek to save a dishonorable man by making me more dishonorable than he is." He tilted the book in his lap and returned his gaze to it. "Permit me some scruples, finally, where you are concerned. Now, please return to your chamber."

It was a dismissal, and not gently spoken. Her courage shook. Her whole body did. Being close to him caused that more than the rejection did. Embarrassment at being rebuffed was overwhelmed by disappointment that he did not want her enough.

If she had known more about these things she would not have failed. If she were prettier, or more worldly, or more seductive, he would choose differently.

She should retreat with what pride she had left, but she could not. She might never be this close to him again, might never see the candlelight shading his face like this. Once she walked away, his aura would never surround her as it did now, compelling her to stay even as he repudiated her.

He turned a page. "Leave now. I want you to go."

Trembling, barely keeping her balance, she lowered to her knees beside his legs and sat back on her feet. He still read the book, but he might see her over its edge.

She released the top pearl button at her breast. It took too long because her fingers did not want to work right. Not only nervousness made them clumsy. Being mere inches from him affected her.

She finally managed it. The gown and its lace parted a little. She worked quickly on the next button.

"Slowly, darling. Seduction is not something that one does in haste."

She looked up.

The book lay on the table beside the candles. The prince of temptation watched.

His attention held her spellbound.

The other buttons went very slowly since she barely noticed what she was doing. It appeared he did not either. Their connected gazes were all that existed, linking them together, creating admissions and anticipations that should have never been acknowledged. She knew that he wanted her, that was obvious. It was less clear that he would accept her bargain.

With the last button near her waist, she tore her gaze away from his and looked down. The satin gaped, barely covering her hard nipples pressing against the shiny fabric.

She looked back at him. He seemed to be waiting for something.

Swallowing hard, she eased the gown farther apart. The satin glossed against her skin. She moved the fabric farther so that her breasts showed.

The sensation of kneeling there, exposing her nakedness, sent an erotic glow through her. Her breasts grew heavy and full. Her nipples hardened more, sensitive now to the air and his gaze and even the light. Tremors of excitement obscured her embarrassment. The satin's caress on her skin became a little waterfall of sensuality.

His expression hardened. She sensed a battle being waged. The tension of it charged the air between them.

"I should let you strip completely, so there is no mistaking what is happening, and why."

"There will be no mistaking."

Averting her gaze, afraid to see his reaction, she raised her hand and watched, astonished with herself, as she laid it on his bare leg and caressed up to his knee.

The world spun. In a startling, dizzying move, he pulled her forward, into his arms and lap, and took her mouth in a savage kiss.

The satin offered little protection from the warm roughness of his embrace. His mouth demanded a yielding more complete than his kisses ever had before. The hard ridge of his arousal, pressing against her thigh, proved she was a better seductress than she had thought.

His kisses coaxed her passion to rise to the level of his. It began doing so as she responded to his hot, possessive demands. The power of the sensations sliding and prickling through her body frightened her.

"I told you to leave. Do not say you weren't warned." His head turned. His soft hair brushed her face. His mouth moved down her neck. Her breasts swelled and tingled as a maddening desire for him to move lower filled her head. She instinctively arched, to encourage that.

He kissed the side of her breast in response. "I am glad that you want this, so it is not too much a sacrifice."

"I also want you to stop this duel." She hardly got the words out, barely remembered to demand the promise.

"Do you really think that you could leave now if I refused?"

It sounded like a threat, but he slid his thumb against her nipple to make it clear that she could not leave because she did not want to. Her whole body flexed. Her breaths shortened.

"I give you his life, and you give me yourself. It is a devil's bargain that you demand, Diane, and we will both soon regret it, I think." His dark eyes looked right into hers. "Right now, however, I don't give a damn. You have seen to that."

He rose with her in his arms. He strode to the bed and dropped her on it. Grabbing the shoulders of her gown, he pulled it down her body and cast it aside, leaving her naked.

Looking down at her, he began untying the sash of his robe.

She almost changed her mind then. The moments beat by, too sharp and real. The sensual frankness of his gaze made what was going to happen undeniable. Lying naked and vulnerable on the bed, covered with nothing but the male power pouring out of him, she knew he had been right. She had not fully understood what she was offering.

She looked away when the robe fell from his shoulders. It was cowardly and he said nothing, but seconds later the room darkened as the candlelight disappeared.

She heard him approach the bed and her heart pounded with a flurry of panic. She almost jumped when she felt his naked body suddenly warming her side. Her eyes grew accustomed to the dark and she snuck a glance.

Propped on one straight arm, he looked down at her. The dark made the bed a small, mysterious place, full of a shadowed intimacy. Not a dream, though, even if the night obscured the world. Dreams were never this tangible and defined. She felt more awake than ever before in her life. The soulful liveliness he always inspired became a physical alertness.

Lowering, he pulled her into an embrace. He caressed her body as if he could see better than she could. She embraced him back, clumsy and unsure and too aware that her surprise at feeling his skin and touch all over her could be heard in her catching breaths.

Kissing her hard, as if impatient with her fear, he caressed more intimately. Her inner thighs. The swells and cleft of her bottom. The free way he handled her body insinuated ownership. His boldness kept shocking her, but that only increased the thrill of the new sensations, and her reactions startled her even more.

He circled his fingertips over her breast. This pleasure she knew. He had already taught her this and she had no defense. The slow caress might have been internal, so directly did the teasing strokes send tremors to her lower body. A fullness grew until a deep, insistent palpitation in her pelvis echoed deep between her thighs.

He kissed her other breast. His tongue flicked, making her tense. His mouth made her nipple so sensitive she could hardly bear it. The combination of caress on one breast and his teeth and lips on the other sent her reeling. She grasped his shoulders and tried to hold on to her trembling, cracking control.

She couldn't. The fear fell away, and the shock, and the strangeness of being here and doing this. Her mind grew foggy and focused. The lower pulse built and built, intensified by the sensations on her skin and in her body, sensations that began to own her.

The itching, moist throb between her legs became uncomfortable. What he was doing only made it worse. Her hips rocked, to relieve the odd hunger building there. She bit back little whimpers of frustration.

His hand left her breast and caressed down to her stomach. It rested there as her body involuntarily raised and lowered, seeking something.

"This is you wanting me," he said, gently pressing against the rhythm, guessing her dismay and embarrassment. "But I need you to want me even more."

His hand stroked lower, to her thighs and their wetness.

To the private place that tortured her.

The shock returned, forcefully. She pressed her thighs together, to stop him.

"You will let me," he said. "You are mine tonight, and I want this. You want it too."

He lightly squeezed her thigh in a wordless command and pushed her legs apart.

His caress stunned her. She held him tighter and sought his kiss so she would not cry out. The sensations possessed her, making her want more. She tried to contain what they did to her, but she could not. The pleasure was too concentrated, too direct, almost painful in its intensity. Her physical reaction confused her. The primitive demands in her head frightened her.

He moved on top of her, a strong dark shadow full of physical warmth, part stranger but all male. He continued touching her, coaxing her abandon, forcing her to want him even though doing so terrified her.

"Part your legs more. Bend your knees."

She did. Her thighs flanked his hips and her arms clung to his shoulders. He pressed against her, slightly filling the throbbing void and relieving the craving. For a few wonderful, perfect seconds she knew a lovely bliss of having him closely bound to her, in her arms and close to her heart. His passion seemed to retreat a little, overwhelming her less, so that she could bask in the intimacy.

It did not last. A raw pain ripped as he pressed farther. A sense of being violated obliterated the tenderness. She grit her teeth and clung to him viciously so that she would not cry.

He stopped and did not move. The pain lessened but was still there. She accepted his kiss, but could not escape the fear that she had just given a part of herself that she could never reclaim. She could run to the ends of the earth, but something of her would always be his.

She thought it was over, but it wasn't. He moved, and she realized that the initial joining was the least of it. Rising over her, dominating her, his body commanded hers with every reentry.

Pressing one hand against the bedboard for leverage, he took her in a rhythmic, rocking possession. Whatever else this act meant, she could tell that it was a primitive claim of rights. Worse, his moves lured her and demanded that she surrender to that claim.

He moved harder, taking everything, giving meaning to every intense look he had given and every unsettled reaction she had experienced. She tried to block herself from the power, from the aura it created and the emotions it evoked. She concentrated on the pain, to protect herself. It affected her anyway, astonishing her, reminding her again of his warning that she did not know what she offered, or what he would expect.

His head angled back. A hard, deep thrust penetrated her. He stayed deep inside her, frozen for a second. The coiling danger that defined his persona tightened. Tension hardened his muscles beneath her hands. Then suddenly both spun away, into the air.

He moved no more. He looked down at her too long, breathing deeply. She could not see his eyes, and wondered if they contained intense attention or the distracted coolness that she knew too well.

He rolled away, separating their bodies completely. He sank onto the bed, beside her.

Humiliation wanted to slide through her. It could not make any headway. She was beyond embarrassment. Her emotions had been pummeled. Everything still felt too real, but also irrevocably changed.

She experienced neither regret nor triumph, only a sharp sense of the present. It would take time to absorb and understand what was in her heart now.

The silence became strained and awkward. She guessed that he did not speak because there was nothing to say. Well, she had known what she was going to do when she came. She would not pretend it had been other than it had been, or expect him to either.

Leaving the bed, she groped on the floor for her gown. She pulled it on and fumbled with a few buttons as she walked away.

"Was it worth it?"

She turned. He had not moved. He did not even appear to be looking in her direction.

"Was it worth it, Diane? You must care more than I realized, to do such a thing."

It surprised her that he broached this. The physical intimacy probably demanded that something be said.

"It was worth it. It was a small price to pay to save the man I love." She found it amazingly easy to say that word, to be honest about her feelings, even if she knew he did not share them. What had happened in that bed had stripped her of more than clothes and innocence. It had also peeled away all of the reasons people guard the truths in their hearts.

"He was not worthy of your sacrifice." He rose on an elbow and looked at her. "I can't let him have you, even if you think you love him. Especially not now. You must know that."

He?

She walked to the door. "You misunderstand. I did not do this to save Andrew Tyndale."

He watched the door close on the column of rose satin, then sank back on the bed.

He saw her again, kneeling by his chair, so beautiful his heart had stopped beating. With that first button he had known she would not back down. He had known he had lost.

And he had been glad for it, and so hungry for her that nothing else had mattered. *Nothing.*

He swung his legs off the bed and reached for the robe. He tied the sash and went over to the window.

He had compromised everything tonight. Her. Him. His whole life.

He opened the window to the silent, sleeping city. He knew the view from this spot very well. Many nights he had stood here, his mind planning, waiting. He had strategized a little war at this window, infiltrating the enemy camp, picking off the guards, watching his back while getting closer to the goal.

Tonight, a woman had lured him to complete defeat without even knowing it.

It was worth it—

She had done it to save a man.

Not Tyndale.

He should have known that. Maybe he had. But if he had admitted it, he could not have accepted her bargain. He could not have carried her to that bed and ravished her. He needed to be angry with her to do that.

And all through this last day it had been essential he not accept that if this duel occurred, it might not be Tyndale who would die, who needed saving.

It was worth it—

He fixed his gaze on the street. One of the lamps had a shorter post than the others. He had never noticed that before. He had looked down from this window for years and never really seen those posts.

His gaze darted around, seeing other oddities he had missed. One of the roofs had an odd bulge in its cornice, and the lower side window of another house appeared to be boarded over. Tonight all these details jumped at him, distinctions long invisible but now demanding attention.

Better to focus on them than face the more critical matters at hand, such as how this bargain that Diane had bought with her body would tie his hands with Tyndale.

Such as how the old memories had swarmed in on him as he lay on that bed beside her, making him disgusted with himself and furious with her.

Such as how he had not treated Diane especially well tonight. She may have been foolish and bold, and he had been hungry and angry, but he could have been more careful with her. He could not have spared her the shock or the pain, but he could have been gentler, even if he lacked the strength and honor to refuse her completely.

It was worth it. It was a small price to pay—

More details loomed in the lamplight outside. One of the houses only had four steps leading to its door, instead of five. He pictured visitors not noticing their steepness, and tripping every time they came.

He realized that two buildings that he had always assumed were identical in fact had slightly different heights.

It was a small price to pay, to save the man I love.

Her words barged into his head, breaking through his attempts to keep them out. He stared at the street, suddenly seeing nothing as her words repeated again and again, leaving him immobile. The tone of her voice, the calm acceptance and resignation, echoed in his thoughts, making his chest fill with an odd heaviness.

He had been right about one thing. The man she had sought to save had not been worthy of her sacrifice.

And it had been a huge sacrifice, given in simple innocence to a man who did not even treat it as valuable. A man owned by the past, who fueled anger and hatred because he feared having nothing inside him if they disappeared. A man who had tempted her long before she tempted him, and then resented her using his own lust to thwart the goal born of that hatred.

She was an idiot to care at all for such a man, let alone love him.

His throat burned, and he heard the cruel silence as they lay next to each other. He saw her walking away, proud despite her desolation.

It was a small price to pay, to save the man I love.

Jesus.

He turned away from the window. He made his way to the door of a chamber he had wanted to visit many times in the dead of the night. He entered and went over to the bed.

She lay on her side with her knees drawn up, wearing a white nightgown. She looked alone and defenseless, as if she huddled under the sheet to protect herself against an indifferent world.

Lifting the sheet, he eased down beside her. She startled enough for him to know that if she had been sleeping she no longer did.

They lay beside each other again, in a different bed and a different silence. There was much that he could say to her, but very little that would not hurt her more. She did not deserve any more wounds. She was an innocent prisoner in this war, not a soldier.

"I am sorry that I hurt you, and that I was not more considerate." He spoke to her back.

Her shoulders shrugged a little. "It probably can't be helped."

"Not completely, but—"

"It was not entirely horrible. Do not feel bad."

How like her to worry about *him.* He almost laughed, and also came close to crying. "Well, I am glad to hear that it wasn't *entirely* horrible."

"But if you have come here to do it again, I don't think that I want to."

"I am sure you do not. I did not come here for that."

"Then why?"

"To tell you that I am honored that you cared enough, and to stay with you for a while, if you will permit it."

She went very still. So still that she might have stopped breathing.

"Will you permit it?"

She nodded.

He touched her shoulder. "Will you lie in my arms, so that I can hold you?"

There was a pause, as if she had to think that over.

She turned. He pulled her to him.

"Do not worry. I will be gone before the servants are up."

She nestled close. He embraced her gently and kissed her cheek. His lips touched wetness. She had cried since she returned to this chamber.

That broke his heart. He tucked her closer, protectively.

It felt good holding her as she fell asleep. He had never done that before with a woman. He never shared beds with his passing lovers.

He found her feminine warmth and softness surprisingly pleasing, even soothing, and not intrusive as he had always assumed sleeping with a woman would be.

chapter 19

She woke up alone to the smells of cocoa and lilacs.

The cocoa was on a nearby table, as it had been every day since she first tasted some out of Daniel's cup. The lilac sprigs lay right near her nose, tucked in a crevice between two pillows.

A servant had brought the cocoa. Daniel must have left the flowers.

She held them and sniffed. They came from a bush that grew in a sun-filled corner of the garden. She pictured him going down there in the dark to cut the little cluster.

He had stayed with her most of the night. She had felt his embrace whenever she stirred.

It had been wonderful being held like that. The long, comforting contact had moved her more than what had happened in his bed. For one remarkable night, that emptiness in her heart had disappeared. Vanished. Even in her sleep she had marveled at its absence.

A maid arrived to help her dress. When they were finished, Diane wrote a hasty note to the Countess of Glasbury, brought it down to have posted immediately, and then went looking for Jeanette.

She found her in her chambers, in the same sitting-room chair where she had been yesterday. Jeanette appeared so worn and tired that Diane wondered if she had ever gone to bed.

"It is happening now. Right now," Jeanette said.

"What is happening?"

"The duel. I expected tomorrow, or the next day—not this soon."

"I am sure you are wrong."

"The chevalier came. Daniel left with him. They are meeting now. I know it in my soul."

"I do not believe this, Jeanette. He told me he would stand down."

Jeanette's gaze darted to her. It examined her much as it had that first day in the porcelain chamber in Paris. "When did he say that?"

She felt herself flushing. "Last night. He promised."

"Last night? Tell me, where was this promise made? When?"

Her face burned hotter.

Flames of understanding and anger flickered in Jeanette's eyes. "When he was making love to you? Do not look so surprised. I have known of his interest in you. I saw it from the start." She shook her head and muttered a curse. "A man will say anything at such times, Diane. Worse, he will mean it when he says it. Then the light of day dawns and he regretfully changes his mind."

"He will not go back on his word."

"There are older words he is obligated to keep. My brother has never allowed any woman to interfere with what he swears to do. He stands down from nothing. If he seduced you with this promise, it was despicable of him, and I will say so when he returns." Her harsh expression cracked. "If he returns."

"He did not seduce me. Nor will he fight this duel." She said it as firmly as she could, to reassure the woman in front of her, who looked to be grieving already.

Jeanette held out her hand, seeking comfort. Diane grasped it and laid her other arm around Jeanette's shoulder.

"Was last night the first time with him?"

"Yes."

"He promised me he would not pursue you. Anticipating the duel, he must have grabbed at the chance to live. I am sure he would not have acted so dishonorably to you otherwise."

Diane was not convinced of that. The way he had kissed her at the brook implied that he had abandoned whatever assurances he had given his sister.

"We must decide what you are going to do now," Jeanette said after taking a composing breath. "I will tell Daniel that he must settle something on you. Enough so that you can marry. There have been men who would be suitors if you had some fortune."

"I do not want to marry any of those possible suitors."

Jeanette patted her hand. "Right now you may not. Consider it carefully, however. You will see I am right."

"After what happened with Mister Tyndale, I do not think it likely there will be any suitors anyway."

"If the settlement is sufficient, there will be, trust me."

"If the settlement is sufficient, Mister Tyndale himself would take my hand. I do not like the idea of being bartered like used goods."

Jeanette looked up. Sadness and sympathy filled her eyes. "Have no illusions that there is a future with my brother instead. There is very little room in his heart and his life for the kind of affection a woman expects. He is closed to such emotions. He knows that, you see. He chose for it to be that way, because anything else would make him weak."

Diane knew that there was no place in his life for her. Daniel was much more complicated than Jeanette thought, however. He was not the cold, closed man Jeanette described. Such a man would not have come to comfort her and to hold her through the night.

She had experienced a beautiful and trusting peace in that sleeping embrace. It had produced a special intimacy, both different from and connected to the physical ones they had shared in his bed. She wanted to hold on to that special glow. She wanted it to fill the void for as long as her memory would let it.

Deep in her soul, however, she knew that she could keep it alive only if she did not reach for more. She did not want to risk learning that he had only been moved by pity or guilt, not affection.

She definitely did not want to take the chance that they might ever make love again. She could not bear it if they did and, instead of that warm intimacy, she again endured the empty, embarrassing silence.

"I have already decided what to do, Jeanette. I think that I should leave this house. There will be no duel, but there will be talk. I do not want to live this lie any longer, that we are cousins. I do not want to attend parties where people will be whispering about what happened with Mister Tyndale, or wondering about what exists between Daniel and me."

"Where will you go?"

"I will ask the countess to allow me to stay with her while I arrange things. I will ask her to contact some of her friends in the country, and give me a reference as a governess. Or perhaps there is a school where I can teach, one far away from London. If I disappear before a scandal starts, maybe there will be little scandal at all. I will be easily forgotten."

Jeanette nodded. "I have some money. I will tell Daniel to give you more."

"I cannot take his money now, in any way."

"Will you visit me? While I am here, before I return to Paris?"

"Of course." She bent and embraced her.

Jeanette kissed her cheek. "If he does not return, perhaps you can come back to Paris with me. Promise that you will consider it."

"He will return today, you will see. He has not gone to fight a duel."

• • •

A return letter arrived from the countess, inviting Diane to join her in a visit to Laclere Park, her family's country seat. Penelope explained that it would be impossible to hide out anywhere in London, and proposed this as a better solution, adding that she felt some need to hide out herself.

Diane went to her chamber and packed. It was harder to do than she had expected, and she sent the maid away so that her reactions would not be watched.

All the while she listened for the sounds of Daniel's return. What would be reflected in his eyes when they faced each other again? She suspected it might be very awkward.

How would he react to her leaving? Would he be surprised? Accepting?

Relieved?

She knew he would understand that if she stayed here, dependent on him, it would eventually become unpleasant. All the lilacs in the world, all of the love in her heart, would not make it other than it would truly be.

Her trust in his promise wobbled as the hours passed. By the time she left her chamber and went down to the library, it had gotten very shaky.

She opened a window that faced the street and waited and listened so hard that her head hurt. As more time slid by, worry grew, making her nauseated and sick at heart.

Carriages and horses passed, and she heard each one. Finally, when she had almost given up, when she had begun grieving, a horse stopped in front of the house.

She identified the sounds of a groom leading the horse away.

Jumping up, she ran down the corridor until she saw the entry.

It was Daniel.

Of course it was. Who else would it be?

The relief that made her heart race answered that question. She had been afraid it was the chevalier, coming to bring bad news.

"Go up to your sister," she said. "She is sick with worry for you. Go now. I will be in the library."

He mounted the staircase. She waited until the last sight of his boots disappeared, then went back to the library.

In her mind she again saw his face when he noticed her. The memories of last night had been in his eyes, but also something else. She had recognized a touch of the old distraction.

That made it harder to look at him when he finally entered the library. He came in quietly and closed the door.

There was no distraction now. His eyes burned with that total attention he could summon. His mouth formed a hard line.

"Jeanette is reassured?" she asked.

"Yes. Louis and I met with Tyndale and his second. It has been resolved honorably."

"You withdrew?"

"I said that I would."

"I did not doubt it."

"The hell you didn't."

Her worry must have been on her face when she rushed to the entry. "Jeanette is very relieved, I'm sure."

"I do not think that is her reaction at all. She is astonished, however. It has been a long time since I have been able to surprise her, so there is some satisfaction in that."

But in little else. He had not liked doing this. It had hurt his pride to appear the coward and withdraw. He resented that she had forced him to it.

"Thank you."

She got a dark glance for that.

"My sister said that you are going to visit the countess."

"I thought it would be for the best to—"

"Where did you ever get the idea that I would let you leave now?"

He spoke as if he found the notion more curious than anything else. She could not ignore the coiling anger seeping out of him, however, much as it had at the brook. He restrained it, but the restraint itself only intensified its effect on the air, and her.

He walked toward her. "I just went to a man whom I despise and declined to kill him because you demanded it of me, and while I did so, you were packing your belongings."

"I can't stay here now. You know that."

"I don't see why not." He moved close to her. "In fact, you must stay here now."

"You know why I cannot. It would be wrong."

"Was last night wrong?"

He was confusing her, standing so close like this. Making her mind muddle. "That was different."

"Perhaps you think that last night was not wrong because you gave yourself in a noble cause. To save a life. Well, if you have a taste for such sacrifice, you must stay. Tell yourself that you do so to save my soul this time. There is a lifetime's worth of sacrifice in that endeavor."

He spoke sardonically, but the warmth in his eyes and a gentle resonance in his voice contradicted the lightness he forced.

She stared at him, unable to think of an answer to such a challenge. It crossed her mind that the devil might seduce people this way. How effective it would be to use someone's own inclinations to lure them to hell.

"When did you make this decision to go?" he asked. "Last night? Was coming to me the final act of friendship?"

He unsettled her more than he ever had, gazing down at her, commanding her attention. She had trouble thinking straight. His references to last night only made her heart jump around.

"Before," she said. "After the brook, and the game of cards."

"Because you realized how much I wanted you? Did that frighten you?"

She turned from his gaze and took a few steps from his closeness. She did not like this conversation, and the way he persisted in peeling away at her motives and resolve.

"It could not have frightened you too much, if you came to me last night."

"I had a reason for last night. A good reason. I offered one night, however, no more. I am not going to be a Margot to you. I can't. I learned that last night, if I learned nothing else. I think that these things are different for women than for men. Now, I have made my decision and you should be kind enough to accept it."

She felt him behind her, too close. Then his hands were on her arms and his breath in her hair. A small, light kiss on the back of her crown sent rays of lively sensations down her body.

"I am not so kind as that. I do not easily give up what I want. Nor am I asking you to live here as my mistress, Diane."

She pivoted out of his hold and faced him. "You aren't? Then you do not want . . . Of course, it probably wasn't what you expected. . . . You want me to stay here as it was before, as Jeanette's companion only. . . ."

Her flustered response amused him. "You can never just be Jeanette's companion now. Not ever. I intend to make love to you again, and that is definitely one reason why I cannot let you go. Since I am not a man who importunes guests or corrupts innocents, there is only one way to resolve things. We will get married."

The announcement left her dumb.

"It is the only solution, Diane."

"It is not. We both know it isn't."

"True. I could have Hampton change that trust so that you get the income at once. That is what Jeanette just commanded."

"I could not accept it now."

"Because I am inconveniently alive? How unfortunate for you that I did not die in a duel today, then. Your future would have been comfortable and secure. You should have given more weight to your own interests last night."

"Stop twisting what I say. I did not—"

"I have no intention of settling anything on you, despite my sister's insistence. I will not make it easy for you to leave. We will marry."

She guessed the reason for this decisiveness. It was the same guilt that had probably brought him to her chamber last night. She would have preferred not to see evidence of that. "I see. You have decided to do the right thing. I understand. However, that is not necessary. I did not expect—"

"You expected nothing. I know that. It does not speak well of your opinion of me. A young woman has the right to expect something of the man who takes her innocence."

"It was not your fault."

"I have refused more blatant offers before."

A marriage of obligation was the last thing she wanted with this man of all men. "This is kind of you. Very decent. I do not think that we should do this, however. You don't really want to, and I'm not sure that I do either."

"Diane, there are many reasons why this may be a mistake, and most of them have to do with my character. But you must do it, even if you are not sure. It will silence the rumors about Tyndale, and about you and me."

"So would my absence. My disappearance."

"I have already told you that I cannot let you leave."

She resented the way he kept saying that, as if he controlled everything about this. "*I* have the say in that. It is *my* choice. I do not need any money from you to do it, so you cannot stop me if I am determined."

"That is true. I can only do my best to make sure you are not determined." He laid his hand against her cheek and looked into her eyes. "Do I have to show you how it is in my power to ensure that you are not?"

His touch alone showed her. Warmth flowed down her neck to her breasts, and his gaze forced the time to slow. She realized that he had always known his effect on her. His indifference had protected her, serving as a shield that he wore for her sake, because he knew the easy pickings she had always represented.

"Do you have misgivings because of last night? It is often not pleasant for a woman the first time. It will not be like that in the future."

She felt her cheek blushing under his palm. She lowered her gaze and shrugged. She did have misgivings because of last night, but not the way he meant. The pain had been the easy part. "Not all of it was unpleasant."

"So you said. *Not entirely horrible.* I promise it will not be at all horrible next time." He lifted her chin with his finger so she had to look at him. "Do you accept my proposal, Diane?"

The way he looked at her, so handsome and promising in his warmth, so appealing in his dark power, lured her to cast caution aside.

Her heart wanted to accept. Her love yearned to be euphoric. Both were eager to be overwhelmed by him and the magical, enlivening spell that he now spun.

Her better sense would not permit total capitulation. It whispered that she did not really know what she got in him. Jeanette's warnings echoed in her ears. She was out of her depths with this man. There were layers in him that she did not know and possibly never would.

"You are very wrong about something," he said. "I am not only doing the right thing. I want this. I am hoping that you spoke honestly last night, and that you want it too."

He spoke roughly, as if the words were difficult to utter. It sounded as though the declaration was not one that he welcomed admitting to, and had been torn from his heart.

Tilting his head, he kissed her. It was the gentlest kiss he had ever given her. It offered care and comfort and a hint of future excitements. It promised affection if not love. It filled her heart the way his long embrace had last night.

That reassured her as nothing else could. The dark, unknown fathoms did not matter suddenly. Nor did the danger she had sensed in their lovemaking. No matter how this unfolded, she knew at that moment that his intentions were good.

"Do you accept?"

Despite the sensation that she took a reckless step, she nodded. In the daze he created, it seemed the only right thing to do.

He smiled as if her decision had been important to him. "I will tell my sister," he said, stepping away. "We will go to Scotland, if you are agreeable to that. The marriage will be legal, and our ambiguous histories will not interfere. I would like her and Paul to accompany us and stand as witnesses. Is that acceptable to you?"

"Of course. However, since you barely asked if the marriage was acceptable, this new solicitous manner is a delightful surprise."

Her words caught him as he walked to the door. He paused and glanced back at her. "I regret to say that it probably will not last."

She had just been given fair warning and she knew it. "I am quite sure that it will not. People do not change so quickly."

"No, I suppose that they do not."

chapter 20

Paul carried Jeanette into the chapel in the tiny hamlet near Dunbar. The clean scents of spring blew in the windows, and the vicar waited at the end of the nave.

Diane sneaked a glance at Daniel. He appeared calm enough. Having made a decision, this was now merely something to see through to the end for him. He had not spent the three days' journey here so unsettled that he could not eat. During their meals at the inns along the way, his manner had been astonishingly relaxed, even lighthearted.

So had Paul's. It had been Jeanette and herself who lived in tense silence. The two of them had taken one carriage, accompanied by Jeanette's maid, and Paul and Daniel had ridden in another. That had left Diane with many hours to think, because Jeanette said very little the whole way north.

Paul settled Jeanette on a chair near the vicar and stood beside her. Daniel offered Diane his arm. They walked forward.

The vows were a blur. As if from a distance, she heard herself saying the words. It all seemed so much a dream that when they left the chapel the glare of the sun stunned her and seemed to snap her awake.

"We will return in ten days, I expect," she heard Daniel saying.

Over at the carriages a coachman was lifting her trunk up onto the equipage Daniel and Paul had used.

Jeanette gave her a kiss. Then Paul carried her away, placed her in the coach where the maid waited, and climbed in with them.

"Where are they going?" Diane asked.

"Back to London. Jeanette will announce the marriage, and by the time we return it will be old news."

The coach rolled away. Diane looked at the one remaining. "Where are *we* going?"

"I have a small property nearby."

"We are going to hide out until the whispers die?"

"I think of it as having you alone for a week."

She had been nursing a knot in her stomach since they left London, and now it twisted. The coach's open door waited for the bride. She felt much as she had when she faced the front of Daniel's Paris home, paralyzed by a fear that she had gotten herself into something that she had not planned out very well.

A life with Daniel St. John waited in that coach. She only knew one thing about marriage, and she guessed it was all that would matter for the next week. If she were still ignorant she would be less nervous.

His arm slid across her back. "Come with me now. I promise not to ravish you on the way, so you do not have to look as if you are facing the noose just yet."

The property might be small to Daniel's mind, but she thought it was charming and just the right size. Nestled at the base of a low hill and flanked by a copse of trees, the old stone house looked out over a small lake. Two levels in height, it offered four chambers below and four above. The man and woman who cared for it lived in a cottage nearby.

She and Daniel had not been expected, and they went for a walk as the couple rushed to prepare things.

"They seemed astonished to see you," she said as they strolled around the lake.

"I rarely come here anymore. It has been some years since I visited. I lived here for a few years as a boy, but that was before Harold and Meg came. To them, I am an absent owner and the place is more theirs than mine now."

She looked around the property with new interest. "You lived here? After you came over from France?"

He walked a silent twenty steps before answering. "Yes."

"Was this your family's, then?" She pictured the house filled with people, and a very young Daniel running in the grass.

"My mother's family had owned it for generations. I do not know how they even came to have it. Probably from the time when France and Scotland plotted together against England."

"How old were you when you came? When you left France?"

"Eight."

"That was the same age I was when I left England. What an odd coincidence. You left France to come here and I left England to go there, at the same age. I always thought we had nothing in common, but it seems we do."

"I suppose so."

They left the edge of the lake and followed a path into a small woods. Soon they emerged on the other side. A stone wall enclosed a graveyard near the edge of the trees. Daniel aimed north, toward the hill, but Diane entered the graveyard, curious.

He followed and stood beside her as she scanned several dozen stones rising out of the ground. "They are old servants and such," he said.

"They are the history of this place, and the families who lived here. I find such things fascinating, since I have none of that myself." Her gaze slid over the names that defined the lives lived here. McGregor and Graham, LaTour and Mirabeau and Jervais. Smith and Johnson and Scott. "There is no St. John," she said, starting to walk so she could examine the rest."

His hand took her arm. "It was my mother's family who owned it, not my father's, and I said that it is mostly servants buried here. Let us go now. I do not care for graves as much as you do."

She let him lead her toward the hill. They went to its top and looked down on the house and the lake.

"Thank you for bringing me. I like that you lived here as a boy, and that your family owned it for generations. It is not my family, of course, but I am officially connected to it now, aren't I?"

He gave her a speculative look. "It appears that you are now. Officially."

"You do not like to do this, do you?"

"Nonsense. It is great sport. I don't have the chance to enjoy it often enough, and welcome the opportunity."

They were fishing.

After their dinner she had asked Daniel to teach her. Readily agreeing, he had found some poles, baited the lines, and now they stood side by side, waiting for something to happen.

Something was what had not happened for a long time.

"Perhaps it is supposed to induce meditation, much like watching the waves of the sea," she said.

"No doubt. Only less sublime."

"Yes, fishing in a small lake on a cultivated property isn't very sublime at all, is it? A vista needs to be full of grandeur and power for that." She glanced at a small volume poking out of his pocket. "If you prefer to read your book, I won't mind."

He bobbed his line up and down a few times. "You are sure you can manage alone? They won't be too much for you? Won't pull you to the depths while you fight them?"

She laughed. "I think I am safe."

"If you are sure, perhaps I'll sit under that tree until you have had your fill."

He laid down his pole and strolled away.

She played with her rod and line, trying to catch one of the silvery, slithering forms in the water.

She decided that it was one of the best afternoons of her life. When he had spoken of having her alone, she had assumed he meant in bed. She had not expected this quiet companionship that they had shared during these hours, imbued as it was with the intimacy of that long night in his arms.

The fish simply did not want to be caught. She knew that if she could get her line farther in the lake, her luck would improve. Looking back at Daniel, she saw that he was involved with his reading.

Sitting on the ground, she peeled off her hose. Skirt bunched to her knees in one hand and rod in the other, she waded into the lake and cast her line.

The hook sank. She stood as still as she could, with the cool water lapping at her, dampening the edge of her dress. She hitched it a bit higher and tucked the pole under her other arm.

A sharp tug told her a fish was on her hook. There was no way to bring it in, however, without dropping her skirt into the water. Excited by her success, she turned and walked back to the lake's edge, dragging the squirming weight behind her.

She stepped onto the grass, water dripping down her legs, her skirt scrunched in her hand and up her thighs. She examined her muddy feet, and then looked up, right into Daniel's eyes.

He no longer read. He watched her, and she guessed he had been doing so for some time. She let her gown drop and turned to bring in the fish.

"It isn't nearly as large as it felt on the line," she said as she pulled it out of the water. "I think I should put it back."

"I will do it." He got up to come and help.

She had already taken care of it, however. Without thinking, she grasped the fish and removed the hook. By the time he reached her, the little fish was flying through the air, back to the water.

"You did that very well. Most women do not like to touch them."

She gazed at her hand where the fish had just been. She *had* done it very well. Nor had the feel of the fish been a surprise. "I think that I did it before. As a child. Certainly not since, or I would remember. I will smell of fish now, I'm afraid."

He took her hand and sniffed it. His breath sent chills up her arm.

"Not a bad smell. All the same, we will bathe you." He took the rod from her hand. "Let us go in now. It is getting late."

She grabbed up her hose and shoes, and walked barefoot back to the house. The grass felt familiar beneath her feet. She had done this before too. It was another little echo from her lost childhood, she was sure.

Daniel spoke privately with Harold before joining her in the sitting room. As he sat by the window in the late-afternoon sun's glow, numerous bootsteps sounded on the back stairs.

A Chinese urn stood on a table in a corner. She examined it. "One of yours?"

"Yes. I brought it back from one of my first journeys to the East."

"Ming?"

He laughed. "No. You can break this one. It was made for export and is not very valuable. I did not know what it was at the time, but it appealed to me and I began learning more about them."

"You have many Oriental things. Your chamber in London . . ." She caught herself as memories of that chamber blocked her throat. "Is that what you carry in your ships mostly? Urns and such?"

"Sometimes. Often less interesting things."

"They must have been valuable even if less interesting, if they made you wealthy."

"Luck played its role. So did big risks that turned out well. For years I did not carry other men's cargo, only my own. If one ship had gone down I might be plying the waters today, hauling nothing but dried fish."

"Why didn't you avoid those risks?"

He shrugged. "I was very young when I started, and very impatient."

How young? She swallowed the question, but she wanted to ask it. After all, he was still fairly young. He must have been very young when he brought her to Rouen, but he spoke of knowing her father through shipping, so it had to be after some of those big risks. But that would make him ridiculously young when he began making his fortune.

She glanced at him. Maybe he was older than she thought. Some men look younger than their years. His life had not been pampered, however. For a long time he was at sea and traveling around the world.

"You say very young as if you are an old man. You can't be more than thirty-two or -three."

"When the years are full, it takes longer to live them."

It was a good answer, but not the one she wanted. He had neither corrected her, nor agreed.

"There are rumors about you, besides those involving me. Did you know that? The countess told me that some say you were a pirate in the eastern seas. Were your risks as big as that?"

"You worry that you have married a pirate? Nothing so dashing, I'm afraid. Why, there were not more than two or three episodes in all those years that could be described that way."

He was teasing her. Mostly. She suspected that there had been episodes that might indeed be described that way.

She perused the books in the case on one wall. She did not really see the titles and bindings. She pictured him in the chair by the window, his booted legs crossed, his cravat indifferently tied, his elbow propped on the chair's arm, and his chin in his hand.

She felt his attention on her.

Harold appeared at the door, caught Daniel's eye, and made a vague gesture to the second level. He disappeared. Other sounds from the back of the house, of Meg moving about the kitchen, stopped.

"Your bath is ready upstairs," Daniel said.

A bath would be welcome. She still stood in bare feet, and the lake's mud had crusted on her legs. Her hand still smelled vaguely of fish.

She turned to leave the room. He sat there, much as she had seen him in her mind. He appeared so handsome that she did not want to move. His presence charged the air in the chamber, flustering her even though he merely looked at her.

"How do you want to do this, Diane? Would you prefer to bathe alone before I come up?"

A stimulating stab jolted her low and deep as her body understood the implications of what he said.

He had been so mild all day. He had barely touched her. She had assumed that this would be delayed until after supper. Until tonight.

She just stood there, feeling stupid and nervous.

He rose and came over to her. Her heart began a slow, rising spin. "Meg has left with Harold and returned to their cottage. You will probably need some help with lacings and such."

He took her hand. Resisting the urge to dig in her heels, she let him lead her from the chamber. She plucked up her courage and tried to contain the muddle of reactions swimming through her. They were married now, and she would not act like a foolish girl. She was not even an innocent, and would not behave like one.

Climbing the stairs with him close behind, she told herself all that. Feeling him back there unsettled her, however. It entered her mind that it might have been better if he had just ravished her in the coach. Daniel succumbing to rough passion was something she knew. This quieter, calmer, contained sensuality seemed more dangerous.

And more exciting. She could not deny that. By the time they reached the upper chambers, her senses were sensitive to everything, especially his proximity.

A long metal tub had been set in one chamber behind a low hearth screen. A small fire burned, removing the building's light chill.

She dipped her fingers into the bath water. "Just right."

She felt him behind her. His hands began working the tapes on her gown. She instinctively stiffened, to suppress a visceral tremble that threatened to shake her whole body.

"Do you mind that I am doing this?" he asked.

"I am very unsettled, that is all."

"Is it unpleasant, being unsettled?"

She realized it was not unpleasant. Not really. She shook her head.

Her gown gaped open in the back and sagged on her shoulders. With no effort from her, it slipped down her body, leaving her in her underclothes and bare legs. He kissed the skin of her naked shoulder.

"You are not unsettled, darling. You are aroused. You are feeling how much we want each other."

Giving a name to it only made it stronger. The sensation turned more physical. Her body became even more conscious of him. The parts of lovemaking that were not entirely horrible, not horrible at all, began flitting through her mind.

He went to work on the lacings of her stays. She sensed the garment slowly releasing her, too aware that soon she would have almost nothing on. If the first time was any indication, she doubted she would have a bath after all.

She was not even sure that she wanted one now.

The stays fell to the ground too. She only had her thin chemise on now. It was daylight still. There were no candles to snuff out.

Embracing her, he turned her in his arms and kissed her. He did not overwhelm her with his passion as he had in his chamber, but it affected her just the same. Everything that she was feeling, the delicious excitement and the physical thrills, grew tenfold, burying fear and wariness.

He slid the chemise off, his gaze following its slow descent. An echo of shock sounded, but mutual desire sang louder. Astonishment at being naked faded. She liked the way he looked at her. It woke that deep pulse, and the throbbing seemed to spread to her whole body.

She wanted him to kiss her again. Touch her. She wanted it enough that she could not pretend she did not. She imagined him doing so, and that created an anticipation that aroused her more. The power of what she was experiencing was all that surprised her now. Admitting that they wanted each other was turning her wanton.

Instead of that kiss and caress, he handed her into the tub.

The water felt sensual and cool, lapping gently over her warm skin, showing her how vivacious her senses had become.

He handed her the soap.

"Are you leaving?" she asked as she raised and lathered a muddy leg.

His gaze meandered up her leg, and then up the rest of her body. "Do you want me to?"

She suddenly saw him as she had in his chamber while she lay naked and waiting. The same sensuality stretched between them now, and a little of the old fear returned. "I don't know."

"Yes, you do." He smiled, and walked around the screen.

She scrubbed the other leg, disappointed in herself. She was such a coward. He was being so patient with this slow seduction, and she had backed down—

He was behind her suddenly. She felt him by her head, kneeling by the tub. "Give me the soap."

Glancing back as she handed it to him, she saw that he had removed his coat and shirt.

He looked wonderful. So handsome and warm, so appealing in his lean strength. Images of embracing him entered her head, making her breath catch.

He dipped the soap into the water at her side. The action brought him closer. As he joined his hands to make a lather, his flanking arms enclosed her in a vague embrace.

"You are too beautiful for me to leave you to your privacy. If you could see yourself, you would understand. I think that bathing a wife may be one of the rights of a husband." He spread the lather down her arms in a soapy caress. Stroke after gentle, slow stroke, his fingers and palms moved the white foam over her skin.

Luxurious, soothing stimulation lapped over and around her hips just as the water did. She leaned against the tub's back, into his chest and support, and submitted to the seductive caresses. She watched his taut muscles stretch as his splayed fingers slithered the soap up and down, up and down.

"This will also help me to discover which parts were not *entirely horrible* for you." He washed the lather up to her shoulders and onto her chest. His palms skimmed her breasts as he covered her torso with the soap.

The washing slowed. His hands moved deliberately. They slid below her breasts and around them, teasing her. She closed her eyes and waited.

"Is this what you want?" he asked, his mouth right near her ear. His caresses stroked her two breasts in languid, circular movements. The sensation was incredibly sensual. When those smooth hands focused on her nipples, the pleasure sharpened, shortening her breaths, making the arousal almost desperate.

She watched through lowered lids, biting her lip to hold in gasps of pleasure as his fingers circled gently on her nipples, intensifying the pleasure.

"Kneel. Face me."

This felt so good that she did not want it to end. He lifted her shoulders however, and guided her into position up on her knees, rising out of the water, facing him.

Not only she had been affected by this. His stern expression reflected his own arousal and his awareness of hers. She expected him to lift her up and carry her away. Instead he took the soap and made more suds.

He caressed her breasts again, and then lower. While he kissed her his hands moved to her back and down to her bottom. He stroked over its swells every way possible, making the deep pulse of arousal throb until it owned her mind.

The hot feeling down there maddened her. Holding his shoulders, accepting his kiss, she arched her bottom to his hands, urging him with her body to touch lower and deeper.

He took her hands and lowered them to the edge of the tub. He moved to her side, still washing, now down the backs of her thighs and up between them, now over her bottom and down low, everywhere but where she wanted him.

It was slow, wonderful torment, and she was helpless against what it did to her. She shamelessly hung on the tub's edge and raised her hips as she arched her back and lowered her shoulders.

He bent and kissed her back. His hand soothed between her upper thighs. "You did not want this last time. Do you now?"

He had made sure she would. She wanted it so badly that she grit her teeth, to hold in her cries.

"Do you?" He made one light touch, like a question mark.

A cry did escape then, one of relief and affirmation. A low series of them followed when he responded with direct caresses. The sensation built and built, turning so intense it pushed her into total abandon.

She rose and grabbed him, pulling him to her so she could hold him. His passion burst free to join hers. He enclosed her in a tight embrace and took her in a deep, possessive kiss. All the while he touched and stroked until nothing mattered to her, nothing existed, except him and that focused sensation so full of unbearable pleasure.

Rivulets of water streaked down his chest from her wet arms. She kissed at one to stop its path, and then another. She playfully licked at the tiny stream. Her tongue followed it all the way up to his shoulder, flicking at his skin. Turning her head slightly, she saw a new kind of passion in his eyes. Proud of herself, she kissed him.

His lips parted and suddenly she was invading him as he had her. The boldness of it gave a triumphant thrill to the desire.

Water slapped around her body. He rinsed the soap off her with one hand while he held her to him with the other, encouraging her in her daring explorations. He lifted her out of the tub and pulled her closer yet, in an embrace that seemed to completely enclose her.

Still bound together, still joined by hot flesh and cool water, he released his lower garments and let them fall so that the embrace could be complete.

Firm holds on her hip and shoulder confined her. His deep kiss commanded less physical yieldings. The sense of being absorbed swam through her. Of no separation. Of being controlled in the most benign way, but dominated all the same.

Her feet left the floor. Still holding her, still kissing her, he carried her to the bed.

In the early, cool twilight he knelt over her, his knees flanking one of her thighs. No black night hid her sight of him. The image he created, of lean muscular strength and stern control and passion, left her heart pounding and her body eager. His dark eyes reflected the confident knowledge that she wanted him and that he would have her soon.

He came to her, taut arms flanking her, kneeling still, and kissed her. His head dipped, and his tongue flicked at her nipple just as hers had at his chest.

The pleasure had eased to a deep, flowing excitement, but his mouth sent her reeling again. With his fingers he aroused her other breast. She grasped at his shoulders and her sanity, but the unceasing intensity of the pleasure meant she lost the latter. Closing her eyes, she submitted and spun into a place where nothing else existed but sensation.

Her mind swam with cries for relief and pleas for more. She clutched him harder, wherever she could, unable to keep her hands any stiller than her body. His arms and sides. His torso and hips. She caressed his chest, trying to return to the absorption of that kiss near the tub. Her body became a void that needed something to be complete.

Her hand brushed his phallus in the space between their bodies. Even in her madness she could tell he liked it, that he wanted her to caress him that way.

He gazed down at where her hand moved. Reaching between her legs, he touched her too.

They shared a moment of erotic, heavenly pleasure. Then he touched her differently, very specifically, and her breath left her. She began spinning in a tightening coil of unbearably focused pleasure. Knowing he watched, that he saw the way her body begged and heard the wanton cries and gasps, only increased his control of her.

It turned excruciating. She had been here before, the last time. She tried to retreat, to find relief.

He eased down along her side and she was able to embrace him. It did not help for long. He kissed her and the sense of torment softened a little. He stroked long and deeply, spreading the sensation from that one intense spot.

His mouth brushed against her ear. "Give in to it. If you surrender to it, it will be wonderful."

She was not sure that she could. She was not sure that she wanted to. She only knew that she was close to crying.

He kissed her breast. "You will surrender, darling. I want you to know what this can be."

A new touch made her breath catch and her mind go blank. A tension of precise pleasure made all thoughts of retreat disappear. He forced her toward something that she grasped for.

The tension got stronger, excruciating. A high pitch of wonderful sensation shot all through her, making her scream. Perfect pleasure held for an unearthly moment, then burst into a million pieces that flowed through her body.

He was in her when her mind came back to her, settled between her legs. There was no real pain this time, only relief, as if her body had been incomplete and needed the way he filled her.

She had no resistance this time. She could not protect herself from anything, least of all her own heart. She could not block the way he possessed her. He filled all the voids, even the oldest one in her heart. It vanished the way it had in her chamber that night. She was helpless against the emotions evoked by the intimacy.

She gave more than he did. She knew that. Even when he paused and looked in her eyes and she thought that she could see his soul, even then he reserved something to himself. She could not do the same. She did not know how to. She did not even want to, because her heart had never known such wholeness.

The pleasure returned, quivering where they were joined. She lifted her legs to draw him in more and moved in response to both him and the sensation. He thrust harder, deeper, and the power beckoned her. She rocked into his movements and swept into his passion so that even the desire and hunger and madness were mutual.

At the end she encouraged him, raising her hips to the final hard thrusts. She relished the evidence that he was as helpless to the passion as she was.

For that tiny slice of time, when the surrender was mutual and he was as much hers as she was his, she understood what this could be.

chapter 21

Spring was beautiful this year. Daniel decided that as he rode his horse through London's streets, aiming for an appointment he did not much care about.

He *should* care about it a great deal. It promised a small victory instead of a large one, but it would be something. Instead, when he received the letter requesting the meeting, his reaction had been boredom rather than anticipation.

He laughed at himself as he maneuvered his horse around wagons and carriages. The last two weeks had turned him soft. He had always suspected a woman might do that to him.

He could not regret it. He would not have missed one moment of those days by the lake and those nights in her arms.

Memories of Diane's beauty and passion, of her eagerness and ecstasies, distracted him. Of long hours of incredible pleasure and early mornings of astonishing peace. London had been a world away and the past in another lifetime.

He had come very close to telling her everything. There had been times when the contentment was so complete he had been sure nothing could ruin it. He would look at her while the confessions and apologies tickled his tongue. Each time an image of her, hurt and confused, and of her eyes, wary and cautious, kept him silent. *Later,* he always decided. When we are back in the city.

The dreamy mood had lingered upon their return, however. He had surrendered to it and gladly kept reality at bay.

Even the letter, and this meeting, had not been able to intrude.

Without knowing he had stopped his horse, he found himself in front of the house he sought.

His soul gave a sigh of resignation, not triumph as it should. He dismounted and went to the door.

The butler led him through an expensively appointed home to the back garden. Like the house itself, the plantings had been arranged with an eye to effect rather than beauty. Lilac bushes, clipped into perfect mounds, lined one wall. Many beautiful blooms had been sacrificed to maintain those globes. A small fruit tree in the corner could have been painted by a salon artist, so artificial was the careful way its budding limbs sprang. The paths appeared as if someone had spent hours chiseling each stone.

It reminded him of a toy he had seen in a shop once, composed of tiny iron bushes and flowers and pavers that a girl could arrange. Now he stood amidst gigantic versions of the same tight shapes.

Andrew Tyndale sat in a chair by an iron table, sipping tea and reading a volume of ancient Greek philosophy in Latin translation. Daniel found that amusing. He doubted Tyndale had ever read such things, even when in school and required to.

"Ah, here you are," Tyndale said. He smiled broadly and gestured to another chair.

Spirits were offered. When Daniel declined, tea arrived.

"Back from Scotland, I see." Tyndale's jovial tone implied that he had heard all about the marriage.

Of course he had. Upon returning to London, Daniel and Diane had discovered they were the talk of the town. In their absence, the Countess of Glasbury let the true story be known. She said that Daniel had stood down because the challenge had led him and Diane to recognize their feelings for each other.

The gossips now speculated on what might have been occurring in Daniel's house these last weeks. Tyndale's role in things was all but forgotten.

"Congratulations on your recent nuptials." He made it sound like an acknowledgment of defeat, as if they had met in a duel of a minor sort and Daniel had won.

Daniel accepted the good wishes and then waited. He was not here to exchange pleasantries, and did not want to be in the man's company more than necessary. Already their proximity, and seeing Tyndale's bland, false manner, was shading the last week's sunshine with a cloud. Other memories, old ones, threatened to push away those of Diane.

"I thought that we should discuss the matter of that debt," Tyndale said.

"A bank draft would be fine."

"Of course. However, I would like to propose an alternative, one that may interest you a great deal."

"If you want to deed me land in South America, I have no interest in such things."

Tyndale's tight smile showed he knew he had just been insulted. "It is more complicated than that, and has significant potential. There are men who would kill for this opportunity."

"I am listening."

"Do you know how steel is made?"

"As it has always been made."

"That is correct. Forged in small batches, with great labor. It is too expensive to be used in most industry as a result."

"There is always iron."

"It has limitations. Cast iron is weak and wrought iron presents problems in its manufacture and its weight. Imagine if steel could be made much more quickly, with no labor at all. What do you think the value of such a process would be?"

Daniel had to struggle not to show his surprise. At least now he knew who Dupré's partner was. "It would be impossible to calculate. Are you saying that you have such a process?"

"Yes. I will have the proof in a day or so."

"Is this proposal of yours connected to this process?"

"I had intended to exploit this myself, but have concluded it might be good to have a partner."

"And you generously thought of me?"

"I like the cut of your coat, so to speak. Oh, I know we had that little problem over a young lady, as men often do. It was all a misunderstanding, and it has turned out with no one any the worse and you very well off. I am able to look beyond that, and I hope that you will be too. I think that we have much in common, actually. I see something of myself in you."

It was all Daniel could do not to smash his fist into the earnest and sincere face across the table. He gazed at the row of soldier bushes and leashed the seething anger that ripped through him.

"Why do you need a partner?"

"It has occurred to me that the most lucrative exploitation of this will require some contacts in the industrial community. I think that a partner would be more effective at finding and dealing with such men."

"In other words, you would prefer only to be an investor, and not become such an industrial man yourself. You offer this in order to avoid that necessity."

"Yes."

"Of course, you also do so because you owe me twenty thousand pounds. I assume that is the price of this partnership?"

Tyndale beamed, pleased and surprised by Daniel's quick wits.

"How do I know that it is worth so much?"

"If you think about it, you will realize it is worth much more."

"That depends upon the efficiency of the process and the size of the piece I am buying."

"I should think twenty-five percent could be arranged."

Daniel looked to the garden and contemplated this offer and the comical irony that it was being made to him.

"I want to see this proof you speak of."

"It will be ready tomorrow or the next day."

"Today. If it is not ready, I want to see how it is being made ready."

"That is a secret. Surely you must realize that I can't allow you to see the process unless you are committed."

"And I can't commit myself unless I see the process. I am not so stupid as to be handed a hunk of steel and take your word on how it was made. If that is inconvenient, you can always give me that bank draft instead."

Tyndale appeared less pleased at quick thinking this time. A thoughtful frown broke upon his brow. Daniel suspected it was the first time anyone had seen a false expression on the man's face in years.

"I suppose I can show you, but there are things I cannot explain at this point. There are details I must keep from you."

"That is fine. There is one other thing. Are there any other partners? I would not like to learn at some point that I own twenty-five percent and five others do too."

Tyndale laughed, but anger made it sound hollow. "No, only you."

Daniel hoped that was true. He did not want any innocent fool being lured into this scheme. "What about the inventor. I am sure that you did not discover this process yourself."

"I will compensate the inventor in my own way. The process belongs to me alone, and absolutely no one else will have a share of it except you. Did you ride here? I will call for my horse, and take you to see the process."

Daniel followed him into the house, thinking about Gustave Dupré, whom Tyndale would compensate in his own way. Whom exactly did Tyndale intend to swindle, Dupré or Daniel St. John?

Both, most likely.

Tyndale withdrew three keys from his coat and worked the heavy locks on the shed's door.

"Are those the only keys?" Daniel asked. He had been peppering Tyndale with suspicious questions the whole way to the Southwark alley. Tyndale had interpreted the interest as reflecting a sense of ownership, and welcomed the inquisition.

"Only I and the inventor have keys."

"All the same, if I agree to this, I will want a guard here. One of my men."

The second lock loosened. "You imply that I may be lying, that I will bring others here as I bring you."

"I imply that this is a rough area of town and anyone could break into this shed. You may have the keys but it would take only an ax to cut down the door itself."

They entered the damp, shadowed space. Over on the table were the cylinders, each with its pan of liquid.

Tyndale gestured to Daniel to take a look.

Daniel peered into one of the pans. "I thought you said it would not be completed until tomorrow at the earliest."

Tyndale glanced. His eyes widened. He stuck his head very close. "I was told . . . of course, the calculations on mass and weight could only be approximate . . . and the effect's power only a guess . . ." Using a stick of wood, he yanked some wires out of the pan and gingerly stuck his fingers into its liquid.

His hand rose, holding a sleek steel bar. His eyes narrowed with excitement. He might have been a man discovering gold. "It appears to make the transformation even quicker than we anticipated. The physical reaction must increase in speed with a larger mass."

Daniel took the wet bar in his own hands. "How is it done?"

"Those cylinders hold voltaic piles that generate electricity, the powers of which are only beginning to be understood. This discovery that it can alter the properties of metal is a major scientific advance."

"Why hasn't it been published? Such things are normally reported through one of the scientific societies."

"This was too valuable to disseminate. We do not want everyone in the world to know of it before we can patent it and put it to practical use."

"What is in those pans? Water?"

"Yes, and chemicals. I cannot tell you which ones. Not until you are committed."

Daniel balanced the bar on his palm. "Is there any chance that this is a fraud? Could your inventor have switched them? Taken out the iron and replaced it with steel?"

"He is not so clever. However, I will know for certain in one moment." He lifted the wires out of the third pan, grabbed the bar, and ran his fingertips over its base. "Here it is. I made a mark on this without telling him, just to be sure it was the same bar at the end as it was when it began."

Daniel paced around the table. "It needs to be done again on a larger scale. It could be that if the iron is too large, it will not work. Small bars will be of little use in industry." He gestured around the shed. "Several more need to be set up, with different amounts of the chemicals and different numbers of cylinders, using large, heavy bars. There is no way to calculate the costs of the process, its timing, and its profitability, otherwise. It may be that the cost of production will exceed the finished steel's value, so we also need to determine how small the cylinders can be for it to still work on good-sized iron."

Tyndale nodded. "Yes, I can see what you mean." He looked at Daniel with new respect. They might have never quarreled over a woman. "I think it is good that you are involved. My instincts were correct, that this could use a man of practical cut as a partner."

"I am not a partner yet. Until I see the results of what I describe, it will not be my investment being spent in this shed. And my man will be outside once the new demonstration is begun, to be sure that no steel enters by mistake."

That gave Tyndale pause. "I see. I suppose that makes sense. But in your opinion, what do you think the gain will be if the process is shown to be profitable?"

Daniel set the steel bar back down in its liquid. He shot Tyndale a conspiratorial smile. "Even if the profit per pound is mere pennies, I think that we are talking millions."

"Such a story! Ah, Diane, it is like a tale told to children, with a perfect ending." Margot patted her chest as if her heart gave palpitations.

They sat side by side in Margot's chambers. In London Mister Johnson kept Margot in style, but not in luxury. The love nest was in a building close enough to Mayfair to be respectable, but in a neighborhood not truly fashionable.

Still, the sitting room had been appointed very nicely, as had Margot. On returning home from Scotland, Diane had received a letter from her schoolfriend and decided that it would be rude not to call on her.

"How do you enjoy married life?" Margot smiled suggestively and raised her eyebrows.

Diane felt her face turn red. She laughed. "Well enough."

"That is good. Keep him happy at night and all will be well. If you do not, he will come looking for someone like me. It is not wise to be too much the lady in bed. I think that English mothers teach their daughters stupid things about that. It is all about duty, not pleasure."

How? Diane could not bring herself to mouth the word. How do you keep Mister Johnson happy at night? She had not been raised by an English mother, or any mother, but she felt awkward speaking of this.

"I asked M'sieur Johnson about the Devil Man," Margot confided. "They had never met before that time in the Tuileries, but your husband was known to him. He began hearing of St. John about eight years ago, from men who had dealings with him. He went to sea on merchant ships when just a youth, it is said, then one day got his own ship. From there his fleet just grew. His success at such a young age is much admired, as is he. The smooth way he inserted himself into better circles is envied, I think."

How? The word popped into Diane's mind again. How did he insert himself so smoothly?

Margot gave her the answer. "The ladies helped with that, it is said. He is very discreet, very polished, but is legendary as a seducer."

That only raised the question again, of how an ignorant girl could keep such a man happy. She pictured the gorgeous, worldly women they socialized with, and wondered which of them had helped Daniel's entry into those better circles, and who had been the seducer's lovers.

Margot's story prodded other questions, however, and they rapidly replaced the ones about women. How did he get that first ship? How youthful was he when he had success?

Curiosity about that had been nibbling at her since the day she asked Daniel about the urn in the Scottish house.

"You take good care of him and you will have anything you want, I promise," Margot said, patting her hand.

How?

She thought about that all the way home. Daniel appeared contented enough when they were together. He did not appear to be expecting anything that she did not give.

Perhaps that was because he thought of her as Margot said these English husbands did their wives. As ladies who gave duty, and could not be expected to know about pleasure.

She remembered Madame Leblanc's exhortation that mistresses did the things in that book. She had implied that wives did not. According to Margot, that was why men had mistresses. Not, as Daniel had said that day at the Tuileries, because their wives were cold or sick or far away.

She went to the library and peered at the shelves of books, searching for a small, thin one with a red cover.

It was not there. Perhaps Daniel had burned it after all.

She debated that as she strolled down the corridor. She paused at the door to his study.

She slipped in. There were not so many books here, and the shelves held mostly ledgers and portfolios. Scanning a shelf right above her head, however, she spied a bright red strip of leather.

She pulled it out and went to the window. Page by page she turned the plates. The images did not look as bizarre as the last time she had viewed them. Most were still embarrassing, but the flush she felt did not only come from that.

A sound jolted her. She spun around to see the door opening and hid the book behind her back.

Daniel walked in, appearing as distracted as she had ever seen him. It took him a moment to realize she was there.

He cocked his head curiously. A question entered his eyes.

As he walked toward her, he glanced sharply to the desk and the papers laid out on it. "Did you want something, Diane?"

She shook her head and backed up against the window. Perhaps she could just slip the book behind the drapes, onto the sill. . . .

"What do you have there, darling?"

"Have where?"

"Behind your back."

"Nothing. I merely had not been in this room much and thought I'd see what it was like. If I shouldn't have come in, I am sorry."

"You can come in. I am just wondering why you look as if you have been found stealing." He caressed down her two arms. All the way down, to her hands behind her back. He pried the book away.

Suddenly he was holding it, right in front of her.

He looked at the book, and then at her. "It appears that you have decided it has some value after all."

"The plates are somewhat artistic. There is a virtuosity in the use of the gravure." It did not sound as objective as she wanted. In fact, she heard her voice squeak.

"Ah. So you are studying this to improve your appreciation of artistic technique."

"It is a subject often discussed at dinners and such."

"Art is not only about technique, of course, but also content. Have you found the content shown in here shocking or interesting?"

She swallowed hard. "A little of both, I suppose."

He strolled over to the desk and picked up two scraps of paper. Opening the book, he paged past leaves, stuck the scraps in front of some, and came back to her. "Why don't you decide if you find those more interesting than shocking."

He tipped the book with its marked pages toward her. She wondered if it would be a mistake to take it. He smiled that private smile, and warm amusement lit his eyes.

He was teasing her. Daring her. But she sensed that he wanted her to take it. He would not mind if she found some of it more interesting than shocking.

She snatched the book and, with what she hoped was a sophisticated expression, flipped to the first scrap of paper.

Well, now, that one wasn't all *that* shocking. In fact, there had been times when they made love when she had wondered if he would do that.

Smug now, she flipped to the next one. It was farther along in the book, on plate XVI. She contemplated the image. It wasn't entirely clear what the engraving portrayed.

She turned the plate this way and that, puzzling over it. Surely the man was not—

"What is he doing?"

"Kissing her."

"Oh." The image suddenly made shocking sense. "It seems an odd place to kiss someone."

"It is a very special kiss."

"I can't imagine the man likes it much."

"I think he does. Perhaps more than the woman does."

She nervously fingered the paper scrap marking the plate. "Do you intend to kiss me like that some night?"

"Yes. Unless you forbid it."

She wondered if she would.

She opened the book again. Her initial astonishment had worn off, but it still seemed a very odd thing to do. "Can I decide later?"

"Nothing will ever happen between us that you do not want."

Her thumb slid off the edge of the page and the plate flipped. The next image was somewhat similar but also more complicated. "Look here. The woman is kissing the man too."

He angled his head to see the picture. "So she is."

"But you did not mark that one."

He did not reply to that.

"I suppose that means that you found it more shocking than interesting."

Silence.

"Don't men enjoy being kissed like that?"

He just looked at her.

"You are very selective in which parts of this book you want me to consider, Daniel." She tapped the binding's edge against his chest in a scolding manner. "I am supposed to allow you to give me peculiar kisses, but you are spared such things. Perhaps *I* want to kiss *you* in a special way too. What would you think about that?"

"I expect that I could be convinced to allow it."

"I should hope so. After all, if there are going to be odd doings in that bed, it seems to me that you should be subjected to them as much as I."

"You are absolutely right. I stand corrected." He took the book, tore the second marker in half and placed one half at plate XVII. "Actually, should you ever decide to subject me to this, I think . . ."

"You think what?"

"I think that I would probably buy you a diamond necklace the next day."

Diane sat near the window, watching for the signs of Daniel's return. The lamps in the street threw halos of eerie light into the night, and the few passing carriages and horses appeared and disappeared as they moved from one to the next. She did not know where he had gone tonight, but he had said he would not be too late returning. She had foregone a visit to the theater in order to be here when he got back.

Finally she spotted him. He was just a shadow down the street, but she knew it was him because the rider wore no hat.

Biting her lip, she left the sitting room and went to her chamber. She let the maid remove her dress and stays and then sent her away.

Once alone, she went to her wardrobe, opened a drawer, and withdrew the little red book.

She turned to the first plate that Daniel had marked. She had examined it several times since the afternoon. At some point, she did not know when, it had begun to be much more interesting than shocking.

It really did not depict anything odd. A little different, but hardly debauchery.

Taking one last look at the plate for reference, she put it back in her drawer. She began to blow out the candles, then paused. There had been a few candles lit in the picture.

She removed her chemise. Wearing only her hose, she climbed onto the bed. She pushed all the pillows away, except one big one. She knelt with it in front of her, and then lay down so that it formed a mound beneath her hips and raised her bottom on a little hill. She reviewed the engraving in her mind, and parted her legs.

It felt very wicked lying like this.

Sounds in the next chamber heralded Daniel's presence. She listened to his movements as he undressed, and to the low mumble of his conversation with his valet. Just hearing him and expecting his arrival excited her.

So did her position. She was surprised at how arousing it was. The anticipation and vulnerability were incredibly erotic.

The mumbling stopped. The movements grew fewer. She heard steps outside the door that joined her chamber with his dressing room.

Daniel paused at the adjoining door and contemplated sleeping in his own bed tonight. His mood had turned dark and edgy. The memories were back all the time now. Every time he thought of Tyndale, or saw Jeanette, they would swarm into his head, ugly images that froze his blood.

Diane deserved better. He did not want to bring this to her. He did not want to learn that even she could not defeat it.

He really should not go.

He opened the door anyway.

Candles still burned. Normally she snuffed them on going to bed, so there would not be a risk of fire later in the night.

The soft glow illuminated the chamber with faint, mysterious light. He entered, and saw her.

She lay on the bed in an erotic pose. He realized it was the one in the book. Hose still clad her legs up to her thighs, but she wore nothing else. Her naked back dipped to the base of her spine and then curved up to the erotic swells of her raised bottom.

He stood behind her, entranced by the inviting, abandoned image of her waiting for him. Hunger ripped through him, and his mood and her submissive pose gave it a savage strength.

He removed his robe. "You must have seen into my mind tonight."

"I decided it was not so shocking."

He could see the side of her face where it rested on her joined hands. "Look at me, Diane."

She raised her head and looked back, down her body. The lights in her eyes were unmistakable. Surprise at the excitement and anticipation made her expression as inviting as her pose.

He climbed onto the bed and knelt over her. He kissed down her spine. "Have you been waiting for me long?"

"Not too long."

"Does it arouse you, being like this?"

She rested her head back on her hands, and nodded.

He knelt behind her and caressed her bottom with both his hands. Her back dipped and her hips rose in response. She bit her lower lip.

"Are you already wet?" He could tell that she was, and was glad for it. His mood would not tolerate long loveplay now. He wanted passion to burn away everything else that owned his soul tonight.

She nodded again.

"Good. Because I want you now, at once." He entered her.

Raw pleasure took over, obscuring everything just as he had hoped. Only her velvet hold on him existed.

"You are lost in your head," Diane said.

Through the open drapes he could see a bright moon in the dark sky. A gentle breeze cooled the sweat glossing their skin.

"It took me a long time to realize what it means when you get like this. Your mind is a world away, isn't it?"

A world away. A lifetime away. She was right, and he resented the way it had claimed him again. "I am sorry."

"I don't mind. I am sure that your business affairs must preoccupy you. I know that I can't have all of you all of the time."

He kissed her crown and drew her closer. She tucked herself against him with her head on his chest and her arm embracing his torso.

He thought of the day's meeting with Tyndale. He should have refused the offer to get involved in that scheme. He should have demanded the money and been satisfied with the small victory. Instead, he had not been able to resist the chance to thoroughly bring the man down.

He felt like a victim of his own game. He had spent years seducing men with prizes that appealed to their greatest weakness. Today, without intending to, one of those men may have done the same thing to him.

We have much in common, I think.

Diane's pale shoulder peeked through her flowing tresses. He watched his hand move over it, feeling her luminous skin. He did not risk normal ruin in succumbing to temptation today. Not financial disaster. The real danger lay here, in this embrace. The real loss might be the contentment he had now with this wife, and the freedom his spirit felt when he was truly and completely with her.

There are things I need to tell you. Things that you should hear from me and not someone else. The words were in his chest, then in his throat. They would go no farther, however. She would never forgive him once she knew.

She tilted her head so that she could look at him. In the moonlight he saw a smile before she stretched to kiss him.

"I am thirty-two." He did not even know why he said that. It just came out, a half-measure to encourage her to ask for the truth, perhaps. "In Scotland you were curious about my age. I am thirty-two."

She looked at him thoughtfully. "And you came here when you were eight? Then perhaps the countess was correct. She said it is rumored that you were an émigré during the revolution. Were you?"

"Yes."

She rose up on an arm and looked at him. "Was your father an aristocrat? Were you fleeing?"

"My father was not an aristocrat. He chose to leave, however. It was not a good time, and no one was safe."

"So you came here, and lived in that house in Scotland. Where are your parents now?"

"My mother was dead when we came. My father died soon after we arrived. Louis was with us. The chevalier had helped us get out, because he was an old friend of my mother's. He saw to my care until I was old enough to fend for myself."

"Margot said that you went to sea very young." She sounded like someone finishing a story, content she had read the whole book.

She settled back in his arms. "Do you remember much from back then. Coming here, and your life before, in France?"

"I feel as though I remember all of it." Every day, and every sight. Every loss and every fear. He remembered too well.

"I remember almost nothing. We both left our homes as children and went to new ones. Why should you have such clear memories and I have so few?"

"Memories are capricious. Some disappear, and others, insignificant ones, stay forever. Perhaps the difference is that I did not feel very much like a child by the time I made that journey."

He had not felt at all like one. Life had already made him old and tired and hard. There had been nothing of childhood left when he followed Louis onto that small boat.

The conversation produced an intimate mood, such as only night confidences could. It made the day and its distractions disappear. He relished their retreat.

Her arms tightened and she kissed his chest. "Daniel, I want to tell you something. I came to England looking for something. There was this . . . hole in me, this gap, that never seemed to go away. I thought that if I found my relatives, my history, that it would be filled. I think I thought that being loved would fill it."

His heart hurt for her unhappiness and the years she had lived with that hole. He wished to God he could change it for her, but he knew that he of all men could not.

"I have found what I was looking for." Her voice barely surpassed a whisper. "I had it all wrong, you see. I thought that being loved would fill that empty place. I have discovered that it is loving someone else that does it." She paused, and the silence begged for more words. "I know that you do not feel the same way, and I do not mind. I think that I am supposed to, and maybe one day I will. Right now, loving you fills me so completely that I am grateful for that alone."

Her words touched him so deeply he could not speak. He moved her until she lay on top of him, with her head on his shoulder and her face against his. He could embrace her totally this way and feel her body all along his skin.

It would be wise to be more careful with your love. He wanted to say it, to warn her. He did not. Instead he lifted her body so he could enter her again, and so their passion could obscure the warning, and even the reason for giving it.

He eased her shoulders up until she sat, straddling his hips, snugly connected. Her dominant position confused her. She appeared unsure of what to do, and surprised to find them together before she was wild with need.

"This was not on a plate that you marked," she said.

"No. Do you dislike it?"

"It feels different, having you inside me before I . . ." She checked the situation again. "Do we just stay like this?" A little squirm accompanied the question and answered it at the same time. She leaned forward to resettle herself.

"Stay like that, so I can touch you." He reached to caress her. With his touch he felt her arousal begin, tightening her hold on him. She looked so beautiful, like a dark statue touched by faint moonlight. Her eyes watched his hands smooth over her body.

The languid build of pleasure created a blissful intimacy. He was aware of every reaction she had, every breath she breathed.

She straightened and slowly ran her smooth palms down his torso. She said nothing, but her earlier declaration of love was in her touch and the way she gazed down at him.

That made his heart burn painfully. Beautifully. He leaned her forward again so he could kiss her lips, then farther still until his mouth could touch her breasts.

He did not have to show her what to do. Pleasure did. She propped herself over him as his tongue teased at her breasts. Her hips moved in response to the deep, delicate tremors binding them as closely as their bodies did.

The ecstasy came slowly, in a long climb out of the world. Her cries, the way she moved, her astonishment at the intensity—it offered a complete escape for his spirit and heart.

He did nothing to hasten the end. He held off the beckoning climax, not wanting to relinquish the soulful layers beneath the pleasure. In her arms, for a while, he was no longer a slave to memories and anger.

chapter 22

Dupré is spending money like a man with great expectations," Adrian reported. "Going back to all the places I first took him for supplies, ordering zinc and copper and silver disks, pans and chemicals and iron. Lots of iron."

Daniel stripped off his shirt and hung it on the dressing chamber's hook. He walked with Adrian out to the hall.

"I worry about this partner of his, Daniel. I agreed to help you in Paris because you got me out of that trouble in Syria. You spoke of settling a score without bloodshed, and it seemed little more than a prank. I do not like the idea that someone is being ruined now, however."

"I will look into it, and make sure that no innocent is harmed."

Daniel had not explained to Adrian that the partner was Andrew Tyndale. He had certainly not laid out how the plans for Gustave had taken on a new and different life.

"I think that we should expose the whole thing, to be sure of that."

"In time, but not just yet. I relieve you of responsibility for any of it. I know who the partner is, and neither he nor Dupré is worth your concern. Believe me when I tell you that their crimes are so great that even their deaths would not repay them."

"I would feel better if you told me all of it, Daniel. It is clear now that I know very little."

"Trust me, you do not want to know all of it."

Nor did Daniel want him to know. If Adrian learned all of it, he would probably feel honor bound to warn Tyndale. The son of an earl would feel obligated to protect the son of a marquess.

Adrian looked highly skeptical. "I fear this has turned into a fraud."

"It was always a fraud, only now money is at stake and not a reputation. It is not our fraud, however. I did not lure Dupré into what he does now. Greed did. And his partner is a thief, as is Dupré, and you cannot cheat swindlers. There is no sin in lying to the devil."

"It gets a bit murky, doesn't it? Which of you is the devil and swindler?"

Daniel saluted with his sabre. "Not at all. We all are. I have no illusions about that."

Diane strolled down the garden path in a daze of contentment. Bright flowers peeked up at her, and the pear tree was in bloom. She loved this garden, and this house, and her life. She marveled at how she had been reborn in this love she had. It made her feel safe and warm, wanted and complete. All of the things she had never known, she enjoyed now. The girl at the school might have never existed.

Jeanette sat under the pear tree. Since the marriage, Jeanette had been happier too. They were sisters now, and Jeanette often asked about the parties and theater performances Diane attended. Diane hoped that one day soon Jeanette would give up being so reclusive and join her and the countess or Daniel when they left the house in the evening.

"Perhaps when the weather gets too warm this summer we can all go up to Scotland," Diane said. She handed Jeanette some pear blossoms as she picked them. "I expect that you would like to visit the house there while you are in England."

Jeanette half-shrugged as she held the little blooms to her nose.

"Were you left alone there when Daniel went to sea? It must have been very lonely. Very isolating, what with your father dead too."

"Being alone has never made me lonely or sad."

"Who cared for you? Was Paul a friend already?"

"The first few years that Daniel was at sea, two women took care of me." Jeanette made a gesture of impatience. "It was long ago. I do not think of that time anymore. Once Daniel made his fortune, he got me back to France, which is where I belong. Unlike my brother, I can never be comfortable here. In fact, I will be asking him to arrange for my return to Paris soon. I have been overlong in this city."

"I wish that you would stay with us. I do not like to think that marrying your brother means that I lose your company."

"You will come to Paris often. You must insist that Daniel bring you. He does not care for that city any more than I care for this one, but if you ask it of him, he will come. I would say that you could visit alone, but I think that he needs you more than I do."

That was an odd thing for Jeanette to say. Daniel needed no one, from what she could tell. He had lived an independent and adventurous life. He appeared contented in the marriage, even happy, but he did not need her. He enjoyed her company, but he did not require it.

The mail was brought out. Jeanette glanced through a few invitations and set them aside with a mutter of exasperation.

Despite her being reclusive, invitations had always arrived for Jeanette, daily little proddings that irritated her. More had come recently, and Diane guessed it was curiosity on the senders' parts. The story of Daniel's marriage had made this invisible sister a subject of speculation. A few ladies had even called, but Jeanette had not received them.

"You will disappoint them," Diane said. "It has become a game, to see who can snag you first. If you should decide to accept one, I hope it will not be from any woman who has been unkind to Pen."

"Should I ever change my mind, only the countess would be worthy of such a triumph, I assure you. But I will not be put on display for these women."

Diane flipped through her own letters. "Will you accept my invitation, at least? I think that I will give a dinner party soon. A small one, with Pen and her brothers and perhaps Mister Hampton, not that he is very good company, since he so rarely speaks." Toward the bottom of the stack was a letter on paper less fine. She slid her thumb beneath the plain seal. "What do you think? Can I pull it off without making a mess of—"

She froze and her voice died on her lips. Her gaze rested on a very surprising word at the top of the paper in her hands.

It was the name of the town from which the letter had been sent. The town in which the writer lived.

Fenwood.

The first line of writing revealed that this letter had come from Fenwood's vicar, Mister Albret. Within five words she realized that Andrew Tyndale had never visited the vicar. This letter was in response to the one she had sent while at the house party.

She read the letter quickly. Her heart began pounding, first a low, rapid beat, then a loud, clamoring one. Her head throbbed with the sensation that an anvil was inside it, clanging to the same rhythm.

She got the gist of the letter, enough to leave her struggling to breathe. She returned to the beginning and read again. As she absorbed the implications of the contents, the drum of excitement slowed to a painful pulse.

She read it yet again, trying to make it say something other than it did. Her heart hurt so badly she thought it would break. It was all she could do to hold it in one piece. She knew that if she did not, the shattered bits would get smashed even more by the waves of confusion crashing through her head.

"Jeanette, where is Daniel today?"

"What is it, dear? You look as though you are going to swoon."

"Where is Daniel?" She glanced up from the letter to see Jeanette frowning with concern at her.

"Where?"

"I think that he rode to Hampstead. To the chevalier."

Diane crushed the letter in her fist and rose.

The house in Hampstead was quiet. Daniel's horse was tied in front. No sounds of ringing steel came through the open windows.

Diane did not wait for the coachman to open the door. She did for herself, impatient to be out of the confining space. On her command they had made all possible haste, and now the horses panted and snorted and dripped with sweat.

The fury that sent her rushing out of London had subsided to a sickening desolation. She looked at the letter, still crumpled in her hand. If she had never spoken to the servant . . . if she had never written to the vicar . . . if, as the letter said, he had followed his first inclinations and not responded . . .

If any of those things had not happened, she would have been happy a while longer.

Her heart hurt. Her whole chest did. Hot tears stung her eyes. She wished that she had been allowed more time to be complete before the truth came crashing into her dream, emptying her out again.

She wanted to discard the letter and pretend it had never come. Her love wanted to, desperately. She could not ignore this, however.

She turned away from the house. She had come to speak to Daniel, but it could wait. She was not so brave that she welcomed asking him the questions that she had, and hearing the answers he would give.

Entering the woods, she followed the path. Her feet just knew where to go. Of course they did. They always had. She had not gotten lost the first time she came here. Without even thinking, she had found her way from the big house to the cottage.

It came into view as the clearing neared. There was no sense of a moment relived this time. It appeared crisply familiar. Snips of memories flashed in her mind, of the bushes smaller and the path wider.

She walked over to the well and peered down. The echo of a woman's voice called in her head, warning her not to climb up because it would be dangerous.

She turned, half-expecting to see an old woman wearing a cap and simple garments at the door.

The door opened, but no woman appeared. Instead it was George, the man who lived here now. He paused and studied her.

"Do you want something?" he asked curiously. "You look ill."

"I am not ill." She stared at him, begging her mind to cooperate. "You said when we last met that you had been here for years. Did you always live in this house?"

He shook his head. "Used to be up there, at the stables. Was a groom in those days, when there were lots of horses here. Head groom at the end. Then, when it was empty and everyone else had left, I became caretaker, as I am now."

Horses. Yes, of course. She saw George in her head, years younger, his hair not so white and his beard not so full.

"And the woman who lived in this cottage before you? The old lady. What became of her?"

"Alice? You know of Alice? I'll be damned—um, sorry, you just surprised me. She stayed on a bit, but passed away, oh, ten years it is now, so I moved myself down here." He cocked his head. "How do you know Alice?"

"I am Diane."

His mouth fell open, and then formed a big smile. "Well, I'll be dam— I thought you looked familiar last time. Couldn't place it. Just a certain something. 'Course, you were just a tiny thing when you left. Quite the lady you are now, eh? Well, who would have thought it."

Yes, quite the lady. Only one person would not be surprised by the transformation.

"Would you permit me to see the house? The inside?"

He stood aside and gestured gallantly. "Well, of course. Was your home as a child, now, wasn't it?"

She paused at the threshold and took a deep breath. *Her home.* She stepped inside.

Memories assaulted her, hooking themselves to what she saw. Not to the whole space, but to details and sensations. The way the light fell on the floor from the open window. A scent, such as every house had, distinct to this place alone. The beams of the ceiling, and the way one had an edge that had split away.

The hearth. The sight of it brought complete and precise memories suddenly. The hearth in summer, cold and lifeless, and in winter, a source of warmth and rocking embraces.

She did not stay long or ask to see the other chambers above. She could not do that today. The recollections offered her no peace. They did not fill the sick emptiness inside her. Another time perhaps they would. Another day, when her heart did not know that dreadful unhappiness waited, she might enjoy finding this history that she had so long dreamt of discovering.

Steeling her courage, she returned to the house. She walked through the woods and her feet made no wrong turns. The path caused her to approach the house from an angle that showed a bit of its side and back. That image, of the half-timbers angling away from the corner upright, might have been branded on her brain.

The familiarity startled her. If the last time she had returned this way and not another, if she had not been distracted by Daniel's kisses by the brook, she would have realized what this place was to her.

Daniel's kisses . . . She stopped and closed her eyes and forced down an unbearable sorrow.

She found him in the house. She heard a mumble of voices and followed it to a chamber in the back of the house. Small and tidy, with a few elegant items of furniture, it appeared to be the chevalier's private sitting room.

He and Daniel sat in two chairs near the window, sharing a bottle of wine. Both had removed their coats. They made a picture of relaxed friendship, of complete trust.

They had heard someone coming. Their talk ceased before she arrived. When she found herself at the threshold of the chamber, looking at them, they were looking back.

"Diane." Daniel's inflection revealed surprise and curiosity. "We had assumed the coach was one of Louis's students."

"It is only me." The sharp and clever accusations had deserted her along with the initial fury. She could only look at him and wish this day had never begun.

"What is it you want, darling?"

"I came here to visit my father's home."

Daniel's expression fell.

The chevalier pursed his mouth and rose. "I will leave you alone."

She stood aside so that he could pass, then went over to Daniel. He had turned his gaze out the window, to the woods and meadow rolling down the back hill.

"Do not do that," she said, her hand still clutching the letter. "Do not ignore me in that way. Not now."

He looked back. She saw his expression and knew that he felt as she did, and that he also wished this day had never come.

"I am not ignoring you. I have never ignored you. You have never once been in my presence when I was not totally and completely aware of you, even when you were young and I wished I could block you out."

He reached for her but she stepped back. With a sigh, he let his hand drop. "How do you know this was your father's home?"

She opened her hand to show the crushed letter. "My grandfather wrote to me, in response to my letter to him. He was not going to. He does not even know who I am, but I do now. He explained enough for me to understand it."

"What did he explain that has you so distressed?"

"That he had a daughter who died in childbirth. That she had not been married to the father of the baby. That the father took the child into his care, at a house that he owned in Hampstead."

Her voice was rising. The words poured out, madly.

"That the man who had seduced his daughter was in shipping, but was ruined over a dozen years ago, and that he and the child disappeared."

Daniel watched her, waiting.

"That the man's name was Jonathan. Jonathan *Makepeace.* Not Jonathan Albret, as you let me believe. Albret was my *mother's* name." The inner agitation got the better of her. She wanted to hit him, pound him. She threw the letter at him instead. It bounced off his face and onto the floor. "You deceived me. You let me look for his family without even knowing his right name."

"Yes, I deceived you." He rose and came to her.

"Do not touch me." She paced away, around him. She swung her arm at the chamber and everything beyond. "How did you come to have this place?"

"I came to have it because of a night of cards."

"You got it through gambling?"

"I was very young and Jonathan just assumed he would win. It started out simply, and grew."

"As it did with Andrew Tyndale?"

"Much the same. By the end I was far ahead. Your father was a reckless man. He bet everything he had left—his two ships, his London house and this one—on one cut of the cards against everything I had won."

"I have been living in my father's house in London too?"

"No. I sold that one and bought another some years later."

"And you let him do this? Let him bet everything?"

His lids lowered. Darkness flashed. For a moment, he was the Devil Man again. "Oh, yes."

"No wonder you made your fortune so quickly. You stole it from another man. You took everything from him that night! That is how you got your first ships, isn't it?"

"That is how I got my first ships."

"How could you do that? Ruin him like that. You did not have to agree to that last bet."

"I was glad to agree to it. I did not like your father. In fact, I despised him. He had a weakness for gambling and that is what ruined him, not me."

She could not believe the way he said it. Flatly. Coldly. "You astonish me. You destroyed his life and ruined mine, but you have no remorse. None at all."

"I have no remorse for him. I regret that an innocent was hurt. The way it affected you was an unfortunate consequence."

"*An unfortunate consequence!* That is a neat way to put it, Daniel."

He stepped forward, to block her pacing. His hands closed on her arms and he looked down at her. "I knew nothing about you. He was not married; he had no family. I did not know there was a daughter until I saw you."

Something in the way he looked made her wary. There was a softness in his expression, and real regret, but not for the past. It was the way he had looked that day in the carriage on the way to the Tuileries, when she had demanded information.

She opened her mouth to speak, but the question forming stuck in her throat. She knew in her heart that she would not want to hear the answer. "How did you come to have *me*?"

"The last bet included this property, and everything on it. When I arrived to take possession, I found you here."

The devastating truth hammered away at her composure. Her father had abandoned her. Walked away and left her to fate's whims.

She should probably be grateful that Daniel had not foisted her off on the local parish. Perhaps one day she would be. Right now the devastation was getting so vast that there was no room for gratitude, or for anything except a hundred questions.

Some of those questions prodded insistently. "Why did you deceive me? Why not just tell me this in Paris? I do not think it was to spare me the pain. If you let me think he had another name, if you let me ask for information on the wrong man, you must have had a good reason."

He walked away and faced the window. Not ignoring her. She could tell that, despite his gaze on the hill beyond, his mind was completely with her.

Her anger rose, as if to form a shield against the blow that her soul knew was coming.

"It was not in my interest to have anyone realize that you are Jonathan Makepeace's daughter."

"Why?" It came out a frustrated yell.

He turned. "Because Jonathan was an old friend of Andrew Tyndale, and I did not want Tyndale to know that I had met Jonathan, ever. I did not want Tyndale to know who you are, and surmise there was a connection to that night of cards all those years ago."

The admission only confused her more. Her head swam with bits and pieces of things, with impressions and words all jumbled together.

She crossed her arms over her chest, to hold herself together. "The duel. You said it was not only about me. You said Jeanette would not object because she knew the whole story."

Her heart screamed with silent yells, some accusatory, others beseeching. "Was it your plan from the start, to find a way to challenge Tyndale? Not really because of me, but for other reasons? Is that why you did not want him to know of my connection to Jonathan? Daniel, did you bring me to London and make me a lady to lure Tyndale into that duel?"

She caught a glimpse of the answer in his expression. Then his face blurred as stinging tears overflowed from her eyes.

"It was my plan at first, Diane, but I could not do it in the end. That it turned out that way after all was not my intention."

He had not only deceived her. He had intended to use her.

She could not bear it. She could not stay to hear more.

Crying so hard that she could not see, she stumbled from the chamber and ran out to the coach. Daniel's voice followed, calling her name.

chapter 23

The ragged man was following him again.

Gustave glanced back. It was the same thief whom Adrian had pointed out, the one with the beard. The man seemed to loiter around the district where Gustave had taken his rooms. No doubt Adrian had been correct, and this was a pickpocket who preyed upon the men of business and law who walked these streets. He must have recognized the foreign cut of Gustave's coat and decided he would be easy pickings eventually.

It was unnerving to feel one was being watched. Gustave did not like the notion that there had been times when this man may have been following him and he had not been aware of it.

Perhaps this thief even knew about the shed across the water.

The thought appalled him. That could be disastrous.

Enough was enough. He would let this thief know that he had been noticed, and that it was time to shadow some less astute man.

Gustave slowed to a stroll. He finally stopped to examine the books outside a printer's shop. From the corner of his eye he saw that the thief did not move on, but merely paused and waited. That was bold.

Annoyed, Gustave walked rapidly. He put some space between himself and the man, and entered a coffeehouse. Taking a table near the window, he watched as the man came into view and walked by.

And turned and entered the coffeehouse too.

And walked over and sat at Gustave's table.

Really, it was too much.

"If you expect me to pay you to leave me alone, you have misjudged your prey, m'sieur." Gustave spoke angrily, only realizing at the end that he had spoken French and this criminal would never understand. He trusted that his tone conveyed the message well enough, however.

The man smiled and removed his hat. "I thought that it was time we spoke."

To Gustave's amazement, the reply came in French as well.

"I seriously doubt that you and I have anything to speak of."

"We have much to speak of. For example, we can speak of how you are being led to the slaughter."

"See here—"

"No, you see here. Right here." He pointed at his eyes.

Puzzled, Gustave peered closely at the man's eyes. A jolt of astonishment made him dizzy. "My God, it is you! But you are dead!"

"Not dead. Just buried for a long time in drink and stinking poverty."

"This is such a shock. . . . What do you mean I am being led to the slaughter?"

"You are being used. You will be ruined." He leaned across the table. "First me, then Hercule, now you. Lured to ruin, one by one."

"How preposterous. I am not being lured to anything."

"Aren't you? Then why are you in England?"

Gustave looked down his nose. "That is my affair alone."

"Yours alone? No one else is involved in your affair?"

Gustave shifted, suddenly uncomfortable. "You were not lured to ruin. Your character brought you to it, as did Hercule's. You always wanted easy wealth, and he always wanted glory."

"And what have you always wanted, Dupré? Are you in England seeking it now?"

A stab of concern made Gustave shift again. "Of course not."

"Then I am mistaken. I am just a man too fond of spirits, who has seen schemes that don't exist." He rose. "And to think that I came all this way to warn an old friend. Had to stow away under a stack of canvases to cross."

That concern pricked again, ruining Gustave's contentment that this ghost was departing.

"Wait. Sit. Have some coffee. Tell me what scheme you see."

They waited until the coffee came, and the ragged man called for some cakes and let Gustave pay for them.

"Speak," Gustave demanded, getting suspicious that he was being fleeced for a free meal.

"When I lost everything, I fled to the Continent. There were debts in England— Well, it is an old story. I lived in Naples. One day over two years ago, right after Napoleon went to Elba, I was at the docks and I saw one of my ships. Oh, it had been changed somewhat over the years, but I knew it."

"So you saw the ship. What of it?"

"I lost the ship to Edward St. Clair. The ship was now owned by the same person, only older and with a different name. Daniel St. John."

Gustave startled.

"When I made my way to France, I heard about poor Hercule. Strange that a private confidence to an English officer became public knowledge."

"And you think that St. John—"

"He often dined with the officers in that regiment. I think that this one, when in his cups, was indiscreet. Odd to learn of that connection between St. John and the officer. That is what got me thinking."

"I am sure that you are building castles out of air. It is too much a coincidence. You and Hercule—it was years apart."

"Perhaps. But I ask you this—are you a coincidence too? You are in England suddenly, very busy with something. Have you ever met this St. John, or St. Clair, or whatever his name is?"

Gustave's mouth felt peculiar. Too moist.

"Is your current affair connected to a meeting with St. John?"

Gustave swallowed. "If you are right, why?"

"Me, Hercule, and now you. There are only two explanations. At first, I thought St. John was someone who knew about our connection, from when we were young. However, I wonder now if he merely is an agent for someone who does."

"An agent? It is a long time to be an agent."

"Not if he works for someone with power. Someone who can be his patron. This St. John has had great success. He is well received here in England."

"But who?"

"Someone, perhaps, who would prefer that our association to him was buried with our fortunes and reputations. Someone with ambitions, who would not like the world to know about certain things that happened long ago."

Gustave was sipping some coffee as the implication hit him. Suddenly his stomach felt sour.

"Tell me Dupré, have you had any dealings here in England with Tyndale? Is that little shed you visit across the river his shed too?"

"Shed? What shed? You are mistak—"

"The reason I ask is this: St. John has had dealings with Tyndale recently, and St. John knows about that shed. I know because I saw him there one day."

Diane found herself adrift as she had never been before. She experienced the rootless, aimless existence that she had always feared. She had left the school, trusting that the truth would spare her from such a life. Instead, the truth had thrust her into it.

She never returned to Daniel's house. Instead, she directed the coach to a street where she changed to a hired vehicle, and took that one to Margot's house. The next day she sent for a trunk of practical clothing, and instructed Margot's servant to refuse to say where the trunk was going. She did not want Daniel knowing where she was yet, although she sent a letter assuring Jeanette that she was safe. On learning that she had left Daniel, Margot left her to heal and plan.

She was not ready to do either. A horrible ache numbed and distracted her. It was as if the void had returned and come alive and taken over her body and spirit. She veered from anger to desolation to wrenching disappointment. She saw her time with Daniel, every detail, over and over in her mind, despite her efforts not to think of him at all.

Beneath the heartbreaking anguish there flowed another emotion, just as devastating. A longing for things to have been different. A wistful regret that even her memories of gentle intimacy had been ruined.

She did not accompany Margot to parties and calls. When Margot entertained, Diane remained in her own room. She did not belong in Margot's world. She did not belong in any world.

All the same, one of those worlds found her in the other.

Three days after she had received the vicar's letter, Margot hosted a party. Diane remained out of sight, but late in the evening she slipped down to the kitchen to make herself some tea. In the corridor outside the chamber where Margot's little party played cards, she almost walked right into Vergil Duclairc.

He was very surprised to see her, and a bit chagrined that she had seen him. Before he quickly closed the door on the party, she glimpsed the face of a certain opera singer.

"So, you are here. St. John is—well, your husband is distraught. He visited my sister at once, looking for you."

Which was why she had not gone to Pen. "He knows I am safe."

Vergil managed to look both strict and kind at the same time. "This will not do. You know that."

"It is not so rare. Pen—"

"Pen's husband is a scoundrel of the worst order."

"Perhaps mine is as well."

"That is not true. I know St. John and—"

"I think that you and I are too young to ever *know* a man like St. John. Now, please allow me to pass. You are interfering, as men are wont to do."

He glanced to the chamber door, behind which Margot and her friends laughed and played. "You cannot stay in this woman's home. It is not proper, and you do not belong here."

"I do not belong anywhere. At least here there are not friends of my husband scolding me every day. It is my misfortune that your paramour made Margot's acquaintance or I might have been spared any scolds at all."

At mention of his opera singer, he reluctantly stepped aside.

"I ask that you do not tell St. John where I am."

He said nothing, which meant that he would indeed tell Daniel.

She did not sleep that night. Her mind played over the confrontation that was coming. She did not know what she would say to him.

Early the next morning, well before calling hours, a visitor was announced for her. Not Daniel. A lady had called, but no name was given. Expecting that Vergil had sent the countess to cajole her, Diane left her chamber and went to the sitting room.

She arrived just as a very large man was placing a veiled woman in a chair. Jeanette peeled back the veil and gestured for Paul to leave.

Diane bent and kissed her. "I am astonished to see you here, Jeanette."

"*I* am astonished to see *you* here, in the home of a courtesan."

"I could hardly go to the countess. She has enough trouble without it being known that she gave refuge to a woman who has left her husband. People will say that she is forming a Society for Disobedient Wives."

Jeanette did not find the little joke amusing. "You should be with your husband, not here and not with the countess."

"Jeanette—"

"Sit."

It sounded much like Madame Leblanc's command that last day in the school. Diane obeyed.

"What was in that letter that you read in the garden the other day? What evil was written to you, to make you abandon my brother?" Jeanette demanded.

"It was not evil. The man who wrote it did not know the meaning of its contents for me. He assumed he was merely explaining that I was wrong to think he and I had a relationship. I will not tell you what it said. I do not want to speak badly of Daniel to you."

"You want to spare me? That is charming. There is nothing that you could tell me about my brother that would surprise me. No, I am wrong there. The affection he feels for you, the changes it has made—I suspect that you have known a side of him that I never will. Now, tell me what you have learned about the other side, the one that I know very well."

Diane described the contents of the letter and the evidence of Daniel's deception. She explained the revelations learned during their confrontation at Hampstead.

Jeanette appeared unsurprised by the story. "Yes, you were to be a lure. Blame me as well as him. I did not stop it, and I aided him. He at no time intended for you to be harmed, nor would you have been. It was perfect. You were perfect. Tyndale likes girls young, refined, and innocent. He has an unhealthy weakness for them that he dare not satisfy with the daughters of his own class. He would not be so constrained with the cousin of a shipper. It unfolded just as Daniel had foreseen, except for one snag."

"What was that?" The confirmation that Jeanette had known all along only made Diane's sick heart sicker.

"My brother fell in love with you."

"I do not believe that. I think that he concluded that the plan would work even better if eventually Tyndale importuned a *wife,* and not only a cousin. I think the plan was not over yet. I think, having been forced to stand down because of what happened with me that night, he found another way to eventually have it happen anyway." The words poured out from the saddest place in her heart.

"What nonsense." Jeanette waved the notion away. "If my brother was so lacking in honor, he would not have upheld the bargain he made with you."

Diane bit her tongue before she could blurt out that Jeanette herself had not expected Daniel to uphold that bargain and be honorable.

"He did not explain why he wanted a way to get to Tyndale, did he?"

"I did not want to hear it."

"It does not matter. He would have never embarrassed me by revealing that tale. I think that is why he did not come here last night to bring you home, after learning where you were. However, I can tell you the part he never would."

She spread her arms with a dramatic flourish. "Andrew Tyndale is responsible for *this.* For the fact that Paul had to carry me here, instead of my walking in on my own. He is the reason I do not visit England, and why I have not left that house."

"Are you saying that he knows you?"

"He knows me. Whether he would recognize me, I cannot say. He might, however. After all, twenty-four years ago I was his lover."

"His lover!"

Jeanette noted Diane's surprise with dour satisfaction. "I was a girl, seventeen. My family was trying to leave France and he offered to help. He smuggled me to England first. I carried jewels and money, so that when the others arrived a place would be waiting for them. I was ignorant and trusting, and when he seduced me I thought it was love."

Diane had no trouble seeing Tyndale's face, years younger, kind and concerned, speaking of affection and alluding to marriage.

After all, he had said the same thing to her.

"He brought me to an obscure property. Time passed and no word came from my family. Whenever he visited I asked him about it, and he would say that such things take time. I was isolated and had no news of what was happening in France. Still, I grew suspicious. Finally, I confronted him and demanded to be brought to London. From that day on I was a prisoner, but then I had been all along. His use of me continued, but there were no illusions after that."

"I dreaded his visits. I loathed his touch. Finally, one time he visited and I could not bear it anymore. I stole a horse and ran away. It was winter, and the horse threw me. I landed on my back and could not move."

Her voice gave the dreadful facts in flat, clipped statements. Diane got the impression Jeanette had rarely spoken of it before, and only kept her composure now through force of will.

Jeanette looked straight ahead, her eyes suddenly flaming. "He followed me. He found me there, on a barren field, crippled. I still remember his words. 'Well, like that you are no good to me at all anymore.' He left me there. He took the horse."

"You could have died."

"He probably assumes that I did."

"You think that was his intention?"

"Why else leave a woman in the cold with no way to save herself? However, a farmer happened to pass that evening, and I called out. He put me in his wagon and brought me to his home. His wife and sister took care of me. I lived with them for years, bedridden. Then one day Daniel walked into the house. I had not seen him since he was a boy. He had been searching for me. Whenever he was in England he would seek out the properties that Tyndale's family owned, and ask in those regions about a young, dark-haired French woman. Finally, he found me and got me to France."

She opened her hands, announcing the story's end. Diane could barely absorb the horror that must have been Jeanette's life. Years of fear and helplessness.

"When Daniel was looking for you, why didn't he just confront Tyndale and ask where you were?"

"There were good reasons why he could not, but that is my brother's story, not mine."

She called for Paul. He had been just outside the door, as always. He had heard everything. From his expression, Diane guessed that he already knew this story.

He lifted his mistress into his arms. From her perch, Jeanette looked down on Diane. "You are pale and wan. Tomorrow promises to be a fair day. I think that you should walk in St. James's Park tomorrow morning. Paul tells me there is a little lake surrounded by jonquils. A visit there will do you good. One should not become a recluse unless there is an excellent reason for it."

Dupré was acting very odd. Normally Andrew would not take note of it, because even at the best of times Gustave was a peculiar man. He was the sort of fastidious fool who took great pains with his appearance but managed to appear pinched and tucked rather than fashionable. All of those years peering into books had left him with the face of an old woman, and he had a host of mannerisms that were barely tolerable.

Today, however, Dupré acted unusually guarded. He paused before answering any questions. He fidgeted even when he stood still.

Andrew surveyed the elaborate demonstration in the shed and his concerns shifted from Dupré to the money these cylinders and iron embodied. It had cost a fortune to satisfy St. John's demands for proof. The man had damn well better be contented when it was done.

Dupré frowned down at a huge hunk of iron in a deep metal kettle. "I worry about this one. The copper of the tub may affect things."

"Maybe it will do so for the better. Perhaps we will learn that the process improves if copper is used."

"I still do not know why you insisted on such an elaborate and expensive experiment. The last one proved things, as I said it would."

"This way we can calculate the cost better, and assess the profit. It would not do to start selling steel that we cannot make quickly or that will cost more than we can recover."

Dupré fussed like an agitated old woman. "That big man out there. Why is he here?"

"To protect the shed, as I told you."

"I do not like it. He does not speak French. I came yesterday and he would not allow me to enter."

"If you had informed me that you were coming, I would have alerted him."

Dupré folded his arms, unfolded them, and folded them again. "I do not like that you are making these decisions without me, as if you are hid—as if you do not trust me."

Andrew had been eyeing one hunk of iron on which he had made some private markings. Dupré's half-spoken words riveted his attention, however. *As if you are hiding something,* he had almost said.

Yes, Dupré was acting very peculiar today.

He went over and slid his arm around Gustave's shoulders. "What is distressing you, old friend?"

Gustave's mouth pursed, making him look very prim. "Nothing distresses me. I simply did not anticipate this stage. I did not expect it to take so long." He gestured to the cylinders. "And all of this. I gave you the proof you wanted. Suddenly we are making a demonstration as if more proof is needed. You insisted that I use what little fortune I have to build all of this."

"Most of the funds were mine. It was not unreasonable that you also take the risk."

"So we agreed. I find myself wondering why you wanted this, that is all."

"You sound as if you are suspicious of me. That is not good in a partnership."

"I merely wonder if you are telling me everything."

Fortunately, Dupré was not as subtle as he was peculiar. "You sound as if you believe that I have not. What makes you think so?"

"I do not—"

"Come, come. With such a fortune at stake, we should not have a falling out over some minor matter. Let us speak frankly."

He watched Dupré's debate. The choice made, Gustave's expression assumed a haughty, superior countenance. Yes, the fool could never resist the chance to display his brilliance.

"I have reason to think that you have let me risk everything, deliberately. I suspect that this iron will mysteriously not turn into steel. You will do something, add a new chemical perhaps, that will abort the process."

"Why in God's name would I do something that stupid?"

"So that I will think we have failed and return to France, ruined just as the others were ruined, and the discovery will be yours alone."

Andrew laughed. "What an elaborate schemer you think I am."

"I *know* how good a schemer you are."

"If I schemed this well, I would own the world. You came to me, Dupré. Or have you forgotten that? And only you know the chemical formula. Remember?"

"I am not sure that I do."

"What?"

"I am not sure that you do not also have it. After all, I received it myself from your conspirator."

Dupré looked insufferably superior as he said that. Very confident. Andrew would have laughed again but for the gleam of satisfaction in the man's eyes.

"My conspirator?"

"Your secret conspirator. The man you sent out to ruin us, to protect this fine reputation that you have."

"Dupré, if I thought that you or anyone else could harm me, I would not stop at ruin. I would simply kill you. If I have the formula as you suggest, I did not have to lure you into discovering it on the chance that you would come to me to finance this project. Think, man. You are speaking nonsense."

The word "kill" made Gustave's eyes bulge. His gaze darted to the door, as if checking a way to escape.

"Calm yourself. I merely point out that this plot you see is too unlikely, even for me." Andrew tightened his grip on Dupré's shoulders. "However, now I need to know why you believe I have a conspirator who knows this formula."

A line of sweat moistened Dupré's forehead. "I was told that someone else had been here, besides you and me. Another man was seen. And this same man sold me the manuscript that contained the formula and most of the process. He is also the same man who ruined the others."

Andrew gazed at that line of sweat and found himself counting every tiny bead. A vicious chill took over his mind. "Who told you this? Who saw this other man?"

Dupré sealed his lips together. Idiot. As if he could keep silent if Andrew wanted the information.

"You say that a man sold you the manuscript that contained *most* of the process. Where did you get the rest? Through experiment?"

Dupré nodded, but the truth was in his eyes.

"Where did you get it, Gustave? This is not some mathematical proof that no one cares about. Our fortunes may depend on your telling me."

Dupré squirmed away. His eyes widened. "How did you know? The proof—I got the calculations on the number of cells from the library, just as I did the proof."

Jesus.

"And who sold you the manuscript?"

"Your friend, Andrew. Daniel St. John sold it to me."

Jesus.

Andrew had a sudden mental image of a tunnel made up of sections, each of which was one of his recent connections to St. John. At the end of the tunnel, staring at him, were the contented eyes of the devil himself.

"You fool, Dupré. You absolute fool."

"*I* am a fool! How dare you insult—"

"Put that worthless and questionable brilliance of yours to work for something practical for once."

"Why are you shouting? I am the one who should be angry. It is clear that you have taken this St. John as a conspirator."

"Not as a conspirator, as an investor. But you are right, he did lure you to ruin, and now you have pulled me in as well."

"How did this become *my* fault?"

"Think. *Think.* Who would have known that the rest of the process was somewhere in that damn library?"

"It was a coincidence. It happens in science all the time."

"It was no coincidence. You were sold the manuscript by someone who had known the man who used to own the library. Someone who knew that another man had begun working out the process, and that his notes could be found in that library." He grabbed Gustave and gave him a firm shake. "Someone who knew how *you* came to own the library."

chapter 24

He came looking for her in the dawn and dew, striding through the park with a serious, determined expression. It was the face of Daniel distracted and attentive at the same time.

Diane watched from behind a tree. The concern in his eyes increased her confusion and undermined her resolve. Whoever thought she would see the day when Daniel St. John appeared worried.

He stopped where Jeanette had told her to be, where the lake was framed by yellow flowers. When he did not see her, he peered down at the water and waited.

Her bruised heart fluttered. He appeared so handsome. Great care had been taken with his appearance. His cravat was tied to perfection, and looked suitable for a portrait sitting. His boots shined in the morning sun, making the droplets of moisture on them sparkle like diamonds. He even carried a hat, which he moved from hand to hand as if he did not know where to put it. She suspected that his valet had been both delighted and undone by the sudden fastidiousness.

She was not sure why she had come. It had been an impulsive decision. Jeanette's revelations explained Daniel's actions, but that was not the same as excusing them. Her heart could not absolve him completely, much as it ached to.

Perhaps it would be better to slip away, or just wait until he tired and left himself.

Without knowing why she did so, she stepped silently from behind the tree. His body stilled as he sensed her presence. He held the pose for a five count before turning around.

She wondered what he had been suppressing during that little pause. Relief? Anger?

"Jeanette said you might be here this morning. She thought that you might agree to speak with me."

"I am here, although I am not sure why."

"Whatever the reason, I am grateful."

Daniel St. John, grateful? She wanted to believe that, but a new wariness, one that made her feel old and jaded, kept her cautious.

"And I am thankful that you did not try to force me to come back."

"I almost did. I think that I may have, eventually."

She did not miss the implications of that. He still might, eventually. At least he was honest and did not claim an equanimity about this that was not true.

"Jeanette told me about Tyndale and what he did to her. She explained why you intended to use me to get to him."

"I can only ask your forgiveness for that. I know that I have no right to expect it."

"I think that I understand. You had a goal and I was the means to achieve it. I was merely a lure, and not in danger. My role was a small thing compared to the luxury and comforts I received."

"Yes."

"You waited a long time to have your revenge. Years, it seems."

"Yes."

"Is it your only purpose in life? Does it own your soul?" It blurted out, revealing the pain that wanted to break her heart, and the suspicion that had grown all night. *Is there room for nothing else, not even me? Was it only passion and pity that you gave me?*

"Why don't we let heaven and hell judge my soul." Annoyed, he looked to the ground for a moment, and then into her eyes. Fires that she knew and feared had flared. The Devil Man had emerged, called forth by her questions.

"My sister told you too much, but still not everything. Tyndale's crime with her was actually the least of it."

"I'd say it was great enough. I understand your hatred of him."

"You are incapable of comprehending my hatred of him. You are too good."

"Not so good. Not so innocent anymore, either. Two days ago I hated you a little, so I have even begun to learn about that emotion, just as I have learned about love. Perhaps you should trust me to understand. It is why you came, isn't it?"

"I am not sure why I came. Probably in the hopes of seeing something on your face besides the disillusionment it wore when you ran away in Hampstead. I cannot bear to have that be my last image of your looking at me."

The sad way he said that touched her. She went to him and gazed up into his eyes. He would not see disillusionment. Her reactions had become more complex and confused than that.

"You could have told me, Daniel. It would have been less of a shock then. If the confidence had come from you, my feelings for you may have conquered my dismay."

"I almost did, several times. I intended to.

But something had stopped him. "Perhaps it is time to do so now. Jeanette said there is more."

He looked to the water again. "I am not accustomed to speaking of it. You know my sins, or most of them. The rest does not reflect on me too much."

"I suspect that the rest reflects on you a great deal. You will always be a mystery, Daniel. I think that a man like you is never really known. However, this mystery is one I cannot let continue, unless keeping it is more important to you than I am."

He nodded, and breathed a sigh of resignation. "Tyndale was supposed to use the money and jewels that my sister brought to England to smuggle my family and others out of France. It was a good plan, his own, neatly worked out and sold to desperate people. Others helped him, but it was his idea."

"So your sister said. And you came to England, but he kept her from your family."

"That is not how it happened. Tyndale took everything, kept it, and abandoned thirty people to their fates. We waited on a strip of coast for the ship that would save us, and it never came. Instead the French army arrived, and almost all of those helpless people were taken." His jaw clenched. "I was a boy, but I remember it clearly. Every detail. I dream about it. I see the faces, hopeful and waiting, and then in despair. The guillotine waited for most of them."

Unlike Jeanette, he did not tell his story calmly. He snarled it, as if the pageant of betrayal played out in his head as he spoke.

"Were you taken with them?"

"I was with Louis, away from the others when the army came. We watched it all happen and then made our way back to Paris to see if my parents had been released. My father had been, but he was a broken man, his mind gone. My mother—"

He abruptly turned his gaze to the pond, looking over its water with that expression of intense distraction.

She stepped closer until her body almost touched his. For the first time she saw the pain flickering behind that veiled expression. It broke her heart, so completely did she absorb the anguish.

The pain had always been there. She had been blind, that was all. She had only seen the face he showed the world and not the emotions that the mask hid.

"What happened to your mother?"

"She died."

"How?"

His jaw tightened. "My mother came from a family targeted by some revolutionaries. It had not mattered earlier, but then, during the terror—" He glanced at her, then away quickly, as if facing another person would make the revelation too hard. "She was executed. I walked beside her cart, although Louis tried to stop me. I was the last thing she saw before they tied her to that plank and tilted her to the blade."

She had stopped breathing and now gasped deeply so she would not swoon.

He had watched. A child, he had watched it all.

"She had nothing to do with any of it," he said bitterly. "But the country had become mad for blood, and she had the wrong name. It was that simple, that merciless." He looked at her again. "I still see faces. The ugly faces of the crowd, eager to see one more head drop. The bored faces of the executioners. Her face, her terror at the end—yes, avenging that, and my sister, and all that happened, owns my soul. It has been the only purpose in my life." He snapped the declaration so crisply that it rang like an oath.

"No wonder you did not hesitate to ruin a man at cards, to procure his wealth, or to use me as a lure. I don't think I can blame you for any of it. After such a betrayal, and such a horrible result, I understand how the goal is more important than anything else."

The anger and bitterness disappeared with her words, as if she had called him back from another place. His face softened so much that he appeared boyish. He took her hand in his. "Not more important than you. It astonished me to realize that you mattered more."

"I think that you always reach your goals, Daniel."

"Not this one, I think. Nor will you ever be the means to achieve it now."

"I am not sure I believe that."

"So my sister said. She told me you suspect that I married you in order to have an even better cause to challenge Tyndale later, when he continues pursuing you. You are wrong. That is not why I married you."

"I do not expect you to admit such a thing."

"Then do not take the word of your husband, but that of the man you now know I am. Tyndale has no interest in married women. When I took your innocence, I destroyed his fascination with you."

"So, for a few moments of passion you ruined a great plan. No wonder you resisted me so well. I seduced you into a very bad bargain, didn't I?"

"It was the best bargain of my life, darling."

"No, it was not. What I offer cannot stand against the emotions bred by years of anger. I think that with time you will resent me for it." Suddenly she realized the truth of something. "The silence that first night, after . . . you were already resenting me then, weren't you?"

He raised her hand to his mouth and kissed it gently. "Yes."

She had not expected that word. That honesty. It stripped away her defenses as nothing else could.

"Look at what is between us, Daniel. Deception and mysteries. You ruined my father, left me orphaned, and now I have interfered with your dark dream."

"I cannot excuse the deceptions, Diane. I can only promise you that I do not regret the interference."

"Truly? This must be a heavy burden. Can you live with it unresolved?"

"I think that I can live with anything if you are with me." He kissed her hand again. "I want you to come home. Now. Say that you will."

His closeness, his lips on her skin and his warm breath fluttering over her hand, made her dizzy. Just his presence lured her, as it always had. She sensed that he had turned the full force of his magnetism on her, deliberately and shamelessly.

She almost succumbed. Her love responded to all the parts of him that she knew to be good. But the mystery and darkness had a reason and purpose now, and could not be ignored. It excited her before and still did, but she recognized the danger in it for her love and her happiness.

"Daniel, can you abandon the revenge that you seek? Is having me so important that you will do that?"

"Is it the price you demand?"

"I am not sure that I can live with it as you have, knowing it is always in you now."

"It is not always in me. Not anymore. When I am with you it goes away. With time, it will become a small thing."

"Or perhaps not. Maybe someday I will awake to find you gone, and learn that you died in a duel with him, that you finally had your accounting."

She imagined that morning. She imagined waiting for it, year in and year out, and watching the distraction in his eyes that said the day would come eventually. "I do not think that you want it to become a small thing either. Not really. So, yes, I am afraid that it is the price of having me with you."

The ultimatum angered him. She expected him to deny her, and stride away. For a long pause there were no sounds or sights around them, just Daniel weighing and deciding as his lips pressed the skin of her hand.

Her heart beat painfully. She did not want him to walk away. Her breath caught as she comprehended just how big a choice she had given him.

His arm moved to surround her waist. He pulled her to him, so their bodies touched. Other visitors now strolled near the lake, but he did not care if they were seen.

Her breath turned ragged, as if she were being crushed even though he held her gently. Panic beat lowly in her chest. She knew her good sense would be no match for her soul's desire to believe anything he told her.

"I do want it to become a small thing, darling. I never thought that I would. I assumed there would be nothing to replace it. I have learned that is not so." He kissed her sweetly, as a boy might a girl. "Come home with me. Lie in my arms, and let us build a future together. We will discard the past. If you are with me, I can give it up. For you I can. If it is the price of having you, I will."

His belief in her left her trembling and afraid. She was not sure her love could replace the hatred. It was inconceivable that she had such power. It was impossible that he wanted her enough to discard the purpose of his life.

He raised one hand in a beckoning gesture while he kissed her again, deeply. His hold became an embrace. In her daze she vaguely heard the sounds of a carriage slowly approaching and the *tsk* of a woman strolling by.

His kiss led her into euphoria. His promise dislodged her worries and she released them gratefully. He was right. They could build a future together. She could forget what he had done and make him happy, so that he never wanted to finish this long quest. Of course she could. They could. His kisses said so. His embrace demanded it. She was his and nothing else mattered.

He turned her in his arm and guided her to the carriage. She did not hesitate to enter it. Her soul wanted to believe everything he said. Love left her weak-kneed. Physical desire had begun its focused pulse.

The carriage door closed. He lifted her onto his lap and wrapped her into an embrace that pulled her close. He neither kissed nor caressed her as the carriage moved. He merely grasped her to him, his breath warming her temple, his firm hands permitting no release.

The slow, silent ride excited her. She needed no demonstration to know how much he wanted her. It was in the air and in his silence. She could feel it in the tautness of his body and in the steady rhythm of his heart.

She glanced up at him. His expression said where his thoughts were, no matter what restraint he showed. Anticipation enlivened her body more than a hundred caresses. The mix of sensual arousal and emotional intimacy made her heady. Whoever thought that confidences and quiet silence could create such a powerful seduction.

Seduction. The word caused a little flash of reason to penetrate her stupor of excitement.

He had offered her exactly what she wanted. He had seduced her back by giving her what she craved most—the promise of himself.

No servant opened the door. No sounds came from the chambers. Daniel led her inside by the hand, as if guiding her to a place she had never been before.

"Is everyone gone?" she asked.

"No."

"Only out of sight?" He had given instructions on this. He had wanted to spare her any ceremony or embarrassment when she returned to him.

He had also assumed that she would be coming back.

His embrace inside the entry insured she did not mind his confidence too much. The memory of his face as he waited for her at the pond said he had not been truly confident at all.

His possessive kiss gave expression to the hunger that had made the ride slow and sensual.

"Do not leave me again," he muttered between kisses as he held her face in his hands. She heard a plea below the command.

Suddenly she was cradled in his arms, moving up the stairs through a blur of lights and shadows.

His instructions had been obeyed. They met no one in the house. He would not have cared if they had.

He carried her to the bedroom. Only there would he be able to fill the ghastly void inside him that his promise had carved.

The chamber's draperies and shutters had been closed, sealing it from the city. He kicked the door closed. His blood raged and he wanted to lay her down and tear off her clothes and bury the hungers roaring within him.

Acknowledging their violence made him pause. If he followed those impulses, she might misunderstand. Nor could he explain what was in him. He only knew that it was not physical. Mere sexual arousal would never create this kind of need.

Her arms still encircled his neck. Amusement entered her eyes. "Are you inclined to ravish me?"

"Yes."

She glanced to the bed and then up at him quizzically. "You have changed your mind?"

He laid her down. "Today deserves better." He flipped her and released the tapes on her gown. Sitting beside her, he worked at her corset's lacing.

She looked so lovely, lying there in the cool, filtered light. Her skin seemed paler, her eyes darker. The unlacing aroused her. He could tell that from the way her lids lowered, and he felt it in her body's subtle flexing.

He caressed her back through the thin chemise and traced the same path with kisses. Containing his desire was not easy, but this patient path gave the maddening urge a special power.

His slow kisses reached her shoulder and nape. "Wanting you, especially now, is about more than pleasure." She deserved to know that, especially since he did not trust that his behavior would prove it. "I do not want you to think that I am only reclaiming my rights as a husband here."

She rolled onto her back. "You have never made me think it was only that. Even the first time. That is what frightened me."

And later, when he was cold, that was what devastated her.

"It is never only pleasure with me, either." She spoke reassuringly, as if she worried he did not know that. "I do not think it ever could be." She smiled. "It is a good thing that you want me and I want you, because I do not think I could ever be a Margot."

He traced the sloping line of her loose gown's edge. "It is good to hear you say that."

"That I could never be a courtesan or mistress?"

"That you want me."

"You doubted it? I told you that I love you."

"For women there can be love without desire."

"You surely can tell. When we are together—"

"I can make you feel pleasure, but that is also a separate thing."

"*I* came to *you* that first night."

"You had an ulterior motive."

Glints of understanding entered her eyes. "I have no ulterior motive today." She scooted off the bed, pulling her disheveled garments around her.

She stood in front of him, inches away but not touching. Her hair had gotten tousled and mussed. Curls and tendrils fell around her face and shoulder. He was glad she did not move to take it down completely, because she looked lovely just as she was.

She lowered the gown seductively. "If I have come back, it is only fair that you know all the reasons, Daniel. You wanted me to know that you don't only want me for pleasure. I need you to know that pleasure is most definitely one of the reasons I am here."

The gown fell to her feet, forming a froth from which her lithe body rose. She looked so lovely that his whole being ached. He wanted to grab her.

She noticed. "Do not. Not yet. Not until I am sure that you understand how my love and desire are braided together, and not separate things for this woman."

Elegantly, she began peeling her chemise. She eased it off her shoulders and down her luminous skin. Her expression mesmerized him as much as her body. Half-worldly, half-shy, all loving, she gazed at him and let her expression reveal her delight in his attention and in the incredible currents streaming between them.

She made him burn. This time he reached for her. She stepped back and shook her head. One delicate foot rose and nestled itself between his thighs. With a naughty grin she snuggled it deeper until her toes rested at the base of his erection.

Her fingers played along the top of her stocking. Blood thundered in his head. Her foot maddened him more. He contained it and slid his hands up her leg. "I will do it."

He caressed to the top of her stocking, then higher up her thigh. Her breath quickened as skin touched skin and his fingers slid over the moistness at the top. She moved her leg just enough to permit him to touch the dark, shadowed spot that was barely visible, but compellingly available.

He caressed close enough to make her want it, to arouse her more. Her gaze, locked on his, reflected how the seduction had now become mutual. She waited for the next touch with parted lips and glistening eyes, ready to succumb to passion.

If she did, they would be entwined on the bed in mere seconds. He realized that he did not want that yet.

He moved his hands down and began sliding the stocking off.

The sensation and delay made her toes curl so intimately that he had to grit his teeth for control.

She must have seen his reaction. When she removed that leg and propped the other, those toes wiggled even more.

His vision blurred. "Stop that now."

She smiled impishly, wickedly, as her foot made one more devastating movement.

He did not bother with the stocking. He pulled her to him, impatient to touch her. She demanded to do it her way. With a gentle climb, she sat on his lap, facing him, her bent knees flanking his hips and her bottom nestled on his knees.

He kissed her to release some of the mind-splitting hunger. It only made him want more. Instead of a delay, the kiss sped things forward. Holding her naked body, feeling her soft skin and smelling the faint musk rising from her parted thighs, sent him reeling. Her own embrace and kiss were just as aggressive. Together they spun up a tight little coil of pleasure and anticipation.

She pushed his coat off his shoulders, and he shrugged it away. While she kissed and moved to the rhythms of her arousal, she removed his cravat and waistcoat. Together they got the shirt off, but he did not know how. All the while they stayed together in the hot, unending kiss, taking turns, until finally he was able to hold her against his chest so that her naked skin warmed and caressed his.

He broke the kiss and held her, feeling her heart beat, hearing her breath. Beneath the violent need there flowed the most exquisite sensation. Contentment. Gratitude. It awed and humbled him, and filled the ugly emptiness he had battled as they returned to this house.

The new feeling fascinated him. It was not a thing apart from his wanting her. It never could be. Nor would it die with the end of today's lovemaking. It would be another thread in the braid. Its power suggested it would be the strongest one.

He loosened his embrace and set her back on his knees. That confused her. She frowned, a little hurt.

"Not yet." He smoothed his fingertips over her breasts. Her breath caught and she grasped his shoulders. He teased at the tips until low cries escaped her. He loved hearing her passion. Loved the way her body moved, and the sensual sparkle in her eyes. He loved how both her body and heart had returned to him and wanted him now.

The madness began spinning again. She reached down and fumbled with the buttons of his trousers. With new boldness her hand groped and closed on him, and then stroked low to where her foot had nestled.

She watched his reactions just as he had watched hers. "Do you believe that I want you now?"

"Yes."

Her fingers slid up and down, making him insane. "Even when we sit at meals, I want you. When you are gone and I think of you, I want you. When you are near, you have only to look at me for my body and heart to react. Even before I knew what to call it, I felt it." Her finger began a devastating circling of the tip of his phallus. "I'm glad that you know. I do not want you thinking of me as these Englishmen do their wives. I do not want you believing it is only duty. I do not want you looking for a mistress in order to find pleasure."

"I would never do that."

"I intend to see that you don't." She took his face in her hands and kissed him. "I have been studying how to see that you never want to."

She eased off his lap. He did not realize why until she lowered herself to her knees. Anticipation shouted in his head, drowning everything else, even his surprise at her confident expression.

The pleasure almost undid him. It might have, if the unbearable sensations had not created a new hunger and a new anticipation. Even as his awareness swam in a delirium of torment, a primitive compulsion beat within it.

He reached for her, raising her up, kissing her too hard. Standing, he laid her on the bed and stripped off his lower garments.

Everything about her revealed that passion had crazed her as much as it had him. Her parted legs and expectant expression, her full breasts and hard nipples, even the flush of her skin and the low, quick breaths were those of a woman in abandon. Her gaze took him in, slowly and completely, in a frank manner that showed there would be no notions of innocence inhibiting them any longer.

He spread her legs more and knelt between them. He gave her the caress she had wanted from the start. Her hips gently rose as she invited his touch. A low chant of passion flowed quietly on her frenzied breaths. He touched in ways that made her cries rise and beg.

He lifted her hips. He did not ask permission. Her own special kisses had already given it.

The scent and taste of her obliterated everything but his sense of her reaction. He heard and felt her shock, and then her acceptance, and finally her moans. He used his tongue to tease lightly at her excitement until her surprise disappeared, and then more deliberately as they both succumbed to the savage pleasure.

Her climax came violently in shudders that shook them both, in a scream that no walls would hold. It tore at his control and made him crave different kisses and different abandon.

She grabbed for him as he moved into her. She clutched him madly, her cries still riding on every breath, the climax not ending her need. "Yes, yes." She pulled him to her waiting body. "Yes, fill me up, Daniel. Fill me."

She did not only speak of her body. He knew that because she filled him too. She no longer obscured the angry past as she had before, but replaced it. Her love poured into him with every desperate kiss and clutching caress and breathless cry, promising there would be no gaping emptiness.

In that bliss where they possessed and completed each other, he finally believed that he could fulfill his rash promise to her.

chapter 25

"Wait here. I will call you later to bring out my trunk." Diane issued the instruction as the footman handed her down from the carriage in front of Margot's building.

It was a glorious afternoon, cool and bright. Since Daniel had gone to Hampstead, Diane had taken the opportunity to reclaim her belongings. Margot had sent a letter asking her to visit and explain all that had transpired.

There was not much that could be told. All the same, Margot had taken her in when she ran away, and deserved some accounting.

Diane contemplated what that would be as the front door opened.

The house sounded very quiet. The silence was so complete that as she followed the servant to the drawing room, a footfall back by the door sounded extremely loud.

Margot sat on a chair, upright and stiff. Her eyes reflected worry.

Diane hurried over to her. "You do not appear well. What has happened since you wrote to me, to cause this?"

Margot took her hand in a crushing grasp.

Diane embraced her. "Is it Mister Johnson? Has he ended things with you?"

Margot shook her head. "Forgive me. I fear that I have done something that may cause more trouble between you and your husband," she whispered. "He came early, and insisted I write and invite you here. He spoke of love making him rash. He said St. John had forced you to return, and that you would want to see him." Her brow puckered. "If I made a mistake, I am very sorry."

Diane looked down, not comprehending. As she did, the air in the chamber subtly changed.

She suddenly sensed a new presence, and pivoted.

They were not alone. Someone else stood in the chamber now, near the door. Diane instinctively took a step back.

"You are looking lovely, as always, my dear," Andrew Tyndale said. "How thoughtful of you to respond to your friend's summons so quickly." He walked toward them. "Also, how convenient. It will make everything much more efficient for us."

"You are off today, St. John," Vergil said. "Keep making mistakes like that and I will inadvertently draw blood."

Daniel stepped back and lowered his sabre. He *was* off today, and his sparring had grown clumsy and dangerous. His heart was not in it. Neither was his soul or his head.

He had spent years perfecting this skill, but the reason for doing so was gone. This might be sport to the young members of the Dueling Society, but it had never been that for him. It appeared that he could not make it so, either.

He gestured for Vergil to begin again and tried to concentrate. Beside them Adrian and Hampton sparred, and by the wall Louis was giving young Dante his first lesson.

Daniel managed to keep half his mind on Vergil's sabre, but the rest worked at the conundrum facing him. He had promised Diane that he would give up his plan for Tyndale, only that was easier said than done. The plan had taken on its own life and progressed apace in that shed in Southwark with no effort on his part. Extricating himself from that scheme seemed nigh impossible, short of meeting with Tyndale and confessing the whole ruse.

That would surely result in the duel that Diane wanted to avert. It appeared that the only solution was to let the demonstration run its course and fail. At which point, he supposed that he would have to propose that Tyndale deduct the costs of the equipment and chemicals from the gambling debt.

That struck him as a suitable recompense, and one that Diane would accept as just. It would kill him to do such a thing, but that was the whole point of penance.

Of course, Diane might suggest that the gambling debt itself should be forgiven. It would be just like her to do so. Daniel debated whether that was really necessary.

Vergil abruptly paced away, and then turned with a scowl. "What are you laughing at? Not me, I hope. I am no expert at this, but you are hardly the grand master today either."

"I am not laughing at you, but myself."

"St. John, you have never laughed at yourself in the three years I have known you, so I doubt you have begun today."

"Perhaps I am no longer the man you have known. Maybe today I begin a new life." The notion struck Daniel as a wonderful joke and he laughed again.

That distracted Adrian and Hampton. They paused and looked at Daniel curiously.

Vergil gestured and rolled his eyes. "He is drunk, I think."

Daniel walked over and clamped his hand on Vergil's shoulder. "Not drunk. I am trying to determine how I can extricate myself from a devil's trap."

"And you find that amusing? You *are* drunk."

"Since the trap was of my own making, it is enormously amusing."

Vergil began to respond. Something distracted him. His gaze snapped to the hall's entry and he groaned with exasperation.

"Hell, she is here again. Once is a mistake, twice is too bold. If her husband was not such a bastard, I'd insist she return to him so he could keep her out of trouble, because the task is too great for me." Shrugging off Daniel's hand, he strode toward the threshold, where the Countess of Glasbury stood.

"We have been favored by a visit again," Adrian said. "Who is that stunning blonde with her this time?"

Daniel had not noticed the blonde, who stood behind the countess, with her head barely visible. Now the head moved into his view.

"That is an old schoolfriend of Diane's." He handed his sabre to Adrian, just as Vergil turned and gestured for Daniel. "One of you fetch my shirt, please."

Foreboding grew in his heart as he approached the doorway. The women's expressions caused it, and the mere presence of Margot made it worse.

Diane was supposed to visit Margot today.

By the time he reached the door, he knew that this intrusion heralded danger. What was left of the man he had been for years began rising above the giddy mist of love to deal with it.

He did not wait for an explanation. "Duclairc, bring them to Louis's study. I will come as soon as I am presentable."

Adrian arrived with his shirt and coats as soon as the women disappeared. Daniel pulled them on and followed.

"I apologize for pulling your sister into this," Margot was saying to Vergil. "I learned that M'sieur St. John was coming to this place, but did not know how to find it. His butler said that he was meeting you here, and I called on Lady Glasbury in the hopes she would know the way."

"Do not apologize," the countess said. "Of course you had to come. I am grateful that you did, if it will resolve this more quickly. Here is St. John now. Give him the letter."

Daniel held out his hand and Margot placed a sealed letter into it. He recognized Diane's writing on its back.

"Where did you get this?"

"From her. It was waiting for me after he took her away."

"Andrew Tyndale is whom she means," the countess inserted with excitement. "Daniel, it appears he may have abducted her."

Daniel's heart made a sickening fall, then filled with anger directed mostly at himself. There would be no escaping the devil's trap now.

"Damn the man, that is bold," Vergil said.

Yes, it was bold. But, knowing Tyndale, well thought out. "Do you know what it says?" he asked Margot.

She shook her head. "He made me leave the room when she arrived. Her carriage was right outside, and if I had known he was going to take her I would have—but I thought he would leave alone, of course. They went out through the garden and were gone before I could alert your coachman."

"He said that they were lovers and that Diane would want to see him," the countess said angrily. "He has made it appear that she has run away with him."

Margot was close to tears. "At first I believed him, so I wrote the letter asking her to come. But as I thought about it, I was suspicious. She had not sought him out while she stayed with me. She had not written to say you had made her return—I have been very stupid, and when I found them both gone I knew something was amiss."

"I thank you for finding me with such speed, and I thank you, Countess, for showing her the way. You have both been true friends to my wife and I will never forget that."

He carried the letter over to the window and slid his thumb to break the seal. Behind him, he heard the movements that said the others were leaving the chamber.

Tyndale had dictated the letter, that was obvious. Diane declared that she was leaving for good, and would be staying with some friends in Kent. Nothing in the letter could be used as evidence of the villainy at work, just as Margot's belief that Diane had been abducted would not be believed. If it came to the word of a courtesan against that of the brother of a marquess, there was no doubt who would win.

The letter left the husband in question with no alternative but to track down the lovers.

Diane was being used as a lure. Again. Only a different man used her this time. One who would not care whether she was hurt.

He closed his eyes and said his first prayer in years. He silently begged that once Tyndale had the man he wanted, that he would allow Diane to leave.

A sound jarred him. He looked over his shoulder. Louis stood ten paces away. He held a sabre in one hand and the box of dueling pistols in the other.

"How much do you think he knows?"

Daniel shrugged. "It is probably only about the steel. That would be enough."

"Bring some of your young friends."

"What would I say to them? That I defrauded a prominent scientist and the brother of a peer? That a respected member of Parliament has abducted my wife? No one but she and I know that she willingly returned, and that she did not love Tyndale before our marriage."

"They are your friends. They will believe you."

"They are acquaintances, and when it comes to something like this there are no democratic circles. Blood will count more than the loose friendships I have with them. That is how it works, Louis. We both know that." He folded the letter. "I never expected Gustave to admit that the discovery was not his own. I depended on his pride keeping his connection to me a secret."

"What will you do when you find them?"

"Give Tyndale whatever he wants, if it will buy Diane's safety."

"It is obvious that what he wants is you."

"Then he will have me."

"If you will not bring the others, I will accompany you."

"If I ride up with a companion, we will be told neither Tyndale nor Diane is there. I fear that if I do not play this game his way, he will do her harm." He also feared that even if he gave Tyndale satisfaction, Diane was in danger. He would not want her telling the world that he had abducted her, even if he thought his reputation could survive the accusation.

Louis ceremoniously laid the sabre and box on the table.

"I doubt it will be so honorable," Daniel said.

"Bring them. It is the safest way for him. He will not want suspicions and accusations of murder. And such a man never believes he can lose."

"Then it will be pistols. He has no advantage with sabres." Daniel smiled bitterly as he lifted the box of dueling guns. "I had promised her to give it up."

"She will not want you to give it up so much that you are dead."

"No, I expect not."

"When you see him, remember—a clear head. A cold heart. Sangfroid is essential."

"So you have always taught, old friend."

Daniel tucked the box under his arm. "Years ago I asked you to leave this to me, but I now have a favor to ask of you."

"Certainement."

"If I fail, and she is harmed in any way, kill him."

"*D'accord.* Of course. It will be a privilege, and a pleasure."

"She is so lovely. So young. Like a little sparrow."

Diane did not stir or open her eyes. Upon waking, she had decided to pretend that she slept on. She did not want Andrew Tyndale to see her fear.

She had not intended to sleep, but had nodded off anyway. It had been delicious to escape like that into her dreams. She wished she could have stayed there until Daniel came.

She could smell the damp of the cottage. Even the little cot on which she slept had a musty odor. The humble home had not been aired in months before they arrived.

She guessed that they were on one of Tyndale's properties. He had not brought her to the big house where there would be servants, but hidden her here instead.

The man who spoke was not Tyndale. It was the other one, the funny little Frenchman named Gustave, who had been waiting in the carriage outside Margot's garden. She guessed that Gustave did not speak English, because Tyndale had only used French with him, and sometimes English with her when she guessed he did not want the Frenchman to comprehend.

The threats had been in English.

"So innocent. So—"

"Oh, hell, enough. You sound like a swooning fool. She is his wife, and, like all women, she is a whore."

"You are barbaric to speak of her like that. I do not like this. A woman—it is not honorable," Gustave said. His voice was very close. She could feel him leaning over and peering at her.

"I told you, once he arrives we will let her go."

"When will that be?"

"I *told* you. Tonight."

"It may not be until tomorrow or the next day," a third voice said. "It may take him some time to discover where your Kent holding is."

Diane barely suppressed a startle. She had not realized that there was someone else in the chamber. This other man must have arrived while she dozed.

He also spoke French, but, like Tyndale's, it was not native.

"He damn well better not keep me waiting," Tyndale said.

"He may not come at all," Gustave fretted.

"He'll come." Movements at the other side of the chamber reached Diane. "I will go to the house to wait for him, now that you are here." Tyndale switched to English. "If this French fool decides to be heroic for his new lady love, take care of it. If he tries to interfere, kill him."

A hand caressed her hair. Gustave's hand? No, a different scent floated to her, of a different man. Tyndale. She almost recoiled physically when she realized he had touched her.

"Yes, lovely," he muttered. "But spoiled forever, and of no good to me at all anymore, except to get her husband here."

A shiver chilled Diane. *No good to me at all anymore.* Jeanette said Tyndale had spoken the same words to her when he found her.

She heard Tyndale leave the cottage.

"I do not like this," Gustave fussed again. "She is sleeping too long. He gave her too much, I am sure. *Just a little,* he said, *so that she sleeps and is not a nuisance,* but it looked to me that a good deal went into the tea."

"It is not a mistake he would likely make."

"He is not a god. He makes mistakes."

"Not this kind. Besides, she is no longer sleeping. She has been awake for some time now. Haven't you, madame?"

It shocked her to be addressed directly. She debated whether to attempt to continue the ruse. With Tyndale gone, she was not so afraid anymore.

Besides, she was curious about this third man.

She pushed herself up. Her head felt odd, as if someone had stuffed it with cotton. She rubbed her eyes and oriented herself to the wood plank floor, and the two windows with open shutters. The light showed that it was early evening.

Gustave sat in a chair near her cot. He smiled with relief.

"See, she is fine," the other man said. He sat at the table near the windows, a silhouette backlit by the setting sun.

"Who are you?" she asked.

"Just another man who badly wants an accounting with your husband."

She took in his beard and dark hair and pale, sickly pallor. Peering harder, she tried to make out the details of his face.

Her inspection amused him. He turned.

Suddenly, shockingly, she found herself looking into her own eyes.

He sensed something was wrong. His smile disappeared and he cocked his head curiously.

She could only gape at him.

"She is going to swoon," Gustave cried.

She held up a hand. "I will not. Do not concern yourself." Composure returned. "Who are you?" she asked again.

"That is not *your* concern," the man said.

"I should say it is. You have helped abduct me. You lie in wait for my husband."

"Tell me, madame. Who is your husband? If you satisfy my curiosity, perhaps I will satisfy yours."

"Daniel St. John."

"I knew him by another name."

"You are mistaken."

"Not about this man. I think that *you* are mistaken, which means he cannot be your cousin."

She gazed at his eyes. It was as if the shadowy images from her mirror, the phantom face that would emerge sometimes, had come to life. "No, he is not my cousin," she said in English so that Gustave would not understand. "When I was a child, he found me abandoned on a property he had acquired. He put me in a school, and saw to my care and education even though I was not his responsibility. Every year he journeyed to visit me, even when it meant returning from great distances to do so, and risking his safety to enter France during the war. By whatever name you knew him, that is who he is to me. He is the man who gave me a life after another man had thrown me away."

His smile disappeared before she was done.

"What did she say?" Gustave demanded.

"Nothing of interest to you. Go outside, Gustave. Get some air."

"What? Why? I do not think that you should be alone—"

"*Leave.* Good God, man, what do you take me for? Just go. *Now.*"

Alarmed by the outburst, Gustave rose like a puppet yanked up by strings. "I will be close by," he assured her. "Just call if you have need of my assistance."

With his departure, a heavy silence filled the room. Diane watched the man who sat at the table. She let her memories, what few there were, attach to his eyes and his mannerisms.

"He told you about me," he said defensively. "That is how you know about—you are using that now, to confuse matters."

"He told me very little about you. I am telling you who I am, and who he is to me."

His glance darted around, as if his mind sought some escape from this conversation.

"Where was this property where he found you?"

She almost felt sorry for him. "If you are Jonathan Makepeace, you know where it was. Hampstead."

His eyes closed. "Hell."

He sounded angry and resentful. That hurt. As a girl she had dreamed of finding him. She had imagined running to him and jumping into his arms. Maybe when he visited Hampstead that was how she greeted him when she was a child. She had always heard laughter in her fantasies of their reunion, not an angry, startled curse.

"He let me think you were dead," she said, wanting to hurt him too. "I realize now it was a kindness. He let me believe that the card game with you had been by chance. He never told me that you were involved with Tyndale, or that he deliberately ruined you."

"So now you know the kind of man he is."

"Oh, yes. He is the kind of man who would omit the truth about you, to spare me my small childhood dreams. He never let me know that my father had been part of Tyndale's scheme to rob those people of their lives and property. It was your ship that was supposed to find those poor souls on the coast, wasn't it?"

He said nothing. He did not look at her.

"Did you even set sail, to try and save them?"

"The gold and jewels were in hand. Tyndale . . . if they were not rescued, we could keep it all, far more than the payment we were to receive. It was decided early on. We all knew how it would be. I had debts . . ."

He shrugged, as if to make light of the decision. Diane could see his eyes, however. She could see the guilt. The shrug itself appeared tired and heavy, one of resignation rather than indifference.

"I could not have changed things," he said. "Tyndale had arranged everything. He would not even give me the final destination, lest I decide to go for them anyway."

She doubted he had argued with Tyndale very hard, if at all. His tone indicated he had not.

"It is a wonder my husband did not kill you."

"Better if he had, maybe. He took everything, even you."

"You *left* me. And it seems to me that he took what you had built on that betrayal."

A flame of anger lit his eyes. The energy died almost immediately, however. They sat in silence, strangers in every way except the most important one. Diane could feel the familial bond tugging her. It kept her from hating or fearing him. It made her ache for some acknowledgment.

It broke her heart.

Gustave's face suddenly peered in the window. Jonathan snarled a curse, and the face disappeared.

"Who is he?" she asked.

"A scientist. A great mind, to hear him tell it. A fool, if you ask me."

"What was his gain in this betrayal?"

"A library."

"A library? He allowed people to die for some books?"

"Those books included a treatise with a mathematical proof. He was not sorry that the man for whom he kept the library, and to whom he was to send the treatise, died. The proof became Gustave's own, and secured his reputation. He scoured every page in that library for whatever else its owner had written and noted, and built his fame upon another man's brilliance. No, Gustave was not sorry the ship did not come, even if he had been the one to introduce Tyndale to those people."

He focused his attention on his fingers, as he tapped them against the tabletop. Gustave's sins had ceased to interest him.

"He put you in a school, you said. You were well cared for, then."

"Yes."

He tapped some more. "The midwife wanted to give you to a farming couple when you were born. But I had loved your mother, and could not give you up. In the long term, it would have been better for you. I did not see you much, but you seemed happy enough when I did, but . . . Then, after that card game—I could not take you with me. I did not even know where I was going."

"I understand." And she did, in her head. Her heart was less rational. The fact that he had abandoned her still made it burn, but this new evidence, that he had wanted her enough to keep her when she was born, muted it with something that resembled forgiveness.

"Where was the school?"

"In Rouen."

He smiled, and shook his head. "I often thought about you, and wondered . . . and the last two years, you were no more than a day's ride away." His gaze sharpened, just enough to make her cautious. "Do you know who he is?"

"Daniel St. John."

"There were no St. Johns or Saint-Jeans among the people Tyndale promised to save. No St. Johns, or St. Clairs, the other name he has been known by."

"Well, it is the only name I know."

He looked at his tapping fingers again. "Do not let Tyndale and Gustave know you are my daughter. I do not know how they will react. Especially Tyndale."

"You think it would put me in danger?"

"You are already in danger. If he does not know, however, I may be able to help you." He made another vague shrug, as if he had not quite decided that he could, or would.

It was a small offer, and not a promise, but her heart tightened. She rose and walked to the table and stood beside the stranger who was her father. She looked down into her own eyes.

Years fell away during that long, connected gaze. Accusations and resentments and denials and forgiveness all flowed silently on the odd, visceral knowing that they shared. Her eyes misted, and it seemed that his did too.

She placed her hand on his. It seemed very natural to touch this sickly, wan man, because the eyes had not changed and she knew them. A small smile formed on his mouth, and she knew that too.

His hand turned so that he was holding hers.

"Will you tell me about my mother?" she asked. "And about my childhood, and all of the things that I have forgotten?"

chapter 26

Daniel was not accustomed to bargaining from a position of weakness. He followed the servant into the library on the Kent estate, too aware that he was at Andrew Tyndale's mercy.

Tyndale appeared as bland and harmless as ever. Only when the servant left did the nasty lights enter his eyes.

He gestured to the box that Daniel carried. "Pistols?"

"I expected you to choose them as weapons."

"You came here for a duel?"

"Of course. You have abducted my wife."

"She came with me gladly."

"No, she did not. In any case, I have come to demand satisfaction."

"I will give it to you, but only if you give me what I demand first." He examined Daniel from beneath lowered lids. "You must think that you are a very clever man. Certainly you are a patient one, ruining us one by one over the years. Oh yes, the others have realized how long you have been at this and your role in their misfortunes. Now you concoct this elaborate scheme for Gustave and me."

So, this was not just about the steel. The revelation increased the danger, and the stakes.

"My plans for Gustave were very simple. I never expected him to come to England and involve you. He had not sought to enrich himself with money before."

"You thought that he would let such an opportunity pass by, and content himself with the small fame that comes from a scientific discovery?"

"The fame is not so small in his world. The scorn would not have been small, either, when he was shown for a fool."

"True. It would have destroyed everything that mattered to him. Very neat," Tyndale acknowledged. "And very apropos."

"I thought so. As for his partnership with you, and then your offer of one to me, that was a gift from Providence."

"A gift from hell, actually, since it led to our realizing your scheme." Tyndale smiled slyly. "If you did not expect Gustave to pursue the profits of his discovery, you must have had other plans for me. Diane? A duel over a woman? How crude. Also risky. I would have won. Better to have caught me unawares and slit my throat."

"I considered that."

"I'm sure that you did, and still do. I don't care for that notion."

Tyndale walked over to the desk and removed a pistol from one of its drawers.

"You have no intention of killing me here, now, in this library," Daniel said. "You are not that stupid."

"If I have to, I will. There are few servants here. I had most of them sent away, except for several men who owe me their lives." He pushed some papers to the edge of the desk. "You will sign these now. If you do, we will meet for your duel, and you will have your chance to kill me before I kill you. If you do not, I will shoot you like a dog."

Daniel examined the papers. They deeded over to Tyndale everything Daniel owned, to repay debts unspecified.

"I would be an idiot to sign these."

"You will be dead if you do not."

"I think that you expect me to be in either case, since my signature will be worthless if I am not, procured as it was with a pistol to my head. I think that I prefer dying rich, thank you."

"*She* will also be dead if you do not sign."

"For all I know, she already is." He gestured to the pistol. "Either let me see that she is unharmed, or use it. If you expected me to sign those papers, to buy the chance to save my own life, you have miscalculated badly. Perhaps age is dimming your wits."

"At sixty my wits will be three times as sharp as yours have ever been."

"If so, Diane is here, and safe."

"That she is. I will send for her. Spare me any sentimental reunions, won't you?" Tyndale went to the door and spoke with a man waiting outside.

Daniel had donned the armor of cold emotion before journeying to this manor, but now cracks appeared in it. Relief that Diane was safe, and anticipation of seeing her, briefly flooded him, followed immediately by ruthless anger that Tyndale had dared to threaten her safety.

He turned away so that Tyndale would not see either reaction. "This is an impressive property," he said. "I could not help but admire it as I rode in."

"It is not as large as my family's seat, of course. That would never do, but in many ways it is a superior holding."

"Has your brother, the marquess, ever seen it, so he could admire that fact?"

"Once, soon after I bought it twenty odd years ago."

Twenty years ago. It had been purchased with those jewels and gold. Tyndale was goading him by letting him know that they now played the final hand in a game begun long ago. A hand that Tyndale expected to win, as he had all the others. Daniel swallowed the fury and memories that wanted to rise in response to the reference.

"You do realize that others know I have come here."

"Your wife's letter said nothing of this estate. You could have gone anywhere in Kent."

"Others were present when I received the letter. They know I came looking for you."

"You came here, but did not find me—that will be the story the servants give. I was not here, nor was Diane. You left, and looked elsewhere."

"Margot knows that you took Diane."

"The word of a courtesan, and one kept by a merchant at that, will have no weight. As it happens I am spending today and the next several days with an old friend, who will swear I was with him the whole time. The Earl of Glasbury. He owes me the favor. As for your wife, she ran away from you, you forced her to return, and she ran away again." Tyndale paced as he spoke, until he forced himself into Daniel's view. "Did you think that I would forget to see to such things? I am insulted."

Daniel was glad that he was, for the simple reason that it had him alluding to his plans and intentions. Thus far, the revelations had not been encouraging. Diane might be safe now, but if Tyndale intended murder he could not leave her alive as a witness.

He regretted demanding to see her. It could have forced Tyndale's hand with her. If she remained ignorant . . . From the corner of his eye he noticed Tyndale studying him. No hand had been forced. Tyndale had decided how he would do this from the start.

"I would have my curiosity satisfied on one point," Tyndale said. "Who the hell are you?"

"I am the son of your past and the witness to your sins."

"Spare me the bad poetry. Who are you? You knew what was in the library, but I remember no child in that family."

Daniel had dreamed of the day when he would let this man know who had brought him down. He had lived for the moment when Tyndale's nose would be forced into the hell his own actions had wrought. Now, suddenly, it did not matter.

Let Tyndale wonder. Let him worry. Let him always wait, lest another son of the past arrive.

"My father had been given liberty to use the library and had commented in my presence on its owner's experiments. Scientists enjoy discussing their theories to any who will listen. Dupré can explain that to you. After all, he knew that an important mathematical proof would be found in those papers and notes."

Tyndale's lids lowered. "You could not have been more than a boy at the time. What would you understand about proofs and theories of electricity?"

"What I did not know or understand, others have explained. Not everyone who waited on that coast died. Not every person you betrayed was executed. I am not the only one who remembers what you did. Kill me, but you will not kill the past. The war protected you, but that is long over now. Others will come for you now that they can."

Tyndale's expression both fell and hardened. Daniel saw a speck of doubt join the uglier lights in his eyes.

A commotion in the hall drew their attention. The door opened and Diane walked in. Before an arm pulled the door closed, Daniel caught sight of one very worried French scientist and of another man with a beard, probably one of Tyndale's servants.

Diane walked over to Daniel and gave him a light kiss. Her eyes met his with a wonderful expression of warmth and love, but she also conveyed a message of caution in that brief look.

She turned to Tyndale. "I trust that you will not return me to that crude, musty cottage."

"You will stay here. The servants have been dealt with, so I do not need to hide you any longer."

"I do not understand why you ever did. If you merely desired a meeting with my husband, you could have called on him as other men do."

"I do not call on such as your husband. I call *for* them." He turned a sly smile on Daniel. "You never told her, did you?"

"Told me what?"

"Your husband is a swindler, my dear. Also a fraud and a cheat. He is an imposter, taking names as they suit him, seducing his way into fine circles so he can rob people with his schemes. Did he find you in some alley and pay you to help him? I doubt that he is your cousin, you see, so I have a passing curiosity about your relationship to him."

The string of insults had Diane's expression hardening.

"Do not allow your pique at losing her make you a fool," Daniel said. "Insult her further, and you will get nothing from me."

"I will get everything I want from you," Tyndale snarled. "Everything you have, including her if I choose." He closed his eyes, and forced the spurt of fury down. "Of course, you had to go and ruin her, so she is of no interest to me anymore. Unless you refuse to do as I say. Then I'll be forced to shoot her in the head."

Diane tried to show Tyndale no fear, but Daniel saw that the threat stunned her.

He slid his arm around her protectively. "You have a chamber prepared for her, I assume. Let her go there now so that you and I can complete our conversation."

"Of course. My man will show you the way. My apologies for the lack of a woman to assist you, but they can never be trusted. Oh, and the locks—well, it is important that you not leave just yet, so do not bother trying to open the door."

Diane turned her back on Tyndale. She looked up at Daniel.

Nothing could be said with Tyndale watching. Diane's face was not visible to their captor, but Daniel knew his was, and he dared not reveal the pain burning his heart. For all he knew, this would be his last sight of her. He should be telling her things, speaking words not spoken yet and begging forgiveness for endangering her, but that was denied him. He could only gaze into her moist, expressive eyes and trust that she understood all of it.

A small, wavering smile formed despite her tears. She rose on her toes to kiss him. Her whisper barely sounded, but it reached his ears anyway.

"I know that you love me," she said.

Diane did not undress. She had no intention of remaining the night in the chamber where they had locked her.

She strained to hear sounds that would tell her what was happening. Surely if a pistol fired the sound would reach her. With every minute that passed in silence, her belief grew that Daniel would find a way to outsmart Tyndale.

Through her high window, she watched the sliver of moon rise in the sky. She stayed awake as the night slowly slid past, thinking of Daniel. She kept all of her concentration on memories of him, as if her thoughts alone could protect him.

When half the night had passed and she was convinced that she was the only one left awake in the house, a sound outside her door told her that was not true.

She jumped from the window bench and grabbed a heavy candlestick. Tyndale had said she was of no use to him now, but she did not trust the man. He might harm or misuse her merely to torture Daniel.

Keys sounded in the locks. The door eased open. A shadow slipped in.

She began to raise the candlestick, but stopped. Her soul recognized the intruder.

"Come with me," Jonathan said quietly.

"Where?"

"Gustave is waiting at the cottage with a horse. He will get you away."

"You must free Daniel too."

"I cannot do that. Nor do I want to. Neither Gustave nor I wish to see you harmed, however. If you stay, I fear that you will be."

"Perhaps you will be as well. Free my husband. Let us all leave together. If Tyndale is thinking of murder, neither you nor Gustave will be safe if you know what he has done. You will never be missed. No one even knows that *you* are still alive."

"You know it. If you escape, Tyndale will have to reorder his plans, whatever they may be." He eased the door open again. "More than locks guard your husband. I cannot get to him, even if I wanted to. Now come quickly, before Gustave loses his courage, or decides that between the risk of a noose or facing Tyndale's wrath, he would prefer the former."

She joined him at the door, but touched his arm, stopping him. "Why don't you take me away instead of Gustave? Whoever remains will face the most danger."

"It must be Gustave. I am a better liar than he is, and stand a better chance when Tyndale begins asking questions." He covered her hand with his. "As for any danger—allow me to be a father this once. Finally."

His skin felt rough on hers, and moist in a way that revealed his bravery had not come easily. He was afraid. She pictured him these last hours, weighing her against everything else, knowing he should not respond to that primal connection they had, but succumbing to the demands of fatherly duty all the same.

She embraced him in gratitude for the hard choice he had made. "Do not lie too well," she said. "Let Tyndale think that I am going for help. Let him know that I will tell everyone what I saw here."

"The *idiot.*"

Andrew could not believe he had been cursed with such a fool as Gustave Dupré.

The irony was unbearable. The man was a scientist, but he proved incapable of rational judgment. The absence this morning of both Gustave and Diane proved that.

The little man had helped her to escape.

"Whatever she says will implicate *him,*" he said. "He is riding to his own hanging. Is the man too stupid to see that?"

Jonathan shrugged. "I think he fell in love with her. He kept calling her a little sparrow yesterday. It distressed him that your plans put her in danger."

"She was in no danger, merely a lure to get her husband here." Tyndale decided to ignore how thin the lie sounded. If spoken sincerely enough, and he now spoke most sincerely, lies became truths to the people hungry to hear them.

"You should have explained things better, then. Gustave could not see how you could allow her to leave, knowing her husband had met you here. I was at a loss on how that would work myself and could not help him. Still, I never expected him to be so bold. Well, there wasn't much moon and Dupré is no horseman. Maybe they fell down a hill and broke their necks."

Andrew hoped so. He could not count on it, however. Nor did he know just when the two of them had left. With the estate emptied of most servants, no one had seen anything.

His gaze fell on the documents stacked on the corner of his library desk. He had spent hours last night trying to get St. John to sign them. Hours of promises about Diane, and oaths of honor, and arguments and threats. He had played on St. John's concern for his wife. In offering a path to salvation for the only person who mattered to his prey, he had expected to obtain the signatures. It had worked before. Instead, St. John had remained adamant that he would sign nothing until Diane was released.

He would not have held to that if a pistol were aimed at her heart. Which it would have been this morning, Tyndale had decided.

And now Gustave had run off with the girl, complicating everything.

Well, if it had to be a duel, so be it. It wasn't as if St. John would win.

"Will you let him go too?" Jonathan asked.

"And spend the rest of my life looking over my shoulder? I will handle this a different way, that is all. Bring him these documents. Tell him she is gone, and if he signs them we will meet with honor to settle things."

The door to Daniel's chamber opened. The bearded servant he had seen in the corridor yesterday entered. He carried the documents from the night before.

"Tyndale wants to meet with you," he said.

"Until I have proof my wife is safe, he and I have nothing to discuss."

"As it happens, your wife is gone. She left during the night. He does not want to discuss anything. He wants to *meet.*"

The news surprised Daniel. He refused to believe it even though profound relief shook through him. It would be just like Tyndale to lie about this, to get those deeds signed. No sooner than the ink was dried it would turn out to be a ruse.

As he forcibly controlled the vain hope that she was actually gone, he saw a small smile form above the man's beard.

He inspected the man more closely. "Do I know you?"

"Why do you ask? Do I appear familiar?"

He did, in vague ways.

"I am an old friend of Tyndale's, and an old victim of yours, St. John. Or should I say St. Clair?"

St. Clair. Daniel suddenly saw this man in the lamps of a Parisian street, lunging with a knife. He saw him again, slipping away on a Southwark alley. Finally, with total clarity, he saw him without the beard and sickly pallor, smiling with confidence over a hand of cards.

He watched the man's eyes. He knew them very well because he had seen them often, recently, on another face.

"Did you get her away?" he asked, as the hope began rising again.

"Yes."

"Then you realized who she is."

"She recognized me. Can you believe that? I only saw her a few times a year when she was a child, but she recognized me."

"She kept the image of you alive when all other memories deserted her."

Jonathan nodded. "Well, she is gone, and out of this."

"I thank you."

"I did not do it for you. As far as I care, Tyndale can cut you into pieces. Still, it will not be murder and that is just as well. Whatever plan he had hatched, I suspect that Gustave and I would have been surprised by the parts concerning us. Now he must deal with you honorably." He dropped the documents on the bed. "If you sign these, that is how it will be."

Daniel did not expect this duel to be honorable at all. The witnesses would all be Tyndale's. Still, it was a chance, which was more than he had expected.

He pulled on his coat. "You are sure that she is away? That she is safe?"

"As her father, I swear to you the truth of that."

The relief had its way this time. It flooded him, washing away a night of worry and self-recrimination. Later, if he survived, he would face the latter again, but he could not allow it to distract him now.

He picked up the documents and carried them to a table. Using a quill and ink pot there, he scrawled his name on each one.

"Let us go down. It is time to finish this."

chapter 27

They waited in the park behind the house as the silver sky lightened. The morning held a mystical quality. But for the chorus of birdcalls, there were no sounds as the earth revealed its beauty. Daniel breathed in the fecund smells and noticed all the details as he never had before.

Peace saturated him along with the new light.

Knowing Diane was safe made all the difference. He would not be distracted by worry for her, at least.

Jonathan walked over from the tree where he had been standing with the three footmen who guarded Daniel. "He should come soon."

"What will you say when questions are asked? Surely you know that he has no intention of making this fair. Tyndale will make sure that this duel ends only one way."

"I owe you nothing. Those papers you signed will give me back my life," Jonathan said. "If you die, I saw a fair duel."

"What of your daughter? Diane will know the truth. She is aware of all of the strings in this knot of betrayal and revenge that we have tied."

"I lost her long ago. I have no dreams about that."

A door opened up at the house. The dot of a blond head appeared and moved toward them. Two other men walked alongside. As they neared, Daniel saw the box of pistols he had brought from Hampstead in one man's arms. The other carried a silver tray loaded with cups and a coffee urn.

Daniel's mind flew through a whole life of emotions. He did not see Tyndale, but harsh images from his boyhood and youth. Anger began to rise in him. Then his thoughts veered to more recent memories, of Diane and her gentle love, and the sweetest, most profound nostalgia and regret flooded him.

He had lived for this moment, for this chance to settle the past with

Tyndale. Ruin had been enough for the others, but he had dreamed of killing the man who had been the instigator of that betrayal all those years ago. He had expected it to be hatred that filled him when the time came.

Instead, all that mattered now was the terrible awareness that he might never hold Diane in his arms again.

Sadly, he forced his thoughts away from her. He doubted that he had much chance of surviving today, but he would have none at all if he dwelled on what he might lose.

The sun broke over the trees. Golden light spread on the park, displaying the perfection of Tyndale's appearance. Daniel struggled to put on the armor of cold concentration that he would need soon.

The sun brought sounds as well as clear light. Nature came alive to join the chorus of chirping birds. Beneath it all, the vague noise of wheels and horses leaked into the air.

That sound got louder with each step that Tyndale took.

Tyndale heard it. He stopped and looked quizzically back at the house.

The sound abruptly stopped. Birds filled the hole it left, so that one wondered if it had ever been there.

Tyndale came forward, his expression as open as ever. He gestured for his man. "Coffee?"

Daniel looked past the tray and over the shoulder of the man who carried it. A movement had caught his eye. A figure appeared on the side of the house, then disappeared.

Tyndale's gaze followed Daniel's up to the house. "It appears we have a guest." A sour note punctuated his tone.

"That would be my second," Daniel said. "The Chevalier Corbet."

Tyndale set down his cup on the tray. "It appears they did not fall and break their necks, Jonathan. Nor did Gustave have the sense to keep her in confinement."

"He was very smitten. She must have worked her wiles on him."

"Well, it changes nothing."

The figure of the chevalier appeared again. He was not alone this time. A small assembly surrounded him. They all strode toward the tree.

Tyndale watched. "The idiotic, French fool."

"Perhaps you would like to stand down," Daniel said.

"The hell I will."

The group drew near. The faces of Vergil and Adrian and Hampton grew clear. A diminutive figure broke through their ranks from the rear and ran across the grass, skirts hiked high so she could move fast.

Diane looked like an angel descending on the morning's light. Daniel's heart swelled with joy at the sight of her. He strode forward and opened his arms to receive her.

Her embrace warmed him as no sun could. He closed his eyes and savored the scent and feel of her. Her heart beat rapidly against his body as she clutched him.

"Jeanette sent for the chevalier, and we came by coach, but I sent word to the others and they followed and caught up with us on the road," she whispered in a rush, pressing her face to his shoulder, twisting to kiss him. "They came to stop this."

Daniel gazed over her head, to the faces of Louis and the Dueling Society. Each of them knew something about his argument with Tyndale, but only Louis knew it all. Their expressions revealed that they guessed this could not be stopped.

They had not come to stop a duel, but to witness one and to ensure fair play.

As they reached the tree, another figure appeared near the house. Paul trekked through the park, carrying a veiled woman in his arms. Without a word, he set Jeanette on the ground beneath the tree and she arranged her long shawl over her lap and lifeless legs.

"She would not stay in London," Paul said to Daniel.

Louis went to the man holding the pistol box and gestured for it to be opened so the weapons could be inspected. Hampton came to Daniel and spoke lowly.

"Your ship at Southampton—I sent word to the captain to leave with the tide and anchor off the coast. A boat will be waiting to row you out to her."

Diane's head snapped around. "Why?"

"Duels are accepted for gentlemen, madame. For your husband, however, if he kills the brother of a peer, there is no saying for certain that he will not hang."

"But there does not have to be a duel now. Tyndale cannot force one."

At Daniel's gesture, Hampton retreated. Daniel held Diane closer and caressed her face. "If it is not finished today, it will be another day. He is as tenacious as I am and will find a means to kill me, honorably or not."

"Not if you tell everyone about him. Not if you denounce him for what he is and what he did."

"The fact that I can do so only means that the danger is immediate. Not only for me. That I can live with. He has proven that he might harm you too. I cannot allow that. I will not leave this place knowing that he may take revenge on me through you."

"There must be some other way."

"There is no other way. Tell me that you understand that. I do not want to face him knowing that you are angry with me, or that you believe this is a betrayal of my promise to you."

Worry trembled through her lithe frame. He felt it rise to a maddening level. Then it died as she conquered it.

She gazed up at him and only love could be seen in her eyes. "I understand. I know this is not your choice."

He kissed her. Soothing peace and calm filled him as he lost himself in her. The whole world retreated and they were alone in the beautiful present, where he dwelled only with her, and where no dark past and no old hatreds could intrude.

"There is something I must say to you," he said. "You have stolen my heart. You are my world now. I love you so much it astonishes me."

"And you are my world. I told you last night that I know you love me. There is no doubt in my soul about that. Now, do what you must do. Should I leave? I do not want to watch this, but I cannot go if it might be—"

If it might be our last minutes together. He should make her leave, but his awareness that it might be a final farewell hurt his heart. "It is your choice, darling. Women do not attend duels, but this is no normal duel."

"Then I will stay, if it will not interfere. If you make it my choice, I choose to stay with you."

She slowly extricated herself from his embrace. He was grateful she mustered the strength for that, because he doubted he could have let go on his own.

She went to stand beside Jeanette. He walked over to the young men of the Dueling Society. Vergil appeared extremely sober, his blue eyes full of concern.

"Is this necessary, St. John?"

"It is necessary, I assure you."

Adrian looked more calm, but then Adrian had seen men die before.

"The head or the heart, Daniel," he said quietly with a small smile.

"My horse is waiting," Hampton said. "When it is done, ride for the coast immediately."

Daniel removed his coat and handed it to Adrian.

Louis came forward.

Tyndale waited out in the sun.

"A cool head," Louis said. "Sangfroid is essential."

Daniel looked at Diane and allowed his love for her to scorch his soul.

Then he summoned the cold blood that Louis advised, and that would be necessary to survive.

. . .

She could not bear to watch. She could not bear to look away.

How calm everyone acted, as if such things were commonplace and one saw two men shoot at each other several times a week.

The stoicism infuriated her. There should be some acknowledgment that a life would end soon.

She prayed that it would not be Daniel's.

Tyndale chose his weapon from the box and Daniel took the other. The chevalier asked if the duel could be averted, and Tyndale snickered.

Diane did not like the confidence in that reaction. She did not like the vacancy in Daniel's expression any better. He should be angry and intense. Those devil eyes should be burning. Instead he appeared as if he were gazing out a window.

The men began pacing away. Diane's heartbeat slowed to the rhythm of their steps. Tyndale walked toward her.

When he had paced six steps, a movement beside Diane distracted him. His gaze darted over to her hip even as he walked.

Diane looked down to see what had caught his attention.

Jeanette had lifted the veil from her face.

Tyndale frowned. One could almost see his mind searching, as if prodded by something he did not understand.

Suddenly he stopped walking and stared at Jeanette. Amazed recognition flared in his eyes.

Jeanette returned a level gaze, while her hands rearranged the large shawl over her lap.

It had only taken a few moments, but in that time, Daniel had completed his own pacing and turned. Now his pistol was aimed at Tyndale's back.

"Andrew," Jonathan hissed in warning.

Tyndale pivoted and faced the pistol. His own hung loosely at his side. He had not even completed the ritual steps. Unprepared, no longer confident, he fired.

The sound made Diane jump. She stared, waiting to see Daniel fall. He did not even flinch. He still stood rigidly, legs apart, the gun in his hand.

A horrible, long count passed with everyone immobile, watching, listening for the next explosion that would shatter the morning.

Diane ceased breathing. It seemed that the whole world did. Daniel's arm stiffened straighter. He was not at all distracted now. Despite his cool expression, burning lights flashed in his eyes.

She guessed what memories and hatreds had called them forth. For an instant he was the Devil Man again, contented that he was about to fulfill his dream and send Andrew Tyndale to hell.

His gaze shifted slightly. He saw her now. The sharp lights died and very different ones took their place. The strict line of his arm wavered.

The report of a pistol cracked the silence. A ball entered Tyndale's body.

Daniel stared in her direction, but not at Tyndale. She looked down in dazed confusion, to see what compelled his attention.

Jeanette held a smoking pistol in her hand.

As a crowd formed around Tyndale to check his state, Daniel threw his weapon away and strode over to Jeanette. He crouched beside her and eased the gun from her shaking hands.

"You should not—"

"Better it was me. As for how I did it, I will let heaven judge me. My mother will speak on my behalf, along with all the others he betrayed." She patted his face. "Besides, I did not think you were going to do it. You had lost your heart for it."

He had no answer for that. Diane remembered the moment of wavering, and wondered if Jeanette was right.

"Do not feel guilty, brother," Jeanette whispered. "I am glad that he did not succeed in crippling us both for life. When they hang me, I will be more contented than I have been in years, knowing that you are happy and free."

"You will not hang." He rose and clutched Paul's shoulder. "Get her away from here, to Southampton and the ship. Now. Take her to France."

Paul scooped her into his arms and began striding away. Jeanette made him stop and gestured for Diane.

Diane went over for her sister's embrace. "We will see you soon," she promised. "I do not think Daniel will mind visiting Paris now."

Jeanette looked over at her brother. "Is that true, Daniel? Is it finished?"

"Yes, it is finished, darling."

As Paul carried Jeanette away, Hampton came over with Daniel's pistol, peering into its chamber curiously. "It appears a little damp in there." He pointed the pistol in the air and pulled the trigger. It sputtered rather than cracked. "Tyndale must have tampered with it. Louis is too inexperienced with guns to notice. Good thing we arrived when we did, or you were a dead man even if you had fired first."

"Don't tell anyone. That pistol is all that stands between my sister and the gallows if she is caught."

"How is that?"

"If she does not get away, you saw me fire. You saw me kill Tyndale."

Diane's heart flipped. Alarm that Daniel was still in danger shuddered down her back. Suddenly Paul's progress up the rise of the park seemed very slow.

Hampton gestured over his shoulder. "I think it is safe to say that she will get away."

Louis and the other members of the Dueling Society had circled Jonathan and the servants. Their expressions said that no man would leave this estate for a good long while.

Daniel's eyes glistened. His arm stretched in Diane's direction and she stepped into his embrace. "They don't even know why she did it. They do not understand who Tyndale was to us."

"They know you," Hampton said. "They trust that the story, when told, will exonerate you both. If not in the eyes of the law, at least in those of honor and justice."

"And you? You are the law's man, Hampton."

He favored them both with one of his rare smiles. "Today I am your friend, St. John. We all are."

chapter 28

The Marquess of Highbury appeared nonplussed as he received the news of his brother's death. Julian Hampton told the story in his best solicitor's voice.

The marquess surveyed the visitors who had intruded on his London house. His lazy gaze drifted over the son of an earl and the brother of a viscount and the French chevalier. It came to rest on the least significant man in the study.

"So, you are St. John. I heard the rumor of my brother's doings with your cousin. My wife told me you stood down and married the girl. I try not to listen to her gossip, but it is so incessant that some leaks in anyway. Decent of you to handle it that way."

"Unfortunately, as you have just heard, your brother was not so decent," Daniel said.

Vergil, standing beside him, gave a subtle but sharp nudge.

The marquess shook his head. "Abducted her, you say. Well, I always knew what I had in him."

Daniel doubted that, but the rest of the story, the oldest parts, would not be told in this room unless it became necessary. They had all decided that back in Kent.

"You all swear it transpired as you say? That St. John's pistol misfired and his sister shot to protect him when Andrew did not stand back?"

Vergil, Adrian, and Julian all muttered vague assurances.

"Who else was there, besides the two women? Hell of a thing, women watching a duel—"

"Some of his servants," Daniel said.

"Well, they can be bought off." He rose from his chair. "Gentlemen, my brother died in an accident. That is the story I will give out. He was at his property in Kent and died in a hunting accident."

Daniel did not doubt that a marquess could find a surgeon who would ignore that a pistol's ball had entered Tyndale from the back.

"I do not want the rest of this, the business over this woman, the duel, any of it known. I a pistol's bury my brother quietly, with his good name intact."

"The local justice of the peace—" Hampton began.

"Let me explain it to him. I relieve you of any responsibility, since officially you were not even there. The matter is in my hands now."

There was nothing more to say. Led by Louis, the Dueling Society took their leave and filed out of the study. Daniel was the last in line.

"St. John," the marquess said, stopping him.

He turned and faced Tyndale's brother.

"I know about you. All that chattering gossip, you see. Know how you seduced your way into some of his circles, how you mesmerized certain ladies several years ago to get where you are. My wife spoke of you so much that I wondered if you were pursuing her."

"The marchioness and I have never met. Her world is too selective for me."

"I see to that. I don't approve of these new notions of mixing the classes, as some do. It is merely a passing fashion, and one I will be glad to have end, as all fashions do."

One could hear the low rumble of a demonstration riding the breeze entering the open window. Its rise and fall mocked the marquess's words.

The marquess's face fell. "There is more to this than I have been told, isn't there?"

"Yes, but believe me when I say that you do not want to know any of it."

"Then let no one know of it. If I hear any slurs on him, any hints of scandal because of this, I will have to crush you."

The four men who had just left already knew all of it, but they would be discreet. "I have no more interest in your brother. He is dead, and it is over. I cannot guarantee that some of his other sins won't be exposed in time, however. If you truly knew what you had in him, you'd understand what I mean. If I were you, I'd lay aside some money to pay whomever is necessary to prevent that."

What a mess this library was.

Gustave clucked his tongue as he worked his way along the shelves. He had been at it for hours, since waking from the deep nap his adventure had demanded. Since the footmen in this house would not let him leave, he had to do something.

Examining St. John's library took his mind off things too. Not entirely, unfortunately. Even as he read titles on bindings, he worried. What if Tyndale came looking for him? What if St. John's sister went to the authorities? What if the little sparrow swore evidence against Gustave Dupré, even though he had risked his life to save her?

The books had no organization. Unlike Tyndale's library, they had all been read, however. On pulling a few out, he had seen that some even had margin notes.

He moved along, critical of the varied subjects. St. John's mind was that of an amateur, veering this way and that. No focus, no specialization. There was more poetry than Gustave approved of. At least the man seemed to favor the old French poets, and not the messy, meandering, emotional nonsense popular of late.

"Have you found what you are looking for, Dupré?"

Gustave jumped. He turned to see St. John and Jonathan by the door.

"I was only browsing to pass the time." He pointed to the shelves. "It is customary to arrange them by some system. You would find that more efficient."

"They are arranged by a system. They are in the order in which I obtained them. The most recent ones are down here. For example, Volta's paper on creating electrical effects from metallic piles is on the next to bottom shelf."

It appeared that St. John intended to explain himself. That boded well for how this unpleasant episode would end. Apparently there had been no murder, but rather negotiations. Now St. John was ready to rectify his criminal behavior rather than risk exposure.

"Volta's discovery is well known and your knowledge of it does not surprise me. However, you were aware that speculations regarding the effect of electricity on metals could be found in my library. That is more provocative."

"Not your library. It once belonged to my tutor, who was in correspondence with Volta and knew his theory before other scientists. He drew an image in his notebook, to show me how such a pile might work, and told me his ideas about how chemical and physical properties might be isolated once electricity could be produced at will."

"Are you saying that the rest was yours alone, built on these conversations with your tutor? But the other manuscript—"

"A forgery. A fake. The rest of it was all a product of my imagination."

Gustave had held on to the slim hope that the theory had some merit, and that he had not invested his fortune and reputation in a total hoax.

Despite Tyndale's conviction that they had been duped, he had hoped that with a little experimenting, a little tinkering . . .

He regretted having interfered with Andrew's plan to kill this man. Right now he would shoot St. John himself if he could. The man had seduced him to ruin, and he had followed the lure as a dog tracks the smell of meat.

The door opened and another man entered. It was Adrian, his secretary.

"What are you doing here?"

Adrian smiled at St. John.

Really, it was too much.

"Are you in this swindler's employ? How diabolical is this plot?" The answer rushed in on him before the question was asked. "The experiment in Paris, the iron's markings—you told him everything. Traitor! I will tell everyone about both of you. You will learn that Gustave Dupré has influence. You have ruined my fortune and now I will ruin you."

A snickering laugh greeted his outrage. It sputtered into coughs as Jonathan dropped into a chair and doubled over.

"Dupré, you are such an ass." He barely got the words out as the coughs and laughter racked his body. "We abducted the man's wife, you fool. Be glad you are still alive. You will probably write your next treatise from a prison cell."

Prison?

"Do not swoon on me, Dupré. I have no plans for you," St. John said. "Adrian, will you see to them? Diane is waiting for me, to learn what transpired with the marquess."

After St. John left, Gustave turned on his secretary. "I am very disappointed in you."

"He told me everything," Adrian said coldly. "I know about your old history with Tyndale, and how you got that library. So I know how you came by that proof that bears your name."

"You would never—" But he might. St. John probably would. There would be those who had always been suspicious, who would spread the rumor.

Gustave had never felt so helpless in his life. Not only his fortune but his reputation was destroyed.

"We are caught, Dupré," Jonathan said. "You are ruined, as I was. Well, it could have been worse for us. After all, Tyndale is dead."

"Dead!"

"Mmm."

He was cornered. Doomed. "I may as well shoot myself. I haven't a franc left."

"That is not entirely true," Adrian said. "There is a shed in Southwark full of metal. Those piles contain copper and zinc, and there is a lot of iron there too. When it is sold, you and Jonathan will be better off than when this started. Let us go there now and see what can be salvaged."

Jonathan appeared incredulous. "St. John will permit this?"

"His wife suggested it and he could not refuse her, since you helped her escape last night."

"I am overwhelmed," Gustave said, heady with relief. The little sparrow had done this. He knew she had a special affection for him, but such a gesture— The room swam as this unexpected salvation made his blood rush in all the wrong ways.

"Hell, he is going down," he heard Jonathan yell, right before oblivion swallowed his consciousness.

Diane took Daniel's hand as soon as he entered the garden. "Later. Tell me later," she said.

She led him to a corner farthest from the house and embraced him under the stars while she hungrily sought his kiss. "Just hold me now, so that I am sure we are both here and that it is over."

"It is very over, darling."

She grasped him to her, desperate for contact. All of the worry of the last two days threatened to flood back, and only holding him kept it away. "Kiss me. Love me." Her hands moved over him, feeling his body, searching for all the warmth she could touch. She held his hips to her own, so that she could feel his desire for her.

She wanted no words now. All of that could wait. She needed him, his love and his hunger and the passion that would convince her soul that he was here and safe and that this was real.

His embrace absorbed her. His kisses consumed her. It was not enough. She needed more. Everything.

"Here. Now." She gasped the pleas between savage kisses. "Love me. Fill me up, darling."

He lowered them both until she lay on the spring flowers. He settled between her legs, surrounding her totally with his embrace, and covering her with his body. Sweet scents rose up from the crushed blooms, intoxicating her more.

She savored the reality of the scents and sky, of his weight and wanting, of the passion binding them totally. There were no words and no need for any. She felt everything in him, all of the love and relief.

He began raising her skirt. She helped, eager to complete their unity, desperate to be together.

He caressed her, to make her ready. She did not want that, did not need it. "No. Just come to me, darling. Fill my body and heart, fill all of me as only you can."

He looked down at her, his head framed by the night sky. The frenzy calmed, but not the passion. It filled and surrounded them like a spiritual wind.

The beauty made her want to weep. When he entered her, silent tears dripped down her temples. In their union she knew him completely. Her soul understood the mysteries that had no words. Her heart felt the cautious wonder in his soul.

He made love to her slowly, wonderfully. He held nothing back. The pleasure was the least of it, a mere metaphor for the more important sharing. They poured love into each other, reaffirming their alliance against an indifferent world.

The ending was powerful, mutual, mystical. They melted together for a long moment of fulfillment. In her ecstasy she knew that the best parts of this night's loving would go on forever. She would never be alone again.

Afterward he stayed inside her, the two of them pressed to the reawakening earth. He quietly told her about the meeting with the marquess, and the way that Tyndale's brother had erased all of them from the story of Tyndale's death.

"So you were right when you told Jeanette it is finished," she said. "All of it might have never happened. Can you accept that the world will never know what he did?"

"I never sought to have the world know."

"Why not? Why didn't you denounce him?"

"I had no proof of what he had done, or even who I was. Who would have believed me? He was the brother of a peer, and a powerful man in his own right. Even if I had shouted the truth for years, his world would have ignored me. So I handled it a different way."

Yes, a different way. A subtle way. A duel over a young woman. Not Jeanette, though. There was no proof on that, either, except the word of a shipper and a crippled woman.

"You brought the others down in ways that echoed the past, and what they had done. I think that you wanted to do the same with Tyndale."

"Perhaps I did."

She stroked her fingers through his hair. "So I know everything now. There are no more mysteries. Except one."

"What is that?"

"My father said that there were no St. Johns waiting on the coast all those years ago. Nor any St. Clairs, the name you used when you ruined him. So, tell me, husband, who are you? If your history is to be my history, I want to know."

He rose up on his arms and looked down at her. "Today, now, I am Daniel St. John. However, I was born Daniel de la Tour. My father taught ancient languages at the university in Paris."

"And your mother?"

She sensed an echo of the old anguish quake in him, and instantly regretted the question.

"My mother was the youngest daughter of a baron. She married far below her family's station and was disowned by them. That meant nothing in the end, however."

"You told me in Scotland that your father was not an aristocrat. You neglected to mention that your mother was."

He settled back down into their embrace. "An oversight."

She laughed. "Have there been other oversights?"

He shrugged. "I should probably mention that I am the last of the line, except for Jeanette."

"That means that you are now the baron."

"I suppose so, if I want to try and claim it. Louis's word on my identity may be enough."

"Do you want to claim it?"

He did not answer for a while. She sensed a new shadow in him.

"It will be some time before I know that. My family did not believe in such privilege. Like many intellectuals, my father approved of the revolution, and as a boy I thought it a good and necessary thing, a blow for equality. We never expected it to eventually devour us, too, of course."

She did not know what to say. She had thought that she knew all of the mysteries, but she had not guessed that this final one lurked in his soul. The great cause he had believed in eventually took away all he held dear. It added a dark nuance to his boyhood experiences, and another snarl to the tangle of emotions that had driven him all his life.

The final confidence lightened his mood. He kissed her cheek. "Such things are not so important anymore. I have other things to occupy my thoughts now."

"What things?"

"You, and the gift you have given me in your love. Without you, I would be bereft today. Empty, with one life over and no new one waiting. Instead I am glad it is finished. Relieved. We will build a new life together, anywhere you want. All that matters to me is that you are with me and that your love is mine."

"It is yours forever. Loving you makes me whole. If not for you, I would still be an orphan with no history or family. Even finding Jonathan could not have filled the void I once lived with. Only loving you did."

"We were both orphans, Diane. But that is over now. We will make our own family, and a new history."

Hearing the confidence and certainty in his voice moved her more than she could contain. Her heart swelled, filling with the promise their love offered.

"Diane, the night before the duel, when you came to me—that was very brave and generous. Telling me that you loved me—that broke through clouds in my heart that were dark and old. Until that night, I had not even realized how they dimmed the world."

It had not been brave. It had been necessary, for herself and her own heart.

He looked down with his body still pressed to hers. Night hid his expression, but she could feel his total attention on her.

He kissed her. "Thank you."

the SAINT

chapter I

~1823

Vergil's grudging appreciation of Jane Ormond's aria did not salve his anger one bit. He resented like hell that he couldn't have her thrown into Newgate Prison where she belonged.

She had costumed herself like a French queen from the previous century, but she appeared uncomfortable with the illusion. She held herself stiffly whenever she moved, as if she expected the high white wig to topple off or the padded, hooped gown to tip her over. The confidence of her voice contrasted with her physical awkwardness. Poses of professional self-possession contrasted with short strolls of vulnerability.

He was not fooled by her calculated charm. With her wide eyes and full lips and intimations of frailty, she affected the most dangerous type of innocence. It was the kind that prompted a man to want to lay down his life to protect it, but which provoked another, darker part to imagine stripping off her clothes and destroying it.

She moved in his direction, raising her head for the high notes of a vocal display. Her gaze met his. A flicker of curiosity passed, as if she perceived that he would not be here if duty did not demand it.

He knew that nothing in his appearance told her that. This gaming establishment had added staged shows to cater to men of his class. They took breaks from their gambling to eat in this salon and enjoy a concert of opera, or, later, entertainment of a much baser sort.

She looked longer than she ought, boldly meeting his inspection with one of her own. He suppressed the alarming combination of protective and erotic inclinations that those wide eyes summoned, by concentrating on all of the trouble that she had caused him the last two weeks.

Morton slid into the other chair at his table. Morton did look out of place with his bearish form and unfashionable beard.

"The girl is here," he said. "In a room in back. Miss Ormond brings her every night, to wait there while she sings. I spoke with the man at the door and he saw them come in together tonight."

Vergil rose. "Miss Ormond sings an art song after this aria. Let us do it now. We will have the girl out before she finishes." The unsuspecting Miss Ormond warbled on. "If she is smart, she will run for the coast when she learns her plans were foiled. As for the girl, we will bring her to the country to recover, and no one will be the wiser."

He was assuming, of course, that Miss Jane Ormond had not already sold the girl to the highest bidder. He narrowed his attention on the deceptively ingenuous face beneath the towering white wig. There was something intelligent in those eyes. No, she wouldn't have risked all of this for so small a prize as a virgin's price. Perhaps she had planned to ask for a ransom, but most likely her intentions were to sell the girl in marriage. Since she had served as the girl's maid and they had traveled from America together, she undoubtedly knew about the inheritance.

This all might have been avoided if Dante had been more alert. His own fault that, sending his brother to meet their ship, but whoever expected this chit of a maid to dare such a thing.

The seedy back corridor contrasted with the opulence of the dining salon. Morton gestured to a door tucked beneath a stairway. Vergil turned the handle.

He had visited singers' preparation rooms before and they were normally disasters of confusion. This tiny space had been carefully organized. A brace of candles sat on a small table that also held a mirror and containers of paint. Costumes and day clothes hung from a row of hooks on the wall. A chair crowded the shadows to the right of the table, and a young woman sat mending there with her needle and cloth held close to the flames.

"Miss Bianca Kenwood?"

She looked up in surprise and he immediately began calculating how much he would have to increase the bribe to Dante. She could well be a sweet girl, but Dante judged females by appearance, not character, and hers was not impressive. The brown wisps of hair escaping her cap looked more frizzy than curly. Her nose turned up at the end, which might have been charming if the nose had been less broad.

"Miss Kenwood, I am Laclere."

"Oh!"

"This is Morton, my valet. I have a coach behind the building and we will take you there at once. Your ordeal is over, and I assure you that no one will ever know about this unfortunate interlude."

"Oh! Oh, my . . ."

"If you will come at once, please. I will deal with Miss Ormond later. Right now it is best if we remove you from here."

"Oh, I don't think . . . that is . . ." She cowered back, making gestures of resistance and confusion. He bent toward her and smiled reassuringly. He noticed that her gown was of the most common sort, a gray simple broadcloth. Evidently she had no sense for fashion, either.

"Come, my dear. It would be best if we left before—"

"Who are you?" The voice asking the indignant question was feminine, melodious, and young.

Vergil pivoted to see Marie Antoinette standing in the doorway, hands akimbo on her little waist, the broad-hipped gown flaring out to span the threshold. "Well? Who are you, sir, and what are you doing here?"

Miss Kenwood leapt up and darted over to Miss Ormond, who embraced her protectively. So that was how it was. Of course she had befriended the girl. It wouldn't have worked otherwise.

"Your concert is finished?" he asked.

"The *lieder* are brief works. Now, if you would leave please. My sister and I—"

"Miss Ormond, this young woman is not your sister. She is no relation to you whatsoever. You may have convinced her to come with you, but your behavior has been nothing less than abduction and will be seen as such by the magistrate."

Miss Ormond eased the girl away, then pressed her gown so that she could squish into the room. The breadth of the ridiculous skirt forced Morton against the wall.

She crossed her arms over her chest. The gesture brought Vergil's attention to the upper swells of firm breasts crushed under the top of her stiff bodice.

"Which one are you?"

"Vergilius Duclairc, the Viscount Laclere. Miss Kenwood is my ward, but then you know that."

Her gaze drifted down, then up. "I know nothing of the sort."

Her poise, despite being caught at this crime, annoyed him to no end. "Do not think to play a game of wits with me, young woman. Your betrayal of the trust that made you her companion on the crossing is abominable. The danger and potential scandal to which you have subjected her these last weeks is inexcusable. I will not stand for any interference now. If you act quickly, you can be on your way back to America before daybreak, but I only make this concession for Miss Kenwood's sake."

She didn't even blink. She stepped forward until her flounces brushed his leg, and looked up in a considering, curious way. "Ah. You are one of those."

He stared her down. If she were a man, a good thrashing would be in order.

She glanced at the distraught girl, cowering against the doorframe. "It appears that it is over, doesn't it? Too bad, I really thought that I might pull it off." She gestured, and Miss Kenwood joined her while she began removing the garments from their hooks and folding them.

He stepped between them, took a gown from his ward's hands, and cast it aside. "We will leave now. If Miss Kenwood has belongings here or at your lodgings, I will send for them."

Miss Ormond smiled in a damned insolent manner. "Oh, you are most definitely one of those. Very sure of yourself. A man who sets his course and always knows it is the right one. I was warned that this country has a lot of men like you, men who are positive that they never make mistakes."

He felt his face flush at this soiled dove's presumption. Enough. He took a gray broadcloth arm in his hand.

Miss Ormond shifted and blocked his retreat with the eternal span of her gown. Her warm, soft hand covered his and gently pried his fingers loose. The gray broadcloth slipped away.

Blue eyes looked up with mocking delight. "Well, this time you *have* made a mistake, Vergilius Duclairc, Viscount Laclere. In fact, you have got it all backward. She is not Bianca Kenwood. *I am.*"

He had a moment of incomprehension before the meaning of her words struck. Intimations of trouble flurried through his mind, a light snow of foreboding that suggested fairly simple arrangements had just become dangerously complicated. He glanced to the timid gray wren kneading her hands together, and then at the self-confident, painted bird of paradise, and wondered how Dante would react to this shocking development.

Thwap. Thwap, thwap.

The riding whip slapped against the high boot of the Viscount Laclere while he paced in front of the fireplace.

Bianca embraced Jane on the chaise longue, patting her shoulder. Across the drawing room, the Countess of Glasbury, the viscount's sister, blinked with drowsy dismay in her Oriental-style green dressing gown.

Bianca thought it had been very rude of Vergil Duclairc to rouse the countess from her sleep when he dragged Jane and Bianca here to the countess's town home. If he would stop brooding and pacing she could clear this up in a snap and they could be gone.

Thwap. Thwap.

"You don't plan to use that do you?" Bianca asked. Her voice cracked the tense silence that had ensued with the end of his explanation to the countess about where he had found his missing ward after two weeks of searching.

He pivoted in midpace and glared at her. He was a tall, lean, well-framed man in his middle twenties, with startling blue eyes and wavy dark hair dishevelled in the current fashion. Attractive, actually. Perhaps even handsome when he wasn't scowling, but then she wouldn't know.

"The whip," she said. "You don't plan to use it? I should tell you that I am twenty years old and Jane is twenty-two, which makes us far past the age for such things. Although my aunt has a maid who was courted by an Englishman who told her that there are quite a few men who whip grown women here in England, which I found very peculiar, and others, it turns out, who actually want women to whip them, which I don't think makes any sense at all."

The countess gasped. She appeared fully awake suddenly.

Vergil turned to his sister with strained forbearance. He threw out his arm toward the chaise longue in a gesture that said, *"See?"*

"Really, Miss Kenwood," the countess said with a wavering smile. "Of course my brother has no intention of . . . of . . ."

Vergil's lids lowered as if there were no "of course" to it. He clasped his hands behind his back and studied her severely. "My brother came to meet your ship in Liverpool. How did you miss him?"

Bianca considered whether to use the elaborate history of misadventures that she had concocted in the event things ever went this wrong. It suddenly struck her as very thin.

She examined the blue eyes piercing her. Aunt Edith had said that the English aristocrats were an overbred, indolent people, and a bit stupid, and Bianca had counted on that being accurate. Unfortunately, this one appeared the exception, at least with regards to the last descriptive. He didn't seem likely to be bought off with confused tales of hapless innocence.

"There was a sailor on board who helped us remove our trunks and find a hired coach before anyone came and called for us."

"You befriended a sailor?" The countess glanced askance at her brother, who briefly shut his eyes.

"Miss Kenwood, perhaps there has been a misunderstanding. Your grandfather's solicitor contacted a Baltimore attorney, a Mr. Williams, to handle this matter. He did come to speak with you, did he not? I was not misinformed, was I?"

"He most certainly came. He is a very nice man. In fact, he secured our passage on the ship."

"As he wrote to me that he would. Did he explain to you that a member of our family would meet you in Liverpool?"

"He explained it very clearly. My aunt would never have permitted me to come if she were not reassured that I would be met."

"So you admit that you disembarked on your own without waiting for an escort, that it was no accident that my brother missed you?"

"It was no accident. It was very deliberate."

For some reason her frankness left him speechless. He looked at her as if she were incomprehensible.

"I think it would be best if you sat, Vergil, so you do not fluster her by hovering like that," the countess said. "Then maybe we could discuss this calmly. I'm sure that Miss Kenwood has an explanation for everything."

Vergil sat on a small bench, but he still managed to hover in her direction all the same. "Do you have an explanation?"

"Of course." Jane had fallen asleep on her shoulder and the dead weight distracted her. Their embrace had unsettled the wig and she could feel it tilting askew. These old gowns were not designed for sitting, and the pads formed a platform all around her. The stays under her costume dug into her waist and side.

She felt a little ridiculous and very uncomfortable, and annoyed that this high-and-mighty viscount had not given her time to change or wash before hauling her into his coach.

"The explanation, Miss Kenwood. I should like to hear it."

"Actually, Mr. Duclairc, I really do not think that you would."

His eyes narrowed. "Let us try, anyway."

She tucked one leg up under her rump, to prop herself up more. The countess's lashes fluttered. The viscount cocked an eyebrow censoriously. Realizing that her dangling leg was uncovered to midcalf, Bianca smiled apologetically and pushed the skirt hem down.

"Mr. Duclairc, I was aware of the plans arranged for my visit here. I simply decided to make a few alterations. If Mr. Williams communicated with you about me, you may know that I lived with my great-aunt Edith more as her companion than her ward. I traveled extensively when my mother was alive, and learned to take care of myself. I am regarded as very mature for my years."

"He only wrote that your aunt is a bulwark of Baltimore society and that you are a well-bred young woman." His tone implied that Mr. Williams had some explaining to do.

"I know that my grandfather named you as my guardian in his will. It was a charming and quaint gesture. He probably wanted to cover the eventuality that I actually needed a guardian, which I obviously do not.

Besides, I am American, so I do not see how an English will can establish that kind of authority over me."

"I will be happy to explain that later."

She already knew the explanation. She just did not accept it. "At Mr. Williams's urging, I agreed to come here to see matters regarding my inheritance settled in person. I never actually agreed, however, to stay with your family." She omitted the minor point that she had never disagreed, either, and had boarded that ship with both nice Mr. Williams and old Aunt Edith assuming that was exactly what she would do.

"With whom did you intend to visit, dear?" the countess asked. "See, Vergil, I told you there was an explanation. She expected other friends to meet her and they didn't show."

A peculiar wariness entered his expression. "Is that so, Miss Kenwood?"

"No," she admitted. Oddly enough, he looked relieved. "It is my intention to live by myself, with Jane as my companion. The offer of accommodations at your country home . . . well, I would feel like an intruder and besides, I prefer city life. And, of course, I did not want to have to delay my lessons."

"Lessons?"

"Singing lessons. That is why I have come. To procure professional training for the opera. My instructors in Baltimore have told me that they have taken me as far as they can, that I need better teachers. My plan is to arrange for that in London until the inheritance is settled, and then use the income to go to Milan."

The viscount sighed, rose, and paced to the fireplace again. The countess leaned her dark-haired head forward confidentially. "I think it is wonderful that you are devoted to your music. How accomplished! When we come up to London for the season, I'm sure that we can find a voice master. I know quite a few people in the art and music circles."

"Thank you for the kind offer, but I do not want to wait for the season, whenever that is. This really was my purpose in coming, and I intend to start right away."

Vergil rubbed at shallow creases between his eyebrows. "Miss Kenwood, I do not want to embarrass you, but I need to know how you came to be singing in that establishment."

"Vergil . . ."

"No, Penelope, it is best to have it out now and learn exactly what we face. Miss Kenwood?"

"Well, hiring that coach all the way to London was very expensive. It cost most of what I had with me. When we arrived in London I found employment singing, to support us until I could obtain money from my grandfather's estate."

"How very clever and capable of you," Penelope said.

Vergil looked as though "clever" and "capable" were virtues he neither admired nor expected. "Are you aware of the reputation of that place? Do you know what occurs on that stage after your arias?"

"We never stayed afterward. It seemed a common music salon to me."

"Very common. We can only hope that your costumes obscured your identity and that no one who meets you in the future recognizes you from this last week. It is scandalous for a woman to sing on a stage of any sort, but one like that, painted and frilled as you are . . ." He made a gesture toward her gown, her face, her wig.

"My mother sang onstage, Mr. Duclairc, and these are her costumes."

"I'm sure that she was a lovely singer," Penelope inserted quickly.

"Stop humoring her, Pen. That may be acceptable in the United States, but not in England, Miss Kenwood."

"Since I am not English, that doesn't bother me. I think it would be best if we avoided any social connection so that you are not embarrassed by my performances, don't you?" She forced a smile, to encourage him to accept the undeniable logic of it. "Since you have executed your duty by assuring that I am safe, please return Jane and me to our lodgings now."

"You will remain here tonight. Your belongings will be sent for, and I will have the proprietor of the gaming rooms informed that your performances have ended."

"I must decline your offer, Mr. Duclairc. I will not impose on your sister, and I intend to continue my employment. As a singer, I need experience with audiences and—"

An autocratic slice of his hand cut her off. "No. Absolutely not. You will not live independently of mature chaperons, nor will you parade yourself on a stage. While you are here you are my responsibility, and you will conform to the behavior expected of a young lady."

Bianca glared back at the intractable, towering viscount. That an old miser, whom she had never met, could complicate her life with a few scratches of a pen struck her as intolerable. She hadn't expected the viscount to find her so quickly. She hadn't planned to have this conversation until she was ready for him.

Vergil crossed his arms over his chest. The pose made him look very tall and powerful. It was the sort of stance a king might take when he ordered someone's head chopped off.

"Tomorrow my sister will accompany you and your maid to the country," he intoned, stating the lord's will. "You will not speak of this experience, not even to the other members of my family. As far as the world is concerned, you were met at the ship and have been in our protection from the start."

"If you take me out of London, you do so against my will. As you noted earlier, that is abduction. I, too, can complain to the Justice of the Peace."

He faced her coolly. "It is legally impossible for me to abduct you, Miss Kenwood. I am your guardian. Until you turn twenty-one or marry, you are under my complete authority. Pen, have the housekeeper show Miss Kenwood and Miss Ormond to their chambers."

Dismissed like a naughty schoolgirl, Bianca found herself and a drowsy Jane handed over to a woman in the corridor. Vexed that her plan had failed, and confused by this stranger's determination to take up a responsibility he surely could not want, she followed the woman up the stairs.

Something about the end of their confrontation troubled her. It wasn't until she reached the top landing that she found the vital omission. *Until you turn twenty-one or marry, you are under my complete authority.*

Or until she left England, of course. Right?

"Don't you think that you were a little too firm with her?" Penelope asked.

"Not at all." Vergil watched Bianca Kenwood tottering up the stairs on her dainty silk mules. The snow shower of foreboding had turned into a blizzard.

What a disaster.

"She is a stranger here, Vergil. Ignorant of our proprieties. No doubt, behavior is less formal in America."

"Don't believe it, Pen. She knew precisely what she was about." Which was doing exactly what she wanted, and guessing that the doing of it would induce him to wash his hands of her, so she could go on doing it.

He turned away, thinking that a glass of port was in order before he left. He needed to plan how to prepare his brother, and how to curb Miss Kenwood so that even a rake wouldn't be shocked by her.

Penelope touched his arm, stopping him. "It was kind of you not to say anything about how she addressed you, to understand it was only her naivete. All of those Mr. Duclaircs. She was embarrassed enough as it was, and you were quite generous. I'll explain it to her tomorrow."

Is that what Pen had seen in those big blue eyes? Naivete? Embarrassment? Normally his older sister was more astute than that, despite her good-natured optimism.

"Explanations won't be necessary, Pen. I will wager one thousand pounds that Miss Kenwood knows full well the proper way to address a viscount."

chapter 2

Vergil threw his soaked hat to his valet and tore at the knot of his cravat. "Whisky for both of us, Morton. After that journey, we need it. Then show Hampton up when he arrives."

Within ten minutes Morton had not only produced the spirits but also some cold fowl and cheese, built a low fire in the library, and gotten Vergil dry and presentable. Not that there was anyone to present himself to. Only a few rooms in the expansive London house were open anymore and, in addition to Morton, there were only two servants.

Nor did he have to be presentable for Julian Hampton. The family solicitor had seen him most unpresentable before. Still, the life he lived here in London demanded that appearances be maintained.

He sat by the fire, sipping his whisky with two ledgers on his lap. He already knew what these documents would show and what Hampton would say. The Duclairc family finances were not healthy. Only Vergil's careful stewardship this last year had prevented a total fall.

Recently, however, he had not had as much time to devote himself to such things. Other matters, more pressing and also more interesting, demanded his attention. Matters such as the one he had just attended to up north.

And now, of course, he needed to deal with the new matter of Bianca Kenwood. The potential complications that she presented made him close his eyes.

Her image flashed behind his lids, as it had too often the last two weeks. He saw her sitting in Pen's drawing room in that absurd costume, with one slender leg dangling down the front of the chaise longue and the silk mule arching her little foot just so. She had been most *unpresentable.* Also irredeemable and impertinent and sly and fascinating . . .

Fascinating? What a peculiar thought. Wherever did it come from?

"Mr. Hampton," Morton announced.

Julian Hampton entered, wearing his solicitor's face. He always did that when they met for business reasons. Since he was an old friend it was probably necessary, especially when it came time to discuss bad news. Vergil had seen that expression a lot in the last year.

"Have you studied them?" Hampton asked, gesturing to the ledgers as he took a chair and accepted a glass from Morton.

"I expect that little has changed."

"A bit. Solvency beckons. If your sister would live at Laclere Park—"

"I cannot ask her to be that dependent."

"Or if Dante would live within his allowance—"

"He never has, so there is no hope there."

"You could consolidate the farms and lease the land."

"This is an old litany, Hampton, and you know my answers. My father and brother did not displace those families, and I will not, either."

"Well, at least you no longer live on the brink."

They were closer to the brink than even Hampton knew, in ways these ledgers would never reveal. However, Vergil had a plan to deal with that. Unfortunately, an essential part of the plan might cause trouble. The part named Bianca Kenwood.

Hampton smiled. That was never a good sign, especially when he had on his solicitor's face. "You might improve things the easy way. The traditional way."

"Yes, I expect that Fleur's father would be very generous. I should be grateful that my value has risen so much with my brother's death. With time, I expect that I will agree to marry. Right now, however, other entanglements make that impossible."

Hampton was not an expressive man, so the light of curiosity and concern that flickered in his eyes let Vergil know that he had said too much. "Can I be of assistance? I have some experience in negotiating my clients out of entanglements." He stressed the last word in a way that alluded to problems of a romantic nature.

The entanglement that Vergil found himself in would take more than Hampton's skill to unravel. "You are unsurpassed at that, and I would hand mine to you if I thought it would help. I can only imagine how you convinced the earl to release my sister."

"All men have secrets that they want to hide. The Earl of Glasbury simply had more than most. How is the countess faring?"

"She is happy enough, and has come to prefer those social circles that accept her."

"Her fall would have been far worse if not for you."

Vergil knew that. Through ostentatious correctness he had managed to blunt the impact of Pen's separation from the earl, and of Dante's various sins, and even partly rectified the age-old reputation of the Duclaircs for unconventional behavior and ideas. Instead of his family pulling him down, he had managed to keep them afloat. Barely.

"Are we done?" Vergil asked, lifting the ledgers.

"It appears that you are."

He dropped them on the floor. "You can explain the sad details another day. Tell me what you have been up to, besides advising fools like myself."

"If all my clients were so foolish as you, I would starve."

Hampton's expression dropped its seriousness and he became the friend whom Vergil valued.

It turned out that he had been up to very little. Hampton did not seek out society much, and participated on the periphery when he did. Women thought him brooding and mysterious, and men considered him proud and dull. With his dark hair and sharp, perfect features, Hampton looked like a figure drawn in pen and ink by an illustrator. The problem for most people was that no captions came with him.

"St. John has come up to London," Hampton said. "Burchard and I are meeting him at Corbet's tomorrow. Witherby and the others will probably come too. Since you are back from wherever it was you went, why not join us? The Dueling Society will be whole again."

He was referring to the group of young men who had been meeting in Hampstead at the Chevalier Corbet's fencing academy for five years now. Vergil had not partaken of that sport or company in months.

His absence was all the odder because he had been the hub that had brought all those spokes together. He had known Hampton since boyhood, and become friends with Cornell Witherby while at university. Adrian Burchard, an earl's son, had been found in the circle of the peerage. Even Daniel St. John, the shipper, had been appended to the Dueling Society through Vergil because of St. John's friendship with Penelope.

"I wish that I could, but I must find Dante and bring him to Laclere Park. There are matters to attend there."

"Burchard will be disappointed. He has been looking for you, to discuss something that he will not divulge. I assume that means it is political."

If Adrian Burchard was looking for someone, he would soon find the man. Adrian was the last person Vergil wanted curious about his activities. "I will write and invite him down to visit. I expect to be there for several days."

"Why not invite Witherby as well? The prolonged absence of the countess from London has turned him melancholy."

"Perhaps it will inspire him to write another ode. Witherby will have to bide his time. Miss Kenwood has arrived in England, and Penelope has taken her to the country for a long visit."

"Any trouble there?"

It wasn't clear whether Hampton referred to Bianca Kenwood or the way Cornell Witherby had been dancing attendance on Penelope. Although the former promised nothing but trouble, Vergil could also do without the latter. Having a good friend develop a passion for your older sister, especially when that sister was estranged from her husband and lonely and vulnerable—it was the kind of situation that could ruin a friendship.

"No trouble at all. Miss Kenwood is a delight. I look forward to your meeting her."

That was how entangled his entanglements had become. He was lying to a man he had known half his life.

Hampton turned the conversation to politics. As they talked of Whigs and Tories, of violent demonstrations and of the adjustments still occurring after the death of the last Foreign Minister, Vergil's mind dwelled on the private matters waiting in the country.

Over and over there appeared in his head the image of a young woman dressed like a French queen, challenging him with too much self-possession, and of a pretty leg dangling below a hem that had been hiked improperly high.

"I still don't understand your impatience," Dante said. He flicked cigar ash out the coach window. "No reason to drag me back from Scotland. She doesn't come of age for almost a year."

That was an eternity by the way Dante calculated his calendar with women. Normally he would court, seduce, bed, and discard two mistresses in that time. Vergil studied his younger brother's beautiful face and limpid eyes and dark brown hair. Dante's history with females had almost been inevitable with features like that. Vergil had seen ladies of the highest breeding lose their breath when Dante approached.

"The season starts well before her birthday, and with Charlotte coming out, we can hardly leave Miss Kenwood here while we all pack off for town. You need to be married before then, not just engaged."

"Why? Do you think some fortune hunter will cut me out?" Dante's tone implied the notion was preposterous.

No, I think that if she is married we can prevent her from going up to London at all, if necessary, Vergil thought. The very notion of Bianca Kenwood in polite society, calling dukes and earls "Mister," and announcing that she intends to study performance opera, was enough to ruin his spirits on this late August day.

But Dante's question also pricked at the foreboding that had continued plaguing him since he had left Penelope's house that night. It might be best for Dante to get this over while the field was clear.

Dante looked him squarely in the eyes. "We are almost there. Don't you think that you should tell me now?"

"Tell you?"

"You haven't said much about this Miss Kenwood, whom I am expected to marry. I find that suspicious. After all, you have met her. We both know that I have no choice except to agree to this, but if warnings are in order, you are running out of time."

"If I have not described her in detail it is because it would be indelicate to do so. This is not one of your racehorses."

"You have not described her at all."

"Very well. She is of middling height and slender, with blue eyes."

"What color hair?"

Damned if he knew. What color hair had been hidden by that ridiculous wig?

"Just how bad is she?"

Vergil had fully intended to warn Dante, but had failed to come up with the right approach. A tinge of guilt colored his reflections while he debated the appropriate one now. After all, he had practically forced his brother into this. Not that Dante had resisted much once he learned that over five thousand a year came with her.

"It is not her appearance. Her manner, however . . ."

"Is that all? Just like you to get stuffy about a few *faux pas.* What did you expect? She is an American. Pen will shape her up in no time."

A few *faux pas* did not do Bianca Kenwood justice, but he let it pass. "Of course. However, even so, she is . . . distinctive."

"Distinctive?"

"One might even say unusual."

"Unusual?"

"And perhaps a bit . . . unfinished. Which can be remedied, of course. Pen has her in hand even as we speak."

Dante peevishly looked out the coach window at the passing Sussex countryside. Vergil hesitated continuing, but they *were* almost there and he *was* running out of time. "She may need a strong hand. She is a bit independent, from what I could tell."

His brother's gaze slid back to him. "Independent, now."

"She has certain notions. It is her youth, and they will pass."

"It would help immensely if you would balance some of this by adding how beautiful she is."

No doubt. The problem was, he didn't know if she was beautiful. He only remembered big eyes, interesting because of that intelligent and spirited spark in them.

What else could he offer? All that stage paint had been obscuring. The possibility of a lovely complexion, but who could be sure until he saw her washed? A nice form, but that may have been the costume. The suggestion of an underlying sensual quality . . . not something one noted about a brother's future bride.

"Damn it, if she is vulgar I won't go through with it, Vergil. Nor should you want me to. Aside from the fact that she would reflect on me and this family, I could hardly avoid her completely once married, even living in town and leaving her out here, which is how I plan to arrange things. And until you marry Fleur, which you are taking your damn sweet time doing, and set up your nursery, I am your heir and this American could end up the Viscountess Laclere."

Vergil did not need his younger brother to list the pitfalls dotting this path. Pits much deeper and more numerous than Dante imagined. A honeycomb of them. If he could think of an alternative, he would use it, but two weeks of debating options always led him back to the same conclusion. Bianca Kenwood needed to be bound to this family with unbreakable chains.

Dante bit his lower lip and again looked out the window from beneath heavy lashes. "The income from her funds will be mine? As trustee, you will not interfere? And my allowance continues until the wedding, enhanced as we agreed?"

"Of course. I also promise to continue management of the financial investments, as you requested. The income from the funds is secure, but the others require occasional oversight, and I know that you hate such things."

Dante gestured dismissively. "Sordid and nettlesome things. I doubt they are worth the trouble. Sell them out or hold them, as you judge best. After how you scraped us through when Milton died, I would be a fool to question you."

They rode in silence through the oak and ash forest filling the back of Laclere Park. Vergil much preferred this approach to the broad sweep of landscape facing the front, and always instructed his coachman to take it. Normally it served as a transition space for him, a few miles in which to prepare himself for the role of the Viscount Laclere and the responsibilities that it entailed.

He had first come this way when summoned by news of Milton's death, choosing the longer route in order to delay that arrival, churning with conflicting emotions and spiking resentments at the changes in his life suddenly decreed by his older brother's demise.

It was in this forest that he had finally accepted the new reality and its attendant restrictions. Little had he guessed how complicated his brother's death would make his life. Along with restrictions, mysteries and deceptions had waited for him at journey's end.

Dante suddenly leaned toward the window. He squinted. "What the . . ."

"Is something wrong?" He pushed Dante's head a bit and stuck his own to the opening.

"There, over in the lake. Wait, some trees are in the way. Now. Isn't that Charlotte?"

The trees thinned while they began to pass the lake. Two women bathed in the water, laughing and splashing. *Naked,* for all intents and purposes, since their chemises had gone transparent from the water. Hell, yes, it was their younger sister, Charlotte, with that maid, Jane Ormond.

The water broke and a third feminine body rose up. A soaked chemise adhered to her skin and obscured little. Pretty shoulders . . . tapered back . . . nipped waist . . . graceful hips . . . finally the tops of enticing rounded buttocks slid into view. Long blond hair fanned in the eddies and then sealed to her body in a thick drop from a well-formed head.

Her slender arms began skimming the water's surface, creating waves in the direction of her playmates. The other two squealed and started a massive counteroffensive of splashes, sending sprays of water all around her until she appeared like a vision emerging out of a misty dream.

A shriek of joyful protest reached them. Laughing, she turned to run from the assault.

Vergil could not be sure that those large blue eyes actually saw the passing coach with its two stunned occupants. But she paused, and one arm slid across her breasts and the other hand drifted to the shadowed triangle just above her thighs. For the briefest instant before she turned and knelt, she assumed the pose of a Botticelli Venus, a goddess lovely of face and luscious in form, dripping wet, still virginal and modest, but ripe and waiting. The combination of protective instincts and erotic suggestions that he had experienced in the gaming hall surged with force.

He and Dante found their sense at the same instant. They straightened and sank back into their seats.

His brother eyed him with suspicion. "Who was that?"

"I cannot be certain, but I think it was Miss Kenwood."

Dante closed his eyes and rested his head against the seat's back. "Let me make sure that I understand my position, Vergil. I am required to marry *that*? I am to be sacrificed on the altar of the god of financial stability and be forced to take as my lifelong partner *that* female we just saw? A girl so *distinctive, unusual,* and *independent* that she bathes almost naked in full view of a road, in broad daylight, and influences our sister to do the same thing? You intend to coerce me, if necessary, by threatening my allowance? *She* is the bride whom you have chosen for me?"

"Yes." There really was nothing else to say.

Dante held his pensive pose a moment longer. His eyes opened. Their limpid warmth glowed. A very male smile slowly broke. "Thank you."

"Very good, Pen. *Very* good."

Penelope flushed an even deeper pink than the hue her skin had assumed while he told his tale. "Do not blame *me.* I certainly did not countenance such a thing. She has been the most gracious guest. Her behavior has not been untoward. Well, to my knowledge, at least."

She added the last with a little grimace. Penelope was smart enough to recognize that today's lark indicated that she might not know the full extent of Miss Kenwood's activities. Vergil imagined a whole string of scandalous episodes played out under the unsuspecting Penelope's nose.

"Our time here has gone swimmingly well."

"Under the circumstances, *swimmingly* is not the best choice of words, Pen."

She hung her head, embarrassed at failing at her charge. He patted her shoulder reassuringly. She simply did not have it in her to see the worst, and was always too understanding.

Bianca Kenwood probably had seen immediately what she had in Penelope, and had taken advantage of it.

What was needed for Miss Kenwood was an old harpy of an aunt whose force of will would brook no defiance, whose steely gaze would make young women tremble, whose strict admonishments would summon immediate submission.

Unfortunately, no such aunt existed.

"Perhaps bathing thus is common in America."

"*Please,* Pen."

"I will speak with her, and give Charlotte a good scolding."

"You will do no such thing."

"You intend to instead? Oh, Vergil, I wish that you would not. She gets a peculiar look on her face whenever your name is mentioned. I suspect that she sees you as a gaoler, and if, on meeting you again, the first thing you do is lecture on behavior . . ."

"I won't say a word about it. No one will. Not to Charlotte, either. To mention it would be to admit Dante and I had witnessed it." He didn't even want to contemplate *that* confrontation. To mutually acknowledge what had occurred would create an impossible awkwardness and a difficult . . . intimacy. "We are left with no choice but to ignore it. I will speak with Charlotte in more general terms about not permitting herself to be influenced."

Dante joined them, looking happy and refreshed in a change of clothes, perfectly pressed and exquisitely tailored. His expression glowed expectantly beneath carefully mussed hair, slightly long in the romantic fashion.

"It was kind of you to join us for a few days," Penelope said, rising to give him a kiss.

"One misses the family sometimes, Pen. In fact, I shall probably stay, oh, about a week. Yes, a week should do it." He cast Vergil a wink that made Penelope frown curiously.

Vergil returned a reproachful glance. Penelope did not know about their plans for Miss Kenwood. Also, for some reason, his brother's self-confidence rankled him.

"A whole week? That is wonderful, Dante, and very kind. I know how you hate the country unless there is good sport."

"Well, Pen, there is sport and then there is sport. I'm told Verg has bought a new horse that needs breaking and I felt obliged to help him, since I have such a hand with the animals and it is a gift to me besides."

"A new horse? Vergil, you didn't tell me."

"It arrives in a few days," he muttered. Clever Dante. Enjoying his metaphor and getting a horse in the bargain. Not such a bad metaphor. Miss Kenwood did not really strike one as unfinished so much as unbroken. Just like Dante to size a woman up in a few seconds from seventy yards, and delight in the challenge awaiting him. No wonder he looked so insufferably content.

The filly in question joined them shortly, arriving with Charlotte in a faint rustle of petticoats. Charlotte looked charming as usual, her willow-thin elegance still softened by childish innocence. Beside Charl's dark hair and white skin and pale pink dress, Bianca Kenwood appeared a bit of a country miss.

Her blue dress was a little dated and plain. Her skin bore a light, unfashionable tan, but his sense of its flawless beauty had been correct. Her golden blond hair was coiled into a simple knot that emphasized the feminine but firm jaw outlining the bottom of her heart-shaped face. She hardly fit the definition of a fashionable beauty, but she possessed a singular prettiness and exuded health and carried herself with mature grace.

Dante studied her with calculating eyes during the few moments before Penelope called him over for an introduction. That examination made Vergil uncomfortable. Suddenly he felt soiled by this business. Ridiculous. Such things were arranged all of the time, and usually with less subtlety.

Dante advanced on his prey. His success with women resided less in pursuit than in magnetism. A lady had once blurted out to Vergil that when Dante looked in a woman's eyes, she felt as if he could see her soul, and his attention absorbed the breath out of her body.

If so, Miss Bianca Kenwood's soul was not easily observed. She took Dante's greeting with ease and didn't appear the least bit breathless. Vergil could not help but admire her poise, even though the plan had been for her to fall in love at the first sight of Dante.

"And you remember Vergil," Penelope added quickly, gesturing in his direction.

"I could hardly forget Mr. Duclairc. I am delighted to see you again. Perhaps before you leave we might have some conversation."

"Of course, if you wish it."

Oh, she wished it. She had been saving speech after speech for two weeks now. She had hardly buried her resentment of the imperious interference that had sent her here.

She realized that she was glaring at him, and that everyone else was watching her do so.

"You are finding your stay pleasant?" Dante asked, guiding her toward the settee.

"Very pleasant, thank you."

He sat beside her, giving her his full attention. He was a handsome man, but a little fine in form and face, as if God, in sculpting the bones of his older brother, had used up the best materials and then had to make do. Beautiful brown eyes regarded her from beneath thick lashes. A spark of inappropriate familiarity glowed in them.

Yes, they had seen. She had argued with Charlotte that no one had looked out the carriage that passed. In truth, she thought that she *had* seen faces peering at her for a moment, but when nothing was said during the hours since their return, she just assumed . . .

"So you are named after the Italian poet," she said, very discomforted that Vergil Duclairc had gazed upon her practically naked body. Oddly enough, the fact that his brother had also done so didn't bother her much at all.

"It was my father's unfortunate idea. He fancied himself an epic poet and named his sons after the great ones. Our eldest brother was Milton."

"It might have been worse. He could have chosen your names from among the heroes and not the authors."

Charlotte giggled. "That would have been horrible. Ulysses and Aeneas and such."

"Or he could have moved into his fascination with the Arthurian tales sooner than he did," Dante agreed. "Lancelot, Gawain, and Galahad."

They played with that awhile, Penelope joining in. The man at the window did not, but Bianca sensed him following the banter with more interest than his occasional look indicated.

She could see her adversary clearly from her position. He cut a fine figure, tall and lean, but with shoulders and legs that suggested more strength than obviously visible. He did not scowl now and, yes, he was quite handsome in a strong-boned, harshly chiseled way. The blue eyes still startled, piercing out from beneath dark eyebrows.

They pierced now, catching her looking at him. She turned her attention to Dante, managing, she hoped, not to flush. She had the uncomfortable sensation that in that glance the viscount was remembering what he had seen by the lake.

Dante had been saying something to her. She responded with a question of her own, falling back in her ill ease to the sort of small talk typical at home. "And what do you do?"

Total silence faced her.

"Do?" Dante repeated after a ten count.

"Your brother sits in Parliament, as I understand it. What is your occupation?"

Charlotte giggled. Vergil's jaw looked more set than usual, but a glint appeared in his eyes while he turned his full attention on his brother.

Dante smiled. "I am a gentleman."

"I would never suggest otherwise, but how do you employ yourself?"

"When my brother says that he is a gentleman, he does not beg your question, Miss Kenwood. He answers it," Vergil said.

In other words, being a gentleman meant that one had no gainful employment. The refined young man beside her suddenly appeared as foreign as the Indians she had seen on occasion when her mother toured the towns near the frontier. This was another example of what Aunt Edith had meant when she had warned that Bianca would find this country familiar in some ways, but very odd in others.

"Surely you have gentlemen in the United States," Penelope said.

"We have men of great wealth and position. There are estates as large as this. But a man who does not work . . . well, it is considered almost sinful."

She immediately wished that she hadn't put it quite that way, even though such indolence was evidence of a serious fault in character. She had no desire to insult these people, three of whom she had no argument with.

The one with whom she did have an argument broke the awkward silence. "How quaint. But then your country is young still."

Coming from any of the others, she would have let it pass.

"Old England is learning that there is strength in youth."

"You refer to our last war. A minor skirmish. It would have ended differently if Bonaparte did not occupy us as well."

Somehow, barely, she kept a civil tone. "My father died in that skirmish, Mr. Duclairc."

Another thick silence fell. Penelope smiled weakly and rose. "Why don't we go in to dinner?"

Dante demanded Bianca's attention during the meal. The viscount did not speak much. She looked over several times to find him scrutinizing her, as if he wondered what he had. Nothing but trouble, she wanted to warn him. You really should send me packing at once.

She had every intention of cornering him after dinner in order to make that clear, but Vergil excused himself as soon as they returned to the drawing room. Dante stayed, however, and joined them for cards.

He complimented her play far more than her skill deserved. With familiarity and the passing hours, his smiles assumed an unsettling warmth. She began to get suspicious that Vergil was avoiding her, and using Dante as a distraction.

"Where is the viscount?" she finally asked Charlotte. "Perhaps he would like to take my place here."

"He is in the library, I expect. Or his study."

She rose. "Excuse me. I will invite him to join us."

She did not wait for permission, but walked from the drawing room and aimed down the corridor for the library.

He was there, sitting at the desk and poring over some papers in a folio. He glanced up at her entrance and rose.

"You appear startled to see me. Have I done this wrong? Am I supposed to apply for an audience?" she asked.

"Of course not. I assumed that my brother and sisters would keep you entertained this evening, that is all."

"Cards do not amuse me long if the hands are thrown to me. If we were playing for money, I would have already won your brother's entire fortune. I decided to give his pride and generosity a rest."

"He is only trying to make you feel welcome. However, I am glad that you sought me out. I want to apologize for my careless comment in the drawing room. I should have been more sympathetic to the possibility that you suffered in the war. I did not intend to demean your father's sacrifice."

The sincerity of his expression disarmed her. He did not appear nearly as stern as was normal for him.

"Perhaps now you understand why I do not welcome a long visit in this country, Mr. Duclairc, and why I do not want to partake of the society for which your sister tries to prepare me. I want to return to London so that I can tend to my affairs there as quickly as possible."

"The war is long over, Miss Kenwood. Our countries are friends again. As to your affairs, I am tending to them for you." He said it with a firm smile that indicated he considered that particular direction of conversation ill-advised.

"You are convincing me that I made a mistake in coming to England. I should have followed my first inclination and told Mr. Williams to have the investments that I inherited sold out."

"That cannot be done. Most of it is in trust. Short of petitioning the Chancery Court, a very lengthy process that would take years, it is impossible to break the terms."

"So he explained. My second inclination was to have him arrange to send the income to me in Baltimore."

"Then why didn't you? Especially if you blame us for your loss?"

"As I explained in London, I had reasons for coming."

"Yes. Your opera lessons." His tone managed to convey relief that those plans were now dead.

It would take more than this man's disapproval to kill them. They were very much alive, and she was desperately impatient to progress with them.

"Whatever my reasons, I am in England for only a short spell and I have interests that cannot be satisfied while I am in this house. I do not accept your interference. I do not need a guardian."

"Considering how I met you, I think it is obvious that you do. Today has done nothing to change my belief in that."

He was referring to the lake. Nothing in his expression really changed, but a provocative ripple eddied from him to her. It entered her body and shivered down her limbs. Yes, he had seen her in that soaked chemise. Despite his dispassionate demeanor, he was seeing her in it again right now.

For an instant, lights entered his eyes that said he knew that she knew. That acknowledgment added a dangerous nuance to his masculinity. She suddenly felt at a disadvantage and had to struggle to regain her indignation.

"I fail to understand why you are so determined to take on the trouble of me."

"Your grandfather's will gave the responsibility to the Viscount Laclere. He had intended it to be my brother, but since he did not change the will after Milton's death, it falls to me. I do not shirk my duties, no matter how troublesome they may be."

"I relieve you of the duty. Now, I demand that you allow me to leave for London in the morning."

"No."

She waited for more, but nothing else came. That one word was his entire response. No.

She glared at him, searching for a way to win this stupid battle. He gazed back like a general who knew he had the superior army.

She turned on her heel. In a few days she expected her reinforcements to arrive. She looked forward to throwing them at him.

"Miss Kenwood, if you are returning to the drawing room, please tell Charlotte that I would like her to join me here before she retires."

Bianca mounted the steps and strolled her way through the huge Gothic-style house, to her room. It was the largest and most luxurious bedchamber that she had ever used, with a gilt-framed mirror and heavily carved furniture.

Jane moved toward her, to begin unfastening her gown, chattering away with gossip about the servants and tenants. That lower world sounded a lot more fun and interesting than the high one in which Bianca lived out her days.

The last two weeks had felt like two months. They took walks. They arranged flowers. They exchanged visits with neighbors she didn't know. They talked about fashions and who was who in society. All the while Pen instructed the American savage on the proper address and acceptable behavior here in England.

Bianca had gotten to where she envied the servants who polished the silver. Finally she had arranged a few ways to break the monotony for herself.

Charlotte arrived just as Bianca drew on her batiste dressing gown. It had been a short meeting with her brother.

"He didn't say one word about the lake." She scooted onto the bed while Jane began brushing Bianca's hair. "Actually, he wanted to talk about you."

"Me?"

"Asked what you had been up to. He did not put it that way, of course. He inquired if you were content and occupying yourself."

Why, the intruding . . .

"I think that he knows about the lake and blames you, and wanted to know if you had done anything else scandalous."

The arrogant, self-righteous . . .

"Then he gave me a lecture. How you were raised differently and permitted more freedoms than is proper, and how I am not to be influenced by you to do things that aren't proper. I counted at least ten propers before he had finished. I had to promise him to behave very correctly while you were here." Charlotte giggled. "I think that you have my saint of a brother very concerned."

Bianca didn't know what to say. She *had* been raised differently, and permitted more freedoms than Charlotte would ever know, but there had been nothing improper in any of it, just unconventional, even by America's standards. She also planned a life fated to be unconventional but not at all improper, although Vergil Duclairc would probably assume that it was.

Charlotte laid back on the big bed. "I am glad Dante came to visit. He doesn't much. He prefers London." She looked over slyly. "I am not supposed to know this, but I think that he has a mistress there. I have surmised this last year that my brother may be a rake. What do you think? Would Dante make a good rake?"

"I wouldn't know," Bianca said, but she guessed that Dante would make a magnificent rake. It also occurred to her that this rake had seen her almost naked and had spent the evening giving her intent looks and warm smiles.

"I always thought Vergil would make a good rake, too, so long as one never actually met him. He looks like he might be one, but of course he is *so* proper. He has been courting Fleur for over a year and I have never seen him do more than touch her hand."

Bianca had heard all about the perfect, ethereal, very wealthy Fleur, who was Vergil's presumed intended. They expected a visit from her and her mother soon.

She did not intend to be here when they came. "Charlotte, is this the only property that your family holds?"

"There are several others here in Sussex, but no one visits them except Vergil. They are not in the best repair. Father let some things go, what with his writing and then rebuilding this house. Vergil also has a manor up north. It was his portion from our mother."

"Do any relatives live at these other places?"

"There are none there, or any with whom we are close. Father was reclusive and we lost contact with them while he was alive. Milton was a bit odd too. Vergil isn't the least eccentric, but he has not revived the connections."

No close relatives. No aunts or female cousins on whom to foist an errant ward.

"I think that my brother likes you," Charlotte said.

Which brother? Bianca caught the impulsive question before it left her throat, shocked by the jolt of excitement that had accompanied it. "I am sure that he just felt obliged to entertain me."

"Dante rarely feels obliged to do anything. He let you win at cards and he kept smiling at you."

"You are mistaken, but if you are not and he is a rake, I am hardly flattered."

"Oh, you do not need to worry about *that.* He knows that you are Vergil's ward and our guest." She slipped off the bed. "I had better get some sleep. Dante is going to take us for a carriage ride tomorrow. It should be fun. He is a crack whip, and always drives fast."

"Will the viscount accompany us too?"

"You don't need to worry about him spoiling the fun. By the time we rise, he will have lived a whole day. He rides at dawn, and then tends to the estate affairs."

When she was gone, Bianca sat on the bed and embraced her knees.

So, Vergil Duclairc worried that Miss Kenwood might badly influence his sister. He had warned Charlotte to be on her guard. What would the saint do if he became convinced that Miss Kenwood was not just a little different, but quite unconventional, and a bit wild?

No other relatives to send her to. Too dangerous to keep around. No remedy but to sever all social ties and let her go her own way. It would be the only responsible decision for a very responsible brother.

She would have to make sure that this viscount concluded that her presence and influence were totally unacceptable.

"Jane, I want you to borrow a few garments from the servants for me. The male servants."

chapter 3

Vergil took the polished boots from Morton and pulled them on. He accepted the starched white linen and adroitly tied his cravat in a conservative knot. Morton held out a black riding coat.

These morning preparations were a routine at Laclere Park or in London, and Vergil performed them instinctively while his mind organized plans and duties. It still amazed him that he had no trouble abandoning certain details of these habits when circumstances demanded it.

Light had barely broken when he let himself out a side door and walked through the dew to the stables. He much preferred these silent, solitary rides at daybreak to the official circuits that he made with his estate agent later. It was one of the few habits continued from those free years as the second son. He could sometimes recapture that youthful belief in unfettered opportunity permitted by his insignificance back then. He could simply *be,* not the lord surveying his domain, but merely a man riding through the countryside, admiring its beauty and dreaming in time to its rhythms of life.

Sounds came from the stable. George, a lanky red-haired young groom, was laughing while a younger boy in breeches and a straw hat mumbled something. Together they were fitting the bridle on a chestnut mare.

George heard Vergil's bootstep and jumped back with a flushed face.

The younger boy merely stiffened. Vergil noted a familiar something in that slender back, and took in the peculiar way the breeches stretched over curving buttocks. He had seen this form before, rising all but naked out of water.

"Miss Kenwood, I see that you rise early too."

She turned with nonchalance, as if no one should be surprised to find her like this because she donned breeches every day. Maybe she did. Who would know? Pen, Charlotte, and Dante probably would not emerge from their rooms until noon.

"I thought that a morning ride would be pleasant." She fit the bit like she knew what she was doing.

"George offered to escort you? How chivalrous of him."

"I planned to ride alone."

"Well, we cannot have that at such an early hour. You can ride with me, however." He examined the mare. "You have made an error, George. If that is Miss Kenwood's animal, it will need a sidesaddle. Then you can prepare my horse. We will wait outside."

Bianca paced into the yard with him. He stepped back in the silver light and raked five and a half feet of trouble with his gaze.

Her cotton shirt bagged around her body, but managed to drape revealingly over the swells of her breasts. The breeches hung loosely from her thighs to the boots into which they were stuffed, but were loose nowhere else. The straw hat crushed low over her brow emphasized her eyes.

She looked thoroughly disreputable and provocative as hell.

He walked away and slapped his whip against his leg. The slight sting distracted him from the flaring impulse to . . . not something to contemplate and certainly not to name. "It will take George some time with the horses. Go back to your room and change your clothes."

Her lids lowered at his order. He expected her to refuse. What the devil would he do then? No one under his authority ever defied him, least of all a woman. Fortunately, she turned on her heel and strode off in the direction of the house.

He went back into the stable.

"Does Miss Kenwood ride alone often?" he asked George.

George shrugged. "Just the last few mornings, m'lord. Heard some noise in here last week, and found her saddling up that mare, so I helped, didn't I?"

"And the garments?"

"Showed up in them this morning. Makes sense, since she always rides astride. She be a good sort, just a little free-minded for these parts. They's different, them Americans. Talk like they know you right off." He bent to check a hoof.

"Yes, they are different. Do not let me suspect that you misinterpret that familiarity."

George shot him a glance of horror, as if the insinuation were too shocking to contemplate. Vergil took the mare's reins and led her out to the yard.

Miss Kenwood emerged from the house just as George brought

Vergil's gelding out. She had dressed in a violet riding habit of severe cut and little decoration. A tidy high-crowned hat perched on her sedate hairstyle, its brim skimming her eyebrows.

"Where were you planning to ride?" he asked after they had mounted.

"Oh, I just wander about."

He led the way into the park. She kept fussing with her position on her saddle, scootching this way and that while she frowned down at her legs.

"You are not accustomed to it?"

"I did not live on the edge of civilization. The dreadful, dangerous things are given to women in Baltimore too."

"Did you ride astride there?"

"Yes." She glanced a challenge at him, then grinned. "Aunt Edith forbade me to use a sidesaddle unless I just poked along, and I was not inclined to do that. She knew too many women who had fallen from one when doing serious riding."

"And what was the reaction when you rode astride through the city, with breeches and boots?"

"If I had been anyone but Edith's great-niece, some might have been scandalized. Her position is unassailable. As a young woman she was active in our war of independence. She knows all the great men from that time. If presidents pay calls on a woman, no one else is inclined to criticize her much."

"She sounds very interesting. It is a pity she did not accompany you on this journey."

"If she were not so old, she would have. She would be back there now, lecturing George on how he is your equal and should not grovel."

"England hardly needs to import radicals. We are growing plenty of our own. Nor did George grovel. He retreated because he knows it is suspect for a man to be alone in such a familiar demeanor with a young lady, especially at such an hour."

"I see. However, you are a man and now I am alone with you, aren't I? Is that suspect?"

The insinuation took him aback. Her mocking smile hinted that Miss Kenwood was not some naive schoolgirl who remained ignorant of what might occur between a man and woman alone together for hours.

"I am your guardian. Like a parent."

She broke into low peals of laughter, melodic like her voice. "Heaven spare me, Mr. Duclairc. With a father like you, I would have grown up to be the dullest of women."

"Are you implying that dull fathers make for dull daughters?" *Are you insinuating that I am a dull man, you vexing piece of baggage?* An inclination to show her just how undull he could be had been trying to poke into his awareness since he saw her in the stable.

"No, sir. I am thinking that strict fathers make for very narrow daughters."

"Your less orthodox upbringing did not leave you narrow, I assume."

She turned those big blue eyes on him for a long, knowing look, as if she could see inside him and identify the veiled, improper images creeping around the edges of his mind and alluded to by his impulsive, indelicate question. The impact of that naked gaze was so staggering that she might have caressed his thigh.

"I have had experience in the world, Mr. Duclairc, and that is why I am not narrow. When my father died, my mother needed to support herself and me, so she returned to singing. I was eleven at the time, and for the next six years we lived a peripatetic life, traveling part of the year."

Experience in the world. Bianca would have been seventeen before her mother died, a pretty girl traveling in the wake of a mother whose profession was sure to attract men.

"I would have thought that she would leave you with your aunt, and not drag you to strange cities and towns."

"*You* would, wouldn't you?" She implied he was so predictable as to offer no surprises whatsoever. "I wouldn't have it, not after just losing Father, and Mother needed someone to look after her. She was not a very practical woman. It was left to me to make sure that she got from one place to the other."

"An odd role to give to a child, surely."

"Not a child so long, and it wasn't planned. I found myself taking care of it because she was so bad at it."

Not a child so long. "Life must have become very dull when you went to live with your aunt."

"I was ready. Mother's death knocked the life out of me, and I needed time to sit in one place and sort things out. Only when Aunt Edith employed a music tutor for me did I begin to feel normal again."

Vergil pictured them, the precocious child and flighty mother, arranging subscription concerts in the churches and halls of rough towns, roles reversed while the little blonde girl negotiated for transport and managed their funds. Exciting perhaps, and obviously maturing.

Not a normal childhood, however. No hours of carefree play, and probably no friends. No protection or security except what she created for herself. He felt a little sorry for her and admired her strength, inconvenient though it promised to be.

Their wanderings took them to the southern edge of the lake and he began the route around it. Miss Kenwood appeared annoyingly indifferent at finding herself at the location of yesterday's indiscretion.

"Our family has lived here since Norman times," he explained, deciding he should impress her with the family history and prime her for Dante's attentions. "Both our name and the estate's derive from this water. Clear lake. Duclairc is a corruption of *du clair lac,* as is Laclere."

"Norman times. Back then, the ancestors of the Kenwoods probably lived in hovels."

"Well, money has a way of leveling such differences."

"What a democratic notion, Mr. Duclairc. Almost American."

He pulled onto a path leading to the farms. "You can stop that now. You have made your point."

"Stop what?"

"Mr. Duclairc."

"It is not intended to offend you. Aunt Edith made me promise to bow to no aristocrat, not even your king."

"Your diplomats conform when they are here, as do most visitors."

"I am not a diplomat. And Aunt Edith—"

"Yes, yes, the Revolution and all. If addressing me as Lord Laclere will bring the ghost of Washington down on you, you may simply call me Laclere."

"How generous of you. Then perhaps you should call me Bianca."

He would rather not. Really. Even vague familiarity with this young woman was breeding uncomfortable feelings in him. She was his ward and would soon be his brother's wife and he found her exasperating, to say the least. All the same, an alluring, disconcerting simmer flowed in him. Boiling bubbles broke to the surface on occasion, tiny little explosions not at all acceptable under the circumstances. Under any circumstances. To call her Bianca would only make another bubble pop each time he did so.

"I think that would be too familiar."

"Well, then, perhaps Laclere is too familiar as well." She cocked her head. "I know. I will call you Uncle Vergil. Despite what you say about a guardian being like a father, 'Papa' would be ridiculous."

Uncle Vergil, indeed. He glanced under that brim and caught a fleeting smile. She was deliberately teasing him and he kept rising to the bait.

Worse, her provocative ambiguities and sidelong glances gave her a very worldly air, and made that simmer relentless.

"Uncle Vergil, are we near the border with Woodleigh?"

"It is just over that hill. You can see the house from its top. Would you like to go up?"

She accepted. It did not miss Vergil's attention that she knew how to find the easiest path without his help.

• • •

She reached the crest of the hill that overlooked the fields leading to Woodleigh. In the distance she could see the gargantuan bulk of the classically inspired mansion that Adam Kenwood had built.

"It is very big, isn't it?"

"Yes." He said it quietly, but she heard a criticism. Too big. Too much. Vulgar in its mass, especially for a newly minted baronet. *Nouveau riche* from its foundations to its cornices. He must have been Adam's friend or her grandfather would have never made him guardian, but that did not spare the old financier from the judgment of this aristocrat who dated his lineage back to Norman times.

She did not resent that censure. In fact, she welcomed it. Adam Kenwood may have left her a fortune, but she hated him anyway. If he had bequeathed this house to her, she would have burned it to the ground. He had committed one great sin that she knew of, and she did not doubt that others shadowed his entire life.

She cantered down the hill and over the fields. Vergil pulled up alongside her when she stopped in front of the house.

"Help me to dismount, please."

"Miss Kenwood, your cousin inherited this property, and he has not returned from France yet. You should wait until he has taken up residence before you visit. The house has been closed for months, and there are only a few servants tending the property now."

"Actually, my cousin returned a week ago, but has gone up to London for a few days. Either help me down or I will jump and be ungraceful."

He helped her off the horse. "You intend to go in, don't you?"

"My cousin, Nigel, may have gotten the house and lands, but I was left my grandfather's private effects. I want to see what they are. Once you explain who I am and what my rights are, the servants will allow me to do so."

He accepted her plan more quickly than she expected, and talked their way in. He accompanied her to Adam Kenwood's study.

Bianca stood in the chamber's center and breathed in the scent of her grandfather's presence. Wainscoting covered the lower walls, and a huge desk angled off one corner. Some shelves held folios and ledgers, but other records had been heaped into wooden crates that lined one wall and surrounded a small trunk.

She felt Vergil watching her from the threshold.

"Did you know him well?" she asked.

"After he built Woodleigh, he formed a friendship with my older brother, Milton. With Milton's death, I came to know him fairly well."

"You have the advantage on me there. I knew there was the grandfather in England, but my parents never spoke of him. As I grew older I realized that this old man had left my father to live in poverty while he himself amassed this." She swept her arm to indicate the luxurious house.

Vergil strolled into the chamber and peered at the crates. "Your grandfather built a lot of wealth in shipping and other trade. During the early Napoleonic Wars, his ships were of great service to the government, and the king gave him his title of baronet. Like most such men, he planned for his son to be a gentleman and gave him the education for that. I gather that your father had other ideas and went to America."

"I think that his decision to go to America did not create their estrangement, but rather his decision to marry my mother. She was not a suitable wife for the son of a man clawing his way up in your society."

He pulled a folio out of a crate and flipped through it. "As I explained, such a profession carries a certain taint here."

"I suspect that it does everywhere. My mother was less tainted than most, in part because of her relationship to Aunt Edith. She stopped once she married my father. He served as a tutor, and she kept a proper house despite our circumstances. That was not good enough for this old man."

That folio went back, and after further inspection he lifted out another. "Well, he remembered you in the end."

"Unfortunately, the end came a little late."

"You sound bitter."

She did sound bitter. She could hear the resentment in her voice. "A tiny fraction of this inheritance would have spared my mother much grief, and probably saved her life. She died from a fever contracted while we traveled."

He looked up from the folio as if she had said something of singular interest. "I see. So now you will take revenge on Adam for her death by using his fortune to become a performer like the woman he repudiated."

His accusation made a little fury spin in her head. "You trivialize my purpose. I set my sights on an operatic career long before I heard of the inheritance." She surveyed the chamber again. "However, now that you point it out, there is a certain justice in using his money to become what he despised."

"It sounds more like a great joke than it does justice. Before you enjoy it too much, I should explain that one part of your knowledge about your grandfather is wrong."

"What is that?"

"From what he said to me, I am sure that he did not break with your father. Your father broke with him."

"I do not believe that."

"Believe what you choose, but that was Adam's memory of it."

It did ruin the joke, and the justice. It fractured the soul-chilling resentment that had formed in her heart while she watched her mother cough her life away in that rented lodging on the edge of the world.

"He only told you that so you would not think him cold and heartless."

"My opinion was not of great concern to him."

"Then he lied to himself, so he could die without guilt."

"Perhaps."

She looked at the records in the chamber. The truth was probably in them somewhere. She might find letters from her father. There could even be some from her mother, asking for help when she was widowed.

It should not really matter how it had been, but it did. If she was going to build a life on this man's wealth, she wanted to know whether she should be grateful or laughing while she did so.

"Is there any way to know what in here is mine?"

"His solicitor separated his papers. These crates contain the personal ones, while the estate accounts are on the shelves." He pointed to the small trunk. "I assume that the contents of his desk and anything of value are locked in there."

"I want to read these personal records. I will ask my cousin if I can visit and do so."

"It would be more convenient to move it all to Laclere Park. Then you could peruse the materials at your leisure. I will arrange for that."

"I am sure that my cousin will not mind if I do it here."

"I will mind."

She looked him right in the eyes. "There is no point in moving it twice. I will wait until I can send it all to my private lodgings in London."

He looked straight back. "You have no London lodgings, nor will you for a long time."

She did not expect it to be very long at all, but he hadn't realized that yet. "Fine, as a start, let us bring it to Laclere Park."

As they left the house, she noticed that he still carried a folio. He saw her glance curiously at it.

"There are some letters from my brother in this one. I hope you do not mind if I borrow it so I can read them."

"Not at all." It touched her that he wanted to do that. It was more sentimental than she expected of him. "When did your brother pass away?"

He helped her to mount her horse. "Just under a year ago."

"Perhaps there are other letters. When we get it all to Laclere Park, we can see."

As they paced their horses toward the fields, a fair-haired young man galloped toward them, hailing with his arm. He looked like a figure out of a fashion plate, with his elaborately tied cravat and beaver high hat and fashionable coat.

The young man pulled up his horse and whipped off his hat. "Miss Kenwood! A happy coincidence to see you again. To think that if I stayed in London another day as I had planned, I would have missed you."

Vergil didn't turn a hair at the *again.* "You must be Nigel Kenwood, my ward's cousin. I am Laclere."

"A pleasure to finally meet you, Lord Laclere."

"I would have called if I knew that you were in residence at Woodleigh. I thought that you were still in France. My apologies."

Nigel smiled at Bianca. They resembled each other a little. His eyes were the same blue and his hair the same gold. A nice-looking man, she had decided, except that his expressions hinted at a tendency toward moodiness.

"I have only been back a week. Just sorting through Woodleigh's affairs has occupied me, but life is settling down now."

"Then you must call at Laclere Park soon. I am sure that the ladies would be grateful. There are so few new faces in the country."

"Thank you. I shall do so."

Nigel smiled appreciatively at her again. Bianca smiled sweetly back. Vergil smiled thinly at the two of them.

She gave Nigel her rapt attention longer than necessary.

Thank goodness Vergil was an intelligent man. She had no intention of lying, just planting enough concern for him to decide not to risk sweet Charlotte to her influence.

They declined Nigel's offer of refreshments and took their leave. Vergil pulled up beside her. "You have met the new baronet before. You did not mention that."

"Didn't I? Several mornings ago I rode down to take a closer look at Woodleigh and he was out. It seemed only polite to stop and speak since he is my relative."

"Did he show you Woodleigh itself?"

Did you enter the house? Were you alone with him in his domicile? His expression remained so carefully impassive that she wanted to laugh. "Yes, he did. It was my grandfather's property, so of course I am curious." In fact she had only surveyed the gardens, but she felt rather smug at leaving another ambiguity for the viscount to chew on.

"It was your intention all along to visit Woodleigh and investigate

Adam's study this morning, I think. I am happy that I could accommodate you."

She did not think he was happy at all. He appeared to be contemplating the implications of her visiting Woodleigh in breeches and shirt on a day when perhaps she knew Nigel was not in London after all.

On the whole, she decided that this had been a very successful morning ride.

They took a more direct route back. Feeling more secure on the sidesaddle now, she galloped through the park and did not slow when they entered the woods. Rosy sunlight dappled through the branches, creating marvelous blurred blotches while she sped along. The visual effect distracted her and she was unprepared when suddenly, inexplicably, her horse violently reared.

A different blur now, of trees and ground swirling while she struggled to control the animal. It acted berserk, and twisted on its hind legs. The sidesaddle could not hold her. She landed on her stomach with an impact that dazed her senses.

More shocking was the weight immediately pressing her back, and the forearms bracing the ground on either side of her head. Vergil was on top of her, covering her back and head with his body. She struggled against him with indignation and opened her mouth to protest.

A crack split the morning quiet. Vergil pressed firmly between her shoulders and pushed her back down into the dirt.

"Watch your fire," he shouted angrily in the direction of the sound. His right hand grasped the ends of reins and both horses whinnied and pranced.

She suddenly did not care that they must look ridiculous, sprawled together like this. "Who would be shooting?"

"Poachers, most likely after fowl. Very bold of them to use guns instead of traps. They would only dare it in early morning. We are several miles from the house and they expect the family to still be abed."

Another crack rang. This time she heard a little *thump* as the ball landed in a tree to their left. The horses reared and almost broke loose. Vergil cursed and shouted again.

He still pressed against her, his weight all along her back. His breath tickled her nape. The cloth of his sleeves flanked her cheeks, brushing them softly.

She did not feel in danger at all, but secure and protected in the warmest way. The intimate proximity kindled a glowing response in her.

She inhaled his scent of soap and leather, and a strange little flutter scurried from her heart to her stomach.

"Now you see why you should not ride at this hour. It is dangerous," he said.

"*You* were going to ride."

"That is different." The words were spoken near her ear, as if he had moved his head closer. He had her hugging the ground, her chin crushed in the leaves and soil. The warm breeze of his breath caressed her temple, making that flutter beat its wings furiously.

He rose up but he did not move away completely. He still hovered. Something she could not name poured out of him and into her. It frightened her. The flutter rose and filled her chest.

She rolled onto her back and looked up at him, right into his eyes. No one in her life had ever looked at her so . . . specifically. At least not from this close. That gaze seemed to penetrate right into her mind and explore at will.

She did not feel protected and secure anymore. Rather the opposite. The flutters multiplied and beat a frantic, humming rhythm, taking over her body and limbs. Wings of warning. And excitement.

His tight expression made him astonishingly handsome. He pushed away from the ground and knelt to offer his hand, to help her to a sitting position. "Did the fall hurt you?"

She moved her limbs gingerly. "It just knocked the breath out of me. I was not really thrown, but I will be a little sore in the morning." She scrambled to rise. "As guardians go, you are superior, Uncle Vergil. Not many men would throw their bodies between a musket ball and a woman whom they barely know."

"All honorable Englishmen would do so, Miss Kenwood."

They walked the horses for a while to get them calm, then rode the last miles back to the house. His silent company unsettled her and that strange excitement still hummed. At the stables, he swung down and walked over to help her dismount. She paused when his arms reached up to guide her.

He noticed her hesitation. His blue eyes met hers in a most startling manner. She became breathless and incapable of looking away.

Strong fingers closed around her waist and lifted her down. It seemed to take a long time for him to release her, a stretched moment when he held her mere inches from himself. The subtle pressure of his hands and the closeness of his tall body shook her.

"Thank you. I enjoyed the ride very much." She collected her composure and turned away.

"I am glad that you did, especially since it will be your last one."

She whirled around to face him. "Are you saying I can never ride while I am here?"

"Of course you can, with company and later in the day. However, I will inform the grooms that you are not to be given a horse this early again, nor any time when you plan to go alone." He acted as imperious and calm as ever, but a tense power surged across the ground at her. "Nor are you to arrange any more morning assignations with your cousin Nigel. You may see him when he calls here, or if Penelope decides to call on him."

Assignations? His imagination had explored those ambiguities more thoroughly than she had intended.

She walked away without correcting him.

Let him think the worst.

Vergil pulled a chair next to the bed, sat in it, and raised his boot to give his brother's hip a good nudge.

Dante groaned and threw an arm over his eyes. He peered out below it, saw Vergil, and groaned again in resignation. With an irritated sigh, he pushed himself up against the headboard. "Morning, Vergil."

Vergil took in his brother's naked chest and noted the two glasses and empty wine bottle on a nearby table. "Up most the night with Marian, I gather. I have told you to leave the servants alone, Dante. I will not have them molested."

"A man does not molest Marian; he fights for his life. But then, you wouldn't know, even though she fancies you. Not discreet enough."

"Not discreet enough for you, either. Your intended is in the house."

Dante rested his head against the board and smiled. "Ah, yes, the fair Bianca. Your description did her a disservice. She is really a sweet young thing, just a bit naive is all. It is charming to watch her grapple with our ways."

A bit naive? "I just took a long ride with your sweet young thing."

"From the condition of your coat, it looks more as if you took a crawl with her."

"Some poachers were shooting and we ended up unhorsed." Not exactly how it had happened, but there was no point in inviting detailed queries about it. "I am glad to hear that Miss Kenwood suits you. However, I should warn you that you have competition."

"Nothing serious," Dante said as he yawned.

"You haven't even heard who it is yet."

"Not you, I trust."

Vergil shot him a scathing look that hid an uncomfortable spike of guilt.

"Just joking, Verg." Dante laughed. "It is so clear that you two don't rub well together, that she all but despises you, that I could not resist."

Unless he had misread things entirely there on the ground, they rubbed together disturbingly well. "Not me, but a title."

That checked his brother's mirth. Dante may have supreme confidence in his ability to attract women, but as a younger son, that did not translate into the ability to marry anyone he chose.

"Which title?"

"Her cousin, Nigel Kenwood."

"The second baronet of Woodleigh? All but newly patented, and very minor a title at that."

"She does not care about the finer points of birth and rank, and they are related, which gives them a natural bond. I thought him safely in France, running through whatever old Adam left him, but I fear he ran through it faster than I calculated. He has returned and taken residence as our neighbor. I suspect he did so hoping to find her with us. She got most of what wasn't left to charity, after all. To his mind he is practically entitled to her, I would guess."

Dante didn't exactly look concerned, but Vergil had his attention. "What do you know about this cousin?"

"He is the grandson of Adam's brother. They had started in business together, but the brother got into some financial scrape and Adam bought out his share. Nigel's father would not touch the trade, although Adam offered to take him in. Nigel fancies himself an artist and has lived in Paris since he attained his majority."

"A dabbler? Be serious, Vergil, I don't think—"

"Not a painter. A musician. Adam groused on occasion about the boy and his pianoforte."

"Oh, well, a musician. Now *there* is cause for alarm."

"Miss Kenwood is a musician, too, so there may be reason for concern, if not cause for alarm."

Dante raised his eyebrows at this new tidbit.

"A singer," Vergil explained. "She prefers opera. So you see Nigel's potential attraction. Similar interests and common blood."

"You make too much of both. We are talking marriage here, not a lover's liaison. Did mother and father have similar interests? Do you and Fleur have similar interests?"

He and Fleur had the most basic of similar interests, but that was beside the point. Vergil pushed himself to his feet. "Well, you had better move fast. I will try to discourage frequent visits from Nigel, but I can hardly bar him from the house."

He walked to the door. Dante's voice followed. "Well, now, big brother, just how fast do you want me to go?"

Vergil looked back at Dante. Pictures of those naked arms and chest embracing a barely clothed Bianca burst into his mind, inciting an ugly reaction. He did not respond for a moment, while he suppressed both the images and the anger. That embrace would be inevitable. And necessary.

"Do not even consider dishonoring her," he said. "And keep your hands off Marian while you are in this house. I will not have the ladies scandalized."

chapter 4

Penelope visited Vergil's study that afternoon, to inform him that she had received a letter in the day's post saying that Fleur and her mother would visit in ten days.

"I will be gone for the week prior, but I promise to return by then," he reassured her.

"I think that I will invite a few friends down from London too," Penelope said. "It will give Bianca a chance to try her wings."

"Not too many, Pen. And choose carefully."

"There is something else, Vergil. I suspect that Dante is developing a *tendre* for her."

He tried to focus on what Pen was saying, but his mind's eye was seeing Miss Kenwood lying on the ground and looking up at him with a startled blush that produced a charge through his veins. His hands felt her feminine waist once again and his body warmed from the closeness when he brought her down from her horse. The shadowy scent of lavender filled his head.

"Do not concern yourself, Pen. Dante will not get himself entangled inadvertently."

"I am not concerned about Dante. Bianca, however, strikes one as so guileless."

Guileless?

"And Dante . . . Vergil, I do not know if you are aware of this, as I am sure that no one speaks to *you* about it, seeing as how you are such a . . . but it is said that he is a merciless rake."

He wondered what Pen thought men talked about when they got together after dinner with their port and cigars. He had spent years being goaded about his brother's conquests, and on more than one occasion had been forced to stare down an irate husband.

"Even Dante respects the basic rules. If he has an interest in her, it is an honorable one, I am sure."

She blinked stunned eyes at him. "You will permit that?"

"Why shouldn't I?"

"She is very ignorant of the ways of the world and will be very disillusioned when she learns the truth about him."

"I would not interfere, Pen. Let things develop as they might. If he wins her, they will work things out the way couples always do with such things."

"If you say so, but I always resented that no one warned me about Anthony."

He had wanted to, but as a mere youth it had not been his place, especially with their mother alive and managing things. A boy did not go to his older sister and inform her that her wonderful earl had a reputation as a libertine, and that shadowy allusions suggested his sins were not typical ones.

Someone should have, however, and he remembered well his sister's unhappiness. Pen's formal separation from the earl these last five years had brought her some peace, but at the cost of her social standing and a perpetual loneliness. The reminder that a bad marriage could be hell made him ill at ease about Bianca, and he wished Pen had not brought up her own loveless, childless union.

She gave him a look of female skepticism. "I will hold my tongue and see how things develop, but if I suspect that he toys with her, I will scold him severely, Vergil. That is something I will not tolerate."

"Do as you think best, Pen."

She left, and he lifted the letter that he had been reading when she entered.

He scanned its contents again. The biggest problem with a secret was that it always demanded your attention at the most inconvenient times. He had planned to stay here as long as Dante did, but that would not be possible now.

He left the study and went to his chambers to tell Morton to expect a journey the day after next.

The next afternoon Bianca sat in the drawing room, tapping her foot impatiently. She expected a visitor sometime soon. Unfortunately, the one whose card the butler delivered to Pen was not the one she anticipated.

Nigel breezed in, looking very romantic in his nip-waisted Parisian frock coat and dark muffler and tousled shoulder-length hair. He bestowed a warm smile of familiarity on Bianca while Pen greeted him.

"You are recently returned from Paris," Charlotte said. "You will have to tell us all about it."

Nigel obligingly entertained them with some descriptions of the latest fashions. Bianca barely heard, even though her cousin directed most of his attention to her. She listened for sounds of another arrival.

The doors opened, but it was only Vergil and Dante.

"I hope that you plan to make Woodleigh your home, at least through the autumn," Penelope said.

"It is my intention to do so."

"I will be hosting a house party here soon, and I will count on your riding over to join us whenever you can."

"That is most kind of you. I rarely visited my great-uncle, so I am all but new to these parts."

"You have not spent much time in England these last years, have you, Kenwood?" Vergil asked.

"I have preferred Paris. I found the culture there to be of surpassing quality. The artistic life is very rich."

"You have an interest in the arts?" Penelope asked. "Then you will enjoy the company of my party. Your cousin is no mean artist herself. She sings like an angel and has graciously entertained Charlotte and me on occasion."

Nigel's expression showed polite interest, but also carried a patronizing tinge. Bianca guessed that he had met many young women whose friends believed they could sing like angels.

"Let us cajole her to sing now," Charlotte said. "Vergil and Dante have never heard her."

"I would be honored to accompany you," Nigel offered. "I am passably competent on the pianoforte."

Bianca felt a little cornered. She had only entertained Penelope and Charlotte with popular drawing-room songs, and had managed little serious practice over the last two weeks. All the same, the opportunity to sing, even if it couldn't be her best effort, excited her.

They all went to the music room and Nigel took his position at the pianoforte. "My repertoire of popular songs is limited," he warned her in a slightly superior way.

"Perhaps an aria would make more sense, then."

He looked up in delighted surprise. They agreed on one by Mozart, which she had learned just before leaving Baltimore. The prospect of this little performance quickened her heart.

The others positioned themselves on benches and chairs. Nigel played a few measures, to introduce the piece.

Her spirits immediately soared with the notes. No need to restrain her voice like she did in her room while she practiced scales. No cold isolation such as she experienced when she snuck away to sing on the grounds. Her joy in letting her voice vent its strength colored the sounds.

The reactions of her little audience produced a type of power. Penelope looked stunned, Dante enthralled, Charlotte confused, and Vergil sharply interested. She glanced aside at Nigel and saw surprised approval. His skill at the pianoforte was considerable, and she suspected that he understood that the audience gave the skill meaning.

When she finished, the room was so silent she could hear insects through the open window. She held the swelling euphoria for a priceless heartbeat and then released it.

"That was astonishing, dear cousin," Nigel said quietly. "You have been training in earnest."

"You amaze us all, Bianca," Penelope said. "And your playing was masterful, Sir Nigel. I can see that music is a serious interest for you."

"Not an interest, but a passion." His eyes met Bianca's with a glimmer that said they shared a secret these others could never understand.

"You must promise to play when my guests are here. Perhaps we can induce Bianca to sing as well. It will make for a wonderful evening."

"I would be honored."

He began to take his leave, imploring Penelope to visit Woodleigh soon. The butler entered before Pen called for him, carrying a card.

"A man has arrived, my lady. He requests to see Miss Kenwood."

Penelope examined the card and raised her eyebrows when she handed it to Bianca. Bianca knew the name before she read it.

The visitor she had been expecting had finally arrived.

"It is business, Penelope. Is there someplace where I may meet with him alone?"

"Put him in my study," Vergil instructed the butler. "Miss Kenwood can conduct her business there."

Bianca saw Nigel off and then ran down the corridor to the study, still feeling lighthearted from singing.

She had never visited the study before. It faced north, and the light coming through the pointed Gothic windows offered veiled illumination of the dark wood desk, the wall of books, and the watercolor landscapes.

Her visitor rose from a chair near the window.

"Mr. Peterson, I am delighted that you came."

"I was relieved to receive your summons, Miss Kenwood. When you did not make our last appointment I grew concerned."

"Lord Laclere found me and had other plans for my visit in your country."

She took a place on the padded window seat. A deep sill ran inside the window. It held an assortment of what appeared to be unusual toys. One was a wood-and-chain catapult. Another was a wood-and-leather carriage. A third appeared to be nothing in particular, just a series of grooved ramps leading one to the other, decorated with chains and wheels.

Their construction was somewhat rustic. She guessed that Vergil had made them when he was a boy. The notion that the proper and stern viscount preserved memories of his childhood in his inner sanctum charmed her, even though, for the life of her, she could not imagine such a man as ever being boyish.

Mr. Peterson was a man of middle years, balding and pale, with gray eyes that could look shrewd or deferential depending on the circumstances. When she had first visited him in London, the shrewd side had been quick to understand her explanation that, while she could not pay his fees now, she had expectations that would ultimately settle things quite nicely.

"You have reviewed the will?" she asked.

"I have. I met with your grandfather's solicitor. He seemed surprised that you had engaged me, but cooperated to the extent he was obliged to. No more, however."

"What did you learn? Can Lord Laclere's rule be broken?"

"If you are not cared for, or if there is evidence of fraud, it is possible to have that provision set aside, but the court will not permit you the independence that I think you seek. If the viscount is not your guardian, someone else will be named. With a man of his stature, any abuse of his position would have to be egregious before a court took action."

She fumed with disappointment. The pointless toy caught her attention and she noticed a little lead ball at its base. Debating her next move with Vergil, she absently lifted it and dropped it on the uppermost ramp. It rolled its way down from one to the other, back and forth, setting off little wheels and pulleys when its weight hit different levels.

"Miss Kenwood, it is not a permanent situation—less than a year. You are a wealthy young woman, and it is understandable that your grandfather did not want to leave you the unprotected prey of unscrupulous fortune hunters."

"How wealthy?"

"Excuse me? I assumed that you knew."

"I know in general terms. Exactly how wealthy?"

"The income from the amount invested in the funds should reach at least three thousand pounds this year."

"That is a fortune in itself, and far more than enough for my purposes."

"Your guardian will control it, releasing funds to you as necessary, to cover your expenses. He is required to be reasonable regarding your requests."

She doubted that Vergil would be so reasonable as to hand her several hundred so that she could escape to Milan. If he controlled her income, he controlled her movements. In point of fact, he controlled her life.

"Now, the other part of your inheritance is more complicated," Mr. Peterson said, continuing his report.

"What other part?"

"Your grandfather was a man of business. Toward the end of his life he sold out of most of them. However, he held on to three partnerships. Two were minor holdings in transportation companies, and the third was a majority in a cotton mill in Manchester. You were also bequeathed his interest in those businesses, less ten percent of the mill, which was given to your cousin."

"The viscount is also my trustee, however. He manages those investments."

"These partnerships are not a part of the permanent trust like the funds are, however. If you marry or come of age, he must relinquish control of them. Actually, it surprises me that he has not sold out of those businesses. They represent a threat to your wealth. Should anything go wrong, all owners are fully responsible for debts incurred."

These business did not really interest her much, unless . . . "Is there income from them as well?"

"The solicitor was not inclined to let me see those records. I think that the mill does pay."

"What will happen with that income?"

"It will go to your trustee, who presumably will invest it in more funds. Or it will be sent to your guardian."

Who was the same person. Trustee. Guardian. Everywhere she turned in this conversation she kept bumping into Vergil Duclairc.

"Mr. Peterson, I would like you present while I speak with Lord Laclere. The situation he has created is intolerable. I am being kept a prisoner here."

She sent the butler to request Vergil's attendance. Mr. Peterson looked very discomforted at the notion of the upcoming interview. By the time Vergil came through the door, deference had replaced shrewdness in those gray eyes, and the balding pate showed tiny beads of sweat.

"Lord Laclere, this is Mr. Peterson. He is my solicitor."

Vergil coolly examined the attorney with bored, aristocratic hauteur. Mr. Peterson dissolved into an obsequious fluster. Bianca fought the urge to scold him to be a man.

Vergil turned critical eyes on her. "I did not know that you had engaged a solicitor, Miss Kenwood."

"It was one of the first things I attended to when I arrived in London."

"Your grandfather's solicitor, or mine, or I myself, would have been happy to explain anything that you needed to know."

"I thought it best to have my own representation and to decide for myself what I needed to know."

"I trust that Mr. Peterson has satisfied your curiosity on all points."

"Almost all. He has explained about the business partnerships that I have inherited, and suggested that you should have sold them out, for safety's sake."

"I did not put it that way, my lord," Mr. Peterson rushed to explain. "I only explained the law regarding a partner's financial responsibilities."

"As you should for your client. I am obtaining information about the value of the partnerships. As trustee, it would be irresponsible for me to give them away. There have been several inquiries regarding purchase that I will pursue when I am in a better position to judge their fairness. These things take time, however. It is difficult to obtain honest information from the managers and other owners."

"Excellent, my lord. Just the sort of careful oversight one would expect. I think it is obvious that all is in perfect order, Miss Kenwood, and that you are fortunate to have Lord Laclere taking care—"

"When do the companies pay out the profits?" she asked.

Steely forbearance set Vergil's jaw and mouth. "If there are profits, the companies pay out once a year. It will be reinvested in government funds."

"Have the funds themselves paid since my grandfather's death?"

"They have."

"Has that income also been reinvested?"

"Most of it."

Most, but not all. "Mr. Peterson, would you be so kind as to wait for me in the library?"

Mr. Peterson was delighted to do so. He almost stumbled in his hasty retreat.

Bianca took a chair facing Vergil. "I want you to arrange for the income to be at my disposal."

"I have no intention of doing so."

"It is *my* inheritance."

"Even if you were the most sensible of young women, I would fail in my duty if I handed it to you. As it is, you have expressed intentions that would make me a conspirator in your ruin. It is out of the question."

"Mr. Peterson explained that a guardian is expected to be reasonable in releasing those funds."

"A sum is available to meet your needs. Tradesmen need only send their bills to me. Modistes and others who cater to women are accustomed to that. Barring extravagant spending on your part, we need never speak of this again."

"Since there are no modistes in this house, I am in no danger of being accused of extravagance."

His expression cleared a little. "My apologies. Of course you would like to enjoy the fruits of your good fortune. I will arrange for Penelope to take you up to London in a few weeks."

"Thank you. However, I would like some pin money now. I need to purchase a few items of a personal nature."

As she expected, the word personal kept him from probing. He opened a drawer in his desk.

"I expect that twenty pounds should suffice," she said.

"That is a lot of pins, Miss Kenwood."

"I will use some of it to pay Mr. Peterson."

"Mr. Peterson can send his bill to me."

"I prefer he does not. I prefer that he remembers just who has engaged him. Nor do I think it right that I ask him to await my expectations."

Vergil removed several notes from the drawer and placed them on top of the desk. He walked to her chair, no longer hiding his irritation. He towered above her and she barely managed not to cower.

"I am not accustomed to such blunt discussions of money, especially with women. Nor am I accustomed to questions that imply suspicion regarding my honesty and judgment in managing your estate, especially in front of a man with whom I have no acquaintance."

He bent and grasped the arms of her chair. She shrank against its back, away from the sparks flashing in the eyes just inches from her face. "The fact is, Miss Kenwood, right now Uncle Vergil is thinking that his disrespectful ward could use a good spanking."

Her mouth fell open in indignation. He whipped away and strode to the door.

As soon as he departed, she scooped up the notes and joined Mr. Peterson. She handed him ten pounds. "This is to pay you for your fee and expenses so far. I want you to take what is left and establish an account for me at a bank. Use your own name if necessary."

"Surely Lord Laclere has an account on which drafts can be written."

"I want my own, and I don't want him to know about it. Write to me with the information once it is done. I also want you to find out about these offers to purchase the business partnerships."

"If you insist, I will see what I can learn. Should I write to you here?"

"Yes. I don't think the viscount intends to allow me to go anywhere for a very long while." Probably not until she married or turned twenty-one.

She had no intention of doing the former, and refused to wait for the latter. If Mr. Peterson obtained the names of the parties interested in her partnerships, she might find a way to procure the funds necessary to go to Italy, despite the obstacle of Vergil Duclairc.

Vergil had barely cooled his temper after the surprise meeting with Mr. Peterson when another unexpected visitor arrived late that afternoon. Adrian Burchard, one of Vergil's friends, entered Vergil's study, mercifully distracting him from insistent, erotic images of taming Bianca Kenwood.

"It has been too long, Burchard," Vergil said, welcoming him.

"If you spent more than a few days in London at a time, it would not have been so long. Where have you been keeping yourself?" Adrian's dark, foreign-looking eyes revealed no expectation of an interesting answer.

Nor did he get one. Vergil gestured to the desk. "The family's affairs occupy most of my time, I'm afraid." The statement was true, but not the gesture and its implications. He spent no more time at Laclere Park than he did in London.

Of all his friends, Burchard was the most likely to become aware of the gaps. "I escape north frequently, to my own property there. I do not have to be a viscount then," he added, to cover that eventuality. "It is good of you to ride down and save me from being one this afternoon."

"I regret that this is not a social call. Let us walk outside, and I will explain."

Curious, Vergil accompanied him out the drive. Adrian led him to the spot where another lane broke off to circle the property. There, in the shade of a tree, a carriage waited.

A graying man with a prominent hooked nose sat inside it.

Vergil pulled Adrian aside. "You could have warned me that you brought Wellington with you."

The duke overheard. "I told him to bring you here without announcing my presence, and Burchard fulfills his missions to the letter," he said as he climbed out of the carriage.

"Your Grace honors us with this visit."

"This isn't a visit, which is why I had Burchard bring you to me here. It is no insult to your sister, Laclere. I merely don't have the time today for drawing room chats." He gestured with his walking stick. "This appears a pleasant, shaded path. Let us take some exercise."

Vergil fell into step, with Adrian alongside. Adrian had become a protégé of Wellington's. The great man's patronage had secured a seat in the House of Commons for the Earl of Dincaster's third son.

The rhythmic fall of their boots beat out a few minutes of time. The duke did not even try to fill it with pleasantries.

"I have come to speak of a delicate matter," he finally said. "There is no good way to broach it, so I will be blunt. I have come to ask you about your brother's death. I am always curious when men accidentally inflict mortal pistol wounds on themselves. I am in a position to know that it is not an easy thing to do. I want to know if, in your brother's case, it was not an accident, but suicide."

Vergil gave Adrian a resentful look, only to have his friend subtly shake his head. The evidence that Adrian had not been disloyal or indiscreet checked the anger.

"Yes. Only the family and a few friends know."

"I appreciate your confidence in my discretion as well, but receiving confirmation of my suspicions is hardly good news. Tell me, did you never think it odd that we had two prominent suicides in the same week? Your brother's and Castlereagh's."

"My brother was prone to fits of deep melancholy. The Foreign Minister was deranged. It was a coincidence."

"Laclere, I am not convinced it was a coincidence. Is there any chance that your brother was being blackmailed? Did you find any evidence of that? I ask because there is some indication that Castlereagh was."

"I thought that suspicion had been laid to rest. By you."

"Considering his position, I could hardly let it stand. The man was clearly delusional, so I gave it little credence. However, the last time I saw him he did say something to me about receiving a letter. He alluded to fears of exposure."

Exposure. Vergil suspected where this was going and he did not want to tread that path. "As you said, he was delusional."

Wellington paced five steps before he spoke again. "The letter writer claimed to have proof of certain criminal activity."

Vergil stopped, forcing Adrian and Wellington to as well. "And so, after months of mulling it over, that detail led you to see some connection to my brother?"

"Laclere, hear him out," Adrian said.

"I'll be damned if I will."

"I understand your anger, Laclere. I assure you that the only connection I saw was two suicides, one of which may have been the result of blackmail." Wellington's voice got stern. "I ask you again, do you have reason to think that your brother was being blackmailed too? Lest you be tempted to lie to protect his name, let me say that I think that others are being victimized now, that Lord Fairhall's hunting accident in May was not what it seemed, and that we will see more ruin and death if we do not get to the bottom of this."

The fury spun out of Vergil. It was not the Iron Duke's severe tone that caused that. He had been carrying this secret for almost a year, wondering if the pattern and connections that he suspected were his own delusions.

"Yes, I think that Milton was being blackmailed. I think that is why he killed himself."

"He left a letter. I found it in his papers, where he knew I would look after I took up the reins of the estate. It alluded to a betrayal, whether his or another's, I do not know. Mostly it spoke of the family, and how it would be better if he left the stage before we were ruined. I wanted to believe he meant the finances, which were in dire condition by then. However, I have wondered if his hand was forced."

They had sat down on a fallen tree while he told his story. Wellington drew pictures in the dirt with his walking stick as he listened.

"Let us assume that it was blackmail in both cases. Was the goal their deaths?" Adrian asked.

"That is the question, isn't it?" Wellington said.

"For my brother, it may have only been money. There would be no way for someone to know that he could not pay. Our financial condition was not obvious. He spent as if there were no problem."

"Normally, one would assume that a blackmailer only wants to bleed his victim. However, the timing—we have had evidence that there are radicals trying to assassinate members of the government and House of Lords. How much easier, and safer, to affect things this way."

"My brother was not prominent in the government."

"He had an interest in politics."

"A theoretical interest."

"A radical theoretical interest. It may have brought him into contact with men who espouse violence, and who would entangle him, and, through him, others," Wellington said. "He may have innocently communicated or associated with such men, only to have them use the connection against him later."

The comment hung in the air, begging a response. The duke had neatly articulated Vergil's own fears about the reasons for Milton's death.

"Did you find letters to indicate a friendship between your brother and the Foreign Minister?" Wellington asked.

"I did not look for any." It was a lie. A damn lie. He would not allow supposition to become fact so easily, however.

"Perhaps you should."

"I have been pursuing other directions. I do not think there is any direct connection between these deaths, except perhaps the same blackmailer. I am more interested in finding that man than in learning the sins he discovered."

"So that is why you have not been in London much, nor here," Adrian said. "Have you made any progress?"

"A little." Damn little, considering how much of his time and his life he had invested in the search.

"There is nothing that I can do in this, except observe men's demeanors and wonder if they are worried," Wellington said. "I have reason to think that several are. It is a diabolical notion, that someone is ferreting out secrets and using them to intimidate or extort your friends. Or worse, that men are being pressed so much that they take their own lives to escape."

"And you, Burchard? What is your interest in this, or did you only come today to arrange a private meeting for His Grace?" Vergil asked.

Wellington answered as they all stood to make their way back to the hiding coach. "He is making some discreet enquiries for me regarding Lord Fairhall. Since you know him to be trustworthy, it is my hope that you will share anything that you learn with him so that we can resolve this quickly."

"Of course."

It was another bold lie. Adrian was a friend, and experienced in both enquiries and discretion, but Vergil had no intention of telling anyone what he learned if it would reflect badly on either Milton or the Duclairc family.

He suspected that the truth would, for all of the reasons he had carefully avoided discussing today.

chapter 5

Do you see what I mean?" Charlotte whispered.

She sat with Bianca in the drawing room while the house-party guests arrived.

Vergil stood by the mantel, chatting amiably with Fleur and her mother, Mrs. Monley. They had arrived just after midday, pulling up in a magnificent carriage.

"Nothing," Charlotte muttered, shaking her head. "No . . . well, I do not know what. Vergil may as well be talking to me, and Fleur to her father."

Sitting on Charlotte's other side, Diane St. John, one of the countess's dearest friends, patted Charlotte's hand. Her soulful eyes showed amusement as she glanced to the mantel. "I would not worry for your brother or Miss Monley. Things are not always what they appear to be in such matters. They look perfect together, don't they? A matched pair."

They did look well matched. Fleur was all grace and elegance, tall and slender, alabaster-skinned and dark of hair. Ringlets falling from a little beribboned topknot framed her oval face, which possessed a rose of a mouth. She had struck Bianca as an intelligent, soft-spoken person whose deep brown eyes did not miss much.

Bianca experienced a vague disappointment that she could not instantly dislike Fleur, as well as an inexplicable pang of melancholy whenever she looked to the group by the hearth.

"I fear that Vergil is sacrificing himself for her fortune," Charlotte said. "He looks happy to see her, but considering that her family left London eight weeks ago and they have been apart all that time . . ."

"You do not know that," Mrs. St. John said. "Perhaps when he is not here or in London, he is visiting her sometimes."

"I think not. He goes to his manor in Lancashire, mostly. He has to tell his agents and Pen and the governess who comes to stay with me where he can be found. If it were anyone but Vergil, one might suspect that he visits a woman up there. Someone he loves but cannot marry."

Bianca snapped her head around and stared at Charlotte's wistful expression. "That is a scandalous thing to suggest."

"Such arrangements are very common, I have gathered. Pen has even suggested to me that I should expect my husband to form other friendships on occasion."

Mrs. St. John lowered her lids. "I think that too many people have been very indiscreet when speaking around you, Charlotte."

Bianca noted that Mrs. St. John did not say that Charlotte was wrong, or that her ignorance had led her to misinterpret Penelope's instruction.

"It *would* explain a lot. *That,* for one thing." Charlotte nodded her head toward the mantel. "The delay in announcing a formal engagement for another. With her beauty and portion, she does not have to wait for him. The odd thing is that Fleur does not seem to mind how things stand. It is her mother who grows impatient."

Yes, the mother was growing impatient. The eyes of Mrs. Monley were the brightest pair by the fireplace. She followed her daughter's conversation with a lovely smile and a cocked head that set the feather in her silk, corded turban at an inquisitive angle.

"The evening promises to be full. You should retire and rest," a male voice said.

Bianca tore her attention from the mantel to see that Daniel St. John had joined them, and was addressing his wife. A handsome man who could quickly slip from passive coolness to intense attention, he now focused the latter on the subject of his interest.

"Daniel is very protective when I am in the family way," Diane confided to them with a smile. "After two children, you know I am not very frail, my dear."

"All the same, some quiet is in order." He held out his hand to escort her.

Bianca did not miss the look that passed between them. Warmth, humor, and total absorption flowed in that fleeting connection. It was as if years of memories colored how they saw each other, and enriched even this commonplace exchange.

She glanced back to the mantel, and noticed how the demeanor that Vergil and Fleur displayed contrasted with this other couple's. She comprehended Charlotte's comment in new ways. There need be no overt demonstration to show passion and affection. In silent ways that involved no physical contact, a man and a woman could be intimately connected.

Diane St. John accepted her husband's command and rose. "I suppose a short rest would be a good idea." Side by side, saying nothing, but speaking volumes, they strolled from the drawing room.

Activity in the hall heralded another carriage.

"Finally the last." Charlotte rose to her feet. "This must be Mrs. Gaston. She is one of Pen's friends and a great patroness of the arts. She stood by Pen when others forsook her after the separation. I think Pen invited her just for you, because of your singing."

Bianca and Charlotte followed Penelope and Vergil out to meet the new guest.

Mrs. Gaston had come in a large coach. Pen advanced with outstretched hands of welcome. "So good of you to make time for our little party."

Mrs. Gaston was a beautiful woman with a winning smile, high cheekbones, and coppery brown hair. She carried herself with prideful elegance, and wore a dress with an exotic pattern and a bonnet with extravagant feathers. "It is you who are good to give me a chance to escape the city for a few days. I fear, however, that I have committed a *faux pas* and must beg your indulgence for it."

"A *faux pas*? You? Never."

"Alas, yes. You see, I have brought a friend with me."

"I wrote that your friends were welcome."

"So you did. Normally I would have written to alert you all the same. This friend, however, arrived in town unexpectedly."

A footman reached through the open door of the coach. A gloved hand and a sleeve *en gigot* emerged. An elaborately coifed and hatted dark head ducked as the friend in question bent to step down.

"Maria," Pen cried, embracing the statuesque figure swathed in pale blue muslin. "No one said you were coming to visit this year. This is a wonderful surprise for me."

The woman's face was not beautiful, with its prominent features, but her manner possessed solid dignity and confidence. "It was an impetuous decision on my part, *cara mia.* Milan is horrible with heat, my musicians are acting like spoiled children, and the tenor for the next production is an arrogant young idiot who will not take direction. I simply left them all. Let them see how they fare without Catalani."

"Oh, my, what fun," Charlotte whispered to Bianca. "Do you know who that is?"

Bianca knew. For years the preeminent opera singer in England, Maria Catalani had returned to Italy six years ago and now managed an opera company in Milan.

What a wonderful twist of luck. With Mrs. Gaston and Catalani here, this house party promised to be vastly more interesting than she had expected.

Vergil stepped forward to greet Catalani, and kissed her hand smoothly. She said something quietly that brought a smile to his face.

If the unexpected visit of an opera singer to Laclere Park distressed him, he did not show it. Probably he would take the matter up with Penelope later.

Penelope brought the newcomers toward the house. Bianca's knees wobbled with excitement.

"This must be Charlotte. A young woman now, and so lovely," Catalani said. "Are you out yet?"

"Next year," Pen explained. "Vergil does not approve of the young age some girls come out these days."

Catalani glanced back at the trailing viscount and her lips pursed with humor. "A good ploy, and it will be very effective. Let them wait for such a diamond. You will be the sensation of the season, Charlotte. I predict that your brothers will need four extra footmen just to guard the garden walls."

Pen drew Catalani toward Bianca. "This is Bianca Kenwood, from Baltimore. She is Vergil's ward."

"I have never had the pleasure of visiting your country. We will be sure to talk. I have many questions for you."

"And I for you. I will be visiting Italy very soon."

"You plan a grand tour for your sister and ward, Lord Laclere?" Catalani asked while Pen guided her into the house. "Ten extra footmen, then, if you send such beauties to my country."

Bianca scooted to catch up with Charlotte, ecstatic by the turn of events. This party promised to be the highlight of her entire stay in England.

"That is all of them for today," Charlotte explained. "Pen said that Mr. Witherby wrote that he would arrive tomorrow morning. Let us go rest before dinner."

Bianca refused to do so unless it became clear that Catalani herself would retire. She waited until the stately Catalani floated up the stairs with Penelope beside her.

She found herself standing alone in the empty entrance hall, knowing it would be impossible to rest now. Looking for some way to relieve her itching excitement, she went into the library, found the volume of Shelley's poems that she had been reading, and tucked herself into the corner of a divan facing a far window.

This was her favorite spot for reading, especially in the afternoons. Shaded light flooded in the window and the breeze was divine. No one could see her here unless they walked around the divan. It had become one of her little nooks of privacy.

Bootsteps entered the room. She stretched and turned to see who had come. Dante spotted her and walked over, carrying his hat and riding whip. He threw himself onto a chair, facing her, and stretched out his booted legs.

"They are all here?" He had disappeared from the house after Fleur's arrival.

"All but Mr. Witherby."

"I am surprised he is delayed. I would expect him to take advantage of every moment with my sister."

"Charlotte?"

"Pen. He has become a special friend to her during the last year. Or at least he thinks that he has. Don't know Pen's idea of it, although she appears to welcome his company. I'm sure that is why she has invited him, even though he is an old friend of Vergil's as well."

The phrase "special friend" alluded to more than companionship. Dante often lapsed into speaking to her in this familiar manner, as if they shared some secret understanding of the world. His conspiratorial tones implied a type of intimacy.

He lounged casually, looking at her from beneath thick lashes in a way that always made her uncomfortable. They were always alone when he looked at her like that.

"Maria Catalani recently arrived with Mrs. Gaston. It was a surprise for everyone," she said.

That caused his attention to sharpen. "Mrs. Gaston is here? I should have asked Pen who was attending before agreeing to stay myself."

"You do not care for her?"

"Through sheer persistence she has managed to insert herself into many circles. She sees herself as a great patroness of artists, and wants others to know how she advances careers."

"Does she? Advance careers?"

He shrugged. "I wouldn't know. Pen's artistic circles do not interest me much, and that seems to be what we have here. Mrs. Gaston and Catalani, you say. Lord Calne is another patron of the arts. Cornell Witherby will be good company, at least, although with the others here he will probably only talk about his poetry. Hopefully Vergil will distract him from that."

"Do you think that Vergil will allow Catalani to stay?"

"Why wouldn't he?"

"I thought that, perhaps, with Fleur here and Charlotte and . . ."

Her allusion amused him. "This is Pen's party, and my brother knew what that would mean. Vergil may be a saint, but he is never rude. Besides, fame like Catalani's has a way of obscuring the means by which it is achieved." He rose. "I think that I will go for a walk. I would be honored if you joined me. I will show you the ruins."

Bianca had already found the ruins of Laclere Park's medieval keep, and she did not want to visit them alone with a rake. Especially one who looked down at her with the light currently shining in Dante's eyes.

"Thank you, but I think that I will continue reading my book for a while longer."

A subtle annoyance altered his expression. To her astonishment, he reached out and stroked one finger along her jawline. "You do not have to be afraid of me, Bianca."

She angled away from his touch. "Your brother said that it is not customary to address women in such a familiar way here."

"I am not my brother."

No, he was not. The last week had been full of this young man's attention. She had tried to discourage him. Unsuccessfully, so it appeared.

His hand touched her again, cupping her chin. Her eyes widened in disbelief when he tilted her head up, bent, and kissed her lips. It happened so quickly that shock left her immobile.

He misunderstood. Sliding down beside her, he deepened the kiss and moved to embrace her.

She broke away and made it to the window with a staggering lunge. Furious with embarrassment, she faced him down. "Do not dare do that again."

He rose. "My apologies. I should have asked your permission first."

"You would not have received it."

"I think I would have."

"You misunderstand our friendship."

"I do not think so. You are fearful and confused, and that is appropriate in one so innocent. I will not kiss you again without your permission, but when I ask, you will give it."

She groped for a scathing response. He smiled in an insufferably self-confident way and walked out.

She sank back into the divan, pulled up her legs, and huddled in its corner. What had given this rake the idea that she would welcome such a thing? Had he learned about her performances in London? For all she knew, he had attended one.

Just her luck that the wrong brother had concluded that she was a little wild, and careless about proprieties.

• • •

"Hiding from the duties of state?" Dante asked as he strolled into the study where Vergil read his correspondence.

"Resting my face before I must smile so long my lips crack."

"It shouldn't be too bad. She invited Witherby and St. John so you would be diverted."

Vergil was grateful that Pen had invited Daniel and Diane St. John. He had not seen them for months. They were Pen's friends too. She had befriended Diane St. John when the young woman first came to London, and had played a role in the dramatic events that had led to Diane's marriage to the shipping magnate.

As for Witherby, he suspected that Pen had offered that invitation for reasons other than her brother's diversion.

Dante lounged against the window frame and absently dropped the lead ball onto the ramps of its toy. "Fleur is looking lovely as always. Should we expect an announcement some night after dinner?"

"I do not think so."

"It is past time, Verg."

"Of all the people to lecture me, Dante, you are the last. My responsibilities to the living members of this family far outweigh any to those of the future."

"Are you saying that we are so expensive that you cannot afford a wife?"

"I am saying that any woman who marries me will have certain expectations that I cannot fulfill at this time. Which brings us to the matter of your own marriage, which will significantly relieve the financial burden. I turn the question back to you. Should we plan an announcement? I recall a confident young blood saying smugly that a week should do it."

"Damn it, these things take time. Furthermore, she is . . . confusing."

He pulled a chair over to the desk and sat flush along its other side, his arm resting on its edge, propping up his head, his booted legs crossed. It was the pose of Dante settling in for a "man to man."

Since the topic of conversation was Bianca Kenwood, Vergil wished that he could be spared any confidences. Bianca continuously intruded on his thoughts, and last night, after his return to Laclere Park, he had found himself loitering in the drawing room with the ladies until she retired.

"I often think that I have gained some ground, only to find it is an illusion. She appears very warm one morning, but that afternoon I hear her being just as warm with a servant. She turns those big blue eyes on me and I think I should propose then and there, only to have her ignore me for the next hour. Sometimes I think that I am dealing with a girl so ignorant that she does not even notice my interest, and other times . . ."

"Other times?"

"Sometimes I wonder if she is far from ignorant and leading me in a fine dance. Forgive me, but we are speaking frankly here."

"*You* certainly are."

"I wonder if she is being deliberately intriguing. Elusive in a calculating way."

"It sounds more to me that you are failing and looking to blame her for it."

"Perhaps. But there is something about her, indefinable . . . an air, a scent, I don't know. I look at her and see a springlike innocence, and then all of a sudden she will look back and I find myself thinking that she would make a splendid mistress. It is a confusing and compelling combination."

So Dante had finally sensed what Vergil had that first night in the gaming hall, and too often since. "I trust not too compelling."

"Of course not. But it puts one off one's game. There is an art to this, and knowing the woman is essential."

"I am always grateful for your instruction on these matters, Dante, but let us get to the point. If you proposed tomorrow, do you think that she would accept?"

"Damned if I know."

Which meant probably not. "Does she even know that you are interested? She might interpret your attention as mere friendship, a helping hand in a strange country."

"She knows now."

"What is that supposed to mean?"

"I just saw her in the library."

"You declared your intentions?"

Dante looked away and Vergil instantly knew that the interest had been articulated with actions, not words. He almost reached across the desk to strangle him. "Let me rephrase that. Does she know that your intentions are honorable?"

"What else could they be? She is your ward."

Vergil rubbed between his eyebrows. "Well, let us just suppose that she has heard about you—"

"From whom? Pen would hardly go telling tales."

"From anyone else. A servant. Her maid, Jane. Nigel Kenwood."

"She hasn't seen Nigel all week but once, when Pen went to call on him, and they weren't alone, so he could not—"

"From *whomever,* Dante. Suppose someone has told her. If you did not express honorable intentions, she may think that you pursue her for other reasons."

Dante straightened. "If so, I am insulted."

"All the same—"

"I am not a scoundrel."

"I recommend that you clarify things. If she has misunderstood, she will only avoid you now."

Dante rose and paced back to the window. "Of course, you are right. However, if I propose and she turns me down, the game is up. Explaining my intentions, short of a proposal, does the same thing. Girls get these notions, and a man who pursues despite them looks a fool. I sat there in the library and I found myself wondering, what if it isn't contradictory?"

"You are not making much sense."

"What if she is in fact innocent, but has the other inside her? The man who tapped it would be in a very strong position with her. Talk about an inside track, why—"

"No."

"I am not talking about anything really dishonorable, Vergil. Just a mild dalliance that would save a lot of time."

"You will do nothing that even remotely compromises her."

"You are being impractical and too concerned with proprieties. This was your idea, remember? If I did compromise her, marriage would be inevitable."

It was not his much-vaunted sense of propriety that rebelled against Dante's insinuations, but something more visceral, having to do with a relentless simmer and the scent of lavender and a melodic voice that had sung in his memory during a week of travel and duties. Still, being a saint had its uses. He would not abort these arrangements, but he would not allow Dante to trap her.

"Winning a woman's honest affection may seem a long, tedious effort to a man accustomed to exploiting quick passion, Dante, but if you intend to have her, that is how you will have to do it."

"At least someone in this family has some passion, damn it. Between you and Milton . . ."

At their brother's name, Vergil's whole body tightened. "I would think that you would be very careful not to mention Milton and your reckless appetites in the same breath."

Dante's face darkened with resentment. "You still blame me for something I could not foresee."

"You are wrong. I do not blame you. There was no way for you to know what he intended to do. But do not pull him into these discussions. Insult me as cold, if you want, but leave our brother and his memory out of this. All of that has nothing to do with Miss Kenwood and your behavior toward her."

"Ah, yes, the lovely Bianca. You are drawing some fine lines in your concern for her, Verg. Your protection is oddly selective and shortsighted. You will not have your ward compromised, but you would tie her for life to a man whom you despise."

His words found their mark for reasons Dante would never know. "I do not despise you."

"Do you not? You may not blame me, but you have never forgiven me."

Vergil saw pain in the beautiful face that never showed a care. He should have been more perceptive to the guilt that Milton's death must have caused Dante. Odd that the discussion of a girl who had nothing to do with that episode was drawing this out.

"I may criticize how you live your life, but it does not reflect my feelings about the role you inadvertently played in the disaster last year. You do not need forgiveness for that, Dante. Ignorance is not a damnable offense. If I never spoke of this with you before, it was not because of blame, but only because I do not seek reminders of it. Perhaps my reticence on the subject has not been fair to you, however."

Dante's face was a visage of strained composure, but his eyes glowed. "I was here. I dined with him. I should have seen—"

"I am grateful that you were with him during his last hour. I think that he was too."

The air in the room flowed heavily with the raw intimacy born of unanticipated frankness. An invisible barrier had fallen that Vergil had never realized existed. A chasm dug since the crisis of Milton's death had unexpectedly been breached, and all because of the conflicting emotions created by Bianca Kenwood's presence in this household.

He looked at his younger brother with new eyes, and saw a depth carefully obscured by the rake's carefree persona. *She could do worse.*

Dante smiled wryly and sauntered to the door. "I'll do it your way, Verg. Should be interesting, trying to inspire a chaste affection with only intimations of something more later. Unfairly limits me, though. Can't play my best card. After all, I have nothing to offer the girl except pleasure."

An hour ago, Vergil would have agreed.

chapter 6

Vergil was the first to the breakfast room the next morning. He wanted to get a ride in before his guests roused themselves.

He had just settled down to his plate when a movement at the window caught his eye. Green and gold flashed by as a blond head and trim figure disappeared behind some bushes.

Bianca Kenwood had risen with the dawn again.

He turned from the window with annoyance. Dante had said that she had only seen Nigel Kenwood once, but Dante wouldn't know about Bianca's early wanderings. The possibility existed that she and Nigel had been meeting secretly for over a week.

He drew a mental curtain in front of the image forming in his mind. There was no evidence that she contrived assignations with her cousin. All the same, whatever her purpose, she had blithely walked into the park at dawn despite the danger she had faced from poachers that day on her horse. That episode would have kept a normal young woman fearful of venturing forth unless half an army accompanied her.

But then, she was not a normal young woman.

Foregoing his meal, he slipped out into the garden and crossed to the path she had been walking.

"Laclere."

Vergil pivoted at the call. Cornell Witherby strode toward him along the lane that led from the stables.

Down the path, gold and green got swallowed by the forest.

"Don't tell me that you rode through the night, Witherby." Vergil noted that the new arrival was well turned out in brown riding coat and fawn trousers. The boots looked new and the sandy locks visible beneath Witherby's hat appeared newly styled.

Witherby looked very dashing and in damnable good humor.

"I rode down most of the way yesterday afternoon, and stayed over at an inn."

"Eager, were you?"

"The city has gotten raucous the last few days. Demonstrations daily. Lots of arrests. Some country air will do me good. The muse gets petulant if there are such distractions."

"I trust that you will not be distracted here. There is breakfast waiting, but you must feed your muse in isolation. My sister has not risen yet to do the hostess duties."

Witherby smiled vaguely at this reference to Penelope. He knew that Vergil knew what was up, and Vergil knew he knew, but a man did not discuss another's pursuit of his married sister, even if they were old friends.

"You will be happy to know that the gathering is artistic, as one would expect from Pen," Vergil said.

"The countess's parties are always delightful. I expect this one to surpass all others."

Vergil decided not to speculate on just how much delight Witherby might be anticipating. A big, quiet country house offered all sorts of opportunities for privacy.

He firmly shut contemplation of that out of his mind.

"You are dressed for riding," Witherby observed. "I am keeping you."

"A walk first, then a ride. Go and settle yourself as best you can. St. John is here, by the way, and he normally comes down early, too, so you should not be bored too long."

With a happy, jaunty stride, Witherby aimed for the house. Vergil waited until he was out of sight, then turned and headed after Bianca.

When she came into view, he slowed so that he would trail behind her.

He followed out of concern for her safety, but admitted that he also wanted to determine whether Nigel waited somewhere up ahead.

A mile into the trees she turned onto a western path. He realized that she headed toward the ruins. Not a good sign. The medieval castle provided an ideal spot for couples to meet.

She was nowhere in view when he stepped into the high grass around the remains of Laclere Park's early fortifications. The keep survived as half a shell, and only one section of the old battlements endured, with the wall down in places and crumbling in others. Large stones scattered the overgrown clearing that had once served as the bailey. Of the whole structure, only a single, square wall tower still stood in reasonably safe condition.

Memories of childhood play tugged nostalgically, reminding him of the easy bond that he had once shared with Dante, and which secrets and neglect had almost destroyed. He scanned for signs of Miss Kenwood.

Suddenly a muffled, sweet sound floated through the morning silence. It rose and lowered like a gentle wave on the breeze, sending eddies out to surround him. He followed it to its source in the square tower and stepped through the stone threshold.

Sound submerged him, pitching off the walls and vaults. Above in the guards' chamber, Miss Kenwood practiced her scales, her voice gaining volume with each recurrent rise. He paused and listened to the repetitious climb of an instrument being tuned and warmed.

She stopped and he heard her speak. To Nigel? The man might use her music to entice her here. If so, she was in no immediate danger. He doubted that she would set aside her primary passion in order to explore other ones right now.

The sound broke again, pouring down the stairs. Not scales now, but a Rossini aria.

The melody washed through him. Precise and disciplined, like a bird's elaborately textured song, it drenched the mind and flooded the heart and churned indefinable sentiments the way the best music always did. The sensual undertones in her voice inundated a hidden reservoir that he had been struggling to keep dammed.

Almost involuntarily, his legs took him up the dark stairway toward the siren who unknowingly lured him toward a forbidden shore.

She stood alone in the chamber, her back to him, framed by the lines of walls tapering up to the stone vaulted ceiling. No Nigel. No one at all. She must have been speaking to herself.

He rested his shoulder against the portal's frame, to watch and listen. He wished that he could see her face, but his memory provided the radiant expression that he had witnessed that day when she performed in the music room.

He did not fight his reactions. He would have been incapable of doing so even if he sought to. Instead he let her notes raise a tide that submerged everything in the world except her pure passion and his own astonished desire.

It felt so good. Transporting. Glorious. Her voice took over her body and dissolved its substance until only the singing existed. The stones enriched the timbre like no other room ever had. She wished that she could bring Catalani here.

It ended too soon, and she regretfully held the last note longer than the score required. It hung above her, dripping like a single bud's nectar into her exposed spirit. And then it was over, leaving her spent and a little melancholy.

She abruptly sensed that she was not alone. Fearing that Dante had followed her, she turned with misgivings.

The viscount leaned casually against the portal opening, arms crossed over chest, watching her. He looked very handsome there, and somewhat intense despite his nonchalant pose.

"Did you follow me here, Uncle Vergil? To spy on me?"

"I thought of it as protecting you, but yes, I followed."

"Surely I am safe at Laclere Park. Your bold poachers must have moved on or switched to traps. There have been no firearms shot this last week."

"If you know that, you must come here often. Always to sing?"

The chamber had a window, no more than an arrow slit. She moved toward it, away from him. The stones heightened nuances in his tone that made her cautious. His eyes carried a hooded expression that she could not read. His presence struck her as dangerous. A ridiculous reaction to have, but she could not shake it.

She examined the view, avoiding his fixed regard. "I do not accept the situation that makes you think that you have a right to quiz me. Yes, I come here often, usually in the morning like this. I found this tower one day while riding. And yes, I come to sing."

"Alone?"

She looked back over her shoulder. "You thought perhaps I arranged assignations here with Nigel? You followed to protect me from any improper intentions?" The notion made her want to giggle. Such careful protection of her virtue on the grounds, while his own brother accosted her in the library. "You missed your ride to no purpose. The convenience of this tower for such meetings never occurred to me. I shall have to keep it in mind for the future."

"I doubt that you will. You would not have time to practice then. I never noticed before, but this chamber affects sound the way the ancient Norman churches do. Whatever your cousin's potential attraction, these stones hold more."

"Perhaps he will come to listen. As you did."

He pushed away from the wall with a little smile. "If so, you will definitely need protection."

He paced casually toward her. She found herself edging away. Silly, really, but there was something different about him today. A compelling something, but also disconcerting.

"Pen announced that you will sing this evening. Are you practicing for your performance, to be sure that you are in top form for Catalani?"

"Yes."

"You spoke at length with her last night. Quite a *tête-à-tête.* I assume that you informed her of your plans."

"Do not worry that I embarrassed you and Pen. No one else heard me and I think she knows the necessity of discretion with a viscount's guests."

He kept moving, looking around the chamber as if he had not been here in a long time. She felt a continued compulsion to stroll away.

"What did Catalani advise?"

"She agreed with me, that if I want the best training I must go to Italy, or bring one of their premier voice masters here. Until then, she gave me the name of a tutor who might work with me in London. She recommended a Signore Bardi, who serves as *bel canto* master to some of the best singers in London."

"No other advice? I would not have expected Catalani to be so reserved."

"She asked if I understood the life, what it would entail."

"Do you?"

"I know about the hard work. The travel. The need to perform despite exhaustion and illness."

"That is not what she meant."

A flush warmed her face. "I *know* what she meant."

"I do not think that you do. Not really. I doubt that you have any idea of what it means to be someone whom respectable women will not have as a friend. This opera singer may visit houses like this one, but there is only one Catalani. It will not be thus for you. There will be no Aunt Edith in England or Italy to blunt the scorn."

Annoyance made her stand her ground. "I know what so-called decent people think about such women. I saw very decent men indeed approach my mother at times. As I grew older I understood what they wanted. I will deal with them as she did. Am I supposed to forego something important to me, *essential* to me, because of unfounded prejudices?"

He kept walking. Circling, circling. If he were not a citadel of propriety, if his demeanor were not so casual, she might succumb to the sensation that she was being stalked. His height kept him to the center of the chamber, and the circle seemed a rather small one now that she stood in its center.

"The prejudices are well-founded for most actresses and singers," he said, as if discussing women of ill repute were a perfectly acceptable topic. "The life is an insecure one, and I expect many performers need to accept the protection offered to them."

"You think that it is desperation that makes such women into mistresses and courtesans, and that your inheritance will spare you? Your judgment is harsher than mine. I assume that it is loneliness. A decent marriage is almost impossible. There are wastrels who will offer, but none whom you will want."

This indelicate conversation had suddenly become personal. "I know that too. Some things are worth sacrifices, however."

"A lifetime of them? You think so now, but in ten years? Fifteen? No marriage, no children, no home. I find it more sad than scandalous that for most of these women the day comes when someone offers the semblance of love and they take it. No matter what their resolve when they start, after a period of virtuous, unnatural isolation, the choice is probably inevitable."

"How dare you presume to predict such a bleak and sordid future for me. You are very cynical to contend that if I pursue my singing my fall is preordained. Not that I can see why it should make any difference to you."

His pacing stopped, leaving him several feet away. "I am responsible for you."

"So you interfere with my life, to protect me from myself. For all of ten months."

"Longer, if I can find the way."

Longer! "Don't you dare try to manipulate further obstacles. I will not tolerate it."

"Your resolve leaves me little choice. You may think that you can live like a nun, but I doubt that you have it in you to do so indefinitely."

"Your implication is insulting and scandalous."

"Not insulting at all. And scandalous only if you end up as some man's mistress instead of some man's wife."

"You have crossed a line, sir. It is improper for you to speak with me like this, even if you are my guardian."

He cocked his head and a wry little smile flickered. "I have crossed a line, haven't I? Rather decidedly. I astonish myself."

He glanced around as if suddenly realizing where they were. "Are you finished, or did you intend to practice further?"

"I want to rehearse the aria once more. I will return to the house shortly."

"I will wait and escort you back."

He settled against the wall again, in a pose of relaxed patience. She experienced a peculiar shyness.

She began to turn away, but he shook his head. "If you cannot practice with one man watching, how can you perform in front of an opera house full of them?"

Because that is different. An irrational response, but it *was* different. The focus of two eyes, *these eyes,* discomforted her more than a sea of faces. The attention of one person, *this person,* unsettled her more than a packed music hall. If even one other body were present, it would dilute the singular connection. After all, he had been present in the music room and she had not reacted this way.

She averted her gaze and tried to erase the awareness of him, but it didn't really work. The aria started weakly, as if her breath dodged an obstruction in its path to her throat. The blockage was her swelled heart pounding nervously. Stupid. *Stupid.* She located some composure within resentment at his intrusion, and hit her stride.

The music took care of the rest. Concentration on technique and expression absorbed her. The exhilaration transported her. It was not like the last time, however. Another spirit joined her on the journey, following, crowding, encompassing. As the song progressed, she could not resist looking at him. He waited with a detached manner, looking down, a man courteously biding his time before moving on to important things.

He sensed her attention. His gaze rose and met hers. She almost faltered into abrupt silence. His eyes were more startling than usual. Their expression glowed deeply warm, subtly savage, and definitely male. Not the least avuncular or aloof, and hardly protective.

Goodness, had her singing done *that*?

Despite her startled dismay, an amazing thrill streaked through her. Instead of stumbling, her voice soared. She could not look away and the aria created a provocative union between them. Spiritual. Sensual. Almost erotic. Perplexed alarm shook her, even while a heady sensation of power grew. The euphoria transformed into something undeniably physical within their mesmerizing link.

She could not have ended it even if she wanted to. Unknown emotions propelled her voice with new passions. She closed her eyes at the end, as much to contain the sensations as to savor the finale. The stones held the last sounds like a silent echo for a long heartbeat.

She did not want to open her eyes. Something had happened here that she did not want to acknowledge, something wordless and touchless, but more improper than Dante's kiss. He should have known better. She should have stopped it. She did not want to look at him until this terrible breathlessness abated.

A breeze of warmth caused her to open her lids a slit and see polished boots very close to her skirt. His fine, strong hand took hers and raised it to his lips for a fleeting kiss. "Your singing is nothing short of magnificent, Miss Kenwood. Catalani should be suitably impressed this evening."

She had to look then. He gestured formally toward the stairs. His expression had resumed its normal restraint and hauteur, but the other still shadowed it, as if the drape of reserve he had drawn was translucent.

He led the way, handing her down the winding stones, a careful representation of detached, courteous concern. As they strolled along the wall toward the path, he paused and looked up at the battlements.

"It is very picturesque," she said, hoping small talk would vanquish the odd mood throbbing between them.

"My father considered restoring and rebuilding it. Just as well he chose to remodel the house instead. This would have cost three fortunes instead of one, and resulted in a dwelling barely habitable."

"I think that it is nicer as it is, with bits and pieces of history breaking through the brush. It would look a little silly all repaired and newly mortared."

"We used to play here as children. Dante and I were the knights, and we pressed Pen into playing the lady imprisoned by her evil guardian." A broad smile broke as soon as he said it. "You can have that role now."

The little argument that he invited might help diminish how conscious she was of him standing beside her, but she simply could not pick up the cue.

"Didn't your older brother join your play too?"

"When we were very young he did. Then he outgrew us, I suppose." His gaze on the battlements turned reflective. "As he got older he retreated into his own interests, and his own mind. By the time he went to university, he was a stranger."

"Is that why you want to read his letters and such now? To get to know him in ways he did not permit in life?"

His head snapped around and he gave her a very odd look, as if she had surprised him. "I suppose so, in part."

His attention called forth the emotions from the tower again. She forced her own gaze away, up the wall. "I would like to explore the keep one day."

"I do not advise it. It has been unsafe for years. The wall walk too. Not all of these stones scattering the ground were here when I was a boy."

As if to emphasize his point, a fist-sized stone plummeted to the earth, landing at their feet. Vergil frowned up, his eyes scanning the battlements. Bianca turned to scoot away.

An ominous scraping sounded above. Another stone fell, hitting her shoulder.

Suddenly everything blurred. He grabbed her arm and swung her around, smacking her against the wall. She found herself wedged between unyielding stone and a hard body, her shoulders embraced by covering arms, her face tucked against his neck while his head pressed down on hers. Her sight had barely righted itself when a lethal avalanche of large rocks fell right beside them, one of them bouncing above their heads before grazing along Vergil's back.

She stared aghast at the shower of death and cringed inside her haven. It seemed forever before the scrapes and rumbling stopped.

Vergil raised his head to examine the upper wall. "A whole machicolation came down."

"An apt lesson to give these ruins wide berth in the future. Who would expect peaceful Laclere Park to be so dangerous?"

She spoke nervously into his starched cravat. The blue superfine of his coat caressed her cheek and her fingers rested on the silk embroidered roses of his gray waistcoat. The shock had made her extra alert and a part of her mind absurdly contemplated the varied textures of his garments. And the blissful protection of his arms. And his masculine scent. "Could my singing have done this?"

"It was most likely gravity finishing off what time began. Still, the odds of witnessing such a thing are rare. It is possible that your voice added a push." He angled his head down to see her face. "Were you injured?"

"I do not think so."

One hand slid along her back to gently press her shoulder. "Does that hurt?"

"It is a little sore. I will probably only have a bruise."

He had not released her. One arm still circled her and his other hand rested carefully on her arm below the injured shoulder. The cocoon of his strength felt very reassuring.

"That is much what you said after the horse threw you. You are supposed to swoon when faced with such danger."

She knew that he referred not to rocks and poachers, but to the physical closeness both episodes had fostered.

His warning sounded as clearly as a horn blowing in her ear. She could not heed it. His masculinity made her feel small and helpless in a sinfully delicious way.

She looked up into his deliberating eyes. "I never swoon."

His expression from the stone chamber returned, filling her with wonderful flutters. The hand on her arm slid down to her elbow, then up again. "Do you not? Never?"

The slow caress glided again. Its gentle friction created a rippling sensation. Inside her. All through her. That aria had left her vulnerable, and fear had stripped her of normal restraint. She should say something arch to end this little game, but she only wanted those fingers to glide again.

"Never."

"Every girl should swoon at least once."

That hand caressed up, not down. A slowly trailing touch. Gently over her shoulder, warmly up her neck, softly over her cheek, firmly into her hair.

She almost *did* swoon when his head angled and his lips met hers.

Warm lips. Firm and controlling like everything about him. Deliberate. Restrained but determined. He brushed her mouth with caresses before playing more seductively. Subtle nips made her lower lip pulse and quiver. Devilish tongue flicks sent scattered prickles through her face and neck. A sensitivity awoke in her breasts and she instinctively embraced him, searching for the contact that their heavy tenderness craved.

He pulled her closer and looked down in a tense, appraising way. A sigh escaped her throat with the pressure of his chest. Kissing her with fierce capitulation, he dragged her back through the threshold of the tower, into the mottled light and cool stones.

He leaned back on the wall and pulled her against his length and into a whirlwind. His arms surrounded and dominated, holding her firmly to his body and the ravishments of his mouth. Fevered kisses assaulted her neck and ears, arousing a frenzied, insistent yearning. His lips seduced hers open for an internal probing of shocking intimacy. She held on to him and submitted, dizzy with amazing sensations, soaring helplessly into a blurred euphoria.

It felt so good. Glorious. Transcendent. The exaltation of her singing made physical. The power and potential of that last aria given substance.

Here. Now. Yes. With an inaudible voice her blood pounded demands between her gasps. *Here. Now. Perfect.* Shocking pulses in her body joined the chant. Even her mind, the part that should know better, echoed a litany of scandalous urgings. Her hands shamelessly slid beneath his coat to caress and clutch his sides and back.

Something tensed within him. She felt a dangerous change and knew that her gesture had been an affirmation of some sort. His arms moved in possessive caresses and her arched body stretched in immodest reply. His hands explored for her through the petticoats and stays. His commanding passion and where it ventured should frighten her, but her excitement only allowed resentment that the layers of cloth interfered and separated and inhibited.

Yes. I want . . . I want . . . She did not know what. A crying hunger pulsed through her, with sources and destinations she did not understand. *Closer. More. I want . . .*

As if he heard her silent begging, his hand slid to her waist. Thumb on midriff and fingers on back, he caressed up the sash of her gown. Begging anticipation reduced her breath to a series of sharp inhales. A surprisingly gentle kiss accompanied the rise of his hand to her breast.

Oh . . . *Oh.* The luscious feelings aroused by his touch stunned her. The sensations streaked and flowed, joining those being stimulated by his inflaming kisses on her neck and his mind-obscuring invasions of her mouth. He gave and took pleasure at will and her limp, overwhelmed body could only accept and submit, too ignorant to offer more than acquiescence to a fervor that both liberated and subjugated.

Fingers playing at nipples grown hard and needful . . . *yes* . . . Searching now at the frill of her neckline . . . *please* . . . Sliding beneath fabric to explore the new wildness of skin on skin . . . *Ah, yes* . . . Arms pulling closer, harder, and a knee pressing between petticoats and skirt, the pressure disgracefully welcome . . . *oh my* . . . *heavens* . . . Dress loosening and puffed sleeve sliding and her naked breast being cupped up to a dark, lowering head . . . *oh* . . . Gently sucking lips . . . *oh* . . . Wickedly titillating licks . . . *OH* . . . Exquisite streams of pleasure descending, filling, demanding . . . *YES* . . .

. . . a movement, a soft crunching, echoing into the stones.

He straightened abruptly, crushing her exposure into the protection of his chest, shielding her with surrounding arms while he listened. The possible meaning of those sounds crashed through her dazed senses, obliterating the dreamy sensual world and plunking her mercilessly back into reality.

"Is someone . . . ?" she whispered, gritting her teeth against the slow unwinding of her physical excitement. She could still hear something, more of a vibration carried through the wall than an actual sound. It intruded like an invasion between the pounding of their hearts.

He pulled up the band of her chemise and the shoulder of her dress, then set her away from him. "Stay here."

He strode out of the tower. She grappled frantically with her garments, managing somehow to refasten the dress, experiencing the stark guilt of a criminal caught in the act. A pit opened in her heart.

If they had been seen, it would be disastrous.

She could hear him outside, walking around. The pit widened until it became a sick, hollow void. The full impact of her behavior hit her. This had been madness. She had been shameless. They didn't even like each other.

She heard him returning and braced herself.

He appeared in the threshold, a lean dark form surrounded by light. She could not see his face well.

"If someone was here, they are gone. It may have just been an animal."

She prayed so, and hoped if someone had come from the house to explore the keep, that they had not peered inside the tower portal.

He held out his hand in a gesture commanding her forth. Wondering what women were supposed to say and do after such brazen behavior, and feeling almost nauseous with confusion and embarrassment, she emerged into the morning. They started back to the house.

He didn't say a word. It was the longest mile that she had ever walked in her life.

She tried to find consolation in the notion that she had proven she was too dangerous to keep around Charlotte, but the idea of leaving Laclere Park unaccountably increased her dismay.

He stopped in the trees near the stable.

"I find that words fail me, Miss Kenwood. My behavior has been abominable, and an apology is not sufficient. I promise that I am not in the habit of importuning young women like that. I have no explanation except that I am clearly not myself this morning."

Aren't you? What had occurred suddenly did not impress her as entirely surprising from this man. It struck her as a natural extension of his demeanor, something controlled but always there, like a subcurrent beneath the calm, a depth one sensed but never saw and couldn't name. It had produced a tension between them from the start, like a dangerous undertow. She had felt its effects, but until today she had not understood them.

He still looked down the path, not quite facing her. His words blamed himself, but she wondered what he really thought. That he had proven she could not live like a nun? That she had the nature of a courtesan and should be permitted the ruination which she sought? "Importune" did not really describe what had occurred and they both knew it.

"I was not harmed."

"If we were seen, you most definitely were."

"I do not think that we were seen. We would have noticed someone at the portal."

"If you are right, that only avoids the worst of the potential repercussions. It does not negate the fact that my actions were inexcusable and dishonorable, most significantly because I am responsible for you. I have compromised you, whether anyone else knows it or not. If you require it, I will do the right thing by you."

"The right thing? You mean . . . Oh, no, that is an absurd idea."

"It certainly promises to be a complicated one, what with . . . well, complicated. All the same . . ."

"Let us not get carried away by your sense of propriety and duty, please. I do not feel compromised or ruined."

She received a sharp look for that. "Do you not? You are a remarkably composed young woman."

So, there it was. The insinuation of unseemly compliance on her part. Of encouragement, if one wanted to face it frankly. That look and question revealed his mind and she was hard-pressed to blame him, considering all those ambiguities she had deliberately dropped regarding her experience.

"Let us say that I do not feel compromised enough to require such an extreme measure as marriage in order to be redeemed. Perhaps we should merely forget about this."

"Your equanimity impresses me. I should be grateful that you prove so forgiving."

She didn't feel at all forgiving. She felt shattered, devastated . . . disappointed. To descend from such glory to this formal discussion on how to expiate that potent sharing . . . It made her want to hurt him, hit him, strike a blow that would defeat his cool deliberations on how to rectify their imprudence.

"I simply do not choose to complicate things further than necessary, especially in a way that removes my future from my command and requires a sacrifice on both our parts that promises a lifetime of unhappiness. I would not marry you no matter what scandal threatened. However, our further relationship becomes awkward. I think that it would be best if you agreed to my preferences regarding my stay in England. Jane and I will find a house in London and—"

"I will be the one to make myself scarce. I expect my visits to Laclere Park will be infrequent and brief during the next months."

"It is hardly fair to your sisters."

"When you come up to the city for the season, my presence will be unavoidable, but by then, perhaps time will have dulled my insult."

He didn't mean a word of it. He knew there had been no insult, not really. He had hardly forced himself on her.

She turned away, both relieved and saddened that after this house party she would rarely see him again.

chapter 7

Dante had been right. She would make a splendid mistress.

He tried to block the thought while he strode back to the ruins. It kept blurting into his head, the thoroughly dishonorable reaction of a man who had succumbed to dishonorable inclinations.

His behavior had been disgraceful. Reprehensible. *Insane.*

Which did not stop him from reliving it in his mind and experiencing anew her joyful consent. Feeling her soft lips and sweet breast with his mouth. Exploring her throbbing arousal with the pressure of his knee.

If the intruder had not stopped them he would have carried her up to the chamber and made love to her until those stones rang with her cries.

And she would have let him.

He stopped and slammed his palm against a tree, seeking a tangible reality that might obliterate his resurgent desire.

Confusing, Dante had said. Damn right, she was confusing.

She didn't even like him. They rarely spoke without arguing. He might have loitered in her presence the last two days, but she never sought out his. To then jump that chasm in such an uninhibited way . . .

He paced with determination through the trees, a dangerous mood gripping him. Her calm at the stables had been further unsettling. Infuriating. Barely a blush. Total composure. He had been a mess of conflicting impulses, but her demeanor had been incredibly calm.

I was not harmed.

I almost stripped your clothes off and took you on a stone floor.

I do not feel compromised or ruined.

Well, damn it, I *do.* Men who seduce their wards are disgusting.

I would not marry you no matter what scandal threatened.

He paused at the edge of the castle's clearing as those words echoed again and again.

He *should* have been grateful for her abrupt rejection. Instead he had experienced an irrational anger. In part because her composure left him wondering if it had all been a capricious game to her. Mostly because her resolve left him with the depressing awareness that he would never have her the way he wanted.

Just as well. She would make a splendid mistress, but an impossible wife.

Let Dante deal with her.

That notion incited a primitive, possessive resentment. He suppressed it by forcing his attention to the castle's battlements.

A stairway rose at one end of the wall, so badly ruined that whole steps were missing. He could only mount it by stretching his legs for perilous footholds. A few small sections of rock fell into the grass while he climbed. He paused each time, trying to identify whether they resembled the distant sounds he had heard while he held Bianca in the tower.

The wall walk at the top existed in gaps. Someone had replaced some missing sections with new wood, but others consisted of remnants of rotten planks, themselves no doubt repairs from the last century or so. He picked his way along until he came to the spot of the wall where one whole tooth of the crenellations had just fallen away. Down below he could see the new pile of stones.

Who would expect peaceful Laclere Park to be so dangerous?

A damn good question.

He examined the rough surface from where the machicolation had lately risen, and probed at the mortar of the stones still standing. Decayed binding fell in a little shower, joining a pile of coarse dust at his feet.

Nothing so extensive could be seen near the other partial crenellations. He examined the surface of the stones again, feeling for evidence of a tool. Did he only imagine subtle scrapes created by a metal implement?

Poachers who used firearms and now a falling wall. Perhaps just a coincidence. No proof of anything else. All the same, he didn't like it.

He climbed down from the wall, looking for evidence that someone else had come this way recently. The sounds picked up by the tower stones haunted his memory. Not the sounds of someone walking on the paths. Still, that intruder may have merely been one of the guests exploring Laclere Park's picturesque castle.

He returned to the house. When he passed the breakfast room he saw Bianca at the table with Cornell Witherby and Daniel St. John.

She smiled and laughed at some joke Witherby made.

Incredible composure.

Possibly it *had* just been a capricious game to her, a way to show the saint he was not so pure. *Perhaps we should merely forget about this.*

He strode to his study, resenting like hell the spot of honesty that admitted she might be able to forget it, but he would not.

I never swoon.

For me you did!

He was reacting like some untried boy and that irritated him even more. He sent a footman for Morton, then threw himself into his chair and pulled out some paper.

Morton arrived while he was finishing his writing.

"I want this letter to Adam Kenwood's solicitor to go to London by express delivery," he said while he sealed the missive. "Take it to the town yourself, at once." He handed the paper into Morton's thick fingers. "I may leave you here when I go north again. I do not like the idea of leaving Miss Kenwood at Laclere Park without someone watching over her."

"You think that she is in some other danger?" By *other,* Vergil knew that Morton referred to any lovely woman's danger from Dante.

Possibly she was in danger. He didn't know. However, between poachers and falling walls and assaults by the Viscount Laclere, her danger from a rake might have become the least of her concerns.

After dinner Bianca found herself sitting between Fleur and Mrs. Gaston, chatting with Pen and Cornell Witherby.

"It will be a series of epics," Mrs. Gaston explained. "Sold by subscription, although I will finance the printing. Mr. Witherby's poem will be first."

Cornell Witherby smiled modestly. Penelope bestowed an admiring gaze on him.

Mrs. Gaston held herself like a queen accepting homage and bestowing favors. Her reddish brown hair glowed like copper in the firelight and her contentment in her significance showed on her face. "The printers are at work even as we speak. I expect it to be a sensation, and for many editions to be required. Not that the profit matters, of course. Exposing people of high taste and sensibility to Mr. Witherby's prodigious talent is my goal."

She spoke as if divine guidance dictated her patronage, but Bianca suspected that Mrs. Gaston's own importance as a patron drove her as much as any love of art.

"Who will the other poets be?" Fleur asked.

A discussion ensued on the merits of young poets who might deserve such patronage.

Bianca barely heard what anyone said.

An afternoon of Fleur's gentle company had induced a horrible guilt. Vergil's cool displays of courtesy had instilled a hollow devastation. An internal clock noted the passage of every minute of the very long day with ticks of agony.

She had tried never to look at Vergil or have cause to address him, but she was aware of him at every instant. She felt him when he was nearby. She heard every word he spoke, if even from across the room.

Two Biancas reacted to his every move. The old one, the smart one, cataloged his deficiencies with a scathing anger. A new one prayed for some sign of the lord's favor. This new Bianca demeaned herself with pitiful sighs, but the old Bianca could not make her disappear.

Somehow, *somehow,* she would get through this day.

". . . there will be hell to pay if we repeal the Combination Act," Lord Calne intoned as he and Vergil and Mr. St. John walked toward their little group. "If the lower classes are permitted to mass, order is threatened. Can't have it. Too dangerous. It could end up like France in '93. You'll be regretting it, Laclere."

Little fires appeared in Daniel St. John's eyes. He looked at Lord Calne as if the man was an ass. "It sounds as if you know little of what happened in France. If you did, you would know that the people cannot be kept under a boot forever."

Lord Calne's face turned red.

Vergil spoke appeasingly. "England cannot create policy based upon the excesses of the French people a generation ago, Calne."

"Oh, spare us all. Politics," Cornell Witherby moaned softly to the ladies. "It is good for nothing but satire."

A special warmth sparkled in his eyes as he turned his good humor on Pen when she giggled. It looked as if Dante had been correct about the special friendship.

Feeling in a critical frame of mind where men were concerned, Bianca gave him a thorough scrutiny. He cut a good figure and was of average height, but his posture possessed a very unpoetic strictness, as if a rod of steel had been welded to his backbone. Blond hair fell around his forehead and cheeks. His face was a bit too long, but he was a nice-looking man of about twenty-five years of age.

That he wooed a woman who was officially married counted for nothing in her deliberations of whether he was good enough for Pen. More significant by far was his thoroughly engaged expression right now as he looked at Penelope.

She had never seen Vergil Duclairc look at any woman like that, not even Fleur. When the Viscount Laclere examined a woman, she got the impression that he was assessing her shortcomings.

Unless, of course, he was listening to her music.

Or deciding to kiss her.

Or pulling off her dress.

Or . . .

"Well, at least these political deliberations keep your printer busy," Mrs. Gaston said.

Witherby sighed. "It was only to support the literary arts that I took on the hobby of that press. I would rather tell the men to refuse every commission that was not poetic. However, the tracts subsidize the important work very nicely. As does the patronage of great ladies like yourself."

Mrs. Gaston appeared pleased with the flattery, and with her success in diverting his attention back to her.

"The repeal is a moral necessity. It is unconscionable to prohibit free men free assembly," St. John was saying to the men standing nearby.

"If they are so dissatisfied, let them leave," Mrs. Gaston said, joining the conversation. "Free passage to New South Wales for malcontents. I do not understand why no one proposes such a bill. It makes perfect sense to me."

"Give all men the vote so they can affect their futures, and there will be less discontent," St. John said.

"Should the rabble of Manchester be making laws?" Lord Calne asked. "The Commons is disrupted enough, what with radicals and Irishmen."

Pen gave St. John a beseeching, quelling smile. The shipper bit back whatever disruptive retort he contemplated.

"The people of Manchester are not rabble," Vergil said. "They are helping England become the wealthiest nation in the world. Industrial cities like Manchester cannot remain disenfranchised because of borough rights drawn up centuries ago. Reform of Parliament is inevitable."

Pen rolled her eyes at her brother, reproving him for encouraging this argument.

Lord Calne looked like he would suffer apoplexy. "I'll be damned first. Support that, Laclere, and you betray your blood. Those northern cities are terrible places. Filthy with mills and machines and base men made rich by stinking trade. Worse than London, I hear. No, give me clean country air and a good hunt. We will never let them take that from us."

Pen saw her chance. "And how is the game at your estate this year? Can everyone expect the usual magnificent shoots?"

"Looks good, looks good. A continuous battle with the poachers, though. Had to bring five men up at the Quarter sessions. . . ."

The shift in topic gave Bianca an opportunity for escape from Vergil's close proximity. She excused herself.

The less politically minded men had fanned out in the room. Nigel spoke with Catalani and Mrs. Monley near a window. Her cousin favored her with a warm, inviting smile as she passed.

She joined Diane St. John, Charlotte, and Dante instead.

They were discussing the St. Johns' two children. Dante displayed more interest in the little boys' antics than Bianca would have expected, but he moved to sit beside her and allowed the ladies to carry the conversation soon after she arrived.

"You have been very quiet today," he said softly. "I hope that you are not distraught by my bad behavior."

She had all but forgotten that kiss in the library. "I am overwhelmed by so many new faces. I have little to talk to them about."

"Well, here comes St. John. He is in shipping, as your grandfather was, so you have a bit in common with him."

Daniel St. John had removed himself from Lord Calne's company and now approached theirs.

"St. John, you knew Adam Kenwood, didn't you?" Dante asked, to make things easy for her.

"I first met him when I was very young. In fact, my first voyage as a boy was on one of his ships. That was long before he moved into finance, of course."

"When did that happen?" Bianca felt obliged to continue the conversation since Dante had started it for her sake.

"Years ago. He sold out his ships, what, ten years back or so."

"Did you sail with him long?"

"No, only that once. I jumped ship in the West Indies and found a berth with another master."

"My grandfather's rule did not appeal to you, I gather."

"Your grandfather was not the master himself. He only owned the ships and arranged for their cargo. I merely decided to sail elsewhere."

He was lying. Bianca just knew that from the overly polite way he spoke.

"Odd that he sold out the whole lot all at once," Dante said. "To own a fleet of ships one day, and then none the next."

"Since I bought two of them, I was glad that he did," St. John said.

"What did his ships carry?" Bianca asked.

"All sorts of things, I imagine, as mine do."

She got the sense that Mr. St. John was humoring them, and not being very forthright. Dante was right, it was odd that her grandfather had sold out all those ships at once, no matter what this other shipper said.

She did not have time to press him for a clearer explanation, because Penelope walked to the center of the room and called for attention. "We are fortunate to have several accomplished musicians among us tonight, and I have imposed upon two of them, Sir Nigel Kenwood and Miss Bianca Kenwood, to perform. Let us regather in the music room and give them our grateful attention."

She led the way out. Dante moved to escort Bianca, but Mr. St. John claimed her attention first. "It appears that Catalani knows when to give way to youth."

"It is kind of you to say that, but I doubt she fears competition from me."

"She has given up performing for a reason. She knows that the instrument is not what it was." He tucked her hand into his arm while they strolled down the corridor. "Nervous?"

"Horribly. I was looking forward to this, and now . . ."

"Then that explains your distraction today. My wife commented on it to me. She is very observant in her quiet way, and worried that you were distressed about something. She will be relieved to learn that it was your fear of blundering tonight's performance. I told her that was so, and perfectly normal."

No it wasn't. Not for her. But this was different. She had dreaded this moment all day. To sing that aria again, in front of all of these people, with *him* sitting there . . . Her insides twisted tighter with each step.

Nigel took his place at the pianoforte. The guests sat in chairs arrayed in front of her. Vergil chose to stand near the wall, next to Fleur's place.

She looked at him, hoping for a smile of reassurance. He didn't notice, as he bent to say something to his intended. Her heart filled. He looked so appealing in his dark green frock coat and cream trousers, with waves of hair framing his face and his blue eyes lighting with humor while he smiled at his lady.

She realized with a start that Nigel had begun the introduction. She scrambled to prepare herself.

From across the room, Vergil looked at her.

She blundered it. That first note simply wouldn't come. She turned to Nigel with a desperate, wordless plea.

He improvised until he brought the melody around to the beginning again. She focused on the floor and pulled herself together. When she looked up again she saw a green frock coat slipping out the door.

Thank you.

She hit every note perfectly, but her soul wasn't concerned with precision. Vergil might not be present in the room, but he was in her head, confusing her with that startling look, spiritually intruding with improper memories. This aria wasn't like the last one at the ruins, with its thrilling exaltation. A different emotion dripped through it this time. A strange hollow existed inside her and the music deepened it and then filled it with penetrating, regretful yearning. By the time she finished she did not know if the performance had been successful or not.

"Magnificent, cousin," Nigel whispered into the silence that followed.

The effort left her in a melancholy fog. She glanced to Catalani's pensive expression even as she accepted the praise of the other guests.

Catalani walked over, took her hands, and pulled her aside. "I have grown jaded, and confess that I expected a pretty voice, suitable for drawing rooms and churches. I was mistaken. You possess great talent, my dear. You are not ordinary."

On any other day Catalani's judgment would have produced euphoria. Tonight it only added one more big knot in the tangle of emotions that confused her.

Pen led the way into the library for cards, but Bianca begged off, saying that she wanted to retire. She followed the retinue down the corridor, but turned away at the stairs.

Nigel held back from the others. "I had hoped that we would find ourselves at the same table, cousin."

"I would have been a poor partner tonight. The excitement of singing with Catalani present . . ."

"Of course. I understand. Still, I would be grateful for some time with you. We have much in common, cousin. I would like to know you better."

All the "cousins" in the world, all the formal, proper address and tones, did not obscure what he meant. His interest glowed in his expression. She suspected that if they were alone right now in the garden, Nigel would try to kiss her.

Three men in two days. She had no idea that becoming a loose woman was this easy.

Her experience this morning was making her cynical. Maybe Nigel's interest was an honorable one.

"Will you be joining the others on the ride in the morning?" he asked.

Pen had arranged for everyone to tour the estate, ending with a luncheon at the ruins. Going back there so soon would be horrible. "I do not think so. I am not feeling well, and will stay here and rest."

The study door opened down the corridor. The tall figure of the Viscount Laclere emerged, heading to the library. He saw them and paused, standing sentry. Nigel glanced to him and gave her a private smile.

"I should like to speak with you sometime when your guardian does not glare over my shoulder. We are both alone in the world, and relatives can be a source of solace for each other. If you ever need my aid, I hope that you will call on me."

"It is very kind of you to offer. Now, you should join the others and I must seek my privacy."

Vergil did not move, even when Nigel passed with a greeting and entered the library. He just stood there, looking at her. She wanted to flip her head and turn away with haughty indifference. Instead she couldn't move.

"You retire?" he asked.

"Yes. The evening has been a trial."

"I think the evening was a triumph. I listened. You outdid yourself. As for the day, I expect it has been a trial, and I apologize for it."

She did not want to hear any more of his apologies.

"Your grandfather's personal papers arrived this morning," he said. "Most of the boxes are in my study so they will not crowd you, but I had the ones from the years when your father lived with him brought up to your chamber, along with the contents of his desk."

"Thank you." She forced herself to move and turned to the stairs.

"There is something else. I must insist that you do not go about on your own in the early morning in the future."

"Do you worry for my virtue?" It came out before she could stop herself.

He didn't even have the decency to look embarrassed. "I worry for your safety."

"I will go where I wish, and practice when I can."

"Not in the morning, and not alone. If you want to practice in private and you worry that you will disturb others in your chamber, use my study. But do not leave the house."

"You keep shortening the leash, Laclere. Why not just tie me to my bedpost?"

His blue eyes regarded her in a way far removed from the day's bland acknowledgments.

"You have a talent for provoking the most astonishing images, Miss Kenwood." He turned away. "Until tomorrow, then."

Jane was waiting in her chamber. It felt good to be alone with someone who had known her for years.

"The guests have certainly livened this old place up, haven't they?" Jane said. "All those handsome men in their fine clothes."

Jane had viewed this journey from the start as a good opportunity to find Bianca a husband. She had never recognized that the lack of suitors in Baltimore was intentional, and the result of careful discouragements.

"That Mr. Witherby looked promising. A gentleman, it is said, and nice-looking enough."

"I suspect that he has an interest in Penelope."

Jane frowned. "A married woman? Separated or not, that is what she is. Well, the viscount is out, what with being all but engaged to Miss Monley. Just as well. Who would want such a strict, stern man? There is always Charlotte's youngest brother, although it is said—"

"I know what is said."

Jane helped her into a dressing gown. "All these unmarried men, and not even a flirtation? Who would expect England to be so dull."

Anything but dull anymore, and a flirtation didn't begin to describe just how undull it had become. "My cousin Nigel has made his interest known."

"I've never liked the idea of relatives. Not good for the blood."

"He is some ways removed."

"True. Only it is said downstairs that he is much like Dante. Lives in debt. Can't afford all those fine things. Your grandfather left you most of the money. It's said your cousin only got enough money to maintain the estate, tied up proper so he can't get it, only the income every year."

"Where do you learn these things?"

"Servants here know the few servants remaining there. Tenants talk among themselves. It is just like one of our neighborhoods. It all comes in through the kitchen door," Jane said. "If he has expressed that kind of interest, you should know that he may be like Dante in other ways too. Seems your cousin is not always alone in that big house. A woman secretly visited last week. Take my advice. That is one man whose interest I don't think we want."

Bianca didn't want any man's interest. Absolutely not. Nothing but distractions, that was what men were. Potentially permanent distractions, the way the world worked. And, as she was learning the hard way, sources of confusion and hurt.

She yearned for sleep, but knew it would only come with total exhaustion. After Jane left, she moved the candles over to the crates and trunk stacked near the hearth, and sat on the floor to see what they might reveal.

A key poked out of the trunk's lock. Turning it, she lifted the top and examined the contents of Adam's desk at Woodleigh.

She fingered the quills and cheap inkwell. She poked amidst scraps of paper that bore cryptic notes. One had the name of Vergil's brother along with some others, and she guessed it had been among the last that her grandfather made.

A stack of letters, tied together with twine, caught her interest. She was about to open them when she noticed the salutation on the top one. Written in a man's hand, it addressed Adam as "My dearest friend."

They could not be from her father, with a salutation like that. Probably they were from the previous viscount. She would give them to Vergil.

In a little leather case she found a miniature of a blonde woman. She guessed that it was her grandmother. She saw a resemblance to her father, which called up memories of his love and noble honesty. Her throat burned as an old sorrow joined the new ones.

A dried flower dropped from the depression onto her lap as she lifted the tiny painting from its velvet nest.

The flower did not look very old. It did not crumble when touched, as it would if it had been in this case for years.

She pictured an old man picking a flower as he walked in the garden and later opening this case to the memories of his wife. She imagined Adam leaving this tiny offering to her.

She snapped the case closed. She did not want to become sentimental about him. Probably the flower had been there forever, and put there by her grandmother herself.

The other trunk held portfolios. Adam had been an organized man, and each year's correspondence had its own, with the year written on its front. She searched for the ones from the years before she was born, when her father had left England.

It took her some time to find the right year. She had not realized that her father had gone to America a full six years before she was born.

It was a thin portfolio with very few letters. Three were from her father. She read them, and learned the reason why Adam Kenwood and his son had become estranged.

It was not because of her mother. It had happened before her parents had even met. Vergil had been correct about how it had happened too. Her father made the break. In a letter refusing Adam's offer of an allowance, he laid out the reasons.

His explanation emptied her heart of its last shreds of joy and confidence. The dream that had sustained her since her mother's death wobbled as if its foundations had been attacked. The inheritance suddenly struck her as an evil joke, a devil's lure to join his sin.

No wonder her father had turned his back on the estate and status Adam had built.

Her grandfather had made his first fortune in the slave trade.

chapter 8

Very early the next morning, Bianca rose and dressed and headed to the viscount's study. He had said she could practice there, which meant that she could enter. She did so, but with no intention of singing.

The rest of the boxes containing Adam's effects were stacked against the window seat. Kneeling, she began to line up the wooden crates so she could examine their contents.

She wanted to know just how much she should hate Adam Kenwood before she made her decision about the inheritance. She ruefully admitted that she hoped to find some evidence of his redemption, so she would not feel obligated to renounce all of it.

Pushing the crates this way and that absorbed her, and she did not hear the bootsteps until they stopped right beside her. Out of the corner of her eye she saw polished boots and doeskin breeches. She trembled with an alert, stupid excitement.

"You were riding again," she said. "At least one of us is allowed to enjoy the mornings."

"You are welcome to join me any morning."

"I do not think that would be wise. Do you?" She fussed with some files, not really seeing what she handled. "If you want me to leave, I will do this later. I am trying to find out if my mother wrote to him after father's death, asking for help."

He walked to the other side of the row of crates and lowered to his knees. "You said it was during the war. Those years seem to be in this crate here."

She scooted over and pawed through it until she found 1814. "He was a slave trader. Did you know that?"

She guessed from his hesitation that he did know.

He poked through another crate. "Many families have that trade in their background. Lord Liverpool's father was a slaver, but he worked for passage of the law that made it illegal."

"Did my grandfather work to pass that law?"

"I do not think so."

"It was why my father broke with him. In America, my father wrote and spoke against it. We almost moved to Philadelphia so that we would not live in a city that had a slave port, but he believed he could do more good in Baltimore." She pulled at the ties binding the two pasteboards of the 1814 portfolio together.

A letter from her mother lay on top of the others. In response to an offer of financial assistance from Adam, she had refused for the same reasons her husband had never accepted any money.

And so, to get his way, to force his son's family to accept who he was, he had left a huge amount to her, his granddaughter.

She knew what she had to do. It saddened her no matter how right and just and noble it was. Without the dream of her singing, she was not sure that she had anything left.

"My inheritance was built on slavery. You were correct, and using it will be a great joke rather than a great justice. The joke, however, was Adam's."

"He sold out of shipping long ago. Most of his fortune came from other things."

But it had started there. She could not reconcile it, much as she ached to. Her conscience forced a choice that she dreaded. To have a dream within reach and then to voluntarily not grab it—

"I cannot accept it. I want you to sell out anything that you can, and give it to charity. When the funds pay out, give that away too."

"It will be reckless to sell out, even if it is your desire. A court oversees my stewardship, not you. A court made up of men who will not understand or accept that I should agree to your direction, especially since it will leave you impoverished."

"Are you saying that you will force me to accept this tainted fortune?"

"I am saying that the fortune will remain intact while I control it. When you begin receiving the income, you can give that away if you choose."

"Fine. In the meantime, there is no reason for me to remain in England any longer. I want you to secure passage for Jane and me back to Baltimore."

"I am not inclined to do that either."

"Your inclinations do not interest me."

"I think that you are making this decision too hastily, and perhaps for the wrong reasons. Furthermore, your first reason for coming, to see the estate settled, is still important even if you have decided the tainted money forces you to abandon the other."

"I said nothing about abandoning my plans to train for the opera. I will find a different way to make it happen. One that does not defy my parents' beliefs and sacrifices."

"Now I am even less inclined to purchase your passage back to Baltimore."

"In addition to being abducted, it appears that I am now a hostage. You merely delay the inevitable, to the vexation of us both. When I decide to do something, I find a way to accomplish my goal."

He had gotten that resolute, stern expression again. It was pointless to try and sway him when he was like that, she already knew. Nor did she have the heart to try now. The last day had pummeled her spirit, and she had little heart for arguments.

To feign acquiescence, she gestured to the crates and changed the subject. "Did you find anything else of your brother's?"

"I have not looked. This is your property."

She rose on her knees. "Let us look now. I will help you. When did Adam build Woodleigh, and the friendship start?"

"Six years ago."

"These will be the ones we want, then." She lifted a heavy stack onto the floor.

Vergil's hands quickly closed on the top four. He sat cross-legged and began flipping through their contents. He appeared so interested that it occurred to her that he had lingered with her now in the hopes that she would make this invitation.

She examined the two that were left. "This is odd. There are letters from Adam himself in these as well."

"They are copies of letters he sent. At some point he probably adopted the practice even for private correspondence."

"Most of these concern the building of Woodleigh. From their tone, I do not envy the architect. Have you found any to your brother?"

"Yes, but nothing surprising." His tone suggested otherwise. She looked over to see him scrutinizing a letter with a frown. He appeared very serious and a little sad.

His honest, revealing expression disarmed her. It was easy to forget that he was not only a viscount and trustee, but also a young man who was never supposed to have the title and responsibilities he now bore. She wondered if he had welcomed that unexpected change in his life. Since it had come at the cost of his brother's life, she suspected that guilt shadowed any joy he took in it.

"You can keep it," she said. "Keep anything of his, or about him."

He looked over at her. "Thank you."

His gaze did not return to the letter. It stayed on her and she could not move her own away. The silence of the study pressed on her, but a primal song sounded like a silent melody that went on and on, taking over the space in which they sat too closely and too isolated.

She might have been back at the ruins, being held by him, looking up at a face made stern with passion. She half-expected him to cast aside the letter and reach for her.

Frightened of that impulse, and of the way her heart begged him to do it, she jumped to her feet and backed away to the door.

She awkwardly gestured to the crates. "You have my permission to examine all of it. We will trade. If I find any letters concerning your brother, I will give them to you. If you find any about my parents, you do the same."

Not waiting for his agreement, she fled the room.

"Laclere."

The melodic voice drifted to Vergil that afternoon while he climbed the steps to the terrace. Maria Catalani stood at the open door.

"Maria. You did not ride this morning?"

"I am well past the age when bumping along on some rude animal is amusing, *caro mio,* and when it comes to ruins, well, my country has them in abundance. And you?"

"I have business to attend."

She fell into step when he passed into the drawing room. "You go to your *studio?* I will walk with you."

The house was silent, emptied of its noisy guests. Catalani strolled beside him as if she crossed a stage. Her form had grown matronly in the last few years and the passionate voice had failed her, but she still knew her worth.

"Thank you for the invitation. I was pleased that you extended it, and Mrs. Gaston was kind to allow me to join her so we could make your little surprise for your sister work."

"When I heard that you had arrived in London, I thought that the country might offer some rest after your journey. Also, as I told you yesterday, I had an ulterior motive besides Penelope's surprise. I need a professional opinion, and yours is the best. What did you think of Miss Kenwood's performance?"

"She is very talented, Laclere."

"How talented?"

"You do not need me to tell you. Anyone with an ear can hear it. Anyone with a heart can feel it."

"Some ears are better than others."

"She needs training, of course. It will take some time. She also must learn the languages so the words have specific meaning for her, but she is intelligent and that will be easy. Her range at the upper levels may prove limited. Roles for *mezzo-sopranos* may prove her strength. She can have many years in opera, however. She has the talent and the determination and, most of all, the heart. Quite a find, Laclere. Are you going to ask me to take her back to Milan as my protégée?"

"Absolutely not, and I must ask that you not make such a suggestion to her." Bianca had spoken of renouncing the inheritance and finding another way. He did not want Catalani to be that other way.

She studied his face. "You are not pleased with my assessment, I think."

"I confess to hoping that it would be less positive. It would have simplified things."

They had reached the library door across from the study. Maria considered him with a tilt of her head. "I think that I understand. You do not intend to allow this young woman her way, and my judgment was going to absolve you. If you have listened to her, your heart knew it would not turn out that way."

Yes, his heart knew that, but he had been hoping that lust had been obscuring his judgment.

"She will not permit you to interfere, *caro.* When we spoke, I was very frank about the sacrifices, but she remains undeterred. Was that also to your plan? That she would seek me out and become discouraged by what I described? As I said, she has the determination. It is hopeless to try and stop her."

"Perhaps, but it is my duty to try."

"Your duty? Ah, I see. You must save her. Very charming and very male. I thank God no man saved me." She shook her head and opened the library door. Hand on the latch, she turned and smiled with a warmth that made the years fall away. "What has happened to you, Laclere? Where is the young man of dreams and passion who came to my door with an armful of roses that day?"

The gentle scold provoked more nostalgia than anger. "Life happened, Maria. Duties happened. I grew up."

"Deadening duties, from what I see and hear. I should have kept you as my lover longer than one summer, if you so quickly surrendered to such a fate."

"I counted myself fortunate to have a summer. You had little taste for boys, as I remember."

She closed the door and leaned against the wall. "You were so moved by the music, who could not be charmed? Have you lost that too? Is that why I had to come and tell you what would have been obvious to you years ago? Does it no longer speak to you?"

"Sometimes it speaks as powerfully as ever."

"I am glad, *caro.* We should embrace whatever makes us young dreamers again, even if it is only for a few minutes now and then."

She did not enter the library, after all, but strolled down the corridor toward the stairs.

Bianca huddled low on the divan, not daring to move. Even after the door closed again and the voices became low mumbles, even after silence fell, she stayed in her ball of arms and legs.

She couldn't believe what she had overheard. Catalani and Vergil . . .

Astonishing. Astounding.

The *hypocrite.*

No wonder he assumed all performers became courtesans and mistresses. He probably had a whole string of them in his background, accumulated after that summer with Catalani. He probably had one ensconced in that manor up north, just as Charlotte speculated. It was isolated and discreet and no one would ever know.

Poor Fleur.

The *scoundrel.*

And yesterday morning at the ruins . . . This certainly shed an unpleasant light on that too. For all she knew, he was a predator keeping her nearby for the most dishonorable of reasons. He could be . . . He could be *dangerous.*

Prolonged silence indicated that Vergil and Catalani had left the corridor near the door. She untwisted herself and tried to accommodate this startling development.

She wasn't going to solely blame herself for yesterday anymore. She had begun to do so, in part because of Fleur, in part because it had seemed an inexplicable lapse on his part when thought of any other way. But if he hadn't been a saint when young, he probably had not truly become one later, and, in light of this news, the lapse had not been inexplicable after all.

It would be nice to blame him completely instead, but her memories wouldn't let her. Fine. They both were to blame then.

Or not, depending on how you looked at it.

She didn't feel inclined to blame anyone. That embrace and those kisses had been glorious and exciting. They had produced an intimacy such as she had never known, and a connection that seemed unbreakable. That was why she sensed his presence all the time, and why her heart beat so hard when he moved nearby. She admitted now that she had been hoping for some recognition that he also felt the invisible links forged by that brief passion.

She threw an arm over her eyes and groaned. An experience like that might transport her, but it would hardly turn a man like the Viscount Laclere inside out. He had once had the great Catalani as a lover. A few kisses and gropes with a raw recruit to passion could easily be forgotten.

She would simply have to forget as well. Clearly he expected her to.

She tried to fix on that decision. Her head was willing but her heart would not cooperate. She kept seeing that look in his eyes and experiencing anew the exciting magic of his embrace. Her chest filled with a hopeful joy that urged her to sing, and then emptied with a disappointing sadness that almost moved her to tears.

She sighed and sat up. She didn't recognize the sad, confused person she had become. She needed to find the Bianca she had been before yesterday.

She would simply step backward and pick up the strands. She would renew her plan to make him send her away, only this time to Baltimore. Leaving had become essential now. She couldn't live the next ten months like this, absorbed by a man who obviously regretted their behavior and only wanted to keep his distance from her.

She needed to settle matters quickly. She would have to do something very shocking, something Vergil could neither ignore or forget.

An obvious solution presented itself. Vergil could rationalize a lapse with himself by blaming himself, but he would hardly miss the implications if she lapsed again with another man soon after. He might have affairs with women like Catalani, but a good brother could not permit a Catalani to live with Charlotte.

Who should the other man be? Not Nigel. Vergil might decide to call him out.

Dante?

She felt more like her old self than she had in twenty-four hours. Planning her next move helped keep her mind off the sadness that nibbled inside her.

Yes, Dante would do very well, and a rake would hardly disappoint her.

The next day the party spread out along the shores of the lake, enjoying a lazy afternoon. They had brought books and sketching pads with them in the carriages, and lots of parasols for the ladies. Dante and Cornell Witherby had stripped off boots and stockings and waded with fishing rods into the low water.

Dante walked out of the lake. She caught his eye while he dried himself. She smiled. After he pulled on his boots he came over.

She had never realized how susceptible men were. If he weren't a rake, she might have felt guilty.

Dante lounged beside her. "You do not sketch?"

"I never learned. My education was not the typical drawing room variety."

She noticed Vergil rising from his spot and meandering into the trees. As if his movement had been a cue, the other members of the party began regrouping. Pen and Catalani carried their parasols over to Fleur.

"Your walk in the lake must have been refreshing on this warm day," she said. "I envy you."

His lids lowered and he regarded her with that private look. She knew he was remembering her own dip in this lake the day he first arrived. It reminded her that she played a dangerous game here. She had better choose her moment with the greatest care.

"I tire of sitting. I think that I will take a turn," she announced.

"May I join you?"

"That would be kind."

The path formed a large circle through the trees and brush. She guided him in the direction opposite that which Vergil had taken.

"Will you be leaving with the others tomorrow?" she asked.

"I think that I will stay a few more days."

"Charlotte says that you find the country boring."

"This visit has been anything but, thanks to your company. And you? Can Laclere Park occupy you during the months ahead?"

"I confess that I doubt it. Fortunately, Pen has spoken of a visit to London soon, so that Charlotte can begin choosing her wardrobe for the season."

"I will make it a point to be there when all of you come."

They strolled into a spot where the trees fell away and only tall grasses and bushes flanked the path. Down a low hill, a little clearing filled with flowers lay near the lake.

"Look, bluebells. Help me down so I can pick some."

Dante was only too happy to help her down the hill. She knelt amidst the fragrance and began plucking up the buds. With an encompassing glance that noted their isolation, he settled down beside her.

She peered toward the tall bushes hiding the path, looking for Vergil's dark hair. He should be passing this way soon.

"You are very lovely there, surrounded by those flowers, Miss Kenwood. They make your eyes even bluer."

"Call me Bianca, Dante."

He looked like a man pleased with a sudden good turn in fortune.

Still no Vergil.

"I am honored that you agreed to walk with me today. I was concerned that my behavior in the library had left you angry and afraid."

"Not angry. But a little afraid, I will confess."

"Such a reaction is what one would expect of an innocent girl. Kissing you like that was an inappropriate thing to do. I can only offer as an excuse that I was overcome by how lovely you looked in that subtle light."

"You do not need to apologize. I was not insulted, just surprised. If I reacted strongly, it was because of that."

"May I take that as encouragement that my addresses find some favor with you?"

It sounded like something Vergil would say. Only Vergil had said nothing of the kind before kissing her, and now this rake did. Men could be very confusing.

"That depends on your intentions."

"Completely honorable, Bianca, I promise you."

He hadn't touched her. He hadn't even moved closer. How much encouragement should a rake need? She glanced anxiously toward the path.

"Not too honorable, I hope."

He smiled in both surprise and delight, but he still didn't move. Where had this sudden inconvenient restraint come from?

"You cannot know how happy this makes me. Now, we should resume our walk and return to the others."

She couldn't believe her ears. "I do not want to return to the others just yet. I would rather stay here with you."

"I am flattered, Bianca, but—"

"I want you to ask to kiss me. You said that you would and that I would not refuse. I have thought about it and decided that you were right. I would not refuse."

He glanced around at their isolation, clearly torn. She did, too, and thought she saw dark hair finally moving between the bushes' branches.

"It would be best if we left now," he said.

What good was a rake if he got all proper just when you needed him to do something outrageous? When you had bluntly invited him to do so? In a few seconds Vergil would move to the top of the little hill and what would he see? Nothing.

Dark hair strolled closer. She stomped a mental foot in frustration. This chance might never come again.

Kiss me, you idiot.

Dante rose to his knees and offered his hand to help her up.

She lunged.

He fell back with her weight and his arms instinctively encircled her. "Miss Kenwood . . . Bianca . . ."

She pressed him to the ground and he grappled in confusion. In the flurry that followed, she rolled so he embraced her reclining body amidst the flowers.

The world righted itself and silence fell. She looked up at a face at first startled, then dangerously sensual.

"Well, sweet girl, if you insist." He lifted her toward a kiss.

Their lips never met. A rampaging animal crashed down the hill. A strong hand grabbed Dante by the neck of his garments and hauled him off her. Furious, savage blue eyes seared into one befuddled and astounded rake.

"I warned you," Vergil growled.

His fist sent Dante sprawling. Then that hand pulled her up, set her right, and brushed the grass off the back of her garment with swipes that stung her bottom.

She looked guiltily at Dante. She hadn't expected Vergil to react so violently.

She faced Vergil bravely. They stared at each other, her glaring a challenge and him barely controlling his fury.

Dante staggered to his feet. "Oh, hell," he muttered.

"Exactly," Vergil said.

That confused her. She looked quizzically from one to the other. Vergil shook his head in exasperation and stepped aside.

Her gaze followed Dante's.

Oh, dear.

Up on the crest of the little hill, Fleur, Pen, and Catalani watched from beneath their parasols.

"I tell you, she literally threw herself at me. One moment I'm offering her my hand and the next I'm sprawled on the ground with her on top of me."

Dante paced in front of the study's window, looking as agitated as Vergil felt.

Vergil stayed behind his desk, because if he got within ten feet of his brother he might thrash him. "Do you expect me to believe that Miss Kenwood jumped you, overpowered you, and then dragged you into an embrace? It is preposterous."

"*Listen* to me. I'm kneeling there, about to get up. She had just invited me to kiss her and I had demurred. Then suddenly she turns into a she lion and—"

"You were *on top of her.*"

"That part is a bit confusing. It all happened so fast. I have to tell you, her behavior has been astonishing. I am shocked, to be frank about it. I can't recall that I have ever experienced anything like it."

"You hardly looked as though you were fighting for your virtue."

"Well, she was so insistent. And I *am* human."

Far too human. He'd like to smash his fist into Dante's face again and then grab Bianca Kenwood and turn her over his knee.

"Nothing else for it, of course," Dante said. "What with the ladies seeing."

"If I discover that you decided to save time as you suggested that day in here, I will—"

"Don't know why you are so upset. It is what you wanted. I'm the one who has to marry a girl with very suspect morals."

"Suspect morals?"

"If she is so bold with me, one has to wonder."

Yes, one did. Especially if one knew for a fact that she had been kissing another man just two days ago. That explained partly why he was so angry. However, it was seeing them embracing that had caused the explosion in his head that still hurled sharp fragments.

She knew that such indiscreet behavior carried extreme consequences. He had spelled it out less than two days ago. How could she be so careless as to . . .

How, indeed?

He sank down in his chair and mulled that over. He had left first, followed by Bianca and Dante. The ladies must have begun their walk soon after. Pen and the others had caught up with him only because he had paused to think some things over. Things about Bianca, as it happened.

It all fell into place. She had planned it. She had intended him to find them together. To make him jealous? She had definitely succeeded there, but he could not delude himself that it had been her intention. A woman's revenge for what had happened in the ruins? A declaration of indifference because she had noticed him watching her? He had tried to be very discreet about that, but he might have failed.

Damn.

"You were right about one thing, Verg. I will have to be very firm with her. No matter what is in the past, I will not have her taking lovers once we are married. She will have to understand that." The censorious line of Dante's mouth would put a bishop to shame.

"You think to dictate her behavior?"

"I'll not be made a fool."

"Dante, you have made a fool of half the House of Lords. Do you think that young woman will permit you to preach morality?"

"A husband has his rights, and I've a reputation to consider. Despite the likely blemishes on her virtue, no doubt the result of lax supervision, she is a sweet and accommodating creature."

Accommodating? "You amaze me."

"As to my own activities, I expect she will remain ignorant of that."

"No one in England is ignorant of that."

"It is obvious that she is in love with me, and she is, in her heart, still a wide-eyed child. I do not doubt that she will accept any arrangement that I present, and submit as appropriate to my supervision."

Wide-eyed child? Submit?

He shook his head incredulously. Dante had assumed the countenance of a *paterfamilias* who took for granted marital devotion and obedience from his wide-eyed, accommodating wife.

He doesn't stand a chance.

"If we ignore what this reveals about her character, one could say things have worked out very nicely. I will take the blame, of course, but she has played right into our hands."

She had certainly done that. He should be gloating in triumph, but the thought of what was to come only sickened him.

"Where is she?" Vergil asked.

"Up in her chamber. Pen has everyone in the library, trying to pretend nothing happened. The rest don't know, but it is bound to get out. I will speak with her at once and make my offer."

"We will speak with her together. She may need some persuading."

"Can't imagine that. Everyone knows the rules."

Yes, everyone knew the rules, but Bianca had not shown any inclination thus far to play by them.

chapter 9

For a warm September day, the study held quite a chill.

That probably had something to do with the icy blue eyes ostentatiously looking away while Dante knelt and proposed.

"Therefore, while I would have preferred to court you and then offer in the normal way, under the circumstances it would be best if we married immediately," he concluded, squeezing her hand and bestowing a reassuring smile.

Vergil lounged in his chair behind his desk, turned toward the window with a distracted, bland expression. He had sat there like a silent witness while his brother performed this most intimate of rituals.

She gave her attention back to the young man balanced on one knee. "Why would it be best if we married?"

"Why?"

"Yes, why?"

"Because, Miss Kenwood, the alternative is a scandal." Vergil's steely tone cut the air into shards. "You were seen with my brother, and as a gentleman, he will do the right thing."

She looked at the beautiful man kneeling by her side. Poor Dante. To have successfully raked all these years, only to get ensnared the one time he had tried to act very honorably.

She patted Dante's hand. "You are very kind to offer, but I must refuse."

"Refuse?"

"You will be relieved to learn that I do not exact such a high wage for such a small indiscretion." *As your brother well knows.*

He rose. He didn't look relieved at all. Incredulous and a bit insulted, but not relieved.

"Vergil . . ."

"I will manage this now, Dante."

Bianca shifted so she faced him squarely. "You will find that I am not inclined to be managed, least of all by you. It is unforgivable for you to force your brother, your own blood, into this for such a little thing."

"I assure you, Bianca darling, that I am not at all unhappy about it."

"A little thing? It was no mild flirtation that the ladies witnessed. You were lying on the ground together. Only if your garments had been in *dishabille* could it have been worse. What would have happened in Baltimore if you were found thus?"

"I imagine if my father were alive he would have shot Dante."

"Are you saying that you would prefer that I shoot my brother?"

"I am saying that I will not accept marriage under these circumstances. The punishment is far too permanent for such a small crime." *I have explained all this before. Remember?*

Vergil began to respond, but Dante cut him off with a quelling gesture. He lifted her hands in his own and gazed into her eyes. "My dear Bianca, I assure you I do not view this as a punishment. Rather, it is a dream come true. For your sake only do I wish the circumstances were different. You stole my heart immediately. I have spent these weeks praying for a sign of your affection. This only gives me my soul's desire sooner than I had dared hope."

Her heart sank into her stomach. He meant it. Not the parts about stealing his heart, but the rest. He didn't mind this development.

Out of the corner of her eye she observed Vergil. He appeared resolute and angry, but not one bit surprised.

Her heart sank further.

This had been the plan from the start. It was why Dante was here, and why Vergil wouldn't let her leave. Dante had been chosen for her. Her whole stay at Laclere Park had been a type of trap, and her own stupidity had sprung the clamps closed.

"So, let us hear no more talk of sparing me from punishment," Dante said, lifting her hands to his lips. "In a few days we will be wed, and I promise to make you very happy, darling. Doing so will be no punishment at all."

His soothing tone carried a note of seduction. Vergil's jaw clenched. Her stomach heaved.

She extricated her hand. "I am honored by your affection, but still I must decline."

A silence ensued, so tense that one expected invisible coils to snap. Bewilderment, then amazement, then annoyance flashed over Dante's face.

"Perhaps you should leave us, Dante. I would like to speak with my ward alone."

"Certainly," Dante said. "Bianca . . . Miss Kenwood." With a little bow he was gone.

She glared at Vergil, daring him to pursue this farce. He rose and paced to the window.

"With your mother long dead and your aunt unmarried, your education has been lacking. Forgive me if I must be blunter than men should be with women. You were seen prostrate under my brother in those flowers, engaged in lovemaking. When that is discovered, the only honorable course for the man and the only redemption for the woman is that they wed. You may not extract such a wage for indiscretion, Miss Kenwood, but society does."

"As I remember it, I was engaged in lovemaking with you and you accepted my refusal of your offer. I suppose that means you got to be honorable but I did not get to be redeemed. Fine. I will accept the same resolution with Dante."

"Do not . . . This is different. You were *seen.* The consequences cannot be avoided."

"So it is being seen that makes such behavior scandalous? How unfortunate for Dante. It is a good thing for him that I am not a slave to propriety."

"You did not hear me. When you lost control with my brother, you also lost control over the outcome should your behavior become known."

"What makes you think that I lost control with your brother? I don't remember it that way at all."

He turned abruptly with an expression of . . . what? Shock? Relief? "Are you saying he importuned you? Forced you?"

He almost appeared hopeful and, for a moment at least, not at all stern. Her chest filled with an astonishing yearning. He looked so . . . vulnerable. An odd thought, but that was what she saw for an instant. It made her wish that she could somehow abort this foolhardy plan. But what good would that do, especially now that she knew why he was so adamant about her staying with his family.

"I am saying nothing of the sort. Would it make a difference to society if I did?"

"No."

Nor would it make a difference to you. Not really, despite that look. Our passion was a blunder that almost botched things horribly. You planned for Dante to have me, after all.

She forced herself to act lighthearted despite the raw hurt ripping at her composure. "I did not think so. The thing is, you keep bringing up scandal and society, while I care about neither. You seem to forget that this is not *my* society."

"It is the one in which you now live."

"Only temporarily. You asked what would have occurred if we had been found thus in Baltimore. A duel or a marriage, such as families demand here, would be two possibilities. Or I might have been sent away. I suggest that we consider that last option now as well."

His expression lightened. Definitely relief this time.

"Ah, I see. Of course. I had wondered why you did it, but it is becoming clear now. Independence was your goal from the start and you still pursue it. But you have overplayed your hand."

And you are glad that I did. Glad that I sprang the trap so neatly. Glad that Dante will have me. Oh, Laclere . . .

"I assure you that I *did* it because I wanted to *do* it. Furthermore, I think that you will have to permit me to leave. I have no intention of rectifying things by marrying your brother. If the result is a scandal, so be it. I expect that it will be a very big one, but it will fall only on me if I leave soon. We will let everyone know that he tried to do the right thing, but that I refused him. Once I have left, it will all be forgotten."

He cocked his head. "Are you so determined that you would invite such scorn to achieve your ends?"

"I would invite even more if necessary. You really should let me go. Otherwise you may find your family the center of all kinds of outrageous behavior." She tossed her head in what she hoped was an imperious manner.

The silence crackled. She turned back to find him suddenly standing right beside her chair.

He did not look amused anymore. "You wouldn't dare."

"I have already dared. First with you and now your brother. It should be clear by now that I am not what you expected."

"What is that supposed to mean?"

"Open your eyes, Laclere. What kind of a woman would hop from one man to the next like that?"

"You tell me, Miss Kenwood." His quiet tone made her very uncomfortable.

"One too free-spirited to avoid scandal in your very proper society, I would say. Wouldn't you?"

"I haven't decided yet."

"What is to decide? You know that my behavior has been outrageous, and I don't even feel remorse. I refuse to be redeemed. The conclusion that you must be drawing is unattractive, but I don't even mind."

"What conclusion is that?"

The scoundrel was going to make her spell it out. She wobbled to her feet, trusting she would feel more brave if she felt less small.

"That I like men far too much for a decent woman. That I am too . . . experienced to remain part of English respectable society."

He cocked an eyebrow. *"Experienced?"*

"Dangerous, it is said in Baltimore."

"*Dangerous* now."

"Yes. *Dangerous.* In fact, there are those who say . . . I have even heard that some people think that I am . . . wicked."

"Are you saying that there have been other men?"

It had become difficult to act casual and flippant. He was making her uncomfortable, but in a foolish, flustered way. Something of the expression at the ruins seemed to have deepened his gaze. Ridiculous, of course. He was probably just suitably appalled with her confession.

"Other men? You mean besides Dante and yourself?"

"I mean besides myself. My brother has told me how little actually occurred today."

That detail seemed to please him far too much. A flood of irritation emboldened her. She raised her chin at him. "Of course there have been other men. You don't think that the English air has suddenly made me lose my head, do you? Of all the atmospheres in the world, the stuffy one here would be the last to cause a woman to do so. There have been lots of other men."

He didn't like that. Good.

He hovered more, bending his face to hers. *"Lots?"*

"Many. Dozens."

"Dozens?"

"Hundreds."

They stood there toe to toe and nose to nose, glaring at each other.

A smile twitched. "*Hundreds*? You are a superb actress and would have been magnificent on the stage, but *hundreds*?"

"Yes, *hundreds.*"

He laughed. "You should have stopped at *lots.* Or at least *dozens.* But *hundreds* . . ."

"You do not believe me?"

"Not at all."

He looked so handsome with the smile softening his mouth and humor sparkling his eyes. Incredibly handsome. And reassured. Triumphant, if the truth be told. It vexed her to no end, and she suppressed the odd swell of emotion foolishly glowing in response to that smile.

She had gone to all this trouble, had risked being assaulted by a notorious rake, had created a scandal that for all her posturing would be hell to face, and he was refusing to see her disreputable character even when she threw it in his face. It infuriated her, even while her heart stupidly beamed with gratitude.

"You do not believe me because your male pride does not want to accept that you were merely one of hundreds, that is all."

"I am confident that I was not one of hundreds, or even dozens. I strongly suspect that I was not even one of lots, and quite possibly not so much as one of two. You will drop this ridiculous act at once."

Something dangerous burst inside her. Something rebellious and furious and even a little wicked.

She reached up with both hands and grabbed his head. She pulled him down and planted a very firm kiss on his lips.

She held him until his stunned shock began to pass, then released him and stepped away before he had completely recovered.

"Hundreds, Uncle Vergil. I am infamous for ruining saints."

She turned to exit upstage.

A firm hand closed on her arm.

With a gasping swirl she found herself turned and pulled into arms, which encircled her waist and shoulders. The Vergil of the ruins looked down at her. Dangerously.

"You make me wish that were true," he said, lifting her until her toes scraped the floor, lowering his head.

She should push him away, but her arms would not obey her command. Her suddenly foggy mind scrambled for words to put him in his place, but her heart beat so loudly that she couldn't hear herself think. His warm lips touched hers and she didn't have a mind at all anymore.

He ravished her mouth with demanding lips and nipping teeth and exploring tongue. Disgraceful sensations cascaded through her and, heaven help her, she reveled in them, savoring his encompassing strength, losing herself in a warmth that obscured considerations of anything else.

He buried his face in the crook of her neck and kissed and bit a pulse there. It sent shocks to her breasts, her thighs, and all the way to her toes. He took her mouth again with a burning insistence. She welcomed him this time, parting her lips, inviting the arousing invasion.

His embrace moved into astonishing caresses, pressing to her hips and back and buttocks through her garments. The recently awakened, shameless Bianca thrilled at each possessive touch. His hand slid toward her breasts and her reckless passion lilted a plea for him to hurry and release the desire aching through her consciousness, building a breathless craving.

He stopped abruptly, like a slap had made him sane.

His lips parted from hers. His head rose. He did not release her, but held her in a silent embrace, caressing her back with slow, soothing strokes.

The frenzy leaked away, leaving the Bianca Kenwood whom she knew too well in the arms of a man whom she should hate. But even this Bianca did not want to separate. She rested on his chest and floated in the friendly tenderness of that touch, because it kept the worst of her confusing emotions at bay.

Finally, she tilted her head. He gazed out the window with a sightless expression.

He looked down, touched her face, and set her away from him.

"I seem to have forgotten myself again."

He wanted them to retreat once more to their roles of dictatorial guardian and rebellious ward. Of course. What else would he want? Just as well. If he kissed her like this every day and held her with such gentleness afterward, she might decide that nothing else mattered in her life.

She saw no criticism in his face, but considering what she had just told him, she could imagine what he might be thinking. Even if he really had not believed her, she had undoubtedly just changed his mind.

Say something.

Of course he would not. But, oh, how her heart wished that he would speak whatever he thought right now, good or bad. She wanted with an inexplicable yearning to know this man, whoever he really was, sinning paragon or sordid fraud. She longed just once to enjoy the special intimacy of sharing his confidences along with his passion, even if the result was hearing condemnation for the woman she pretended to be.

The acknowledgment that he would never open to her in that way, that he responded to her with lust but nothing more, left that newly discovered corner of her heart anguished with regret.

"You really must permit me to go," she said softly. "You should be concerned with my influence on Charlotte, but perhaps you should worry for yourself as well, if I provoke you like this. It is abundantly clear that I must leave this family now."

He only glanced at her, that thoughtful expression still deepening his gaze.

"I will not marry your brother. If you do not let me leave, the scandal will encompass your whole family. You will be the talk of society for harboring such a female, and Charlotte will be tainted by my friendship. In your sister's interest, if not in mine and yours, allowing me to leave is the only decent choice for you."

Still he said nothing. Perhaps because there was nothing to say.

Somehow she turned away from him. Half-blind with tears, she found her way to the door.

• • •

He experienced no self-recrimination this time. No guilt or shock. No regret.

He was glad her brash kiss had destroyed the dam filled to bursting. Glad she had provoked him to release his tenuous hold on control. That was all her kiss had really been, an excuse that he had ruthlessly grabbed. He would not demean her by pretending it had been a deliberate invitation on her part.

How quickly the mind surrendered to what the passions wanted to do. His blood had roared and the next thing he knew she was in his arms.

She was not wicked or experienced, but she was definitely dangerous. To him at least.

She was right. She really had to leave. Within a day, everyone in this house would know about her and Dante. Within a month, the entire world would be whispering. She had not missed the implications of the lessons Pen had been giving her about the code of discretion in English society. She had deliberately arranged things to use the threat of scandal against him.

But that was only part of the reason why she should leave, and she knew that too. What a picture he must present to her. The saint lecturing her on behavior one moment and then ravishing her the next. A laughable figure at best, a depraved one at worst.

He lifted the little lead ball and sent it down its path on the toy. When it reached the bottom he did it again. The chinks and clanks beat out the pattern of his thoughts.

He should send her away and let her have what she wanted, but he could not do that. As long as possible, he needed to keep control of her, and not only because the relentless simmer had become an enlivening, welcome excitement.

He walked to his desk and fished a letter from amidst the documents stacked there. He flicked it open and reread the information sent to him by Adam Kenwood's solicitor.

What a tangle.

He needed to keep her here because she might be in danger. He needed to keep her here on the chance that he still might bind her to this family.

He needed to keep her here because her absence would create a void in his life, but she had cornered him so he would have to let her go.

He smiled with regret and admiration. In overplaying her hand, she had managed to force his own.

The door opened and Penelope's dark head appeared.

"Vergil, may we speak with you?"

"Of course, Pen."

The other part of the "we" turned out to be Maria Catalani and Fleur. Fleur went to the window seat and the others settled themselves into chairs.

Penelope let forth a deep sigh. "This is a very unfortunate business. You cannot say that I did not warn you."

"That is true, Pen. I cannot say that."

"I expect that Dante offered to marry her when you had them both in here."

"I did not hold a pistol to his head, if that is what concerns you. He has great affection for Miss Kenwood, and had intended to propose, in any case."

"Did he? That is interesting, but that is not what concerns me. Or us, rather." She gestured toward Catalani and Fleur. "Bianca is too naive to protect herself from someone like Dante. We really should have warned her. What is worse, I do not think that she has the same *tendre* for him that he does for her and it would be very unfortunate if Bianca is forced to marry him."

"Not *unfortunate.* Tragic." Catalani intoned. "I do not think that marriage to your brother was in her plans, Laclere."

"Plans sometimes change."

"That is a man's arrogant dismissal of a young woman's preferences. And this marriage—a man takes advantage of a girl's innocence, and the response of everyone is to marry them. Barbaric. It is worse in my country, but still it is barbaric."

"So you see, we do not think marriage is the solution," Pen said.

"Well, ladies, I suppose that I could defend her honor by killing Dante if you would find that more to your taste."

Catalani actually began to nod, but Pen looked aghast. "You misunderstand us. We have talked it over, and the point of their marrying is to blunt the scandal. We have come here to tell you that there can be no scandal."

"I would say there can be a very big scandal."

"Not at all. Maria and Fleur and I have realized—"

"That we did not see anything." Catalani finished triumphantly.

He settled into his chair and looked at them. "You did not see anything?"

"That is correct, Laclere. Nothing. So much for this talk of marriage. *Abbastanza.*"

"As I remember it, you saw quite a bit."

"Oh, no," Pen said. "Maria was explaining a new sleeve becoming fashionable in Milan and we were engrossed. Until the three of you came up that hill, we were not even aware that Bianca and Dante were there."

"You think to contain this among yourselves?"

"Yes, not that there is anything to contain. But if there were, we would never speak of it after leaving this room, even to one another. The fact that we saw nothing, that is."

He should resist this solution and hope that Bianca would change her mind, but the relief with which he heard Pen's scheme told him that he would have embraced this offer of silence even if Bianca had submitted to the marriage at once.

In that instant he knew that he did not want Dante to have her. Nor any other man. Except himself.

Which was impossible.

He turned to Fleur.

She noticed his attention. "I am the last woman in the world to force a girl into marriage, Laclere."

He considered this reprieve. She would not have to leave. She would be safe. He might yet rearrange those plans.

He would still see her.

"I have yet to hear of women keeping silent about such things, or men either. However, if you think you can do so, perhaps disaster can be averted."

"I can be a citadel of discretion when it is warranted," Catalani said with a meaningful arch in her eyebrows.

"Well, now that is settled, we must go dress for dinner," Pen said, rising. "It is very generous of you to be so understanding about this, Vergil. I promise you, no one will ever know that you bent the rules just once."

"Very good, Pen. We certainly wouldn't want anyone to know that."

He found Dante alone in the library.

"It appears that you have been spared. The ladies insist that they saw absolutely nothing. Assuming Miss Kenwood does not start rumors about herself, which despite her boldness is unlikely, there need be no marriage."

Dante threw up his arms in exasperation. "Are you forgetting that we do not want me to be spared?"

"I made it very clear that I did not want the girl trapped against her will."

"I did not trap her, damn it, she trapped *me.*"

"It would be best if you left tomorrow with the others. Some time apart and she may welcome your attention again."

"You have more tenacity than I. The girl just refused me, in case you didn't hear it as clearly as I did."

"I heard a young woman refusing to be coerced by circumstances."

"I do not care for the way she dismissed me. It was insulting, especially since the alternative was rather bleak. She all but implied that marrying me was a fate worse than death, and while I may not be some great prize . . . If it weren't for her inheritance, I would tell you to go to hell."

"Pen will be taking her and Charlotte up to London soon. I expect they will remain there at least a fortnight. I will accompany them and stay a few days, but it would be best if you took over when I left. Whether Miss Kenwood welcomes your interest or not, I do not like the idea of her alone in the city with just Pen watching out for her. She is too independent-minded, and may attempt to go about on her own."

"I daresay there will be men enough to watch over her once Pen starts taking her around."

"Exactly, Dante. If she does not marry you, I would prefer that she marry no one for some while yet. In particular, I do not want Nigel alone with her at any time. I want you there to see that she has no opportunity to get into any more trouble. With any luck, however, she will allow you to pick up the pursuit of your case."

He didn't really believe that, but if Dante continued to court her, it would mean someone was nearby who could be trusted. After what had just happened again in the study, it had become imperative for that someone to be other than himself whenever possible.

All the same, Dante's lack of enthusiasm heartened him, and relieved him of one potential opportunity for guilt. If Dante had fallen in love with her . . .

"It may be best if you made any new overtures very subtle," he added.

"I know how to handle women, Verg."

"Of course. My apologies."

"I will be subtle. Damned subtle. I don't fancy having the girl make me look like a fool again."

Vergil turned to go find Fleur. With any luck, Dante would be so subtle that Bianca wouldn't even notice him keeping watch.

Fleur was sitting on the bench in the garden where they met sometimes for conversation away from the hopeful eyes of her mother. She appeared, as always, utterly beautiful, like a figure molded in porcelain or painted by a great master. She turned at his footfall and her mouth pursed into a wry smile.

"I hope that we did not disrupt your plans too much."

He sat beside her. "Not really. Catalani's idea?"

"Pen's, although the solution had crossed my mind. On my own, however, I would have never proposed it. I did not know if you welcomed the development or not."

"The match would have been convenient, but the circumstances did not appeal to me."

They sat in the contented silence of friendship. He studied the serene, delicate profile that he had always admired with a peculiar objectivity. He had never felt any passion for this exquisite woman, even before he learned that she was incapable of feeling passion for him.

"My mother is letting her impatience show, isn't she? She has said things this visit."

"She has been more pointed sooner than I anticipated. I do not think there is cause for concern yet, but—"

She held up a hand to stop him, then let it fall helplessly to her lap. "Which means others are saying things to her. I know that it has been almost a year, but I had hoped to get another season out of it."

"As had I. That may not be possible."

"No. Oh, how I resent this, Laclere. Last season was the first one I enjoyed. No suitors bothering me with their silly petitions. No endless speculation about this match or that. No pressure from father, and best of all, a good friend with whom to enjoy the balls. A woman should be allowed to have such peace all the time if she chooses."

Her fervor would have surprised anyone else who knew her. However, he had seen her in tears, confessing the fears that led her to resist marriage, admitting that she could not contemplate the love of any man without freezing with terror. A deep friendship had emerged from that unexpected confidence, and a casual association had become a calculated deception. Such a ruse had a limited life, however.

"A woman with your beauty is bound to attract suitors, Fleur, especially if she has your fortune. If you looked more gently on them, perhaps one would—"

"Not you, too, Laclere. Please, do not. Forgive my outburst. You have been very kind, dancing attendance in a waltz you knew would end."

"Not kindness, Fleur. Remember that it also spared me the tribulations of the marriage mart. For my own reasons I would like to avoid pressure to take a wife right now as much as you would a husband."

"You never told me why. Not fair, to share confidences only one way. I was tempted several times to try and learn your secret. It is nothing sordid, I trust."

"That depends on what you call sordid."

"Nothing you would do, I'm sure." Her laugh turned into a sigh.

"What a pair we are, Laclere. Do you think anyone has guessed our little arrangement?"

"No, but some have probably begun to wonder."

She turned thoughtful eyes to him and the frown returned. "I suppose so, especially if mother has grown so bold. It has been falling on you, hasn't it? The suspicion that you are behaving less than honorably toward me."

"Nothing has been said, Fleur, nor do I think that my reputation has been affected."

"But mother . . . yes, people are beginning to wonder. I will tell mother after we leave that you offered and I refused you. I will let it be known that it was my decision, as I always promised I would. Father will be furious, of course. He always is when I let a title slip away." She cocked her head. "Unless, of course, you have decided to accept the arrangement I proposed last spring."

He couldn't help but smile. "It had its appeal. A permanent solution for us both, and your inheritance as well. But I cannot marry right now, Fleur. If the day comes when I can, I will want children. A white marriage is not for me. No doubt you can find another man who will accept it."

"I will make that offer to no one else. I would trust no other man to honor the terms. Nor do I expect to find another whose company I enjoy enough to contemplate a lifetime with him. I think that once I break things off with you that I will go on a grand tour. A very long one. By the time I get back I will be old enough to be on the shelf."

"There is no need to tell your mother immediately. Take your time if you want."

"I may put her off another month or so. Express some reservations first, that sort of thing."

He patted her hand. "There is no hurry, as I said."

Her soft palm turned up and grasped his with a child's desperation. "I do not fancy facing the loneliness again," she whispered. "Promise me that we will always be friends."

He wished he could spare her. He would obliterate her fears if he could, and send her off to find happiness with a good man.

He held her small hand tightly, to reinforce his words. "Of course, Fleur. I am always here for you."

chapter 10

The sabres clashed and rang under the watchful eye of the Chevalier Corbet. Vergil met the challenge of Cornell Witherby. On the other side of the large chamber in the Hampstead manor, Julian Hampton sparred with Adrian Burchard. Adrian's brother, Colin, and Dante formed a third pair.

"You have improved," Vergil said as he caught Witherby's sword making a new move.

"You have not."

No, he had not. It had been months since he had met the others here. What had been a regular sport before he became viscount had turned into a diversion that he had little time to enjoy anymore.

Not only his skill had suffered, but also the friendships that he shared with these men. Today he had made time for both them and the exercise.

The practice continued, with the old French chevalier snapping praise and criticism.

"Have your sisters come up to town with you?" Witherby asked as they paused and faced off again.

The light in Witherby's eyes revealed more than Vergil wanted to know. But then, he had seen how Pen's demeanor had changed since the house party. Her glowing happiness made it easier to accommodate himself to their escalating intimacy, but there was a husband who never would. Vergil trusted that if a love affair began, his friend would be carefully discreet, and not only because of their old friendship. No man wants to be named in court for criminal correspondence with an earl's wife.

"They have both come. It is time to prepare for Charlotte's first season."

Witherby rolled his eyes. "I have always considered it a gift from heaven that I had no sisters demanding such an expense."

"Well, we all find our way into debt, and a sister is as good a path as any."

"Speak for yourself. I am happily solvent."

No doubt he was offering reassurances to the brother of the woman he pursued, but Vergil found the admission interesting. It appeared that Witherby's printing establishment, which he liked to treat as no more than a gentleman's hobby, served the baser purpose of supplementing his income.

They engaged again, but the sounds beside them stopped. Hampton and Burchard strolled toward the entry to prepare to leave.

Vergil made a better show during the ensuing minutes. His lack of practice hampered him less with each move. He forced himself to concentrate on the task as well, and that made a significant difference. Instead of contemplating his unproductive investigation into Milton's death, or exploring improper thoughts about Bianca Kenwood, he honed his attention on the moves of his sabre.

The chevalier called a halt and treated them both to little lectures on how to improve. They joined Hampton and Burchard in the chamber used for dressing, while the chevalier turned his attention to Colin and Dante.

"I am glad that you could join us, Duclairc," Hampton said as he tied his cravat in the reflection of a small mirror tacked to the wall. "Will you be coming back to the club?"

"I need to escort my sisters this afternoon. Pen will be commissioning Charlotte's presentation gown."

"Say no more. Even with your oversight, the cost will be obscene. Left on their own, they will ruin you."

Adrian had already dressed, so he sidled over. "Will you be in town a few days now?"

"Two or three."

"I will call on you."

Vergil knew why Adrian planned to call, and what he intended to discuss. While Vergil wanted to know what Adrian had learned on his mission for Wellington, he had no desire to reveal his own investigations.

Hampton and Adrian left to claim their horses. Within a minute of their departure, the sounds of an altercation poured in the window of the dressing chamber. A carriage clamored up as a man's voice shouted curses.

Vergil grabbed his coat and headed out to the front drive with Witherby on his heels. They joined Hampton and Adrian just as a slender man with graying hair jumped out of the coach.

It was the Earl of Glasbury, Penelope's husband.

"Fiend," he snarled, striding to the men arrayed in front of the building's door, pointing with a walking stick. "You despicable scoundrel."

Witherby tensed. Vergil stepped closer to him, to form a human shield, and Adrian closed in from the side.

The earl advanced with the walking stick thrusting like a sword. His slack mouth formed a flaccid, scowling line and his face flushed redder with each step.

The tip of the stick did not seek its mark on Witherby. Instead, the earl thumped it against Julian Hampton's chest.

"I'll not be your prey," the earl said, poking the stick with each word. "Who do you think you are, daring to try and make a fool out of me?"

Hampton barely reacted. His hand grasped the stick's tip where it rested on his chest. He did not even remove it. He merely held it and walked forward, forcing the earl backward.

When he had him twenty yards away, he yanked the stick out of the earl's hands and thrust it aside.

A conversation took place that Vergil and the others could not hear. Vergil could not see Hampton's face, but he witnessed the earl's reactions. The man looked half-mad, and more than anger made him so. A frantic terror fired his eyes.

The earl turned on his heel and gave Vergil a pointed, disdainful glare as he climbed back into his coach. Insignia flashing in the morning sun, the coach pulled away.

"I'll be damned," Witherby muttered with annoyance. "Hampton? Who would have thought—"

"It had nothing to do with the countess," Adrian said.

Hampton's expression showed no reaction to the drama as he rejoined them. "A misunderstanding," he said blandly.

They all claimed their horses, to ride back to the city. As Vergil prepared to mount, he caught Adrian's eye. It was not hard to do, because Adrian was in the process of trying to catch his in return.

They soundlessly acknowledged their mutual conclusion regarding what had just occurred.

Someone was trying to blackmail the Earl of Glasbury, and the earl thought it was Julian Hampton.

Bianca shuffled through the fashion plates and plucked one out to set aside.

Very casually, Diane St. John removed it from the preferred plates and returned it to the original pile. "The waist is too high."

Across the elegant sitting room, Penelope and Charlotte bent their heads in consultation with Madame Tissot, debating designs for Charl's presentation gown. Diane had joined the party to offer her opinions. She and her husband frequently visited the house they owned in Paris, and she knew the latest developments even better than Madame Tissot.

Vergil patiently waited. Mostly he ignored the proceedings, while he gazed out the window or paced around the room.

"What is he doing here?" Bianca muttered to Diane. "Surely he could trust Pen's taste in these matters."

Diane cast Vergil a sidelong glance with her soulful eyes as she tilted her chestnut head toward an image of a morning dress. "Perhaps his attendance has nothing to do with taste in fashions."

"Well, he is underfoot all the time now. He left Laclere Park with the rest of you after the house party, but then inexplicably returned in time to travel with us up to London. Now every day he shows up at Pen's house, always in time to accompany us. These visits to the modistes must be boring him."

"His sister will represent the family when she is presented. However, perhaps he finds female company other than boring. Many men do." Diane spoke quietly and casually, but her little smile left Bianca wondering if Mrs. St. John referred to the company of one female in particular.

It horrified her that someone may have guessed about that, especially since Diane had probably heard about the episode with Dante by now.

Bianca was very sure that the viscount's presence had nothing to do with his desire for her company. Vergil was hovering about for some other reason, probably to keep an eye on the expense of Charlotte's new wardrobe. However, as a result, Bianca had not been able to slip away as she needed to. Worse, she had been forced to bear the discomforting presence of a man with whom she had twice now been shockingly out of control.

He did not appear at all discomforted. He acted so calmly one would think he had forgotten those embraces.

Except for the moments when she caught him regarding her with eyes that said he remembered all of it. Those looks served as little pokes at her composure. Scandalously exciting provocations.

A male hand reached around her shoulder and plucked a plate from the pile. "This one. Without the lace on the sleeves and in this rose color here."

With a fluid movement, Diane St. John rose and strolled across the room to where Madame Tissot was unfolding silken evening wraps.

"I rather thought this one," Bianca said, pulling out a flamboyant ball gown with an excess of frills. "In scarlet red."

"No wonder Madame Tissot has taken no orders from you. She has her standards."

"Then I will have to find another modiste to dress me as society expects. There will be no point in swathing myself in sedate rose if everyone sees scarlet anyway."

"You do not need to worry about that. It is clear that the episode with my brother remains unknown."

She looked up at him with surprise. She had assumed that the force of his reputation had merely delayed the storm.

"It has been a fortnight, Miss Kenwood. If anyone in that house learned of it and intended to speak of it to others, they would have done so by now. You have been denied your scandal."

"Perhaps *I* will speak of it."

"I do not think so. Suffering shots from others' guns is one thing. Turning the pistol on oneself is quite another. It takes hopeless despair to do that. Stubbornness will not suffice."

He was right. She had steeled herself for the onslaught of scorn, in part by concentrating on her escape from it. It would take more determination than she possessed to deliberately provoke the gossip that might free her.

She suspected that he had found a way to thwart her. Just as well, then, that she had an alternate plan.

Madame Tissot unfolded a shawl with a flourish. Woven of the finest deep sapphire silk with violet undertones, it fluttered over Charlotte's lap like an eddy of water. The modiste cocked her head critically, then shook it with a sigh. "The hue is not right, mademoiselle. Since it is not a fashionable color this year, it must be just right for the woman who wears it."

Vergil walked over and lifted the exquisite shawl. It cascaded from his hand like a waterfall.

Madame Tissot noticed his appreciation. "However, with the right gown, a violet one perhaps . . ."

"It would suit my ward."

Madame Tissot turned to Bianca with new eyes. Within moments the little French woman had draped the shawl over her back and arms.

"It is lovely on you," Diane St. John said. "You have an excellent eye, Laclere."

Charlotte clapped her hands. "It is beautiful, Bianca. You must have it. See what it does to her eyes, Pen."

"Yes, you must have it," Vergil repeated. "The violet gown too, Madame Tissot. Something modest and understated."

"Of course, Lord Laclere."

Madame Tissot escorted Bianca back to the inner sanctum, and a whirlwind of measuring and draping ensued. An hour later Bianca emerged into the front room again, to find only Penelope, Diane, and Charlotte waiting for her. The guardian who had just imperiously spent a sizable chunk of her income for her had disappeared.

Which meant only Penelope stood between her and a few hours of freedom.

"Let us walk back," she suggested while Roger, Pen's footman, carried the wrapped shawl to the carriage.

"Heavens, no," Charlotte said. "I am exhausted. Where do you get your vigor, Bianca?"

"It has been a curse all my life, and I really grow troublesome if I cannot walk it off."

Pen blanched at the word troublesome. "We are supposed to attend the theater tonight. Surely you would like to rest."

"I really feel the need for a good walk, Pen. A nice long one. Why don't you and Charlotte take Mrs. St. John in the carriage, and I will follow. I know the way."

Pen glanced around the street, as if hoping to see reinforcements. Bianca had already determined that the general had left the field.

"If I was not expected by my husband, I would join you in this walk," Diane St. John said, giving Bianca a private wink. "One absorbs the life of the town when one strolls its streets. Why not permit it, Pen? Especially since it will avoid her becoming *troublesome,* as she says."

"If you insist. I must require that Roger stay with you, however. Please do not tarry, and be sure not to get lost."

"I can hardly get lost with Roger as an escort."

The other ladies left in the carriage. Bianca began walking away from the direction they had just ridden. Roger fell into step behind.

"May I ask where we are going, Miss Kenwood?" he ventured after a good half hour.

"To the City."

"The City? Nothing to see there and it is too far. Best if we turn back now. My lady said you should not tarry."

She began to respond but a passing carriage caught her eye. She turned and watched its progress down the street. Surely that had been Nigel by the window. And across from him, the shadowed figure of a woman.

Roger waited with strained forbearance. He appeared ripe for negotiation.

"No doubt this excursion keeps you from other duties, Roger. Perhaps it would be best if I found a coach. Show me where to hire one, and then you can return to the house."

He began shaking his head even before she finished. Sighing with defeat, she turned and led him down the street. She would prefer to do this alone, but even if Roger spoke of it and word reached Vergil, she still would have accomplished her errand.

Like magic, his name summoned his memory and his memory summoned his presence. A curricle slowed into pace beside her. She glanced over to find Vergil holding the reins.

He had a whole city to ride in. He might have taken another street to wherever he was going.

He stepped out of the carriage and Roger rushed to hold the horse.

"I will take Miss Kenwood home, Roger. You are released of your charge."

The footman turned on his heel. Vergil gestured to the curricle.

"I am not returning to the house yet, Laclere, so I will continue walking."

"No, you will not. Whatever your destination, I will accompany you."

She let him hand her up. He settled beside her. "Where can I take you?"

"To the City. I wish to see Mr. Peterson."

He didn't turn a hair. "It is good that I happened by, then. Pen would have worried with your delayed return. It will not do for you to absent yourself for so long, even with a footman for protection."

A red arrow shot through her head. This man had the effrontery to scold her for not accommodating herself to the restrictions he created.

She welcomed the old vexation. Like a suit of steel for her heart, it blunted other reactions evoked by being alone with him again.

Embarrassing, confusing, dangerous reactions.

"I think that my cousin Nigel is in London," she said as they rejoined the other vehicles crowding the streets.

"He arrived a few days ago."

"It is odd that he has not called on Penelope."

"He called yesterday."

"It is odd that Pen did not mention he had left his card."

"She never saw his card. I procured it from the butler."

She turned in surprise toward his impassive profile. "Your sister will be insulted that you presumed to do so."

"I doubt that, since he did not call on Pen."

He said it with utter calm, as if the implications should not bother her at all.

"You discovered that my cousin called on me, and you removed his card so I would not know? How dare you?"

"Compose yourself. Anyone who sees us would think we were having a row."

"We *are* having a row. It is time that we had a right understanding on a few things, Uncle Vergil."

"Call me Laclere. It is disconcerting to have a woman whom I have kissed address me as Uncle Vergil."

She stared at him with astonishment. "You amaze me. You refer to that with equanimity even while you assume a posture of authority."

"I neither refer to it nor think of it with equanimity. I merely point out that Uncle Vergil has become a peculiar form of address. As for your cousin, I do not approve of his interest in you."

"Considering the man who did meet with your approval, your lack of it might be treated as the highest recommendation, and suspect in its motivations."

"I will not spar with you over this. I forbid you to ever see your cousin alone, and I must insist that you do nothing to encourage him. I do not take this course to further my brother's cause, but to protect you. I do not think Nigel Kenwood is what he appears to be."

He must have heard about Nigel's secret woman visitor.

"Not what he appears to be? Oh, my, dear me, goodness, goodness, what a shock." A storm of confusion, hurt, and resentment that had been gathering for three weeks broke and she let fury fly. "A fine observation coming from you. Excuse me if I am not undone by this stunning news, but I think that there is not a single man in your fastidious society who is what he appears to be. Aunt Edith warned me about the corrupt, immoral underbelly of the English aristocracy, and I begin to understand her. How dare you judge Nigel. If he is not what he appears to be, he is no more a fraud than you. Less of one, because he does not set himself up as some saint. Much less of one, because the last I heard, he did not make love to his ward *even* while he courts a fiancée *and* keeps a mistress up in Lancashire."

He almost didn't react. Almost. The slightest flicker of dismay lit his eyes, however. That instant of concern told her more eloquently than words that she had hit a mark with her last accusation.

Charlotte had been correct about his journeys north. He kept a woman there.

It sucked the fury right out of her. She sank back into the seat, overwhelmed with a sick desolation.

The depth of her disappointment staggered her. This detail irrevocably turned those kisses from impetuous passion into sordid follies.

"Fleur is not my fiancée," he finally said.

"A minor point, Laclere."

He drove slowly, as if some contemplation distracted him.

"Who told you that I keep a mistress?"

"Do not worry. No one at the house party made insinuations about it. The servants are not gossiping. Only those closest to you suspect. Your visits to her have been noticed. What attraction could draw you north so frequently? Charlotte suggested the explanation, but I would assume that Penelope and Dante have guessed."

She ached for him to deny it. She even wished he would lie. What could one more deception hurt?

He began navigating the City's narrow streets without a word, but a frown continued to crease his brow. Considering her own devastation, she was glad that she had given him something to worry about.

A public scandal about Dante would have been easier to bear than this private humiliation.

She entered Mr. Peterson's chambers with renewed resolve to shed herself of Vergil's presence in her life.

The solicitor smiled with relief when he saw that she was alone. Vergil had escorted her to the outer chamber and then gone off to conduct some business of his own.

She hurried through the usual pleasantries. "I do not want to appear abrupt, Mr. Peterson, but I expect the viscount to return for me quickly. When last you wrote, you indicated that you expected some news soon, and since I am in London I thought it easiest to come and hear it myself."

"As you requested, I have obtained the names of some of the men who have expressed interest in purchasing your business partnerships. Most were only tentative inquiries, but one was very firm."

He pawed through some documents. "Here it is. It is for the mill. That is the investment already yielding income. For one thing, the business has established itself. For another, you own forty-five percent of it. The mill's manager, a Mr. Clark, owns another forty-five percent. Your grandfather stood him to over half of the initial capital some six years ago when it was built."

"Who owns the rest?"

"Your grandfather was the majority owner. He left the remaining ten percent to his grandnephew, Nigel Kenwood. He intended the income to help maintain Woodleigh."

"Someone wants to buy the mill now?"

"Learning the details took a few pints of ale cajoled down the throat of a clerk to Adam Kenwood's solicitor. There has been a serious offer from a Mr. Johnston and Mr. Kennedy. Nigel Kenwood is eager to agree, but the manager has refused to entertain the offer. Mr. Johnston and Mr. Kennedy demand majority ownership and control of the business, so the new baronet's ten percent is worthless to them without the agreement of one of the principals."

She lined the details up and saw them paving a road back to Baltimore. "And I am the other principal. If I sell, and Nigel sells, the manager loses control of the mill."

"That is correct. He will still enjoy its success, assuming that the new owners pay out honestly, but there are many ways to see that minority investors do not reap the same benefits as those in control. It is easy to claim costs that do not exist, and divert funds accordingly. Not that I would cast any aspersions upon Mr. Johnston and Mr. Kennedy, but they *are* managers of mills. Unsavory types, for all the wealth they accrue."

He made it very clear such men were definitely beneath Mr. Peterson himself, who was hardly to the manor born.

"What has my guardian's reaction been to this offer?"

"The viscount is considering it and has asked for financial figures, which Mr. Clark has delayed in sending. No doubt the man plans to be an obstruction whenever possible. Still, the clerk with whom I imbibed indicated that the viscount seemed inclined to hold the investment. It does pay handsomely."

Which meant that it would pay handsomely again. Who was to know if part of the next payment got "diverted" now to the account Mr. Peterson had established for her? Not much, just enough to get her and Jane back to America.

If she promised the manager not to sell when she turned twenty-one, he would probably grab at her suggestion and see it as a mutually beneficial business arrangement.

"Mr. Peterson, I would like you to write out the information on this mill for me."

That night Bianca attended the theater with Vergil and Penelope. She wore the blue silk shawl for what she expected to be the first and last time. She intended to leave it behind when she sailed from England.

Its luscious fall reminded her of the life her inheritance offered, and that she would soon reject.

She did not want to return to Baltimore without visiting Milan. For all of her brave resolve with Vergil, she was not sure that she would find another way to affect her dream and plans. She pictured herself at Aunt Edith's age, always wondering what might have been.

Perhaps she did not need to repudiate the entire inheritance. Maybe, if she gave away half . . .

She mentally castigated herself. If she began making excuses for using some of Adam's ill-begotten fortune, she would probably end up seduced into the luxury the whole amount afforded. Baltimore it would be, and she would return as poor as she had left.

She noticed little about the performance on the stage down below. Not only her moral debate occupied her attention. So did the man sitting beside her. His mere presence made her warm. His smallest movement made her heart jump. Considering what she had learned about him today, her susceptibility infuriated her.

Yes, Baltimore it would be, and very soon too. When she was back home she would be able to forget this man who had her reacting like a fool, even though she knew he was a scoundrel and a fraud.

That night when she retired, she found a letter waiting for her in her chamber. It was one that Adam Kenwood had written to Milton.

In it he agreed to Milton's suggestion that he give to charity an amount that equaled what he had reaped when he sold his shipping business, to make reparations for the profit he had accrued through the slave trade.

Another note had been folded into the letter, this one from the current Viscount Laclere.

"I found this among my brother's papers and thought that you would like to see it. Today I visited Adam's solicitor to verify that the intentions expressed in this letter were carried out. They were, some three years ago. Therefore, the portion of his estate that you have inherited is not tainted. There is no guilt in accepting it. It appears that Adam came to see his son's rightness on this matter."

She stared at the letters as their implications sank in. Her heart beat rapidly with reborn joy and excitement. It would not be Baltimore, after all.

She pictured Vergil leaving her with Mr. Peterson and going to the solicitor to verify what had happened. It was not in his interest for her to know about this. The truth gave her back her dream—a dream that he did not approve of.

His generosity touched her profoundly. Her annoyance at his interference disappeared and her suspicions about his character became insignificant. Even the dream lost importance. Vergil's gesture of discovering the truth turned her heart inside out.

He might be a fraud, and he might be dangerous, but she would miss him badly when she was gone.

chapter II

Vergil poured two glasses of port and handed one to Dante. His brother had discarded his frock coat and now lounged contentedly in a chair in front of the study's low fire. He looked for all the world like a man whose various appetites had been sated. Vergil surmised that he had spent the evening with his current mistress.

"I expected you to join us at the theater tonight."

"I got distracted, and then the weather turned raw. It is bad enough that I have to start playing nursemaid tomorrow. No need for both of us there tonight."

No. No need. However, Dante's presence might have distracted Bianca, and pulled her out of the subdued mood into which she had retreated since their argument in the afternoon.

It had been an uncomfortable night. Bianca had cloaked her reactions in serene composure, but he had felt her thoughts, and even seen them on occasion in the lidded glances she gave him. By the time he escorted the ladies back into Pen's house, he had come close to pulling her aside and blurting out an explanation and begging her forgiveness.

Pointless. Hopeless. What could he say?

She had concluded he was the most dishonorable of men, not because of the mistress, but because of the implications regarding his behavior toward her. She had decided he was a predatory monster. Maybe she was right.

Certainly he felt a predatory desire with her continued proximity.

"Nigel Kenwood is in town. It is very important for you to stay in London until the ladies leave," he said to Dante. "It would be best if you resided here. I have instructed Morton to open your bedchamber."

"Laclere House is uncomfortable out of season, what with most of the house closed and most of the servants in the country. You may not mind living like a monk in a few rooms with only a valet, but I think that one of my clubs would be preferable."

"I want you near Pen's house, not in a club."

"You are acting like a fussy old aunt, Verg. What can Kenwood do? She cannot marry him without your permission, unless you fear them bolting to Scotland."

"That would not be beyond the imagination. However, I must confide in you that my concerns are more serious now." He went to the desk and retrieved the letter he had received at Laclere Park from Adam Kenwood's solicitor. "Read this."

Dante lazily flicked the paper open. "Seems common enough to me. Miss Kenwood's inheritance is entailed. If she dies without children, it goes to her closest relative."

"Yes, common enough. Except for the clause that limits the relative to someone with Kenwood blood. I had barely noticed that when I read the testament, but the solicitor's letter makes it explicit. That rules out the great-aunt in Baltimore, and leaves only Nigel."

"So?"

"She is more valuable to him dead than as his wife."

"Barely, considering a husband's rights. Are you saying that you think that musician would harm her? Your imagination has gotten the better of you."

"Most likely. I may be doing Kenwood a disservice in my suspicions, but I would rather take a cautious stance. I have asked around, and he is thoroughly in dun territory both here and in France."

"Which is why he wants to marry her. Hardly a criminal offense. If I stood to inherit with her death, would you assume that I contemplated murder?"

"Of course not. Nor would I suspect it of him, if she had not come close to being killed twice in the last month."

That wiped the amusement off Dante's face.

"There were two very close accidents at Laclere Park. Unusual accidents, Dante, and I am not entirely convinced that they were accidents at all." He briefly described the incidents.

Dante pondered the tales. "Could have been nothing, of course. Just coincidences. Still, I can see where one might raise the caution, just to be safe."

"Exactly."

"Wouldn't it be best to warn her?"

"I can't impugn the man on such flimsy evidence, and I may be wrong. I suspect Miss Kenwood would attribute my warning to a desire to keep her and Nigel apart. If so, it could have the opposite effect."

Dante frowned at the fire for a spell. "Old Kenwood did you no favors in naming you her guardian, Verg. I am concluding that she is nothing but trouble. A firm hand doesn't begin to describe what is needed with her. I had thought that little episode in the lake was a charming misstep, but you tell me now that while at Laclere Park she slipped out alone in the early mornings for long rides and walks, unaccompanied. She is found rolling in the grass in my embrace and flouts all sense of decency by refusing to marry me. She has shown evidence of a very loose upbringing and unacceptable notions of independence, and in all likelihood she left her virtue behind long ago."

Vergil noted his brother's uncompromising, male expression. Did the Viscount Laclere look like that to her?

You do not know her. She is not trouble or indecent. She is a young woman with dreams, fighting for her life.

"I will tell you now that I am no longer amenable to marrying her, and to hell with her inheritance. However, I will see to it that she does not stir from Pen's house without a chaperon, and not only because she may be in danger. The fact is, Verg, I do not think that you have been strict enough with her. If we are not very careful, she might bring this family down."

Miss Kenwood's safety accounted for, they moved on to other things. But in the flames that he watched while they spoke, Vergil saw her body turned away while she watched the play tonight. She had worn the blue wrap, and its fluid silk cascaded in swooping curves along her back and over her arms, picking up the theater's low lights, bringing out the blond of her hair through a lovely contrast.

He had envied the way it caressed her, and was glad she had worn it. Madame Tissot's account would not be settled from Bianca's income, but she would never know it. He had taken enormous pleasure in seeing her wear his secret gift, even if her icy manner indicated that she would throw it in the fire if she knew he had paid for it.

Just as well that Dante had arrived. He had been enjoying her company too much, and contemplating her far too often. She had become a dangerous fascination. An impossible hunger.

He narrowed his eyes on the dancing flames. Time to be off again. To Lancashire. To his mistress.

"Then it is settled. You will host the reception next week." Mrs. Gaston made it sound as though she bestowed a great favor on Penelope.

Penelope lifted a beautiful little book off the table beside her chair. "I could hardly refuse, since Mr. Witherby saw fit to dedicate the volume to me. That honor should have been yours, as patron of the series."

"It would be vulgar for *all* of them to dedicate their poems to me. I prefer less ostentatious acknowledgment anyway. Nor would we want anyone to infer that the genius of our poets was being bought like so much ham in a market."

Bianca watched Mrs. Gaston's face as she demurred her significance. Her high cheekbones appeared more prominent today, as if her skin strained against them. Bianca wondered if Mrs. Gaston had been nearly as delighted as she now professed, to find that her patronage had not been celebrated in Mr. Witherby's brief dedication.

Penelope, on the other hand, glowed with delight. Her gaze kept returning to the book's brown leather binding, and her fingertips drifted over the tooled decoration again and again.

"He would do better if you hosted the reception, I fear. There will be those who will not accept my invitation."

"Nonsense. I will see to it that the people who matter come. This will be an important event for you, my dear. A first step, as we relaunch you into the circles you deserve. Your situation has lasted long enough. Even transported prisoners eventually can come home."

Pen's wavering smile revealed skepticism, resignation, and hope. Bianca's heart twisted at the emotions flickering on the countess's face. Penelope always appeared accepting of her social fall, even glad for it, but it was obvious right now that she merely hid the pain.

Bianca looked to Mrs. Gaston with new eyes. She had not warmed to the woman before, but she did now. Mrs. Gaston had continued her friendship with Pen when many others did not. Now she was plotting Pen's rehabilitation. Small wonder that Pen counted her as a dear friend despite her vain, overbearing manner.

"I will ask my brother if I can use Laclere House." Pen spoke with firm decision. "It will take a lot of preparation, of course, but perhaps he will agree."

"Make him agree," Mrs. Gaston said. "Explain what is at stake. More than a poet's success. Witherby is his friend, so Laclere should come around." She rose. "Now, I must go and make my other calls. I think that Mr. Witherby will arrive soon. He allowed me the honor of bringing you this first printing, but no doubt he wants to witness your pleasure in it."

She left Penelope gazing at the book, stroking its cover again.

Bianca went over to admire the little volume with Pen, and then sat nearby. She would have preferred broaching her request on a different day, when Pen was not so absorbed in the compliment of that dedication.

"Penelope, I would like to return to Laclere Park tomorrow."

That pulled Penelope's attention away from the book. "Are you saying that you are not happy here? I thought that you preferred the city."

"I do. However, I am very uncomfortable with Dante in attendance so much."

"Goodness, are you saying that he has—"

"His behavior is above reproach. I know that we are fortunate to have him escort us to the theater and such, and yesterday's excursion to the British Museum was very enjoyable. It is just . . ." She let her voice trail off.

Pen had never spoken of that day by the lake and what she had seen, but her expression indicated that she understood Bianca's reason for wanting to leave London.

"It wouldn't do to ask Dante to make himself scarce, Bianca. Charlotte rarely gets to spend time with him. As for departing the city, I have just promised to give Mr. Witherby the reception to honor his new book next week. I wish I could accommodate you, but until the reception is over, we are rather stuck here."

"I could return myself tomorrow with Jane, and you and Charlotte could follow as planned."

"I do not think that would be wise."

"Jane and I crossed an ocean. The ride down to Sussex is a minor thing, especially if we go in your coach. Once back at Laclere Park, we will be well cared for."

Pen began wavering.

"Please. The alternative is for me to take to my bed here and pretend an illness. With time I am sure that Dante's company will not embarrass me, but right now, so soon after . . . it is difficult to face him."

Pen patted her hand. "You are always so composed that I never realized how awkward it is for you."

"Very awkward."

"I think that I will permit it. Still, I will be giving my coachman strict instructions to take you directly to Laclere Park, and he will carry orders to the butler and housekeeper to see that you remain there. Vergil can hardly object with those precautions in place."

"Thank you, Pen. Will you make some excuse to Dante?"

"I will find something to say when he comes tomorrow. Eventually he will know that you have left, of course, but not right away." She bestowed a sympathetic smile. "He really is very gentle, Bianca, despite his naughty behavior. I hope that you will be at ease with him in the future. Vergil tells me that Dante holds the most honorable affection for you."

"Do you really think men are capable of that? I wonder if their affection is ever really honorable."

Pen shook her head with a little laugh. "I am the last woman to give advice on the topic." She caressed the book of poems with her fingertips.

"Although, I find myself wondering if it might not be possible in a few rare cases."

The mail coach careened around a bend and its passengers braced to keep from crushing to the left. Bianca huddled inside Jane's light cloak, seeking some shelter from the damp chill that had reached her bones hours ago.

She had not expected this journey to be this miserable. The speed of the coach created a jaw-jarring ride despite the good roads.

There had been no alternative. Not only did she need to make this journey a fast one, but the money she had hoarded out of the twenty pounds extracted from Vergil would not pay for a private coach. She had permitted herself one break last night at an inn, and would do so on the way back, but she doubted that Jane could maintain the deception longer than three days.

She pulled the cloak snugger. Just her luck that the only hooded outer garment that Jane had brought to London was lightweight wool.

The request for Pen's coachman to stop at a coaching inn near Laclere Park so that Jane could detour to visit an ill friend had not raised any suspicions. Nor had her own excuse to seek relief at the necessary. Back behind the building, she and Jane had exchanged cloaks and the wrong woman had returned to the carriage. Even the weather had cooperated, providing a light rain to explain the obscuring hoods pulled low over their faces.

Hopefully, when Jane arrived at Laclere Park, she had managed to retire abruptly with complaints of a chill. Snuggled in Bianca's bed for a few days, wrapped and capped and sleeping off an illness, she might just avert discovery of her true identity.

If not, Bianca expected to return before a full alarm could be raised.

The biggest inconvenience in the plan, besides her numb extremities, was the fact that she had not been able to bring any baggage with her. The only items of toiletries and clothing that she carried were stuffed in her reticule and inside her bodice.

The coach sped into the environs of Manchester, making a series of quick stops as the countryside gave way to sprawling villages that then bled into the edges of the city itself. An odd combination of raw newness and old squalor flanked the residential streets. Perhaps on sunny days, and if a visitor weren't bone-chilled and hungry, it would not appear such a dreary place. One knew without being told that this was a growing city. The congestion spoke of too many people cramped into too few domiciles.

Their pace slowed until the driver pulled to a halt. Two other passengers gathered their belongings. "If you want Manchester, this is it," one said. "Coach heads to Liverpool now, and the mail for the city will be picked up here by others."

Bianca stepped out into the drizzly mist. She entered the coaching inn and asked the man in charge where she could hire a gig and driver for a few hours.

Soon she was back in the damp again, this time squashed beside a portly driver snapping the gig through the city streets. She huddled inside her thin cloak with the hood pulled low against the mist.

"Is the Clark mill far away?"

"East a bit. Newer mill than somes the others, and a bit off on its own. Hard to believe it was almost open country there just ten years ago. City just keeps getting bigger, like a spider getting fat from eating those coming in from the land." He pointed to a young man standing against a building. "Like him. Can always spot them. They have that bewildered look. Then, if they find work in a good mill, they grow contented, and if they don't, they get mean."

"What is a good mill?"

"One with decent wages, such as they are. Where the machines are kept safe. Where families work the same times." He cast a sidelong look at her. "None of my business, but you sure you want to go to this mill today? There's been a spot of trouble popping up here and there the last few months. Been gettin' worse, it's said."

"I must go today. I am sure that Mr. Clark has one of the good mills, so there should not be a problem."

He laughed. "When trouble spreads, there are no good mills."

It took almost an hour to make their way to the eastern environs and the long, low buildings of the Clark mill.

The driver hopped down and helped her descend. "He would be in there." He pointed to a two-storied stone square. "Manager's house. Not as fancy as some." He raised his head like a dog sniffing. "Seems quiet enough."

"Wait here, please. I will want to go back to the coaching inn for tonight."

She gathered her limp cloak around her and marched into the house. A young man sat at a desk in the building's first chamber.

"I have come to see Mr. Clark," she explained.

He gave her the once over and was not impressed by Jane's serviceable cloak. "He is in the works right now. Perhaps I can help you. I am Mr. Thomas, his secretary."

"Thank you, but it is Mr. Clark himself with whom I must speak."

He examined her critically again. "They don't usually send such young ones. Which reform group are you from?"

"I am not from a reform organization. I have business of a most critical nature with the manager."

"Tell me your name and I'll go see if he knows of this business."

"Mr. Thomas, I have no intention of giving you my name. I will wait on Mr. Clark's return. I promise you that he will not thank you for any interference."

His startled reaction hovered between a laugh and a frown. Amusement won. He showed her into the office.

A fire burned in its hearth. She stood close and savored the warmth that began burning away the damp.

She turned to give her back a little roast, and surveyed the office. The furniture was solid but plain. The desk's surface held only writing implements and a neat stack of documents. The whole room appeared rather blank. If it reflected the manager's personality, he was a colorless, uninteresting man. Hopefully that did not mean that he lacked imagination. She needed him to see that her proposal actually gave him what he wanted.

And gave her what she needed. The chance to get away.

She turned back to the fire. She pictured herself walking sunny streets and being gay and happy and singing for hours. Her life would be so bright and exciting that she would never think about this horrible interlude in damp, cloudy England, and how it had scrambled her emotions and turned part of her into someone she didn't recognize.

This would all become a brief memory, a stage stop on her journey to womanhood. Once she was gone, the ache that she carried inside her chest would disappear. A wonderful future waited. She would grab it bravely and not look back and—

A sound behind her broke into her hopeful reveries. A door opened and one footstep fell.

"Mr. Thomas said that you wished to see me, madame."

Images of Italy fractured like a hammer had smashed them. The fragments rained through her stunned mind.

Her mouth dropped open as she swung around and looked into the blue eyes of the Viscount Laclere.

chapter 12

"Hell."

The low curse floated on his delayed exhale. They stared at each other for a dazed interval.

Slowly, her wits absorbed the implications of his presence.

Vergil and Mr. Clark were one and the same.

What a stunning discovery.

What an incredibly bad stroke of luck.

Then again . . .

He recovered first. "What in damnation are you doing here?"

Amazement left her speechless. Amazement, plus the fact that her explanation would hardly soften his expression. To say that he was less than pleased to see her was putting it rather too finely.

He looked subtly different. Still Vergil. Still tall and dark and stern. Still chiseled face and startling eyes. But his black frock coat was cut more austerely than usual and seemed of poorer quality. His collar points were less perfect somehow, and he wore a black cravat tied in a casual knot, something she had never seen him do before.

He was presentable enough in a dark, menacing way, but she couldn't shake the sense that he appeared a man new to fine garments, who didn't quite know how to put them together yet, and who lacked a good valet to show him. A wealthy man, but not born to it.

"I asked what you are doing here, Miss Kenwood?"

Despite her cursed outspokenness, she knew that there were times when silence was the best course. It would hardly do to blurt out that she had come to extort money from Mr. Clark so that she could escape her evil guardian.

"How did you get here?"

"The mail coach."

"That explains why you look half-dead. Is that your gig outside?"

She nodded.

"Where is your baggage? Did you leave it at your inn with Jane?"

Oh, dear. "No."

He frowned. "You came all this way with no baggage?"

Her lack of response did not delay the conclusion. He raked her with a very sharp look. "In fact, you came without Jane, too, didn't you? You made this journey alone."

She would have spun a story, an outright lie, if she could think of one. Her mind simply wouldn't cooperate.

"That was very, very reckless of you, Miss Kenwood." He abruptly opened the door and left.

A few minutes later he returned.

"I expect that you are tired and cold, but I must delay your comfort for a while longer. I have paid your coachman and sent the gig away. My carriage will be here shortly. While we wait, I want you to tell me how you arranged this journey, so that I can determine just how large a calamity you may have created."

Feeling more like a naughty schoolgirl than she liked, she explained the brilliant plan that had abruptly lost its luster. "So, if Jane remains undetected, there may not be any calamity at all," she concluded.

"And if your ruse was discovered, Penelope might already be raising the hue and cry all over England."

"She will know once she speaks with Jane that I was not abducted. I expect she would wait a few days for my return."

"Does Jane know where you went and why?"

"I did not confide the details to her. If you send me back at once, no one will have reason to seek out Mr. Clark. No one will know your secret."

"*You* will know. Until I decide what to do about that, I have no intention of sending you back. However, we cannot discuss that here."

The sounds of the coach rattled outside. Vergil disappeared into a side room and returned with his great coat. He draped the heavy garment around her shoulders and escorted her through the front office to the door.

Morton held the reins in the coachman's seat of a vehicle that bore no aristocratic insignia. The mouth buried between his beard and mustache opened in surprise when Vergil guided her out of the building.

"Well, now, my lord, this is an inconvenient complication."

"You have a gift for understatement, Morton."

"Rather bold of her, if I may say so."

"Yes."

"On the other hand . . ."

"Exactly."

What was that supposed to mean? The way she saw it, all of the "other hands" belonged to her.

Vergil settled across from her. He found a coach rug and tucked it around her legs. "Your shoes are damp. Silly, flimsy things to wear on a mail coach." He unstrapped both shoes and slipped them off, then swathed her feet in the fur rug.

He tucked and wrapped like she was some child. He pulled the coat snugly around her until her head stuck out of a huge bundle. It was very disarming of him to fuss like this, especially since the light in his eyes suggested that he thought she deserved it if she caught a fever from this escapade.

Morton guided the coach across a bridge and they headed south.

"Where are we going?"

"I have a manor nearby. We should reach it in less than an hour."

The manor. She wondered if the mistress was in residence. Since she already knew about that woman, she wondered if he would bother to keep her hidden for the few hours they might need to settle this "inconvenient complication."

He kept regarding her with intense speculation. It was the sort of calculating expression one sometimes catches on a person who thinks no one is looking. Having it directed at her for this extended length of silent time was very unsettling.

She felt no danger for her safety. Quite the opposite. But she couldn't shake the notion that the man sitting across from her had become very unpredictable all of a sudden, and that Mr. Clark might not play by the same rules as the Viscount Laclere.

"Unless you want me to conclude that you made this journey because you could not bear to be parted from me, you had better explain yourself."

The cool allusion to that other part of their relationship sent a peculiar alertness blotting through her.

"I came to see Mr. Clark."

"Why?"

"To have a little chat. To make his acquaintance."

"I am not in the mood to have my wits insulted. Since I am Mr. Clark and we made our acquaintance long ago, you will state your business now."

"Well, if Mr. Clark had been amenable, and I'm sorry to say that I do not think he will be, I intended to propose a mutually beneficial arrangement. Mr. Peterson told me about the offer to buy the mill and how Mr. Clark—that is, you—did not want to sell, and how if I sold and Nigel did, too, then . . . oh . . . *oh,* so that is why you tried to force me to marry your brother. To secure ownership of that mill. Really, Laclere, I am very disappointed in you."

"You have many reasons to be, but this is not one of them. I never tried to force you to marry my brother. You were supposed to be a meek, provincial orphan, who, like all women, would swoon with delight every time Dante smiled. You would fall in love, marry him, and that would be that. There was nothing dishonorable in the plan. As for what happened later, may I remind you that if you had not thrown yourself at Dante I would not have—"

"I hardly think *thrown* myself is a fair way to put it."

"*—thrown yourself* at Dante, I would not have found myself in the contradictory situation of trying to negotiate your way out of a marriage that could only benefit me."

"Why did you, then?"

The look he gave her knocked the breath right out of her. *You know why,* those eyes said.

"It has never been my intention to trap you into something that you did not want."

They were speeding past farms clouded in mist, leaving the city far behind. Potentially perilous did not begin to describe her situation. But this was Vergil Duclairc. A saint. Besides, he would hardly importune her when his mistress resided in the house.

"Morton obviously knows who Mr. Clark is. Does anyone else?" she asked.

"No."

"No one? Penelope or Dante?"

"No."

"Fleur?"

"Least of all Fleur."

"You will have to tell her. A man can hardly hide such a thing from a wife any more than he can from his valet."

"Fleur and I will not be getting married. She has no interest in it. Our courtship has been a feint to remove her from the marriage market for a while. I expect in a month all of society will know that she broke it off."

"I am sorry. I would never have expected her to deceive you."

"You misunderstand. I knew from the start. So you can acquit me of at least one crime. I did not make love to you even while I courted a fiancée."

She could do without him blithely repeating references to that. "It is odd no one ever found you out."

"The ease of the deception surprised me at first. But Mr. Clark keeps to himself mostly, and lives out of town. Refuse social invitations often enough and eventually they stop coming. I am not unknown in Manchester, especially among the other men of business, but I avoid gatherings where I will not know who will attend. Of course, the *haute ton* do not mix with mill owners, and the city has no representation in Parliament, so there were no members of the Commons about who would recognize me."

"Maintaining a double life must be very difficult and uncomfortable. I do not understand why you have done this. Why not be open about it?"

"Surely your perceptions are more astute than that. Gentlemen do not engage in trade, least of all this one. We invest in certain ones, shipping and canals, but the mills are too sordid. And we never actively manage those businesses."

She remembered Mr. Peterson speaking of mill owners as beneath him, and Lord Calne calling their owners base. It would probably be very scandalous for a viscount to take his place among such men. Scandalous enough to ruin the social standing of his whole family.

Dusk was falling when the coach lumbered off the main road. They slowed as they passed some farms.

"Are these yours?"

"They are attached to the manor but are mortgaged to the hilt."

"Is Laclere Park mortgaged too?"

"The estate is entailed to prevent that, not that I would have ever done so anyway. A man does not gamble with his family's patrimony."

She kept her gaze out the window, looking for signs of a village. With an inn.

Morton took a turn and they trotted up a hill. An old Tudor manor stood at its top. In the waning light she made out a rambling collection of half-timbered beams crossing plastered walls that rose up from a stone first level.

Vergil hopped out as soon as they pulled up in front of the house. Not a single light shown through any window. The place possessed an eerie mood. It looked like the sort of manor one read about in the more fantastic stories. The sort where young innocents came to no good.

Vergil waited as if he knew that, whatever her misgivings, she would conclude that she really did not have any choice except to go in.

She fought her way through the swaddling coat and rug only to remember that her shoes were off. He fished for them, slipped them on, and buckled them as if she were incapable of dressing herself properly.

An old man led the coach away and Morton hurried inside ahead of them.

"It looks deserted," she said as Vergil took her arm to support her under the weight of the clumsy coat.

"I do not keep staff here, except for old Lucas to tend the horses and serve as caretaker. When I am in residence, Morton does for me. He was army in his younger days, and is amazingly competent even in a kitchen."

No servants. She glanced askance at him. In the dusk his expression appeared dangerously alert.

The large, square entry hall held a hearth and chairs and settee. Old armor glimmered in the corners and an ancient tapestry hung on the wall leading up the stairs. Overhead one could see the beams that supported the second floor. Everything appeared in decent, if worn, condition. All this dark wood could use a good polishing, but Morton had managed to keep things clean.

Morton moved two chairs near the fire he had built. She swayed under the great coat while she walked around and peered through open doors into the rooms giving off from the hall. There was a library at one end and a proper drawing room at the other end beside a dining salon.

Vergil watched her inspection. "Are you looking for my mistress? I keep her chained up in the attic. Morton, don't forget to bring my love slave her supper."

"That is not humorous, Laclere."

"She thinks that I am making jests, Morton. The thing is, that wench upstairs begins to bore me. Perhaps I will send her home and keep Miss Kenwood to take her place. What do you think, Morton?"

"A bit sharp-tongued, my lord, but a comely young woman."

"The luck of it is, no one will ever know. No doubt you will find it difficult to believe that any woman could be so foolish, Morton, but she snuck away from Pen and Dante and came north all on her own. Told no one where she was going. Left herself with no protection whatsoever. If she disappears, who is to say what happened? All sorts of accidents and mishaps could have occurred on this adventure. They won't even know where to begin looking for her."

"You astonish me, Laclere. This is very vulgar, and not at all like you," Bianca said.

"It is not the Viscount Laclere who contemplates your future. It is Mr. Clark. It is said that he is a strange man, not much given to society and friendships. Whoever would have expected an intelligent woman like yourself to put herself in the power of a man whom she knows nothing about? Yes, Morton, I think that she will do very well. She will need a bit of taming, of course."

"I hope that you are both enjoying yourselves. The potential danger in what I have done has been amply communicated. I am not amused by your insinuations, Laclere, nor the least bit frightened."

"Aren't you? You have more faith in my honor than I do, then."

He said the last in a thoughtful, musing tone. The rest had been a teasing scold, but that had not.

The silence of the manor suddenly pressed on her.

He stepped behind her. His hands settled on her shoulders and the skin from her neck to her waist prickled. His touch briefly lingered before he lifted the coat off her shoulders. "Go sit by the fire and get warm. Morton, would you prepare a hot bath for Miss Kenwood? It will be the only way to get the chill out of her. See about some other garments too. Her gown is holding the damp."

"No things here but yours and mine, my lord."

"Something of mine, then. Miss Kenwood is no stranger to breeches. And do whatever one does to prepare a chamber for a lady. It will have to be mine. None of the others are suitable."

His last order made her trip on her way to the hearth. He certainly did not expect her to remain here tonight, in his chamber.

She sat and unfastened the neck of her cloak.

He threw himself into another chair nearby. "You are warm enough? Morton will fix supper soon, but I could find something if you are hungry."

"I will wait." She pulled off her gloves and smoothed them together on her lap. "There is no mistress, is there? All of the journeys were because of the mill."

He just looked at her in that considering way he had used in the coach. Finally he shook his head with an exasperated sigh. "What am I going to do with you?"

"The first thing you are going to do, is instruct Morton to drive me to an inn."

"I do not think so. Rain is falling, there is no moon, and the closest inn is miles away."

"I hardly need to remind *you* that it is unacceptable for me to remain in this house tonight. There are not even any servants here."

"Which means no one will ever know. Now, if you were some blushing innocent, I might be concerned for your delicate sensibilities. However, since you are so *experienced, wicked,* and, some in Baltimore even say, *dangerous,* we can dispense with inconvenient gallantry. I will not risk either Morton or my horses to cater to any concerns about propriety that you have suddenly discovered this evening. Besides, a woman who admits to having *hundreds* of lovers can hardly be reduced to the vapors by the notion of being alone with a man for a few days."

"A few *days*?"

"I cannot let you leave until we have come to some understanding."

"That should not take long at all. I promise to tell no one about your secret. See? All settled."

"Hardly all settled, as you and I both know."

His meaningful glance stunned her into silence. He was not only talking about his management of the mill.

The hall grew very quiet. His implications hung in the air, filling the gap between them with connections and memories, forcing the attraction to quiver more insistently than it ever had before.

The fire crackled, illuminating the two of them in a cozy glow. It created a little world of protection and warmth in the cold cavern of the hall. No, it was not the fire doing that. It was the presence of the man sitting a few feet away. She had always experienced an alluring security with him. Especially when he held her. He offered for a short while, just a little, that she could let someone else make the decisions and do the worrying. Not since she had been a young child had she been allowed that respite.

She nervously smoothed her gloves some more. She felt as though his silent contemplation was deliberately stripping away layers of camouflage, revealing something carefully hidden behind anger and resentment and clever sparring. It was leaving her terribly exposed to an intimacy that spread like the fire's warmth, circling their chairs, subjugating the adversarial postures they took with each other as surely as the hearth did the chill.

Did he sense it too? She snuck a look at him. He gazed into the fire with a face subtly expressive, its stern planes reflecting annoyance, but also something else. It was as if a transparent mask had been removed.

He turned to her. His eyes glimmered with anger and warmth and a flicker of vulnerability. Not a guardian's eyes. Not a saint's, either. Just a man's. The man who had kissed her at the ruins and held her in the study. Every piece of her remaining armor dropped and every ounce of defense disappeared under the honesty of that gaze.

"You might have been harmed. If that coach had gone into a river, I would have never known what happened, just that you disappeared one day," he said resentfully.

It was the first indication, the first admission, that he cared about her.

"Is that why you are so angry? I thought it was because I had discovered your secret."

"Give me some time and I will work up some ire over that too."

"I should have been more considerate of the worry I might have caused Pen and you. I am sorry. It's just . . ." To explain it would leave her even more vulnerable to the seductive familiarity she suddenly felt with him. In an indefinable way, she understood him much better than she had ever realized. In front of this hearth, with her protections peeled away and his mask shattered, she knew the important part of him as well as she knew herself.

"It's just that you saw a way around your interfering guardian and back to the pursuit of your dream," he finished.

"Yes. There was that."

"It's just that you saw a way to escape the hypocrite and fraud who forced his attentions on you when he was supposed to be protecting you." He voiced her thoughts in a frank way that suggested he intended to clear the air. "Perhaps that is why I am so angry. It is really directed at myself, and it is unfair to lash out at you instead. I cannot escape the conclusion that if anything had happened to you, it would have been my fault."

"Not entirely. Nor did you really force your attentions on me. I have never lied to myself about that. But, as I said in the study, I decided it best if I left."

"As any sensible woman would have. Now you have discovered that your brave plan has only led you directly back to me. You must be dismayed."

"Not so dismayed. Better you than Mr. Clark, whom people say is a bit odd."

He laughed quietly at that. "So you came to Manchester to chat with Mr. Clark. Did you plan to threaten him?"

"Certainly not."

"Negotiate, then, if you prefer that term. Let me guess. You would promise not to sell the mill when you came of age if he gave you some money. The implication being that if he did not hand over the blunt, you would promptly throw in with Nigel once you turned twenty-one and sell out. Am I correct?"

"You do not have to make it sound like highway robbery. The money I wanted was mine anyway. Some of the profits, to be diverted to me and not sent to . . ."

"To your unreasonable guardian. Your solicitor did well by you, getting the information you needed. A brilliant plan, Miss Kenwood. You have my admiration."

"Would it have worked? I mean, if you hadn't been Mr. Clark, that is."

He smiled with stunning warmth. "It is charming of you to think that it makes a difference that I am he. You have me at a distinct disadvantage. I do not hurt myself by pointing it out, since it was only a matter of time before you realized it."

She had already realized it, as soon as she saw him in the office.

"Once you procured your funds from Mr. Clark, what then? Off to Italy, I expect. Immediately? With no baggage and no Jane?"

"I had intended to go back to Laclere Park, to fetch Jane."

"I suppose you would have had to leave without saying so. A letter propped on your writing table for Penelope is the best I could have hoped for." He pressed the fingertips of his hands to each other and studied her over the peak they made. "I am a little insulted at how this plan of yours did not take me into account at all."

"It certainly did not take into account that you might be Mr. Clark."

"I do not mean that. Perhaps I foresaw your scheme. Maybe I fed Mr. Peterson the information in order to lure you up here. Has it not yet occurred to you that the man whom you castigated in the coach that day might be that nefarious? Perhaps you do not think me clever enough to have plotted it."

It had occurred to her, poking into her mind with a momentary, silly caution. "Clever enough, but not nefarious enough."

Her judgment seemed to please him. "If this had played out as you intended, what did you expect me to do?"

"I expected you to be relieved, and to recognize it was for the best."

"Of course. The saint could return to his courtship of the lovely Fleur, and the fraud could return to debauchery with his mistress. A comfortable life again, with the troublesome, provoking Miss Kenwood out of the way."

"Something like that."

He angled toward her. "Shall I tell you that I anticipated some new attempt on your part to leave? I even warned Catalani of dire consequences if she should aid you. I have St. John checking the passenger lists at the shipping companies to see if you tried to arrange for berths."

"I planned to take the packet to France and travel overland, so you would not have been able to stop me that way."

"Then I would have followed."

"I see. You would not have wanted the mill's future depending upon someone you could not control, and you still had nine months to convince me to wed your brother."

He looked to the fire with renewed irritation. "Fetching you back would have had nothing to do with Dante, and very little to do with the mill. Furthermore, my legal rights as your guardian would have only provided the excuse."

His words and expression insinuated more than responsibilities and manipulations, although he appeared less than happy with the notion. The new Bianca flushed with delight at this evidence that she had been right about him and the old Bianca wrong.

A cough drew their attention to Morton on the landing halfway up the stairs, holding a candelabra.

"I have the chamber and bath prepared, my lord. If Miss Kenwood is ready, I will show her the way." He turned and retreated upward.

She rose and Vergil did too. She regretted having to relinquish the fresh honesty that had begun between them. They would probably resume to their old poses when she returned.

She mounted the stairs, sensing his attention on her. At the landing she glanced down to see him watching her.

"No."

She paused at the simple negative, even though it had not been a command for her to stop.

"No," he repeated. "To your question earlier. You were correct. There is no mistress. No mistress and no fiancée." He paused. "There is only you."

She thought that her legs would give way. The new Bianca wanted to climb over the banister and jump down into his arms.

"Since we are being honest, I should admit that you were correct too. There were not *hundreds,* or even *dozens.* Not even several, I'm bound to say. Only you."

He turned away with a wry smile. "Go to your bath, Miss Kenwood. Since I had intended to seduce you, I will need some time to decide if I am glad to hear that."

chapter 13

Vergil crossed his arms and stared out the dining-room window into the wet, black night.

If Bianca had any sense at all, she would never leave that chamber upstairs.

She was a virgin. Of course she was. He had known that almost for certain. However, the simmer had encouraged enough doubt so that he could ignore his better judgment and speculate on the possibilities that her arrival presented. Maybe she wasn't and then what he contemplated would be a bit less unconscionable. Perhaps, if he were to make love to her and do it well enough, then hopefully she . . .

Only you.

Two words had demolished all the "maybes" and "possiblys" and probably any "hopefullys."

He shook his head with a quiet laugh. Just his luck, and wonderfully ironic. He never thought he'd see the day when he regretted learning that the woman he had decided to marry was an innocent.

She would make a splendid wife. Bright and interesting and, in her exasperating way, unpredictable. The kind of wife one looked forward to spending time with and did not merely tolerate. The sort of woman who enlivened one's existence beyond the bed where you joined her for pleasure and procreation, although his determination to have her there played no small part in his attraction.

A perfect wife for him in other ways too. Not only because she would bring forty-five percent of the mill with her, although that would be convenient. The best part was that he would not have to hide his double life. She came from a country where men of business were not scorned. She already knew his secret and there would be no need to keep it from her.

That the woman whom he wanted should also be the only woman he could risk marrying struck him as a generous gift from Fate. It was during the coach ride that he had realized how her discovery had freed him to pursue her.

The Rossini aria that she had sung in the ruins began filling his head. He imagined the body that he knew better than he should, stretched out naked on that bed upstairs. She rested on her stomach, shoulders raised and weight propped on her forearms. The sheet hid her lower body to the middle of her bottom, the way the lake's water had. She watched his approach with teasing blue eyes that managed to combine worldliness with innocence. His hand caressed down her soft skin and his mouth found her lips . . .

Only you. After playing out such a long and elaborate act of worldly experience, she *had* to go and admit that tonight.

"You are already grinning and you haven't even seen me yet," her voice said. "Did you catch my reflection in the window?"

He turned and choked down a laugh.

The frock coat dropped off her shoulders and its sleeves buried her hands. The trousers were so long that she had rolled up their bottoms into thick, clumsy cuffs. The whole ensemble immersed her in an ocean of cloth out of which her head bobbed and in which her body swam.

She stretched out her arms and flapped the coat's sleeves. "I feel like a little child dressed in my father's clothes. I must look bizarre."

He thought that she looked adorable. "The blue of the coat becomes you."

She held up her arm and tried to scrunch down the sleeve so her hand could emerge. "It may be impossible to eat supper, and I am very hungry."

"Then I will have to feed you." A delightful thought. "Or, we could build up the fire and you could remove the coat." That was an alluring notion as well.

"Would you? The fire, that is."

He got it to a high inferno just as Morton arrived with some soup.

"This should help warm you, Miss Kenwood, but I am sorry that the rest of the meal is a cold platter. We eat plainly here in the evenings. I will do better tomorrow night," Morton explained.

"I would not lay in stores, Morton. I expect to be on the road tomorrow night."

Morton shot him a look such as an officer would give a soldier who was shirking his duty.

"Why don't you bring the rest now, Morton. Miss Kenwood will forgive our informality."

"Certainly, sir."

Bianca shrugged off the frock coat and laid it on a chair. Her dark gray waistcoat also hung loosely, but its lines and fabric could not totally obscure her form. Vergil beckoned her to a place set at a right angle to his own at the end of the banquet table. Morton had made her place as close as possible without appearing too obvious. Certainly within easy reach.

She looked around at the mirrors and inset paintings and gold leaf that glimmered in the light of hearth and candles. "This is an odd room to find in such a manor."

"My maternal great-grandmother loathed this house for the primitive place it was, but her husband insisted on coming here. She decided that they would at least eat as civilized people, and she had this room done in the current fashion. He permitted it, but only for this chamber and her own."

She dug into her soup. Her full lips parted delicately to accept the warm broth, and the tip of her tongue swiped an errant drip. Her mouth mesmerized him, spoonful after spoonful.

This was going to be a very long night. A paragon's purgatory.

He guessed that she hadn't eaten a decent meal since leaving London. Rectifying the problem absorbed her attention for a while. When Morton brought the ham, she methodically tucked hers away. Vergil speared another slice and placed it on her plate.

She flushed a color that looked incredibly lovely in the candle glow. "I am being rude."

"You are being human. We should have fed you before you went upstairs."

She looked down at her garments and grinned. "Do I get port when we are done?"

"You do not drink strong spirits, and tonight is not the time to start."

"If I am dressed like this, I think that one glass of port is almost obligatory."

"If you insist, but only one very small glass. I do not want you accusing me of getting you inebriated."

She looked to her ham with a peculiar smile. "I am sure that you would never do that."

Oh, wouldn't he?

A small roll and a slice of ham later, she finally stalled. He practically saw her mind snap back to attention regarding the matter at hand.

"How did it happen? You and the mill?"

"It was another responsibility that I inherited from my brother. He, in turn, got involved in response to a dare."

"A dare?"

"From your grandfather. Adam Kenwood and Milton formed a strong friendship, despite their disparate ages, backgrounds, and politics. Milton found him an interesting man with a mind as sharp as a honed sword. Very ambitious and very clever. You have a lot of him in you, by the way. Milton once said he found Adam a wonderful contrast to the philosophical abstractions that had filled his own life."

"So Milton left the manor to work in the factory?"

"Four years ago there was a demonstration in Manchester that turned bloody, one that has been dubbed Peterloo. The deaths of those people shook my brother badly. Milton was not so much of the tower that he could not see that the country was changing profoundly. Adam and he got into terrific rows about the moralities of what was happening in the new industries. Milton believed that the problem was the character of the men running them. Better men, less absorbed by greed, would mean better conditions and less unrest among the people. Adam challenged him to face the same risks and choices and see what he would do. He dared Milton to throw in with him on a new mill."

"It sounds like a very sly, and very expensive dare. However, I can almost picture the two of them, worlds apart, sparring over such things, and others as well. The influence went both ways, I think. Your brother convinced my grandfather of the error of his early trade, and Adam made your brother see how impractical some of his ideas were."

Her expression softened as she referred to her grandfather's slave trade. The way she looked in his eyes conveyed her gratitude for being informed that Adam had expiated that sin, and that her inheritance could be kept.

"It was foolhardy for my brother to agree to the dare. The family finances were already a disaster. Adam stood him to a large part of the financing, and offered to advise him, but it would be my brother's business. No doubt Milton saw it as a grand experiment, but also counted on Adam's business acumen to keep it from failing."

"Perhaps Milton thought it was not foolhardy, but a way to save the family."

"If so, he was correct. It turned out to be the only sensible decision about money that he ever made, and, with Adam's help, he made the mill profitable. He was the first Mr. Clark, you see. I think when he donned that identity, he literally became another man."

"Then when Milton died, Mr. Clark's brother, which was you, inherited his share. Did your double life begin then? Have you been managing that mill ever since?"

"With my brother's death, I began traveling north, relying heavily on your grandfather's advice while I learned what to do. Eventually the decisions became mine. It was essential that I manage it closely. The income from the mill had kept us from financial ruin."

It had also been useful to spend time in the north as Mr. Clark. Mr. Clark could go places and hear things that the Viscount Laclere never could. Mr. Clark could try to learn if the answer to Milton's suicide could be found somewhere in Manchester, where Milton also visited, and among the political radicals whose ideas Milton had supported.

He realized that he wanted to tell her about that, too, and regretted that he could not.

She inclined forward with her elbow propped on the table and her chin resting on her hand. He could see Adam Kenwood's shrewd mind working behind the thoughtful expression in her eyes.

"You said it scraped you through some bad years. Why don't you sell out now? The offer from Mr. Johnston and Mr. Kennedy is waiting. You could be free of this deception."

"Johnston and Kennedy run the worst mill in Leeds. Ours is paradise by comparison, even if it is still a hard life. If I sell the mill, I also sell any chance for a halfway decent future for the people who work there."

Morton had found some little cakes to present with the meal. She reached for one. Her small white teeth bit carefully, but some sugar topping smeared her lips anyway. Still thoughtful, she seemed unaware that her tongue snuck out to wipe up the sweet grains. She missed a few and they glistened against the pink swells, like an invitation for him to finish the job.

"You could sell to someone else. There must be other mill owners who are decent."

"That is true. I could probably do that."

"But you do not want to."

Perceptive woman. Delightfully so. Dangerously so.

"No."

She sat back and absorbed that. He wondered what the admission would cost him.

She smiled as if she had learned what she needed to know. "Can I have my port now?"

"I keep it in the library."

She walked beside him through the hall to the library. He noticed that she had cinched the trousers to her waist with a cord from the bedchamber's drapes. The white sleeves of his shirt floated around her arms and the collarless neckline showed a fair amount of skin despite the waistcoat.

He pictured her in nothing at all but that shirt hanging loosely from her shoulders and breasts, skimming her body with soft fabric, revealing naked thighs and legs.

Morton had built up the library fire. She sank into a corner of the settee and accepted the port he offered her.

He sat in the chair across from her, wondering when she would get around to negotiations. It was why she had come down for supper, after all.

Not yet, it seemed. She popped up and began perusing the volumes in the bookcases flanking the hearth. Her brow puckered. She reached for a candlestick on the mantel, lit it off the hearth flames, and held the light to the bindings.

"There are some volumes here by Edmund Duclairc. Was that your father?"

"Yes. The fat red one is his epic about Alexander's march to the Indus River. The brown one is an Anglo-Saxon view of the Battle of Hastings. Milton's literary efforts are in that blue folio on the bottom shelf. Unpublished, since he did not have the chance to finish them. Not poems. He was writing a comparative analysis of your country's revolution and that of the French."

She had pulled out the brown volume. "It all sounds very erudite. Do you also pen great works?"

"My interests have been in other things, to my father's dismay."

"You were at odds with your father? Somehow I cannot picture you as less than dutiful."

"Like all youths I had my own ideas about my future. I wanted to join the army. Not the cavalry, which would be acceptable, but the engineers. Machines, buildings, earthworks, those things fascinated me. As a child I loitered around the carriages, not the horses. My request to have a commission was soundly rejected by my father. Off to Oxford for me, to study the poets and philosophers."

"Were you miserable?" Her face showed genuine concern.

"No young man is miserable at university. It is a free and privileged life. Those poets and philosophers had a thing or two to teach me. The experience influenced my thoughts, but not my natural inclinations. Your grandfather recognized that, I think. He and I became more familiar after my brother died. On occasion I went with him to see some of the new machines being built. I watched my first working steam engine with your grandfather by my side. When we left, he spoke his mind. 'Your world is dying,' he said. 'It will never be the same again.' "

"It sounds to me that he enjoyed your company." She slid the book back onto its shelf. "I think he was impressed by your interest in machines and how things work. It was unfair of your father to interfere with that."

Clever, clever girl. Subtly laying the foundations before she began constructing her argument.

She strolled back to the settee and perched herself carefully in the corner again. She appeared vulnerable and desirable in her baggy clothes and simply bound hair. The firelight broke her form into lovely glows and mysterious shadows.

He looked at her and she looked right back. Innocent wariness flickered despite her falsely carefree smile. Only a saint could ignore the anticipation pulsing through the air, and he was hardly that where she was concerned.

He found himself swimming against an incoming tide of indifference to notions of honor. The exhaustive effort began to seem increasingly futile.

Yes, she should have never left that chamber.

He kept looking at her. Directly. Intently. As if he waited for something. She suspected that he knew what his prolonged attention was doing to her and drew it out deliberately. Maybe he heard that physical hum drumming louder.

The silence became dangerous. Her skin flushed and her mouth dried. She kept expecting him to get up and come over and . . . but he just sat there. Waiting.

This would never do. Besides, they had business to settle. It was why she was here, wasn't it? She forced some semblance of composure.

"Well, Laclere, what are we going to do about this?"

He favored her with a small smile: "I would say that is up to you. What do you want to do about it?"

"I think that any understanding that we reach should be a mutual one."

"I am at a disadvantage here, and we both know it. Any resolution of the situation must be your initiative."

"The course is obvious, I think. It is unfair of you to demand that I spell it out."

"I suppose that it is, but I am incapable of stating a rational case for myself, because there isn't one. The only thing I want right now, the only obvious course that I can see, is to take you to bed and trust that a mutual understanding can be reached tomorrow."

Her heart skipped and then rose to her throat. "You misunder . . . That is not . . . We are speaking about the mill."

"No, we are not."

"*I* am."

"Are you? My apologies." He rose and paced to the hearth. She would have preferred he remain seated. He gazed into those flames for a while before turning. "Fine, let us discuss the mill and your discovery first."

First?

"My disadvantage in that matter is even more acute than in the other."

"I have already said that I will tell no one."

"I thank you for that. Now, what will it cost me?"

"Nothing that is not already mine. What is my income from the mill?"

"This year, at least four thousand pounds."

"Goodness. You must be a very good manager, Laclere."

"Thank you. However, since it grew to that amount two years ago, neither Adam nor Mr. Clark took it all out. We have been reinvesting in an expansion. If you demand the whole sum, I have no choice but to give it to you, however."

"How much did you reinvest?"

"Half."

"That still leaves quite a lot. More than enough."

"More than enough for what?"

"For me to live in Milan, of course."

"So the true cost of your silence is that I permit you to pursue this rash plan. If I refuse, you will announce to the world that I am Mr. Clark."

"I did not say that."

"No, you did not. Your blackmail was more clever than that. You will keep my secret, but if I do not agree to your terms, you will sell your interest when you are of age."

It would help her to concentrate if he didn't keep pacing around the settee. Circling, circling. It reminded her of that morning in the guardroom of the castle. So did his manner, and his eyes.

"The problem, as I see it, is that you cannot guarantee your side of the bargain," he said.

"Do you doubt my word?"

"I doubt your ability to foretell the future. If you marry, the decision whether to sell or hold that investment will cease to be yours."

"I will not be getting married."

He paused behind her. "You think not now."

"I know not, ever." She twisted and looked up at him. "You yourself pointed out that no decent man would want me if I performed. Besides, a woman cannot be a wife and mother and also an opera singer, no matter what society will permit. With babies, the career must end."

"You may change your mind someday about what is important to you."

Twisting to see him was uncomfortable, and he seemed disinclined to move. She turned and knelt on the settee. It brought her closer to him than she thought it would. "I told you once, this is essential to me. I must do it if I have the talent to even try. I will die if I do not. No husband will interfere with our bargain."

"I find that hard to accept."

"You doubt my resolve? You of all people have seen evidence of it."

"I do not doubt your resolve, but it has never been tested. Time has a way of turning life's blacks and whites into grays. The singularity you describe is a freedom that grows heavy and dull with the years. Trust me, I know. I think that the bargain that you offer in good faith tonight will one day become meaningless."

"You treat me like some silly child playing a game. It is as if you assume I am too ignorant to know my own mind. I realize that men think women are too stupid to think things through and weigh their decisions, but your attitude is very insult—"

Suddenly his hand pressed on her cheek, startling her into silence. He looked down with an expression that suggested he had not heard one word.

"A mistake, Miss Kenwood. Letting your annoyance show. Innocence I am duty bound to respect. Worldliness I am adept at resisting. But the light in your eyes when you fly at me reveals a passionate spirit that provokes me until nothing else matters except possessing it." His thumb seductively brushed her lips. "Which brings us to the rest of what must be settled between us."

That thumb stroked and stroked, as if preparing her for him. She knelt dumbfounded, on wobbly knees, staring into a face darkly pleased by her mesmerization. Her lips tingled under the subtle caress. He coaxed a gap so he could skim the moist inner edges.

"Do you want me to kiss you?"

He had never asked before. She could not summon enough breath to respond. Her lips pulsed with swelling sensitivity at his luring touch. Her whole being trembled with anticipation, as if the expectant tension in the room had entered her body.

"Do you?"

"Yes." No sound came out, but her lips formed the word.

He did. Wonderfully. He cupped her face in his warm palms and his mouth replaced his thumb in those caresses. She grasped the back edge of the settee to keep from wilting right into him. The new Bianca soared with triumphant relief.

Gently, carefully, he obliterated thoughts of anything but him and the pleasure he created and implied. He tasted and savored with firm, acquisitive, titillating nips and slow, shallow, sweeping invasions. This was a different path to passion than the abrupt release in the ruins and the study, and she instinctively knew, a more dangerous one. His tender exploration of her consent aroused her emotions as well as her body. She wanted him to kiss her like this forever, even while that inner voice began its chant for more closeness, more pleasure, more giving.

The luring warmth hypnotized her. She could not move, even to embrace him. When he broke the kiss she could only look wordlessly into blue, deliberating eyes.

He caressed down her neck, his fingers splaying over flesh, pressing beating pulse, exploring trembling shoulders. He watched his hands' progress. That expression of hooded contemplation still veiled his eyes. It dully occurred to her that her mind might be blank to everything but this entrancement, but his was not.

Hands and gaze lowered to the valley between her breasts. She felt the top button on her waistcoat loosen. Then the next. She gripped the back of the settee harder.

The waistcoat fell open and he brushed the sides away. She glanced down. Hard nipples pushed against the shirt fabric like proud announcements of desire. He caressed around the sides and bottoms of her breasts, outlining their swells. Her eyes blurred as all of her body and mind and heart narrowed into one tiny, intense ache of waiting and want.

"Do you want me to make love to you?"

She almost didn't hear him. Her eyes met his and she struggled to recover the capacity to think and speak. He still stroked her breasts, distracting her, making her helpless. He studied her face as if he sought to read her mind.

"Do you know what it means if I do?"

She heard her voice speak. "I am not ignorant of such things."

Her words might have been sharp tools poking holes into their trance. Rationality leaked in. He smiled with amusement, and regret. "I was not talking about that."

He walked away. She sank around into the settee, flooded with confusion and a visceral disappointment.

He retrieved her candlestick from the mantel and brought it over. A strong hand beckoned her up. Her thoughts still were muddled, but her body practically shrieked with relief.

With disarming courtesy he led her to the door. Placing the candlestick in the hand he held, he closed her fingers around it.

"Go up now. Quickly."

She glowed at his thoughtfulness. Grasping her light, she scurried to the stairs. As she mounted them her thoughts unscrambled and the last minutes began making sense.

By the time she reached the landing she realized what had just happened. He had not sent her ahead to prepare for a bed that he would share.

He had no intention of following, now or later.

chapter 14

Bianca twisted restlessly. She punched the pillow, pulled another over to make a high mound, and flopped onto her back.

She certainly was fortunate that Laclere was such a decent man. Yes, indeed.

The nightshirt that Morton had laid out rucked up. Her exposed hips felt annoyingly titillating. Leveraging them, she pulled the fabric down.

A very decent man. Very honorable. A saint, by God.

Any other man would have ravished her right there on the settee. Any other man would have carried her up to this chamber and would be lying beside her right now. . . .

And she would be facing the morning, knowing that she had made a mistake, probably worrying about all kinds of things.

Then again, any other man would be holding her in his arms, soothing her concerns with his embrace.

She could not get comfortable. She should be exhausted, but she was horribly awake. All of her. Awake and alert with a huge portion of her still waiting.

Half the night must have passed. Hours with her contemplating what he had meant by that last question. Endless minutes with her secretly wishing he had never found that decency.

Silence filled the whole manor. Somewhere Morton slept in his chamber. Somewhere else, in one of the rooms too unsuitable for her, Vergil did too. No doubt he snoozed the calm, deep slumber of the righteous. Even the ghosts dozed. She was the only soul wide-awake, twisting on this big bed, torn between gratitude and regret.

She flung back the bedclothes. Maybe if she read for a while it would distract her enough to aid her repose.

The nightshirt was warm enough in the bed, but a chill hit her once she stood. No one would see her, but she felt exposed in it too. She dragged a blanket from the bed and draped it like a cape. She grabbed the trousers and pulled them on.

She bent the candlestick to the coals in the hearth. She pushed her hair over her shoulders and carried the small spot of illumination while she clutched the blanket. Treading silently on bare feet, she descended the stairs.

The library's fire had almost died. Her little circle of candle glow barely penetrated the darkness. She skirted along the wall and made for the books beside the hearth. Holding the flame near the bindings, she searched for something dull.

A low noise crunched and a burst of light suddenly broke the shadows. She jumped in surprise and turned. Vergil crouched in front of the hearth, watching the flames climb from a new infusion of fuel. A dark counterpane lay rumpled on the settee where he must have been reclining.

He rose and her heart flipped. Coats and collar had been discarded. He stood in a shirt showing a lot of neck and a V of chest. Snug trousers delineated the lean strength of his hips and legs. She stared like an idiot at the magnificent image he presented. He examined the hearth with a casual stance while he waited to make sure the fire had taken.

Finally he turned to her. Flaring eyes raked her from head to toe and then met hers. He reached for a glass of port that he had set on the mantel.

"I thought that I would read for a while and . . ." She stammered and flustered and held the candle toward the books, pretending to examine them.

He strolled over. "Poetry or prose?"

"Um, prose I think. Maybe your brother's."

He set down his glass and took the candle from her. "Allow me. You are in danger of setting your lovely hair on fire. You want the blue folio on the bottom."

He stood behind her, holding the candle to her search. She reached to pluck out the thin volume. Her hand shook beside his steady one.

"The treatise may not induce somnolence, if that is what you seek. My brother was brilliant."

She clutched the folio to her chest. She could not walk away without turning, and she feared facing him. A power poured out of him, exciting parts of her spirit and unnerving others. "I thought you would have retired by now," she said, thinking it a good idea to clarify her presence.

He did not respond at first. He just stood there closely, as if he tested the attraction he could wield if he chose, even when he was invisible to her.

"I decided to wait, for you to return to me." Firm fingers fell on her right shoulder in a caressing hold. "For you to realize that sending you upstairs was my last bow to the gods of propriety where you are concerned."

The candle flickered away while he placed it on the mantel's corner. He reached around and removed the folio from her grasp and set it next to the glass of port on the book ledge. He stepped closer so that he entrapped her against the stacks.

Warm breath flurried through her hair. Two arms circled her shoulders. He gently pried her hands from her chest and spread them wide. Like a curtain the blanket opened, stretched, and fell. She found herself grasping at bookcase uprights to her right and left.

"I thought . . . I came for a book," she said a little desperately.

Hands on her waist held her to her vulnerable position. Kisses on her neck and ear lit shimmering lights in her body.

"No, you did not. You came here to give yourself to me."

It embarrassed her that he knew her heart better than she did. She *had* hoped he would not be gone. The dark room and dying hearth had provoked a spike of disappointment.

"No more facades, Bianca. No more pretending. That is one thing that this means."

It was the first time he had ever used her name. That, even more than his decisive handling, told her where he was leading her. He caressed up her back and around her neck and pried the top button of the nightshirt free. Its neckline slinked loose. He eased the fabric down her shoulder and kissed the exposed skin, finding spots of unexpected sensitivity.

So strange to feel protected and helpless at the same time. Her skin awoke with a thousand sparkles as the suppressed anticipation surged into a hunger crying for resolution. She dropped her hold of the bookcase and sank back into his surrounding embrace.

"What else does it mean?" Coming down the stairs had made negotiation irrelevant, but she should know what she agreed to.

His hands moved over her sides and midriff, learning the parts previously encased in her stays. "That you are only mine. I do not share. That you give yourself to me when I want, how I want. That . . ." He broke the explanation with a tingly nuzzle on her nape.

It was a lovers' pact that he sought. "Perhaps I will not like it."

"It is for me to make sure that you do."

He turned her. Holding her with one arm, he dipped his finger in the port. Like a painter working a delicate canvas, he smeared the rich liquid across her lips and down her neck. He lowered his head to taste.

It was a wonderful kiss, full of complex flavors and mysterious emotions. He licked the streak marking her neck, kindling tiny flames of giggly pleasure. The light glowed brighter in her breasts and thighs, a suffusing inner warmth anxious for more fuel.

His hand moved to the port again. She waited for the drips to heat her lips. Instead he drew the lines of his own mouth.

She had never kissed him before. She sensed that complying meant crossing an invisible line. Accepting was one thing and sharing was another.

The port glistened.

"I thought you said that I could not have more than one small glass," she said, trying to hide her fear that he lured her into deep water.

"A drop or two will hardly turn you into a Bacchic maenad."

"I'm not so sure."

"I will not ask anything else of you, but I want you to kiss me, Bianca."

And she wanted to. Very much so. That frightened her too.

She slid her hand behind his neck and pressed him down. She pursed her lips on his and then ventured to flick up the port. His mouth parted at the touch of her tongue and suddenly she was inside him. He pulled her into a tighter embrace and a quickly escalating response. His reaction incited a different type of pleasure, and a reeling sense of power.

She watched her own fingers dip in the port and followed their path up to his neck. The liquid streaked down and meandered to the wedge of chest exposed by his shirt. With kisses and toothless bites she followed the daring stream. Her fingers pressed the taut skin beside her mouth while she lost herself in the sensations of touch and taste. Even her ears fed the sensuality, hearing the heartbeat and tight breaths that revealed what she was doing to him.

Yes, yes. Need me and want me like I do you. Fear me a little, like I do you. Lose part of yourself, as I have with you.

He took her hand and kissed her palm, her pulse, and the soft flesh of her inner arm. "I ask you again. Do you want me to make love to you?"

Tonight, in this manor, in this room, she wanted it desperately. An important part of her had never wanted anything more, not even success in her art. Admitting that startled her, but still she nodded.

"You are very sure? There will be no going back to innocence for you."

At this moment she had never been more sure of anything.

He backed away, leading her toward the hearth. "Here, then. The first time I saw you I thought of firelight and velvet counterpanes."

He pulled the coverlet to the floor and lowered her until she sat on his lap, encircled by the warmth of the hearth and the strength of his arms. It was bliss to melt into him and yield herself to his support. He looked at her in that considering way while he stroked her hair.

He tilted her to a long, ravishing kiss. Luscious sensations cascaded and her expectant senses whirled. The world constricted to the five feet of light and warmth in front of the hearth. The only solidity became the body of the man who cradled her on his crossed legs.

Yes, yes. So good. So delicious. Her heart reveled in the intimacy, and her stomach and loins tightened with that marvelous tension. *Ah, yes.* He kept his need in check, but she could feel it, a power coiling out of him and pulling her into its spiral. *Please.* His arm arched her back, raising her body to him. His kisses explored down the gap in the nightshirt, to the skin above her breasts.

She wanted his touch so badly that she let out a little cry when his hand enclosed her breast. He caressed softly and then teased at the nipple until she could not keep her body still.

"Do you think that you will like it?" He nuzzled at the other breast, warming her through the cloth with his breath.

"If it is all like this."

The gentle friction of his palm warmed her skin through the cloth. "It is better than this before the end."

Firm lips took hers in a gently exploring kiss. It was so good and right to be in his arms. She experienced utter peace with her decision.

"What do we do now?" she whispered.

"Now I give you the pleasure that you already know, and while I do, I undress you."

"Completely?" The notion of being totally naked for him both dismayed and excited her.

"Completely. Eventually. Right now I think that I will unfasten these buttons. You look very beguiling in my nightshirt, by the way."

"I feel a little wicked in it. It is modest enough, but knowing it was yours made putting it on more daring than if it had been the most shocking silken boudoir gown."

"I look forward to seeing you in one of those sometime, but I find this very charming tonight."

He released the second button and worked on the third. He took his time and his hand nestled tantalizingly between her breasts. The thin opening grew down the front of her body, revealing a line of skin and then the top of her trousers.

He laid her down, and brushed the halves of the shirt aside, exposing her body to her waist. The fabric hung off her shoulders and sagged along her sides. She doubted that being completely naked would prove more startling.

He caressed the soft skin of her breasts and circled and rubbed her nipples, unleashing a craving sensitivity that almost made her jump. Her back arched involuntarily, invitingly. *Yes, oh, yes . . . more . . .* She returned his kisses with increased vehemence, in an effort to assuage the pressure building and filling her. *Yes, yes . . .* Her hands and arms scrambled to find a hold on him that could not be broken. His shirt did not obscure his body the way the coats had, and the delight of feeling him only made her want more.

He took her breast in his mouth and sucked. The pleasure grew so excruciating that she wanted to weep. She clutched and his shirt became a frustrating impediment. Pulling it loose of his trousers, she dragged it up his body.

He released her to draw it off.

He really was quite magnificent to look at. She could not resist running her fingers along the ridges of the muscles defining his chest and shoulders.

He came down to her, sealing their bodies skin against skin. New astonishments spilled through her, of touch and scent and mingling breath and long caresses that learned and possessed. The intimacy left her helpless and tight.

He broke their fevered kisses and nuzzled her ear. "Now I give you the pleasure that you do not know yet."

"I do not think it can be any nicer than this."

"It is the difference between a drawing room melody and an aria." He untied the cord at her waist while he spoke. The trouser buttons loosened. Unspeakably wicked excitement charged through her while he pushed the garment down her hips and legs. Stomach and tuft of hair flashed through the nightshirt's low slit.

He pushed the hem up, covering her most intimate parts, but fully exposing her thighs. He stroked her legs like he molded their shape. A different demand fired, internal and hot and focused on the forbidden landscape he explored. *Yes, yes. Oh, goodness . . .* A trembling shook her that could only be relieved through movement. Her hips rocked silkenly, pressing into masterful caresses. *Yes . . . higher . . . so close. I want . . . I want . . .*

"You must trust me now." He peeled the shirt down her shoulders and lifted her into an embrace that made the sleeves fall from her arms. It became a rumpled white drapery around her loins. He slid it down.

Off. Gone. She looked at her naked body and realized that he did too. The exposure carried its own excitement. The heady eroticism of the moment intoxicated her. In a few moments he had kicked off the rest of his own clothes. She did not have the courage to examine him as he did her, but her furtive glances absorbed the strength of the body lined against her, skin to skin all the way to her toes.

A dreamy intimacy permeated her. Her body and soul waited within their harmony. Waited as they had all day and night. As they had for weeks. She wanted to hold him as closely as possible, so that she might possess a part of him no matter what happened beyond this fire glow and after the power of this precious night.

He gazed right into her eyes. She knew the next kiss would be different. He might have led her to this point with sweet seduction, but it would not end so restrained.

The passion of the ruins instantly swept her into a tempest. With fierce possession he kissed her senseless, his mouth and tongue conquering hers before joining his hands in their merciless stimulation of her body. Insistent need and an itching hunger joined her pleasure, converting it into something seeking a goal. Yearning pushed and ached with escalating intensity.

He boldly explored her nakedness, learning its secrets and feeling its tremors. Startled gasps leaked out amidst her ragged breaths, and that only seemed to coil his tension tighter. He took her breast in his mouth and sucked until she cried out. The pleasure turned toward a center, twining and twisting, wanting and waiting with a power that tormented.

Yes, please . . . She held on to him as if her sanity depended on it, grabbing frantically at his shoulders. *Oh, God, please . . .* He led her toward something dangerous and wonderful and she wanted both to rush forward and beat a retreat. *Give me . . . I want . . .* His caresses moved lower, to stomach and thighs. He firmly pushed her legs apart. *Oh, oh . . . yes, I want . . . please, higher, there, oh, I . . . I . . .*

He brushed his fingers through her lower hair, stroking down between her thighs. When his hand answered her plea, an acute spike of pleasure made her stretch away. He threw a leg over hers to hold her in place. His hard phallus pressed into her hip, startling her more.

"I am not taking you yet. You will enjoy this, I promise you." His finger slid down her cleft into slick moisture and hidden folds.

Oh. Touches. Strokes. The intensity of the sensations assaulted her in a relentless series of pleasurable shocks. The places he explored were scandalously sensitive. She lost sense of everything else but a groaning craving that left her begging.

Yes, yes, ah, yes. Desperate want vanquished virginal fear. She spread her legs and moved into his touch, rocking closer. *Please . . . ah.* The pleasure only got stronger, sharper, worse. Building, building spinning out of control now, crying her single-minded thoughts, the flesh that he caressed, pulsing in time with her speeding heart. *I . . . I . . . oh, God . . .* Her awareness shattered into bright shards, blinding her senses. An unearthly pitch of shrieking pleasure exploded into an instant of suffusing bliss.

He moved on top of her and she clawed him to her. In her sated stupor he was the only reality besides her own physicality. The whole world existed in him.

He entered her carefully. A vague awareness of pain penetrated her concentration on his scent, his skin, and her relief. He lifted one of her legs up over his hip and that eased the tightness. *Yes, yes, so good . . . I want this. I want you.*

He pressed until he filled her. Controlled power poured out of him, tensing the shoulders above her and the arms flanking her. A sensual severity sculpted his face. She found his rhythm and rocked up to accept each filling penetration. *So good, so close. In me, with me. I want you. I love you.*

The end came too soon, but then morning would have been too soon. Holding her leg to his hip, he leveraged her up and thrust even deeper, ravishing her in a flurry of hard moves that incited a renewed wildness in her. A final savage kiss, a visceral tremor, and suddenly he was gone from her, leaving her arms full of him, but their joining over.

She drifted in a sweet cloud, dazed and stunned. Her arms gripped him long after his own embrace had slackened. Newborn emotions saturated her and she did not understand them all.

Her mind slowly comprehended the end. He had withdrawn to protect her from pregnancy. His thoughtfulness touched her, but she also experienced a stab of inexplicable disappointment.

He brushed the hair away from her face and pressed a kiss to her cheek. "You never cease to astonish me, Bianca."

Slowly the sacred intimacy changed to something less holy and more solid. His possessive embrace broke and he shifted off of her. They lay together for a long while, and she sensed contentment luring him to sleep. She hopped up and scurried over to the bookshelves.

"What are you doing?" He watched her naked body in a way they both assumed was his right now. How quickly one became shameless about these things.

"Getting the port. I think that I should be allowed some more." She also snatched up the glass, and on second thought, lifted the blue folio as well. Back in their nest, she snuggled down and he tucked the coverlet around them until they were cocooned together.

He poured the port and shared it with her. He gestured to the folio that she had set aside. "You are in the mood to read? I can see that I will have to do better next time."

"If you should fall asleep I will need something to do, because I am very awake. I would like to read this someday, and see what your brother wrote about my country. Both you and Charlotte speak of him with pride."

"Pride to be sure, but Milton was not without his faults. He possessed an intellectual arrogance that managed to offend without intention. Also, he could be very impractical sometimes."

He might not have revered Milton, but she could hear his sadness, timeworn but still keen, when he spoke of him. She understood too well the quiet poignancy that grief assumes over time.

She moved the folio out of view, hoping the painful subject could be dropped as easily. To her surprise, he stretched for it and flipped it open. He ran his fingers down the large sheets, as if by doing so he could connect with the hand that had held the pen that wrote the words.

Her gaze followed his fingers, and she noticed the way the ink formed the letters beneath his touch.

"So, they were not from him," she said.

He looked at her curiously.

"There were some letters from Adam's desk at Woodleigh in the trunk in my chamber. I assumed they were from Milton and had intended to give them to you, but with the events of our last days at Laclere Park, I forgot. However, if this is your brother's hand, the letters were not from him after all."

"Did they bear his signature?"

"I did not check. I did not even read them."

"Why did you believe they were from Milton?"

Why had she? "The salutation on the top one, I suppose. It was something like 'Dearest Friend,' and you had spoken of their fast friendship. It was stupid of me to assume they came from Milton. I expect that Adam had other friends."

He ran his fingertips over the page again. "Where are these letters now?"

"Still in my chamber at Laclere Park."

"I would like to see them, to be sure they were not from Milton."

She understood that. Didn't she clutch the little bits of her father's and mother's lives that she found in those papers? "It is always tragic when one so gifted dies young. Some claim that God takes the best the fastest. Everyone said that about my father, but I do not believe God to be so selfish."

Vergil looked to the hearth with a sightless frown. "God did not take Milton, Bianca. He died by his own hand."

"Oh, Vergil. I am sorry that I spoke of it at all."

"You could not have suspected."

"Do you know why?"

"I am trying to learn that. He could be melancholy, but I do not think that drove him to it." He paused in a way that caused her to think that he was picking his words carefully. "Like many men born to his station, my brother assumed the rules were necessary but intended for everyone but himself. He pursued his own interests quietly, secure that the world would leave him alone if he did not demand attention. He was correct, up to a point. However, some of his ideas and behavior left him very vulnerable, and the day came when someone exploited that vulnerability."

"He was being blackmailed?"

"I am all but certain of it."

"You said that some of his political views were radical, but—or was it his involvement in the mill?"

"I had assumed it was the former, because Milton would never have found the latter so damning it demanded his death. There are those who advocate violence as the way to solve our current troubles, and there have been assassination attempts on government leaders. If my brother had any connection to the men who planned such things, any at all, and it became known— It was one reason why I took his place here. It was a way to gain entry to his life, and the radicals in this region. But I wonder sometimes if it was not politics that he was threatened with, but something much more ordinary."

"So the answer may not be here, you are saying, but somewhere closer to home."

His expression changed, as if she had startled him. "Yes. Closer to home."

She kissed his shoulder. "Is that why you became such a saint? To compensate for the scandal used to threaten your brother, should it still become known? I thought it was to deflect attention from your secret life."

He gave a slow smile. "Perhaps I became a saint because it is in my nature to be one."

She giggled and pointedly looked at their discarded garments. Sneaking a hand around his waist, she tickled him and he jumped. "It does not appear to be in your nature at all, by my reckoning of things."

Maybe, just maybe, she enjoyed the next hours even more than she had the physical pleasure. In their little world of firelight, they told stories from their past and discussed people they knew. Bianca learned of his concerns for Charlotte's future and his hope that she would marry happily. She told him all about Aunt Edith, and how she once scolded John Adams at a formal dinner. They speculated on how Pen and Cornell Witherby had *tendres* for each other, and whether Dante would ever find happiness.

Finally, shortly before dawn, he bundled her in the blanket and carried her up to the lord's chamber. He unwrapped her and warmed her and made slow, soulful love, so beautifully that it wrung her heart.

When her emotions and body were sated, he showed her the final, most dangerous pleasure. That of falling asleep in the security of her lover's arms.

chapter 15

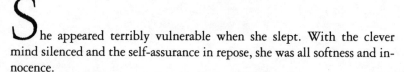

She appeared terribly vulnerable when she slept. With the clever mind silenced and the self-assurance in repose, she was all softness and innocence.

He had spent the last hour looking at her, delighting in the little twitches of her eyelids and lips, drinking in the sight of her, like some country boy enraptured by the first girl who had finally said yes.

Making love had only further confused the tangle. It might have helped if she had been less open and passionate. Less joyful. Whatever defenses he had retained against his feelings had been demolished by the pleasure.

Astounding pleasure. Incredibly intense. If he had ever experienced anything like it, he didn't remember. Even the few great infatuations of his younger days, of being mesmerized by Catalani and others, paled as superficial and immature in comparison. Certainly the efficient sensuality practiced in recent years had produced nothing remotely similar. A man did not permit true intimacy with professional women.

Was she even aware that she had gasped out audibly in her frenzy? Her melodic groans and urgings had filled his ears, making his hold on restraint tenuous at best. *Yes . . . I want this, I want you.* The echo had his mind reeling and an erection hardening. *I want you. I love you.* Did she realize that she had even thought that, let alone said it? He knew better than to put much stock in words spoken in the throes of passion.

Dante had been right. She would make a splendid mistress. He strongly suspected that she would agree to be his lover, for a while at least. Which was the problem that awaited him all too soon and tinted his preening contentment with misgivings.

He did not want her in a love affair smothered by discretion. He wanted her for a wife. He was not at all convinced that she would agree to that, in which case he had corrupted her last night, and possibly initiated her to the very life he had been warning her about.

Later. He would stretch what happiness he could out of this interlude first. There would be time enough to explain that she had to marry him now.

He laughed aloud. Leave it to Bianca to end his grand seduction with the tables completely turned. He was damn close to waking her and demanding that she do the right thing by him.

"What are you smiling about?" She stretched and blinked like a kitten awakening. Her sleepy smile turned up to accept his morning kiss.

"Just watching you and enjoying you beside me."

She nestled against his shoulder and peered around the bright chamber. "The rain has stopped. The sun . . . everything looks and feels so different."

"Not too different, I hope."

"Not too, but a little." She snuck a glance up at him. "Should I be embarrassed to find myself here with you?"

"That depends on whether you have regrets. Do you?"

She thought about that. "No, even though I am supposed to."

"I have always suspected that all of the 'supposed tos' were decided by people who lacked experience in the situations they pronounced upon."

"Aunt Edith says much the same thing, about different situations, of course. I think that you would like her. She does not much hanker to people trying to tell her what she is supposed to do or think. Mother may have been the same way, but since I was her child, she would not have voiced such ideas to me. Edith is too old to know restraint in her opinions, however."

He would like to meet the aunt, and regretted that he would never know the mother. He would enjoy seeing the city where Bianca had lived and the streets where she had walked as a child and a girl.

She tucked the coverlet up around her neck. Despite her brave front, she was not completely without embarrassment, and her vulnerability touched him.

"What do we do now?" She kept looking around the big chamber.

We get dressed, ride to York, procure a special license from the archbishop, and get married. "Whatever you like. I think that we can put off returning you to Pen for another day if you want, or I can order Morton to make the carriage ready at once."

She bit her lower lip. "Do you want me to stay?"

He realized that her embarrassment had to do with him. She wondered what morning-after judgments he was making. He should have considered that the new day might require some reassurances.

"I want you to stay as long as we can manage it, and heartily wish that nothing existed to put limits on our time alone together. If you want, we will take this day and make the most of it and decide about the waiting world tomorrow."

A beautiful smile lit her face. "I would like that. Is it very late? Have we slept most of the day away and wasted it?"

"Not so late. Not yet noon."

"Do we have time to go to Manchester? To see our mill?"

With any other woman, he would suspect that she flattered him by expressing interest in his life.

"If you do not want to, I understand, Laclere. After all, there is the risk that people would see me with you."

I would have the whole world see you with me. "I would very much like to show you our mill. We will go this afternoon. Is there anything else you would like to do?"

Mischievous lights flickered in her big blue eyes. She ran a finger along his collarbone and blushed prettily. "Well, it is still a little different and strange, what with the sun and day and all. Not too much, but a little. Maybe if you were to . . . if we were to . . . that is to say, it might be less so then. Different and strange feeling, that is."

He eased her head toward his kiss. "Except that I worried for you feeling overused, I would have, we would have, as soon as you opened your eyes. It pleases me that you want me, Bianca, and that you tell me so."

"Oh, yes," she whispered. "I do."

He inclined his shoulders up against some pillows on the headboard and showed her how to straddle his lap. Savoring her weight lying against his chest, adoring the face turned to his kisses, he embraced and caressed her like the precious gift she was. He slid the bed coverings away so he could gaze over her shoulder at the sinuous lines that dipped down her back before curving gracefully up her bottom and snaking back and forth along her bent legs. His hard phallus nestled between her thighs and he felt the wetness of arousal seep out of her.

He eased her upright so that he could see her body and her passion. A little different, what with the sun and the day and all. Not too much, but a little, and wonderfully so. He loved watching her ecstacy grow while he touched her.

He inclined her so that he could lick and suck her breasts. Her frenzy broke and those erotic affirmations began sighing out of her. Like flames, they set his blood on fire.

"Bring me inside yourself," he said, bracing himself against the explosive urge to have her every way imaginable before accepting release.

She straightened with dazed confusion.

"Stay where you are and take me inside you. This is how I want you this time."

She looked down at his phallus nested between her thighs, its tip pressing visibly against her cleft. She had never touched him before. Her hesitation reminded him of the recent ignorance that her quick passion made easy to forget.

He was about to take over when she rose up and grasped him firmly, like a woman determined to meet a challenge. Then he was sliding into her tight velvet warmth while her eyes closed with contentment and a melodic groan of relief escaped her. He pulled her down and held her motionlessly in a firm embrace so he could merely revel in the feel of her for a spell.

She pushed up and squirmed until he was deeply imbedded. Her hands drifted down his chest in two slow inflaming paths. Cautiously, curiously, she rose up and lowered herself and blinked with astonishment.

She found a rhythm and he let it last until she began moving and frowning as if she searched for something out of reach. Her cries and gasps and hard absorptions singed his constricting consciousness. He slid his hand to her cleft and touched the spot that would bring her to climax. With increased wildness she rode him harder until she screamed a release that filled the chamber and drove him to his own completion.

He had to forcibly lift her in order to withdraw in time. She collapsed on him, her head resting against his chest and her body wrapped in his arms. The sweat of her passion glistened all along her back.

Holding firmly to her warmth and heartbeat and slowing breaths, he dragged the coverlet over them both. He pressed his lips to her damp hair and allowed his soul to taste the rare, deep flavor of love.

Morton had disappeared. Like a busy ghost, he executed his duties but never showed his face. When they finally descended for a late breakfast, the meal was ready, as if he had divined the exact moment it would be needed. Hot water awaited their return to the bedchamber, and the carriage and its horses were prepared just in time for the trip to Manchester. Old Lucas sat at the reins because, as he explained to Vergil, the valet had some business to attend in the manor.

Bianca appreciated the total isolation that Morton's absence created. Not because of shame. She experienced none of that at all. The old manor had become theirs alone, a little world existing in dream time, and the solitude intensified their deepening intimacy.

It was Sunday, and Vergil escorted her around an abandoned works. He showed her where the raw cotton was received and cleaned, and the long, low buildings filled with steam-powered spinning machines. His commentary became animated and detailed when he described the improvements he had invented, and she delighted in the quiet pride he found in his achievement. Finally he took her to a new structure, larger than all the others.

"You should see this, since you will be investing in it," he explained.

The building held rows of large looms connected by vertical arms to iron bars overhead.

"They will be steam-powered, like the spinning. Only a few others have done this yet, and not on this scale. The engine is being built in the next room." He showed her the way and explained the huge metal cauldron and water pipes and valves that would make the metal arms move the looms' parts as required. "Most weaving is still done in homes. This will be much faster and more efficient. I have promised the jobs here to any home weavers who want to learn the new ways."

"Some will not want to."

"They will manage for a long while yet. The change will not happen overnight, but the craft will not exist for their sons. It is for them, much as your grandfather said it was for me and my kind. Their world is dying."

"It does not appear to me that your world is dying. I think that my grandfather was premature."

"Prophecies are always premature. As with the weavers, the change will not be overnight, and two hundred years from now Duclaircs and Calnes will still be lords with privileges. But we will be as quaint and picturesque as the medieval ruins in Laclere Park, I think. In my lifetime I expect our hold will be circumscribed as the cities like Manchester demand their say. My hope is that the change comes peaceably, and not with the violence that already tears at the country, reflecting the people's impatience."

He checked his office for any materials Mr. Thomas might have left for his attention. She peered over his shoulder as he sat at his desk and flipped through some letters.

"Mr. Thomas wrote these?" she asked, picking one up to examine it. "Well, that explains it, then."

"Explains what?"

"Those letters in my grandfather's desk. The ones I told you about last night, that I had thought were from Milton. This is the same handwriting. They must be letters regarding the mill, that Mr. Thomas wrote to Adam."

Vergil went very still. He no longer read the pages in front of him. She sensed a distraction that took him far away from her, to some place in his head where she did not intrude.

He turned a thoughtful gaze on her. "How did you say the salutation read? The one on the top letter that you saw?"

"My dearest friend."

"An odd way for an employee to address Adam Kenwood, don't you think?"

"They may have formed a fast friendship. Such things happen."

The frown turned into a scowl. "All the same, I want to know about those letters, and I don't intend to wait until I return to Laclere Park." He rose. "Mr. Thomas lives in the local village. If I am here, I may as well go speak with him about it now. It should not take long."

The village was a quarter-mile west, a single lane of cottages pressed shoulder to shoulder. The age of some of them indicated this spot had been inhabited for generations, and had been a farming community before the mill was built. Now many of the homes burst with people, and the lane this Sunday showed the community relaxing from the week's work.

"There are a lot of men here," Bianca said as she craned her neck to survey the commotion through the window. "It appears that some of these homes are crowded."

"We have been building new cottages, but give them to the families first. The men who come from elsewhere have to make do for now."

"I think that we will have to build faster, Laclere, if you intend to bring weavers in as well."

"If Adam Kenwood's granddaughter has decided to remain a partner, I'm sure that we can afford to build faster."

She smiled contentedly, in a way that reassured him. However, the points he had made last night, about her marriage to another man jeopardizing control of the mill, had not disappeared with their passion.

He really needed to settle their future together. Not now, however. Now he needed to have a conversation with his secretary, a young man who probably knew far more about the mill and the Duclaircs than previously suspected.

"I should speak with him alone," he said as the coach rolled to a stop in front of an old stone cottage that had seen recent improvements.

"I understand. We can hardly go calling together."

It wasn't that. He did not want her hearing this conversation. In fact, he could not even have it if she were present.

He walked to the door quickly. All the same, he was noticed. He sensed the lane go quiet, and felt eyes watch his progress.

Mr. Clark never visited this village, at least not in ways that its inhabitants noticed. His inspections had been as subtle and secret as the rest of his life in this region.

His secretary showed astonishment equal to the villagers. Taken aback at the call, he brought Vergil to a little sitting room and quickly took a chair near a table.

Vergil noted the man's guarded expression. "I have not come to criticize or chastise, Thomas, and certainly not to release you. This is a social call."

Harry Thomas was a large-framed, fair-skinned man, the sort whose face colored easily when he was angry or ill at ease. It was very ruddy now. His pose in the chair, with legs and arms crossed, made it appear that he braced himself for unpleasantness, or restrained himself physically from revealing his reactions.

He knew that, social call or not, the unexpected presence of his employer was not good news.

He was correct about that, but Vergil guessed that the news would be worse for the employer than the secretary. Rather than delay the pain, he threw himself right on the blade after they had exchanged some banal talk about the fair day and the village's growth.

"You know who I am, don't you?" he said. "You knew who the last Mr. Clark was, too, I think."

The face got ruddier. The eyes glazed with caution. "He confided in me. I kept it to myself then, and I still do with you."

"I believe you." Did he? Was he looking at the answer to it all, right here in this chamber? Did Harry Thomas betray Milton's confidence and threaten to reveal the viscount's déclassé dabbling in industry?

It might have been Thomas, but the mill was not reason enough. Not for Milton. It was something far more damning.

The solution wanted to force itself into his mind, and his heart's rebellion barely kept it at bay.

Vergil strolled around the chamber, wondering how to proceed. His gaze lit on a low case of books, and one caught his eye. He slid the volume out of its spot. As he did, he heard a movement behind him, that of a man shifting in his place. He felt Harry Thomas's alarm.

"Homer's *Odyssey.* My brother loved this work." He cradled the book in his hands. He recognized the binding. This had been Milton's book, a part of his private library. It had been given to Milton by their father.

And now it belonged to Harry Thomas.

"He loaned it to me. I should have returned it. Take it now."

Vergil came close to accepting the explanation. He wanted to nod, take his leave, and stride back to the coach and Bianca.

Except this had been no loan. He just knew that. He suspected if he opened the cover he would find an inscription that made it a gift.

He kept the cover closed and looked at the other books, all of them new and with impressive bindings. Too impressive for a secretary of dubious fortune. He scanned the authors. Poets, philosophers, and historians. Milton had given Harry all of these, he was sure.

Had it been an exercise in education? An attempt to improve a naturally sharp mind with some culture? A Voltairian experiment?

The answer, he guessed, was inside the volume that he held. Milton would not have given away his own boyhood treasure to a mere student of literature.

"I have come to ask you some questions about my brother," he said, setting the book down on the table where they both could see it. Harry looked for all the world like a man who would like to snatch it and hide it under his coat.

"There are some letters from you to Milton. I am wondering about them."

"I wrote to him. Was my job, wasn't it? He came here less often than you do, and after Kenwood got ill, the mill was left to me to manage day to day. I had to keep him informed."

"I saw those letters. They were among his business papers, and sent to a London address, and addressed to Mr. Clark. I speak now of different ones, probably sent to Laclere House in London, and to Laclere Park in Sussex. These were kept separate from the others, and saved together. In them you address my brother as 'Dearest Friend.' "

Harry's face turned so bland it might have been made of stone. "We formed a friendship. Here, at the mill, in the works, he was not such a grand man. Not the sort to think he was better than such as me."

No, he had not been that sort at all. Nor had he been the sort to worry that his friendship might be betrayed.

Vergil laid his hand on the volume. "I want you to think now. Were any of these letters indiscreet?"

"What are you insinuating? I'll not be—"

"*Do not* feign indignation with me. I was his *brother.* I may have ignored what I saw, but I saw it all the same. I need to know now if anyone who read those letters might surmise the depths of your friendship."

Harry's jaw tightened in anger, but his eyes were those of a man trapped and frightened.

"You are safe with me. I would never do anything to harm his name," Vergil said quietly.

Harry's stiff pose slackened, more in defeat than relief. "I suppose, it is possible, if they were read—but I thought they were destroyed."

"A sensible man would have burned them, but my brother could be foolish sometimes, and sentiment ruled him in this."

Beneath his dismay, the notion that his letters had been saved seemed to touch Harry. He nodded his head toward the bookshelves. "Had me reading philosophers and such. Wanted to open the world to me, he did." He smiled nostalgically. "Interesting stuff, but not much help when the workers got mad after he decided no children could work. They depended on the wages, those families did. I got him to agree to let the boys stay on for some hours, at least. Kenwood couldn't get through to him on some of his notions, but I could. Real life isn't so neat as in those books, I told him. Even good deeds can have bad results. You are more practical than he was. Kenwood said so too. Said this was in your blood more, and not only an experiment for you."

"It is good that you were here to help him. When he came north, did he visit you in this house?"

"None saw him. He was discreet. Didn't come up in a fancy coach as you just did."

In villages such as this, no discretion was great enough. "Did you and he ever visit Manchester together?"

"Sometimes. Nothing untoward was seen, if that is your question. It was natural for us to be together at meetings and such. We worked together."

That was true, but one wrong glance, one wrong laugh . . . "I regret that I must return to those letters. Did you ever write another sort of letter to Milton, asking for something of value from him?"

Harry's soft expression snapped away. "What are you saying?"

"Did you make any demands on him? His friendship with you made him vulnerable to anyone who knew of it, including you."

"Made me vulnerable as well. No point in my making demands."

"That is not true, and we both know it. He was a peer. Any scandal, let alone a trial, would affect him more. Men no longer hang for such things, but they can be destroyed. You could disappear if it came out, but he could not."

"Damn you. Damn all of you. Assuming that I'd be grasping, just because I'm not born to silver as you are. It wasn't like that, but I'd never expect the two of you to understand."

"What do you mean, the *two* of you?"

"You are not the first to come have this chat with me, *Mr. Clark.*"

"Another man has approached you about this friendship? Who?"

"Not a man. A lady came, all veiled and sneaky. Said she knew about the mill, and me, and worried for his reputation and that of his family."

"She knew who Mr. Clark really was?"

"To be certain. She said he was careless, and asked if there were letters to him as the viscount that should be destroyed. She was going to do it, you see. To protect him. Before she left she threatened me. Said if I ever told anyone, if I ever tried to use this for my own gain, she'd see me hang."

"Was this before or after my brother's death?"

"A good four months earlier. I didn't want him to know that she had figured it out. If he knew, he might . . ." He shrugged.

"She may have been veiled, but you must have known who she was if you spoke of anything at all with her."

Thomas sneered at him, as if he were an idiot. "I knew who she was, because she told me straight-out. It was your sister, the Countess of Glasbury."

The child peered at Bianca and Bianca peered back. The little girl had been scrubbed for Sunday, and her red hair blazed in the sun. Her big eyes examined Bianca's garments with astonishment, then she ran back to her mother who watched from the doorway.

Their cottage was small and tidy and new. A little row of them flanked the lane, facing the older homes that showed their age and indifference to care.

Vergil came out of Mr. Thomas's house and noticed her down the lane. He walked toward her with a troubled expression.

"Did you learn what you wanted?" she asked as he joined her.

"More than I wanted." He appeared tired and lost.

"The letters were from Mr. Thomas?"

"Yes."

"See, they were friends, as I said."

"They were not to Adam, but to my brother."

She shrugged. "A different friendship, then. Charlotte always speaks of Milton as being reclusive, so it must have been a joy to him to have some dear friends. It must make you feel better to know that he did, that he wasn't lonely in his life."

He gave her an odd look. "Yes, I suppose it makes me feel better knowing that. Now let us return to the house. Of the many lives I find myself living today, the one that includes you is the one I need right now."

As soon as they entered the coach, he took her hand and pulled her across the carriage to sit on his lap. "What did you think of your mill?"

"I think that perhaps I will let the manager continue for a few more years, at least. I am not sure that Nigel will be so sanguine, however. How have you managed to keep him ignorant of your role in it?"

"He was in France, and since his return Mr. Clark has dodged meeting him. We have a lively correspondence going. I am counting on him being content if his income surpasses what he could get in the funds, but if necessary, I will offer to purchase his share at a generous profit."

"Why not do so right away?"

"The offer from Mr. Johnston and Mr. Kennedy will give him fifty thousand pounds. I cannot raise that without mortgaging the mill itself."

"Fifty thousand . . . Why, that means that my share must be worth . . ."

"Over two hundred thousand. The value is in the equipment and the land and the accounts more than the annual profits. Are you sorry that you have promised not to sell?"

"I wouldn't know what to do with that much. You say the profits are better than the income from an equal amount in the funds, so I am better with the mill it seems."

"One bad decision by your manager and the mill's value diminishes."

She pecked his nose with a little kiss. "I think that I will take my chances. I trust my manager. Not because he is hungry for the gain, but because he has a passion for what he is doing and therefore will do it well."

One eyebrow arched rakishly. "Does passion lead to superb performance? I think that theory should be tested more."

A long kiss made his meaning clear. She emerged breathless. "Lucas . . ." she gasped while he untied the neck of her cloak.

"He won't hear a thing with all the noise the carriage makes."

It didn't seem to make much noise at all suddenly, but then his mouth was raising sensations that had blood pounding in her ears. "If we are stopped . . ."

"No one will do so except a highwayman, and these parts haven't seen one in a decade."

"We are almost home."

"At least twenty minutes away. But you are right, we wouldn't want to pull up at the wrong moment, and I am not inclined to make love to you quickly. Quite the opposite. I will have to pass the time with more leisurely pursuits."

"A game of cards?"

"I was thinking more in terms of discovering just how wild I can make you between here and the manor." His expression gave lie to his teasing words. The concern she had seen when he found her on the lane still veiled his eyes. "I am very grateful that you are here with me now, more than I can ever explain."

It turned out that he could make her very wild. Incredibly so. Sensations piled up and split and multiplied. Pleasure layered upon pleasure. She was not even undressed, but his hands found and touched with wicked precision through her bodice and under her skirt. The end never came and the frenzy doubled in on itself, pitching her up to a crazed peak of need. With observant deliberation he kept her balanced on a point of exquisite torture.

When they arrived at the manor he assisted her dazed body from the carriage. He guided her to the door with such nonchalance that Lucas could have assumed they had passed the time discussing roses.

The cool aristocrat disappeared as soon as the manor's door closed. In an instant she found herself pressed against the paneled wall of the hall, his mouth on her breast and his hands pulling up her skirt. In a blur of primitive need he opened his trousers and lifted her so that her legs encircled his hips.

Her arousal immediately centered on the glorious relief he gave. She felt him as she never had before and she wanted nothing else, no other touch, just this hot pressure, thrusting and filling. Desperate now, she urged on his feral power with bites and crazed kisses and clawing holds. *Yes. Love me. More. Harder, deeper. Yes.* Tremors awoke where they joined, and quaked and spread. A different end beckoned, almost terrible in its power. *Yes. Come with me.* His voice, not hers, against her breast, repeated again and again, the command emphasized by the rhythms of their violent passion. The spinning ecstacy frightened her and she grasped him like a mad woman. *I love you. I love you. Do not leave me this time. I love you.* She lost hold of the world and spiralled into a crescendo of pure sensation.

It took forever to find herself afterward. Neither of them moved for a long time. They remained entwined and pressed against the wall, with Vergil supporting her weight on his arms and hips. He was not inside her anymore, but she could not remember if he had obeyed her plea not to withdraw.

In her bliss she discarded any concern that she had just flirted with pregnancy. All she wanted now was for him to keep holding her, to never let her go, and to never stop filling all of her.

"I took the liberty of preparing the next chamber yesterday, my lord." Morton set down the breakfast tray on the bedchamber's table. Bianca still slept behind the bed's drawn curtains. "I thought that the lady would want some privacy on occasion. To wash and whatnot. I am preparing a bath for her in there now."

"You went to a lot of unnecessary trouble."

"It was my pleasure to arrange for her comfort. With your permission, I thought that I would go to the village and see if there is a suitable girl to come here and serve her."

"Also unnecessary. Miss Kenwood and I will be leaving today."

"York is a short enough journey. After procuring the special license, you may choose to return this evening."

"It is not at all clear that Miss Kenwood will agree to go to York, Morton."

The valet smiled indulgently. "Of course she will. What other course is there now?"

Obstinacy. It was past time to take matters in hand.

She hadn't once broached the subject herself as he had hoped, damn it. Nor had she picked up on his own allusions to continuing what they had begun. She appeared to accept that he would keep her here two days, take her virginity, make love to her repeatedly, and then blithely return her to London with no further ado. He would be insulted if he let himself contemplate her attitude very long.

He paced around the chamber, waiting for her to wake. The course was clear, obvious, inevitable. If she didn't see reason right away, he would have to be very firm with her.

Not that doing so had ever been effective before.

He heard her stirring behind the curtains and resisted going to her. He would not make love to her this morning. He did not want what might be the last memory to be one heavy with solemn emotions. If it came to an end, let last night's laughter and games and easy confidences be the closure.

She poked her head through the curtains, wiping her eyes with a charming gesture that made his heart ache. "You are up and dressed already," she said.

"There is breakfast here, and a bath waits in the next chamber for you after you have eaten."

The realization that the idyll was over dulled her eyes. She pushed the curtains aside and reached for the bedrobe of his that she had been using. "Of course. We need to be off early. You should have woken me."

"Come and eat something."

"I will just take some tea into the bath. I am not hungry." She marched over and poured. "Where is the tub?"

"This way." He opened the door that joined the two chambers.

He had not seen the mistress's bedchamber prepared for use in years.

The white covers had been removed, the hearth cleaned, the gilt furniture polished, and the cloth beaten of its dust. The large room glimmered yellow and white and gold, its mirrors reflecting the clear morning light streaming in the washed windowpanes. Morton must have spent all of yesterday preparing this wedding bower.

"It is very grand. It looks like a queen's chamber." She advanced on the tub, plucking at the tie on the robe.

The midnight-blue silk flowed down her back much the way the water had done that day he saw her in the lake. He memorized every curve her body made while she bent and stepped into the bath. The possibility of losing possession of her beauty did not trouble him so much as giving up the easy familiarity that permitted her to undress with a total lack of self-consciousness.

She began to wash.

"We must talk now," he said.

"At the least, we need to get our story straight, don't we? Have you thought how you will explain finding me?"

"I would like to talk about other things." He began to move a chair closer.

The faintest rumble, like a small tremor in the manor's structure, stopped him. It grew in intensity until it became a commotion pouring down the corridor outside the chamber.

"Damn." He pivoted and strode to his bedchamber. He stepped through and closed the connecting door.

The commotion burst into audible voices muffled by the walls.

"I tell you, my lord is not receiving," Morton announced with furious desperation.

"He'll be receiving for *us.*"

"Dante, we should let Morton wake him, and wait down below."

"I've spent the last fifteen hours in a hellish coach ride. I'll be damned if I'll await the lord's pleasure this morning."

The door flew open. Dante strode into the chamber, with Pen in his wake.

"Bianca bolted, Verg. God knows where the devil she's gone, or which scoundrel she is with."

chapter 16

Evidence of a female visitor dotted the room, but neither Pen nor Dante noticed.

"Bianca disappeared three days ago," Dante said. "I was keeping a close watch, but she talked Pen into letting her return to Laclere Park."

"She was distraught with Dante's continued presence, you see, and she requested . . . It seemed safe enough . . ."

"Face it, Pen, she is too sly for you. Anyway, on the way down she snuck off in Jane's cloak and then that maid hid in her chamber, pretending to be her. The housekeeper realized the ruse yesterday and word was immediately sent to us in London and we started out as soon as we heard."

"We thought it best to let you decide what to do," Pen concluded.

"As you should have," Vergil said.

Dante threw himself on the settee, right next to Bianca's discarded chemise. He actually pushed it aside without realizing what he touched. "There is more, I'm afraid. Nigel has left London, too, and is not at Woodleigh. I think that we should ride with haste up to Gretna Green. If they thought themselves safe, they may not have pushed the journey and there is still the chance that they haven't married yet."

"Why don't you start for Scotland immediately while I go visit the shipping offices in Liverpool," Vergil suggested. "She may have decided to sail home."

"I don't think so," Pen said. "She took almost nothing with her, and she would never leave Jane behind."

"If she is with Kenwood, one hopes the man waited to—" Dante glanced at Pen and caught himself. "I apologize for not taking your concerns about Nigel more seriously, Verg. Presumably they have just eloped, but if it is the other thing . . ."

"I am confident that Miss Kenwood is safe for the time being, in that respect, Dante."

It had been at least fifteen years since Pen had visited the manor. She toured the chamber, distracted by her worry, absently fingering objects and touching furniture. Her aimless stroll took her near the table.

"We should decide our course at once," Dante said. "Who knows what has happened . . ."

Pen was vaguely admiring the silver service on the breakfast tray.

". . . especially since there is no guarantee that Kenwood is even the man . . ."

A frown puckered Pen's forehead. One could practically hear her counting the two plates and knives and forks. A blush rose up from her neck. "Why don't we go and discuss this down below," she interrupted, turning with a stricken expression.

"The way I see it, we don't have time to discuss anything," Dante said. He rose and paced to the window. The window directly above the bench still piled with the garments that two lovers had pulled off each other the night before.

"Dante, Vergil needs to finish dressing. You and I can plan the next step while he does so."

"He is impeccably dressed and shaved already. Probably has been since dawn. Now, Verg—"

"In any case, I think that I shall go below."

"Do as you wish, Pen. Now, Verg, the odds of Scotland are better than Liverpool, so it makes more sense for you to go north if anyone does—" His voice halted as his eyes fell to the garments at his knees. His head angled curiously.

"I'll be damned," he muttered, fingering the edge of a petticoat. "My apologies—" His voice stopped again as shock lit his eyes. He reached into the pile to touch a green sleeve. "Hell, this looks like one of . . ."

His exclamation halted Pen's retreat. She glanced back and saw the sleeve's color. Frowning deeply, she marched to the window, pulled out the garment, and held it up for inspection.

Of course they both recognized it. Bianca's wardrobe was not large and she had worn this many times in their presence.

Dante stared at him in astonishment. Pen appeared as if she might swoon. She turned with the gown displayed like the irrefutable evidence it was.

"Vergil," she began.

"Yes, Pen?"

She shook the gown at him accusingly. "Vergil, I think that you have been a very naughty boy."

Hell and damnation.

"Yes, Pen."

"Jesus." Dante paced with his arms crossed over his chest, the image of a man too staggered for words.

Pen had collected Bianca's garments and disappeared into the neighboring chamber.

"Hell."

"Is that all, Dante? If so, you must excuse me, as I need to speak with Bianca."

"Not yet, you don't, and do not presume to take that superior tone with me *ever again.*" He gestured erratically. "Have you gone insane? Lost your wits completely?"

"In a manner of speaking, I suppose that I have."

"Please tell me that she lost her way to wherever she was going and somehow landed on your doorstep this morning and has not been here all this time."

"I would not insult you with such a preposterous story, nor would you believe it."

"Damnation, Verg, this is the sort of thing *I'm* supposed to do, and even I would not be so bold. She is *your ward.*"

"You do not need to remind me of how dishonorable my behavior has been."

"Don't I? *Don't I?*" Dante peered at him furiously. "Badly done, very badly done. Clumsy and risky. If you intended to initiate an affair, why not do so in London or at Laclere Park? Having her sneak away to join you here . . ." Insight flashed in his eyes. "Yes, clumsy and risky. Too much for my careful, discreet brother. You did not plan this at all, did you? It was her idea. She followed you here and . . ." He drew himself into a posture of righteous outrage. *"Hell."*

Vergil did not like being upbraided by Dante of all people, but if he described how and why Bianca had really made this journey, it would scandalize his brother more than any affair.

"No wonder she turned me down. She had her eye on your title. To trap you like this, to take advantage of your fastidious honor . . . the mind reels that one so young could be so ruthless."

Upbraiding him was one thing. Insulting Bianca was quite another. "You will not say another word against her, Dante."

"Still has you addled, does she? Turns out you are only human, too, it seems. Wipe the fog of passion from your eyes, big brother, and look at the facts. Unless you intend to submit and make this lightskirt your viscountess, we had better put our minds together and find a way to thwart her."

To hell with protecting secret lives. "She did not come to this manor uninvited, nor was our time together planned by either of us. We met by accident when she came north in order to—"

"It is chivalrous of you to try to protect me, Laclere, but that will not be necessary," Bianca's voice interrupted.

She stood at the connecting threshold, in her green dress. Pen stood beside her.

Vergil went over and took her hand. She squeezed his gratefully, then released his hold.

"I have always been too impetuous. Penelope can attest to that," Bianca said to Dante. "As can you. But following your brother here was part of no plot. I am not that clever, nor do I seek to trap him into marriage. I came to demand my independence. The rest that occurred was not planned at all."

Not a word of it was a lie, but it obscured the details and protected his secret. Still, her story hardly absolved them.

"For your brother's sake, I ask that you both be discreet about what you have stumbled upon. I am sure that you do not want him ruined because I am too headstrong. Now, I think that I would like some time alone. I also expect that the three of you will want to make some decisions without me present."

She walked proudly out the door, but Vergil could see the humiliation below the surface of her bravery.

"Follow her, Pen, to see if she will accept your company. I will come down shortly," he said.

Pen was happy to escape. Vergil closed the door behind her and turned on his brother. "I may never forgive you that Bianca heard your damning words, Dante."

"Perhaps it is for the best that she witnessed that there will be some rational influence on you. I thank God that we got here before she bewitched you all the way to the altar."

"Do I look like a man bewitched and addled? You have got it backward. I brought her to this manor, and with the full intention of seducing her. Your arrival interrupted *my* attempts to cajole *her* into matrimony."

Dante's surprised reaction melted into amusement. "Why would you want to do that? She is pretty enough, but no great beauty. She is hardly suitable for you, and her free manner would only embarrass you and affect your position. Fleur will make a far superior wife, and you know it. If you found Bianca passionate and want to keep her for a while, it is obvious that you do not have to marry her for that."

"You are in grave danger of finding my fist in your face again, Dante."

Dante's lids lowered. "If so, it may end differently today, Vergil. After all, I will not be caught unawares because I am sprawled atop Miss Kenwood this time."

Vergil did almost hit him then. Biting back his fury, he walked to the door. "I am going to propose now. If by some gift of grace she accepts, and even if she does not, you will never again so much as raise one eyebrow where she is concerned. If you do, I am finished with you."

"For a man not bewitched and addled you are playing the fool. There are times to put honor aside, such as when you have been manipulated by a woman with her character."

"I have already put honor aside, and now it is time to take it up again. Are you so jaded that you cannot see the truth of what happened here? Her character was unblemished before she met me. She entered this manor an innocent and I deliberately seduced her even though I knew that."

He swung away from Dante's gape-mouthed shock and strode down to the hall. Pen sat in front of the hearth, looking tired and spent.

"Where is Bianca?"

"In the library." She held out a hand and he took it between his in a gesture of reassurance. "This had been a tremendous shock, Vergil. Even with Dante one would not expect . . . but *you.* I do not even begin to know what to do."

"Just promise to be a friend to her, no matter what happens. Will you give me that?"

"Of course." She looked up with a faltering smile. "Are you going to marry her?"

"Yes, if she will have me."

"Thank goodness. Of course you would do the right thing, especially after being discovered like this."

"It is the right thing, Pen, but not because honor dictates it, nor because you and Dante discovered us."

She paced the edges of the library, gazing at the chair where he had sat that first night. She could feel again the exciting anticipation that had pulsed between them, and then the bonds of intimacy that he had forged later on the floor. She blinked the heartrending memories away.

She had known when she woke that their dream world was dying. She had felt it in the empty space where Vergil's body should have been. Then she had seen him, dressed already, proud and tall and thoughtful. Nobility clothed him as surely as the frock coat and impeccably tied cravat. It imbued his casual stance with the magnetic self-confidence born of generations of privilege. *The Viscount Laclere,* her heart had whispered. Neither Mr. Clark nor Vergil her lover had smiled at her, but a peer of the realm.

She had looked at him and known that the freedom of their passion had ended with the night. He had said that they would decide what to do about the waiting world this morning. That waiting world was the viscount's world, and with the dawn he had left her side and dressed to meet it.

But the world had not waited after all. It had crashed in the door and robbed them of whatever soft moments were left. And the very honorable viscount had almost invited his family's censure in order to spare her a small fraction of the scorn, as if the circumstances that brought her to this manor and to his bed made any difference at all.

She could not remember ever feeling this wistful. Her heart ached, for reasons she could not name. It reminded her too much of grief's nostalgia over losing something important forever.

The door opened. It was not Dante or Pen, but Vergil. She should be relieved, but instead that pang throbbed again.

"You look very lonely, Bianca. May I join you?" He offered his hand. "Will you come and sit with me, darling?"

She let him guide her to the settee, where he enclosed her in a gentle embrace. She rested her head against his chest and went boneless in the sweet security of his strength. For these precious moments she would pretend that he could make everything right and perfect and would carry her off to a secluded world where rules and shame never intruded. For this brief spell of quiet peace she would close her mind to everything but the reality of him, and his closeness and comfort and soft kisses pressed to her hair.

"I am very sorry that Penelope and Dante arrived as they did, Bianca. If I could undo the last hour I would, not because I want to hide what has occurred, but to spare you any embarrassment. I must be honest, however, and confess that I cannot find it in me to want to undo anything else about these last three days."

She had to grit her teeth to keep from weeping. He had spoken the only words that she wanted to hear. The slightest reference to regrets would have been horrible.

He looked so serious. Every crease of his concern was for her, not himself. Gratitude that he worried for her crashed headlong into panic over how he would try to save her.

"If they had to arrive today, I think when they did was much preferable to an hour earlier. I would rather have Pen discover me dripping wet in your robe than have Dante find me stark naked in your bed."

He smiled and caressed her cheek. "You are still astonishing. Your composure surpasses mine this morning. Most women would be in hysterics."

She did not move her head. Not even a fraction. She wanted and needed the warmth of his hand. She was desperate for any connection to him right now, because she was holding on to her much-lauded composure by a very thin thread of pride. Her heart cringed because she knew where this gentle conversation must inevitably lead.

He had come to offer more than apologies and warmth. He was an honorable man. This could only end one way now.

The wrong way, to her mind. For the wrong reasons.

"Are you disappointed that I am not in hysterics?"

"Well, I might find reason in your overwrought condition to thrash my brother, who certainly has it coming."

"I did not like hearing what he said, but considering what he discovered and how I behaved in the past, I cannot blame him."

"I have warned him to display only respect for you in the future. If he ever insults you, even subtly, you must tell me."

He dropped his hand down to hold hers. He thoughtfully watched his thumb caress the back of her palm. "I would not undo anything about these last days, but I would add a few things. Words that should have been said and offers that should have been made. Pen and Dante interrupted my efforts to say it when you woke. Now I wonder if you will believe that I am not coerced." He kissed the inside of her wrist. "I would like us to be wed at once. You believe that, don't you? That I speak with sincerity? Will you marry me?"

So there it was. Of course. What else could he do?

His words unleashed a battle in her heart. Pride and love clashed with confusion and fear. She hung her head, wishing the love did not fight with those other tumultuous emotions.

"Not entirely," she said.

"*Not entirely?* An odd answer. You do not entirely believe that I speak without coercion, or you will marry me, but not entirely?" He teased, but cautiously.

"The former. Although, if I could manage it, I should like the latter. That would settle things in an ideal manner."

"You think it would be ideal to find a way to be married to me, but not entirely so?"

"If you think about it, you would agree. We could go on as we have been here the last few days. We could both be free to live however we want, and still be faithful lovers with no scandal attached. We would be married and thus acceptable and proper, but not *married.*"

"I do not agree that would be ideal. I want to be *married.* Entirely so. In fact, I would like to be more married than most couples are." He sounded a bit like Laclere the autocrat. Two days of passion did not change a person completely, of course. Considering the declaration being announced, she found his tone more charming than exasperating.

The sweet happiness of love wanted to obscure her confusion. She yearned so much to submit, it pained her. But her glowing heart also knew that this offer contained serious consequences. The shadows of what he gained and what she lost with this marriage crept around the edges of her love.

"I expect that maybe you would enjoy being very married. No matter how married we were, you could still do whatever you want and continue much as you do now. I am the one for whom everything changes. Which is why I wish Pen and Dante had not arrived today. If they had not, I think that you would have agreed to being not entirely married, or even not quite married."

One eyebrow rose suspiciously. "Not *quite* married, now."

"Two nights ago I specifically asked what making love meant, and you only demanded fidelity. If you had expected marriage, you could have said so then. That is why I do not entirely believe that you are not coerced by propriety now."

"I admit that the honest course would have been to state my intentions right then when you asked. However, I did not want to surprise you with the idea at that particular moment."

"I understand completely. You did not want to risk scaring me off and being left unsatisfied. I truly do understand, because, you see, at that moment, right then by the bookshelves, if you *had* said that making love meant marriage, I was in no condition to negotiate or walk away."

His lids lowered. "You would have agreed?"

"Undoubtedly. I had already lost my senses."

"And subsequently, if I had started making love and then made continuing contingent upon an agreement of marriage—"

"I wouldn't have stood a chance. Which is why I do not really think that in your heart you want to marry me."

"Bianca, men do not trick women into marriage that way. We are almost physically incapable of doing so."

"Then how do you trick women into marriage? By intoxicating them with pleasure and trusting they will come back for more?"

He exhaled heavily and looked away in that exasperated way he had used with her from the beginning. "Bianca, this is me, the Viscount Laclere. If you have seen below the surface these last days, that does not mean the surface is entirely false. You must have realized that I would never have touched you while you were in this house if I did not intend to marry you. You cannot think me such a scoundrel as to seduce an innocent and then cast her aside. You must have understood what making love would mean, what that question meant, even if I did not spell it out."

Maybe she had understood. Possibly she had chosen to ignore the inconvenient truth in order to have him for a while. "Perhaps it would be best if you spelled it out now. What this marriage means, that is."

He did not respond at once. He knew what she was asking. "What it usually means, Bianca," he finally said.

"And my singing?"

"I do not want to keep you from what you love. You can train. We will bring the best voice tutor in Italy here for you. You can perform for our guests, and the ladies of the *ton* will often ask you to sing."

"But I will not perform in an opera house, in a full performance, with full accompaniment. I will not be known for my art, but only as your accomplished wife. I will not be respected by my equals in music, because they will not know me as a professional."

"You speak as though I am asking you to give up your soul. Would marrying me be nothing but sacrifice for you?"

"Hardly, darling. Marrying you has enormous appeal. I would have never permitted this intimacy if I did not feel that it was natural and inevitable to lie in your arms. So I face this choice with a heavy heart, because, no matter what I decide, it means giving up half of what I want, and, yes, half of my soul."

"You astonish me more than you ever have before, Bianca. You overjoy me by speaking of profound affection, and then dismay me by speaking of loss. You make me feel more of a scoundrel in offering marriage than if I had raped you and left you by the side of the road."

"You should not feel like a scoundrel at all. I wanted this. I came down to you that night. But I did not agree to marriage in doing so."

"So you ruthlessly used me for your pleasure, and now refuse to do the right thing by me." A wry smile played on his lips, but the lights in his eyes burned deeply.

"I have not refused you anything yet. I want you to understand why I do not fall into your arms at this offer. I do not want you to think that I played you false these last few days. My happiness was no act. If I marry you, I do not want to regret my decision, however, nor would you want the misery for us both if I did. I do not think that I should have to make this choice right now, with disaster raining down around us."

He did not like it. "And if I require that you do?"

"I would probably wonder about your motivations in forcing me to make a decision when I am at a disadvantage."

"My motivations?" An edge of ice sharpened his tone.

"Can you honestly say that my partnership in the mill does not enhance my appeal as a wife?"

He rose and paced to the hearth. "Have you concluded that this was all about the mill? Do you think me capable of such a cynical pretense of affection?"

"I have drawn no such conclusion. I do not really think—"

"You may have as long as you need to decide, of course." He spoke brusquely. "Since you will remain in England until your birthday, perhaps I can hope for a decision by then, if not before."

She did not think the mill had been his primary motivation, but it must have entered his head. His sternness now hid guilt as well as insult.

"I will speak with Pen and ask that you live with her. She will help you to procure a tutor in London until we invite a voice master to come from Milan. Staying in England until next June will not interfere with your plans, nor delay your development. I hope that you will forgive me this last exercise of my authority, Bianca. I will not let you leave until I must."

She went to him and slid her arms around his waist until her palms rested on his abdomen and her head pressed against his back. "I had no intention of demanding to leave right away. I think that I would like to stay in England until June. Living with Pen will suit me fine, and make it easier for us."

He turned in her embrace and cupped her chin. "Do you think that I am making these arrangements because they will facilitate an affair with you? Pen will hardly countenance such a thing, no matter what my intentions toward you. Nor would I risk your reputation in that way."

"But I thought—"

"That your choice was between marriage or a love affair. *Not quite married,* as you put it before? It is out of the question, darling. You are not a woman of mature years and experience, but an unmarried girl. All of the discretion in the world would not save us if anyone guessed."

"Yesterday . . . last night you spoke as though . . ."

"I referred to the marriage that I have just offered you, Bianca, not a sordid affair."

"Sordid? Is that what you think this has been? What you think I have been?"

"Never. But the world will make it so, and we will both feel it. I will not live the way required to hide such a liaison, pretending indifference in public, slipping in your back door in the dead of night. It would debase what we have shared here, and ultimately smother it. Continuing what began here is no more practical for you outside of marriage than within it. I may well get you with child. For all we know, I already have, despite my efforts to protect you."

She had dreaded that he would take this stand. Her heart began tearing with a sharpness that left her physically pained. The tight burn of suppressed tears strangled her.

He pulled her into a comforting embrace. She buried her face in his chest. "Why did you protect me? If you wanted marriage, why did you always . . ."

Strong arms surrounded her and those firm, gentle hands stroked her back. She savored every detail, knowing it might be the last feel of him.

"I told you why. It was never my intention to trap you into something that you did not want, Bianca."

Vergil handed Bianca up into Pen's carriage. His sister smiled feebly from the other seat and then turned her confusion toward the girl who was proving oddly obstinate about having the right thing done by her.

Dante stood in the manor doorway with an expression of barely suppressed shock. Learning that his brother had seduced a virgin had undone him. That the virgin then refused to be redeemed by her seducer, who had the good fortune to be a landed lord of the realm . . . Dante was making it clear that the entire development struck him as madness at best and highly suspicious at worst.

Vergil leaned in the coach and pulled Bianca toward him for a long kiss that demonstrated to his two siblings that this sinner regretted his behavior not one whit.

He let it linger, absorbing her breath. Her spirit rose into it, a small reminder of the abandon of her passion, to add torture to the farewell. He tore himself away and closed the door. The wheels began to roll.

Vergil watched until the coach completely disappeared. That kiss might have to last him a very long time. Quite possibly the rest of his life.

Dante came down from the house to join him in staring at the empty drive. "None of this makes any sense, Verg."

It made perfect sense. He had interfered with Bianca's plans and proposed a different life than she expected. She understandably wanted to think before replying. Contrary to most girls, her dream had not been one of marriage and family. In fact, she had accepted that as impossible if she pursued her art. Even if she had swooned with happiness when he proposed, the excitement would not have lasted long before she debated the consequences.

What would she see when she stepped back from the passion and weighed his worth? She did not need his money, which was hardly plentiful, and his position meant nothing to her. She required no financial protection, and very little of any other kind. Her piece of the mill tainted the purity of his intentions.

He was in the position with her that Dante had once described for himself. He had nothing to offer the girl except pleasure.

It appeared that might not be enough.

chapter 17

The cool garden outside Daniel St. John's London house beckoned Vergil. So did Adrian Burchard.

He had been avoiding Adrian, but could no longer. Nor did he want to anymore. He needed to speak with someone about the things occupying his mind.

Not all the things. Not Bianca. If he ever confided to another man about that, it would not be Burchard. Daniel St. John, maybe. St. John's marriage had been preceded by an affair, Vergil was almost sure.

Vergil remembered how disapproving he had been when he suspected that. He had considered ending his friendship with St. John over the matter. It had seemed unforgivable for a man to seduce a young cousin who lived in his house and for whom he was responsible. That he now knew Diane was not really St. John's cousin did not change matters.

That the two of them were deliriously happy in marriage did, however. So did the fact that the Viscount Laclere had behaved just as unforgivably himself, and heartily wished that he could continue doing so.

The weeks since leaving Lancashire had been slow torture where Bianca was concerned. He had gone to Laclere Park to find Thomas's letters and make some inquiries, and she had filled his head the whole time, creating a distraction he could not shake.

The days since his return had been much worse, however. Seeing her in Pen's house, watching her accept callers, listening to her train with her voice tutor in the drawing room—he kept hoping for evidence that she was miserable. Instead he saw a rising star of the artistic circles reveling in her independence.

He followed Adrian out the doors at the end of the dining room, leaving the rest of the Dueling Society to their port and cigars. St. John had invited them all to dinner, and it had been a joyful and raucous meal shared by men who had known one another for years and trusted one another completely.

"Have you discovered anything of interest?" Adrian asked.

"I have evidence that Milton had a relationship that would have been very damaging if others knew of it. A group of letters were found in Adam Kenwood's papers. They were letters to Milton from this other individual, and their contents would have caused trouble."

"How would Kenwood come by them?"

"Kenwood found my brother after his death. He came for a meeting, and entered the study looking for him. He was there first. I think that he quickly looked for anything that might have caused the suicide, found the letters, and took them, to protect Milton's name."

"But he never gave them to you."

"Most likely he wanted to protect my brother from my scorn as well. In any case, if such letters existed, and I now know that they did, someone could have obtained one and used it to blackmail my brother."

"The contents would be enough to do that?"

"Yes."

They stopped in the moonlight. In an upper window the form of a woman passed behind the curtain. It was St. John's wife, Diane, and she carried one of her children as she strolled back and forth.

The graceful, feminine image captivated Vergil. He watched, distracted, envying St. John his domestic contentment.

"Why didn't Kenwood destroy them?" Adrian asked, calling him back.

Vergil turned away from the window and continued their stroll. "I don't know. I believe, however, that he also saw a pattern of extortion and may have been looking into it. In his desk, along with the letters, was a paper with my brother's name and some others. Castlereagh's, for one. Also those of two other men who have sold large amounts of property in the last year."

"A pattern, or a list of his victims. That is what this discovery implies, isn't it?"

"I considered that Kenwood could have been the blackmailer, but I don't think he was. Lord Fairhall died after Kenwood, for one thing, and the Earl of Glasbury could not be his victim now, either."

They paced back up the garden, then turned and paced down again. Fallen leaves blew around their legs and the breeze moved ghostly clouds across the moon.

"I think that we are reaching the same conclusions, Laclere," Adrian said. "That episode with Glasbury in Hampstead was telling."

"I agree. I am just not sure what it told."

"It indicated that two of the people who have been blackmailed have connections to your family. That can't be ignored. It also suggested that the blackmailer is probably not from the north, nor from the known and predictable radicals."

"Someone closer to home, then," Vergil said, repeating the observation that Bianca, in her clear-sighted way, had made that night by the fire.

That one sentence had thrown light into the shadows of his search. Had he avoided seeing that conclusion? Had he ignored the evidence that said he had wasted his time looking for a radical such as those who had conspired to kill government officials in the past?

Had he secretly hoped that Milton's secret would be treason, rather than what it had been?

"It could be a coincidence that two of the victims are related to the Duclaircs, but let us assume not for now," Vergil said. "That means someone in our circles."

"Or someone who knows someone in your circles. Or we may be seeing a pattern where none exists. After all, if Hampton could discover the Earl of Glasbury's secrets, anyone could."

Julian Hampton had already discovered those secrets, however. Also, Hampton had known Milton well, had been his solicitor, and could have easily examined more than ledgers while in Milton's study either in London or at Laclere Park.

The profile of the man in question could be seen through the door. Vergil disliked the sense of betrayal he experienced in calculating his friend's connection to the blackmailer's victims.

"Hampton knew Castlereagh as well. And Lord Fairhall." Adrian spoke offhandedly, but with an edge of determination, as if the subject could not be avoided.

"You also move in the right circles, Burchard. His ability to learn things is surpassed by yours. I know this man. I have since I was a boy. Furthermore, he would have no political motive, and in Milton's case, he knew there was no money."

"If you say he has no political motive, I believe you. I myself have no notion of where his beliefs are, or if he even has any."

Adrian made a good point. Hampton was a cipher in many ways, and Vergil's knowledge of him was more instinctive than based on any explicit discussions.

"I prefer Nigel Kenwood," Vergil said. "I have been asking about him in Sussex. He did not stay in France all those years. He visited Woodleigh at least a few times a year, and even accompanied Adam on visits to Laclere Park several times."

"It is far-fetched. He has no connection to Castlereagh, for example."

"We do not know that. Furthermore, there is something else." Vergil hesitated revealing this part. It could so easily be misunderstood. "I think that if Castlereagh was blackmailed, the information used to do so is also connected to my family. I think it came from Milton."

Adrian stopped walking. He just stood there, looking down the garden path, waiting.

"My brother and the Foreign Minister had a closer friendship than I realized. They had a rich correspondence," Vergil said. "I lied about this when I met with you and Wellington, because the letters I saw were political arguments, mostly. I have reread them, however, and if one was of a mind to, and if one had other evidence about my brother that encouraged a certain type of interpretation—it is possible that a letter existed that could be used badly."

"How badly?"

"On its own, I doubt it would have any special meaning. If Milton had already been disgraced, it might be enough to bring down another man."

Adrian did not move. Castlereagh had given him employment when Adrian was a young man whose father had cut him off without a pound. His loyalty to the late Foreign Minister was understandable and his stillness conveyed an icy anger.

"Let us speak frankly, Laclere. We are not talking about political embarrassments now, are we?"

"No."

"The letters to Milton that you found in Adam Kenwood's things were not from a radical, and do not indicate that Milton had gotten deeper into such things than we thought. The blackmail concerned private matters."

"Yes."

"And you are now suggesting that there may have been other letters, from Castlereagh to your brother, of a similar nature."

"No. I am saying that an expression of friendship between men that would mean nothing in most cases could be used to threaten a man in other cases. I am saying that the perception of something more could be read into some of these letters if one had reason to do so. It would be enough to make Castlereagh very worried if he was unstable to begin with."

Adrian crossed his arms and stared at the ground. "Damn."

"I am telling you this in privacy, of course."

"Hell, yes, you are. Do you have any idea whom we are looking for?"

"It may not be only one person doing this. I know now that a woman is involved."

He felt Adrian staring at him through the night. "That certainly makes young Kenwood a better possibility, if he has had help. Who is she?"

"I don't know yet, but I may have a way to find out." He had been avoiding that discovery for weeks now. He had tried to convince himself he need not pursue this evidence, that all could be resolved without learning this one piece of the puzzle. That appeared unlikely, however, and his gut twisted at the prospect of facing this part of the truth.

"Laclere, if what you suspect is true—if someone can damage the last Foreign Minister's name in this way, it must never come out, and not only for the sake of his memory and his family."

"That sounds like Wellington speaking."

"It *is* Wellington speaking. Castlereagh represented this country after Napoleon's defeat, and his reputation is tied to that of Britain in the capitals of Europe. Even his death does not sever that connection."

"Is that your mission, Adrian? To protect his name from this particular taint? If so, Wellington must have suspected how this might unravel."

Adrian hesitated, then spoke lowly. "When Castlereagh spoke with him before his death, he mentioned someone claiming to have a letter that could ruin him. He alluded to one such as you describe, one that could be misunderstood."

"We should not have avoided honest talk that day at Laclere Park. It would have saved us some time."

"No one can blame us for avoiding talk of it. Even now we do so, don't we?"

They aimed back to the house. Through the open door they heard St. John say something and Hampton respond. The whole table broke into laughter.

"What will we do when this blackmailer is discovered?" Vergil asked.

"I turn it back to you. What did you plan to do when you discovered his identity? Swear evidence against him?"

Vergil had faced that question long ago. Before Wellington had shown interest, and before he met Bianca. Whether the reasons for Milton's death were political or personal, he had decided there would be no trial of the blackmailer.

Milton's secrets would be buried in the sepulchre at Laclere Park, and the man who had all but killed him would be silenced.

chapter 18

"If the St. Johns visit our box, can I tell them?" Charlotte popped the question while Penelope inspected Bianca's hair. Jane crimped some more curls.

"Absolutely not." Pen reached over and tweaked a strand into place. "Not one word to anyone, Charlotte."

Charlotte slouched with a pout. "Being part of a big secret is a lot less fun if you cannot tell anyone. Usually you tell at least one other person, and this secret is the best one I've ever had. That my friend is going to perform onstage, in an opera . . . It is so deliciously daring."

"*You* only know about it because there was no way to keep you in the dark."

Bianca pursed her lips. Pen was not making any effort to pretend that tonight did not carry risks for their reputations.

"Go and finish dressing, Charlotte," Pen instructed. "Signore Bardi will be here soon, to escort us to the theater. Bianca must arrive early."

Bianca waited for Charlotte to leave and then dismissed Jane as well. There were some secrets too big for an innocent ingenue or a maid who might one day report to great Aunt Edith.

"Is he here?" Bianca asked.

"Signore Bardi? Not yet."

"I am not speaking about my music master and you know it. Is Laclere here?"

"My brother is in London, but I would be surprised if he shows tonight, Bianca. You know that he does not approve."

No, he did not approve. Signore Bardi, the *bel canto* tutor recommended by Catalani, had been impressed enough with her training to think that she was ready for some minor stage exposure. He had arranged her inclusion in the chorus of several performances. Vergil had reluctantly permitted it, but demanded that the exercise remain a secret.

She prayed that he would come anyway. She wished that he could take some joy in this night with her. It was the first time that she had ever sung in a real theater. It was an important night for her, even if she was only an anonymous member of the chorus in a minor comic opera.

"You repudiate his affection with this decision," Pen said. "He only permitted it because he is weak with you."

"I repudiate nothing, and it would appear that he is not very weak at all, since he has no trouble staying away from me."

"Should he sit on my doorstep and pine? The two of you have gone too far for that, and displaying his interest would only raise dangerous speculations. But I saw how he kissed you when we left the manor, and I see how he looks at you now, and I tell you, Bianca, that nothing has changed."

It seemed to Bianca that in the last few weeks everything had changed. She saw Vergil when he was in London, but not often. He would visit Pen and Charl and sometimes join them at entertainments. In front of everyone, even his sisters, his behavior was so reserved toward her that no one would ever suspect that they had been lovers. Certainly the other young men who visited Pen's house never guessed. Even Charlotte and Nigel thought the two of them still at odds.

Only when they had brief moments alone did he let her see his feelings. The pending question burned in his eyes, and unfulfilled passion electrified his discreet touch. Whenever they parted he kissed her hand as gently as he had once kissed her breast. That brief contact had the same effect on her that his more intimate kisses once had, leaving her breathless and frustrated.

To make matters worse, she could not cry on the shoulder of the only person to whom she could confide. Pen continued to be a friend, but she had only supported this debut in the hopes that a few nights onstage would satisfy Bianca forever.

Would it? She almost hoped so. She had grown miserable with how things stood. She missed Vergil terribly. A part of her spent their long periods apart merely waiting. It did not help her anguish that one word from her could end the waiting forever.

A footman announced Signore Bardi's arrival and Pen called for the coach. Bianca dawdled in finding her wrap, hoping that another announcement of another man would be made. It never came. Wobbly with excitement, she joined Pen and Charlotte and gray-haired Signore Bardi for the ride to the English Opera House.

They separated at the door of the opulent theater. Signore Bardi directed her toward the costume room so that she could be transformed into the village woman whom she would portray.

A half hour later she snuck onto the side of the stage and peered out at the gathering crowd. A curving wall of boxes towered to the ceiling, surrounding the orchestra and pit. The din of revelry echoed around her. The eerie glow of the gas lamps tinted the audience an unnatural hue. She squinted, trying to make out the faces in Penelope's box.

Her heart sank. Vergil still was not there.

She returned to the chorus room. Finding a corner for herself, she joined her voice to the others being tuned and warmed. She followed the exercises instinctively. Her enthusiasm felt dull and forced, as if she watched someone else prepare for this debut.

If only he had come to watch, maybe . . . maybe what? Maybe it would be a sign that they could have some kind of life together? A life that need not sever her soul in two and then make her throw away one of the halves.

The bodies around her began rearranging. She joined the chorus filtering onto the stage and assumed her position in the rear. With the abstracting light and her costume and the crowd, it was unlikely that she would even be seen, let alone recognized.

Her melancholy thoughts instantly disappeared when the chorus joined in song. Thundering, joyful, exuberant voices surrounded and matched her own. Her spirit leapt with startled delight. Leapt and then soared.

She had never experienced such sound. It inundated her with a huge wave of sensibility. The curves of the stage and theater seemed to imbue the music with a complex resonance. She glanced around at her fellow singers and realized that they felt what she felt and that the density of their voices compounded the euphoria she had only known privately before. A few caught her eye and smiled at her awe.

Her blood pounded. The song took over. She had not felt this alive since . . . She looked to Pen's box. *Be there, please be there. Share it with me.* Nigel stood in the rear, speaking with Cornell Witherby. A tall dark figure hung in the shadows and her heart skipped. It moved into view and her disappointment was so intense that her voice faltered. It was not Vergil, but instead that Mr. Siddel who had insinuated himself into Pen's circle the last month.

The performance seemed to go on and on but still ended too soon. She loved everything about it. The singing, the waiting offstage, the camaraderie with the others, the glow of the gaslights, and the damp of the back rooms. The theater became a separate place, where life and emotions intensified, much like the manor had been during those days of intimacy.

She savored every detail and ignored the cutting disappointment that Vergil had forsaken her tonight.

Finally, after the last curtain, she found herself crushed into one of the chorus rooms with the other women, changing into her own garments. Excitement turned everyone's exhaustion into giddiness, and most of the giggles had to do with the rumble of male voices out in the corridor.

"The boys are waiting and restless," a sloe-eyed soprano beside her said. "You are new, aren't you? A mother or sister waiting for you?"

"My tutor will be waiting."

"Just as well. Pretty thing like you . . . they don't know the difference, do they? Think we're all of a piece. Forget their manners sometimes."

She doubted that anyone would forget their manners with Signore Bardi around. His black eyes became satanic when he got angry.

Unfortunately, Signore Bardi was not outside the chamber when she emerged. At least twenty young men were, however. Students, clerks, and young solicitors milled in the corridor, waiting for their favorite songbirds to try and fly. Flowers, endearments, and blunt advances were pressed on her. They surrounded her two deep.

"You will allow the young lady to pass, gentlemen," a cool voice commanded from the periphery.

She looked through the confusion to see blue eyes regarding her. He had come after all. She would have flown into his arms, but his expression pulled her up short. *See?* his eyes said. *This is what you will subject yourself to.*

Mumbles passed. "Laclere . . . viscount . . ." Some of the young men drifted away.

Disappointment stabbed her. His intention in permitting this performance had been to show her the indignities, not the joy. That saddened her so much that she succumbed to an impulse to strike back and deny him satisfaction.

She ignored Vergil's proffered hand and turned to a short red-haired student on her right. He held two yellow roses toward her. She decided that she might be flattered that, of all the female singers, he chose to give her this precious gift.

She took the roses with thanks. Encouraged, and shooting cautious glances back to where Vergil still hovered and watched, two other young men advanced to compliment her singing.

An older man inserted himself into the group. He pierced her with a demanding look and then cast Vergil a scathing glance. For all of his love of music, cousin Nigel was not amused to find her here.

"I thought that it was you, but could not believe it," he said, shouldering an anxious young admirer aside. "Really, Laclere, you must remove her."

"I am prepared to escort my ward home, but it would hardly do to pick her up and carry her away."

"I would not have expected you to react so strictly," she teased Nigel. "You of all people know the importance of performing."

"Performing is one thing, doing so here is another. What were you thinking, Laclere? I trust that tonight will be the end of it."

His scold was interrupted by another man oozing forward. It was Mr. Siddel. He was of Vergil's age and similar in build and coloring. Perhaps he was even more handsome. He had made his interest in her known during the last month while he drifted around the edges of Pen's circle. Pen's warnings that he was dangerous had been unnecessary. He possessed a talent for making even subtle attentions invasive.

"I thought that I recognized you, Miss Kenwood." He took a position in front of her that left no room for anyone else. "I knew that you studied with Signore Bardi, but I had never heard that you performed." His tone conveyed speculative delight in the discovery.

Four steps away, Vergil's profile grew stern.

"See here, Siddel," Nigel blustered.

"It is an experiment, so that I can see how it feels to sing with a large chorus."

"Certainly. Why take lessons with Bardi unless one is very serious? Perhaps one day we will see you be the supreme performer in one of London's great houses."

He said nothing improper. Even his tone could not be faulted. But she heard a difference in the way he addressed her, and did not miss the insulting double entendre.

Suddenly Vergil was eye-to-eye with Mr. Siddel. "You will have to excuse us. My sister is expecting Miss Kenwood."

"Of course, Laclere. I wondered, at first, whom you came back here to see. Not your style anymore, is it? I should have realized that only duty would be cause to make a saint's protection public."

He played with the words like he engaged in a game of wit, but almost every one held a double meaning. Vergil assumed a cool hauteur, to match Siddel's own.

"You go too far, Siddel," Nigel said, scrutinizing her with a sidelong, suspicious glance. "You come close to unpardonable insult, and if Laclere will not call you on it, I will."

"Siddel means no insult. His tongue merely runs more quickly than his brain. It has been the bane of his life since he was a boy, but the brain usually catches up in time to avoid a challenge." Vergil's lids lowered. "I am sure that his lack of judgment tonight can be attributed to imbibing too much port. Aren't I right, Siddel?"

"Undoubtedly. My apologies, Miss Kenwood. I would be wounded to learn that my poor attempt at humor in any way offended you, or alienated your affection." He bowed with a wry smile and sauntered away.

Nigel hustled after him. " . . . inexcusably rude . . ." she heard Nigel say.

"Open your eyes," Siddel replied with a laugh.

Vergil held out his hand again. "Are you quite done here?"

"Yes, I think that I am now."

He deftly extricated her from the crowd. His coach waited.

"Did you enjoy yourself?" he asked after he had handed her in. It disappointed her that he sat across from her. In the dark he became an insubstantial shadow barely articulated by the dim light that occasionally swept through the window while they rode.

"At first I was not nearly as excited as I expected, but once we were onstage, it was so thrilling I thought that I would burst."

"I was not speaking of the performance, Bianca."

No, he wasn't. His tight tone had told her that. "I do not think that those men even knew who I was, other than a singer who came out the door when they were nearby. Aside from Nigel and Mr. Siddel, I doubt that anyone noticed me in the back of that chorus."

"You were so exuberant that I expected you to take to flight. You may not have been recognized, but you were most definitely noticed."

"You saw?"

"I was in a friend's box."

"Was I . . ." she caught herself and laughed. "I was going to ask if I was any good, but of course there was no way to tell."

"You were magnificent, darling. It would seem that half of Oxford and Cambridge and most of London's articled clerks agree."

"You sound jealous, Laclere."

"I do not think that is the correct word for tonight, Bianca. Jealousy is what I feel when I see the attention that Pen's friends give you, and I know that I cannot stop it, short of a marriage that you will not accept. Jealousy is what I experience when I see your cousin openly court you. Tonight I was not jealous. Tonight I was raw with outrage when I saw the familiarity strangers felt free to show you outside a chorus room. Tonight I was furious when I heard the insinuations a drunken rake like Siddel made, and all because you dallied in that corridor in order to flaunt your independence in my face."

Tense anger poured across the coach, carrying the hard words. At first her heart sickened while she absorbed the onslaught, but then annoyance of her own began seething through her dismay. "I thought that you wanted me to dally. I thought that you wanted me to see it all, to face the reality of the life and taste the degradation of leering admirers."

"I never want to see men look at you the way those boys did."

"Then why didn't you stop them?"

"The bigger question is, why didn't you? I stood there expecting you to make a fool of me if I tried to pull you away. I found myself wondering if you were telling me through your behavior that you had made your choice—"

"No!"

"—and that I could publicly claim you as your protector or not have you at all."

Her eyes blurred. This was not Vergil. It was his phantom, demonstrating a man's reaction when his pride is wounded.

"I do not want to speak of this any longer," she whispered, praying it could be stopped before they said the sort of words that can never be retrieved.

"I do. We have much to speak of, it seems to me."

The coach had stopped. She waited for the footman to set down the steps. "No, Laclere. I will not have a row with you. The evening has tired me. I bid you goodnight."

She swept to the door. He followed two steps behind.

"You will not dismiss me like one of those spot-faced supplicants, Bianca."

"Pity." She led the way into the candlelit entry. The first floor had been closed up. Everyone else must have retired. "Since this is your sister's house, I cannot deny you admittance. However, I will not submit to your scolds and insinuations, Laclere. I am too tired to spar and too hurt to be clever. You have taken one of the most important nights of my life and reduced it to something shameful and sordid. It was glorious, and like a fool I thought that only your presence could make it better. Instead you ruined it. I may never forgive your cruelty."

Her accusations pulled him up short. A few of the storm clouds blew out of his eyes. "If I have been cruel, I apologize. Let us go into the library, Bianca. I want to speak with you."

"Pontificate and lecture to yourself, dear guardian. I am going to bed."

He grabbed at her as she mounted the stairs. "Come back down here, Bianca."

"Go away, Laclere. Do not make a scene or you will wake the household."

"I will wake the whole damn city if I want."

She shook her arm free. "Oh, stubble it, Vergil. Goodnight."

• • •

Stubble it. Where the hell was she learning words like that?

He knew where. From the soulful, adoring, perfect-image-of-romantic-sensibility young bloods who gravitated to Pen's house like so many bees discovering a newly blooming garden. He spent most of his time swatting them away when he visited, but they always buzzed back.

He strode into the library. No fire or candles burned, but he found the port anyway. It didn't taste nearly as comforting as he thought it would, nor did it relieve his annoyance.

His mood was not only because of Bianca, he had to admit. Tomorrow he faced an unpleasant task in his search for the truth about Milton's death. The prospect of the waiting interview sickened him, and he had entered the opera house resentful and angry about that as much as Bianca's performance.

His world threatened to fall apart. Every friendship and love at its center seemed to have become as insecure, duplicitous, and masked as his own life.

Tonight had shown that Bianca was slipping from his life too. She lived here and practiced with Signore Bardi and made new friends and enjoyed her youth, and every new experience pulled her further away from him. He could feel the gulf widening. Sometimes he wondered if she remembered that she was supposed to be considering marriage to him.

He would have forbidden this debut if he could. He would have strangled Bardi, or at least bribed him, if he had surmised the tutor would propose such a thing.

She had loved it. Of course she had. Catalani had once told him that the magic created for the audience was felt ten times over by the performers themselves. What must it be like to stand surrounded by the sound booming off the ceiling? Like being submerged in an ocean of the senses. He had watched Bianca's amazement and known with certainty that in one night the odds had tilted against him in this competition for her life.

His mind recalled her excited smile when she saw him in the corridor, and then her retreat into cool poise when she noticed his anger. He had been so preoccupied with his resentments that he had not noticed at the time how beautiful that smile had been, nor that it had existed solely for him.

The worst of his bristling mood snapped and died. He set down the port, feeling subdued for reasons that had nothing to do with the spirits. He pictured that smile again and again, replaced by hurt.

His behavior had been inexcusable. Deliberately heartless, if he wanted to be honest with himself. He had reacted to tonight's events as if they had all been about him, when in fact he was merely a guest at another person's party. But for her happiness in his attendance, it really had not mattered if he were there at all. Maybe he had known that. Perhaps he had invited this argument to ensure that his supporting role would not be reduced to a walk-on.

The house throbbed with silence. He wished that one of the servants was about. He would send him to ask Bianca to come down for a short while. He did not want to leave tonight with things the way they were.

He strolled out to the corridor. Someone had locked the front door, a sure sign that no servant would appear. No more candles waited to light the way, but he knew this house as well as his own and could navigate it blind.

Silence pulsed. She might not be asleep yet. He would go and apologize, and then leave through the garden door.

She was not asleep. She had not even prepared for bed. She sat in an undressing gown in a chair by the hearth. When he entered she did not demonstrate the slightest surprise, just raised sad eyes. It was as if she had been waiting for him.

She acknowledged him, then looked down at her lap. Her hands lay twisted together there. "No more lectures, Laclere."

"No."

"What, then? It is dangerous for you to be here."

She looked so unhappy. He would take her in his arms, but he did not trust himself to touch her. "An apology. I did try to ruin tonight for you. Your pleasure in it . . . frightened me."

She rose and paced thoughtfully around the room's edges. "It frightened me too. All of this frightens me. It is a torture. Do not tell me that I can end it with one word. I know that." She cast an accusing glare at him. "You spoke of me tonight as if you did not know me at all. If I have become a stranger to you, do not blame me. I am not the one who stays away."

"I do not stay away."

"You do. I have rarely seen you the last few weeks. You sent no word that you would come tonight. I am left to wonder if you have forgotten me, and to be grateful for your small acknowledgments when you do visit."

"You knew that it would be like this, Bianca. I can hardly display my affection and announce to the world what has occurred. Since I cannot, I do not relish sitting in Pen's drawing room with other men who are permitted to openly court you while I must play the guardian."

"You could arrange—"

"No."

"You could at least kiss me when you leave. You could give me just a brief kiss to show that you have not grown indifferent."

"I am far from indifferent, which is why I could never give you *just* a brief kiss."

She still paced, like a restless spirit drove her and she found the chamber too small. She eyed him with a glint of defiance.

"I did it on purpose, you know. Encouraged those young men. Took the roses and spoke with them. I wanted to show you that they represented no danger to me or my virtue. That is how my mother treated the men who pursued her. Politely enough, but keeping a firm distance. Surely it could work for me as well."

"Undoubtedly it could, but the world's assumptions will carry more force than your actions. In any case, I cannot bear to watch it."

Her brow puckered. "You made that clear. Which is the other reason why I did it tonight, I think. To make you jealous."

"To make me jealous?"

"Yes, I think so. I really do."

"Bianca, I have been castigating myself for reacting badly. I have apologized for misjudging this evening and you have accepted that apology. Now you blithely add that perhaps I was correct all along?"

She shrugged. "I cannot honestly say that making you jealous had nothing to do with it, that is all."

"Other than our unhappiness, what could you hope to gain by that?"

She strolled so close that her perfume and silk robe clouded around him. "Well," she said, plucking at ribbons on the robe with slow, taunting pulls, "for one thing, it seems that I got you into my bedchamber, doesn't it?"

Her sly smile almost stopped his heart. The door stood five feet behind him, but suddenly it might have been miles away.

The bedrobe fell. She was not naked. Stays cinched her from midriff to hips. Chemise and pantaloons created a thin film of fabric over her breasts and thighs. White stockings remained gartered above her knees.

The world constricted to her and him and the space between them. The bold challenge in her eyes made desire scorch through his body.

"It is not wise to tempt a man who is hot with jealousy, darling."

Her lids lowered. "Just as long as you are hot, Laclere, I don't care why."

Damn. He walked over to her. "It appears that you are dangerous and a little wicked, after all."

"Only with you, Laclere."

"You just admitted otherwise."

"That was different, wasn't it? I wasn't really wicked with them. But I did use them to affect you, which was unfair."

They were as close as possible without touching. "Most unfair."

"Was it really very naughty of me?"

"*Very* naughty."

"I suppose that there is nothing for it, Laclere. You will just have to punish me."

With a pout of contrite resignation she climbed onto the bed. She pulled a mound of pillows over and settled herself with them under her stomach, raising her bottom in penitence.

She glanced back at him, and her expression aroused him more than her erotic position. The erection of a lifetime strained against his clothing. His blood pounded without mercy.

He caressed up her leg, grasped the edge of the pantaloons, and ripped. Gossamer shreds flew away from her buttocks and thighs. He flipped her and the pillows raised her hips so that she had to bend and spread her legs to stay balanced. Kneeling beside her, he kissed down the straps of her chemise until her naked breasts peaked high and hungry above the top edge of her stays. He licked and gently drew on each one.

He rose and undressed, never taking his eyes off the lovely body laid out with abandon for him. She watched the coats and collar drop, with eyes as hot as his. The musk of her arousal wafted to him. Just lying there, vulnerable and exposed, already had her hips subtly flexing with a sexual rhythm.

He removed his pocket watch from the waistcoat and checked the time, then placed it near the candle by the bed.

"Hurry," she whispered, reaching a hand in his direction.

"No." He discarded his shirt and stripped off his lower garments. He knelt between her knees. Lifting one ankle onto his shoulder, he began kissing along her leg's inner flesh. "This is not going to be hurried at all."

He rubbed his face against her back and kissed down the length of her spine. The tantalizing stays had been discarded sometime during the night as too warm. His kisses trailed over her bottom and down her thigh to the stocking still gartered on one leg.

She was not asleep, and she sighed in her contentment and shifted her legs, reassuming the position on the pillow with which this had begun, welcoming him to repeat the new intimate kisses he had taught her tonight.

The fall of her arms around her head, the press of her cheek against the sheets, the arched offering of her body—to his amazement, the sensuality of her repose had him hardening yet again.

"It will be dawn soon. I must go." He rolled onto his back and pulled her into his arms. The beckoning day reminded him of the meeting he had arranged for this morning. He did not want to go to it, and not only because it meant leaving Bianca.

She sighed petulantly, as if the revolution of the earth were an inconvenience designed only to limit their time together. "Will you come back tonight?"

"No."

"No one will know. You stayed last night and—"

"And if we are lucky, all will be well. Repeating this will only tempt fate. Nothing has changed, Bianca."

She did not like hearing that. She kissed him sadly. "It seems to me it would be difficult to tempt fate more than you just have."

"I decided that if I was going to hang, it may as well be for a pound as a penny."

He gently lifted her away and swung from the bed. She watched him dress with a sleepy expression. He tried not to reveal his distaste for this part of it. The watched time, the secret departure, the strangling discretion—it reminded him too much of visits to the kind of women who never became wives, and of how she fluttered like a moth around the flame of a life that often led in that direction.

He stood beside the bed and looked down at her. Images of the night passed in their mutual gaze. He had taken liberties with her that many men never expect of their wives, further blurring how he should view this affair and his rights with her.

He brushed her cheek with the back of his fingers. She was so lovely. So joyful and innocent in her passion. He had met women who could degrade the sensuality of a simple kiss. Bianca's sense of wonder could turn the most exotic loveplay into a sacred ritual.

"Do you mean it? When we make love, you cry out that you love me. Every time you have done so. Do you even know that you say it?" It surprised him to hear himself voicing the question out loud.

"If I did not mean it, you would not be standing by my bed right now. I know what I risk. I would have never done any of this only for pleasure."

He supposed that he had known that. Still, it was nice to be sure. It gave him a bit more hope about how this would end, and love made a better rationale than lust if their behavior ended up destroying them both.

"Well, if you think that you love me, I expect that I can wait a little longer, darling."

Her eyes glittered with affection and concern. No one had ever seen him as clearly as she did. "Wait for what, Laclere? To decide to give up on me, or to decide to love me back?"

She could still astonish him. "Both, I suppose. It will probably have to be one or the other for me soon."

He stepped out into the dark corridor and silently closed her door behind him. Only the vaguest light penetrated from some lower windows. He found the banister and glided down the stairs, then crossed to the servants' stairway. Down again, this time to the kitchen.

He was less sure of his way in the lower chambers, and he felt his path along the walls. Near the spot where the door should be, he stumbled into another groping body.

"What the . . . Who the hell . . ."

"Damn! Watch where . . ."

They both froze.

"Witherby?"

"Laclere!"

"Arriving or departing, Witherby?"

"Oh, God. Laclere. This is most awkward."

"Leaving, I assume at this hour. The door is over here."

"Of course. Jesus." Cornell Witherby backed away a few steps and righted himself.

"Are you coming? I think we should discuss this outside."

With the cold air came Witherby's attempt at explanation. "I know how this must look."

"It looks as if you have initiated an affair with my sister, Penelope. It is Penelope, isn't it? Because if it is Charlotte I will have to kill you, and I'd hate to do that to an old friend."

"Charlotte! Zeus, man, what do you take me for? As for Pen, I assure you that she has my deepest affection and admiration. A goddess could not be adored more than I do her. She possesses such a sweet, gracious, lovely soul, and—"

"Yes, yes. The garden gate is over here, or do you know your way in the dark?"

"I assure you that I have never before—"

"I am sure that you understand that discretion is essential. If the earl discovered this affair, he would use it to remove her support, which is hardly substantial as it is."

Their boots kicked along the rocks, punctuating the silence.

"You are being very understanding about this, Laclere. I am, of course, overjoyed that you approve, but we thought you to be less sympathetic."

Vergil paused where the alley met the road. "I would have preferred not knowing enough to approve or disapprove. My sister has had too little happiness in her life, however. If she wants you, I will not interfere."

Ever so subtly, the night had grown less dark. He could make out Witherby's tall, slender form distinctly now, and even something of his expression. "This is not what we expected, Laclere. I daresay Pen will be as astounded as I."

Vergil turned to walk home. "Just make sure that I do not regret my liberal-mindedness."

"I will make her as happy as I am capable," Witherby said. "And since you are so generous, I will refrain from wondering why you were departing from that house at the same time and through the same door as I was."

The pistol cracked the autumn day. The ball *thwacked* into the tree trunk in the woods behind the Chevalier Corbet's fencing academy.

"You haven't been practicing enough," Vergil said.

Dante stood aside and began reloading. "It is only sport for some of us, Verg. I have no intention of killing a man in a duel."

Vergil sighted his aim. "And if some man intends to kill you?"

"I daresay if no husband has challenged me by now, none ever will."

Vergil fired his own pistol. It hit dead center on the paper tacked to the tree.

Dante whistled with appreciation. "You *have* been practicing, I can see."

"Anything worth doing, is worth doing well."

Dante laughed. "I agree. You and I just prefer to do different things."

He took his place again. Vergil watched his careless stance. It had only been by the grace of Providence that Dante had never needed this skill.

The pistol fired. Dante moved aside. "You haven't reloaded."

"No."

The word riveted Dante's attention. The hand holding the pistol fell to his side. "You have that look on your face. What is it this time? Did someone come to dun you for one of my debts again?"

"It is not that."

"Well, it is something, so out with it. You suggested we come and shoot, but I don't think two balls justifies a ride to Hampstead, do you?"

Vergil set his gun in the box. "I need to ask you about something. It is important that you answer me honestly."

Dante's head cocked back and his lids lowered. "Then ask."

"I have been trying to discover the truth about Milton's death. I have spent months doing so. I am convinced he was blackmailed."

"Blackmailed! What secrets could Milton have had? His politics were extreme, but he published his ideas in letters and such, and everyone knew he was really harmless."

"It was not politics. I think that I have discovered why and how he was blackmailed, but the details do not matter. There is a piece missing, however. I think that you can supply that piece."

"You think that I had a hand in this? That is a damnable thing to suggest. It would be a hell of a thing if the only time I challenged a man it was you, Vergil."

"I do not think that you had an intentional hand in it. Trust me, if I could avoid this conversation I would. I *have* avoided it, too long."

"Maybe you should continue doing so. You can't bring him back."

"It goes beyond him."

"Hell." Dante scowled and dropped his pistol into the box. "What do you need to know?"

"I have been asking the servants about things. I am told that a year ago you brought a visitor to Laclere House in London. A woman of good breeding. Who was it?"

"I do not discuss my women with other men, not even you."

"That is commendable, but this time you must. Did you ever have a woman in that house overnight?"

Dante's face assumed a mask of resentment. "If I did, you can be sure it was not an American virgin."

"This is not about our private failings, Dante. I want to know if someone besides a family member had access to Milton's chamber and study prior to his death. Were you in the London house with a woman while he was down at Laclere Park?"

"What are you implying? That she—"

"That someone, somehow, procured letters to Milton. Letters from a lover. A woman went to the lover, claiming she was Pen, to confirm what she already suspected, and then found a way to get her hands on the evidence. Then she blackmailed Milton."

"Letters from a lover? Milton? He lived like a monk where women were concerned. Really, Verg—"

"We are not boys anymore, Dante. Not children. Do not pretend that you are ignorant. Despite his care and discretion, I suspected. I think that you did too."

Dante glared at him. "If you are suggesting what I think—"

"You know what I am suggesting. It was our brother's tragedy to live in a world where even his family had to deny the man he was. He had to hide this part of himself even from us, and so, as we grew older, he retreated from us as from so much else."

Dante turned away and stared at the paper tacked on the tree. "Damn it. *Enough.* I do not want to talk about this."

"No one does. We would prefer that men blow their brains out when their secret is discovered and exposure is threatened. It is a sinful waste, and the silence and shame killed him as surely as that gun. I'll hang before I will let the people who hounded him get away with it. Now, tell me, damn it. Who was she?"

Dante shook his head in dismay. Anger and astonishment fought a battle over his expression. "A lark, she called it. She said she was always curious about the old pile, and had never seen the inside of the house. Well, there hadn't been parties there for as long as I could remember. Asked if I would show her the interior."

"She stayed?"

Dante smirked with disgust. At himself. "Of course."

"All night?"

He nodded.

"While you slept, perhaps she did not."

"I don't believe it. I am sure that you are wrong."

"Are you? Truly?"

Dante crossed his arms and looked to the ground.

"Her name, Dante."

He sighed, and vaguely shook his head again. His jaw tightened and fury flared in his eyes. "If you are right, the bitch used me to destroy my own brother."

"You were unawares. Do not blame—"

"Don't," Dante snarled. He furiously raised a hand to halt the excuses, and also in warning. "Just, *don't.*"

He dropped his hand, and his anger. Only pain remained in his expression.

"It was Mrs. Gaston, Vergil."

chapter 19

Nigel had said that he planned to go down to Woodleigh once again, so Bianca was surprised when he was announced several days after her secret debut.

He entered the drawing room, wearing a serious countenance. He chatted with Pen and Charlotte for a short while, but it was obvious that an important mission distracted him. Finally he asked Pen if he could speak with Bianca alone. Bianca could tell that Pen feared Nigel intended to declare himself. Reluctantly she collected Charlotte and left.

Nigel paced in front of Bianca. He looked more like a man set to scold than to propose. "I trust that you have not repeated your stage performance."

"Once more, the next night. No others are planned for some time."

"Siddel has been telling people. He frames it as a girl's harmless caprice, but I fear that society will be shocked all the same."

"Do not concern yourself for my reputation, Nigel. I already have all of the Duclaircs doing that for me."

"It is precisely the Duclaircs' management of your reputation that concerns me." He faced her and took a deep breath. "What I am obliged to say cannot be discussed without some indelicacy. You are in the power of a man who is duplicitous and dangerous, and who has designs on you of the most dishonorable nature."

"I am? Of whom do you speak?"

"Laclere, of course. I had suspected that he intended you for the brother, and that was disturbing enough. Dante would have only brought you unhappiness. But it was a feint, I realize now, to obscure a much more disgraceful plan. I curse myself for not seeing their game earlier and for letting things get as far as they have."

"This family has shown me only friendship and affection."

"You are not one of them. Not of their blood or world. The honor that they give their women does not extend to you. You are a foreigner of lower social station, and that makes you vulnerable."

"The viscount has never behaved in any way that I consider dishonorable."

"He played the role of a singer's protector the other night. That he permitted you to be there and then called for you like his mistress—"

"It is his duty to protect me. I am his ward."

"Which makes his misuse of you all the more reprehensible." He resumed pacing. "I am your only relative here in England, Bianca. It falls to me to do what I can to prevent this. I had planned to wait until your birthday to ask, because I knew that Laclere would not approve. I think that it is essential for me to remove you from his influence at once, however. I think it best if we married now."

She was getting tired of men proposing like this. For the third time there had been some external coercion that required her reputation to be saved by hasty matrimony. Didn't Englishmen know how to do it the usual way? Was it necessary for events to wrench the offer out of them?

"Nigel, you are overwrought."

"Hear me out, Bianca. I am very fond of you, and I think that you care for me too. Furthermore, we have similar interests. I am sure that your grandfather saw the possibility for mutual sympathy and hoped that we would discover each other. It was the only reason to make Laclere your guardian instead of me. To leave the way free."

"You may be correct, Nigel, but we would be ill-advised to marry in order to fulfill a dead man's wish."

He heard the overture of rejection in her response. It provoked a sharp look as he halted his pacing. "I think that you should seriously consider my offer, cousin. It is in your best interests."

Something in the way he looked at her frightened her. A little flurry of warning fluttered up her spine. "I will consider it, and I am flattered, but I am obliged to say that it is unlikely that I will accept."

His mouth twisted into a sneer. "It is because of him, isn't it? You think you are in love with him, don't you?"

She wanted to deny that, but the lie died in her throat. His expression said that he would not believe her anyway.

"I saw you. When he met you behind the stage, I was in the corridor. I saw you when you realized that he was there." He stepped toward her and she instinctively tilted away. He cupped her chin and lifted her face so that he could inspect her. "I cannot permit it. He cannot have you as a lover. Or has he promised to marry you?"

"I do not intend to marry anyone right now. I will be continuing my training."

"It is as I thought. He has already corrupted you. Damn the man. We must get you out at once."

"I am going nowhere, Nigel."

Her firm tone caught him up short. He studied her from beneath lowered lids. A thin smile formed, which made him appear reptilian.

"I must insist. He will surely break your heart, Bianca. The best that you can hope for is that he keeps you like a caged bird who sings only for him. More likely he will coarsen you until you agree to sing for any with the right price or the right lies."

"You are the one being coarse, Nigel. I recognize gross insult when I hear it. I will not listen to you speak like this of him, or of me. I must ask you to leave now."

His agitation had transformed into a cool, sly swagger. "Do not get high-and-mighty with me, cousin. You are the great-grandchild of a man who began as a costermonger, same as me. Your father was a third-rate Latin scholar, and your mother sang in as many taverns as she did churches. You do not belong with Laclere, and he knows it, if you do not. If he offered marriage, it was out of the sentiment of the moment." He flicked a bit of dust off his sleeve. "Now, as I see it, we should not go to Scotland. The Continent makes more sense. We can be married in France."

His proposal was preposterous, but the confidence with which he pursued it frightened her. He acted like a man holding more aces than the pack should contain. "I have no intention of marrying you in any country."

"You will not be bound by English law once you leave these shores. You are American, and Laclere's authority ends at the coast. After France, we will go down to Italy if you like."

"I will not be going to Italy with you."

"I am afraid that I am part of the package, dear girl."

"Then I will stay here."

"If you do, I will destroy him. I will tell the world about him."

He made the threat so calmly, so normally, that he might have been observing that the weather promised to be fair today. She faced him down, but her throat tightened. He looked so sure of himself. Too sure.

"No one will believe you. You are guessing and have no proof."

"Rumors are usually enough. People love to watch the self-righteous fall. You have never seen how this society can kill people with cuts and oblivion. Imagine little Charlotte suddenly without friends or decent marriage prospects. Pen snubbed even by her artists. Laclere himself a social outcast."

"If you destroy him with rumors, you also destroy me. A fine proof of your affection. I will deny everything. I will return to America before you can hurt him, if you begin spreading such damaging tales."

"A charming sacrifice, but unnecessary. Ultimately, seducing you is not the sin that will bring him down." He smiled smugly. "You see, I know about Manchester. I know about Mr. Clark. For that there is proof, and no forgiveness, especially on top of his dishonor toward an innocent."

He might have punched her, she felt so shaken.

"Manchester?"

"You do not know about it? I will have to explain on the way to France. Suffice to say that I have the means to ruin Laclere and his family completely and thoroughly. Do not doubt it, Bianca, and when you hear the truth of it, you will thank me. Your viscount is duplicitous in the literal meaning of the word. His interest in you is wholly about a mill up north. He wants to control you because of the share that you inherited. He needs to be able to dictate to you."

"And you, Nigel? My property and income play no role in your offer?"

"My primary concern is your safety and reputation. The property is obviously of interest, but at least with me you will be allowed to enjoy it. Once married to me, you can sing as you wish, and train properly, and perform with triumph."

She did not believe him. She doubted that she would enjoy her inheritance at all, or be allowed to use it to train in Italy. He wanted it. It was why he was here.

To blackmail her into marriage, and get at her inheritance.

Had he also blackmailed Milton? Was she looking at the man responsible for that? Had he seen or heard something during one of his visits to Woodleigh, and then used the information to try and bleed Milton? If Milton ever had an unsuitable lover visit, word could travel among the servants and tenants, just as she had learned about Nigel's own female visitor.

She saw him with new eyes, ones that perceived the danger beneath the fashionable persona. His life stood for nothing except his own indulgence. Yes, he could do it. He could dangle destruction with one hand while he held out the other for a bribe.

It was what he was doing right now.

He gazed down at her the way one would peruse an interesting new possession. "I think that you will agree that it is settled. There is little point in further discussion. You are going down to Laclere Park soon, are you not?"

She nodded numbly. She had been looking forward to several weeks in the country. Vergil had promised he would be there most of the time. In such a big house, with such extensive grounds, surely they could find some time alone together.

"We will leave from Woodleigh, then. I will send the instructions to you." He bent and brushed his mouth on hers. Her lips stretched against her teeth in disgust. "Not a word about our plans, Bianca. Do not tell anyone, not even your maid, and definitely not the Viscount Laclere. Do not doubt that I will ruin him if he interferes, and enjoy doing it. I must leave you now, but I look forward to when we are together forever."

He left her limp with helplessness. She had no time to compose herself before Charlotte darted in and knelt beside her on the settee.

"Did he offer? He looked very handsome today. Pen was sure he came to offer, and was fussing that Vergil would like as kill him rather than permit it, but I don't think my brother is *that* strict and unreasonable. You are almost of age, after all. If you are determined, what can he really do. So, did he?"

Charlotte's face flushed so prettily when she was excited. Her eyes, brown and limpid like Dante's, glowed with deep lights. She exuded purity and sweet innocence and would not begin to know what to do if her world turned upside down.

Which it would, if Nigel held good to his threat. In a way, Vergil's secrecy had mostly been for Charlotte's sake.

"No, he did not offer," she lied. "He came to scold me for the chorus performances."

Charlotte's eyes sparkled with mischief. "It was very exciting knowing someone who dared something so naughty. A bit like getting to be naughty oneself without really having to be. I am still amazed that you got Vergil to agree to it. Perhaps he is growing to like you a bit more. Maybe someday you and he can even be friends."

Bianca laughed to hide her tears. Her mind raced, calculating the time left with the man who should not like her much. She prayed that he would visit, even while she dreaded his arrival.

Except for the dream days at the manor, the shadow of eventual parting always tinged her emotions when he was near. The drop of melancholy did not make the wine of love distasteful. It enriched and mellowed the flavor. But it would be different now. Nigel's blackmail made the separation imminent. The days remaining could be counted, and Vergil's surprise when she left could be imagined. How would she face him without his guessing?

She found out sooner than she wanted. He arrived the next afternoon. She remained in her chamber, attempting to muster enough composure to hide her distress. For the last twenty-four hours she had experienced the panic of a woman cornered by a predator. Every scheme for escape that she considered was hopelessly flawed.

Charlotte came looking for her. "My brother is here. He is wondering why you have not come to the drawing room."

"I am not feeling very well." That was the honest truth.

"He does not look as though he feels well either. He appears distracted and displeased. He asked Pen where Mrs. Gaston has gone, and then barely heard the explanation that Mrs. Gaston has left London to visit friends in the country. Now he has ordered me to come and call you to the library." Charlotte arched her eyebrows. "Have you done something else a little naughty, Bianca?"

She sorely wished that all she had to worry about was a little bad behavior.

He waited in the library, looking thoughtful and windblown and devastatingly handsome. A dark lock fell over his forehead, and she itched to caress it back into the thick tumble of his hair. His cravat's folds were not perfectly centered, and she almost reached out to straighten them. His burning eyes and straight mouth made her worry that he had heard about Nigel's blackmail and planned to berate her for not calling for his help.

He closed the library doors. "This will not do," he said.

"What will not do?"

"This." His arm gestured around the room, at the house in general and at her and him specifically. "You. Me. You fill my days, my nights, my thoughts, my heart. I cannot bear the torture of your presence, nor can I survive the hell of staying away. I cannot live like this. We must come to some resolution."

Laclere, no, please no. Leave it alone and give me the few days left. "You promised that I could have some time."

"You misunderstand me, darling. I did not come to press my advantage, but to admit that I have none. My feelings for you have rendered every other concern insignificant." He reached out to her. "You win. We will do it your way. Whatever arrangements you want. If you only want me for a lover, we will try to be discreet and hope for the best."

Devastation paralyzed her. She longed to grasp that hand and press it to her heart. Love and gratitude spilled through her, but she could not demonstrate it.

She had hoped to run away and never see his reaction. To toy with him now would be inexcusable. He left her no choice but to throw his generosity back in his face.

He noticed her hesitation. His hand fell. "Of course, if you have decided that you do not want me at all, we can make arrangements regarding that too."

Not want him? Surely, no matter what she said this day, he would know that could not be true. He would realize that she did not follow her heart and that something else drove her.

Yes, if she was not very careful, he would indeed realize that. She could not allow it. She had to make him believe whatever story she gave.

She lovingly studied every angle of his face. Crystalline blue eyes regarded her carefully, curious about her reticence. She wanted to fly into his arms and tell him everything. But how could he get them out of this?

She turned away. "I have been thinking."

He became utterly still. He waited so silently that he might not have been in the chamber. She forced herself on.

"What has occurred between us . . . It is dangerous. Ruinous. We must have been mad. I have been thinking . . . you know that I have always believed that marriage was too permanent a punishment for so temporary a crime."

"The punishment would not be mine, so do not pretend that you spare me, Bianca."

His tone chilled her. She closed her eyes and grit her teeth. "No, I will not pretend that. It is my life that marriage will change, in ways that I do not want. Considering that, I do not think that any arrangement will suffice. If I want to pursue my music, I must go to Milan, we must part, and we only delay the sorrow by a few months this way."

The words barely made it out. Silence shuddered in their aftermath. She still did not face him, but she could feel him behind her, large and dark and burning. She discerned that he had moved, but whether he had retreated she could not tell.

He had not walked away. When he spoke, his breath touched her hair. "Since I initiated you in love, perhaps I should instruct you in this as well. It is cowardly to refuse to face me, and you are nothing if not brave."

"I am not brave. I am pitifully weak. If this is wounding you, I do not want to see it." She forced down the ripping anguish that provoked the outburst. "And if it is not wounding you, I do not want to see that, either. That is just how selfish I can be, Laclere."

His firm hand took her shoulder and turned her around. A crooked finger tilted up her chin.

Oh, how he looked at her. Not in anger. His eyes glittered with the memories of their intimacies. He looked at her so completely and openly that she knew it was the last honest look he ever planned to give her.

"It is always a lady's prerogative to end an affair, Bianca. A gentleman does not upbraid her for it or demand more explanations than she chooses to give."

How could he accept this so easily? It was as if he had never believed in his heart that they might stay together. That was her own fault if true, but the thought produced a scathing disappointment. "You are being too kind and generous and making it too easy for me. I would prefer that you yell at me and accuse me of being wicked and flighty and bad."

"You are none of those things. I am sorry that you have made this choice, but I knew it was possible."

Unshed tears burned and knotted her throat and chest. *Do not look away. Do not listen to me. Take me in your arms. Make love to me here, now, on the floor. Refuse to accept this, please.*

He lifted her hand to his lips and held it there, closing his eyes. "My dear girl."

And then he was gone, walking away.

"Laclere." His name tore from her as the tears overflowed. "I was not false. I did not lie to you. It is just . . . it is just . . ."

He paused at the door. "I know that you were not false, Bianca."

Words choked her breath. "I did not lie to you. I do love you, I do . . . only . . ."

His expression revealed some anger now. Of course there would be some of that too. "I believe you. I think that you do love me. Only . . . not enough."

chapter 20

She did not sneak away this time.

She waited at Laclere Park until she received Nigel's letter, telling her when to come. Then she packed her valise, gave Jane a note for Pen, and the next morning at dawn called for the curricle to drive her to Woodleigh.

She had kept to herself the week since they had returned to Laclere Park. Pen knew that she had broken with Vergil. The awkwardness about that had made it easy to create a distance. Charlotte was so distracted by daydreams about her impending debut season that she did not notice Bianca's reserve.

Contrary to his initial plans, Vergil had not accompanied them to Sussex. Affairs suddenly demanded his continued presence in London, he had explained to his sisters.

Well, what had she expected? That he would absolve her inconstancy and rise above the insult?

The curricle rounded a bend and pulled onto the road that led to Woodleigh. Gray brush and dull fields fell away on either side of the road. Low clouds muted the light, leaching the color out of everything, blurring distant forms into one depressing mass. Woodleigh loomed ahead, its huge bulk barely alleviated by the elegant classicism of its design. A hired coach and four waited in the drive.

Nigel emerged from the house in time to meet the halt of her carriage. A footman removed her valise, while another helped her down. It appeared that Nigel had hired a staff of servants since her last visit.

"You simply rode away?" he asked as her carriage departed.

"You wrote that we would leave immediately upon my arrival. It seemed overly dramatic to lower myself from my window by the bedsheets and trudge through the forest. Pen will be told when she wakes that I came here, but I trust we will be long gone by then."

"Yes, long gone, and on our way to the packet at Dover."

"I should warn you that I have very little money with me. I left most of what I had with Jane. Since I am abandoning her, it seemed only right."

"Laclere will see that she gets back to Baltimore. Jane is no longer your concern. Nothing is. I will take care of you now."

He escorted her into the house. More new servants were carrying down trunks and tying them onto the coach.

"I will make a poor showing in France, cousin. I only have the garments in that valise," she said while she warmed herself near the drawing-room fire.

"You will look lovely in whatever you wear, and we will have a wardrobe made for you by the finest Parisian modistes."

He smiled and flattered as a fiancé should, as if he expected them to pretend that he had not coerced her into this.

The activity in the hall ceased. Nigel extended his hand. "We should be off, Bianca. We would like to avoid a race to the coast with your guardian in pursuit, if possible."

"He is not even at Laclere Park. But, yes, let us depart."

The coach was luxurious as hired vehicles went, newer than most, with four matched horses. Nigel was already making headway into her inheritance by way of credit on her expectations.

A footman opened the door and set down the stairs. Nigel handed her up. She halted halfway in.

A woman waited inside the coach.

Mrs. Gaston smiled a welcome.

"Please, darling, seat yourself. I will explain," Nigel said.

Bianca settled next to Mrs. Gaston. Nigel sat across from them.

"Mrs. Gaston has been kind enough to agree to accompany us and serve as your chaperon until we marry," Nigel said.

"How generous of her."

Mrs. Gaston patted her hand. "It is exciting, isn't it? Such a match this will be. Two musicians. Ever since I watched you both perform at the countess's party, I have thought this was fated."

"I did not realize you and Nigel were such good friends."

"We have had the pleasure of each other's company on occasion these last months, since meeting at Laclere Park. Your cousin is an accomplished musician, and I collect such stars in my circle."

"Mrs. Gaston has proposed a subscription series of concerts for me next spring," Nigel said with a broad, flattering smile at the great patroness.

"Goodness, Mrs. Gaston, your generosity to my cousin knows no bounds. Such an offer of patronage is extraordinary. Unfortunately, this elopement will ruin those plans. We will be in Milan in the spring. Isn't that so, Nigel?"

Nigel's smile turned a little crooked. "Of course."

Mrs. Gaston smiled benignly and patted Bianca's hand again.

Bianca bit her tongue.

She did not believe that the two of them had met at Laclere Park. She suspected that Mrs. Gaston was the woman who had secretly visited Woodleigh. There was no other explanation for her presence in this carriage and on this journey. Mrs. Gaston, patroness of the arts, would not interrupt her plans to serve as chaperon for two unknown, unestablished musicians.

Nigel appeared contented, as well he might. The scoundrel was blackmailing her into marriage and would soon control her fortune, and he had not even bothered to get rid of his mistress for the elopement.

He misunderstood her expression. "All will be well, cousin. We are safe. Laclere will not interfere."

Laclere. She wished Nigel had not mentioned him. Pen would send word to him in London. He would know by tonight.

What would he think? That she had truly forsaken him for Nigel? If so, it would change the way he remembered everything.

The coach rocked with a rhythm that timed out her seething frustration. Across from her Nigel relaxed and closed his eyes. Blond hair wisped around his face. He might have been a child sleeping, he looked so untroubled.

She would allow him to enjoy his triumph. She would wait until they were in France before she let him know that she had laid a few plans of her own.

Vergil wanted to smash his fist into something. Pen's footman guessed as much and darted away so the something would not be his jaw.

The little bitch. That a grown man of his age, a respected member of the House of Lords, a confidante of the king's advisors, *a saint, damn it,* should have been made such a fool by a little colonial was bad enough. To now learn that her love had been a game, an elaborate jest, and that the whole time . . . his head split from the intensity of the outrage.

The footman tried to melt into the door.

"Damn it, go back to Sussex. I have no message for my sister."

The footman beat a retreat. Vergil slammed the door after him with enough force to shake the books on the library's shelves.

He stared down at Pen's note on the floor, and then at Bianca's letter, crushed in his fist. He uncrumbled the latter and pressed it out.

It was ostensibly written to Pen, but he could hear Bianca talking to him.

My dearest friend,

When you receive this, I should be on my way to France. I apologize for leaving this way, but I thought it unlikely that I would receive your approval if I announced my plans. I thank you for all of your kindness toward me, but it is time to do what I left Baltimore to accomplish, and there is no reason to wait any longer.

Nigel has graciously offered to accompany me. He anticipates marriage, but I do not see how such an alliance will benefit me. However, in the eventuality that he can persuade me otherwise, I have taken measures through Mr. Peterson to ensure that such a development does not create difficulties for any of my friends in England. For the next few months, I will no doubt have to live off my expectations unless Laclere agrees to forward me funds when I contact him. I daresay that Nigel will be an excellent tutor in delaying payment to tradesmen.

Please address my heartfelt thanks and love to your family, Pen. I hope to see you again, if you have room in your circle for one more artist and room in your heart for one troublesome girl.

Please convince your brother that he must not follow me.

Your errant friend,
Bianca

He could hear her enunciating each word. He pictured her writing them. She did not sound or look smug or even excited. She appeared serious and determined and worried. She should be. She had no idea of the danger she may have put herself in by placing herself at Nigel's mercy.

What the hell was going on? Was she the most shameless of flirts, conducting an affair with one man while she rehearsed with another in the wings? This flight with Nigel suggested so, especially since she indicated that she might not bother to marry him, either.

He read that section again and experienced both delicious relief and dreadful misgivings. Shrewd, clever Bianca. She was absolutely right about the alliance benefiting her not at all. On the other hand, marriage to Bianca would settle things very nicely for Nigel.

Her cousin would be most displeased if she refused him. That displeasure, and the conclusions which it could suggest, kept presenting themselves to Vergil with merciless explicitness.

There had never been any proof that Nigel had tried to harm her. But over in France, if she blocked one path to her fortune . . . No one even knew her in that country. Who would voice suspicion if an accident should happen?

With a new, cold calm he read her letter once again. Its full implications unfolded. She made reference to arrangements having been made to prevent difficulties. His dread deepened. If that meant what he thought, she could be in grave danger when Nigel learned what she had done.

It also indicated that this had been planned while she was still in London, perhaps even before she had ended their affair. He tried not to put too much stock in the notion that Nigel had somehow forced this course on her, but a ridiculously heady beam of hope broke through the darkness that had filled his heart since that day in Pen's library.

Convince your brother that he must not follow me. The order read like a desperate warning.

He called for Morton. "Prepare for a journey of about a week. Also, send for Dante, will you? He is still in the city. I need to speak with him."

"Certainly. We will be going north again, I assume."

"No, we leave for France. I must go to the City now. See that Pen's footman is fed and rested before he heads back. Tell him to inform my sister that I will be following Miss Kenwood despite her instructions that I not do so."

"Mrs. Gaston is gone?" Bianca pulled her cloak tighter, to ward off the sea breeze blowing through the cottage garden. Nigel's great coat flapped around him.

"She has gone into Cherbourg to visit her friend."

"I should like to be in Cherbourg myself, Nigel, and not this rustic farmhouse. Actually, I would like to be in Paris. I do not think that we should have to stop here for days because Mrs. Gaston has a sick friend."

"It would be inappropriate for us to travel without her, Bianca. Unless you have changed your mind about marrying right away."

She broke the dried head off a spindly stalk of dead sunflowers. "Let us go for a walk, Nigel. Actually, I welcome her absence today, and the chance to have some private conversation with you."

He strolled beside her out the gate and through the orchard. They crossed the field of clover to the cliff walk. The wind whipped stronger here, icy from the water. It blew Nigel's hair into a tempest and ruddied his skin.

"I have changed my mind about marrying, Nigel."

"You are tired from the journey, Bianca. Once we are settled in Paris you will see things differently. More clearly."

"You mean that I will remember your threats about Laclere? I find myself thinking that the viscount can watch out for himself, dear cousin. And I am seeing things most clearly. Mrs. Gaston, for example. I see that she is more than an acquaintance to you. You must think me insufferably stupid if you believed I would not recognize the neat arrangement that you have made for yourself."

He exhaled a laugh of defeat. "I will admit that she is an old friend. We met over a year ago when she visited Paris, and . . . But it is in the past."

"After hearing the noise coming from her chamber last night, I am not inclined to believe that."

He had the decency to flush at least. Either her frankness or her worldliness had caught him off guard, which was exactly where she wanted him right now.

"Did you assume that I would be asleep, or that I would be too ignorant to understand? The two of you might have waited until I was not under the same roof."

"It was impetuous and indiscreet of us. I never thought that you . . . I will explain to her that our friendship cannot go on."

"I would not be so fast to throw her over."

"Between her and you, there is no choice. It does sound as if you expect me to choose. It is very provincial of you, Bianca. Very American."

"You choose me so quickly? That must mean that she does not have a fortune and that her income is too small."

"Now you insult me. I understand if you are vexed because of last night, but my first concern is your safety and my second is my affection for you. Your income is the least of it."

"My income is hardly the least of it, although it surely comes after a few other things. The Manchester mill, for example. I know about the offer from Mr. Johnston and Mr. Kennedy. A very large sum of money just for your small share. With my forty-five percent under your control, not only could you sell them a majority ownership, but you could become very wealthy in the process. My yearly income is insignificant in comparison."

Nigel's expression darkened. Down below, the sea roared against the shore. Gulls glided overhead, and the snapping wind bore the scent of ocean salt.

"I will not deny that it would be convenient for me to sell my share of the mill, Bianca. I have some debts. Great-uncle chose to leave me virtually nothing besides the estate, and barely enough income to maintain it. I had expected more."

"You had expected everything, and lived in Paris as if it were already yours."

"I certainly did not expect him to renew a connection severed long ago and give so much to the daughter of—"

"Of his only son and the woman whom he loved," she interrupted. "That is not how you planned to say it, of course. You almost betrayed your true intentions for me, as well as your prejudices. That is the reason I will not marry you, aside from the fact that I can feel no love toward a man who is a blackmailer. You would never allow your wife to perform. If I were willing to be some man's caged bird, as you so aptly phrased it in London, I would have gladly chosen Laclere."

He faced her squarely, blocking her progress along the cliff path. "Your feelings for him are those of a child infatuated for the first time. They will pass. You will be happier with me. We have much more in common."

"How would you know what I have in common with him? Do you think that you know either one of us?"

"I must insist on the wedding, Bianca. It is not open for negotiation. If you doubt my affection or find none of your own for me, we need not share a bed, but we will marry."

"You cannot insist on a wedding, Nigel. Even in France the woman must agree to it."

"You agreed to it by coming with me."

"I only came with you to get you out of England."

"Do you think it makes a difference where I am? I said that I would ruin him if you did not cooperate and I can do so from Paris as surely as in London."

"I do not think that you can. I think that his reputation will take more than one letter to an acquaintance to destroy. He is not his brother. He will not break so easily. You need to be there, stirring the pot, spreading the word."

"If so, I will return and spread it during high season. Do not play games with me, Bianca. I am not a man to cross."

Her resistance brought out the sullen aspects of his temperament. His expression had grown saturnine and his tone prickled with resentment and menace.

"I do not think that you will spread stories, Nigel. You see, I am prepared to pay you two thousand pounds a year to keep silent about what you know."

"As your husband, I would have much more."

"You will never be my husband, and if you ruin him, you will have nothing. If you demand one shilling more, I will give you nothing and let you do your worst."

He paced away in annoyance and cast her a hooded, inspecting sneer. "Who would have thought such a sweet face hid such a cunning mind, cousin? Mrs. Gaston said not to underestimate you, that you could not be all childish innocence if Laclere was interested in you, but I only saw those big blue eyes." He strode back and peered at her dangerously. She stood her ground. After all, when it came to hovering, Nigel could not begin to compete with Vergil.

"It should all be mine," he snarled. "Your father was dead to him, and I was all he had. If Milton had not stolen his affection he would have been kinder to me, but instead, all I heard about was that high-blooded Duclairc until I couldn't bear to visit the old man anymore. Then, with his death, he shackles me with Woodleigh, but makes sure that I don't have the money to enjoy it."

"Perhaps he challenged you with his bequest, to make something of the estate and thus of yourself. You could hire a good manager and learn. Laclere would help you."

"I do not want Laclere's help!"

"Then take the two thousand that I offer or be damned!"

He paced away and back again. Winter fields spread beside him on one side, and the cliff dropped to the sea on the other. This time he strode up so close to her that they almost touched.

She looked into his hard countenance and a tremor chilled her spine.

He had passed from annoyance to cold fury, and from resentment to bitterness. She glanced askance at her position on the cliff path. Very casually she tried to step away from him and into the field.

His arm swung up and blocked her. He swaddled her in the embrace of his great coat and studied her face as if he weighed a great judgment. Ten feet away, the ground disappeared where the cliff dropped to the sea.

"Unfortunately, Bianca, two thousand a year does not begin to solve my financial needs."

His apologetic tone made panic clutch her heart. The sea and ground appeared to swirl around her. His embrace tightened.

She clawed on his arm. "Stop this now. I am not worth murder, Nigel. The mill is gone."

He entwined one hand furiously in her hair. "What do you mean, the mill is gone?"

"I sold my share to Vergil before I left. For one hundred pounds. The papers were waiting for his signature at my solicitor's."

"You sold a partnership worth almost a quarter of a million pounds for one hundred? Are you a complete fool?" He yelled so furiously that her ears rang.

"Not a complete fool," she said. "Not *your* fool, for one thing. If you forced me into marriage, I had no intention of letting you sell that mill out from under Vergil. Nor would you enjoy the fruits of its sale. And if you chose to expose him out of spite, I made sure that he would at least be wealthy in his social oblivion."

"It is not legal. It cannot be."

"Why not? My trustee and guardian approved, I am sure. And if it is not, I am told that your courts work very slowly on such matters. We will all be dead before it is resolved."

"That is a very real possibility, sweet girl," Nigel snarled. "I was rather counting on selling that mill, you see. You have placed me in an impossible situation."

Her feet left the ground as he began carrying her. Frantic, she kicked and pummeled and bit. Grappling like a madman, he tried to haul her to the cliff.

Suddenly the fight left him. He set her down again and stared at her in shock. His gaze appeared inward, as if what stunned him was in his own soul.

"God, Bianca, I don't know what came over me. I would never—"

Something distracted him. His head turned, and a frown broke over his squinting eyes.

She caught her breath. Heart pounding, she followed his gaze down to the house.

A coach was stopping there. Mrs. Gaston had returned.

Bianca extricated herself from Nigel's hold and ran down the hill. She staggered out of the orchard just as Mrs. Gaston was handed out of the carriage.

The man who offered his help was not the coachman.

Bianca stopped a hundred yards from the house and tried to make sense of the sudden appearance of this visitor.

Nigel caught up. He came up beside her and his expression showed that he had not expected this development, either.

"What the hell is Witherby doing here?" he muttered.

chapter 21

Vergil's hired mount was tiring, but he urged him on. His impatience would not permit rest now. Too much time had been lost in Calais. It had taken him two days to track down the inn where Nigel and Bianca had stayed, and find the servant who had overheard their plans.

The discovery that Nigel and Bianca had not gone on to Paris, but instead had removed to an isolated cottage on the Normandy bluffs, only deepened his misgivings.

Two women were traveling with the man, the servant had said. The news hardly reassured him. The other woman was most likely Mrs. Gaston.

They were playing their old game, but the prize was very high this time. Too high. The value of Bianca's inheritance, hell, the value of the mill alone, exceeded anything they had gotten with their blackmail. If Bianca resisted once in France . . .

For all intents and purposes, they had killed before.

It had not been hard to follow them. Nigel had hired a superb coach for their journey, and such things were noted in villages. In the last one, some farmers had directed him to the cottage by the sea, which had been leased by the blond Englishman.

He angled toward the timbered and plastered farmhouse hugging the rugged rise. A sparsely planted garden cringed inside low stone walls. A screen of bare orchard blocked his view of the coast, but the roar of the sea droned louder as he approached.

No one emerged with his call. He dismounted and entered.

Three people sitting in the cottage expressed no surprise with his arrival. Bianca looked at him fearfully, Nigel only scowled, and Mrs. Gaston smiled with contentment.

Another person waited in the cottage too. Someone Vergil had not expected, and who grinned at the way Vergil reacted to the shock of seeing him.

"It took you long enough, Laclere," Cornell Witherby said.

Bianca jumped up and ran into Vergil's arms. "You should not have come," she said as she kissed him.

"He had to, Miss Kenwood," Witherby said. "Didn't you, Laclere? There was no way you would allow her to leave like that." He turned to Mrs. Gaston. "I told you that he would come."

Nigel rose and distanced himself from the other two. "I want you to know that I had no role in this, Laclere. I did not realize they sought to lure you here. I did not even know Witherby was this whore's cohort."

"To say you had no role is an exaggeration," Vergil said. "You may have been duped by Mrs. Gaston, and this may not be unfolding as you expected, but you did what was needed to get Bianca to accompany you."

"He said that he knew about us, and about you and the mill," Bianca said. "He threatened to ruin you."

He took her face in his hands and ignored the others for a precious moment. "You should have told him to do his worst, darling. If it meant having you with me, I would have gladly been ruined." He embraced her closely and looked at Witherby. "I know how Mrs. Gaston procured my brother's letters, but learning about the Earl of Glasbury— You are the worst scoundrel, Witherby. You befriended my sister and then betrayed her confidences. Only she could have told you about the earl."

"I really wish you had left it all alone, Laclere."

"You killed my brother. I could not leave that alone."

"I killed no one."

"You may as well have pulled the trigger."

"No one was supposed to die," Mrs. Gaston said. "We asked for a little money, that was all. Not even very much. A few thousand. Why the viscount and others felt the need to go and kill themselves—well, that isn't our fault they reacted so rashly."

She appeared annoyed by the bad behavior these men had shown, and the trouble it had caused.

"First Milton and Dante, then Pen. Finally me. You two have used the Duclairc family again and again in this crime of yours."

Witherby got up and strolled over to the mantel of the hearth. A pistol rested on it. "Your family has been limping along for generations. The weakness begged to be exploited."

"It was not weakness that you took advantage of, but trust and affection. Why didn't you make it complete? You knew about Bianca and me, Witherby. Why didn't I get a blackmail note too? Why this elaborate game to bring me here?"

"It would have been just like you to take the fall, Laclere. Or worse, use it to find us out. I have known for months that you were looking for us. Your sister told me. Oh, she does not know the meaning of your absences, but I saw what you were up to when she described your frequent journeys and your deep interest in Milton's life. I knew it was just a matter of time. And that drama with the earl and Hampton—eventually you would remember that one other person knew Glasbury's secret. Your sister." He lifted the pistol off the mantel. "You really should have left it alone."

Vergil watched those fingers close on the weapon. "The accidents at Laclere Park. It was not Nigel trying to kill Bianca, but the two of you trying to kill me, wasn't it?"

Bianca's head snapped around. She looked at Witherby and Mrs. Gaston with shock. Vergil felt the chill of fear shake her.

Nigel's eyes widened. "You thought I was trying to kill my cousin?"

"Do not pretend that you do not have it in you," Bianca said softly.

For some reason, that checked Nigel's indignation. His face flushed and he averted his gaze from her.

"It entered my mind," Vergil said. "However, if Mrs. Gaston was visiting that day that Bianca and I went to see your uncle's effects, I think it is safe to say that the shots that missed us came from her."

Nigel turned in horror to Mrs. Gaston. "You said that you were in the park when I found you gone on my return. That you had slipped out so they wouldn't find you in the house."

"Laclere is guessing, Nigel. He is making accusations without basis."

"The rock fall, that was you, Witherby," Vergil said. "You had just arrived that morning. You saw me following Bianca, and followed me yourself."

"You were getting too close, Laclere. We learned that you had taken Milton's place in Manchester. Eventually you would learn about the visit to Mr. Thomas. I did not make the choice easily." He gestured with the pistol. "Nor do I make this choice easily, either. However, I see no alternative. I think we will all take a walk now. The sea is beautiful this time of day."

Bianca subtly cringed. Nigel went white. Vergil gazed at that pistol, and at the tight resolve on the face of a man he had trusted as a friend.

"Witherby, I did not come to France alone."

"You came *here* alone."

"I am ahead of the others by a half hour, no more. The carriage must stay on the roads, while I rode cross-country. In minutes the others will be here. Even if they are delayed and you succeed in forcing us off that cliff and getting away, they know about Mrs. Gaston already, and will soon learn about you."

"You are bluffing. You would never risk having anyone else learn about your brother, or about you and your ward."

"I can trust the men I told."

Witherby gestured more distinctly toward the door with the pistol. "If what you say is true, I have nothing to lose. I will take my chances. Let us go. You, too, Nigel."

Mrs. Gaston began to rise.

"No," Witherby said. "You stay here."

Turning Bianca under his arm, Vergil followed Nigel out of the cottage. Witherby and the pistol hovered at their side.

"It was her idea, wasn't it?" Vergil asked, glancing back to where Mrs. Gaston sat on her chair.

"Not really. It was a game at first. When it worked with the first one, when this money just appeared so easily—it wasn't hard at all. The wonder is that it doesn't happen all the time. All those secrets that half the world already suspects but pretends they don't—hell, Lord Fairhall wasn't even very discreet about his taste for little girls."

"Are you her lover, along with Nigel?"

Witherby shook his head. "My interest in your sister was not a feint, Laclere. Mrs. Gaston and I are only friends, and business associates."

They approached the barren orchard. The tree branches made a web of snarled lines against the sky. Vergil looked at Bianca's face. She was being brave, but her eyes glistened with worry and fear.

He tightened his hold in reassurance, and stretched his hearing for the sounds of a carriage.

He heard nothing but the close roar of the surf.

"How did you know about my brother, Witherby?"

"His reclusiveness. His lack of marriage, despite being a viscount. It is a common pattern. No doubt many others suspected. As for Manchester, and Mr. Clark, that was an accident. I saw him entering a bookseller almost two years ago, and then leaving with a letter. I merely asked in the shop for the name of the man who had just left, and learned it was Mr. Clark. A pound procured the information that his letters came from Manchester. Well, it was a delicious mystery, and I had to look into it. Imagine my shock at learning how he had debased your family with that mill and that lover."

"And your friendship with me counted for nothing as you exploited that."

Witherby's face flushed. "I did you a favor. You got the title, after all."

"I did not want the title, least of all at such a cost."

Nigel, pacing ahead of them, suddenly halted in his steps and looked east.

"Thank God," he muttered.

Vergil and Bianca turned. The speck of a carriage rolled along the road, growing larger by the instant.

Witherby tensed beside them. For an instant his eyes went wild with panic. Then he sighed deeply and composed himself. The pistol fell, to hang limply from his arm by his side.

"Who is it?" he asked quietly in the voice of a man needing to know what he faced. It was the request of one friend to another, so that preparations could be made.

"Hampton and Burchard. St. John made one of his ships available to bring us over, so he may be with them." Vergil glanced to the cottage, where Mrs. Gaston remained. "I expect that my brother also insisted on riding along, although I suggested he remain in Calais."

"Almost the entire Dueling Society, then."

Not only the Dueling Society. As the carriage rolled up beside the cottage, it was clear that Dante sat up with the coachman because the carriage was full. After Hampton and Burchard and St. John stepped out, a man remained inside, his hook-nosed profile backlit by the far-open window.

The Dueling Society did not react much to seeing Witherby. Vergil could read them reaching the necessary conclusions, however, and saw the dismay in their eyes.

Adrian walked over and removed the pistol from Witherby's hand. "You will not be needing this just yet. If you choose pistols, you can have it back then."

Bianca stiffened under Vergil's embrace. She looked up into his eyes with a worried expression that made his heart clench.

Witherby shook his head. "I will only do it that way if you allow Mrs. Gaston to leave first. Otherwise there will be a trial and all of it will come out, Laclere. Your brother, the earl—all of it, I swear."

Dante overheard. He strode forward with flaming eyes. "She does not go free, Vergil."

Vergil released Bianca and took him aside. "If she goes back to England, if we swear the evidence we have against them—not only our brother's name will be ruined, but those of other men. Your name will come up too. I can't allow it, and if her freedom is the price of silence, I will pay it."

"What about what I am willing to pay? I don't see this as only your decision."

"If you think about it, it will be your decision as well."

Dante's expression turned hard. "Then let me stand to him. It is my place to do so."

"It is not yours any more than it is Pen's."

"I'll be damned if it isn't."

"Dante, you are not a good shot, and if he chooses sabres you will have no chance at all. He will kill you."

"He may kill *you.*"

Vergil looked back at Witherby, whose face had gone impassive. "No, I don't think so."

Vergil nodded to Adrian, who entered the cottage. It took him a while to explain things to Mrs. Gaston, and Vergil wondered just what Burchard was saying to her. When they emerged, her face was flushed and Adrian's dark eyes glowed.

Wellington climbed out of the coach, and subjected Mrs. Gaston to a scornful examination. "I trust that I will not see you again in England, madame."

She turned even more red.

The Iron Duke gestured to the road. "I recommend that you head west. If I catch up with you on the road later, I cannot promise to behave as a gentleman."

Composing herself and assuming a disdainful expression, Mrs. Gaston walked toward the stable where Nigel's hired coach waited. She did not look back.

Wellington turned his attention on Witherby and became the image of barely contained rage. "Tell him to choose his weapons."

Alarmed, Adrian strode over to him and gestured for Vergil to come as well.

"You must not," Vergil said. "If you do, what reason will you give? It will only feed the flames of rumor about the Foreign Minister."

"Damn it, man—what reason will *you* give?"

"My sister's honor."

"Hell, no one will believe that."

"I don't care."

"It must not be you, Your Grace," Adrian said forcefully. "Any of us, but not you."

"Not any of us, Adrian. *Me.*" Vergil said.

Wellington narrowed his eyes on Witherby in disgust. "If you fail, Laclere, he is mine."

St. John had been speaking to Witherby. He came toward them. "Sabres," he said. He reached into the carriage and retrieved two swords.

Vergil returned to Dante. "I want you to stay here with Bianca, so she is not alone. Will you do that for me?"

"Damn it, Verg—"

"I ask for my sake, Dante. Not yours."

He did not actually agree, but he did not refuse, either. The others began walking toward the orchard. Nigel, looking shaken, humiliated, and relieved, sought the sanctuary of the cottage.

Wellington, Witherby, and the Dueling Society disappeared into the trees. Twenty paces away Bianca stood rod straight.

Forcing containment on the emotions trying to submerge his sense of justice and duty, Vergil opened his arms.

She ran to his embrace.

"Do not say anything," she whispered, stretching up to his kiss. "Nothing. I will not lose you today. My heart knows it."

Those big blue eyes could create a world that existed only for them. He savored the bliss that she could inspire in him. "I must speak. I must tell you how much I love you, Bianca."

"You have told me often before, Laclere, in ways more meaningful than words."

"I find myself thinking that if I die today, loving you will have been the best thing in my life. So it is important to me that you know that I love you, very clearly. I would never want you to wonder."

Her lids lowered and she flushed. "As you wondered?" she whispered.

He kissed each lid and her cheek, and held her face so his lips could taste hers. "A man's pride can be a stupid thing. My heart has always understood you. I just did not want to accept what it meant for me, that is all."

He held her to his body, trying to absorb her into his essence. He had not had time to be grateful she was safe, and relief now washed through him, shaking his soul.

She looked at him with an expression of love and trust that obscured the danger waiting.

"Go inside with Dante, Bianca."

He walked away, but she did not go into the cottage. At the edge of the orchard he looked back and saw her still outside, watching him.

From the threshold to the cottage, Dante watched as well.

Vergil's gaze swept the cliff line and the gray void of the ocean beyond. There was something elemental about nature's forces on the coast. The violent abstractness of the sea, the bleakness of the cliffs and beaches—civilization ended where that water began, and man and his rules simply disappeared in a wave.

He joined the others. Witherby already held his sabre, and Hampton walked over to give Vergil the other one and take his coat.

"An appropriate setting," Hampton said quietly.

"Yes, as places for dying go, a seacoast is among the best."

Hampton gave one of his rare smiles. "I always thought so."

St. John came up alongside him. "We seem destined to assist each other in unpleasant matters, Laclere."

"It would appear so."

"The chevalier is not here, so it is left to me to remind you of his first lesson. A clear head, and cold blood. The mind must rule, not the heart."

Vergil doubted his mind would rule entirely. The justice of this course did not make it easy, and the man waiting was not a stranger, nor completely evil.

Hampton and St. John stood aside. Under the watchful gaze of Wellington and the Dueling Society, Vergil walked over to Cornell Witherby.

"Hell of a thing," Witherby said. "To have practiced together all these years, and to now find ourselves doing it for real with each other."

Vergil suddenly saw all those years. His mind pictured Witherby at university, always ready with a joke and indifferent to his studies. He saw Witherby excited when his first poem was published, and bringing life and humor to the meetings of the Dueling Society.

More recent memories flashed through his head too—those of Penelope, happy for the first time in years because of this man.

"You can take comfort in knowing that even if I win, I also lose," Vergil said. "I will be the one who has to return to London and tell my sister that I killed the man she loves."

Witherby's expression fell. In the pure, diffused light of the overcast day, he looked very young and sad. "Let us be done with this, Laclere," he said softly. "There is nothing else for it."

They saluted with their sabres and the roar of the surf entered Vergil's head.

"You aren't going to obey him and wait here, are you?" Dante asked as he strolled toward her.

Bianca watched the spot where Vergil had disappeared into the orchard. "No, I am not going to obey him."

"Of course not. No reason for you to start now, is there? At least your willfulness spares me from playing nursemaid." Dante passed her and headed into the trees. "Come on, then."

They walked quickly through the orchard. Halfway down its path,

Bianca thought she heard the faint sounds of metal on metal. She and Dante broke into a run at the same time.

They emerged onto the field of clover. Up on the rise, near the cliff's edge, the tiny dark spots of six men could be seen against the gray sky. Specks of light flickered off the slashing sabres.

Dante took her hand as they stumbled across the field. She could not take her eyes off those dark spots. Four of them stood like statues, stoic witnesses to the other two's dance of death.

"Laclere is very good at this, isn't he?" she said. "Please tell me he is an expert swordsman, Dante."

"He is better with pistols."

She had never seen Dante so serious. So concerned. He did not look like a man who assumed his brother would win this duel. His expression sapped her confidence and fear took its place.

She stared desperately at the distant drama and ran faster, not knowing what she rushed toward. She doubted her mere presence could stop it now.

Worse, it might even distract Vergil.

That thought made her halt abruptly in the middle of the field. She jerked her hand from Dante's. "You go. I will stay here. He does not want me there for a reason."

Dante nodded as he turned to continue. Suddenly he stopped too. His gaze locked on the figures moving against the sky. Vergil and Witherby's expressions could not be seen, but the progress of the duel was clear.

"He does not want me there, either," Dante said. "We will wait here together."

He backed up and stood beside her. Shoulder to shoulder, down in the field that had ceased to exist to the men on the cliff, they watched the silent, horrible contest.

Suddenly two forms became one. Bianca's heart stopped and her breath left her. She waited, numb with shock, for one man to drop to the ground.

Beside her Dante ceased breathing too. Their hands instinctively sought each other's, and their fingers entwined with all the strength of their shared fear.

Vergil and Witherby separated. One did not drop. Instead Witherby just stood there, as still as the sentries witnessing this ancient form of judgment.

Suddenly he was gone, and only five men stood on the cliff path.

"Jesus," Dante muttered.

It sounded more like a prayer of gratitude than a curse.

chapter 22

He showed some honor in the end," Wellington said.

He was the first to speak after the silent group made their way back to the cottage.

Vergil held Bianca in his arms, not giving a damn who saw. None of that mattered now. He needed to feel her warmth and vitality and the world could go to hell if it objected.

None of the world surrounding them in the cottage did.

"I will send boats out from Cherbourg," St. John said. "If his body is found, there will be no wounds from weapons. We can say it was an accident, that he fell from the cliff. No one will know that there was a duel under way."

Vergil pressed his lips to Bianca's silken hair as he tightened his embrace. He closed his eyes and saw Witherby on the cliff.

The man had lowered his weapon and his defense deliberately, and exposed himself to death.

Vergil had not pressed the advantage. He had not lunged.

He doubted he would ever forget the look in his friend's eyes as they slowly met the gazes of the witnesses, and then Vergil's own. One last sad smile, and Witherby had stepped back, until his boot landed on nothing but air.

"One person will have to know," Vergil said, relaxing his embrace of Bianca, but not letting her go. "I must speak with Pen. I will not live with a lie between us."

"The countess is stronger than most people know, Laclere," Hampton said. "Although, sparing the earl from the fruits of his sins—well, of all the men who were blackmailed, I did not cry for him."

That was the worst of this business, and a miserable irony. Not only had today taken from Pen the man she loved, it had left her shackled to one she hated.

"I will explain it to her," Dante said firmly, darting Vergil a glance that dared him to object. "That way I will be sure that she learns the *whole* truth of it."

"It is getting late, and we should depart," Wellington said. "There is a small matter of transportation now. What with Miss Kenwood and her cousin here, there is not enough room in the coach."

"I will ride Vergil's horse, and Kenwood will take my place with the coachman," Dante said. "Vergil, you and Miss Kenwood will have to wait here until we can send a carriage for you."

Wellington's lids dropped to half-mast. He examined the embracing couple.

Everyone else assumed utterly bland expressions.

"Your Grace?" Adrian said, gesturing to the door.

"Quite." Wellington exited, and a line of men filed after him.

"Why not make a visit to Paris, as long as you are on the Continent?" St. John said as he passed. "My sister, Jeanette, would be happy to receive you."

"Perhaps we will do that," Vergil said.

The rest of the Dueling Society departed, leaving only Vergil, Bianca, and Dante.

"Going to Paris may be a good idea, Verg. Do not worry about Pen. I will take care of her. It is the least I can do."

"Thank you, Dante."

Dante stopped at the threshold. "It may be that the carriage cannot come until the morning," he said. "I trust that you will be a saint, Verg, and that Miss Kenwood is safe with you."

"Of course."

Laughing, Dante left. Vergil and Bianca followed him and watched the men climbing into the coach.

Nigel approached them. "I would like to know if you will be bringing witness against me, cousin. I should like to return to England, but obviously cannot do so if you choose to prohibit it."

"I will not bring evidence. When the choice came, you did the right thing," Bianca said. "The price, however, is that you not speak against Vergil, that you keep silent about what you discovered."

"I intended to do so anyway. I find that I do not have the taste for blackmail that some others do. It brings out parts in a man that are better left buried."

Bianca beamed with approval, but Vergil felt less sanguine. Nigel appeared sincere enough, but who knew what the morning would bring. Good sense and constancy were not this man's strongest virtues.

"Woodleigh is a good estate, Kenwood. With the right manager, it could be productive enough to keep you. Not like a duke, but well enough," Vergil said. "When I return to Sussex I will ask my estate manager to visit you. He may have some suggestions for a good man to see to things for you."

"I thank you for that. Perhaps it is time to put down roots back home. Maybe you were right, Bianca. Your grandfather may have had his reasons for arranging things as he did."

Nigel walked toward the coach and climbed up with the coachman.

"What did you mean when you said he did the right thing when the choice came?" Vergil asked.

"Let us just say that I think that the devil has been fighting for his soul, but did not win." She watched the carriage take him away. "Do you think that he will remain silent?"

"Probably. Not that it will matter, since Mrs. Gaston is certain to tell all to whoever will listen. Eventually her stories about me will get to London."

"Oh, darling, can't we find some way to stop her?"

He placed two fingers on her soft warm lips. "I do not care. I think that I will be glad for it. I am tired of the double life, Bianca. I am tired of denying part of who I am. Doing so left my brother vulnerable, and eventually killed him, and I will not live like that. I am proud of what I have done with the mill. It is important to me, essential to me, and I am not inclined to give it up, either."

"I think that I can understand that."

"Yes, you can. And I can understand you. I understand that embracing your dream and your art does not mean rejecting me, even if it does mean that you cannot stay with me."

She sank against him. It felt so good to hold her feminine warmth. However, her embrace acknowledged that it was time for decisions to be made. The beauty of her sadness made his heart shake.

"What do we do now?" she mumbled.

She was asking for help in seeing it through.

"We will visit Paris and then you will continue down to Italy. I brought a bank draft that you can take. It will see you clear until more formal arrangements can be made. We will send for Jane while we are in Paris and settling the plans for your journey south."

Her big blue eyes widened in her erotically innocent way. "That is not what I mean, Laclere. What do we do *now*?"

His blood fired immediately in response to her quiet invitation. He pulled her to him and kissed her with a ferocity born of relief and regret. "You are a most dangerous lady."

She backed into the farmhouse. "Only dangerous for you, my lord. You have my promise on that."

He followed where she led, over to a sheepskin rug by the fire. With eyes speaking of the passion to come, she dropped her cloak and began to undress him.

"I thought of you often while I walked by the sea." She slid his waistcoat off and plucked at his cravat. "The power of the waves, the rhythm and force of them, the glory of all that untamed nature—it can saturate a person the way love and passion can. Very moving. Like music, actually. Yes, a lot like music. I would watch the sea and want to make love to you and sing my heart out."

"Then we will." He grabbed up her cloak and threw it around her. "On the cliffs. We will make love there and you will sing for me, and we will join our passion to that of creation and remember this day forever."

Flying on desire, they made their way to the cliffs, huddled together against the wind, almost spilling their love in the orchard when he stopped to warm them both in an embrace. They climbed up the walk to the highest point, where the western sun still gave a little warmth and an ethereal pink light bathed an outcropping.

Bianca faced the sea, so close to the edge one expected her to take to flight. The wind whipped her cloak and gown and hair until she appeared like the center of a tiny tempest. She closed her eyes and just felt it, and he felt it through her. Her voice warbled up and down the scales as she announced herself to the elements.

"It is divine," she whispered.

He stepped close behind her. "Sing the Rossini," he said. "Sing as you did the day at the ruins."

"You favor that? Do you know what the words say?"

"The singer explains how she will not marry her evil guardian, but will find a way to be with her true love."

"Very apt that day in the ruins, except that the true love was in fact the evil guardian."

"In his heart the evil guardian wished for it." He embraced her. "Sing it for me."

At first he could barely hear her. The wind stole the sound out of her mouth and carried it to the clouds. But her breath and voice found its strength and the music flowed out of her, another wind blowing its passion, another force drenching his soul. He sensed her with him, pulling him into it, glorying in the elemental energy of her voice and womanhood.

He lowered her to the ground and took her while she sang. The joining left her breathless, unable to sound the notes, but the aria continued silently in his head, filling out the roar of wind and sea. Her soul sang it too. She expressed her ecstacy in her kisses and holds and cries until a completion erupted that merged them into the coast's sublime fury.

She clutched the hearth wall as pleasure of stunning intensity left her limp. Only her grip kept her upright on her knees as Laclere's tongue made her vulva throb with astonishing sensations.

He reached for her waist and brought her down until she straddled his hips on the sheepskin rug in front of the cottage's hearth. She laid against his chest and blinked her senses alert.

In that instant, with the solidity of his body beneath her and the heat of their passion burning, she saw her future. She knew how it must be. No regret tinged the joy that the decision gave her. In the years ahead she might experience some nostalgia for what she relinquished, but she would never grieve.

She felt him hard beneath her, his need intensified by the kisses he had just given her. She rose and sat back on his thighs and looked down at the man who had intruded on her plans, only to become the center of her life. "I want us to be lovers forever, Laclere."

"We will be, darling. I will come to Italy often and the separations will not be too long."

She caressed down his chest, wonderfully alert to the feel of his skin and body. "I want no distance. No separation. I cannot leave you, Laclere. My heart will not let me. I want to get married."

Her declaration surprised him. He gripped her hands to stop their caresses and looked in her eyes.

There was no triumph in his expression. She saw only relief and love and astonishment.

Then a deeper comprehension shadowed the brighter emotions.

"You said that denying your dream would mean giving up half your soul. I do not want that."

"I can sing anywhere, Laclere. In my chamber and yours. In a ruined castle. I do not need to be in Italy for my soul to be whole. I do not need to train for performances in order to have my art."

Her capitulation appeared to trouble him. His fingertips skimmed her breast's swell while he thought, as if its shape aided his contemplations. "You must continue training, darling. When you surpass Signore Bardi's skill, we will bring another voice master from Italy, as I promised."

He pulled her down into an embrace. He pressed a long kiss to her as he smoothed slow caresses over her body. "You will train, and then you will perform when you are ready. If I do something so outrageous as manage a mill, having a wife who performs is almost insignificant."

It was her turn to be astonished. "It will not be so simple, Laclere. There will be a high cost if you permit this. I do not want your family hurt because of me."

"It will be some years before you go onstage. Charlotte will be married by then, so we will not harm her future. As to Pen and Dante, they are hardly paragons of propriety themselves. Maybe everyone will just think I have become eccentric, like my father and brother. If not, I do not care. Your happiness is worth any price, my love."

Her throat burned and her eyes misted. She loved him so much at that moment that holding the love inside her made her heart gloriously full. "Thank you for wanting to do this for me, but you are not being practical. By the time I am ready to perform, I will have children."

"Then we will have an army of nurses and tutors go with them when you travel to your engagements. You will have your dream, Bianca. If you will stay with me, I will not allow our marriage to deny you any of it."

She kissed him. The warmth of his lips seemed to make the sweetest connection they had ever shared. She knew with a woman's certainty that this marriage would indeed deny her part of the dream, but she did not care about that. His desire to give it all to her was what she would always remember.

"I do not expect to travel very much. I do not have to perform on the Continent. I do not want to build a career for the fame, Laclere. However, it will be nice, sometimes, to have the opportunity to sing until hundreds of people weep."

He lifted her body and lowered her so that he filled her. Holding her to his heart he led her back into passion.

Afterward she lay drenched by his presence. The soft words of love that he had spoken at the end still played in her ears, and she slowly realized that he still repeated them. She forced her sated senses back in order.

And realized that for the first time he remained inside her.

She rose up on her forearms and looked at him.

Unconditional love looked back.

They shared a flawless unity in that honest gaze.

What a terribly wonderful thing love could be, she thought. One both found oneself and lost oneself within its quiet power. Love was more transporting than the ecstasies of music and nature. More thrilling than the edge of a sea cliff or the release of passion.

ABOUT THE AUTHOR

Madeline Hunter has worked as a grocery clerk, office employee, art dealer, and freelance writer. She holds a Ph.D. in art history, which she currently teaches at an eastern university. She lives in Pennsylvania with her husband, her two teenage sons, a chubby, adorable mutt, and a black cat with a major attitude. She can be contacted through her web site, www.Madeline-Hunter.com.